TWENTY

ALSO BY JAMES GRIPPANDO

OTHER FICTION

* A Jack Swyteck novel

TWENTY

A JACK SWYTECK NOVEL

JAMES GRIPPANDO

HARPER

An Imprint of HarperCollinsPublishers

HarperCollins books may be purchased for educational, business, or sales promotional use. For information, please email the Special Markets Department at SPsales@harpercollins.com.

FIRST EDITION

Library of Congress Cataloging-in-Publication Data has been applied for.

ISBN 978-0-06-291508-5

21 22 23 24 25 LSC 10 9 8 7 6 5 4 3 2 1

For Tiffany.
Remember that trip to Australia?

TWENTY

CHAPTER 1

"Everything I learned, I've forgotten since kindergarten," said Jack. He was behind the wheel of the family SUV with his wife, Andie, beside him. Their daughter was behind Andie, strapped into her car seat, her curious expression lighting up Jack's rearview mirror.

"What does that mean, Daddy?"

"Oh, there was this book some time ago. It was called—"

"Actually," said Andie, "it was called *Everything I Need to Know, I Learned in Kindergarten.* So I think what your daddy is saying is that he needs to *go back* to kindergarten."

"You mean he wants a do-over?" asked Righley.

Jack smiled. "Yes, honey. Daddy wants a do-over."

"No do-overs! That's our rule."

Jack was the assistant coach of Righley's peewee soccer team. "You're right, honey. That is the rule."

Had a do-over been possible, Jack would have chosen Riverside Day School for his own education. Seated on ten picturesque acres of green space in one of the oldest neighborhoods along the Miami River, Riverside was South Florida's premier K-through-12 private academy. Ninety percent of the faculty had a postgraduate degree, no teacher had more than eighteen students, and every classroom had the latest SMART Board technology. The parent directory read like a Who's Who of Florida business leaders, which left Jack and Andie in the proverbial no-man's-land on the financial spectrum, too rich for financial aid and not nearly rich enough to afford the tuition. So they stretched, remaining conspicuously silent when other parents waxed on about their ski trips over winter break or summers in the South of France.

"Park right there," said Andie, pointing to an open space on the street.

They were still more than two blocks from the campus entrance, just outside the blinking amber lights of the designated school zone. The school had a parking lot, but Jack understood the issue. Andie was an FBI agent, and although she was dressed for a day of field work, she was not yet on duty, and Florida law prohibited law enforcement officers from carrying weapons into school zones if they were off duty. Jack parked the car and unloaded Righley from the back seat while Andie discreetly locked her sidearm and holster in the glove compartment.

It was mid-September, a Wednesday morning, the final week during which kindergarten parents were allowed to walk their children to the classroom. Hand in hand, they entered the campus and went to the flagpole on the quad, where the elementary-level students assembled every morning in a circle, placed their hands over their hearts, and recited the pledge of allegiance. Or some reasonable facsimile thereof.

And to the Republic, for Richard Stanz.

One day Jack wanted to meet this Richard Stanz.

Jack's law office was within walking distance, a historic coral-stone house that, like most residences in this gentrified circa-1920s neighborhood, had been refurbished and converted to commercial use. He gave Andie the car keys and a kiss, hugged Righley, and headed off beneath the sprawling limbs of century-old live oaks. It was a perfect morning, still hours away from the heat and humidity that would return every afternoon until about Halloween, a wet blanket of a reminder that there really was no such thing as autumn in the subtropics. It made Jack think of the walks he would have liked to have taken with his father when he was in kindergarten, when a young Representative Harry Swyteck was away in Tallahassee for legislative sessions and Jack's stepmother was too hung over to get out of bed.

Jack enjoyed his walk along the river, thanking his lucky stars for the life he and Andie had made for themselves and their only child.

The mother-daughter good-bye at the classroom door was without tears, at least not from Righley. Andie's commute to the FBI's field office in North Miami was by way of the dreaded Palmetto Expressway, a miles-long, bumper-to-bumper nightmare of blinking red taillights, the thought of which made her downright envious of Jack's lovely walk from the school to his office. Deciding to let rush-hour traffic subside before getting on the road, Andie joined the other parents in the recreation center for the regular second-Wednesday-of-the-month coffee with the head of school. It was Andie's first, but it wasn't limited to new parents, so it was mostly "the usual suspects." Working mothers dressed for the office in one cluster. Stay-at-home mothers in workout spandex or tennis skirts in another. Off to the side, alone, stood a tech-world multimillionaire who had sold his company and retired way too young, not really sure how he fit into this overwhelmingly female group. Andie felt almost as out of place, dressed in law-enforcement khaki pants and black tactical boots, which made her look more like the head janitor than a Riverside parent. She was relieved to find her friend Molly near the basket of bagels.

"Glad to see you here," said Andie.

Molly had two boys and a girl at Riverside, a senior, a sophomore, and her "happy accident," a daughter in the second grade. After the third, she'd stopped teaching Lamaze, but it was in

Molly's course that Andie had first met her. They'd lost touch after Righley's birth, but she was once again Andie's rock, her only familiar face at Riverside.

"There's a fresh patch of vomit on the gym floor," said Molly. "Could you please fetch a bag of sawdust?"

"Right away, ma'am."

The "janitor look" was a running joke between them. The first few weeks of school were filled with countless orientations and meetings for Riverside parents: meet the math department, meet the coaches, meet the science teachers, meet the alumni parents who are so glad they spent a fortune on private school because their kids are rockin' it at Harvard. At the first gathering of the year, a tenth-grade mother had asked Andie to look into the condensation dripping from the AC vent. Andie had since made a habit of latching on to Molly.

"Have you decided what committee you're going to volunteer for?" asked Molly.

"Committee? I wasn't planning on volunteering."

"Oh, no, no, no, dear. You can attend all the welcome meetings you want. But if you're going to come to the monthly morning coffees with the head of school, you can either volunteer or write a check big enough to have a classroom named after you."

"Jack volunteers. He helps with the soccer team. Doesn't that count?"

"Technically, yes. But that doesn't give you much to talk about with this group of women."

"What committee are you on?"

"Me? Volunteer? I don't think so."

"So you write a check?"

She stepped closer, as if letting Andie in on a secret. "Of course I write a check. But I still come to the coffees."

"Why?"

"Because I like coffee."

Andie laughed, though not everyone at Riverside was as quiet about the checks they wrote, as if they weren't already saying enough with their Cartier bracelets stacked seven or eight high à la Kylie Jenner, engagement rings of at least three karats (extra points for a marquis-cut canary diamond), and sparkling stud earrings that resembled something out of the Milky Way. Andie's entire net worth paled in comparison to the "everyday" bauble collection of the average mother at Riverside.

"Come on," said Molly, still playing the poor-mouth game. "It's time for us commoners to pay our respects to the head of school."

They started across the room, but the sudden blare of a fire alarm stopped them in their tracks. All conversation ceased. The head of school moved to the center of the room and addressed the parents in a calm and even tone. "Everyone, please stay where you are." She quickly made a call on her cell. Despite the pulsing alarm, Andie heard her say into her phone, "Judy, is this a drill?"

The response was heard only by the head of school, but in a moment, every woman in the room had an answer. An unmistakable noise—*pop, pop, pop!*—sounded in the hallway.

"That's gunfire!" shouted Andie.

The screams inside the room weren't nearly loud enough to drown out the blaring alarm or the continued *pop, pop, pop* of semiautomatic gunfire outside the rec center. As an FBI agent, Andie knew that activating a fire alarm to create chaos was a tried-and-true modus operandi in school shootings. The screams of children in the hallway confirmed they were caught in the middle of one. Andie hurried to the door, but before she could open it, the next three pops resulted in three bullet-sized dimples in the bullet-resistant steel.

"This way!" the head shouted. "Follow me!"

She led them to the door on the opposite side of the room, pushed it open, and stepped aside to let parents exit first. It was anything but orderly, elbows flying and parents pushing other parents to the floor in a mad scramble to safety.

"Let's go!" shouted Molly.

Andie switched off the lights. "You go! I got the rear."

The gunfire in the hallway was nonstop.

"Are you crazy?

"Just go, Molly! Run!"

Molly did. Andie was alone in the rec center. As an agent, she was familiar with the active-shooter response protocol. Option one: run. Option two: hide. Last resort: fight. As a mother, the protocol went right out the window. The sound of the semiautomatic gunfire—loud, very loud, then more distant—told her that the shooter was headed south. The kindergarten classrooms were at the south end of campus. Righley was in danger. Andie had no choice.

And no weapon.

Andie spotted a fire extinguisher on the wall. With a tap of the metal hammer, the glass case shattered, and she grabbed the extinguisher. Fire-retardant foam was no match for a semiautomatic firearm, but a sudden burst in an ambush might confuse or blind the shooter long enough for her to overtake him. There was no time to lose. Andie pushed open the door, stepped out of the rec center, and came face-to-face with a stampede of screaming children running for their lives. They were running from a masked shooter at the end of the hallway, a man walking with purpose as he squeezed off round after round from a semiautomatic pistol with an extended magazine. A *long* extended magazine.

To Andie, it looked as long as a child's arm.

"Righley!" she shouted instinctively, and she started down the hallway, braving the noise and the chaos, armed with only a fire extinguisher.

CHAPTER 2

Jack was at his desk preparing for a deposition when an emergency text from Riverside popped up on his cell phone: ACTIVE SHOOTER ON CAMPUS.

"Clear my morning calendar!" he said to his assistant as he rushed out the door, cell phone in hand.

The race back to Riverside was like a high-speed rewind of Jack's lovely walk on a perfect morning, a panic-driven sprint through a parent's worst nightmare. He speed-dialed Andie, never breaking stride, but the call didn't go through. Cell-phone service was already overloaded around the school. Traffic was backed up for blocks, horns blaring. Frightened and frustrated parents abandoned their vehicles in the street and joined Jack on foot. Inside of a block from campus the crowd was so large that people could barely move. Obviously, Jack had not been the first to receive the "Active Shooter" alert by text message. Helicopters whirred overhead, some from law enforcement, others bearing the colorful logos of local television news stations. Jack pushed forward, wending his way toward the police perimeter outside the campus gate.

"You can't go any farther," said an officer in uniform.

"But my daughter's in there!" he said, and it sounded as if a dozen other parents behind him had said the same thing in unison.

"No one goes in," the officer said firmly. "We've locked down the premises."

Locked down the premises. Police jargon seemed only to under-score the insanity of the fact that Righley had skipped through these gates holding hands with her parents, and two hours later Jack was at the gates to hell—parents searching for their children, teachers trying to account for their students, children crying and clinging to one another, ambulances and police cars with beacons flashing.

"Out of the way!" a paramedic shouted.

Jack turned to see first responders whisking a victim from school grounds on a gurney. They nearly had to run over a camera crew to get past the scores of television journalists who had descended on the scene. A sickening feeling came over Jack as the paramedics loaded the unconscious student into the back of an ambulance. The boy wasn't even old enough to shave.

Jack tried dialing Andie again, but the call failed. Righley's teacher had given all parents her cell number on the first day of classes, and Jack kicked himself for not having entered it into his contacts. Not that her cell-phone service would have performed any better. He needed information, and he needed to gather it the old-fashioned way. Down the sidewalk, Jack spotted a field reporter speaking into the camera with a live *Action News* update. He moved closer to hear her report in real time.

"The active shooting from inside the building seems to have stopped," she said in an urgent voice. "A scattering of students have fled to safety, but most are still in their classrooms. The entire campus is on lockdown. Information is spotty. Rumors abound. Some say the shooter is dead. Others say he got away. As best we can piece it together, most of the shooting occurred at or near the rec center."

Jack froze. *The rec center.*

The reporter wrapped up her live update, her crewman lowered his camera, and Jack pushed his way forward to get the reporter's attention.

"Excuse me, but did you say there was shooting at the rec center?"

"You can get instant updates if you follow me on Twitter," she said, but Jack wasn't listening as she shared her handle. His gaze drifted toward the chaos on the campus grounds. More gurneys, flanked by first responders, were speeding toward the waiting ambulances. He was certain that he'd heard the reporter right the first time, and Jack's words came like a reflex.

"My wife was in the rec center."

On a dead run, Andie put herself into a base-stealing slide across the tile floor and hunkered down outside Righley's classroom, still armed with the fire extinguisher. Her shoulder was against the steel door, and the entranceway was a recessed alcove, so she couldn't see left or right down the hallway. It was like peering out from inside a tunnel. She knocked on the door so hard it hurt her hand. The teacher didn't open it, and Andie didn't blame her. No matter: if the shooter was going to get to her daughter, he'd have to get past the mother bear.

Ninety. Ninety-one. Ninety-two.

Andie's estimate of rounds fired was certainly low. She hadn't even started counting until she'd bolted from the rec center, and she'd surely missed a few in the noisy sprint down the hallway. Her singular objective had been to reach the kindergarten classroom before the shooter did. Adrenaline had propelled her. Instinct and training had probably kept her alive. Or luck. The blaring alarm, punctuated by screams and gunshots, made it impossible to think straight, let alone hear. It was the classic fog of war. In a school.

Thirty feet. Andie had switched to counting the 12x12 floor tiles. She was trying to gauge the width of the hallway, trying to guess how far the foam might spray—the range of her makeshift weapon. The sight of a spent ammunition round on the floor made her heart skip a beat.

She checked her cell phone. She'd texted her location to every law enforcement officer on her list of contacts, but reception was spotty, and not one had gone through immediately. She was checking the SEND status when her cop instincts kicked in, and she detected a change in the air—something afoot. She put her phone on silent mode and listened more intently. The fire alarm continued to whine, but the shooting seemed to have stopped. It had been at least a minute since anyone had passed in the hallway from either direction.

Then she heard it—even over the piercing alarm. Footfalls in the hallway. Heavy footfalls, like marching boots on the move.

Is he coming back this way?

Andie gripped the fire extinguisher, not sure if the best defense was to spray the shooter with foam or to throw the entire metal canister like a mortar shell.

"Are you hurt?" a man shouted.

Andie recognized the black uniform of Miami-Dade SWAT in the nick of time, sparing him a face full of fire retardant.

"I'm FBI!" she shouted, as she flashed her credentials.

"Come with me!"

"My daughter's in this classroom!"

"My job is to clear this hallway!"

"I'm not leaving my daughter!"

He seemed to comprehend that the children would be safer with a law enforcement officer there, but it was obvious that standing guard with a fire extinguisher wasn't a viable plan. He reached for the electronic passkey that was linked to his belt and stepped closer, to be heard over the blaring alarm.

"Announce yourself before you enter," he said. "Lock the door and barricade it once you're inside. Don't let anyone leave until I come back with the 'all clear.'"

He inserted the passkey. The electronic lock clicked. Andie called out to the teacher at the top of her lungs.

"Ms. Hernandez! It's Righley's mother! I'm coming in!"

"Mommy!" the reply came, and the little voice from inside nearly crushed her.

Andie turned to thank the SWAT officer, but he was already gone. She opened the door and hurried inside a kindergarten classroom under siege.

CHAPTER 3

Jack watched from outside the campus grounds, having positioned himself as close to the entrance gates as possible without crossing the yellow police tape. The hysteria around him was palpable, the desperate pleas of parents blending into a cacophony of English and Spanish. Jack's español wasn't bad—his *abuela* gave him about a C minus—but in all his years in Miami, he'd never heard it spoken with such urgency. He was pretty sure he'd heard the group of Latina moms behind him correctly, but he needed to clarify.

"Excuse me," he said slowly in Spanish, overenunciating in hopes that the woman behind him would take his cue and answer in the same cadence. "Did you say they are evacuating students?"

The woman's emotions were running too high for her to speak slowly, and Jack's loose handle on Cuban American Spanglish was no match for a native Colombian speaker. But he got the gist: police had begun to evacuate students through the riverside access to campus. The implicit good news was not lost on him.

The police must have been confident that the shooting was over.

The crowd outside the gate was growing larger by the minute, and getting from one side of campus to the other wouldn't be easy. But Jack had still heard nothing from Andie, and he needed to find his wife and daughter. He squeezed his way around one person after another, zigzagging his way past uniformed police, scrambling journalists, and tearful parents. It took ten minutes just to get to the end of the block, where he made a left turn toward the river. With each passing square of sidewalk underfoot, he sensed that more and more frantic people were moving with him in the same direction. News of the evacuation appeared to be spreading. Jack hoped it wasn't just another worthless rumor. He'd heard plenty of misinformation already, everything from "It was just a bunch of firecrackers" to "Dozens of children and teachers dead."

Jack was getting close to the campus's rear exit. The attractive coral-rock wall that protected three sides of the ten-acre campus gave way to a purely functional chain-link fence. On the other side of the fence was an open athletic field, and through the gaps in the eight-foot privacy hedge, Jack spotted lines of students, each line led by an adult, leaving the building. They were moving quickly but in orderly fashion, each student with one hand in the air and the other resting on the shoulder of the boy or girl they followed. Jack found an opening in the crowd and sprinted the last hundred yards to the field exit. A police officer was at the gate.

"Have they evacuated kindergarten yet?" Jack asked.

"I really don't know, sir." A line of older students passed, and her attention shifted fully toward crowd control. "Don't crowd the gate, please!"

"Where would they be, if they came out already?"

The officer's focus was entirely on the students. "Keep moving! Don't stop until you get to the high school parking lot."

It wasn't a direct response to Jack, but it answered his question. He ran ahead of the last line of students, passing a second and third line on his way to the parking lot. The children he saw were too old for elementary school but not yet teenagers. Probably middle schoolers—not a one of them too cool to be caught crying under these circumstances. Jack approached a teacher at the head of the line.

"Has kindergarten come out yet?" he asked, alarmed by the level of desperation he detected in his own voice.

"That's Building G," she said. "We're F. They'd be somewhere behind us."

Jack did a quick pivot and ran back in the direction of the school. The lines were coming nonstop. The school was in full-throttle evacuation mode. Kindergarten had to be part of it. Unless the worst thing imaginable had happened.

The thought propelled him to an all-out sprint back to the rear gate.

The officer stopped him. "Nobody goes in, sir."

"I need to find my family."

"Jack!"

He turned at the sound of Andie's voice. He'd run right past her in the crowd. Righley was in her arms. He ran to them and wrapped his arms around them so tightly that he could barely breathe.

"Are you okay?" he asked.

"Yes. We're okay. Her whole class is okay."

Jack couldn't let go.

"Let's walk to your office," said Andie. "I want Righley out of here."

Righley's teacher was fending off questions from every angle. Jack was able to get her attention long enough to let her know that they were leaving with their daughter. Andie was already on her way and carrying Righley with her. Jack caught up and offered to give Andie's arms a rest, but Andie refused to give up her daughter.

"Have you heard anything?" asked Jack.

Andie threw him a look that said, *Not in front of Righley.*

Jack placed his set of earbuds in Righley's ears, opened the Spotify app on his smartphone, and tuned to the playlist labeled Righley's Stuff.

"How about some music, Pumpkin?"

Righley nodded, and the playful sound of her favorite music took some of the fear out of her eyes. Jack and Andie kept walking toward his office. Andie seemed satisfied that they were free to talk.

"You probably know more than I do," said Andie. "I've been locked in a classroom with zero information. My cell didn't even work."

"I've picked up a few things from reporters here and there."

"Have they identified the shooter?"

"If they have, they're not saying. But all the networks are saying that they recovered a semiautomatic pistol. It's registered to a forty-one-year-old man who has kids in the school."

"Are you kidding me? A school parent?"

"Amir something is his name. Begins with a 'K.'"

Andie brought them to a dead halt. "Amir Khoury?"

"Yes, that's it. Do you know him?"

Andie's expression ran cold. "My friend Molly—that's her husband."

Not another word was said until they reached Jack's office.

The Law Office of Jack Swyteck P.A. was on the first floor of a ninety-year-old house near the Miami River, and, more important, blocks away from the Criminal Justice Center. The first time Jack had set foot on the old Dade County pine floors, this old house was home to the Freedom Institute, a ragtag group of talented lawyers who specialized in death penalty work. It was Jack's first job fresh out of law school. Four years of defending the guilty proved to be enough for Jack, so he struck out as a sole practitioner. A decade later, when his mentor passed away and the Institute was on the brink of financial collapse, Jack bought the building. He set up shop downstairs. His old friends from the Institute leased space upstairs. Jack couldn't remember the last time they had actually made a rent payment.

Jack's assistant met them at the door. Bonnie had been with Jack for years. Andie called her "the Roadrunner," so named because she knew only one speed—full throttle—when zipping around the office.

"Is she—" Bonnie started to ask, but Jack gave her a quick shush signal. Righley was sound asleep in her mother's arms.

"Poor angel," said Bonnie.

Andie took her into what had once been the dining room of the old house—now Jack's private office. Jack cleared away the trial notebooks, and Andie laid Righley on the couch.

"She's wiped out," said Jack.

"Better off in her dreams," said Andie.

They stepped out of Jack's office and into the reception area. Bonnie had the television tuned to the local news coverage. Amir Khoury's name and photograph were on every broadcast in America, confirming Jack's info. But Jack was confused on many levels.

"Your friend Molly strikes me as WASPy enough to be a member of the Daughters of the American Revolution," said Jack.

"She is. She fell in love and married a Muslim."

"Where's he from?"

"What do you mean 'where's he from'? Camp al-Qaeda—is that what you're implying?"

"I'm not implying anything," said Jack. "His gun was found on the scene of a school shooting. I'm just asking the question."

"He's from Fort Lauderdale. Whenever anyone raised an eyebrow, as if lily-white Molly and her Muslim husband were the odd couple, she'd say it was destiny: they were born in the same hospital, Broward General. I cannot believe this is happening."

Andie's cell rang, and she checked the incoming number. "It's Schwartz."

Guy Schwartz was the assistant special agent in charge of the FBI's Miami field office. Jack knew him better as that guy who always called right before Andie had to leave in the middle of dinner, cancel her daughter's birthday party, or disappear on assignment for days or even weeks at a time.

Andie stepped to the other side of the reception area to take the call. It lasted only a minute, and she didn't look happy when it ended. Jack had seen Andie's work face before, and he knew that there would no explanation coming. Just an announcement. It was all part of being married to an FBI agent.

"I have to go," she said.

Andie's partner picked her up at Jack's office. He brought a replacement sidearm, since Andie's was still locked in the glove compartment of Jack's SUV, and the SUV was parked on a street so crowded that it was impassable.

Andie knew Molly's address. Their friendship was precisely the reason for the call from the assistant special agent in charge of the FBI's Miami field office.

"Miami-Dade Police have a no-knock warrant for the Khoury residence," ASAC Schwartz had told her. "No knock" meant that law enforcement would literally break down the door.

"Have they executed?"

"About to. And they want you there when they do."

"Why?"

"No one knows how this might go down. You know the Khoury family. You might be useful in de-escalating the situation, if need be."

Andie could have resisted and said she wanted to be with her daughter the moment Righley woke, but Schwartz's directions had left her no option: "Andie, the bureau could have jurisdiction here, if this turns out to be terrorist related."

Andie's partner turned at Santa Maria Street, one of the most prestigious addresses in Coral Gables that was not on the waterfront. Lined with majestic live oaks and some of the best preserved colonial-style and other historic mansions in South Florida, the quiet old side street bisected the golf course of the famous Riviera Country Club, offering residents drop-dead views of beautiful fairways, not to mention a lifetime supply of golf balls, compliments of innumerable club members with a nasty slice. Molly had joked about not being able to cut a donation check to Riverside on top of three tuitions, but it was indeed a joke.

They parked on the street. Andie and her partner simultaneously climbed out of the vehicle. The front door to Molly's house was wide open. Two police officers were standing guard on the porch. A line of yellow police tape demarked the entire front yard as a crime scene.

"Looks like they executed without us," said Andie's partner.

"Wasn't the whole point that they wanted me here?"

A Miami-Dade police officer approached and explained. "We couldn't wait any longer. The suspect's name has gone viral. The media is hyper-focused on the school, but any minute now this entire street is going to be a mob scene. More packed than Halloween night."

Andie took his point. For Andie, Jack, Righley, and about fifty thousand other annual visitors, Santa Maria was the South Florida trick-or-treating destination of choice. Many a law enforcement officer had done Halloween crowd-control duty on Santa Maria.

As if on cue, the first media van pulled up and stopped across the street from the Khoury residence. Seconds later, Molly's midnight-blue Mercedes arrived and stopped in the driveway. Molly and her three children were inside. The front doors swung open, and as Molly stepped out from behind the wheel, Miami-Dade police officers surrounded the vehicle, weapons drawn.

"Freeze!" an officer shouted.

"Don't shoot!" Molly screamed.

Molly's younger children were in the back seat, the older of the two stunned into silence and Molly's eight-year-old daughter crying hysterically. Molly's oldest son was standing beside the open passenger's-side door with his hands in the air. Xavier was a high school senior at Riverside. Last Andie had heard, he was heading to MIT after graduation.

"Mom, it's okay," said Xavier. "I did it."

CHAPTER 4

Not until late afternoon was the neighborhood around the school clear enough for Jack to walk over and retrieve the SUV. On a normal workday he would never leave his office between four and six p.m., but Righley desperately wanted her mother, so he pushed through rush-hour traffic out of downtown Miami.

Their house was on Key Biscayne, a tropical island community that connected by causeway to the entirely different world of high-rise condominiums along Miami's Brickell-area waterfront. Many thought of "the Key" as paradise. Jack felt lucky to live there. Real estate was priced way beyond his means, but years earlier, before he'd even met Andie, he'd cut a steal of a deal on one of the last remaining Mackle homes, basically a 1,200-square-foot shoe box built right after World War II as affordable housing for returning GIs. Those had to be some of the happiest veterans in the history of warfare. On a day like this one, the fact was not lost on Jack that the Key still had one of the lowest crime rates in America.

Jack pulled into their driveway, a crunchy swatch of crushed seashells that was big enough for just one car. Righley unbuckled herself from her car seat and ran to the front door. Andie met her there.

"Mommy!"

It wasn't the usual "Mommy" of pure joy and excitement. Righley's voice had a more distressed quality. Back at the office, Jack had been under the impression that he and Bonnie were doing a pretty good job with Righley in the wake of trauma. The way she was clinging to her mother, however, made Jack realize that this was going to be a long road.

Andie led Righley back to her bedroom to change out of her school uniform. Jack went to the kitchen, opened a beer, and turned on the five o'clock news. All day long, the "breaking news" alerts had been about the shooting at Riverside. The young reporter on the screen was standing about a block away from the school, not far from where Jack had parked the SUV that morning. This time, the breaking news was actually something he didn't already know.

"Nationwide, this is the two-hundred-and-ninety-fifth mass shooting so far this year," said the reporter, "and it is one of the most deadly. Thirteen are confirmed dead. The identity of the victims has been withheld pending notification of next of kin. Now our sources are also telling us that the terrorist organization al-Qaeda has claimed responsibility for the shooting. Law enforcement has yet to confirm that information."

Andie entered the kitchen. Righley was showered and in her room. The nightly routine of trying on every nightgown she owned, deciding which princess to be, had begun.

"A link to terrorism would change the complexion of this investigation," said Jack. "Is the FBI going to take jurisdiction?"

"I can't talk about that, Jack."

The separation of work and family was standard operating procedure for any FBI agent, and that was especially true when the agent was married to a criminal defense lawyer. Still, Jack thought she might make an exception for a criminal matter that directly affected their family.

"What can you tell me?" asked Jack.

"The standard-issue magazine on the semiautomatic pistol used in the shooting is thirteen rounds. The shooter went through four extended magazines, thirty-three rounds each. Over a hundred and thirty rounds fired in less than five minutes."

"That sounds like a lot. Is it, as far as school shootings go?"

"Not as many as Sandy Hook; a few more than Parkland. But keep in mind this shooter was using a handgun, not an assault rifle."

Jack found it interesting that she didn't refer to the shooter by name. "What's happening with Xavier?"

"He's in custody."

"Are they questioning anyone else in the family?"

"Molly's husband isn't even in the country, if that's what you're asking. He's in London on a business trip."

It wasn't like Andie to sling passive-aggressive reminders of "innocent until proven guilty" in Jack's direction. But nothing was normal about this day. Andie seemed in denial, clinging to the irrational hope that by some miracle things had not forever changed between Molly and her. Jack left her alone for a while and went back to Righley's room. Her wet towel was on the floor, as were Mulan, Ariel, and Jasmine. She'd selected her Rapunzel nightgown and was standing in front of the full-length mirror, trying to run a comb through her tangled, wet hair.

"Let me help you, honey."

"No!"

That took him aback. When it came to girl stuff, untangling wet hair was one of the few things Jack did better than Mommy. He even did it *on* Mommy.

"I just want to—"

"Daddy, don't touch me!"

Jack froze. The day had left even Andie, a trained FBI agent, out of sorts. Righley's outburst was so out of character as to be downright worrisome.

Like a godsend, Jack's grandmother appeared in the doorway.

"Hola, mi vida!" Literally, "my life." To Abuela, Righley was as precious as life itself.

Righley rushed across the room and hugged her. Abuela was too old to pick her up, but as she liked to say, the way she was shrinking and Righley was growing, they'd be eye to eye soon enough. Jack was glad she'd agreed to spend the night. Abuela had a way of shrinking any life trauma down to size. It wasn't exactly a gift. Not only had she lost a daughter—preeclampsia claimed Jack's mother way too young—but it had taken Abuela forty years to escape Castro's Cuba to visit the grave.

"You sure you two will be all right while we're gone?" asked Jack.

Riverside had a satellite campus in South Miami for students with special needs. An emergency parents meeting was scheduled there for seven p.m. If not for Abuela, Jack and Andie probably would have skipped.

"Go," said Abuela.

The drive to the Riverside satellite was thirty minutes. Jack and Andie arrived to a packed gymnasium. This meeting was only for families with children who were neither victims nor eyewitnesses to the carnage; individual counseling sessions were underway at a separate facility for those more directly affected. Still, it was a solemn crowd, easily more than three hundred parents. Jack found two of the last open seats in the third row of bleachers. He and Andie were squeezing into place, bumping shoulders with each other and the parents beside them, when the head of school stepped up to the microphone.

"Good evening. I'm Cynthia Mickelson, and I want to thank all of you for coming tonight."

The first order of business was an ecumenical prayer. The bleachers rumbled as the crowd rose. Leading the convocation were a minister, a priest, and a rabbi. No imam, it occurred to Jack as the prayer ended.

"Amen," the crowd said in unison.

Mickelson waited for all to be seated and then started with a series of announcements. School would be closed for at least a week. Counselors were available to students and parents upon request. Support animals would be allowed in classrooms when classes resumed.

"Also," she continued, "I received a call from the Florida attorney general this afternoon. I have his word that the state will pay all expenses for the funerals of the victims."

"How many are there?" a man shouted. He was a few rows behind Jack.

"Excuse me?" asked Mickelson.

The man rose. "How many teachers and students have we lost? No one will give us a straight answer."

The head measured her words. "The official count has not yet been released. As soon as we have that information, we will post it on the school website."

Another man rose. "It's at least one more than it had to be."

Mickelson hesitated, confused. "I don't understand."

"My middle son, David, was caught in the hallway when this lunatic opened fire. He and his friend Lucas Horne tried to hide in the bathroom. But the bathroom door was locked. My son was lucky. Lucas is dead. So I want know: Why was that bathroom door locked?"

"The bathrooms in our middle school and high school buildings are locked. Students must ask their teacher for permission to use the bathroom, and if permission is granted, they are given a key."

"Why is that?"

"That was a decision we implemented at the beginning of this school year. As a preventive measure."

"Preventative of *what*?"

"Last semester we had to expel two eighth-grade students for vaping in the bathroom."

"So you *locked* the bathrooms? The only place my son and his friend had to hide was the bathroom, and you locked it?"

The pain in his voice drew a rumbling from the crowd. The head of school went into damage-control mode.

"I am so truly sorry, for your son, and for the Horne family. I should point out, however, that if your son was an eyewitness to this unfortunate turn of events, your entire family should be at the other meeting."

"No," he said firmly. "These families here, whose kids will be going back to school in a week with their puppies and kittens for support, need to know the truth. They need to know some of us will be paying the price forever because of *your* stupidity."

"I completely understand your anger."

"No!" he said, his voice booming loud enough to fill the gymnasium. "You *don't* understand. But if you *think* you do, then, by God, you had best not get anywhere near Lucas Horne's father."

He lowered himself into his seat, emotionally spent. His wife slid her arm around his shoulder, as if to say he'd done the right thing.

Another man rose in the next bleacher section. "While we're on the subject of stupidity: Don't we have background checks for families before they are accepted to this academy?"

Mickelson paused, thinking through her response. "As everyone in this gymnasium knows well, the application process at Riverside is highly selective and very comprehensive. And of course we interview all students and their parents."

"What if people lie?" the man asked.

"Lie about what?"

"About who they are?"

"I don't think that's the issue here," said Mickelson.

"I do. Let's say only the mother comes in for the interview and not the father. How much do you really know about that family?"

Jack and Andie exchanged anxious glances. The man might

as well have asked, *How'd you let Molly's Muslim husband slip through?*

"I see where you're going with this," said Mickelson. "And I want to address this as fully and as directly as I can. We all want answers."

"You bet we do."

"Hold on," said Mickelson. "Just because someone called the media to claim responsibility on behalf of al-Qaeda doesn't mean that al-Qaeda was necessarily behind this. And just because the shooter—alleged shooter—has a Muslim father doesn't mean that this shooting had anything to do with radical Islam."

"That's all very nice and politically correct, Mrs. Mickelson. But do you expect us to believe it?"

"I expect everyone in this room to let law enforcement do its job without feeding the rumor mill."

"It's not a rumor. My brother is a cop at Miami-Dade. He says the FBI's Joint Terrorism Task Force is already involved. Why would the FBI's terrorism task force be involved if al-Qaeda's claim of responsibility was not credible?"

"I don't know how to answer that question," said Mickelson.

His gaze swept the bleachers. "Isn't one of our parents an FBI agent? Maybe she can answer it."

Heads turned, and dozens of parents were suddenly looking in Jack and Andie's direction.

Mickelson seemed to sense Andie's discomfort even from thirty feet away. "I don't think it's fair to put Agent Henning on the spot like that. That's not the point of this meeting."

"Maybe we should let her speak for herself," the man said. "It's a simple question. Would the Joint Terrorism Task Force get involved if al-Qaeda had nothing to do with this?"

The crowd fell silent, which sent a clear message. Andie was suddenly the official spokesperson for the FBI. She rose slowly.

Jack heard whispering all around them, which made him wish all the more that they had never come.

Who's she?

Absentee mom. Hardly ever at the school.

I think she's friends with that Muslim boy's mother.

"I can't comment on that," said Andie. She sat down and looked at Jack, but he didn't have to tell her what she already knew.

This crowd had all the confirmation it needed.

CHAPTER 5

Jack and Andie were the last to leave the school parking lot. Not that they weren't eager to get home. After being singled out as the "FBI mom," Andie needed to find a private place and call her ASAC.

"How'd it go?" Jack asked as she climbed into the passenger seat.

"You don't want to know, and I can't tell you."

The drive from the mainland to Key Biscayne was mostly in silence. Crossing the causeway, Andie's profile was a pensive silhouette against the backdrop of city lights in the distance. They were home a little after nine o'clock. Righley was sound asleep in her room. Abuela was nearby in her favorite rocking chair, literally snoring. Andie wanted their little girl in their bed, so she gently picked her up and carried her down the hallway.

Jack heard a car pull up outside the house and then a timid knock on the front door. He went to the living room and opened it.

"May I come in, please?" asked the woman.

Although Jack had met Molly before, it took him a moment to recognize her as the woman standing on his front porch. She was normally a stylish dresser, but the cashmere wrap she wore was better suited for January, and there was nothing stylish about the broad-brimmed hat that left her face in the shadows and the sunglasses so dark that not even eighties heartthrob Corey Hart would have worn them at night.

"It's me, Molly," she said as she removed her sunglasses.

Without them, she looked broken, desperate. Jack couldn't help but feel for her.

"Who is it, Jack?" asked Andie, entering the living room.

Molly went straight to Andie, but it seemed that Molly's need for a hug was not exactly reciprocal. Just a few hours earlier, Andie had been quick to show her support for her girlfriend, at least in conversation with Jack. Maybe it was the phone call with her ASAC, or maybe a gymnasium full of angry parents had unlocked the voices of child victims in her head, but something had changed since the school meeting. Psychologically speaking, it seemed that Andie had already moved from denial to anger.

"Molly, I know you must have a lot to talk about," said Andie. "But right now I just want to lie down with my daughter and thank God she's still here."

"I won't be long."

"I'll let you two talk in private," said Jack.

"No," said Molly. "I'd like you to be part of this, if you would, Jack."

Jack took a seat with Andie on the couch. Molly sat in the club chair, facing them.

"I heard about the meeting at the school," said Molly. "I didn't go, of course. I've been at the jail all night, trying to speak to Xavier."

"Trying?" asked Jack. "Are the police not allowing it?"

"It's a different problem," said Molly. "Xavier refuses any visitors."

"You're his mother," said Andie. "If you want to see him, you have the right."

"I'm told that's not the case. He's eighteen. Since he's no longer a minor, the police are telling me that his parents have no right to visit him and no ability to force him to see us."

"When did he turn eighteen?" asked Jack.

Molly hesitated, then answered in a weak voice. "Today."

The gravity of a high school student embarking on a shooting spree on his eighteenth birthday sent chills through the room.

Molly continued. "I suppose Xavier waited until he was eighteen so that his parents would have no say over what happens to him after the . . ." She seemed unable to even say the word.

"After his arrest," Jack offered.

"Yes," said Molly. "After his arrest."

"Has anyone told you what was said at tonight's meeting?" asked Andie.

"Not directly. But I see the chatter on social media. Not everyone at the school has deleted me from their list of friends yet. They might be surprised to know that I agree with much of what is being said."

"Like what?" asked Andie.

"Al-Qaeda, for one. I'm sure our head of school means well by telling parents not to jump to conclusions about a connection to Islamic terrorism. But al-Qaeda claimed responsibility."

"And you believe that the claim is real?" asked Jack.

"Yes. Someone must have radicalized Xavier to do something as horrible as this. Contrary to what people might say on social media, my son was not 'born to kill.'"

"Molly, if I could give you any advice, it would be this," said Jack. "Don't go on social media. Stay off the Internet."

"I know. It's horrible what people will say. The whole world wants my son executed so he can start burning in hell as soon as possible."

"No one said that at tonight's meeting," said Jack.

"They're definitely saying it online. I can't explain or excuse what Xavier did, but a high school boy who is the victim of brainwashing should not be executed."

"It will be up to the state attorney to decide if she'll seek the death penalty," said Jack.

"Can he be executed?" asked Molly. "Legally, I mean. Can a boy who's still in high school get the death penalty?"

Jack took no joy in being the one to tell her, but soon enough Molly would learn what a difference a day makes. "The Supreme Court has held that the death penalty is unconstitutional under the Eighth Amendment as 'cruel and unusual punishment' for anyone under the age of eighteen. Xavier made the cutoff by one day."

Molly closed her eyes and opened them slowly, absorbing the blow. "So that's the answer? If the state attorney chooses to seek the death penalty, there is no mercy?"

Jack understood the arguments on both sides: What mercy had Xavier shown his victims? "If he's found guilty, there will be a second trial on the issue of sentencing. So it's up to the jury to decide if he gets death or life in prison. Xavier's youth and im-pressionability would be relevant mitigating circumstances that jurors can consider."

"Thank you for that," she said. "I put a lot of stock in what you say. I understand you've done a lot of death penalty work."

"I have," said Jack.

"Some would say too much," added Andie.

"I googled you," said Molly. "You're a very courageous man. You've taken some very tough cases. For some pretty notorious clients."

"Most of those were a long time ago," said Jack.

"Before we were married," said Andie.

Molly paused, and Jack sensed she was building up the nerve to ask him something. Finally, she spoke.

"Could you be Xavier's lawyer?"

Andie answered for him. "No."

"We would pay you, of course."

"Molly, he can't," Andie said firmly.

"I'm sorry," said Molly. "I shouldn't have asked."

"There's nothing wrong with asking," said Jack.

"I wish you would at least think about it. I don't know how I'm going to find a good lawyer."

"You don't have to worry about that," said Jack. "Your son is an adult, even if it is just by one day, and he has no job. It makes no difference that his parents have enough money to afford a private attorney. Your son is indigent for purposes of court-appointed counsel and will be represented by the Public Defender's Office."

"But I don't want him to have a public defender," said Molly.

"The public defender is well qualified to make all of the arguments that need to be made at Xavier's sentencing hearing to avoid the death penalty."

"No, he's not. I spoke to him. He called me earlier today because Xavier wouldn't talk to him and he thought I might have some insight on how to break through. Frankly, I don't trust him."

"Don't trust him in what way?" asked Jack.

"It goes back to what I said before. Xavier wasn't born a murderer. I do believe he was radicalized. But this is key: he was *not* radicalized *at home*."

"Is someone saying that he was?" asked Jack.

"Not yet. But the public defender is already heading in that direction."

"How do you know?"

"It was clear from the questions he asked me. He's going to tell the same old story that lawyers always tell. His client was the victim of his upbringing. The parents are horrible people. How could a boy who was raised in this household grow up to be *anything but* a mass murderer?"

Jack had made similar arguments—the dysfunctional family, physically and emotionally abusive parents—many times on behalf of death row inmates. "The public defender can't make those arguments if they're not true."

"Baloney. My husband is a Muslim. He's a sitting duck for the bogus argument that he radicalized Xavier. It's not fair to Amir, who loves this country as much as any other American. And it's not fair to Xavier's brother and sister, who will have to live with this stigma for the rest of their lives."

"Everything you're saying is valid," said Jack. "But there isn't much you or I can do. It's up to Xavier to choose his own lawyer. He's eighteen."

"What if he called you? Maybe I can get through to him and give him your number. Would you talk to him?"

Jack cut another glance at Andie, who even in her silence was making her position clear.

"I don't know," said Jack.

"I don't expect anyone to prove my son's innocence. That's impossible. All I'm asking is to keep him off death row. And do it without labeling my entire family as Islamic-extremist sympathizers. Is that asking too much?"

Jack considered it. Molly was beyond desperate. "I'm not saying I'll take his case. But if he calls me, I might take the call."

"Thank you," she said. "Thank you so very much."

Molly rose. She and Andie shared a hug more awkward than the first one. Jack showed her to the door. Molly thanked him again, and Jack closed the door. Andie had more to say.

"I don't want you getting involved in this case, Jack."

"I'm not getting involved."

"Xavier is going to call you. How is that not getting involved?"

"I told her I *might* take the call."

"Before you do, I suggest you call Nate Abrams."

Nate was a respected lawyer in town and one of the dads at Riverside Jack had become friendly with. "Why?" asked Jack.

"It was bad enough to get chewed out by my ASAC after the parent meeting," said Andie. "But the reason that call took so long is that he gave me some information that isn't public yet. The names of the victims."

Andie paused, and Jack gave her a moment.

"Lindsey Abrams was shot in the back running from her class-room," said Andie. "She's fighting for her life at Jackson Memorial."

"That's horrible. I'm sorry to hear that."

"Tell it to Nate. Then ask him how he'd feel about your defending the monster who shot her."

It was like a slap to the face. Jack watched as Andie turned and headed toward the bedroom to sleep with Righley.

CHAPTER 6

Jack was in the Richard E. Gerstein Justice Building early the next morning. His client was a nineteen-year-old first-time offender who "forgot" that the recreational marijuana she'd bought legally in Illinois wasn't legal in Florida. It took Jack less than five minutes to get the assistant state attorney to agree to dismissal of the charges upon completion of a pretrial intervention program. Jack had plenty of other work to do back at the office, but he made a stop on the first floor, where it wasn't just the usual courthouse buzz.

"Standing room only," the deputy at the door told him.

Felony arraignments started every weekday at nine a.m. in Courtroom 1-5. The morning docket included everyone in Miami-Dade County who'd been arrested in the previous twenty-four hours on a felony charge. The routine played out in a spacious old room with high ceilings and a long mahogany rail that separated the public seating from the business end of the justice system. A junior assistant state attorney was seated at the government's table in front of the empty jury box, working his way through the stack of files, one at a time, as each case was called. Jack watched from the back of the courtroom, standing, not a seat to be had. The draw was not the usual parade of accused armed robbers, drunk drivers, and others proclaiming their innocence. The crowd had come to see Xavier Khoury. Jack was one of many Riverside parents and supporters in attendance.

"Next case," said Judge Feinstein. He was moving quickly. They were at number nine. Feinstein was the oldest judge on the criminal circuit. Some said he no longer had the stamina for lengthy trials, but he still seemed to enjoy the frenetic pace of arraignments.

"Case number seventeen oh-three oh-one," announced the bailiff. "State of Florida versus Xavier Khoury."

The side door opened, and a pair of deputies brought Xavier into the courtroom. The atmosphere was suddenly charged, as a packed gallery and the rest of the world, via television, got its first look at the shooter in his orange prison jumpsuit and shackles, flanked by muscle-bound guards. Reporters in the designated media section took notes, furiously recording their front-row impressions, as the accused shuffled across the courtroom with head down. The guards seated him alone in the empty jury box, almost separate from the proceeding, as if to keep the prisoner from continuing his rampage and lashing out at the public. Jack had seen that done before, on occasion, with particularly dangerous defendants.

"Mitchell Karr for the defendant," said Xavier's court-appointed lawyer, announcing his appearance.

The junior prosecutor who had handled the first ten arraignments stepped aside and was replaced by the chief prosecutor of the homicide division. "Abe Beckham for the state of Florida."

Jack had squared off against Beckham in several capital cases. The state attorney was bringing in the big gun for *State v. Khoury*.

"Good morning, everyone," said Judge Feinstein. "Mr. Beckham, may I have the date and time of Mr. Khoury's arrest?"

"Yesterday at approximately two twenty p.m."

The judge swiveled his high-back chair toward the jury box to address the defendant more directly. "Mr. Khoury, the purpose of this proceeding is, first of all, to advise you of certain rights that you have and to inform you of the charges made against you under Florida law. Do you understand?"

Xavier was staring at the floor, motionless.

"Your Honor, the defendant stands mute," his lawyer said.

Judge Feinstein recited the Miranda warnings, though it hardly seemed necessary to remind Xavier of his "right to remain silent."

"Mr. Khoury, you have been charged with thirteen counts of murder in the first degree," the judge continued. "As of this initial hearing, those charges are supported by affidavit of the Miami-Dade Police Department. A grand jury will be convened in accordance with Florida law. If the grand jury returns a true bill, your conviction on these charges may be punishable by death. Do you understand?"

No response from the accused. "The defendant stands mute," his lawyer answered.

"Count one charges that without justification Xavier Khoury did cause the death of Kaleb Greene, a first degree felony. Count Two charges that—"

"Your Honor, my client is aware of the charges," said Karr. "We will waive formal reading."

A smart move from the defense standpoint. Tensions were high enough in the courtroom without reading aloud thirteen counts of homicide in the first degree.

"Mr. Khoury, how do you plead?"

His lawyer interjected. "Judge, I have a matter to take up with the court in regard to the defendant's plea."

"Go ahead, Counsel."

"On my client's behalf, we reached out to the state attorney. Mr. Khoury offered to plead guilty to thirteen counts of homicide and seven additional counts of attempted murder—*twenty* life sentences to be served consecutively without possibility of parole—if the government will waive the death penalty. The state attorney has refused that offer. He insists on taking this case to the grand jury, proceeding to trial, and seeking the death penalty."

"Which is the state attorney's job," said the judge.

As a defense lawyer, Jack could only cringe. If the public defender had been hoping that a public announcement might make Judge Feinstein browbeat the prosecution into accepting the proposed plea deal, Karr had badly misread the tea leaves.

"Mr. Khoury, how do you plead?" asked the judge.

The accused didn't look up, didn't move, and didn't say a word.

"The court will enter a plea of not guilty," said the judge, and then his gaze swung to the other side of the courtroom. "Since this is a first-degree murder case, there is no bail. Does the defense have any argument to the contrary?"

"Not at this time," said Karr.

"The defendant shall be remanded to custody. Anything else?"

The state attorney brought up a few "housekeeping matters," as judges called them, but Jack had seen enough. He slipped out the rear exit, continued through the courthouse lobby, and left the building through the main entrance doors. At the bottom of the concrete steps, he stopped, turned, and noticed that another lawyer from the PD's Office, Sheila Kinkaid, had followed him out.

"Buy you a coffee, Swyteck?"

Jack held Sheila in high regard—much higher than his regard for Xavier's lawyer. He was happy to share a coffee with her. There was an old man who sold Cuban *café* out of the back of his truck right outside the courthouse. Sheila ordered two espressos.

"What did you think of round one, Jack?"

"You mean announcing to the world that your client is guilty before he even gets the chance to plead not guilty?"

"The Broward PD did the same thing in the Nikolas Cruz case after the Parkland shooting," said Sheila.

"I didn't agree with it then, either. For one, it all but takes an insanity defense off the table. Anyone who is rational enough to offer a guilty plea in order to save his own life is rational enough to know the difference between right and wrong."

"Good point," she said.

"I can rattle off about ninety-nine other ones, if you have the time."

"No need," said Sheila. "I agree with you. But it wasn't my decision."

"You should be handling this case, Sheila. Not Mitchell Karr."

"Makes no difference in the long run. The PD's Office will be withdrawing as counsel tomorrow."

"On what grounds?"

"Xavier is far from indigent. Independently wealthy, you might say."

The vendor poured two steaming espressos into little poly-paper cups and placed them on the counter at the back of the truck. Jack paid before Sheila could.

"I spoke to his mother last night," said Jack. "She didn't mention anything about Xavier having money."

"She didn't know. We didn't know, either, until we spoke to Xavier's father. Amir Khoury established trusts for each of his three children at birth. The two boys get two hundred grand a year starting on their eighteenth birthday. Their daughter gets hers in one lump sum when she marries."

Jack couldn't even imagine Andie's reaction to a plan like that for Righley. "I'm guessing that's why Amir never told his wife."

"Probably. The bottom line is that taxpayers will not be paying for Xavier's lawyer. He will. Which means he has to find a private attorney."

Jack was on to her, smiling and wagging a finger. "No, no, Sheila. I see where this is headed. Molly Khoury asked me the same thing last night."

"Jack, this is a capital case. Judge Feinstein won't be happy if the PD's Office withdraws without lining up substitute counsel. We want a seamless transition: we're out; you're in."

"I can't."

"Actually, you're one of the few private attorneys in this town who *can*."

"There are others."

"Yes," said Sheila. "But the last thing your school community needs is a grandstanding criminal defense lawyer who parlays this case into his ticket to TV talking-head stardom."

He took her point. Jack had defended one innocent client while working for the Freedom Institute. Out of respect for the families of victims, he never went on television proclaiming the innocence of any other client. "Some lawyers seem to forget that the Constitution guarantees a right to counsel, not to a publicity agent."

"Amen to that."

"But here's the problem," said Jack. "Both Righley and Andie were at the school when the shooting happened."

"So, if they had not been there, you *would* take the case. Is that what you're saying?"

Jack added a little sugar to his espresso. "I don't know."

"Will Righley be a witness for the prosecution?"

"No."

"Will Andie?"

"No."

"Then it's not that you *can't* take the case. You choose not to."

"What are you getting at, Sheila?"

"Look, if I dodged every capital case that made my husband squirm, I might as well hang it up and become an accountant. I know you, Swyteck. You'd make a lousy accountant." She tossed back her espresso and then leveled her most serious gaze at him. "Tell me you'll think about it."

Jack glanced back at the courthouse. Camera crews were at the top of the steps outside the main entrance, and local television reporters were grabbing any available lawyer to comment on the case. There was no shortage of "experts" willing to talk, talk, talk about something that was way outside their sphere of knowledge.

Jack downed his espresso and then noticed the man and woman

getting into their car across the street. The sticker on the bumper read MY CHILD IS AN HONOR STUDENT AT RIVERSIDE DAY SCHOOL.

Was, thought Jack. *Was an honor student.*

"I'm sorry, Sheila," he said, as he crushed the little paper cup into a ball, "I really can't see myself making any other choice than the one Andie and I have already made."

He pitched the ball into the trash basket, nothing but net.

CHAPTER 7

Jack drove straight from the courthouse to UM Jackson Memorial Hospital.

Jackson was Miami's premier public hospital, which meant that in addition to its stellar reputation for groundbreaking research in everything from cancer to spinal injury, its world-class emergency room was the city's go-to trauma center for gunshot wounds. Located just across the river from the Criminal Justice Center, it wasn't at all unusual for the victims of violent crime to land within walking distance of the initial court appearance for the man who'd put them in the hospital. If they could still walk.

"I'm here to see Lindsey Abrams," Jack told the receptionist.

Jack's public-defender friend Sheila had said nothing that made him want to take Xavier's case. Andie's angry reaction—*Ask Nate Abrams how he would feel if you defended this monster*—wasn't the reason Jack went to the hospital. He just felt the need to see his friend Nate.

"She's a minor in the intensive care unit. Are you on the visitation list?"

"I just spoke to her father on the telephone. They're expecting me."

The receptionist called upstairs, checked out the story, and printed out a "visitor" badge that Jack stuck to his lapel. A painfully slow elevator ride took him to the fifth floor. Polished tile floors glistened beneath bright fluorescent lighting. The hallway led to a set of locked doors marked INTENSIVE CARE UNIT. Jack identified himself over the intercom, and a nurse's response crackled over the speaker.

"Room Six," she said, "but only one more visitor can come in now. Maximum of three at a time."

Jack took that to mean that both parents were at their daughter's bedside, which only added to the heartbreak. "I'm alone," said Jack.

The door opened automatically, and Jack entered to the steady sound of beeping patient monitors. In the center of the ICU was the nurses' station, an open island of charts and records surrounded on all sides by a wide corridor. Lining the outer perimeter were the glass-walled rooms for patients, most of whom were in open view. The unit appeared to be full, but in some rooms the privacy curtains were drawn, so it was hard to know. A busy nurse passed with a tray of medications. As Jack approached Room 6, he noticed several visitors outside adjacent rooms wearing hats or T-shirts emblazoned with the Falcon logo—the school mascot for Riverside. The Abramses were not the only Riverside family with a child in the Jackson Memorial ICU.

"Thanks for coming," said Nate.

Jack and Nate were about the same age, but the stress of the past twenty-four hours had already aged him. The privacy curtain prevented Jack from seeing inside Room 6. It made his chest tighten to think of Nate's wife in there with a critically wounded daughter.

"Let's take a walk over to the lounge," said Nate.

Jack followed him around to the other side of the unit, where there was a small room for visitors to catch a moment alone when needed. Nate bought two bottled waters from the vending machine, and they sat across from each other at a small table.

Nate glanced at the calendar on the wall. "Exactly two weeks from today is Lindsey's fourteenth birthday."

It was a painful place to start. Jack wasn't sure what to say, so he simply allowed Nate to continue.

"They tell me Lindsey was running toward the stairwell when she was shot. She had no pulse by the time paramedics finally got to her. They were able to restart the heart with a defibrillator. But . . . uhm . . ."

"You don't have to tell me, unless you want to," said Jack.

Nate looked past Jack, numbness and disbelief leading his line of sight off to somewhere in the middle distance. "I spoke with three different neurologists this morning. Cardiologist came in after that. A pulmonologist is keeping an eye on her to see if she needs any assistance in breathing. Just before you got here, we met a gastro specialist about inserting a feeding tube, if it comes to that. A physical therapist is scheduled to come by twice a day to move her limbs."

Jack said, "They have excellent doctors here."

"Yes, they do," said Nate, and then he took a deep breath. "But not a single one of them can tell us if Lindsey will ever regain consciousness."

"I'm very sorry to hear that," said Jack.

"They say if she lives, she'll be paralyzed from the chest down."

Silence hung between them. Jack suddenly was aware of the hum of fluorescent lights above them. He had no idea how to help. Nate did him the favor of changing the subject. Slightly.

"How did it go in court this morning?" Nate asked.

Jack could have run with it, but he didn't. "A lot of Riverside families showed up."

"Is the state attorney seeking the death penalty?"

"No formal announcement yet. But it's clear enough that he will."

"Such a mistake," said Nate.

Jack wasn't sure he'd heard right. "A mistake?"

"It is in my mind," said Nate.

"Why do you say that?"

Nate breathed in and out. "I remember reading an op-ed that one of the parents wrote in the *Sun-Sentinel* after the Parkland shooting. Of course I never dreamed I'd be in this situation. Anyway, I remember feeling sorry for the man. He'd lost his son. But I didn't agree with what he wrote. Until now."

"What did he write?"

"He started with the fact that in Florida, the average time from arrest to trial in a death penalty case is . . . I forget how many years he said."

"Four years," said Jack, something he knew.

"Right. So this dad pointed out that there would be countless hearings along the way. Worse, the families of all seventeen victims, and every child in that school who witnessed the shooting, would have to relive the experience as witnesses in videotaped depositions and then again at the trial. In the Parkland shooting, the lawyers had to postpone depositions of some of the students because parents were seriously concerned that their child would commit suicide if forced to relive that experience in deposition or at trial."

"So his point was—"

"His point was that the state attorney should accept the shooter's guilty plea and let the court sentence him to seventeen consecutive life sentences with no chance of parole."

"Is that what you think should happen here?"

"I do. And that's why you should take the case."

Jack was dumbstruck. "How did you know I'd even been asked?"

"All of us parents are glued to social media. I saw the update ten minutes before you called. Isn't that what you came here to talk about?"

Jack didn't know who had twisted his words and put it out there. Sheila? Molly? All that mattered was that it was *out there*.

"Please, get involved, Jack," said Nate. "I trust you to convince the state attorney to accept a guilty plea and a sentence of twenty consecutive life sentences without parole. Don't force my daughter and dozens of other traumatized kids to relive this nightmare for the next four years, just so that the state attorney can someday run for governor as the 'pro-death-penalty, tough-on-crime' candidate."

Jack wasn't sure if the allusion had been intentional, but Jack's father had run on that platform twice—and won. "I take your point and can see this in a different light."

"You'll do it?"

Jack paused. "I need to talk to Andie."

Jack met Andie for lunch. He ordered a Cuban sandwich *sin mostaza*, as most of the so-called Cuban joints in Miami didn't seem to know that a *real* Cuban didn't have mustard on it. Andie ordered only an iced tea, having lost her appetite.

Andie was unlike any woman Jack had ever known, and not just because she worked undercover for the FBI. Jack loved that she wasn't afraid to cave dive in Florida's aquifer, that in her training at the FBI Academy she'd nailed a perfect score on one of the toughest shooting ranges in the world, that as a teenager she'd been a Junior Olympic mogul skier from her home state of Washington—something Jack hadn't even known about her until she'd rolled him out of bed one hot August morning and said, "Let's go skiing in Argentina." He loved the green eyes she got from her Anglo father and the raven-black hair from her Native American mother, a mix that made for such exotic beauty.

He hated when she tried to manage his career. But the case of Xavier Khoury was different.

"This one's outside the agreement," said Andie.

The "agreement" was for the sake of their relationship: Jack didn't question her FBI assignments; Andie didn't judge his clients.

"I get it," said Jack. "It affects Righley."

Andie drank from her iced tea. "I'm not going to tell you what to do, Jack. No, let me restate that: if anyone but Nate Abrams had asked, I *would* tell you what to do. But . . ."

He knew Andie would never approve. The question was whether he could live with her mere acquiescence.

"But there's one condition," she said.

"Okay. What?"

"I want to know why that boy wanted to kill my daughter. I want to know what he thought it would accomplish. I want you to ask him. And I don't want to hear any bullshit from you about the attorney-client privilege. You're going to tell me what he says."

Jack didn't say yes. He didn't say no. He wasn't sure what he was going to say—to Andie or to Nate Abrams.

CHAPTER 8

Jack needed some therapy. He drove to Cy's Place in Coconut Grove and took a seat on a stool at the U-shaped bar.

"You look like you could use a Cy Bender," said Theo, offering up his version of a shot-and-beer: craft-brewed IPA paired with 150-proof whiskey.

"Just a draft," said Jack. "No disrespect to Uncle Cy."

The "Cy" in Cy's Place was Theo's great-uncle Cyrus Knight, a saxophonist who'd in younger days—nights, actually—played in Miami's Overtown Village, once known as Little Harlem. It seemed fitting to put his name on the club, the second bar Theo had purchased with the settlement money from the state of Florida—Theo's "compensation" for spending four years on death row for a murder he didn't commit. Cy's vibe and occasional riff inspired the place, drawing weekend crowds from all over South Florida. Creaky wood floors, redbrick walls, and high ceilings were the perfect bones for a jazz club. Art nouveau chandeliers cast just the right mood lighting after dark. It had been Theo's goal to "do something right." He'd nailed it.

Theo placed the draft in front of him. "Funny thing about you, Jack. Whenever there's something on your mind, it's all over your face. Talk to me."

Theo was Jack's best friend, bartender, therapist, confidant, and sometime investigator. He was also a former client, a one-time gangbanger who easily could have ended up dead on the streets of Overtown or Liberty City. Instead, he landed on death row for a murder he didn't commit. Theo was the one innocent client Jack had represented during his stint at the Freedom Institute.

And he was one damn good listener.

Jack unloaded—the plea from Molly, the "ask" from the public defender—and then Nate Abrams, speaking on behalf of his daughter and every other child who might have to relive the nightmare by testifying as a witness in deposition, at trial, and again at the sentencing hearing.

"Nate's the only one who has me thinking," said Jack.

Theo leaned onto the bar top, as if to level with his friend. "Maybe I can get you off the fence. No extra charge."

"Extra?" said Jack. "You've never let me pay for anything here."

It was Theo's way of paying back the young lawyer who'd never stopped believing in him and never stopped fighting to get him off death row—for no pay.

"Figure of speech," said Theo. "Let me tell you this story."

"Only if I haven't heard it before."

"Guaranteed," said Theo. "I used to think my landlord was the most generous man in Miami. When my bar shut down because of the coronavirus, I couldn't pay my staff *and* pay the rent. He said no problem. We'll waive the rent. You don't even have to pay it back."

"That sounds too nice to be true."

"No shit. Here's where it gets interesting. Later on, his partner comes by to check on the place. I thanked him personally. 'God bless you, man,' was all I could say. 'You kept me in business.' He looked at me like I had three heads. That's when I found out the truth."

"Which was?"

"Molly Khoury paid my rent. She told the landlord not to tell me."

"Why would Molly pay your rent?"

"That's what I asked myself. Then I remembered: I coached her son. Xavier was on my eighth-grade-boys basketball team when I ran the program over at the Boys and Girls Club. He wasn't very good. Terrible, actually. But he tried hard, and got nothing in the way of sports from his old man, so I used to run extra drills with him and a couple other kids after practice. I guess that meant a lot to Molly. So when every bar and restaurant around me was boarding up from the virus, I wasn't the one lucky tenant who had a saint for a landlord. Molly paid my rent. It was her way of saying 'Thanks, Coach. Thanks for being the only man who ever cared enough to get my son off the couch.'"

"Wow," said Jack. "She must know we're friends, right?"

"Yeah, we ran into each other at Righley's birthday party. She says, 'Theo, what're you doin' here?' I say, 'I'm Righley's godfather. What're *you* doin' here?'"

"But she didn't mention anything about paying your rent when she asked me to be Xavier's lawyer."

"That's because she didn't help me so that she could call in a favor someday."

"Rare," said Jack.

"Very," said Theo. "So, let me put in my two cents. No one's asking you to put a school shooter back on the street. Nate sure isn't. It doesn't sound like Molly is, either. She's just a mom trying to figure out how to pull her life back together. She needs this to end. We both know that a death sentence is far from 'finality' or 'closure' or whatever you want to call it. It means another fifteen years of appeals and stays of execution. Life in prison without parole: *that's* finality. If you can get that, Molly can put this behind her for herself and for her other two kids. It's step one to getting her life back."

Jack considered Theo's words, and his thoughts kept tumbling back to the way Molly had comported herself in his living room. "She could have easily played that card—paying your rent—when she came to see Andie and me and asked me to defend her son. She didn't."

"I respect that," said Theo.

Jack watched the little bubbles rise up from the bottom of his beer glass and explode at the surface. "So do I."

"Maybe you should go talk to her."

Jack nodded. "Maybe *we* should."

Jack braced his hands against the dashboard as Theo maneuvered around a slow-moving camper with Quebec license plates. "Dude, this is Miami, not Daytona, so there's no need to drive five hundred miles an hour."

"I don't think the Daytona Five Hundred means they actually go five—"

"Just slow down, will you?"

Theo grumbled something to the effect of "old fart" as they joined the normal traffic flow.

The meeting was at the Khoury residence on Santa Maria Street. Law enforcement had finished the execution of the search warrant and allowed the family to move back in that morning. Lamps were aglow inside, situation normal, just like any other house on the street. But the porchlight was out. In the darkness, Jack stepped on a stray strip of yellow police tape that the police had left behind. Walking up the driveway, he felt like the hapless teacher who lights up the laughter by entering a classroom with a trail of toilet paper stuck to his shoe. He finally shook the tape loose, continued to the front door, and rang the bell. Molly answered and invited them into the living room, where her husband was on the couch, waiting. Jack had never met Amir, but he'd gathered as much publicly available background information about him as he could, so it came as no surprise that Molly's Muslim husband spoke with no Middle Eastern accent. According to his online bio, he had a BS from Duke and an MBA from

Wharton. He was fluent in Arabic, French, and English, which was true of many people of Lebanese heritage, especially businesspeople. For the last decade he'd worked at an elite private equity firm on Brickell Avenue, the heart of downtown Miami's Financial District.

"Thank you for taking our case," said Amir.

"I actually haven't decided yet," said Jack. "But I should point out that even if I do defend Xavier, it's not quite accurate to call it 'our' case."

"Excuse me?"

"First thing you need to understand is that I'm meeting with you and Molly as witnesses, not prospective clients. Xavier would be the only client. Everything I discuss with his parents would be useable in court, just like my conversations with any other school parents."

"That seems odd," said Amir. "But if that's the way it is, we'll deal with it."

"Let's start with the search warrant," said Jack. "I've seen a copy of it, but I'm not sure what it turned up."

"The house looked like a bomb went off," said Amir.

"It wasn't that bad," said Molly.

"You didn't see the worst of it, Molly," said Amir.

"The police aren't supposed to break anything, unless it's necessary to execute the warrant," said Jack. "But it happens."

"Happened every fucking day where I grew up," said Theo. "Cops called it tossing the place."

"We got tossed," said Amir. "And please don't use that word in front of my wife."

"Tossing?"

Jack shot Theo a look that said, *Let me do the talking*, and then he turned his attention back to the Khourys. "Have you been able to determine what's missing since the police left?"

"They definitely took Xavier's cell phone and laptop," said Molly. "And the family computer in the den."

"Anything else?"

"Like what?" she asked.

"Weapons? Ammunition?"

"There's none of that in the house," said Amir.

"I don't allow it," said Molly. "Not with children."

"That rule is a little hard to square with the fact that the gun used in the shooting was registered in Amir's name."

"I kept that gun in my car," said Amir. "Locked in the glove compartment."

"Do you have a concealed-carry permit?"

"Yes."

"Do you mind if I ask why you got one?"

"Because I was hoping that my son would someday grow up to be a school shooter."

"Amir, please," said Molly.

"That was clearly the point of his question," said Amir.

"I'm just asking why you had a concealed-carry permit," said Jack.

"Fine. It goes back almost twenty years. Two weeks after the nine-eleven attacks I got into a fender bender. My luck, I hit a monster red pickup truck with a stars-and-bars decal stretched across the entire rear window. When the driver saw the name on my driver's license was Amir Khoury, I honestly thought he might grab the shotgun from his rack and kill me. Anti-Muslim sentiment in this country was out of control. It's gotten almost that bad again. Molly doesn't want a gun in the house. I keep it in my car."

"Did Xavier know you kept it there?"

"Yes. I told him. I took him to the shooting range and taught him how to use it, too."

"For—"

"For self-defense," Amir said sharply. "Not for murdering innocent children."

Molly reached over and took his hand. "Amir, honey. Take a deep breath, okay?"

"I'm sorry I have to ask these questions," said Jack. "But I do have to ask them. When was the last time you saw the gun in your glove compartment?"

"I don't remember. How often do you look in your glove compartment?"

"Fair point," said Jack. He wanted to ask about the extended magazines, but Amir seemed to have reached his limit on guns and ammo questions. "Let's talk about the laptop and family computer taken in the search. Is there anything on those devices I should know about?"

"Can you be a little more specific?" asked Molly.

"Sure. Here's what the police will be looking for. First they're going to check every email, text, and social media post to see if there were any threats or red flags about a school shooting."

"Xavier isn't on social media," said Amir.

Jack looked at Molly, as if the moms always had the real story. "Seriously?"

"We didn't allow it," said Amir. "Social media is a complete waste of time, and Xavier has no time to waste. How do you think he was accepted to MIT?"

"Ordinarily, I'd be skeptical of any parent's blanket claim that their high school student was not on social media. But it's been forty-eight hours, and the media hasn't turned up a single social media post by Xavier. So you may be right."

"I am right," said Amir.

"What about his Internet searches?" asked Jack. "How closely did you monitor Xavier's online activity?"

"As closely as any parent."

"The police will be all over his search history. And so will I, if I take the case," said Jack. "It could be a key part of his defense."

"Part of his defense?" said Amir. "How?"

Jack paused, not sure how his answer might be received. "Let me take a step back and explain the process. A death penalty case has two phases. Guilt or innocence is decided at phase one. If the defendant is found guilty, the trial moves to phase two: sentencing. Both phases are decided by a jury of twelve. Sometimes the strategy in phase one is completely different from phase two. Here, not necessarily."

"What do you mean?" asked Amir.

"Our legal strategy may be to convince the jury in both phases of the trial that Xavier was radicalized. In phase one, proving that Xavier was radicalized by Islamic extremists—perhaps even by members of al-Qaeda itself—is the best shot at proving that he's not guilty by reason of temporary insanity, however slight the chance of success may be. More realistically, radicalization will be a persuasive mitigating circumstance at the sentencing phase of trial and could convince at least one juror that Xavier should not receive the death penalty. One vote is all he needs. The jury must be unanimous for the death penalty in Florida."

"So that's where the Internet comes in?" asked Molly. "Finding evidence to support a radicalization theory?"

"Yes. More to the point, that's where your help comes in. As Xavier's lawyer, I would need to know every possible source of radicalization that Xavier could have been exposed to. Internet. Friends. Relatives."

Amir's eyes were like black, smoldering embers. *"Family?"*

"Is there someone you have in mind?" asked Jack.

"Is there someone *you* have in mind, Mr. Swyteck?"

Molly squeezed his hand. "Honey, you're taking this too personally."

"How else am I supposed to take it? I've seen the posts on social media. They might not come right out and say it, but every parent at Riverside thinks the same thing."

"Thinks what?" asks Jack.

"That—"

"Amir, please," said Molly.

Amir took a breath. "Let me set something straight. Molly and I disagree completely about this being an act of international terrorism."

"You don't think it was?" asked Jack.

"I believe the claim of responsibility by al-Qaeda is a hoax. Al-Qaeda hasn't claimed credit for an attack in the US since 2001. As a terrorist organization, they are yesterday's news."

"Who do you think made the phony claim of responsibility?" asked Jack.

"Some ignoramus racist who hates Islam, that's who."

Jack collected his thoughts, trying not to push Amir into a corner. "First, let me say I disagree with you that al-Qaeda is yesterday's news. They're on a comeback."

"So you're not only a crackerjack criminal defense lawyer, but also an expert on international terrorism, is that it?"

Jack did know more than most people, but he didn't want to bring his wife into this discussion. "You and I just disagree on that point."

"Yes, and we also disagree on the best strategy for my son. I forbid you or whoever defends him to make the argument that Xavier was radicalized."

"I'm sorry, but—"

"No, *I'm* sorry, Mr. Swyteck. Molly and I did not raise a *terrorist*. We raised a *Muslim*. Your strategy plays right into the hands of racists who think every child who is raised in a Muslim household is a terrorist threat. If a white supremacist shoots up a synagogue, not all white people are white supremacists. But as soon as a Muslim opens fire, all Muslims are terrorists."

"That's not the argument."

"That *is* the argument. And it's the same argument the public defender wanted to make. Thankfully, that lawyer is off the case. I hope we don't have to fire *you*."

"You can't fire Xavier's lawyer."

"I can fire anybody I want."

"No. Your son is eighteen. Only he can hire me. And only he can fire me."

"Xavier will do as I say."

"No, he won't!" Molly shouted.

The room went silent. If Molly wasn't about to snap, she was darn close.

"Listen to me, Amir," she said, her voice tight but racing. "This family is never going to be the same. Our lives are never going to be what they used to be. But we have to do what we can do to make things a little better. Talitha is eight years old. I don't want her to be a senior in high school having to deal with the fact that her brother is front-page news again because after ten years of legal gymnastics he's finally being executed. If there is a lawyer on this planet who can convince the state attorney that the death penalty is the wrong decision and that this needs to end *now*, life without parole, you are looking at him. I will *not* let you interfere with that because you have a chip on your shoulder as big as the entire fucking Middle East!"

The f-bomb was lost on no one, but not a man in the room said a word.

"Do you understand me, Amir?"

Her husband didn't answer.

"Amir. Do you—"

"You sort it out," he said, getting up and storming out of the room. Jack and Theo sat in stunned silence, not sure what to say. Molly was about to cry.

"Are you okay?" asked Jack.

She dabbed away a tear from the corner of her eye. "No, I'm really not. I'm sorry. Amir has a bit of a temper. More than a bit, since this happened."

Jack heard little footsteps in a hallway. A young girl dressed in her nightgown took a timid step into the room and stopped. "Mommy?"

Molly smiled. "Come here, honey."

The girl hurried across the room, and Jack was struck by her beauty. She was blond, like her mother, with olive skin and a natural waviness to her hair that hinted at her father's Lebanese ancestry.

Molly wrapped her daughter in her arms. "Why are you awake?"

"Why were you and Daddy yelling?"

"Oh, don't worry about that, honey. We were just talking loudly. Say hello to Mr. Swyteck and his friend Theo Knight."

Jack leaned forward, speaking eye to eye. "Hi, Talitha. I'm Righley's daddy. She's in kindergarten."

Talitha smiled. "I know Righley. I was her reading buddy in library studies last week. I like her. She's funny."

"Yeah, she is funny."

"Are you going to help my mommy?"

"Help her?" asked Jack.

"Uh-huh. I heard Mommy say things are never going to be like they used to. But you could help make it better."

Molly smiled awkwardly. "Kids are all ears, I guess."

"Are you going to help?" asked Talitha.

"Well, I have to think about it."

"Why?"

The question made Jack squirm. "Why do I have to think about it?"

"Yeah. When somebody needs help, why do you have to think about helping them?"

Why? Because I'm a big-shot lawyer, son of Florida's former governor, and I'm worried what people might think if I take this case. Because you're eight years old, toxic, and don't deserve a chance in life because of something your brother did. Because your mother didn't think twice when Theo needed help. Because I'm a piece of shit.

"You know what, Talitha? I've made up my mind. I am going to help you. And your mommy."

CHAPTER 9

At nine p.m. the criminal courthouse was dark, but the lights were burning across the street—Lucky Thirteenth Street, as it was known—at the pretrial detention center. The multistory facility housed roughly 170 inmates awaiting trial on charges that ran the legal gamut, from traffic offenses to capital murder. Among them, in Protective Custody Level One, was Xavier Khoury.

Jack parked in the jury lot, which was empty for the night. With him was Theo Knight.

"Ah, memories," said Theo. He may have been the only innocent man Jack had ever defended on death row, but Theo had grown up no choir boy. He wasn't kidding about his "memories" of the stockade.

"Seems like a lifetime ago," said Jack.

"Yeah, to *you*," said Theo.

They went in through the visitors' entrance on the ground floor. Normal visitation hours had ended, but visits by attorneys—who were apparently something other than "normal"—were allowed anytime. Jack gave his name and his Florida Bar card to the corrections officer seated behind the glass window at registration.

"I'm here to see Xavier Khoury," said Jack.

The corrections officer answered from inside the booth, speaking into a gooseneck microphone. "You his attorney?"

Technically, not yet. The Public Defender's Office had filed the motion to substitute counsel recommending Jack. But Jack had not accepted, and Xavier had yet to say anything to anyone since his arrest, let alone designate replacement counsel.

"Prospective counsel," said Jack.

"Who's he?" he asked, meaning Theo.

"My investigator," said Jack.

The officer shook his head. "I'll let you go, Mr. Swyteck. But until you're officially retained as counsel, no nonlawyers can go with you."

It was a rule that he seemed to be making up on the spot. Jack wanted Theo with him because, in Jack's experience with past clients facing the possibility of the death penalty, there was no better icebreaker than a former death row inmate who swore that he owed his life to Jack Swyteck. But this corrections officer from his throne inside the glass booth had the power to keep Jack waiting for hours, if he chose, so Jack didn't fight the no-Theo edict, however arbitrary. He and Theo took a seat in the waiting room. After about fifteen minutes, a guard escorted Jack to the attorney-client conference room, where Xavier was waiting for him. Jack entered. The guard closed the door and locked it from the outside, leaving Jack alone with someone who didn't look at all like a mass murderer.

Jack introduced himself and offered a handshake. Xavier didn't move or speak. They were surrounded by windowless walls of glossy white-painted cinder block, bathed in the bluish-white hue of LED bulbs that lent the room all the warmth of a workshop. Jack sat opposite him at the table.

Xavier looked nothing like his little sister. Never in her life would Talitha and her golden locks have a problem with airport security. Xavier was the guy who came to mind during media reports of dark-skinned young men who claimed they were being profiled by the TSA. As the father of an only child, Jack was forever amazed how children from the same womb could be so different.

"How are you holding up, Xavier?"

No reply. It was a fundamental problem—the client who would talk to no one, not even his lawyer—but Jack had encountered it before. The only way to handle it was to let the monologue begin.

"You're in deep shit," said Jack. "You need a lawyer. The public defender is withdrawing. I may be willing to step in. But that's hard for me to do if you won't talk to me."

Xavier remained mute.

"The first thing I'd like to do, if I were your attorney, is to have a criminal psychiatrist evaluate you for a possible plea of not guilty by reason of insanity."

No answer.

"It's nothing to get your hopes up about. It's a very low-percentage strategy. Nationwide, about one out of every one-point-two million felony cases that go to trial end with the defendant not guilty by reason of insanity. Florida's legal test for insanity is stricter than most states, so the odds are even worse here. Last time I even attempted an insanity defense was for a client whom the cops dubbed the Fiddler on the Roof. You ever heard of that case, Xavier?"

No answer.

"Maybe you're too young. It got a lot of press. My client was arrested at the murder scene. Above it, actually. He was found sitting on the roof of the house. Masturbating."

Xavier still refused to speak, but Jack had actually drawn a reaction from him. The Fiddler on the Roof was eighteen-year-old boy humor, an icebreaker.

"I'm not going to lie to you, Xavier. Evidence of guilt is strong here. Maybe overwhelming. Other than a long-shot insanity defense, my brain isn't bursting with ideas of how to convince a jury that you're not guilty. But if I become your lawyer, it's also my job to keep you alive. Now, you might be sitting there thinking 'Screw you, Jack, I don't want to live.' I've had clients like that before. But guess what?"

Jack leaned closer, trying to get Xavier to look at him more directly. "When they finally get shipped up to Florida State Prison, and they get assigned to a solitary cell on death row, and they start moving down the line one cell at a time, until there's no more cells between them and the gurney and a needle in their arm . . . that's when a lot of them change their mind."

Jack poured himself a glass of water from the pitcher. He poured one for Xavier, too. Jack drank. Xavier didn't.

"I'm going to ask you a few questions, Xavier. If the answer is yes, just sit there and say nothing. If the answer is no, speak up and tell me no. Got it?"

Silence.

"Good. Here we go," said Jack. "Do you understand that the state attorney is seeking the death penalty in this case?"

More silence.

"Are the Marlins going to win the World Series this year?"

Even *de minimis* baseball knowledge was enough to recognize that as a joke. It drew a hint of a smile from Xavier, like Fiddler on the Roof. Jack seized on it.

"Your mother doesn't want you to die. Does that matter to you?"

All traces of a smile faded.

Jack pushed a little harder. "Xavier, I'm asking: Does that matter to you?"

Xavier sat quietly for almost a full minute. Jack waited. Finally, his client shrugged. Jack smiled on the inside.

It was a start.

CHAPTER 10

Just south of the day school campus, two blocks from the river, was a public playground. Andie had stopped there many times with Righley to push her on the swing. "Higher, higher, Mommy!" she'd shout, hair flying in the wind, toes pointing to the sky. Just when Andie was ready to put her foot down and tell her "That's high enough," Righley would shriek in delight and say, "I see it, I see it, Mommy!" At the high point of her path, at the tip of the invisible arc that stretched like a giant smile from one side of the swing set to the other, Righley could peer over the treetops all the way to her classroom windows. The classroom she loved. A place where, Andie had told her, she would always be safe.

That evening, fifty-some hours after the shooting, Andie went to the park without her daughter. But she was not alone. More than a thousand people had gathered for a candlelight vigil.

"Where's Jack?"

It was Rolanda Suarez, one of the mothers from Righley's class. Dozens of high school students had turned out for the vigil, but for the lower grades it was just parents. Andie, Rolanda, and several others were standing near a chain-link fence that had been transformed into a makeshift memorial laden with so many flowers, crosses, and teddy bears that it might have collapsed of its own weight if not for the support of countless helium balloons of orange and white, the school colors. A sea of glowing candles flickered in the warm night air between Andie and the amphi-theater. On stage at the podium was a grief-stricken father with a microphone. His son, Scott, was in the ninth grade, the shooter's first victim. The man said he wasn't sure if he'd told Scotty he loved him that morning. "My job is to protect my children," he said, his voice quaking. "I screwed up. I sent my kid to school."

His words hit Andie hard. It could have been any father up there. It could have been Jack.

"Jack couldn't come," Andie whispered.

"I heard a rumor," said Rolanda.

School gossip was the extracurricular activity of choice for certain mothers at Riverside. Andie had no use for it, and it bugged her that Rolanda seemed to think it was okay even at a vigil.

"I heard he might be the lawyer for the shooter," said Rolanda.

"He's—" Andie stopped herself. It didn't seem like the right time to tell Rolanda or anyone else that Jack was at the shooter's house. But she wasn't going to lie. "He's thinking about it."

Scotty's father put down the microphone, walked slowly off the stage, and nearly fell into the arms of his grieving wife. Silence came over the crowd, except for the sobbing.

Rolanda looked at Andie in disbelief, but it was the mother right behind them who verbalized it.

"Why on earth would you let Jack do something like that?"

Eavesdropping was second only to gossip in the school-mommy skill set. The chain of whispers hopped from one mother's ear to the next, as Andie's confirmation of Jack's new client spread out of control. Andie felt the urgent need to get away. She excused herself and walked toward the baseball diamond on the other side of the amphitheater, weaving through a mostly silent crowd of parents and teenagers, past a church group embracing in quiet prayer, stopping as she came upon a group of teenage girls dressed in softball uniforms. Riverside had been regional champions two years running. They'd lost their star pitcher in the shooting. The only way her teammates could turn tears to smiles was to tell people about her, tell anyone who would listen.

"She was our MVP," said one.

"She had a ponytail all the way to her butt," laughed another.

"She's not a bragger," added another girl, clinging to the present tense. "She makes us all better players."

Andie moved along, then stopped as a woman stepped in front of her and said, "Agent Henning, I'd like to ask you a question."

Andie didn't recognize her.

"We were in the recreation center with you," the woman explained, and only then in the glow of burning candles did Andie understand the "we" reference. It was a group of women from the rec center, and Andie's read of the body language was that this was not a friendly visit.

"What's on your mind?" asked Andie.

The woman folded her arms, making the body language even clearer. "We've been talking among ourselves a lot since that morning. All of us wondering if there's something we could have done."

"That's a natural reaction to any tragedy," said Andie. "But trust me, there's nothing anyone could have done."

"Well, that's mostly true. But what about you?"

"Me?"

"We all heard the shots right outside the door. You're right. There's nothing *we* could have done. We're not FBI agents. You are. No offense, but why didn't you act like one?"

The *No offense but* qualifier, three words that somehow made it okay to say the most offensive things imaginable. "What is that supposed to mean?" asked Andie.

"I'm just saying. If I'd had a gun and was trained to use it—"

"I was unarmed," said Andie. "I was off duty."

"You were *off duty*?" said another woman, offended. "That's why you did nothing? Because you were *off duty*?"

"Oh, my God," groaned another mother.

"You're not listening to me," said Andie. "I said *I didn't have a gun* because I was off duty."

It was too late. The gossip chain was growing link by link.

Did you hear what she just said?

I can't believe it.

No wonder she's best friends with Molly Khoury.

Did you hear about her husband?

Others quickly piled on, and although Andie couldn't overhear all of it, she somehow knew that she was being compared to that notorious armed security guard at the Parkland shooting in 2018, who'd cowered outside Building 12 and done nothing to protect the children being massacred inside. The distinction Andie was trying to draw—that she was prohibited by law from carrying her weapon onto school grounds—was valid. But no one seemed the least bit interested in hearing it.

Andie hurried to the parking lot, found her car, and headed home, her tires squealing and the glow of burning candles fading in the rearview mirror as she exited the park. She was speeding down the expressway toward Key Biscayne but didn't care. She couldn't get away from that place fast enough. Andie told herself that those women weren't being malicious—that people were so broken and devastated that they just needed to direct their anger at someone. But it still hurt.

Andie was almost home, and Key Biscayne stretched out before her as she reached the very apex of the bridge that arched across the bay from the mainland. She rolled down the window, welcoming the fresh sea air. Questions clouded her mind, and not just the question that had chased her from the vigil. She, too, had been second-guessing her actions that morning. Instinct and adrenaline had propelled her down the hallway to Righley's classroom. But why didn't she rush the attacker? She had a pretty clear memory of at least one momentary pause in the semiautomatic gunfire that must have been a magazine change. In hindsight, that would have been the time to rush him. Maybe she could have saved someone else's child.

Andie parked in the driveway and walked quickly into the house. She dropped her purse on the couch, went straight to Righley's room, and sat on the edge of the bed. It wasn't her intention to wake her, but Righley's eyes blinked open. Andie had been completely unaware of how distraught she must have looked until Righley asked the question.

"What's wrong, Mommy?"

"Oh, it's just been one of those days, honey."

"Do you want a do-over? You can have one. I won't tell Daddy."

Andie smiled sadly. "It's not up to Daddy."

"You can ask God. Maybe if you ask, He'll say I can have one, too."

Andie recalled the conversation Jack and Righley were having on the way to school, and it broke it her heart. "Honey, it's good to pray. But we don't pray for do-overs. Daddy's right. There are none."

"Why?"

Tough question. "Why? Well, I think the reason there are no do-overs, is because . . ."

"Because why?"

"Because we have each other," said Andie. "As long as we have each other we don't need any do-overs."

"Promise?"

Andie brought her closer and held on tightly. "Yeah. I promise."

On Saturday morning Jack took a long bike ride, up and over the Key Biscayne bridge—the only real "hill" in Miami—and onto the mainland. He rode right past Cy's Place in the Coconut Grove business district and didn't stop pedaling until he was in South Grove.

George Washington Carver Middle School is a top-ranked magnet school in an area that was once known as the Grove Ghetto. The Grand Avenue neighborhood isn't the war zone it had been when Janet Reno was state attorney in the 1980s. Back then, butting right up against Miami's most expensive real estate was a ghetto that could service just about anyone's bad habit, from gangs with their random hits, to doctors and lawyers who ventured out into the night to service their addictions. That had been Theo's neighborhood. For some of his friends, Carver Middle had been the first punch in their ticket out. Theo and his brother weren't as lucky, having wandered the streets too late at night for too many years. At least Theo had made it out alive.

The neighborhood wasn't quite so bad anymore, but it was fair enough to call it hardscrabble, especially after dark. One thing surely had not changed: basketball ruled. Jack found "Coach Theo" with his eighth-grade-boys team in the Carver gym.

"Be with you in a minute, Jack," Theo shouted from across the court.

His players were running "suicides" up and down the court, the sprint-until-you-puke ritual that the toughest coaches imposed on the best teams. Jack took a seat in the bleachers, ready to dial 911 or administer artificial resuscitation, as necessary.

"This ain't a walk!" he shouted to his team. "Everyone under thirty seconds!"

Jack's first meeting with the prosecution had not gone well. Abe Beckham was senior trial counsel at the Office of the State Attorney for Miami-Dade County, the go-to prosecutor in capital cases. He'd recently earned the moniker Honest Abe, a courthouse joke that marked an impressive milestone of four-score-and-seven murder convictions without a loss. Two of those victories had been against Jack, and if their first conversation about Xavier Khoury had been any indication, Beckham was highly confident of a third. Jack had paid the prosecutor a visit on

Friday, seeking only to break the ice and suggest that, perhaps, Beckham should at least consider backing away from the death penalty. It had been a short conversation.

"Sorry, Jack. This is a capital case if ever there was one."

"You have to get a conviction before you can get the death penalty."

"Right. See that barrel of fish over there? Shoot one on your way out, would you, please?"

Getting Beckham to budge was going to be even harder than Jack had thought.

"Family on three!" Theo shouted, and his players did their practice-ending ritual, gathering in a tight circle, a mix of black, brown, and white hands at the center.

"Family!" they shouted in unison, and then it was a mad dash to the drinking fountains. Theo walked over to Jack.

"Coming back to be my assistant?"

Jack stepped down from the bleachers and smiled. "I wish."

Theo's team was in the locker room, and it was just the two of them courtside.

"Give me a hand with the equipment?" he asked.

"You got it." Jack draped a dozen jump ropes around his neck, gathered up as many basketballs as he could carry, and followed Theo into the storage room.

"I met with the prosecutor yesterday," said Jack.

"How'd that go?"

Jack summed it up in two words. "Not well."

"You come here to tap my brilliant legal mind?"

"Sort of."

Theo shoved a stack of orange training cones onto the top shelf. "Talk to me."

"The prosecution is way too confident. Legally, guilt or innocence is supposed be a separate question from life or death. But sometimes strong evidence of guilt bleeds over in the prosecutor's mind. The death penalty becomes a foregone conclusion. End of story."

"Why is he so confident?"

"Why?" Jack asked, scoffing. "Well, for one thing, Xavier said 'I did it' in front of three police officers."

"That's bullshit."

"Maybe it is to you. To Abe Beckham, it's a confession."

"Confession, my ass, Jack."

"How do you see it?"

"I see a brown kid looking at three white cops pointing their guns at him. You, his mom, and every other white person in America hears him say, 'I did it, I'm the shooter, I'm a mass murderer.' I hear, 'Don't shoot me, I did whatever you say I did, just please don't shoot me.'"

"I don't know, Theo. You really think I should turn this into Black Lives Matter?"

Theo locked the storage door—three megalocks, Jack noted, a reminder that crime in the Grove Ghetto was not just a distant memory from Theo's youth.

"I'm not telling you to turn it into anything, Jack. Just tell it like it is."

CHAPTER 11

On Monday morning Jack was inside the criminal courtroom of Circuit Court Judge Humberto Martinez, seated at the table for the defense, alone only in the sense that his client was not with him. Xavier had refused to attend, which was his choice, but the gallery was packed with parents, teachers, members of the media, and dozens more. Riverside would not reopen for at least another week, and Jack noticed a few high school students in the crowd.

At 8:59 a.m., precisely one minute before the scheduled hearing, the prosecutor entered through the swinging gate at the rail behind Jack and started toward the other table.

"Good morning, Abe," said Jack.

"Jack," he said, opting for a one-word response that barely passed as a greeting.

"All rise!"

The call to order brought the crowd to its feet, and the packed courtroom fell silent as Judge Martinez ascended to the bench.

With experience as both a prosecutor and defense lawyer, Martinez was a good fit for a high-profile case that demanded an evenhanded jurist. His reputation wasn't one of pandering to the media, but he definitely wasn't camera shy. As a younger man, his good looks and decisiveness had put him on the short list to star in the Latin version of *The People's Court* on Spanish-language TV. It hadn't worked out. "Too polite," the producers had told him.

"Take your seats," he said, and when everyone was settled, he looked straight at the prosecutor.

"Mr. Beckham, I've read your motion. As I understand it, the state of Florida seeks a court order directing Mr. Swyteck to file a formal notice of appearance in this case as counsel for the defendant, Xavier Khoury."

"That's correct, Your Honor. This is a capital case. The public defender has withdrawn as counsel. We are at a critical stage where important decisions are being made. If Mr. Khoury has no lawyer of record, all the work we do to secure his conviction over the coming months will be for naught. His appellate lawyer will argue that the conviction is invalid because he was deprived of his constitutional right to counsel."

"I understand your concern," the judge said. "But what is the basis for ordering Mr. Swyteck, specifically, to be his counsel?"

"On Friday, Mr. Swyteck visited my office and said he's representing Mr. Khoury for purposes of negotiating a plea, but he has not agreed to be trial counsel."

The judge looked at Jack. "Is that true, Mr. Swyteck? Has Mr. Khoury engaged you as his attorney?"

Jack rose. "Judge, I met once with Mr. Khoury. He has yet to say a word to me. I explained that I would be willing to meet with the prosecution on his behalf to try to negotiate a plea. I'm not comfortable saying anything more than that in open court, as what I said is protected by the attorney-client privilege. But I asked Mr. Khoury to nod his head if he would like me to do that for him. He nodded."

The judge leaned back in his oversized chair, looking up at the ceiling, thinking. "So it's your position that you're his lawyer for the limited purpose of negotiating a plea."

"Correct," said Jack. "I have not made an appearance in this case."

"Which is the point of my motion," said Beckham. "He needs to get off the fence."

The judge shifted his attention from the ceiling to Jack. "Seems to me you're splitting hairs, Mr. Swyteck."

"Judge, I have not agreed to defend Mr. Khoury at trial."

"Well, you're here now, and as an officer of the court, you'd be doing this community and the justice system as a whole a great public service by acting as Mr. Khoury's counsel."

"Judge, I—"

"As far as I'm concerned, you're in," said the judge. "File your notice of appearance in the record at the conclusion of this hearing. You are counsel of record for Mr. Khoury until you can demonstrate good cause why I should relieve you of that obligation. Anything further?"

"No, Your Honor," said Beckham.

Jack felt as though he'd been run over by a bus, but he knew the rules. Once a lawyer was counsel of record in a criminal case, it was virtually impossible to get out, even if the client stopped paying. It was the reason defense lawyers asked for the entire fee up front.

All Jack could do was take solace in the fact that this would come as good news to his friend Nate Abrams.

"Judge, there actually is one thing more," he said, casting his gaze toward the prosecutor. "If I'm in, I'm all in. I have a motion for the court's consideration."

"Judge, I object," said Beckham.

"Overruled. As they say, Mr. Beckham, be careful what you wish for. What's your motion, Mr. Swyteck?"

The only way to make death by lethal injection a negotiable item was to take Beckham's confidence down a peg. And that was the point of Jack's first motion before the court—with a little help from Theo Knight.

"Your Honor, both the Miami-Dade Police and the state attorney have stated publicly that Mr. Khoury confessed to the shooting at Riverside. It's our position that this statement is not a confession. Alternatively, if it was a confession, it was obtained in violation of Mr. Khoury's constitutional rights and should be suppressed."

Beckham groaned. "Judge, this is a completely frivolous motion."

"Mr. Beckham, someone who has been in my courtroom as many times as you should know by now that I generally make my decisions *after* I've heard the evidence. Mr. Swyteck, have you any evidence to support your motion?"

Jack's gaze landed on the police officer standing by the door in the back of the courtroom, whom Jack had noticed on the way in. "The defense calls Miami-Dade police officer Glenn Donner."

Beckham rose. "Judge, this is highly irregular."

"Officer Donner was one of the MDPD officers on the scene when my client was arrested," said Jack. "His testimony goes to the heart of the defense's motion."

"Officer Donner, come forward and be sworn," the judge said.

All heads turned as a middle-aged man dressed in the distinctive taupe MDPD uniform walked down the center aisle, his steady footfalls on the tile floor the only sound in the room. He stopped, raised his right hand, and swore to tell the truth.

"I most certainly do," he said.

His embellishment on a simple "I do" was a little thing, but like any good trial lawyer, Jack picked up on the little things. Right out of the gate, this witness had violated rule number one of "Courtroom Testimony for Dummies": never say more than you have to, not a single word more.

"Good morning, Officer," Jack said as he approached.

"Good morning."

The witness was wringing his hands, even before the first question. His anxiety was understandable. It was easy for the prosecutor to dismiss Jack's motion as frivolous, but Donner was the man in the hot seat, and no one wanted to be known as the MDPD officer whose testimony got a confession to a school shooting kicked from the case.

Jack went straight to work.

"Officer Donner, you were one of the MDPD officers on the scene at the Khoury residence on the morning Xavier Khoury was arrested, correct?"

"I was one of four. It was our job to secure the perimeter while the search team entered the residence to execute the warrant."

"You were not part of the search team?"

"No."

"But you and the other officers on perimeter security went there knowing that a handgun had been found on school grounds, and that this handgun was registered in the name of Amir Khoury. Right?"

"We knew the basis for the issuance of the warrant, yes."

"The search team was inside the house when Mrs. Khoury drove up in her sedan?"

"Yes. Her *Mercedes*," Officer Donner added, as if it were a crime to be rich.

"Molly Khoury was driving. Was she armed?"

"We didn't know."

"Her two younger children were in the back seat. Talitha, age eight, and Jamal, age fifteen," said Jack. "Were they armed?"

"There was no way to know."

"Her son Xavier was in the passenger seat. Was he armed?"

"We thought he might be."

"Did he make a sudden move when he exited the vehicle?"

"No."

"Did he have something in his hand that looked like a gun?"

"Not that I saw."

"Did you see anything inside the car that looked like a gun?"

"I don't believe so."

"Did he say he had a gun?"

"No."

"Did he threaten you in any way?"

"Not really."

"But as soon as Xavier and his mother stepped out of the car, you drew your weapon, correct?"

"Yes, of course. There had just been a school shooting."

"You weren't there to arrest Xavier, were you?"

"No."

"No arrest warrant had been issued, correct?"

"That's correct."

"No one had accused Xavier of being the school shooter, right?"

"Not to my knowledge."

"You didn't ask him if he was the shooter, did you?"

"No."

"None of the other officers asked him. Right?"

"They did not."

Jack checked his notes, though they were mostly chicken scratch, since this was a motion on the fly. "So let me see if I have this straight. An eighteen-year-old boy rides up in the family car with his mother."

"Objection," said Beckham, rising. "According to *Roper v. Simmons*, the defendant is an eighteen-year-old *man*."

He was referring to the US Supreme Court decision that prohibited the execution of juveniles as cruel and unusual punishment.

"Let me rephrase," said Jack. "An eighteen-year-old high school student rides up in the family car with his mother. The instant they step out and set foot on the ground, four armed police officers surround the vehicle and draw their weapons."

"As I said, there had just been a deadly school shooting."

For effect, Jack assumed the stance, arms extended, as if he had a gun. "You yelled 'Freeze!'"

"Yes."

"Mrs. Khoury shouted back, 'Don't shoot!'"

"Yes."

"Her two younger children were crying in the back seat, terrified."

"I don't know if—"

"Really, Officer Donner?" said Jack, dropping the marksman's stance and resuming his posture as lawyer. "You don't know?"

"I suppose they were frightened."

"And it was at that moment—with four police officers aiming their loaded weapons at his mother, his sister, his brother, and him—that Xavier Khoury said, 'Mom, it's okay. I did it.'"

"That is what he said."

"And you took that to mean he did *what*?"

The witness hesitated, as if sensing that the lawyer was setting a trap. "I have no idea what he meant."

"Precisely," said Jack, pouncing on the answer he wanted. "You never asked him if he was the school shooter, did you?"

"No."

"You didn't tell him that his father's gun was found at the scene, did you?"

"No."

"So when he said 'I did it,' you had no way of knowing if he meant the shooting at Riverside."

"I—" Officer Donner started to say, then stopped, seeming to sense that Jack liked the way this was going. He was suddenly backpedaling. "I can't read his mind, if that's what you're asking."

"When Xavier saw the police and said 'I did it,' he could have meant that he was guilty of downloading music illegally from the Internet, like millions of other high school kids. Right?"

"I don't think that's what he meant."

"He could have meant he was watching porn the night before, right?"

"Or he could also have meant he did the school shooting."

"Yes, he could have," said Jack. "And he could have thought that a confession was the only way to stop you and three other officers from shooting him and his mother."

"Objection!" shouted Beckham.

"Sustained," said the judge.

Beckham stepped forward. "Your Honor, this charade has gone far enough. Mr. Swyteck knows the law as well as I do. To suppress Mr. Khoury's statement, this court is required to find that the police said something that was likely to elicit an incriminating response before advising him of his Miranda rights. Here, all they said was 'Freeze!'"

Jack had to concede the point—but only half of it. "Judge, I'm not accusing the police of having done anything wrong. This is not a situation where the police said something they shouldn't have said, or did something they shouldn't have done. It's simply a statement that has zero probative value of anything. Xavier said 'I did it,' having no idea what crime he was confessing to."

"I agree with Mr. Beckham," the judge said. "This does not meet the legal standard for suppression."

"Thank you, Your Honor," said the prosecutor.

"Not so fast," said the judge. "I also take Mr. Swyteck's point. This is a high-profile case, and I intend to give this defendant, like every defendant in my courtroom, a fair trial. From day one, we've been hearing from the state attorney and from other sources in law enforcement about a so-called confession. If this is the 'confession' you're talking about . . ." The judge shook his head, measuring his words. "Well, I'm not making an evidentiary ruling today, but let me say this. You need to tone down the rhetoric, Mr. Beckham."

"Understood," said the prosecutor.

"Anything else, Counsel?"

A public admonition from the court was more than Jack could have hoped for. "Nothing from the defense, Your Honor."

"Then we're adjourned," the judge said, with the crack of his gavel.

"All rise!"

Behind Jack, in the packed galley, the bumps and thuds of

a rising crowd thumped like a ragtag army on the march. The judge disappeared behind the paneled door to his chambers, and members of the media rushed to the rail, peppering the lawyers with questions.

"Are you saying he didn't do it, Swyteck?"

"Mr. Beckham, is there another confession?"

Jack didn't answer. It was his job to argue his client's position before the judge. It was not his job to vouch for his client's innocence before the media.

"Swyteck, you got a minute?" asked Beckham.

Jack followed him to the far end of the jury box, where they were out of earshot from the media.

"I don't care how many holes you try to poke in my case. I'm not going to lose, and I'll never back away from the death penalty."

"Killing Xavier won't deter other eighteen-year-old boys," said Jack.

"I'm a big believer in specific deterrence. Your client will never shoot up a school again."

"He won't do it again if he's in jail the rest of his life. This is a case in which life means life."

Beckham glanced toward the gallery, toward the sullen expressions of parents and teachers still in shock from the shooting. "When I hear you defense lawyers say that—life means life—it really bugs me."

"Bugs you? Why?"

"You ever read Vladimir Nabokov?"

Jack had read *Lolita* in high school. The story of pedophilia and serial rape was not his cup of tea. "Not a fan."

"Neither am I," said Beckham. "But there's one thing he may have gotten right. Nabokov said, 'Life is the brief crack of light between two eternities of darkness.'"

"That's pretty grim, Abe. I'm not following your point."

"What your client took away from those thirteen children is unforgivable. Why should his brief crack of light be any longer than theirs?"

"I don't have an answer to that."

"I think you know the answer," said Beckham. "And I'm absolutely certain you know how this is going to end. With or without a confession."

Beckham slung his computer bag over his shoulder and walked away. All Jack could do was watch as the prosecutor stood at the rail, confidence unshaken, and reassured some very concerned parents about the strength of his case.

CHAPTER 12

It was a short walk from the justice center to his office, and Abe Beckham made it in record time. Anger propelled him.

The official name for the main facility of the Office of the State Attorney for Miami-Dade County was the Graham Building, but Abe called it the Boomerang. The building had two wings, and the footprint was angled like a boomerang, but the appellation had more to do with the fact that it seemed he could never leave without coming right back. Ten-to-twelve-hour days were normal. Longer when the lawyer on the other side was as good as Jack Swyteck.

"Mary, I want the whole team in the twelfth-floor conference room," he told his assistant as he hurried by her in the hallway.

"When, Mr. Beckham?"

"Now."

Abe went back to his office to make a phone call. The State Attorney's Office had a victims' relations unit, but Abe had always considered it part of his job to keep families informed. That was especially true in the case of Elena Hernandez, a woman he'd met minutes after rushing over to Riverside on the morning of the shooting. The victims had yet to be identified, but Elena couldn't find her son, and she was convinced that she'd lost him. He was a senior, brave, strong, and with dreams of joining the US Marine Corps, the type of young man who would do everything in his power to save his friends before himself. Sadly, her

instincts had been spot-on. The tributes posted on the fence outside the school included dozens of thank-you notes from students
who'd survived only because her son, Carlos, had held the classroom door shut.

"Call me anytime," Abe said into the phone. "Be well."

He hung up, took a breath, and walked down the hall to the
conference room. The team was waiting for him: Liz Kaplan,
who would sit beside him at trial, and two junior prosecutors
who were relatively new to the adult felony division. Abe grabbed
an erasable marker from the table and wrote on the whiteboard
in big red letters: NO CONFESSION.

"That's how we have to try this case," said Abe.

One of the junior lawyers spoke up. "Didn't Judge Martinez
reserve ruling?"

Abe underlined the word *No* on the whiteboard. "I'm not
talking about the rules of evidence. And your instincts are right.
The judge won't exclude this statement. But we have to be prepared to deal with Swyteck's spin to the jury. Our best strategy is
to move forward as if there's no confession. There's a hole in our
case. How do we fill it?"

Silence.

"Jessica, let's start with the search of the Khoury residence.
What can we pull from that?"

The junior prosecutor checked her notes. "Well . . ."

"Go item by item," said Abe, as he wrote the word *Evidence* on
the whiteboard. "Start with the digital evidence."

Jessica flipped the pages ahead to the forensic report. "The
parental control filters on the family computer were set very
high—keep in mind their youngest daughter is in elementary
school—so that hard drive was squeaky clean, PG-13 at worst."

"How about Xavier's cell phone?"

"Just as clean. No texts or emails of concern. No suspicious
content in any of the files he created."

"No manifesto? No diary?"

"Nope. And his Internet search history shows no visits to the dark web, terrorist websites, or so-called radicalizing elements."

"What kind of music did he listen to?"

"Apparently he was a big fan of Bangtan Sonyeondan."

"Sounds promising. Is that connected to al-Qaeda?"

"No, it's a South Korean boy band. Very popular in the United States. Totally mainstream."

Abe would have laughed if the situation weren't so serious. "What about social media?"

"As best we can tell, he wasn't on social media."

"Huh. So Swyteck wasn't blowing smoke about that, after all. Fine. Let's talk physical evidence."

Jessica flipped to the next page of her notes. "Nothing in the way of weapons. No handguns. No rifles. No ammunition. No magazines. No knives."

"No cache," he said, writing it on the whiteboard. "What about clothing or accessories? Any Kevlar vests?"

"No."

"Anything like the shooter was wearing in the video? Camouflage jacket? Shoe covers? Balaclava? Tactical gloves?"

"Nothing. Well, there was an Elsa ski mask."

"Elsa?"

"The princess from *Frozen*. You know: 'Let it go.' They found it in his sister's bedroom."

"Not helpful," said Abe, popping the cap back onto the marker for emphasis. "I presume the search warrant you drafted specifically asked for each of these items."

"Yes."

"Teaching moment," said Abe, trying not to come down too hard on a newbie. "Never ask for something in a search warrant unless you know it's there. This search warrant is an outline for Swyteck's cross-examination of our lead detective. He'll go point by point: no handgun, no rifle, no ammunition, and on and on. The only answer we have for the jury is that we tore the house apart looking for each and every one of these things and found nothing."

"I'm sorry," said Jessica. "But if you look at the history of mass shootings, the items I listed in the warrant always turn up."

"I understand," said Abe. "It's puzzling. And one more reason this case is not the cakewalk that everyone seems to think it is. Nothing in the hands of a jury is easy."

There was a polite knock at the door. It opened, and Abe's assistant stuck her head into the conference room. "Lieutenant Vega is on the line. It's important. Good news, she says."

Vega was the lead homicide detective on the case. "Patch her through on the speaker," said Abe, which sent his assistant racing back to her desk.

Abe had been just a "pit assistant," a C-level prosecutor in his first year of adult felonies, when he'd met Claudia Vega—"Cloud," as he called her, since she was always correcting gringos on the Hispanic pronunciation of her name: "*Clow*-dia," not "*Claw*-dia." They'd worked at least a dozen homicide cases together. Abe still considered her a friend, though much had changed since the days of double dates to the movies or the Miami City Ballet, the cop, the prosecutor, and their spouses. Samantha loved the ballet almost as much as Claudia's husband did. Abe could take it or leave it. But he would have feather-stepped across hot coals for the chance to sit through another one, holding hands with the love of his life. Abe had always worked long hours, but only after Samantha's death did he come up with the name Boomerang for the building he never left, except to go home and sleep. Alone.

The phone beeped to announce the transferred call. Abe hit the SPEAKER button. "What you got, Cloud?"

The detective's voice filled the room. "The lab finally lifted a print from the murder weapon that doesn't belong to Xavier's father. It wasn't easy. That gun is more than twenty years old, and I don't think Amir ever wiped it clean. Forensics had to deal with fingerprints on top of smeared fingerprints. But finally we got a clean one."

"And?"

"A match," she said. "Right index. One hundred percent certain it belongs to Xavier Khoury."

"Good work," he said with a little smile. "I can't wait to tell Swyteck."

"Wish I could be there," said Claudia.

"Here's what I wish," said Abe. "I wish someone would find the clothes Xavier was wearing when he shot up his school."

"It's not for lack of trying."

"We know exactly what he had on. It's right there on the school security video. Somehow he got rid of everything between the time he left the school grounds and the time he showed up at his house in his mother's Mercedes."

"I printed hundreds of pictures from that video. Teams of officers have checked every culvert, every Dumpster, every alley, every place you could imagine within a mile of the school. Nothing turned up."

"Listen to me more carefully, Cloud. I said somehow all of it disappeared by the time he pulled up at his house *in his mother's Mercedes.*"

There was a pause on the line, and Abe could almost hear the wheels turning in the detective's head.

"You think the mother dumped all the gear?" she asked.

"I don't think a Kevlar vest, camouflage, and all that other shit that makes a punk feel powerful vanished into thin air. But I need evidence."

"I'm on it."

"I'm waiting," said Abe, and with the push of the orange button he ended the call.

CHAPTER 13

Icy glares followed Jack down the granite steps as he left the justice center. The pursuit of justice, whatever that meant, sometimes required a quick exit from the courthouse. Jack needed to clear his head. And fill his stomach. He drove to Coconut Grove for lunch at Cy's Place, pulled up a barstool, and glanced over the menu.

"Try the conch chowder," said Theo. "It's Uncle Cy's recipe. Extra sherry."

"Sounds good," said Jack, laying the menu aside.

Theo put the order in to the kitchen and set up Jack with a cold draft.

"I didn't order a beer," said Jack.

"You look like you could use one," Theo said, in the knowing voice of a bartender. "How did your hearing go this morning?"

"Better than expected," he said without heart. "And worse than expected."

Jack's gaze drifted toward the café tables that fronted the stage, where musicians played till two a.m. on weekends. It was at one of those tiny tables, barely room enough for two pairs of elbows, that Jack had put a ring on Andie's finger, surprising her on what she'd dubbed "the second anniversary of Jack's thirty-ninth birthday." Seemed so long ago. It was sometimes hard to remember life BC, before child. Harder still to imagine life after losing a child, the way thirteen families from Righley's school would live the rest of their lives.

"It's so crazy," said Jack.

"What?"

"If Xavier Khoury had done this one day earlier, I wouldn't be his lawyer. On Tuesday, death by lethal injection was cruel and unusual punishment. On Wednesday, no punishment but death fit the crime. Thirteen life sentences with no chance of parole isn't enough."

"I was sixteen when I was on death row. What do you think the Department of Corrections would have said after I was dead and gone, and the Supreme Court said no executing kids convicted of murder."

"Probably the same thing they said in their press release after trying to execute you three times before DNA proved you innocent."

"Yeah," said Theo, summarizing: "'Oops.'"

Jack turned serious. "To be honest, I do see why a parent would want the shooter dead. My wife and daughter were at the school. How would I feel if Andie and Righley were on the list of victims?"

"You'd want the death penalty?"

"I'm saying that I can understand why someone would."

"Well, excuse me for having strong views on the subject, but I got a problem with it."

"Everybody has a problem with executing innocent people. I'm not telling you my client is guilty, but—well, you get my point." The server brought Jack's chowder. Jack tasted it. "Wow, that *is* good."

Theo didn't want to talk food. "Are you getting out of the case?"

"It's almost impossible to withdraw in a death case. Once you're in, you're in. Unless the client fires you."

"*Would* you get out? If you could?"

Jack put down his spoon. "I'll say this much. Right out of law school, when I went to work at the Freedom Institute, all fired up to seek truth and justice in the world, there was no doubt in my mind that the death penalty was cruel and unusual punishment. I don't know if I'm getting old, or if the world is just becoming a darker place. Maybe the way Andie thinks is rubbing off on me. Part of me almost wants to say that, for certain crimes and certain people, maybe there's room for capital punishment."

"Seriously?"

"Yes," said Jack. "Seriously."

"To me, it's a simple equation. We're human. Anytime you put humans in charge, there will be mistakes."

"I get that argument."

"Maybe you need a little refresher. How many innocent people are on death row?"

"Depends on whom you ask. According to the inmates, probably in the neighborhood of ninety-nine-point-nine percent."

"Let's stick to reliable sources."

"National Academy of Science says four percent."

"There you go," said Theo, doing the math in his head. "Are you okay strapping one innocent man onto the gurney so that you can execute twenty-five guilty ones? Or, to put a more personal spin on it: Is it okay to execute one Theo Knight so you can execute twenty-five Xavier Khourys? If your answer is yes, then get the hell out of the case, Jack. If the answer is no . . . then you're doing the right thing."

Jack actually felt a little better. A little. "You're a pretty smart guy, Theo Knight."

"Hanging around dumb fucks makes anyone look smart."

"Thanks, man. Really appreciate it."

Abe ate lunch in his office. Detective Vega joined him.

"Really, Abe?" she said, watching him unload his paper sack. "Cheesesteak sub, barbecue potato chips, two chocolate chip cookies, and a can of *diet* soda?"

"Gotta cut back somewhere."

It was a working lunch. Abe had watched the video from the security cameras at Riverside at least a dozen times, but he needed to sit down and go through it with someone who could tell him what he was missing. That was Detective Vega.

"What a monster," she said, her gaze locked onto the flat screen on the wall. They were watching the first images picked up on school surveillance cameras, seconds before the shooting started. He did look like a monster, dressed in a camouflage flak jacket and black pants, his face hidden behind a black ski mask and dark goggles, his cloth shoe covers lending a creepy slide to his gait. He had tactical gloves on his hands. In one hand was the pistol with extended magazine. In the other were the extra magazines that had pushed the number of rounds fired to well over a hundred.

"Does that look like Khoury to you?" asked Abe.

"Can't really tell."

The video quality suddenly changed, and there was audio with the next frames. Riverside had no surveillance cameras in the hallways outside the recreation room, so police had patched together clips of video from a handful of students, some on a dead run, who managed to record snippets of the shooting on their cell phones.

"How does a kid get caught in a school shooting and think to record video?"

"It's in this generation's DNA," said Abe.

The image bounced on the screen, but it was taken from behind the shooter. It was utter hysteria, screaming punctuated by the crack of semiautomatic gunfire. A teenage girl came out of her classroom, saw the shooter, ran for her life—and then dropped to the floor. The shooter turned around and faced the student holding the camera.

Abe froze the image on the screen. "There it is. The best look of the shooter we have on video."

The detective studied the image, then looked at Abe. "That's the best we got? A face covered by a hooded ski mask and dark ski goggles?"

"I'm afraid so," said Abe. "What do you think?"

The detective rose, walked closer to the screen, and looked harder, as if trying to see behind the mask and goggles. "One thing's for sure," she said.

"What?"

She turned and looked at Abe. "There's no way anyone could say that's Xavier Khoury."

"More to the point: If someone *did* say it, there's no way a juror would believe it beyond a reasonable doubt."

Abe switched off the screen with the remote.

Vega threw him a puzzled look. "There's more, isn't there?"

"Yeah. Almost two gigs of video from SWAT body-armor cameras when they rushed in and found the victims." Abe tossed the remote control onto his desk. "I don't have the stomach for it right now."

"When are you taking the case to the grand jury?"

It was a good question, as the detective knew that a grand jury indictment was needed in a death penalty case. "Soon."

"Are you going to show them the video?"

"You think I should?"

"You'll probably have them in tears if you do."

Abe walked to the window and peered out toward the detention center where Xavier Khoury was housed. "Might shed a few myself."

Jack was back in his office by two o'clock and spent the rest of the afternoon working only on things that had nothing to do with a school shooting. Not that there wasn't plenty to be done in the Khoury case. The real work would come after Beckham presented the case to the grand jury—it was only a matter of time—but already there were boxes and boxes of materials to comb through. Hannah Goldsmith had offered to take a first cut, and Jack was more than grateful.

"Got a minute, Jack?" asked Hannah, appearing in the open doorway.

"Yeah, come on in."

Hannah's father, Neil, had founded the Freedom Institute in the 1960s. It was Neil who'd found the run-down, historic house made of coral stone and Dade County pine just a few blocks from the courthouse and converted it into office space for the Institute. And it was Neil who'd hired Jack out of law school to handle capital cases at a time when Jack's father, Governor Harry Swyteck, was signing more death warrants than any governor in Florida history. When Neil died, Hannah took over. When Hannah ran out of money, Jack bought the old house, set up his own practice downstairs, and let Hannah run the Institute out of the old master suite and bedrooms upstairs, rent free.

Hannah took a seat in the armchair facing Jack's desk. "I may be on to something."

"Tell me."

"I went through all the witness statements. I count eleven witnesses who say they recognized the shooter as Xavier Khoury. Nine students and two teachers."

"More than I thought there would be," said Jack.

"But here's the interesting thing. I checked the date and time of each eyewitness identification. There's not a single witness who said Xavier Khoury was the shooter until *after* al-Qaeda claimed responsibility for the shooting."

"So your argument is that it's the radical Islam connection that made these witnesses say the man behind the mask and goggles was the eldest son of the only Muslim family in the school. Is that it?"

"Yes, Jack. Have you seen the surveillance camera images that have been released to the media? The shooter is unrecognizable."

"Hannah, that's all very interesting. But I'm not going to cross-examine nine traumatized children and discredit them until they break down in tears and admit they can't possibly be certain that the man behind a ski mask and goggles was my client. I just won't do it. We have to figure out a way to get Beckham to bite on life in prison instead of death. Taking this case to trial is in nobody's best interest."

"We don't have to go after the children," said Hannah. "We need the notes and recordings of the interviews. Let's say the police told the witnesses that al-Qaeda claimed responsibility or that the shooting was an act of radical Islamic terrorism, and only then did they ask the question: Who does this look like to you? The whole preface to the question could have suggested the answer and caused these witnesses to finger Xavier."

"All right. That's an angle that may be worth looking into."

"But not tonight," said Hannah, smiling. "Evan and I are celebrating our one-year anniversary."

"Wow. Has it been a year already?"

"Yeah. One down. Forever to go."

"You make marriage sound so magical," said Jack, teasing.

"What can I say? Mom was a child of the sixties, and Dad was the prodigal son. The apple doesn't fall far from the tree."

"Enjoy your celebration," said Jack.

Hannah assured Jack that she would and nearly collided with Jack's assistant on her way out. Bonnie, it seemed, was always running into or over someone.

"There's a visitor here to see you," said Bonnie. "Nate Abrams."

Jack had not spoken to Nate since visiting him at the ICU. He was happy to talk to the one and only school parent who approved of his defense of the alleged shooter. Jack followed Bonnie out of his office to the lobby. Nate rose from the couch. It was readily apparent that he'd come directly from the hospital, as he was still wearing the VISITOR badge from Jackson Memorial on his shirt.

"How's Lindsey?" Jack asked, but by the time the words crossed his lips, the answer was written all over Nate's face.

"She's gone," he said.

"I'm so sorry, Nate." He lowered himself slowly into the armchair, his heart aching. "I can't begin to say how sorry."

"Her mom and I were with her," he said in a distant voice. "That was good. I suppose."

Jack just listened.

"Her mom is still there," said Nate. "I had to walk. Had to get out of that place. You know what I mean?"

"I think I do," said Jack.

"I just kept walking. Thinking. Walking. Crying," Nate said, adding a little laugh at himself. "And walking some more. I was going to walk over to the school. It's not that far from the hospital, actually. Just on the other side of the river."

Silence hung in the air.

"Did you go?" asked Jack. "To the school?"

"Almost," said Nate. "I got about two blocks away, and I just stopped. I don't why. Honestly, I don't know why I started walking over there in the first place. I don't know why anything happens anymore, Jack."

There was only sadness in Nate's eyes, and Jack could only wish that he had an answer.

"So I ended up here," said Nate. "Lucky you. You're three blocks from the school."

"I used to think of it as a blessing," said Jack.

"Yeah, all us dads married to our hour-long commutes were jealous."

Jack smiled a little, then turned serious. "Something tells me you didn't just happen over here."

Nate shook his head. "No. I came because I'm angry."

"At me?"

"Yes."

"Because of the argument I made in court this morning?"

"No. As a lawyer, I totally get why you're trying to suppress the confession. It's what all trial lawyers do when they have an unwinnable case. Give the other side a little something to think about and make them come to the bargaining table. My anger isn't that focused. I'm mad at you, at the world, at the universe. And mad at myself."

"Why at yourself?"

"I hope I can explain this. And not everyone will agree with what I'm going to tell you now. But this is from the heart."

"Okay. What is it?"

He leaned forward a bit, as if to plead his case. "I want your client dead."

"Are you saying that you take back everything you told me in the hospital? You don't want me to defend Xavier?"

"I'm saying I want to kill him myself. I want to take a hammer and bash his skull in."

It wasn't the first time Jack had heard such words from a grieving father. The popularity of Hollywood revenge stories notwithstanding, real people in real life almost always reached the same conclusion.

"It's not worth it," said Jack.

"That's why I came here. I don't need this, Jack."

"This what?"

"A crusade to put a needle in Xavier's arm sucking the energy out of me for the next ten years. When I asked you to take Xavier's case, I never thought I'd get caught up in it, even if I lost Lindsey. I was wrong. I can tell already. It's going to consume me. That's why I'm angry at myself. I want to focus on something positive. Maybe create a dance scholarship in Lindsey's memory. God, she loved to dance. I'm just thinking off the top of my head. I don't know what my purpose will be. But anything is better than giving my time, my energy, *myself* over to this monster."

Nate took a deep breath, then rose. "I need to get back to the hospital. Left my car there. But that's what I came to say. I want you to stay on the case. Get the prosecutor to agree to thirteen"—he paused, choking back the correction—"*fourteen* life sentences, and let's get this over with. Save me from myself."

Jack walked him to the door. "You're a good man, Nate."

"You're a good lawyer. Put it to good use."

Jack shook his hand, the firmest promise without words he'd ever made to another man. "Can I give you a lift?"

"No, thanks. I need the walk."

Nate walked down the stairs, his footfalls crunching in the pea gravel as he continued down the driveway to the street. Jack went back inside. Bonnie stopped him on his way to his office.

"Oh, Jack, I forgot to tell you. The check came today."

"What check?"

"From the Trustee of the Xavier Khoury Irrevocable Trust."

"How much?"

"Your full retainer. A hundred thousand dollars. Do you want me to split it with the Freedom Institute for Hannah's work?"

Jack thought about it, but only for a second. "No. I want you to take it to the bank and cash it. Then get a money order for one hundred thousand dollars."

"Payable to whom?"

"The Lindsey Abrams Dance Scholarship Fund."

"Oh, how nice. Is there such a thing?"

"There will be now," said Jack.

"Do you want to do a letter with it?"

"No. Just put the check in the envelope. No return address. It's anonymous."

Jack went to the window and looked out toward the street. Nate was long gone, well into his lonely walk back to the hospital, but Jack spoke to him anyway.

"You take care of yourself, Nate," he said softly.

CHAPTER 14

Alone, Molly walked into her living room and stopped.

As in most homes, the Khoury living room was the most underutilized square footage under the roof. The only room Molly had spent less time in—recently, at least—was Xavier's bedroom. He'd told her to keep out, which to her seemed normal for a teenage boy. Everything about Xavier had seemed normal. She no longer knew what "normal" was.

She stepped toward the fireplace. Talk about underutilized. Every expensive home in Coral Gables had one, and Molly couldn't understand why. Amir lit a fire about once every three years, and every time he did, Molly got new draperies because he turned the entire room into a smoker. Worse than useless, as far as she was concerned. It had fallen to Molly to explain to their children why Santa Claus didn't come down the Khoury fireplace.

Slowly, Molly allowed her gaze to drift upward, above the mantel, settling on the enormous family portrait in a beautiful gold-leaf frame. Amir had commissioned an artist to paint the portrait from a photograph taken on the first family trip to Lebanon that included their youngest daughter. Talitha was three. Jamal was nine. Xavier was thirteen. Molly's gaze locked onto the smiling face of her eldest son.

Why?

Before the shooting, removing that portrait from its place of honor above the mantel would have been unthinkable to Molly. But what was she to do now? Take it down immediately? Wait to see if he was convicted? And if a jury said "guilty," would that mean going through every family album and Photoshopping her son out of their memories? Do sons convicted of murder cease to exist? Or would her son continue to exist as captured in the perfect photograph that an artist's brushstrokes had transformed into the perfect portrait. Everything about it was perfect. Her family was perfect. Until it was destroyed from within.

For what?

The front door opened, startling Molly. Amir was home.

"What are you doing?" he asked from the foyer, as if to confirm that she was in the room no one ever entered.

Molly went to her husband and held him. Amir put down his briefcase and returned the embrace. Molly broke away, glanced at the family portrait over the mantel, and then looked into Amir's eyes, unable to speak.

"You're grieving," he said.

"Yes," she said in a voice that cracked.

"You need to stop."

Molly swallowed hard, confused. "Stop? Why?"

"We are still a family without"—he paused, alluding to the portrait—"*him.*"

The pronoun hurt. "You won't even say his name?"

"Do you have any idea what it was like for me going back to the office today? The looks on people's faces? I've spent my entire adult life beating back the notion that Muslims are anti-American. And now this happens."

"That's what really bothers you, isn't it, Amir? Not that our son is in jail. Not that fourteen children are dead. You can't get over the fact that your reputation has taken a hit."

"Reputation? You think hate and prejudice are about *reputation*? I don't want to have this conversation." He started down the hallway toward the kitchen.

Molly followed. "I'm not going to let this go. You need to stop making this about you."

He turned and faced her. "It *is* about me. I'm the father in this family. I'm *the Muslim*!"

They locked eyes for a moment. Then Amir went to the refrigerator and grabbed a beer.

"Do you think Xavier did it?" asked Molly.

The question seemed to annoy him. "I don't know."

"I didn't ask if you *know*. I asked what you think."

"All I can tell you is that if Xavier went into his school with a gun and killed fourteen children, he was not acting in the name of Islam."

"How do you know that?"

"Because I pray, Molly. Try it sometime. It might surprise you to learn the things you can know through prayer."

"Just because I don't kneel down and face east five times a day doesn't mean I don't pray. And my prayers tell me to keep my heart and mind open to possibilities."

"Xavier told you he did it. He said it right in front of four police officers."

"Jack Swyteck explained all of that to the judge. I thought his argument was quite convincing."

"He's doing what lawyers do—the courtroom tap dance. What you don't hear is Swyteck trumpeting his client's innocence, do you? You don't even hear your own son saying he didn't do it."

"We should hire our own private investigator," said Molly.

Amir twisted off the bottle cap and pitched it into the trash. "To do what?"

"The police aren't even considering that someone broke into the glove compartment of your car and stole the gun that was used in the shooting."

Amir took a seat on the barstool at the granite-topped island. "Is that where your head is now? Someone broke into my car, stole my gun, and shot up the school?"

"It's possible, isn't it?"

"It doesn't make any sense."

"As if *any* of this makes sense."

"Molly, think about it. Why steal my gun? It would have been much easier to walk into any gun shop in Florida and buy a shiny new assault rifle—which, by the way, would have done even more damage than my gun."

"Maybe the shooter wasn't interested in 'easy.' Maybe the goal was to make everyone *think* it was the Muslim kid who did it."

Amir drank his beer, thinking. "A setup?"

"It could have been."

Amir narrowed his eyes, the anger returning. "Don't do this to me, Molly."

"Do what?"

"Last week you embarrassed me in my own house in front of Swyteck, accusing me of having a Muslim chip on my shoulder as big as the Middle East. Now you're telling me that our son was set up by an anti-Muslim conspiracy. I can't take your mood swings."

"It's not a *mood* swing! I've had more time to think about it."

"Maybe you should stop spending so much time cooking up conspiracy theories and start worrying about yourself."

"What does that mean?"

"I got a phone call from Detective Claudia Vega at Miami-Dade homicide today."

"What did she want?"

"They subpoenaed my cell-phone records."

"*Your* cell phone?"

"The family plan. Everybody's calls are on it, including Xavier's. The detective is focused on the incoming and outgoing calls on the morning of the shooting."

"And?"

"There was a flurry of calls from you right after the shooting."

"Of course there was. Like every other mother in that school, I was frantically trying to find my children."

"That's what I told her. But here's where I think the detective was going. The police still can't find the clothes and the vest the shooter was wearing. They think he ditched the clothes, but they can't find anything."

"What do cell-phone records have to do with that?"

"Obviously, the police think he coordinated with someone."

"'Someone' meaning you?"

"No. I was out of town," said Amir. "They suspect you."

"That's insane. They think I helped my son shoot schoolchildren?"

"No. They think you're an accomplice *after* the fact."

"That's preposterous."

"Is it?"

"Yes! Amir, I swear. I did not help Xavier in any way. Until the police pointed their guns at us and Xavier said 'I did it,' I didn't even consider the possibility that it was him."

Amir finished his beer and tossed the bottle into the recycling bin. "I'm going to send the phone records to Swyteck. He should have what the police have. Maybe we can stop the bleeding."

"Bleeding?"

"Financial bleeding. If you're a suspect, maybe we can work this out so we only have to pay one lawyer."

"Wonderful, Amir. Our son may be headed to death row, your wife could be charged as an accessory to murder, and all you care about is the two-for-one plan. Do you ever think of anyone but yourself?"

"I'm not making it about me, damn it! I'm trying to salvage what this family has left! I'm just—"

"Just go to hell," said Molly. She turned to leave, but Amir's booming voice—"*Molly!*"—brought her to a dead stop. It was that burst of anger she'd experienced only a handful of times in their marriage, the one that sent a chill down her spine. Molly turned slowly to face him.

"Xavier is *your* son," he said, no longer shouting, but deadly serious. "To me, he no longer exists."

Molly hurried from her kitchen, avoiding even a glimpse of the family portrait as she passed the living room on her way to the master suite.

CHAPTER 15

Jack flipped to the next page of his print magazine, a two-year-old edition of *Sports Illustrated* that he'd picked up in the detention center's waiting room.

Jack did most of his reading online these days, but cell phones were considered "contraband" in the jail visitation lexicon, even for attorneys. Xavier was seated across from him, on the other side of the table. His lower lip was swollen. The left side of his face was bruised. Clearly, he'd been in some kind of tussle, which was why the corrections officer had left him shackled for this meeting—unusual for a prisoner's meeting with his attorney. The guard had given Jack no explanation for Xavier's bruises, and, as per usual, Xavier refused to speak a word about anything. So Jack sat there, reading. Finally, he laid the magazine aside.

"I blocked out an hour for this meeting," said Jack. "You can sit there in silence and watch me read, or you can talk and let me help you."

No response.

"Letting your whiskers grow, I see," said Jack.

It wasn't idle chitchat. Appearances mattered. Jack had cleaned up many a client before letting him set foot in a courtroom, including a former Gitmo detainee.

"Brilliant move on your part," said Jack. "You're accused of carrying out a terrorist plot. Might as well look the part. You going for the al-Qaeda suicide-bomber look, or the Isis foot-solider look?"

The remark was intended to draw a reaction of some sort, but Xavier gave him nothing.

"Some of your fellow students have been telling the media that they saw you on the campus after the shooting. Not that it helps you in any way. Nikolas Cruz did the same thing at the Parkland shooting. Ditched his gun and his 'work' clothes and then tried to blend in with the students as the police led them to safety."

Jack tightened his gaze, trying to force Xavier to make eye contact. He wouldn't.

"So what'd you do with your 'work' clothes, Xavier?"

Jack didn't expect a response. He rose, walked to the other side of the room, and then glanced back to see if Xavier's gaze had followed him. Jack caught him looking, but Xavier quickly averted his eyes.

"The cops think your mother helped you lose the clothes you wore during the shooting," said Jack.

Xavier offered no verbal response, but the body language told Jack that he finally had his client's attention. Jack returned to his chair and laid the Khoury cell-phone records on the table for Xavier to see. It was several pages in length with each call identified by the ten-digit number of the caller or recipient.

"The police have focused on these calls," said Jack, pointing to Molly's phone number. "The ones from your mother to you right after the shooting. I guess their theory is that you were coordinating a rendezvous. Pretty far-fetched, if you ask me. What mother wouldn't be calling her son's cell phone after a school shooting? But this wouldn't be the first time the cops put the pressure on the mother to get the son to confess."

Xavier was staring down at the page.

Jack continued. "I don't know how hard the prosecutor intends to push the idea that your mother helped you. He may just be rattling your cage, hoping you'll sign a nice and clear confession to keep the police from charging your mother with a crime. Or

maybe he really does intend to charge your mother as an accessory after the fact to murder. Either way, your parents want me
to be her lawyer."

Xavier continued his stare at the printed page. Jack laid his
hand flat on the paper, palm down, to break Xavier's concentration.

"Under the professional rules of ethics, I need your consent to
represent both you and your mother. It's called joint representation. Honestly, I don't think it's a good idea. It's not in your
mother's interest to be linked to you in any way, and joint representation only reinforces the link. My advice to your mother
was to get separate counsel. But your father is determined to pay
only one lawyer. So I'm asking you, as my existing client: Do you
object to joint representation?"

Jack waited. Silence.

"I'm not going to take silence as acceptance," said Jack.

More silence.

"Okay, I have my answer. I'll let your parents know that you
do not consent to joint representation. All for the better, as far as
I'm concerned."

Jack shuffled through the next few pages of cell-phone records
until he found what he was looking for. He laid a new page on
the table.

"Here's what interests me," said Jack, pointing. "This number,
right here. It's not your mom's number or your dad's number. In
fact, when I asked your parents, they had no idea whose number this is. Which is interesting because you called it every day.
Multiple times a day. Until five days before the shooting. Then
the calls stopped."

Jack gave him a moment to review the record, to see it in black
and white.

"Whose number is that?" asked Jack.

Xavier was staring down at the page.

"You obviously know," said Jack. "You talked every day. Why did the calls stop? Why did you stop talking just five days before the shooting?"

The silent stare continued.

"Fine," said Jack. He folded the papers and tucked them away in his coat pocket. "I'll pick up my cell phone on my way out of the building and dial the number. Let's see who answers."

Xavier's eyes widened, and for a second Jack thought he might say something, but he didn't. Jack rose, went to the door, and called for the guard.

"I'm not bluffing," Jack said to his client. "I'm giving you this one chance to tell me. If you don't, I'm going to dial that number the minute I leave this building."

He gave Xavier a moment to reconsider. Not a word.

The door opened. "I'm finished," Jack told the guard.

Jack took the elevator down to the lobby and retrieved his smartphone from the custodian. He walked straight out of the building, crossed the street to his car, and got inside. He turned on the air-conditioning but left the car in PARK. Then he made good on his threat. He dialed the number, and the call linked to his Bluetooth on speaker.

"Hello?"

It was the voice of a young woman, which took Jack by surprise. "This is Xavier Khoury's lawyer, Jack Swyteck."

He wanted her name, but fishing for it would only increase the chances of a hang-up. Better to act like he already knew who she was. "Your number is in Xavier's cell-phone records. Are you a friend of his?"

No response.

"Are you still there?" Jack asked.

"What do you want?"

"I'd like to talk to you."

"What about?"

"Xavier."

"I'm sorry. I don't want to talk."

"If you're worried about talking on a cell phone, I understand. I'd be happy to meet somewhere in private."

"I just don't want to talk."

"We could meet wherever is convenient."

"I don't want to meet."

"I'm not asking you to tell me anything that makes you uncomfortable."

"That leaves us nothing to talk about," she said, and the line went silent.

"Hello?"

Jack waited, but she was gone.

"Damn it!" he said, pounding the steering wheel, angry only at himself.

Andie was at her desk, working on a witness statement, when the assistant special agent in charge of the Miami field office stepped into the doorway and invited her to lunch.

"We need to catch up," he said, but Andie sensed there was something more to it. Schwartz was a well-known brown-bagger who ate almost every day at his desk, working. Just before noon, they left the building together and went to Andie's car. She drove in the direction of a local sandwich shop that had the best tuna salad on pita around.

"Tell me something, Henning," said Schwartz.

Andie kept her eyes on the road but braced herself. Her instincts had been right: clearly more to it.

"Do you think the al-Qaeda claim of responsibility is real?" he asked.

She knew exactly what he meant, but she asked anyway. "You mean about the school shooting?"

"Yes. The school shooting."

"Terrorism is not my turf, as you know. So I really can't say any more than anyone else who watches the nightly news."

"What does Jack think?" he asked.

"I don't know what Jack thinks."

"Two possibilities, right? A terrorist cell radicalized the shooter and made him an instrument of al-Qaeda. Or someone wants law enforcement to think it was an act of Islamic terrorism."

"I agree," said Andie. "Which way Jack is leaning I can't say. We never talk about his cases. At least not until the trial is over."

"I find that hard to believe in this situation. A shooting at your daughter's school. You and Righley could have been killed. And you don't talk about it?"

Andie steered into a parking space outside the sandwich shop and stopped the car. "Maybe it is hard to believe. But it's true."

They climbed out of the car, shut the doors, and started toward the restaurant. Andie heard the click of heels on the sidewalk behind them. She walked a little faster, and the footfalls quickened. She turned and stopped. The man kept coming and then stopped.

"Andrea Henning?" he asked.

"Yes."

"This is for you," he said, handing her a large manila envelope.

Andie took it, and the moment she did, the man hurried away.

"What the hell was that?" the ASAC asked.

Andie opened the envelope and looked inside. "*That* was a process server," she said, leafing through the pages. "And this is a civil summons and a complaint."

"Huh?"

Andie looked up in time to see the process server drive away.

"I'm being sued," she said in disbelief.

CHAPTER 16

J ack met MDPD Homicide detective Vega outside the front
gate to Riverside.

The defendant's motion to allow his counsel to tour the
campus grounds had drawn no opposition from the state attorney. Jack had visited the campus before, of course, but only ca-
sually, as a parent. Before the students returned to classes—the
target date was the following Monday—he needed to view the
grounds as counsel for an accused killer. It was an entirely different way of looking at a familiar place filled with mostly fond
memories.

"Here's how we're going to proceed," said Vega.

The detective was in control, and she laid out the rules. The
motion Jack had filed with the court also asked to see any hand-
drawn diagrams or electronic graphics the homicide team had
created to document the shooter's movements. Jack was given an
iPad to use during the tour. A room-by-room simulation would
unfold on the handheld LCD screen in real time, as Vega led
Jack in the shooter's footsteps.

"We'll start in Building E," she said, as she unlocked the gate
and pushed it open.

Jack followed her across the grounds. "Ghost town" was a cli-
ché, but the term nonetheless came to Jack's mind. It was just
after the lunch hour on a school day. In the courtyard, picnic
tables that should have been filled with schoolchildren and their

cafeteria trays were empty. Silence replaced the usual school-day sounds—no bells, no commotion, no laughter, no snicker-ing boys and girls who couldn't heed their teacher's command to stand silent. Even the flagpole was barren.

They stopped at the entrance door to Building E. It was the logical starting point, as Jack knew that Building E was where surveillance cameras had picked up the earliest images of the shooter.

"On my signal, hit the START button on your screen," said Vega. "Just follow me, and walk exactly at the pace I set. Don't stop unless I stop. This tour proceeds at the exact speed of the shooter's movement across campus."

"Got it," said Jack. He checked the screen on the tablet. It was a blueprint-style diagram of twelve classrooms, six on each side of the hallway that ran the length of the building. Inside each classroom were a dozen or more green dots and one blue dot.

"The green dots are students," said Vega. "Blue is a teacher. As soon as we enter the building, you'll see a black dot. That's the shooter. Ready?"

"Yes."

She opened the door. On her signal, Jack followed her inside, and the on-screen demonstration began. A black dot appeared at the building entrance, exactly where they were standing. The de-tective walked calmly toward the fire alarm, as did the on-screen black dot.

"First thing the shooter did was pull the fire alarm," she said, but she didn't actually pull it. On screen, green dots inside the class-rooms formed lines, exactly the way students would in response to an emergency drill. The blue dots went to the front of the lines.

"The teachers opened the doors," said Vega.

They were just dots on a screen, but Jack felt his heart pound-ing as lines of unsuspecting students filed out of the classrooms and into the hallway.

Vega stepped into the stairwell. Jack followed.

"The shooter waited for the classrooms to empty," she said.

Ten seconds passed, and then she stepped back into the hallway.

"And then he opened fire," she said.

The green dots scattered across the screen in every direction, some running away from the shooter, others running toward him in obvious confusion, still others racing back in the classrooms and clustering in the corners.

Before Jack's eyes, green dots in the hallway changed color.

"The purple dots are hits," said the detective.

Jack counted four. The detective continued down the hallway. Jack followed, putting one foot in front of the other, hardly able to imagine what it must have been like for those scattering and screaming "green dots" on that morning. The detective stopped briefly outside the door to Classroom E-101, and then kept walking.

"We don't know why the shooter didn't go inside," she said. "Maybe he was looking for a particular teacher or student. Maybe you can tell us."

Jack didn't acknowledge the remark, but he didn't hold it against her either, given the horror of the virtual reenactment.

Vega stopped at the next classroom. "Seven-oh-three had the most victims."

Vega opened the door, and Jack followed her inside. A blue dot moved precipitously across the LCD screen toward the black one. Blue turned to purple.

"That was Mr. Davis," said Vega. "Science teacher. Thirty-two years old. Wife and three kids."

Over the next fifteen seconds, the dots that had clustered in the corner changed from green to purple, one innocent child at a time, leaving Jack breathless.

"There's more," said Vega.

Jack was all too aware. He followed her out. The virtual hallway on screen was empty, save for the random purple dots that marked the shooter's first victims. Vega continued down the hallway.

"He changed magazines while walking to the south exit. A fully spent extended magazine—almost forty rounds—was found right there," she said, pointing to a piece of ballistics marking tape that was still on the floor.

Jack followed her out of the building, the movement of the black dot on the screen synced perfectly with their walk through the courtyard.

"The shooter's next stop was the rec center," said Vega. "I'm guessing you knew that."

"Yes," said Jack.

Vega opened the door, and they entered a wide hallway. To the left were classrooms. To the right was the recreation center.

"Your wife was in there," said Vega. "Those yellow dots on your screen are the parents who attended the coffee with the head of school."

Vega walked. Three green dots were in a vestibule outside the second classroom on the left.

"By now, word was starting to spread that there was a shooter on campus," said Vega. "Unfortunately, three students didn't make it out of the building with their classmates. They hid right over there."

They stopped outside the vestibule. Two of the green dots turned purple. The third dot moved quickly down the hallway, then stopped. Green turned to purple. Jack could not contain his reaction.

"Lindsey," he said softly.

"What?"

Jack cleared his throat. "That was Nate Abrams' daughter. Lindsey."

"Yes. I was so sorry to hear we lost her. Victim number fourteen."

The screen went dark. The detective took Jack's iPad. "That's as far as our tech team has gotten with the virtual reenactment."

Jack was in some way relieved. He wasn't quite ready to see how close to the black dot the yellow "parent" dot had come after leaving the rec center, racing down the hallway, and standing guard outside Righley's classroom.

"The graphic designers are incorporating new information into the model every few days," said Vega. "You should coordinate directly with Abe Beckham for the latest updates."

"I will," said Jack. "Thank you."

Together they left the building, but instead of retracing their steps, Jack followed the detective on a shortcut directly to the front gate. He thanked her again and walked alone toward his office, just a few blocks away. The front porch outside the old house-turned-law-office was in sight when his cell phone rang. He checked the number. It was the number he'd dialed earlier that morning, the one from the Khoury family cell-phone records. Jack answered eagerly, and her words were music to his ears.

"I've been thinking," she said.

Jack stopped on the sidewalk. Detective Vega's tour had all but convinced him that someone had radicalized his client. The young woman on the line might know something about that.

"Maybe we should talk about it," said Jack.

"Maybe."

"I can come to you," said Jack.

"I don't know."

Jack didn't want to push too hard—but he needed to close the deal before she changed her mind again. "Where are you now?"

"I'm at work."

"Where do you work?"

"Uhm. Little Havana. Do you know San Lazaro's Café?"

"Yes. That's ten minutes from my office. When's your next break?"

"Three."

Jack checked the time. He had twenty minutes. "That would work perfectly for me. How about you?"

"I guess. But . . ."

Jack was afraid to ask. "But what?"

"If you get here before three, take the booth in the back. The one with the old map of Cuba on the wall. Wait there."

He breathed a sigh of relief. That was a but he could deal with. "Got it. Oh, one other thing. What's your name?"

"Maritza."

"Thank you, Maritza. I'm on my way."

CHAPTER 17

Jack made it to San Lazaro's Café with time to spare, ordered a *café con leche* at the counter, and found the booth in the back. Maritza hadn't been kidding about the *old* map of Cuba on the wall. This one was from pre-Castro Cuba, more than sixty years old.

Just after three p.m., a young woman brought him his coffee and took the seat across from him. She was a little older than Xavier, Jack guessed, a dark-eyed Latina with long brown hair and a face like a younger Selena Gomez. Younger and tired. "I'm Maritza," she said.

Jack thanked her and kept the preliminaries short. He had a thousand questions but only a few minutes. "How do you know Xavier? From school?"

"No," she said, scoffing. "I didn't go to Fancy-Pants Day School, if that's what you're asking. I graduated from Miami Senior High two years ago."

"Is that your term or Xavier's—'Fancy-Pants Day School'?"

"Mine. He called it 'fuck-wad penitentiary.'"

She was already more helpful than Jack had anticipated. "How did you meet?"

"Xavier stopped here for coffee almost every day on his way to school. Large American coffee, two sugars. He drives a BMW convertible, so one day I was like, 'Hey, nice car.' We started talking every day after that. Chitchat. It grew from there."

"Grew in what way?"

"We became friends."

"Just friends?"

She smiled. "More than friends."

"Were you his girlfriend?"

"Not officially."

Jack stirred a packet of sugar into his coffee. "What does that mean?"

"Xavier's parents have a problem with Latina chicks. Especially his father. Apparently we're all sluts. His parents are such assholes."

"So you kept your relationship a secret?"

"Yeah. If we went out, it was to somewhere no one would know us. Anyplace north of Miami Gardens was safe."

"His phone had no text messages from you. Did you ever text each other?"

"Never. No Snapchat, no social media. Just phone calls. We had to do it that way. Xavier said he had like a ton of money coming to him in trust on his eighteenth birthday. He didn't want his parents finding a text message and cutting him off over a girlfriend."

"Did anyone ever find out that you two were an item?"

"An item?"

Jack was dating himself with the terminology. "Did anyone know that you and Xavier were, you know—"

"We weren't just fuck buddies, if that's what you're asking."

"That wasn't exactly my question, but thank you for that."

"In fact, that morning was supposed to be 'the day,'" she said, using air quotes.

"Are you talking about the morning of the shooting?"

Maritza was noticeably less cheerful. "Yeah. That morning."

"What did you mean when you say it was supposed to be 'the day.'"

"It was his birthday. The big one."

"I know. Eighteen."

She looked away, then back. "I was his present."

Jack suddenly hoped Righley would never grow up, then shook it off. "I get your drift. So what was the plan? Meet after school?"

"No. Instead of school."

"What?"

"I took the day off. Xavier skipped school that day and came to my apartment. My roommates were at work, so we had the place to ourselves. That's where he got his present."

"I'm less interested in *what* the present was than *when*," said Jack. "You're saying that Xavier was at your apartment the morning of the shooting?"

"Yes."

Jack took a moment to process that answer. "Until what time?"

"Until his phone started ringing. And ringing. And ringing. His mother was psycho-calling him, and he freaked out. He thought his mom was on to him and somehow knew he was with me."

Her story jibed with the cell-phone records, the flurry of calls from a panic-stricken mother to her son. "What did you do?"

"Xavier said he needed to go back to school."

"Go back? I thought you said he skipped school and went to your apartment."

"He parked his car in the school lot, like usual. His father had one of those electronic gizmos on his BMW—the ones the insurance companies have, so you can see where someone drives, how fast they go, and stuff. So he couldn't drive to my apartment."

"How did he get from the school?"

"The parking lot is right next to the athletic field. I picked him up at the back gate."

Jack drank his coffee. "Did you drive him back to school after his mother called?"

"Yeah. Left him off where I picked him up. The back gate."

"What time?"

"I'd say around ten thirty. Maybe eleven."

The shooting had ended before ten a.m. "What did you see when you got there? It must have been pandemonium."

"To me, it looked like there was some kind of fire drill going on. Which I thought was pretty lucky for us. Xavier could just jump the fence and fall in line somewhere. Not until later did I find out this was no drill. People were getting shot."

The café manager approached their table. "Break's over, Maritza. Need you at the drive-through."

"Coming," she told him. She waited for him to leave before saying more to Jack. "Sorry, I have to go. I hope this is useful."

"It's useful," said Jack. "If it's true."

"Why would I lie?"

"Don't take this personally, but girlfriends are the number one phony alibi in the history of homicide. Mothers a close second."

"I'm not a phony."

"I understand. But I'd like to ask you one favor: Would you be willing to sit for a polygraph examination?"

"A what?"

"A lie detector test."

She looked at him harshly, clearly offended. "You don't believe me, do you?"

"I'm just being careful."

"No one will believe me. Even if I pass a stupid lie detector test."

"Passing a polygraph will help."

"No way. You just said yourself that girlfriends are the number one phony alibi. That's who I'll be the rest of my life: the slutty Latina who slept with the Islamic terrorist and then lied to help him get away with shooting up his school."

"I'm sorry. I wasn't trying to offend you."

"My first reaction was right," she said, rising. "I should never have talked to you."

"All I was suggesting is that a lot of people have made up their mind about Xavier. They'll question your story."

"They can't question it if I don't tell it," she said, sliding out of the booth.

"Please don't leave like this."

"Just forget it. This meeting never happened. Don't call me again."

"Maritza, please—"

"I said *forget it*. I won't testify. I won't say anything to anyone. *Ever*."

Jack could only watch as she made an angry pivot and marched back to work.

CHAPTER 18

Jack and Andie were side by side in the moonlight, holding hands, seated in matching Adirondack chairs. A gentle breeze blew in from the bay, adding warmth to the glow of downtown Miami's magnificent skyline on the mainland. Their little vintage-fifties house was tiny by Key Biscayne standards, one of the few remaining Mackle homes that hadn't been bulldozed to make room for elevated three-story McMansions built on concrete pilings. Jack and Andie were among the holdouts. It worked just fine for their family of three, might get crowded if they became four, or might be under three feet of water by the time Jack and Andie were grandparents. The trade-off was life on the Key Biscayne waterfront.

Andie had a glass of sauvignon blanc in her free hand. Jack held the complaint in his, reading.

"Exactly what is a declaratory judgment anyway?" asked Andie.

"The Board of Trustees is asking the court to issue a declaration that the school has good cause to terminate our contract."

"So they can kick Righley out of the school?"

"Yes," said Jack. "And still make us pay the full year's tuition we owe."

"Can they do that?"

"It's frivolous. If the board wanted me to stop representing Xavier Khoury, they should have talked to me about it. Not file a bullshit lawsuit against my wife."

"The lawsuit doesn't have anything to do with your representation of Xavier Khoury."

"It has everything to do with it," said Jack. "They could have
just sent us a letter and terminated the contract. Instead, they
filed a lawsuit and made this a public statement."

"You're talking about the motive. I'm talking about the sub-
stance of the lawsuit. This is serious." Andie took the complaint
from him and read aloud.

"'Agent Henning disregarded the explicit instructions of the
head of school, putting the lives of students in danger. As a law
enforcement officer, Agent Henning was familiar with the well-
established "Run, Hide, Fight" response protocol to an active
shooter in public places. By her own admission, Agent Henning
violated that protocol.'"

Jack stopped her. "There's bogus allegation number one. When
did you admit to violating the 'Run, Hide, Fight' protocol?"

Andie considered it. "I guess at the candlelight vigil in the
park. A few of the kindergarten moms confronted me and made
some pretty harsh accusations. I didn't deny anything. I guess by
not denying it, I admitted it."

"Yeah, you and Jesus."

"But that's not the main point. What this lawsuit is alleging is
that it would have been fine for me to run for an exit. Instead—
well, it says it right here. 'Agent Henning proceeded directly to
a classroom filled with kindergarten students, potentially leading the shooter to the youngest and most vulnerable students in
the school. Agent Henning's negligent and unprofessional actions
caused unknown additional casualties.'"

"That's just outrageous," said Jack. "No one in Righley's classroom was hurt. In fact, the argument could be made that you
prevented the shooter from going in that classroom by standing
guard outside the door."

Andie drew a deep breath. "I just don't believe this is about you,

Jack. These are smart people on the Board of Trustees. Would they file a lawsuit like this just because you're defending Xavier?"

"It's also a proactive move," said Jack. "Yes, the trustees are smart. But the school also has smart lawyers. It's not a pleasant topic while families are still grieving, but wrongful death lawsuits are already in the pipeline. This claim against you is step one in taking control of the narrative: the school did everything it could, and to the extent that any safety measures failed, it was the fault of people like you who broke the rules."

"Maybe it *was* the fault of people like me."

"Stop," Jack said.

Andie turned her gaze toward the distant city lights on the mainland. "The crazy thing is, I had to leave my gun behind in the glove compartment. Not only am I an FBI agent. I was the only one in my class at Quantico who made the Possible Club. You know what that means, Jack? It means I shot a perfect score on one of the most difficult training courses in the country. It means that if you put me at the other end of the hallway with that shooter, I could have shot the teenage stubble off of his chin. I could've put a bullet between his eyes and ended it. Instead, all I could do was hide in a vestibule outside my daughter's classroom, armed only with a stupid fire extinguisher, while he just kept shooting and shooting and—"

"Hey, hey, stop," said Jack. He went to her quickly and held her tight.

"I'm sorry," said Andie, sobbing.

"It's okay."

"It's not okay."

Jack kissed her on the forehead. "You're right. It's not. I was moved when Nate Abrams walked me down the hall from his daughter's room in the ICU and asked me to take this case. Even more moved when he walked all the way from the hospital to tell me to keep on doing what I was doing. But you're my wife. This is our family. I'm not going to do this at your expense. I'll file a motion to withdraw as counsel in the morning."

"That's not what I want," said Andie.

"You don't have to say that. No need to put on the happy mask and play 'the good wife.'"

"It's not that," said Andie, and her expression turned from sadness to resignation. "We never really fit in there anyway, Jack."

"What do you mean?"

"You know exactly what I mean. I'm pretty confident we're the only family at Riverside that uses coupons at the grocery store."

"What's wrong with coupons?"

"Nothing. All I'm saying is that changing schools is not the end of the world. How is Righley going to feel when she's sixteen years old and still riding the bus while her friends are driving to school in a new Audi or Range Rover? We have an amazing daughter who will do amazing things at her new school. And in the long run, she'll learn a lot more from a father who does what he believes in than she would ever learn from attending 'the right school.'"

Jack smiled a little. "Thank you for that."

"I meant it."

Jack held her closer. "One way or another, I have to wrap this up as soon as possible. And it starts tomorrow."

CHAPTER 19

be Beckham and a junior prosecutor entered the grand jury room at eight a.m. Inside were twenty-three grand jurors who had sworn an oath to keep secret all matters that occurred before them, and to consider all evidence presented against Xavier Khoury. There was no judge. The prosecutor was the virtual writer, director, and producer of this nonpublic proceeding.

It was day three of the presentation. It was Abe's decision, with the state attorney's approval, not to call any children as witnesses before the grand jury. Instead, the prosecution team read witness statements into the record, which had taken most of the first day. Day two had been forensic evidence and testimony from law enforcement officers. On Wednesday morning, exactly one week after the deadly shooting, the prosecution was ready to call its final witness.

"Let's get started," said Beckham.

The junior prosecutor opened the door, and a Florida state trooper escorted the witness into the room.

By law, everything presented to a grand jury is eventually disclosed to the defense, and it was usually Beckham's strategy to present just enough evidence to secure an indictment—in other words, only the truly essential witnesses. In some cases, however, it made sense to call a nonessential witness just to see how he performed on the witness stand. Better that he fall on his face in front of a grand jury than before the real jury at trial. That was the case with Simon Radler, owner of Tactical Guns & Ammo in Jupiter, Florida.

"Mr. Radler, how long have you owned your gun shop?" asked Beckham.

"Forty-eight years," Radler said in a strong voice. His weathered skin and his beard the color of driftwood made it no surprise to hear how old he was, yet his solid physique and crusty demeanor would have made much younger men afraid to mess with him. Beckham had seen other men shrink in the witness stand. Radler sat tall on the hardwood chair, like the captain of a ship, his tattoos swelling as he folded his forearms across his chest.

"What kind of weapons do you sell?"

"All kinds."

"Do you sell semiautomatic firearms?"

"Of course."

"Pistols?"

"Yes."

"Rifles?"

"Yup."

"Are you familiar with a semiautomatic rifle known as the AR-15?"

"I am. I own one myself. I take it to the Everglades for target shooting. It's a lot of fun. Arguably the most fun sporting rifle in America."

"Tell the grand jurors a little more about the AR-15."

Radler turned in the chair to face the grand jurors more directly. "First thing you need to know is that 'AR' does not stand for 'assault rifle.' It stands for Armalite Rifle. The first ones were made by Colt, and Colt still owns the AR-15 trademark. So, technically speaking, if the rifle is made by a manufacturer other than Colt, it's an AR-15–*style* rifle. Not an AR-15."

"Understood. Are all AR-15–style rifles alike?"

"Nope. You got your standard full-size rifles with 20-inch barrels, short carbine-length models with 16-inch barrels, long-range target models with 24-inch barrels, and so on. Even more different calibers. Depends on the manufacturer."

"Tell me how the AR-15–style rifle performs."

"It's semiautomatic, not fully automatic. That means to fire a round, you have to pull the trigger. It's not a machine gun or tommy gun like the old Chicago gangsters used in the St. Valentine's Day Massacre."

"But they have been used in mass shootings, correct?"

"I knew you'd bring that up. Yeah, some very sick people have *mis*used the AR-15 and AR-15–style rifles."

"The AR-15 was used in the Aurora movie theater shooting that killed twelve people in Colorado, right?"

"I believe so."

"In the Sandy Hook school shooting that killed twenty first-grade students and six teachers and staff in Connecticut?"

"Yes."

"The AR-15 was the weapon of choice for the husband-and-wife terrorist attack that killed fourteen people in San Bernardino, California. The murder of twenty-six victims at the First Baptist Church in Sutherland Springs, Texas. The massacre of fifty-eight concertgoers in Las Vegas. Am I right?"

"Like I said: It has been *mis*used by very sick people."

"Closer to home, the AR-15 was used in the Parkland shooting that left seventeen students and teachers dead at Marjorie Stoneman Douglas High School. Right?"

"Same answer."

Beckham flashed a photograph on the screen for the witness and jurors. "Let me state for the record that I am displaying the defendant's headshot from his Florida driver's license. Mr. Radler, have you ever seen this man before?"

"Yeah. I have."

"When?"

"About a month ago. He came into my store."

"Let me tell you, sir, that Mr. Khoury's house was in Coral Gables. How far is that from your store in Jupiter?"

"About a two-hour drive."

"So Mr. Khoury drove for two hours to your shop for what? Was he looking to buy something?"

"He said he was interested in a rifle."

"What kind of rifle?"

"An AR-15."

"What did you tell him?"

"He looked kind of young. So I asked if he was twenty-one years old. That's the minimum age now in Florida to buy an AR-15–style rifle. He said he was still a teenager."

"Did you sell him the rifle?"

"No," Radler said, annoyed by the question. "All our sales comply with the law."

"Thank you, Mr. Radler. Those are all the questions I have."

Radler rose, but the prosecutor halted him.

"Just a second, Mr. Radler. A grand jury proceeding is different than a trial. The grand jurors can ask questions. So let me turn it over to these fine ladies and gentlemen to see if there's anything they would like to ask."

A juror in the back row raised her hand, and Beckham acknowledged her.

"I'd like to know if Mr. Radler asked Mr. Khoury why he wanted the AR-15."

"I didn't ask him," said Radler.

A woman in the front row spoke up. "Did you call the police?"

"Excuse me?"

"A high school student who looks like an Arab drove all the way from Miami-Dade County to buy an assault rifle. Did you call the police?"

Beckham interrupted. "First of all, let's be clear that Mr. Khoury is an American citizen born in this country."

"No, *first of all*, let me reiterate that this is not an *assault* rifle," said the witness. "Second of all, I bought my first AR-15 when I was eighteen years old. I've never even aimed it in the general direction of another human being, let alone used it in a mass shooting."

The grand juror didn't seem satisfied. "So the answer is no, you didn't call the police?"

"If I had, I probably would've been sued by the ACLU and put out of business for discriminating against Muslims."

The room fell silent. Another juror spoke up, a man. "When he was in your store, did he tell you his name?"

"No. Or maybe it was on his driver's license. I don't remember. I didn't remember hardly nothing about this until Mr. Beckham showed me his picture and said it was Xavier Khoury."

Beckham interjected. "Just to clarify: I didn't tell you that Xavier Khoury went to your store."

"Well, maybe not in so many words. You showed me a copy of his driver's license with his picture and his name on it, told me he was charged in the school shooting, and asked 'Could this be the guy who came into your store?' I said it could be."

The same grand juror followed up. "How sure are you that it was Xavier Khoury who visited your store? Ninety percent sure? Seventy-five percent?"

"I can't put a percentage on it. I run one of the biggest operations in South Florida. On a typical weekend, over a thousand people come into my store. This was over a month ago, at least. In hindsight, it makes sense that it *would be* him, now that we know he shot up his school. It could be him. That's what I'm telling you."

"Thank you very much, Mr. Radler," said the prosecutor, shutting it down. Beckham was glad he'd taken this witness for a little test-drive before trial. Mr. Radler wouldn't be back.

Radler showed himself to the exit, the door closed behind him, and the junior prosecutor locked it. With a push of a button on the remote control, Beckham darkened the on-screen image of the defendant and queued up the next item. It was the powerful simulation of the shooting that the tech team had prepared—the same one Detective Vega had shown to Swyteck on the school tour.

"Ladies and gentlemen," the prosecutor said in a solemn voice. "Before you retire for your deliberations, there is one more thing I would like you to see."

Jack walked into the clerk's office on the ground floor of the criminal courthouse, affixed his signature to his motion to withdraw as defense counsel for Xavier Khoury, and slid it across the counter to the intake clerk. She thumbed through the pages, cocked her head, and raised an eyebrow at Jack.

"This one'll be in the news," she said.

"I suppose," said Jack.

He could have filed it online, but there was something therapeutic about handing the paper motion to a human being, watching her log it into the docket, and walking out with a file-stamped copy in hand. It felt final. But it wasn't. He was still Xavier's lawyer until the judge granted the motion to withdraw, which was not a given in a capital case. Until then, it was still Jack's mission to persuade the prosecutor to back away from the death penalty—to convince Abe Beckham that the best result was a guilty plea, life without parole, and no trial.

To that end, Jack took a seat on a wood bench outside the grand jury room and waited.

The prosecutor was the only lawyer allowed inside the grand jury room, but the hallway was fair game for other members of the bar. Defense lawyers and even members of the media sometimes parked themselves near the entrance door just to see which witnesses the prosecutor was summoning. This time, Jack had come only to talk to Beckham, and he sprang from his slumber on the bench the instant the door opened.

"Abe, you got a minute?" asked Jack.

Beckham sent his assistant along to the elevator without him and walked toward Jack. They were alone in the long corridor, standing in the shadow of a curiously situated support pillar that blocked the window and the midmorning sunshine.

"What's on your mind, Jack?"

"I don't know how close you are to an indictment, but I wanted to give you a heads-up that I may ask you to present exculpatory evidence to the grand jury."

"You can ask, but you know I'm under no obligation to present it."

That was the law, and Jack was all too aware of it. A defense lawyer could show up with a truckload of evidence that his client was innocent, and the prosecutor could simply refuse delivery. "I hope you'll at least consider it," said Jack.

"Is this what I've seen in the media the last couple of days—students who saw Xavier mixed in with other students during the evacuation? I don't consider that exculpatory at all. That's exactly what the Parkland shooter did to slip through the police perimeter and head over to McDonald's for a burger and fries after a hard day's work."

"That's not what I'm talking about. We may have an alibi witness."

Beckham showed surprise, probably more than he would have liked. "An alibi? Really? Who?"

"I'm not prepared to say just yet. I'm here to ask you to slow down the train for a day or two. I'd like to gather my facts and offer this evidence to you in a reliable way. Then you can decide whether to present it to the grand jury."

"Delay, delay, delay," said Beckham, groaning. "That's the game you defense lawyers always play—until your client is convicted.

Then you file an appeal arguing that I violated your client's constitutional right to a speedy trial. I'm not slowing down. I'm getting my indictment on fourteen counts of first-degree murder today, we're going to trial as soon as possible, and I'm seeking the death penalty."

"That's what I thought you'd say. I understand. Go ahead and announce the indictment. But throw me this bone, will you? Do not make a public announcement that you are seeking the death penalty."

"It's already out there. I've been talking about the death penalty since the arrest."

"Talking, yes," said Jack. "Up until this point, I think it's fair to say that the State Attorney's Office has rejected any request by the defense to take the death penalty off the table. Once you have the indictment in hand and make a formal announcement that you are seeking death, that's a game changer. Politically, it's almost impossible for the state attorney to back away from it in a case like this. So wait a week. Wait a *day*. Just *wait*."

Abe didn't answer right away. "I'll consider it," he said finally.

"Thank you," said Jack.

They walked toward the elevator together, but before Jack could push the CALL button, the bell rang and the chrome doors parted. A gaggle of reporters spilled out of the crowded elevator, and from the looks on their faces, they smelled a breaking development in the case. Jack suspected that Beckham's assistant had put the word out that an indictment was imminent.

"Mr. Beckham!" they shouted. "Mr. Beckham!"

Within seconds the prosecutor was surrounded, the blinding media lamps were up, and the cameras were rolling. Jack watched and listened as the prosecutor spoke into the bouquet of microphones thrust toward his face.

"Let me say this," said Beckham. "The state's presentation of evidence is complete. It is now up to the grand jury."

A reporter pushed forward. "Mr. Beckham, if the grand jury

returns an indictment for first-degree murder, will you be seeking the death penalty?"

"Without question," said Beckham, looking straight into the
nearest camera. "As I've said all along, this is a capital case if ever
there was one. Thank you all very much."

He broke away from the crowd and headed for the stairwell
instead of the elevator, walking right past Jack on the way.

"Thanks for considering my request," said Jack, and he let the
prosecutor go up the stairwell alone.

CHAPTER 20

The package from Abe Beckham landed in Jack's office the next morning.

Federal law referred to it as "Jencks material," so named for the 1957 Supreme Court case that defined the government's initial disclosure requirements in a criminal case. Florida has similar rules, and it was the defense team's first look at the evidence presented to the grand jury. The government was also required to turn over evidence that wasn't presented to the grand jury and that could help the defense. Potentially, it was like Christmas morning; more realistically, like Christmas morning for the kid whose parents didn't get to the store in time to buy the hot new toy. Nonetheless, you open the package, hoping.

"How can I help?" asked Hannah.

They were in the kitchen, the one room in the old house that Jack had left exactly the way it was after Hannah's father passed away. When Jack was a newbie at the Freedom Institute, the vintage-sixties kitchen was not only where lawyers and staff ate their bagged lunches, but it also served as the main (and only) conference room. Hanging on the wall over the old Joe DiMaggio Mr. Coffee machine was the same framed photograph of Bobby Kennedy that had once hung in Neil's dorm room at Harvard. Jack loved that Hannah was filling his shoes.

Jack gave a quick once-over to the stack of banker boxes on the Formica countertop. There would be hours of work ahead of him—if he stayed on the case.

"Let's give it a day or two. See how this plays out."

"See how what plays out?"

Jack had told her about his motion, but Hannah obviously had not given up hope that Jack would change his mind. She was already tearing off box tops, looking for something that piqued her interest and expertise. "What's the name of their fingerprint expert?" she asked, flipping through the printed transcript. "I'll start there."

"Granger, I think," said Jack.

"I'm curious to read his testimony about the extended magazines."

"There were five of them," said Jack. "Thirty rounds apiece."

"What I'm asking is whether Xavier's fingerprints were found on the extended magazines. It's no big deal if his prints are on the gun. His father owned it for twenty years, and he told you he taught his son how to use it, right?"

"Right."

"So we can explain the gun. But if Xavier's fingerprints were found on the extended magazines, that's not so easy to explain. Unless he's the shooter."

"Good point," said Jack. "I don't know if they're on the magazines."

"That's why I'm looking."

Jack's assistant knocked on the doorframe. "You have a call from Judge Martinez's chambers," said Bonnie.

Jack excused himself, went to his office, and picked up the phone on his desk. The judge's assistant was on the line.

"Judge Martinez has scheduled a hearing at four p.m. on your motion to withdraw. Can you please confirm your availability?"

"Yes, I'm available."

"The hearing will be in chambers, not in the courtroom. The judge has granted the request that the hearing be closed to the public."

"I'm sorry, I didn't make that request."

"Ms. Gonzalez did," said the assistant.

"Who?"

"Sylvia Gonzalez. She's an attorney with the National Security Division of the United States Department of Justice. They are opposing your motion to withdraw as counsel."

"Excuse me?"

"That's all I know, sir. Can I tell Judge Martinez you will be here at four o'clock?"

"Yes," said Jack, puzzled. "I'll definitely be there."

Andie was in the field office, working through lunch at her desk, when security called from the main lobby. "Agent Henning, there's a Molly Khoury here to see you."

Her empty stomach filled with pangs of guilt. Andie had always thought of herself as a compassionate person. But Molly was complicated territory. "I'll come down," she said into the phone.

Andie rode the elevator down alone, fairly certain that she knew what this was about. She'd told Jack that he didn't have to withdraw as counsel, but she was happy with his decision. Molly, no doubt, was not.

The elevator doors opened to the lobby, and Andie found Molly seated on the vinyl couch near the window. Molly rose and greeted her with a pained expression. "I'm so sorry, Andie."

They took a seat on the couch. "Sorry about what?"

"The lawsuit. I heard you got sued."

"No need to apologize," said Andie. "I don't see that as your fault."

"As soon as I heard, I had to come and see you. I want to do the right thing."

"I don't really know what that means, but you don't have to do anything, Molly."

"I know how much you and Jack sacrifice to afford the tuition at Riverside."

"Everybody sacrifices."

"No," said Molly. "They don't."

"Jack and I will figure it out. He's trying to set up a meeting with the school's attorney."

"You've been a good friend, Andie. I don't want you to spend another minute worrying about this." Molly opened her purse, dug out a check, and offered it to Andie, who didn't take it.

"What are you doing?" asked Andie.

"Amir and I want to reimburse you and Jack. For the tuition you have to pay to Riverside."

"No," said Andie. "I can't take your money."

"Please," Molly said, pushing it toward her. "We want you to have it."

"Molly, please," Andie said, rising and taking a step back.

Molly rose, too, but she spilled her purse all over the floor. Andie bent over to help gather the mess, but Molly leaned in the same direction, and they bumped heads. Andie laughed, thinking it comical, but Molly shrieked so loudly that it was anything but funny.

"Molly, are you okay?" Andie asked with concern.

Molly was in obvious pain, and she settled back into the couch holding the side of her head.

"I didn't think we'd bumped that hard," said Andie.

"We didn't," said Molly, wincing. "I have this . . . this thing."

Andie took a seat beside her and looked more closely. The knot on the side of her head, right behind the ear, was as big as a golf ball. It couldn't possibly have been caused by their head-to-head collision. It was purple and already yellowing—not fresh—at least a day old.

"Molly, my God. What happened here?"

"Nothing."

"It's *not* nothing. The last time I saw something like this it turned out to be a fractured skull. Did you get in a car accident?"

"No."

"Fall?"

"Uh-uh."

Andie hesitated, but she had to ask. "Did . . . did someone hit you?"

Molly blinked hard. "It's nothing."

"Molly?"

She zipped up her purse and rose to her feet, leaving the check on the couch. "Please keep it, Andie. It would be the first time money made me happy."

It was the saddest smile Andie had ever seen. She just watched as Molly hurried to the exit.

CHAPTER 21

A judicial assistant directed the lawyers into Judge Martinez's chambers for the four p.m. hearing.

"Please have a seat," the judge said cordially. He was behind a massive antique desk, directly in front of which stretched a rectangular table in a T-shape configuration. Jack and Hannah Goldsmith were on one side of the table. Beckham and the Justice Department lawyer sat opposite them. A court reporter was the only other person in the chambers, tucked away in the corner between the American flag and a life-sized plastic replica of Sebastian the Ibis, the sports mascot for the University of Miami—"The U"—Judge Martinez's alma mater.

"It isn't every day that I have a lawyer from the DOJ's National Security Division in my chambers," the judge said.

"It's an unusual and important matter," she said.

"Emphasis on 'unusual,'" said Jack. "Your Honor, I don't see how the federal government has any say as to whether you, a state court judge, should allow me to withdraw as defense counsel in a criminal case prosecuted under state law by our local state attorney."

"Nor do I," said Beckham.

The judge smiled. "Well, Mr. Beckham, not to be cynical, but I can certainly see why you'd want a lawyer of Mr. Swyteck's experience and ability out of the case. But let's hear what the department has to say. Ms. Gonzalez, if you please."

"Your Honor, the federal government is not the outsider to this action that Mr. Swyteck would have this court believe. One of the first things he did as counsel was submit a written request to our office under the Freedom of Information Act."

"Is that true, Mr. Swyteck?"

"Yes," said Jack. "As I'm sure everyone here recalls, within hours of the shooting, the media reported that al-Qaeda claimed responsibility. If that claim is legitimate, my client was obviously radicalized as a juvenile. It's the defense's position that radicalization by a terrorist organization at such a young age is a mitigating factor that should weigh against the death penalty."

"If he's guilty," added Hannah. "It may also be that radicalization will support a plea of not guilty by reason of insanity."

"Got it," the judge said. "So I presume the defense seeks information from the federal government as to the bona fides of al-Qaeda's claim of responsibility."

"Correct," said Jack. "But this issue will be central to the case whether I'm counsel or someone else is counsel. Ms. Goldsmith is prepared to step in as my replacement, and she fully intends to pursue the issue of radicalization."

"Which is exactly why the Department of Justice is here," said Gonzalez.

The judge peered out over the top of his reading glasses. "You're going to have to elaborate, Ms. Gonzalez."

"Happy to," she said. "Ten years after the terrorist attacks of nine-eleven, Mr. Swyteck was appointed to serve as counsel in the case of *Khaled Al-Jawar v. The President of the United States of America*, a habeas corpus proceeding filed in the District of Columbia. Mr. Al-Jawar was a Somali enemy combatant detained at the US Naval Air base in Guantánamo, Cuba."

"No kidding?" said the judge, half smiling. "You're just a veritable box of surprises, aren't you, Mr. Swyteck?"

Gonzalez continued. "The point here is that there is an ongoing investigation into the possible al-Qaeda connection to this school shooting. We recognize that the defendant has a legitimate right to pursue his radicalization defense. To the extent that the federal government is called upon to provide any information relating to 'radicalization,' it is of paramount concern that this information be handled in a way that does not compromise matters of national security."

"So you want Mr. Swyteck to stay on the case?"

"In a word, yes. Mr. Swyteck was thoroughly vetted before he was allowed to travel to Gitmo. He was even more thoroughly vetted before he was allowed to interview witnesses and review classified evidence relating to the accusations that his client sheltered al-Qaeda operatives in East Africa and posed a serious threat to this nation's safety. Simply put, he is no stranger to the NSD, and he has a known track record in litigating a case that raises issues of national security."

"I'm sure Ms. Goldsmith is willing to stipulate to any reasonable protections," said Jack.

"It's not that simple," said Gonzalez. "Mr. Swyteck was even issued 'secret' security clearance under the Rules of Procedure for the Foreign Intelligence Service Court of Review. That's a small universe."

"I take your point, Ms. Gonzalez," the judge said. "Mr. Swyteck, let me ask you this question. Has your client refused to pay you?"

It wasn't the time to mention his donation to the Lindsey Abrams dance scholarship fund. "It's not an issue of payment, Your Honor."

"Has your client asked you to do something unethical?"

"No. Actually, he won't even talk to me."

"So you're seeking to withdraw because . . ."

Jack didn't want to drag Andie into this. "Personal reasons," said Jack. "Withdrawal is in the best interest of my family."

"Well *boo-hoo*," said the judge. "I'm not going to force Ms. Gonzalez to beg you to stay in this case. You know the rules. Courts frown on the withdrawal of counsel in a criminal case. The stakes are even higher in a capital case. I'm denying the motion to withdraw."

"Thank you, Judge," said Gonzalez.

"Sorry, Mr. Swyteck," the judge said. "You're in for the long haul."

Jack felt a congratulatory kick under the table from Hannah, the footsie version of a high five.

"Understood," said Jack.

CHAPTER 22

Jack's court-ordered stint as "counsel for life" to Xavier Khoury began the following morning.

It was not Jack's first visit to a mosque. Some years earlier, after back-to-back mass shootings at two New Zealand mosques claimed fifty-one lives, he and Andie had attended an interfaith memorial service for the victims. But this was his first visit to the mosque in Hialeah, Florida—the one attended by Amir Khoury and his sons. Jack's top priority was to find out whether Xavier had fallen in with the wrong people and been radicalized. Talks with Xavier's father had gone nowhere, so the imam seemed like the next logical interview.

"I've never met an imam," said Theo. Theo was with him, wearing his figurative investigator's hat.

"Treat him the way you would any other leader in a place of worship," said Jack. "And keep in mind this is a Sunni mosque. Not Shiite."

"I know there's a difference, but I can't honestly say I know what it is."

Jack probably could have left it at that, but there was no telling what might come out of Theo's mouth. "Just don't mention the Ayatollah."

Theo parked the car on the south side of the mosque, near the minaret, the tower from which the Muslim crier traditionally called worshipers to prayer five times a day. They walked past the restrooms, past the separate women's entrance to the prayer hall, and then entered the administrative offices. Imam Abbas Hassan greeted them and walked them back to his office, making small talk.

"I know Jack is not Muslim. Are you, Mr. Knight?"

"No," said Theo. "But I did get asked to join a Muslim gang when I was in prison."

Jack could have clubbed him.

"That's not really very funny, Mr. Knight."

"No joke," said Theo. "I did time in Florida State Prison, and they asked me to join. So did the Jamaican gang, the Cubans, the Bloods, the Crips, and about a dozen others who wanted the added status of a six-foot-six brother on death row."

"Theo was innocent," said Jack, quickly in damage-control mode. "It's a long story."

"Gangs are not real Muslims," said Hassan. Then he directed them to the armchairs and took a seat behind his desk. His tone was cordial enough, but he was obviously less than pleased about the purpose of Jack's visit.

"Let me say up front that news of the school shooting made my skin crawl," said Hassan. "What in the world would trigger a young man to do something like that? It makes you sick. We reject it."

"That is the question," said Jack. "If Xavier did it, what made him do it?"

"Is there any doubt in your mind as to his guilt, Mr. Swyteck?"

"I'm not at liberty to discuss what's in my mind," said Jack. "I'd like to limit our discussion to facts. Who were Xavier's friends? Who were his contacts?"

The imam listed several boys, and Jack jotted down the names. For the next few minutes, Jack stuck to that format—just the facts, and strictly about Xavier. Then he shifted gears.

"Is Molly Khoury part of your religious community?" asked Jack.

"No. Amir came only with his sons."

"Was she ever?"

"A very short time. She refused to use the women's entrance. Amir and I had a discussion with her, and that frankly is the last time I have ever spoken with her. As far as I know, she is without religion. I'm sure this was not helpful to Xavier's development, spiritual or otherwise."

"Did you talk with Xavier about that?"

"Those conversations are confidential."

"I'm his lawyer."

"I understand. And as soon as Xavier tells me that I can reveal our confidential conversations to his lawyer, we can talk."

"Got it," said Jack.

"Don't misunderstand," said Hassan. "Nothing I know or even heard about Xavier would have made this shooting foreseeable. Our community director already had Xavier's name on the list of singles for our 'Muslim Matches' under-twenty-one icebreakers. I liked Xavier. We all liked him. This is tragic on so many levels."

The imam appeared truly heartbroken. Jack gave him a minute, then continued.

"What do you make of the claim of responsibility by al-Qaeda?" asked Jack.

"My opinion is the same as Amir's. It's fake. Xavier is from a good family and is part of a solid religious community."

"Do you have any idea why Xavier would have done something like this?"

"None. Why did those boys open fire on their classmates at Columbine? Why did Nikolas Cruz kill all those children at Parkland? Those school shootings had nothing to do with Islamic terrorism. Neither does this. This was a Muslim boy who lost his way in a world that sometimes loses its mind. Not a Muslim boy who was radicalized by his religious community to kill in the name of Islam."

Hassan checked his watch. "I'm sorry, but I have an appointment, and I cannot be late."

"One quick thing," said Jack. "Did Xavier ever mention to you a young woman named Maritza?"

Hassan's expression soured. "I met this Maritza. Xavier brought her to services once or twice. He was quite taken with her."

"You don't seem to approve."

"Not for the reason Xavier thought. She told him that I was opposed to their dating because Maritza was Hispanic. That's not true. In fact, Hispanics are one of the fastest-growing demographics in conversions to Islam."

"I did not know that."

"People forget that Spain has had a large Muslim population for over a thousand years." He checked his watch again, then rose. "I really must be going."

"Sorry," said Jack, "but I have to ask: What was it about Maritza that made her so wrong for Xavier?"

The imam drew a breath, as if reluctant to say. "She's a prostitute."

Jack bristled. "Let's not get into name-calling."

"I'm not calling anyone names. She has sex with men for money. She's a prostitute. A lady of the night. Whatever you wish to call it."

It took Jack a second to comprehend. "How do you know that?"

"Ask her. She'll tell you."

"All right," said Jack. "I will."

CHAPTER 23

Jack was eager to speak with Maritza at the coffee shop, but it would have to wait. He had a two p.m. meeting with Duncan Fitz, the attorney for Riverside Day School in the lawsuit against Andie. Theo drove to Fitz's office on prestigious Brickell Avenue, while Jack rode in the passenger seat, preparing for the meeting.

Theo glanced over from the driver's seat. "What's that famous saying from Abraham Lincoln about a lawyer and his client?"

"'A lawyer who represents himself has a fool for a client.'"

"No, I mean the other one. 'A lawyer who represents his wife is just a fucking lunatic.'"

"I don't think Lincoln actually said that."

"He would have, if Mary Todd had asked him to defend her."

"Hannah will be representing Andie if this case goes forward. This is my one and only shot to see if I can make this go away."

Fitz was the senior litigation counsel at the Miami office of one of the world's largest law firms, Coolidge, Harding & Cash—"Cool Cash," as it was known in the power circles, since every one of its equity partners in seventeen different offices across the globe drew a seven-figure bonus year in and year out. Fitz's typical client was a Fortune 500 company, not a private day school, but his three children had attended Riverside Day School, so Jack assumed he was personally invested in the case against Andie.

"You nervous?" asked Theo, as they rode up alone in the elevator.

"Why should I be nervous?"

"He's a son of a bitch. One of his lawyers stopped in my bar to drown his sorrows. Fitz fired him for missing a conference call to be in the delivery room for the birth of his son."

Jack had heard worse. Fitz actually bragged about his creative approach to settling a "bad drug" case brought by a retired police officer, Gilbert Jones, who was permanently disabled by a weight-loss medication that the pharmaceutical company knew was dangerous. "Mr. Jones, it will take you five years to get this case to trial and through all appeals. You can wait that long for your money or we can end this today. Before you, on this table, are three briefcases. One contains a check for three million dollars, your lawyer's latest settlement demand. One contains fifty thousand dollars in cash, my client's latest settlement offer. The third contains nothing. Think of me as Howie Mandel, and I'm giving you one chance to bring this lawsuit—and the wait for your money—to an immediate end. Deal? Or no deal?"

Gilbert walked out with nothing. The lawyers spent the next two years litigating whether the "settlement" was an illegal form of gambling.

"Mr. Fitz will see you now," the receptionist said. Theo waited in the lobby as Jack followed Fitz's assistant to her boss's corner office on the forty-second floor. Fitz had a drop-dead view of downtown Miami to the north and the blue-green waters of the bay to the east. Jack could almost see his house on Key Biscayne in the distance.

"I've heard a lot about you, Jack."

With lawyers of Fitz's generation there was the usual chitchat about Jack's father, former governor Harry Swyteck, with the added twist of how much money Cool Cash and Duncan Fitz personally had contributed to Harry's gubernatorial elections back in the day. Then the conversation turned even closer to home.

"Andie doesn't deserve this," said Jack.

"We'll see what the judge says."

"I was hoping to stop this case from getting that far."

Fitz chuckled. "What do you want me to do? Take a voluntary dismissal?"

"Yes," Jack said in a serious voice. "If the Board of Trustees is unhappy about my decision to represent Xavier Khoury, this lawsuit is not going to change anything. I filed a motion to withdraw as counsel. The court denied it."

"Is that what you think? That we filed this lawsuit to bully you into withdrawing?"

"The thought crossed my mind."

"Erase the thought," said Fitz. "This is a simple breach-of-contract action. All families execute a binding agreement to abide by the Riverside's rules and procedures. Your wife breached that agreement."

"Then let's address this on a business level. We will agree to leave the school quietly. The school waives its right to tuition for the rest of the school year."

"That hardly leaves my client whole," said Fitz. "Riverside Day School is a not-for-profit institution. The Board of Trustees approves its annual budget based on the number of tuitions coming from enrolled students. Even if one of those students leaves, the school still depends on that tuition to meet its operations."

"You'll find another family to step in. The waiting list to get in to Riverside Day School is as long as my arm."

Fitz shook his head. "That waiting list has evaporated into thin air."

Jack had heard the rumors. "So what people are saying online is true?"

"I wouldn't know what is being said online," said Fitz.

"The buzz is that Riverside is in panic mode. They think families are going to pull out in droves and demand a tuition refund."

"That's a legitimate fear," said Fitz. "Any reasonable parent might ask himself or herself, 'Do I want to pay top dollar to send my child to a school that will forever be linked to a massacre like this one?'"

The lightbulb switched on for Jack. "Now I get it. The Board of Trustees is making an example out of us. The message to the school community is this: every family—even the ones we *kick out* of this school—will be held to their contract for the full amount of annual tuition."

"Plus payment of my attorneys' fees. Which I believe are in the neighborhood of twenty-eight thousand dollars. *Twenty-nine*, once I bill for this meeting."

Fitz rose from his desk chair and offered a handshake, which Jack ignored.

"I can't dismiss the case, Jack. I'm sure you understand."

"I'm trying to," said Jack, leaving the office with the firm impression that everything he'd heard about Duncan Fitz was true—and then some.

"Let's get out of here," he said, as he blew past Theo in the lobby. In five minutes they were down the elevator and in the car. It took another five just to get out of the parking garage and into the stop-and-go traffic of Brickell Avenue, the heart of Miami's Financial District. Jack had no desire to move his office downtown, but it was a beautiful afternoon, and the reflection of palm trees and sunshine against Brickell's glass towers made him long for the old convertible he'd swapped out for life with Andie, Righley, and a golden retriever named Max, who had no idea he was a dog.

"You want me to drop you at your office?" asked Theo.

"Stop by San Lazaro's Café first," said Jack. "I have a few pointed questions for Maritza."

The drive to the coffee shop was just long enough for Jack to call Andie and give her the highs and low, mostly lows, of his meeting at Cool Cash. She took it as well as could be expected, and Jack assured her that Hannah was a pit bull, every bit the match for Duncan Fitz.

Theo found a parking spot next to the one for the Employee of the Month. Jack led the way inside to the booth in the back where he'd met Maritza. Theo's head covered half the map of Cuba. A server approached.

"Is Maritza here today?" asked Jack.

The server suddenly seemed flustered. "Uhm. Maritza? Uh . . . one second."

Jack and Theo exchanged puzzled looks as she walked away.

"Did you see that face she made?" asked Jack.

"That was weird, dude."

The manager appeared a moment later, the same one Jack had met the day before. "You were asking about Maritza?"

"Yeah, I was here yesterday. We talked over her break."

"I remember."

"Is she here?" asked Jack.

"No."

"When will she be back?"

"That's impossible to say. Probably never."

"Do you know where she is now?"

"I'm guessing she's on an airplane to Mexico City. ICE was here yesterday. I'm told she has been deported."

"She was illegal?" asked Jack, though it was more of a reflex than an inquiry.

"Look, I don't know all the details, and I have a café to run. Do you fellas want to buy some coffee? If not, I'd like to turn this table."

"I'd like an espresso," said Theo.

"I'll send your server," said the manager, and he stepped away.

"What do you make of that?" asked Jack.

"It's like the old joke," said Theo. "What's worse than a prostitute for an alibi? A deported prostitute."

"Never heard that one," said Jack.

"A moldy oldie, I call it."

Jack considered how quickly he'd lost his potential alibi witness after mere mention of her to the prosecution. "I call it a little too convenient for coincidence."

CHAPTER 24

I s it safe?" asked Righley.

The question cut to Jack's core. He was leaning over her shoulder at the kitchen table, cutting her toasted waffle—"No black stuff on the edges, Daddy"—into bite-sized pieces on her breakfast plate. Righley was dressed in a blue skirt and white polo shirt, the mandatory uniform of her new school. It was the family's morning routine. Andie got her up and dressed. Jack took Max outside to do his morning business and made Righley breakfast. They'd followed the same routine when Righley was at Riverside Day School, but there was a twist of late, with Righley asking the same question she'd asked every morning since day one at Key Biscayne K through 8.

Is it safe?

"Yes, sweetie. It's safe, it's fun, and you're going to learn so much there." Jack was sure of it. Then again, hadn't every parent at Riverside Day School made the same promise to their children just by virtue of sending them off to school each morning?

Max jumped up on his hind legs, front paws on the tabletop, and licked the syrup from Righley's chin. She laughed the way every child should laugh. There was nothing like an eighty-pound golden retriever licking your face to make you feel safe.

Righley finished her waffle in what seemed like record time, though Jack suspected that Max had claimed more than his fair share. Andie entered the kitchen.

"Ready, Righley?"

Righley looked at Max. "Ready?"

The real winner in the new routine was Max. The best thing about Righley's new school was that it was close enough to walk. The downside was that, with fourteen hundred students, Key Biscayne's K through 8 enrollment was almost triple Riverside's K through 12, which was precisely the reason Jack and Andie had stretched their wallet to send Righley to Riverside in the first place. Andie affixed Max's leash and took Righley's hand. Jack kissed them all good-bye, and the threesome was out the door. He topped off his go-cup with hot coffee and glanced at the newspaper on the kitchen counter. The remaining memorial services for victims of the Riverside shooting were scheduled for the coming week. Jack wondered if his name would come up. He grabbed his computer bag, jumped in the car, and headed across the bridge to Doral.

Most people who'd heard of Doral thought of the legendary Blue Monster golf course, home to PGA events for over fifty years and host to virtually every great player in the sport. Doral was also home to the Forensic Services Bureau of the Miami-Dade Police Department. Jack was pushing Xavier's case forward as fast as possible, and at the top of his priority list was the deposition of the state's fingerprint expert. At nine a.m. Jack was in a windowless conference room, and the stage was set. Jack was on one side of the rectangular table. Abe Beckham was on the other. The witness was seated at the head of the table next to the court reporter. It was Jack's deposition, so he was asking the questions.

"Good morning, Dr. Granger," said Jack, beginning much in the same way he would at trial, eliciting the witness's background and qualifications. Granger was a skinny fellow, mostly bald, save for an exceedingly long wisp of hair that attached at what was formerly his hairline, reached back over his shiny scalp, and disappeared somewhere behind his right ear. It was the gray and self-grown version of the hair extensions that Riverside mothers paid ridiculous sums of money to have taped to their heads, only to lose them in a tennis match or a windy convertible. Granger had a nervous habit of pushing his wisp into place once every minute or so, though it wasn't readily apparent to Jack what was "in place" as opposed to "out of place." That aside, there was no challenging Granger's expertise in his field. He held a PhD and had served as chief of the MDPD Forensic Bureau's Latent Unit for almost fifteen years.

"What is the primary function of the Latent Unit?" asked Jack.

"We evaluate physical evidence from crime scenes for the presence of latent prints through friction ridge analysis."

"What is a friction ridge?"

He used his own hand as a prop. "On the palm side of our hands and on the soles of our feet are prominent skin features that single us out from everyone else in the world. These so-called friction ridges leave impressions when they come into contact with an object. The impressions from the last finger joints are known as fingerprints."

"What is a latent fingerprint?"

"Let me back up a second," said Granger, pushing the wisp of hair back into place. "There are two different types of friction ridge impressions. The first are of known individuals recorded for a specific purpose, like the prints that you gave to the Florida Bar when you became a member, or that your client gave to the police when he was arrested. The second type involves impressions of unknown persons on a piece of evidence from a crime scene or related location. These are generally referred to as latent prints."

"Did you analyze latent fingerprints recovered from the crime scene at Riverside Day School?"

"I did."

"On what piece of evidence were those fingerprints found?"

"From the weapon that was recovered on the scene."

Jack put the next question with some trepidation, as it was a key issue that he and Hannah had focused on. "Were any latent prints found on the extended magazines recovered from the crime scene?"

"No."

"None?" asked Jack.

"No. My assumption is that the shooter wiped those magazines clean after purchasing them, probably with alcohol, and thereafter handled them only with gloves, like the gloves the shooter was wearing in the surveillance video I watched."

It was the kind of long-winded and speculative answer that Jack would have shut down at trial, but he was interested in hearing the expert's assumptions in a discovery deposition.

Jack handed the witness a photograph of the pistol. "Dr. Granger, this photograph is marked as Grand Jury Exhibit Ninety-Two and was produced to us by the state of Florida. Is it your testimony that the only latent fingerprints you examined are those found on this weapon?"

"That is my testimony."

"Were you able to identify any of the fingerprints found on this pistol?"

"Yes. We identified several prints from the gun's registered owner, Mr. Amir Khoury. And one print from the defendant, Xavier Khoury."

"Using the photograph, could you please point to the exact location of these fingerprints?"

"I'd rather use the diagram I prepared," said Granger. "It's in my report."

Jack located it, and reasked the question. Granger first identified the location of Amir's fingerprints, which were not important. "Where did you find Xavier Khoury's fingerprint?" asked Jack.

"There was only one print. It was the right index finger. Found here," said Granger, pointing to the diagram, "on the top of the barrel near the fixed sight."

"Your examination of Mr. Khoury's fingerprint was done in accordance with best practices, correct, Doctor?"

"Of course."

"Consistent with the exercise of best practices, what conclusion did you reach as to the age of Xavier Khoury's fingerprint that was found on the pistol?"

Granger looked puzzled—so puzzled that he pushed the wisp of gray hair back into place when, as far as Jack could tell, it wasn't even out of place. "The age?" he asked.

"Yeah," said Jack. "How long had Xavier's fingerprint been on the gun?"

"I didn't reach any conclusion in that regard," said Granger.

"Why not?"

"There's no reliable scientific test to determine the age of a fingerprint. We can only deduce it from circumstantial or anecdotal evidence."

"How would you deduce the age of a fingerprint?"

"For example, if a latent print is lifted from a newspaper dated June first, twenty-nineteen, you know the fingerprint isn't older than that."

"Let's keep our focus on the weapon at issue in this case. Is there such a way to 'deduce' the age of Xavier Khoury's fingerprint?"

"Not in our lab. The Netherlands Forensic Institute has made progress on a technique that can be used on fresh fingerprints—prints less than fifteen days old. They claim that their technique can pin it down to within a day or two."

"The fingerprints from the weapon found in this case were not examined by the Netherlands Forensic Institute, were they, Doctor?"

"No."

"As far as you know, Dr. Granger, my client's fingerprint could have been a day old?"

"Yes."

"A week?"

"Yes."

"A month?"

"Sure."

"A year?"

"When you start talking years, then it becomes a question of whether the print really could have lasted that long. That all depends on the surface, the firmness of the imprint, and other factors, including the salinity of a person's skin. On porous surfaces, like paper, fingerprints can last forty years."

"What about a gun like the one used in the Riverside shooting? How long?"

"I'm going to object," said Beckham. "That's pure speculation."

There was no judge at a deposition, but the prosecutor had the right to make his objections for the record. Clearly, Beckham didn't like the point Jack was making—that the only time Xavier had ever handled this gun was *years* before anyone had planned the school shooting.

"Let me rephrase," said Jack. "Are you aware of any studies regarding the recovery of latent prints some number of years after those prints were impressed on a firearm?"

"I've read a number of excellent studies. For one, Sheffield Hallam University developed a technique to recover latent marks from spent casings using an electrolysis process. They've examined spent casings and weapons up to twenty years old, in various states of decay, and recovered latent prints that are legally admissible in a court of law."

"In our case, Mr. Khoury's gun is more than twenty years old," said Jack. "In theory, the fingerprints you recovered from Amir and Xavier Khoury could be that old, correct?"

"Not Xavier's. He's only eighteen. And in my opinion the size of the impression indicates that his hands were fully grown."

"So the most your report can say is that Xavier laid a finger on his father's gun sometime after he went through puberty. Say, sometime in the last three or four years."

"Objection," said Beckham. "Dr. Granger has already testified that there is no test to confirm the age of a fingerprint."

"You can answer," Jack told the witness. "Xavier touched his father's gun sometime in the last three or four years. That's all you can say, right?"

"It could have been that long ago."

"And for the same reasons, Mr. Khoury's print could be twenty or more years old, correct?"

"Yes," said Granger. "And the same goes for the unidentified print."

Jack did a double take. It never ceased to amaze him the way smart people couldn't resist showing off how much they knew, even if it helped the other side. It took all of Jack's professional discipline to contain his excitement.

"Dr. Granger, I've read your report. I didn't see any mention of an *unidentified* latent fingerprint on the murder weapon."

"It's not in my report."

"Why not?"

"Additional tests are being run to identify it."

"Where was this unidentified fingerprint found?"

"On the inside of the pistol's slide. I'm not a ballistics expert, but a pistol doesn't have an exposed barrel the way a revolver does. The barrel is inside the slide. So, for a print to be found inside the slide, the firearm must have been disassembled for cleaning, maintenance, gun-safety training—whatever the reason."

"Let me make sure I understand," said Jack. "You've been unable to link this latent fingerprint to any known individual, correct?"

"Correct."

"But you have concluded that this fingerprint *does not* belong to either Amir Khoury or Xavier Khoury."

"Objection," said Beckham. "That was not Dr. Granger's testimony. Your question fails to account for the fact that the impression could have been blurred or smudged, which prevented Dr. Granger from concluding that it belonged to either Xavier or Amir Khoury."

"Is that the case, Dr. Granger?" asked Jack. "Or is the prosecutor putting words in your mouth?"

"I object to that remark," said Beckham.

Jack tightened his gaze, as well as his figurative grip, on the witness. "Dr. Granger, there was nothing wrong with the quality of the fingerprint you were unable to identify, was there?"

"No," Granger said, too much of a professional to mince words. "Actually, it's of even higher quality than the latent print of Xavier Khoury. It oxidized into the metal, which can happen with certain types of firearms or casings."

"In other words, if this fingerprint did, in fact, belong to Xavier or his father, the print was of sufficient quality for you to make that determination. And you ruled them out. Correct?"

He paused, not because he didn't know the answer, but because he seemed to appreciate the gravity of his admission. "That is true. The unidentified print does not belong to either Xavier or his father. As a forensic scientist, I'm certain of that much."

"Thank you, Doctor," said Jack, and he was happy to end it right there.

CHAPTER 25

On Thursday Jack paid another visit to the Miami-Dade Pretrial Detention Center. It was a standing appointment with his client. Sort of.

Jack was fed up with the silent treatment from Xavier. He wanted to talk about Maritza, but the emphasis was on *talk.* So Jack had written his client a letter about his meeting with Maritza and said, "Let's have a real conversation." He'd made it abundantly clear that it would not be another session of Jack talking and Xavier listening. "I will come to the lobby every day at 10 a.m. and wait five minutes. If you're ready to *talk to me,* have the guard send me up." A week had passed, and with each visit Jack had come and gone in five minutes with no word from Xavier or the guard. On a Thursday, fifteen days after the shooting, Jack's conditions were met.

"Your client will see you, Swyteck," the guard told him.

Jack felt optimistic as he rode up the elevator with the guard. Progress, it seemed, was being made. Xavier was waiting for him in the attorney-client meeting room, seated in a chair at the table with his arms folded across his chest. No shackles this time, and no bruises about the face, which Jack took as a sign of Xavier's adjustment to life behind bars, the most important aspect of which was learning how to stay out of trouble. Jack waited for the guard to close the door on his way out. He then pulled up a chair, turned it around backwards, and sat rodeo-style, facing his client.

"Ready to have a conversation?" asked Jack.

Xavier said nothing.

"I know you can speak," said Jack. "The guard told me he heard you praying in your cell this morning."

Jack waited, but it was back to the old routine. Nothing from Xavier.

"You did read my letter, right?" said Jack.

Xavier lowered his gaze, breaking eye contact.

"We had a deal," said Jack. "I offered to come up here if you agreed to talk. You accepted that offer. Now it's time to honor your end of the bargain."

Xavier drew a deep breath and let it out. But no words followed.

It was frustrating, but Jack had dealt with worse. A client who wouldn't talk was probably better than a client who lied constantly or threatened to kill you. Jack had to change strategies.

"Here's my dilemma," said Jack. "The defense has a legal obligation to tell the prosecution if there will be an alibi witness. I also have a legal obligation not to put a witness on the stand who I know is lying. I'm not going to spin my wheels trying to track down Maritza if my own client tells me she's lying." Jack leaned a little closer. "Is she lying, Xavier?"

Again, no reply.

"I think she is," said Jack. "And I think you're the shooter. What do you have to say about that?"

Xavier lifted his gaze and looked at Jack, but that was the extent of his reaction.

"Let's put my opinions aside," said Jack. "This may sound a little far afield to you, but I want to tell you this story. It's about an ol' friend of mine from college. Ray married his college sweetheart and started a family long before I did. He has a grown daughter now who's fantastic. Ray had a son, too. Jason was his name. He died when he was seventeen. Suicide."

Xavier shifted in his chair, clearly listening.

"Jason was a lot like you. Good-looking boy. Excellent student. You were accepted to MIT; I think Jason was headed for Cal Poly or some other top engineering school. Jason never had a girlfriend, though, until his senior year of high school. He was nuts about her, his dad told me. Then she dumped him. Jason was devastated. As much as his dad tried to help him through it, Jason just couldn't get over it. So one Saturday night when his parents went out on their weekly date night, Jason grabbed the keys to his car, closed the garage door, rolled down the car windows, and started the engine. Two hours later his father found him slumped over in the front seat. Jason was gone.

"Terrible story, I know. What his dad can't get over is that Jason didn't want to die. He knows that because Jason recorded a video on his cell phone while he was fading away inside the car. Jason was professing his love to this girl who had dumped him. His dad says that every psychiatrist and health-care professional who watched that video and heard Jason's last words reached the same conclusion. Not only did Jason not *want* to die. He didn't even believe that he was *going to die*. Jason had cooked up this fantasy in his head that his parents would come home from dinner, find him, and rush him to the hospital. And when the doctors revived him and he came to, this girl who had dumped him would be standing at his bedside, and she'd throw her arms around him, kiss him, and say, *Oh, Jason, you really do love me!*"

Jack gave his client a minute to absorb the story, and then continued.

"Like I said, Xavier. I think you did it. But for one moment, let's step into that alternative world of possibilities, the one percent chance you're innocent. Is all of this some kind of romantic fantasy for you? You sit in this room in silence, not helping yourself, not letting me help you. Do you have a tortured vision in your head of this case going all the way to trial, all the way to the *last day* of trial, and it looks like you're going to be convicted and sentenced to death? Then let me guess. Suddenly the doors in the back of the courtroom swing open, and in walks Maritza. She tells the jury that she loves you and that the two of you were making passionate love all morning while the real shooter was murdering innocent students across town at Riverside Day School. You and Maritza lock eyes from across the courtroom, the two of you unable to comprehend another minute apart from each other. Maritza saves you from the needle, and the two of you live happily ever after.

"Is that the game you're playing, Xavier?"

All expression drained from Xavier's face. He was a complete blank.

"I hope not," said Jack, "because that is not going to happen. If you don't open up and talk to me, this is not going to end well for you. I speak from experience. I'm not bragging, but I'm highly regarded in this unpleasant line of work in capital cases. Even so, I have more dead former clients than living ones."

Jack waited, hoping that the weight of his story hanging in silence between them would impel a response. But the ticking seconds turned to minutes, and Xavier said nothing. Jack had one last card to play.

"I spoke with Imam Hassan from your mosque," said Jack. "He told me that he met Maritza."

Xavier didn't deny it, but given the track record, it was impossible to infer an admission from silence. So Jack dropped the bomb.

"He said Maritza was a prostitute."

Jack waited. A slow but steady transformation was underway, right before Jack's eyes. Something at a very primal level was churning inside Xavier, not just in his mind but throughout his entire body, as if those little bubbles that form in a pot of water on the stove were rising ever faster. Xavier didn't speak, but Jack thought he saw him mouth the word *prostitute*—and the pot boiled over. Xavier sprang from his chair, roiling mad, as fifteen days of self-imposed silence erupted from his molten core. He grabbed the chair and threw it across the room, smashing it against the wall.

"Xavier!" Jack shouted.

The door burst open, and two guards rushed in. Xavier was about to slam the table against the wall when the guards tackled him, pinned him facedown on the floor, and cuffed his wrists behind his back.

"Don't resist!" the guard shouted, and Xavier's body went limp.

The other guard checked on Jack. "Are you all right?"

"I'm fine," said Jack.

The guards lifted Xavier from the floor and took him toward the door.

"Wait," said Jack.

They stopped, but only the guards glanced back at Jack. Xavier kept his head down, facing the exit. His anger seemed to be under control.

"We'll talk again, Xavier," said Jack.

"Maybe when he gets out of disciplinary confinement," said the guard.

Xavier was silent, but fully compliant, as the corrections officers took him away.

CHAPTER 26

On Friday Jack was again before Judge Martinez—without Xavier, who was in day two of ten days of disciplinary confinement for his violent outburst. Hannah was at the defense table with Jack. Abe Beckham, on behalf of the state of Florida, and Sylvia Gonzalez, for the Justice Department, shared the prosecutor's table to Jack's right. The proceeding was open to the public, and several rows of seating behind the lawyers were filled with friends and family of the victims. They were almost outnumbered by the media.

"Good morning," said Judge Martinez. "We are here on Mr. Swyteck's motion, is that correct?"

Jack rose. "That's correct, Your Honor."

The judge flipped through the file before him, reading. "The defendant seeks an order of the court compelling the production of all evidence, including forensic reports, concerning an unidentified fingerprint found on the firearm allegedly used in the shooting at Riverside Day School."

"The defense also subpoenaed the federal government to produce any similar records," said Jack.

"Which the National Security Division of the Department of Justice opposes," said Gonzalez, rising.

Beckham rose. "I can simplify matters, Judge. The state of Florida has no objection to turning over whatever records it has in its possession. But the National Security Division has asked us not to."

"On what basis?" the judge asked.

"I'll defer to Ms. Gonzalez on that point," said Beckham.

"National security, Your Honor," said Gonzalez.

The judge threw up his hands, looking at Jack. "Mr. Swyteck, you need to enforce your subpoena against the federal government in federal court in Washington, DC. Not here."

"And I will," said Jack. He stepped to the podium, taking charge. "Your Honor, I'm before you today because the existence of an unidentified fingerprint on the murder weapon clearly raises questions as to the guilt or innocence of my client. The prosecution has an obligation to turn over to the defense all exculpatory evidence. If Mr. Beckham has that information, this court has the power to, and should, order the state of Florida to give it to me. Whether the federal government must give me that information is an argument for another day in another courthouse. But my client has a right to have whatever Mr. Beckham has in his possession."

"I think I understand the issue Mr. Swyteck is raising," the judge said, "and it's an interesting one."

Gonzalez spoke up. "Yes, Judge, it's an interesting issue for a law professor to research for two years before publishing some bleeding-heart article in a highbrow academic journal."

"It goes to the heart of my client's constitutional right to a fair trial," Jack fired back. "Can the prosecutor withhold vital evidence simply because the NSD tells him that handing it over to the defense would be contrary to the interests of national security? The answer has to be no."

"I agree with Mr. Swyteck to a point," the judge said. "Evidence of an unidentified print on the murder weapon is vital evidence. But there has to be a balance of interests. Ms. Gonzalez, exactly what is the national security interest here?"

Gonzalez glanced over her shoulder at the crowded gallery. Members of the media were literally on the edge of their seats.

"Judge, I would ask the courtroom be closed for my response to that question."

A chorus of groans coursed through the gallery.

"Everyone keep your seats," the judge said. "Counsel, let's do this in my chambers."

The judge stepped down, and the lawyers followed. There were no assigned seats, but everyone took exactly the same seats as the last hearing in chambers. Ivan the life-sized Ibis hadn't moved.

"Ms. Gonzalez, let's hear it," said the judge.

"The short answer is that al-Qaeda claimed responsibility for this shooting," said Gonzalez. "That claim is being taken very seriously, and there is an active investigation underway involving multiple agencies. The information sought by Mr. Swyteck goes to the heart of that investigation."

"That's it?" asked the judge. "That's your explanation?"

"That's all I'm at liberty to reveal."

"Ms. Gonzalez, I closed this hearing to the public at your request so that you would be free to convince me that a vital national security interest is at stake. This is your opportunity."

"Your Honor, I'm limited as to what I can say by NSD policies, as well as specific orders entered in this investigation by the FISA Court."

"FISA" was her shorthand reference to the Foreign Intelligence Surveillance Court, which entertains government requests for approval of electronic surveillance, physical search, and other investigative actions for foreign intelligence purposes.

Jack needed to jump in—with both feet. "Your Honor, the government is talking out of both sides of its mouth. Two weeks ago, Ms. Gonzalez opposed my request to withdraw as counsel because I could be trusted to handle sensitive information. Now it's her position that she can't even tell *you* what national security interest is at stake."

"I do recall your saying that, Ms. Gonzalez," the judge said.

Gonzalez hesitated, then replied. "I can tell the court this much. There is a vital national security interest. It is to prevent more terrorist attacks, possibly more school shootings. On behalf of the United States Department of Justice, I'm asking you *not* to be the state court judge who derailed a federal investigation that could have stopped another school shooting."

Gonzalez had the judge thinking, and Jack had to hand it to her: Gonzalez didn't practice regularly in Miami, but she knew exactly the right argument to make in a state where trial judges are elected and can't survive bad press.

"Well, the safety of our schoolchildren is certainly a vital interest," Judge Martinez said.

Jack repackaged his argument on the fly, knowing that he would never get this judge to side with the defense on the issue as reframed by the government. "Judge, I don't want to be the *lawyer* who derailed this investigation, either. But I'm also fighting for my client's life, and apart from the fact that he has not yet been adjudicated guilty, there's something important that's being overlooked."

"Tell me," the judge said.

"The very existence of the unidentified print only came to my attention because I elicited the information while deposing the government's fingerprint expert. That's not the way the process is supposed to work. The existence of that print should have been disclosed to the defense immediately. I'm not sure Mr. Beckham would have *ever* told me about it if his own witness had not let the cat out of the bag. That's a clear violation of the government's disclosure obligations."

Beckham was in the hot seat, and Jack's read of the situation was that he could pull one of two pages from the time-honored, unwritten prosecutor's manual: the Aw-shucks-Judge-I'm-sorry page, or the When-dead-wrong-become-indignant page.

Beckham chose the latter. "For a second there, Judge, I thought Mr. Swyteck was serious when he said he was interested in saving innocent lives. I certainly am. The NSD told me to treat the unidentified print as a matter of national security, so I did."

Jack caught Gonzalez's eye from across the table, and apparently it was enough to get her to do the right thing. "Your Honor, if I may clarify the communication?"

"Please do."

"I asked Mr. Beckham to treat as confidential all matters relating to the identity or possible identity of the person whose fingerprint was found on the gun. The mere *existence* of an unidentified print is, by itself, not a matter of national security and will not compromise the investigation."

Beckham shrank in his chair, and Jack could almost see him shift gears and reach for the "aw shucks" page in the unwritten prosecutor's manual. "Oh, well, my mistake, Your Honor. I'm terribly sorry. It won't happen again. Just an honest miscommunication."

Judge Martinez, too, had apparently "read" the manual and was completely on to him. "It had better not happen again, Mr. Beckham. Because if this had happened closer to trial, I could very well be entering an order dismissing the indictment. Understood?"

"Yes, Your Honor."

"Has this court addressed everything?" the judge asked.

"For now," said Jack.

"Then we're adjourned. Thank you, Counsel."

The lawyers rose, and Beckham was the first one out the door. Jack caught up with Gonzalez in the hallway outside the judge's chambers.

"Thank you for that, Sylvia."

"You're welcome," she said.

"I hope you won't take this as ingratitude, but I do plan to file a motion in federal court. I need to know whose fingerprint is on that gun."

"I would expect no less from you, Jack."

"See you soon," he said.

She just smiled and was on her way.

CHAPTER 27

Xavier waited on the bench for the corrections officer to come. The incident on Friday had cost him two nights in solitary confinement. Unlike the guy in the cell next to him, who'd kept howling like a wounded wolf, Xavier had behaved himself. So he was being moved from solitary to a shared cell, though still in disciplinary confinement. Apparently, it was taking longer than planned to find an open bunk. No shortage of badasses at the Miami-Dade Pretrial Detention Center.

Xavier was on week three as a Level One detainee, and things weren't getting any better. He'd felt untethered from reality the minute he'd set foot in the building. No wristwatch. No cell phone. No talking allowed. Those first few hours had been a blur, but in slow motion. Up and down several flights of stairs. In and out of different holding pens. He'd been shackled, unshackled, and shackled again. The body search had been especially memorable, not so much for what actually had happened, but for fear of what might. Fingerprinting took another hour. Not even the prisoner's obligatory "one phone call" had gone smoothly. Xavier had waited in line for an hour and was reaching for the phone when another inmate came up from behind him and whispered a threat into his ear. "Tanks for holdin' my spot in line, mon—now get the fuck away from me." It had been just as well. Even local calls were collect only, and probably no one would have accepted Xavier's charges anyway.

"Got a bunk for you," said the guard. "Let's go."

Xavier rode up the elevator flanked by a pair of corrections officers. The doors opened to the disciplinary cellblock, where a third officer completed the disciplinary check-in procedures. It had taken so long for a bed to free up that it was already "lights out." The cells were dark, but the long corridor remained lighted. The guards escorted Xavier past one locked door after another until they stopped at cell number 511.

"You're bunking with Roosevelt," the guard said. "It's your lucky day."

Xavier had no idea who Roosevelt was, but the way the other guard snickered at the "lucky day" comment, it was a safe bet he was no relation to the former presidents.

Maybe I should've stayed in solitary.

The cell door buzzed open. The guards removed the shackles. Xavier entered quietly, trying not to disturb Roosevelt on the top bunk as he climbed onto the mattress below. The metal frame squeaked as he settled in. The cell door closed, and then it hit him. This was no ordinary inmate. He was locked in a cell with a man who was being punished for breaking the rules. Maybe it was his imagination running wild, but Xavier quickly convinced himself that Roosevelt had done something far worse than throw a chair against the wall.

"Hey, you that shooter, ain't you, pretty boy?"

Apparently, Roosevelt had only pretended to be asleep. Xavier kept quiet, hoping his cellmate would let it drop. No such luck.

"Yeah, you is. I saw you walk in. Shooter is a fuckin' pretty boy."

Xavier lay still, praying for silence. It was dark. It was scary. His pillow stank so bad that he wanted to throw it on the floor. Maybe Roosevelt had sprinkled it with toilet juice: the joke's on the pretty boy.

A minute later, Roosevelt's voice again pierced the darkness. "Wanna know somethin', pretty boy? You is better off with the death penalty. You get yo' own private cell on death row. Takes years to move on down the line to the gurney. And when you finally get there, you lay down, take a needle in the arm, and go to sleep. That don't sound so bad, does it?"

Xavier didn't answer.

"But a life sentence?" he said, chuckling. "Shit. You in the general population, pretty boy. You understand what I'm sayin'? If you take the needle, you get stuck once. But if you in the general population—shit, a pretty boy like you? You get stuck every night."

Xavier had already gone down that line of thinking, many times, since his arrest.

"You don't talk, huh?" asked Roosevelt. "I get it. You afraid to open your mouth. You don't have to worry, pretty boy. You can open your mouth. I ain't gonna stick my dick down your throat.

"Not tonight."

Xavier froze. This was the first of ten disciplinary nights with Roosevelt. Xavier could ask for a transfer to another cell, but he could end up with worse. Or his request could easily be denied. Either way, he'd need to state the reason for the request, and he'd have to tell the guard that Roosevelt threatened him. Then Xavier wouldn't just be the "pretty boy." He'd also be a snitch who needed to be taught a lesson. "Snitch bitch" was what the other inmates had called that guy in the shower who was down on his knees.

Roosevelt was right. The needle was preferable.

"Hey, pretty boy," said Roosevelt. "I'm gonna do you a favor."

Xavier felt a chill down his spine. Did he mean *sexual* favor?

"Listen good," said Roosevelt. "I don't do this for everyone. And you don't even have to thank me. Just listen real careful to what I'm saying. Then take the time you need to think it over.

And while you thinkin', be sure to pay attention to the schedule
the guards follow to check on us at night. Okay? You listening?"

Xavier remained still.

"I'm gonna tell you how to make a good, strong fucking rope
out of a bedsheet."

CHAPTER 28

Around four a.m. Jack phoned Molly Khoury from his bedroom. She answered on the second ring and sounded wide awake. A good night's sleep was obviously not part of this mother's current existence.

"I just heard from Jackson Memorial Hospital," said Jack. "Xavier is in the intensive care unit. He tried to hang himself."

Molly's shriek on the line was so loud that it made Andie stir on the other side of their bed. Jack went into their master bathroom and closed the door. It took a minute to calm Molly down and tell her what he knew, which wasn't very much.

"They wouldn't give me details over the phone. I pushed so hard to speak to him that I must have ticked off the nurse. She got a little testy and said Xavier couldn't talk to me even if phones were allowed in the ICU. He's unconscious and breathing on a ventilator."

"Oh, my God," said Molly. "Why did no one call me?"

"You're the first person I called," said Jack.

"I mean the hospital or the jail!"

The harsh reality was that Xavier had listed neither of his parents as "contacts," but there was no need to make her feel worse than she already did. "I'm leaving in five minutes. I can meet you at the hospital and we can get a handle on what's going on."

She agreed, and as quickly as Jack could get dressed, he was out the door and on the causeway to the mainland. Molly had a shorter drive to Jackson and was already in the waiting room by the time Jack made it over from Key Biscayne.

"They won't let me go up to see him," she said. "How can they not let his own mother see him?"

Molly seemed to have mentally blocked out the fact that her son was not only an accused mass murderer, but also a Protective Custody Level One detainee who was in disciplinary detention for bad behavior. Jack went to the admissions window. The clerk took the necessary information from him and called for a security guard to escort him to the ICU. Molly was much like any concerned mother, filling Jack's head with her son's complete medical history.

"Xavier had his wisdom teeth removed six months ago. Probably should have had his tonsils out in the fifth grade, but we decided not to. He tolerates acetaminophen well but has trouble swallowing the tablets, so be sure to tell the nurse to break them in half or give him gel caps."

Molly was so scattered that she seemed to have forgotten that, at last report, Xavier wasn't even breathing on his own. "Got it," said Jack.

She handed him the file she'd grabbed from home. "Everything is right here. Please give it to the nurses in the ICU."

"Will do."

The security guard took him up the elevator. They rode in silence, which gave Jack another opportunity to wrestle with the guilt he was feeling. Xavier's attempted suicide had come on the heels of Jack's story about the teenage boy who'd taken his own life—his old friend Ray's son. It was enough to make Jack wonder.

The elevator door opened, and as he stepped into the bright hallway, Jack felt a strange sense of déjà vu. Two weeks earlier, he'd walked down this same hallway to visit Nate Abrams, whose daughter was barely clinging to life. It was almost too bizarre for words. All he could hope was that Lindsey's killer—*alleged* killer—wasn't lying in the very same bed. Jack reached the pneumatic doors and pressed the CALL button, but this time there was no crackling response from the nurse over the intercom. The door opened, and a physician dressed in scrubs walked out.

"Please don't come in," he said.

"Who are you?" asked Jack.

"I'm Dr. Henderson. Infectious disease. I've been with Emily Ramirez almost all night. The infection from the gunshot wound to her abdomen is back with a vengeance. She could easily become your client's fifteenth victim by the end of today."

"I'm so sorry to hear that."

"Her parents are with her now. They don't need to see your face. Please, don't come in."

Jack didn't make an issue of it. "I presume my client is under armed guard?"

"Yes. Two of them. They're posted right outside his bay, which is distressing enough for Emily's parents, not to mention our other patients who have never committed mass murder."

"I don't want to add to anyone's stress," said Jack. "But can someone give me an update? I was told Xavier is on a ventilator."

"Then you got bad information. He's breathing on his own. Vitals are good. Pupils respond to light, so no sign of depressed brain-stem reflexes. Reflexes are normal, and he responds to pinprick and other painful stimuli."

"So, he's going to recover?"

"Let's put it this way: people who want your client to be fully aware and conscious when the executioner sticks a needle in his arm will not be disappointed."

"So he's going to be fine?"

"Yes," said the doctor, and then he glanced back at the ICU entrance. "How the good Lord squares that with the innocent children who didn't come out of here alive is beyond me."

"I understand."

"No you don't," said the doctor. "No lawyer who does what you do understands anything but money and some kind of perverse high that comes from defending despicable people."

"My wife says the same thing," said Jack. "Except the money part. She's on a government salary and makes more than I do."

The doctor didn't so much as acknowledge Jack's attempt to defuse the situation. "I need to get back to my patients."

"One second," said Jack. "Can you give me some idea of what happened?"

"What I know is all after the fact. You'll have to talk to the detention center. I gotta go." As the doctor stepped away, he seemed to reconsider his attitude. He stopped. "Hey, sorry for what I said about what you do and why you do it. It's been a long night."

Jack had been on the receiving end of much worse. "No problem," he said.

Jack was in court before his client was fully awake. Judge Martinez was starting a jury trial in another case that morning, so he squeezed in Abe Beckham's request for an emergency hearing at eight thirty a.m.

The judicial assistant brought a big mug of coffee up to the bench. "Mr. Beckham, I presume this emergency relates to the attempted suicide and hospitalization of the defendant?"

"That's partially correct," said the prosecutor. "The state of Florida disputes that this was an attempted suicide."

The judge reviewed the file in front of him. "The incident report states that the detainee tore off three long strips from his bedsheet, braided the strips together like a rope, tied the rope to the bed frame in the bunk above him, and hanged himself by the neck until he was unconscious. Does that not sound like attempted suicide to you, Mr. Beckham?"

"Things are not always what they appear to be."

"Especially in this town," the judge added. "But why has the prosecution brought this matter before the court? If anything, I would have expected a motion from the defense arguing that Mr. Khoury is mentally incompetent to stand trial."

"I'm being proactive," said the prosecutor. "I, too, fully expect the defense to latch on to this incident and postpone the trial until Mr. Khoury dies of old age. My goal is to nip this stunt in the bud."

Jack rose. "Your Honor, I have to object to the characterization of a medical emergency as a 'stunt.'"

"Yes, Mr. Beckham. Let's tone down the rhetoric, please. Especially in the absence of any factual record to support your allegation."

"My apologies," said Beckham. "With the court's permission, I would like to establish that factual record."

"When?" the judge asked.

"I have Dr. Andrew Phillips waiting in the hallway. He is with the Office of Health Services, Florida Department of Corrections, and oversees the administration of health care at Miami-Dade Pretrial Detention Center."

Jack was on his feet again. "Your Honor, I've had no time to prepare."

"*Prepare*," said Beckham, almost snarling. "Judge, that's exactly why we need to move quickly. We all know exactly what Mr. Swyteck means by 'prepare.' He needs time to prepare his client to say exactly the right words in a psychiatric evaluation. He needs time to find the right psychiatrist who will listen to this beautifully prepared presentation so that he, in turn, can prepare an ironclad report. And Mr. Swyteck then needs time to prepare his disingenuous argument to the court that the trial must be postponed indefinitely because his client thinks the judge is a kangaroo, thinks the prosecutor is from planet Mars, and thinks the FBI is spying on him through a camera implanted in his penis."

"Judge, this is beyond the pale," said Jack.

"Really, Mr. Beckham. What is it that you want?"

"I want the *immediate* opportunity to demonstrate to this court that the defendant is mentally competent to stand trial."

"Judge, I have not yet asserted that my client is mentally incompetent," said Jack.

"But it's coming!" said Beckham. "We all know it. Hollywood makes it seem that claims of not guilty by reason of insanity are an everyday occurrence in a criminal courtroom. They're not. But I can tell you what is: a claim by a guilty-as-sin defendant that he is mentally incompetent to stand trial, followed by a flurry of motions from death row arguing that he lacks the mental capacity to understand why he is being executed.

"Well, what about the mental state of the good people who are grieving for the children who were shot down in their own school, Your Honor? What about *their* mental anguish? I'm here for them this morning. I will not be caught flat-footed and watch the defense use this so-called attempted suicide to delay this trial for months, if not years, which will only deprive the victims and their families of the justice they deserve."

Jack kept his seat. Even at such an early hour, and even for a last-minute hearing, more than a dozen friends and relatives of the victims had gathered in the gallery. They were the core group who had vowed to "be there, no matter what" for a lost loved one—wounded souls who would have shown up in their pajamas at three a.m. if someone in Victims Services at the State Attorney's Office had called to tell them that a hearing was scheduled at the last minute. Finally, the prosecutor had pushed the right button with Judge Martinez: justice for the victims.

"All right," the judge said. "We have time for one witness."

Beckham thanked him, and, as if on cue, Dr. Phillips entered through the rear doors of the courtroom. The witness was sworn and settled into the chair. The prosecutor quickly established his credentials as chief physician at the detention center with more than two decades of experience at the Florida Department of Corrections. The questioning quickly transitioned to Jack's client.

"Dr. Phillips, when did you find out that Mr. Khoury had been taken to Jackson Memorial Hospital?"

"I received a phone call from the warden around one a.m. He informed me that the ambulance was already on the way."

"What did you do?"

"I have staff privileges at Jackson, so I went straight to the emergency room."

"Did you provide any information to the emergency room physicians about Mr. Khoury or the events that led to his visit to the emergency room?"

"Officer Jenkins was the corrections officer who found Mr. Khoury in his bunk. He rode in the ambulance to the ER. He provided that information to the doctors."

"Were you there for Officer Jenkins' report?"

"I was."

"Could you summarize, please?"

"Jenkins was on his regular rounds when he checked Mr. Khoury's cell. Mr. Khoury appeared to be sitting up in the lower bunk. Jenkins called to him, but Mr. Khoury did not respond. Jenkins switched on the light and then saw the rope around Mr. Khoury's neck. He immediately radioed for assistance and entered the cell. He removed the rope and administered CPR. Mr. Khoury was breathing when paramedics arrived."

"Dr. Phillips, have there been suicides at the Pretrial Detention Center in the past?"

"Sadly, yes."

"And I suppose there have been attempted suicides, where the inmate survived?"

"Yes."

"Did any of those suicides or attempted suicides involve hanging?"

"Yes."

"Now, Doctor. Can you tell me if in any of those previous cases, the detainee tried to hang himself while lying down?"

"Lying down," he said, searching his memory.

Jack rose before the witness could answer. "Your Honor, I see where this line of questioning is going, and I object. Any qualified expert on this subject would testify that death by hanging doesn't require a drop from the highest gallows. Hanging is deadly in any number of positions: sitting, kneeling, toes touching the ground—and yes, even in a prone position with nothing but the weight of the head and chest as the constricting force."

"That's not my point," said Beckham. "Judge, may I continue without interruption, please?"

"You may continue," the judge said, "but please make your point soon."

"Dr. Phillips, when you heard that Mr. Khoury hanged himself, what was your first thought?"

"Tragic. We do everything reasonably possible to ensure the safety of our inmates."

"When you heard that Mr. Khoury tried to hang himself while lying down, what was your first thought?"

"Well," the doctor said, almost smiling, "I don't mean to sound insensitive. But we actually have a term for that."

"What is the term?"

"Sympathy hanging."

Jack thought again of the story he'd told Xavier about Ray's son—the teenage boy who didn't really want to kill himself.

Beckham asked, "What does that mean, Doctor? A sympathy hanging?"

Jack sprang from his chair to object, but the judge overruled him. "There's no jury here," the judge said. "The witness may answer."

"It's like the person who takes one too many sleeping pills and then dials nine-one-one before dozing off. They don't really want to die. They do it for sympathy."

Jack objected again. "Your Honor, we are way beyond this witness's sphere of personal knowledge, and ever futher beyond his area of medical expertise."

The judge peered out over the top of his reading glasses, toward the scattering of victim supporters in the gallery, as if to assure them that he'd allowed the prosecutor to go as far as legally permissible. "I have to say I agree with the defense," he said with some reluctance. "Mr. Beckham, if your goal is to convince me that this was all a stunt to set up a claim that Mr. Khoury is mentally incompetent to stand trial, this witness isn't going to do it for you. No offense to you, Dr. Phillips. Counsel, let's schedule this matter for a proper hearing."

"Very well," said Beckham. "To that end, the state requests that the court appoint a psychiatrist to conduct a full competence evaluation of the defendant."

"I'll say it again," said Jack. "The defense has made no claim that Mr. Khoury is mentally incompetent."

"The rules also allow for evaluation at the request of the prosecution," said Beckham. "Why wait for Mr. Swyteck to make his request two hours before the start of trial, which will only delay justice? Let's do it now."

"The state's request is granted," the judge said.

"Thank you," said Beckham. "We ask that the court appoint Dr. Howard Meed."

Jack and every other defense lawyer in Miami knew of Meed. In Meed's judgment, Beckham's hypothetical defendant—the one who thought the judge was a kangaroo and the prosecutor was from Mars—was not only competent to stand trial but also quite qualified to operate his own think tank. "Judge, I suggest that the court direct the prosecutor and defense to confer and select a mutually agreeable psychiatrist."

"More delay," said Beckham. "Dr. Meed is eminently qualified."

"He is, indeed," the judge said. "Dr. Meed's evaluation shall take place as soon as Mr. Khoury's treating physician clears him. Anything further from counsel this morning?"

There was nothing.

"Then we're adjourned," the judge said, with a crack of his gavel.

Lawyers and spectators rose on the bailiff's command, and the judge exited to his chambers. Jack approached his opposing counsel while Beckham was at the table and packing up his trial bag.

"There's still a way to avoid all this," said Jack. "Offer me a plea that doesn't include the death penalty, and I will do everything in my power to make sure my client gives it serious consideration."

"I have no reason to change my mind," said Beckham. "If hanging himself was a stunt pulled purely for sympathy, your client is evil and manipulative. If it was a genuine attempt to kill himself, it shows consciousness of guilt. Either way, he deserves death."

Jack glanced toward the friends and family in the gallery. Some were making their way toward the exit in silence. Others just sat there, staring, as if still coming to terms with the fact that someone they loved was gone, that nothing that transpired in this courtroom was ever going to bring them back.

"I wish I could convince you that this isn't about sparing my client," said Jack. "It's about sparing them."

"You keep on telling yourself that, Swyteck, if it helps you live with yourself."

Beckham turned and exited through the swinging gate at the rail. Jack started back toward the defense table to gather his belongings, glancing once more toward the friends and family who'd come to support the victims, feeling the weight of one woman's stare from the back of the courtroom. Jack averted his eyes—then he stopped and did a double take, his gaze shifting back toward the double-door exit.

The young woman was gone, but Jack suddenly realized that it hadn't been a glare from a total stranger. It had taken a moment for his mind to sift through the confusion and recognize the face beneath the broad-brimmed hat she'd been wearing, but he was certain that he knew her, that he'd met her before.

That it was Maritza from the coffee shop.

Jack grabbed his computer bag from the table, hurried to the exit, and pushed through the double doors to the lobby. He was caught in the nine a.m. rush with hundreds of lawyers and jurors trying to be on time for the start of another day in the justice mill. Jack saw no sign of Maritza in the crowd, and he wasn't sure which way she might have gone. He took two quick steps in one direction, then changed his mind and started in the other, running head-on into a Miami-Dade cop who had apparently missed his calling as a Miami Dolphin running back. He hit Jack so hard that the collision sent his laptop flying right out of his computer bag. It landed with a distressing *crack* on the floor.

"Oh, man, I'm so sorry," the cop said. He helped Jack gather up the pens, Post-Its, and other tools of the trade that had scattered across the floor. "You got it all, pal? Hope you didn't lose nothin'."

Jack glanced toward the escalators at the end of the long hallway. No sign of Maritza.

"No telling what I lost," said Jack.

CHAPTER 29

Andie didn't want her husband in the room with her.

It was Tuesday morning, and Andie's deposition in the school's lawsuit against her was scheduled for nine a.m. at the law offices of Cool Cash. Jack had assured her that he was fully on board with President Lincoln's view, as amended by Theo Knight, as cleaned up by Jack Swyteck, that "the lawyer who represents his wife is an effing lunatic." But on the morning of the deposition, before they left the house, he seemed to be wavering.

"Hannah will appear as the attorney of record," said Jack. "I'll attend strictly as an interested observer."

"You won't just observe," said Andie.

"Only Hannah will speak on your behalf. I promise."

"You lie, Jack."

"Come on, Andie. What can it hurt if I'm there?"

"You said it yourself when we agreed you were not going. All I need to do is tell the truth. The only way for me to get into trouble is if I start worrying how you might react to my answers to Fitz's questions."

Andie had him there. His own words. Jack went to his office like any other workday. It was Andie and Hannah at the deposition—unlike any day Andie had ever experienced.

"Agent Henning, have you ever been deposed before?" asked Fitz.

Duncan Fitz, lead lawyer for the plaintiff, was seated across the conference table from Andie and Hannah, his back to the floor-to-ceiling windows and the view of Biscayne Bay. With him on his side of the needlessly long table were a Cool Cash junior partner, a Cool Cash senior associate, a Cool Cash junior associate, and two Cool Cash paralegals. Andie wondered if the deposition of President Clinton had been this overstaffed.

"I have not," said Andie.

Fitz launched into a five-minute explanation of the rules of a deposition, which included everything she'd already heard from Hannah in their prep session the day before. Hannah had also told her that background questions would come next—education, employment history, current employment, and the like. But Fitz surprised her—as Jack had warned her he might—by going straight to the heart of the matter.

"Agent Henning, you are familiar with the 'Run, Hide, Fight' protocol in response to an active shooter in schools, correct?"

"Yes, I am."

"Let's focus on step one, 'run,'" said Fitz. "I'm reading from the Riverside safety pamphlet that is part of the school information package given to all parents. 'If there is considerable distance between you and the gunfire/armed person, quickly move away from the sound of the gunfire/armed person. If the gunfire/armed person is in your building and it is safe to do so, run out of the building and move far away until you are in a secure place to hide.'"

Fitz handed the pamphlet to Andie and her counsel. "Does that comport with your understanding of 'run,' in the 'Run, Hide, Fight' protocol?"

Andie read it to herself, then answered. "It does."

"The protocol dictates that you *run away* from the sound of gunfire, correct?"

"That is what it says here."

"And that if the shooter is inside the building you run *out of the building*, correct?"

"Yes."

"In fact," said Fitz, "on the morning of the Riverside shooting, that's exactly what the head of school directed every parent in the rec center to do: follow her away from the shooter and out of the building."

"That is my recollection," said Andie.

"Let me ask you this," said Fitz. "If one of the other mothers in that room had decided to run anywhere but out of the building and away from the shooter, you, as an experienced FBI agent, would consider that a violation of the 'Run, Hide, Fight' protocol. Would you not?"

"Objection," said Hannah, though it wasn't at all clear to Andie what the objection was. "You can answer," said Hannah.

"No other mother in the rec center was a trained law enforcement officer," said Andie. "I thought I could help."

"You were off duty and unarmed that morning, correct?" said Fitz.

"Yes."

"So, let's be honest. Did you really think you could help? Or did you think you were special and that the rules didn't apply to you?"

Hannah objected again, but it all seemed pointless to Andie. "You can answer," said Hannah.

"I didn't think I was special," said Andie.

"Well, did you think it was okay to disobey the explicit directions of the head of school to exit the building and follow her to safety?"

"Like I said, I thought I could help."

"All right," said Fitz. "Let's talk about how much help you actually were. After you exited the rec center, did you confront the shooter?"

"No."

"Did you throw anything at him to distract him?"

"No."

"Did you call out to him to confuse him?"

"No."

"The fact is, you did nothing more than run to your daughter's classroom and sit outside the door, correct?"

Andie paused, not liking the way Fitz had phrased it. "I waited outside the door and prepared myself as best I could to confront the shooter if he tried to enter the kindergarten classroom."

"I see. In your view, you committed an act of bravery."

"I think it was pure instinct."

Fitz smiled insincerely. "Well, don't sell yourself short, Agent Henning. We've all seen the diagrams of the shooter's path prepared by the Miami-Dade Police Department. You agree that you ran toward the shooter, not away from him. Correct?"

"That appears to be the case."

"You were putting yourself in danger, right?"

"I suppose so. I wasn't thinking about that."

"Did anyone follow you down the hallway as you moved toward the shooter?"

"No."

"How do you know that?"

Andie understood the question, but she still puzzled over it. "I didn't see anyone follow me."

"So your answer is you *don't know* if anyone followed you because you didn't see anyone."

"Right. I didn't see anyone."

"Someone *might* have followed you, right?"

Hannah interjected. "Please don't ask the witness to guess."

Fitz didn't give up. "Agent Henning, are you going to tell me that it is *impossible* that someone followed you?"

"I would say it's possible."

"More than possible, wouldn't you say? A child is caught in a hallway during an active shooting. Gunfire is popping like an exploding brick of firecrackers. Bodies are on the floor. Students are screaming and scattering in every direction. A lost and confused child doesn't know what to do. The child sees an adult running down the hallway with purpose. The child follows the adult. Wouldn't that be a natural thing for any child to do?"

"Objection, calls for speculation."

"I don't know," said Andie.

"You *don't know*?" asked Fitz, his tone more aggressive. "As an FBI agent and *a mother*, you have no view as to whether or not a terrified child who doesn't know where to run would follow an adult? *That's* your testimony under oath?"

"Objection, asked and answered," said Hannah.

Andie was struggling. She did have an opinion. But clearly her lawyer was sending her a signal not to answer Fitz's question. "I really can't say," she said.

Fitz leaned forward, forearms resting on the table, forcing Andie to look into the eyes of an experienced litigator who knew exactly how to control a witness. He didn't shout. He didn't get nasty. He simply gave the witness no option but to say what he knew, in her heart, she believed to be true.

"Agent Henning," he said in a firm voice. "Let's see if we can agree on this much: if *any* child followed you down that hallway instead of running for the exit, you put that child at greater risk. Didn't you?"

"Objection," said Hannah. "Counsel, now you are simply harassing the witness. Agent Henning, as your lawyer I'm directing you not to answer that question."

"That's completely improper," said Fitz. "If you stick to that position, I will take it to the judge and seek sanctions against you and your client."

The Cool Cash associates at the end of the table were feverishly tapping the keys on their laptops, probably at work on the motion already.

"Do as you think you must," said Hannah. "But move on."

Fitz turned his attention back to Andie. "Agent Henning, are you going to follow the instruction of your counsel? Or are you going to give me an honest answer to a question that you know is fair and proper: If any child followed you down that hallway toward the gunfire instead of running for the exit, that child was at greater risk. Agreed?"

"I object," said Hannah, "and I repeat my instruction to my client."

Andie was thinking—but not about her lawyer's instruction.

"How about it, Agent Henning?" asked Fitz. "Your answer, please?"

Hannah jumped to her feet and said, "That's it. We're leaving. Come on, Andie, let's—"

"Yes," said Andie.

The room was silent.

Then Fitz followed up. "Yes, what?"

He may have been out of line, but Andie felt the need to answer. "If any child followed me, that child would have been at greater risk."

"Thank you," said Fitz. "Now, Ms. Goldsmith, if you will retake your seat, I'd like to ask your client about her educational background and employment history."

"I think my client would like a break," said Hannah.

Andie swallowed the lump in her throat. In the first ten minutes of the deposition, Fitz had drilled to the very core of her own second-guessing of her response to the gunshots that morning.

"Yes, thanks," said Andie. "A break would be good."

CHAPTER 30

Jack worked through dinner and wasn't home until nine. The house was quiet. He assumed Righley was asleep, so he chose not to tap into his half-Cuban roots, play Ricky Ricardo, and announce *Looo-cy, I'm home!* with all the volume of "Babalú." He went quietly to the kitchen, heated up leftover spaghetti Bolognese in the microwave, and took a seat at the counter.

It had been a wasted day at the office. One of Theo's many buddies happened to be a top tattoo artist who'd created one-of-a-kind images for NBA players. Sports video companies paid the players big bucks to use their likeness in their games, and the graphic artists copied the tattoos with impressive precision. Theo's friend thought the video company should pay him for copying the tattoos he created. Jack was no copyright expert, but like most sole practitioners, he thought of himself as a "Jack of all trades," no pun intended. This claim, however, was dead by sundown. Jack found lawsuits over tattoos on LeBron James and other NBA stars, all decided against the artist.

He switched on the TV but kept the volume low. The Miami Heat were battling the Los Angeles Lakers. LeBron was at the free-throw line.

"Nice tats," said Jack.

He ate about half his bowl of spaghetti and cleared the rest into the trash can. It was then that he noticed the empty bottle of wine on the counter. Andie's voice got lower when she was drunk, and Jack heard that voice coming from the dark living room.

"Jack? Is that you?"

She was lying on the couch. Jack went to her and gave her a kiss. She could barely lift her head to meet his lips, and she was still wearing the silk blouse and pants that she'd worn to the deposition. At least she'd removed her shoes. Jack sat at the end of the couch, put her feet in his lap, and massaged the ball of the foot the way she liked.

"Ahhh," she said, almost purring.

"You're drunk."

"Ya *think?*"

"Did you finish that whole bottle of wine yourself?"

"Yup."

"When we talked on the phone, you said the deposition went well."

"It did. I was the perfect witness. I'm celebrating!"

Jack's eyes were adjusting to the darkness, and he could see pain in her expression, feel it in her toes as the phony exuberance faded. "Tell me what happened," he said.

"I don't want to talk about it, Jack."

"Getting drunk isn't going to help."

"Sure didn't hurt."

"Do you want me to call Duncan Fitz?"

"No!" she said, almost jackknifing on the couch, suddenly finding the energy to sit up. "You can't fix this, Jack. Nobody can fix this."

"Fix what?"

"Fix *what?*" she said, overenunciating, her mouth forming the words in such exaggerated fashion that Jack could have understood without a sense of hearing. "You don't think something is *broken?*" she asked.

Jack dropped her left foot into his lap and started on the right, trying to relax her. "Why don't you tell me what you think is broken?"

"Us, Jack. *Us.*"

Jack stopped the foot massage. "What are you talking about?"

"I was talking to Molly."

"Today?"

"No, no. Like two months ago. We were talking about religion. She's not a Muslim, so I was curious to know how that worked for her and Amir."

"The imam told me she has no religion," said Jack.

"That's not true. She's not without religion. She was raised Episcopalian. She just doesn't practice, and she chose not to convert to Islam."

"What does this have to do with us?"

"Just listen to me, Jack. When Molly decided not to convert, she and Amir reached an understanding. Since Molly doesn't practice, their children would go to the mosque with Amir."

"That's the way it is in a lot of interfaith families. You go with the parent who considers religion to be a more important part of their life. But I still don't see how this pertains to us."

"It's . . ." She paused, but it appeared to be just a head rush. "It's like us because they had an understanding, and it doesn't work."

"Andie, we're both Christians. We don't have that issue."

"I'm not saying it's the same issue. But we have the same problem."

"You're drunk, and I'm not following you at all."

"No, don't dismiss what I'm saying. We really do have the same problem. It's like Molly told me. The understanding worked for a while. But as you get older, and you have kids, and things get more complicated, you realize that the old understanding isn't working. You're only pretending it works."

"So religion became more important to Amir as they got older. Is that what you're saying."

"Yes!"

"Fine. That's them. That has nothing to do with us."

"Yes, it does! We have an understanding. It's not exactly like theirs, but it's just as important to our marriage."

Jack finally had a sense of where this conversation was headed. "You're talking about our agreement: I don't ask you about active investigations you're working on; you don't ask me about criminal cases I'm handling."

"Yes! Our agreement," said Andie. "The one that we fool ourselves into thinking can make a marriage work between an FBI agent and a criminal defense lawyer."

Jack was starting to worry. "I don't see the comparison between our agreement and the one that Molly and Amir have."

"Before you agreed to defend Xavier, I wouldn't have seen it either. But now it's so clear to me. After the deposition today, it's crystal clear."

"You're going to have to explain it to me, honey."

"Jack, before I met you, you did nothing but defend guilty murderers on death row."

"Theo wasn't guilty."

"One," said Andie. "*One* innocent client."

"What's your point?"

"It's like a religion for you, Jack. Defending guilty people. Amir went back to his religion stronger, more devoted, as their marriage went on. I'm afraid. I'm so afraid you're going back to *your* religion. Because I can't handle it, Jack. I can't. It's not who I am."

Jack took a deep breath. He'd known this was hard on Andie, but he'd clearly underestimated how hard. "I'm sorry."

"Sorry for what?"

"For all this pain. I can't make it go away now. I'm in this case, and the judge isn't going to let me out. But if it's any consolation, defending Xavier has taught me something."

"What?"

"It's not who I am, either," he said, shooting a quick glance down the hallway to Righley's bedroom. "Not anymore."

CHAPTER 31

Jack drove to work in the morning with one of the biggest songs of the nineties in his head. The one about the guy in the corner. In the spotlight. *Losing my religion.*

Jack considered it a rock trivia nugget to know that the old R.E.M. hit had nothing to do with religion. Not until he went to college in North Florida did he hear anyone say "losing my religion," an Old South expression for losing your temper or feeling frustrated and desperate. "Frustrated" seemed to fit well enough on the heels of Jack's conversation with Andie. Maybe even "desperate." Jack didn't hold out much hope that his meeting with the Justice Department would improve things.

The James Lawrence King Federal Justice Building is a twelve-story government office building in downtown Miami. Glass-and-concrete construction made it a relatively modern addition to a jigsaw complex that included the old and new federal courthouses, all connected by courtyards. Surrounding streets were cordoned off by concrete car-bomb barriers, a part of life across the country after domestic terrorist Timothy McVeigh detonated a truckload of explosives outside the Alfred P. Murrah Federal Building in Oklahoma City, murdering 149 adults and 19 children. Had Xavier been indicted under federal law as a terrorist, he would have been housed in the federal detention center right next door to the US Attorney's Office.

It was Sylvia Gonzalez who'd requested the meeting, and she'd traveled down from Washington to attend on behalf of the National Security Division. Jack assumed it was about federal charges. They met with Jack in the US attorney's spacious corner office, so technically he was the host. The US attorney's post was a political appointment, changing like clockwork with each presidential election, which meant that the best lawyers didn't necessarily rise to the top. Grady Olson was more of a CEO than a lawyer, and apparently he had more important things to manage than this meeting. He was glued to his smartphone, not even trying to hide the fact that he was reading and answering emails, thumbs in high gear.

Gonzalez was in control.

"Let's start with this unpleasant reality," she said. "Because the shooting has been designated an act of terrorism, the DOJ has the power to prosecute your client and seek the death penalty under federal law."

"You also have the power to prosecute my client and seek life in prison without parole," said Jack. "Which is what I hope you'll do. And because I'm feeling particularly lucky this morning, I hope you'll convince Abe Beckham and the state attorney to do the same under Florida law."

"This indeed may be your lucky day, Jack."

Her words took Jack by surprise. He'd come prepared to talk about the dents he'd put in the prosecutor's case, maybe even spring the alibi that Xavier was in bed with Maritza, though he was saving Maritza until he knew whether she was his ace in the hole or a bald-faced liar.

"Come again?" said Jack.

"There's one way to get death off the table," said Gonzalez. "Tell us who Xavier's accomplice was."

"I don't represent Molly Khoury," said Jack, "but I can tell you this much, based on what I know about her. Molly would gladly tell you that she went to Riverside Day School after the shooting;

that she gathered up the shooter's hat, goggles, clothes, and vest and then dumped all of it deep in the Everglades where it could never be found. She would happily plead guilty as an accessory after the fact and even do jail time. And she would do that even if it wasn't true—if it would save her son from the death penalty."

Gonzalez poured a glass of water from the pitcher on the coffee table. Jack declined her offer, and Grady was too focused on his phone to notice, so she kept it for herself.

"We're not talking about Molly Khoury," she said. "And we are definitely not talking about an accessory after the fact."

"I'm listening," said Jack.

"You've seen the evidence Abe Beckham presented to the grand jury. Your client's confession may or may not meet the standard of guilty beyond a reasonable doubt. The gun belonged to his father, so you'll tell the jury that it was stolen from his glove compartment by the real shooter, who is not your client."

"It's more than a colorable argument," said Jack. "The government's own fingerprint expert has confirmed the existence of a print that doesn't belong to Xavier or his father. And the gunshop owner's testimony that Xavier tried to buy an automatic rifle from him is unusable."

"Shaky," said Gonzalez. "I'll give you that."

"There's also no evidence to connect my client to the purchase of extended magazines," Jack continued. "No surveillance video to confirm his identity. No credible eyewitness identification of him as the shooter. No one could have identified the man behind the ski mask and goggles in the fog of war."

Gonzalez chomped on an ice cube from her water glass. "I didn't invite you here to debate the evidence," she said. "Every prosecutor's case has weaknesses."

"These are holes, not weaknesses," said Jack. "More holes than the state attorney wants to admit."

"Not one of these holes, as you call them, will stop a jury from convicting him of murder in the first degree. Nor will they save him from the death penalty. Which leads me back to where I started."

"The accomplice," said Jack.

"Yes," said Gonzalez, placing her water glass on the coffee table.

Grady quickly moved it to the tray, grabbed a napkin, and wiped the condensation from his gorgeous mahogany tabletop. Then he went back to his phone.

Gonzalez continued. "Your client didn't do this alone. Someone planned it, recruited him, educated him, supplied the extended magazines, told him what to wear, and helped him escape. It wasn't Molly Khoury. Tell us who it was, and the United States will not seek the death penalty when we indict him under federal law."

"If you could prove an al-Qaeda connection, you would have already charged him under federal terrorism laws. Without a terrorist connection, you might as well throw double jeopardy out the window and charge him twice for the same crime. Frankly, I'm more concerned about the good, ol' fashioned homicide charges. Beckham doesn't have to prove it was terrorism under state law."

"I believe we can persuade the state attorney to fall in line."

"Let me make sure I understand the deal. If my client names his accomplice, he gets life without parole."

"Put another way, if he doesn't give up his accomplice, he's looking at the death penalty under Florida law and under federal law."

"I don't think he's all that concerned about being executed twice."

"You know what I mean, Jack. At least one of us is going to make it stick."

"I understand," said Jack. "But isn't your offer overlooking one thing?"

"My offer is tailored to what your client is lucky to get."

Jack hadn't pressed the "wrong man" argument so far, but the existence of an accomplice and recitation of "holes" in the government's case had him thinking: *What if Maritza wasn't a liar?*

"Have you considered the possibility that Xavier wasn't the shooter?" asked Jack.

The US attorney chuckled, his second contribution to the meeting, this time without a napkin. "Don't get cocky, Swyteck," he said.

"There's no doubt in anyone's mind who did it," said Gonzalez. "We want to know who helped him."

Jack paused, but only to increase the effect of his next suggestion. "What if Xavier has an alibi?"

"Beckham spoke to me about that," said Gonzalez. "He told me you raised the possibility of presenting an alibi to the grand jury. You came forward with nothing."

"I'm in the process of verifying it. I don't want to put it out there only to have it picked apart. Under the rules, I don't have to disclose an alibi until ten days before trial."

"I'm not going to tell you all of the evidence I'm sitting on, Jack. But know this much: any alibi would be taken not with a grain, but a boulder, of salt."

"We'll see."

Grady rose, as if to signal it was time for his next meeting. "Seriously, Swyteck, do you really believe your client is not the shooter?"

Jack didn't have to answer, and he wasn't sure if the US attorney expected him to. But he gave him an honest one.

"I don't know what to believe anymore," said Jack.

CHAPTER 32

Jack left the US Attorney's Office certain of one thing: if Xavier was the shooter, and if he had an accomplice, Jack wasn't going to get a name from a client who was giving him the silent treatment. The long and impressive run of the Miami-Dade Detention Center Monologues, starring Jack Swyteck, had to end.

The court order directing the defendant to submit to a psychiatric "competence" evaluation was still in effect. Jack had managed to stave off the prosecutor's repeated demands for a firm date, taking the position that he needed to speak to his client—or, more precisely, his client needed to speak to him—before any session with a psychiatrist chosen by the prosecution. Jack's meeting with Sylvia Gonzalez had attached some urgency to the process, so he modified his position: if he wouldn't talk to Jack, Xavier at least had to talk to a psychiatrist chosen by Jack.

"Hypnosis?" asked Dr. Moore. "Really, Jack?"

Elaine Moore, M.D., used hypnosis in her practice, but she used it cautiously. So cautiously that, in one of his capital cases at the Freedom Institute, Jack had called her as an expert witness to *attack* the use of hypnotically induced memory recall in a police homicide investigation. It was Dr. Moore's testimony— "Uncorroborated, hypnotically elicited memories can lead to the wrongful imprisonment of innocent people"—that had won a last-minute stay of execution for Jack's client.

"Can you help?" said Jack. "I'm desperate." *Losing my religion.*
"For you, I'll give it a shot."

Jack arranged for the session to take place the next day in the detention center's police interrogation room. It was a tiny space, the perfect cramped rectangle for one good cop, one bad cop, and any suspect who was pliable enough to trade away the rest of his life for a cheeseburger, fries, and a milkshake. Dr. Moore and Xavier were inside alone. Jack and Hannah were standing in the adjacent room. Hidden behind a one-way mirror and connected by a hidden microphone, they could see and hear the doctor and her patient.

"So this is what it's like to be on the other side," said Hannah. "I wonder where they keep the rubber hose."

"That's not funny," said Jack. Hannah sometimes forgot that Jack was married to a law enforcement officer.

Jack stepped closer to the glass, his gaze focused on his client. Dr. Moore had requested a comfortable cot for her patient, which the warden had denied, so she'd brought a beanbag chair from her office. Xavier was half submerged in a big ball of blue velour, seemingly relaxed, with knees bent, feet flat on the floor, and hands on his thighs. The lights were dimmed to create the right mood. The doctor spoke in a calm, soothing tone.

"Just begin to allow yourself to relax . . . Letting all your cares and worries go . . . And at this moment in time . . . Nothing matters . . . As you switch off your thoughts . . . And let your eyelids close."

Xavier's eyes remained open. The doctor continued in the same even tone, as if her voice were on a recorded audio loop. "Just allow this time for yourself . . . So that you can unwind completely . . . And as you begin to feel more and more relaxed . . . Letting go of any worries or problems . . . That may have been on your mind lately . . . And there is no need to fight any unwanted negative thoughts . . ."

Xavier closed his eyes.

"You think he's faking?" asked Hannah.

"Damned if I know," said Jack.

"Usually you can tell," said Hannah. "My college roommate used to pretend to faint every time her boyfriend broke up with her. We knew she was faking because her eyelids quivered. Xavier's aren't quivering."

They weren't, but Jack was skeptical. "I'm not sure quivering eyelids is a medically sound litmus test."

The doctor's voice continued. "I want you to take me back now, Xavier. Back to that day."

Jack and the doctor had agreed on "that day" as a handle for the shooting. A more explicit reference would have been contrary to the instructions to relax and release all negative energy.

Dr. Moore continued. "You're with your mom . . . In the family car . . . She's driving . . . Your sister and brother are in the back seat."

The clinical approach, as Jack understood it, was to take Xavier back to the last time he'd spoken in the presence of another human being. The hypnosis would elicit the next words out of his mouth. At least that was the plan.

"The car is moving down the street . . . Where you walked the dog . . . Rode your bike . . . You see the house . . . Where you grew up . . . Where your family lives . . ."

Xavier appeared to be very relaxed.

"I don't think he's faking," Hannah whispered.

"We'll see," said Jack, allowing for the possibility that perhaps Dr. Moore had made a breakthrough.

"The car stops . . . You open the door . . . You get out . . ."

She was reaching the critical point, and Dr. Moore had forewarned Jack that even if things were going well, the moment of confrontation with the police could be jarring and might bring the session to a screeching halt.

"Men in uniform approach the car . . . They want some-thing . . . You put your hands in the air . . . You say something to your mother . . ."

Xavier didn't flinch. His eyes remained closed. The doctor gave him a moment and then modulated her tone, as if trying to ex-plore a deeper place in Xavier's psyche.

"You say, 'It's okay, Mom. I did it.'"

More silence. No reaction from Xavier. Best of all, Jack saw no sign of distress.

Dr. Moore leaned closer, further adjusting her tone, probing even deeper. "Tell me why you said 'I.' . . . Did you leave some-one out? Was there someone else?"

Jack watched, hoping to see Xavier's lips move. But he was perfectly still.

"Why?" the doctor asked. "Why did you say 'I did it'?"

It was almost imperceptible, but Xavier's breathing seemed to change. Something about him seemed different, as if he could truly be in a state of hypnosis.

Slowly, he sat up in the beanbag chair, eyes closed, as if rising from the dead. His head turned slowly toward the glass. His eyes blinked open, and he uttered his first words since being taken into custody by police, apparently speaking directly to Jack, as if he were completely on to the fact that he was being watched.

"Because I fucking did it," he said. "That's why."

Jack stared back at his client. Although they weren't techni-cally locking eyes through the one-way mirror, it felt like it.

"Whaddaya know," said Jack. "He speaks."

CHAPTER 33

On Friday morning Jack drove to Miami's Financial District on Brickell Avenue. He had Theo on speaker. Maritza was the topic of conversation.

"Let me get this straight," said Theo. "On Monday, you see a woman in the back of the courtroom who looks like Maritza, even though her boss said ICE hauled her away from the coffee shop and deported her. Five days later you call me and say it's urgent to find Maritza's last name. What's up with that?"

"I was going to do this myself, but I've just been too busy. I didn't want to hire you if I can't pay you. I'm watching my pennies here."

"Bullshit."

"Seriously. I just got the bill from Dr. Moore for her hypnosis session. Blew my budget for the whole month."

"Money's not the reason you're moving so slow on Maritza, Jack. When did you first meet her?"

Jack stopped at the traffic light. He had to think. "A good two weeks ago. More."

"A witness hands you a possible alibi, and you sit on it for over two weeks. That tells me one thing. You don't believe her."

Jack hadn't realized how transparent he was. "You're right. I don't."

"Shit, Jack. When you gonna catch up with the rest of the

legal profession and have no problem putting a liar on the witness stand?"

"Very funny, Theo."

"Dude, I wasn't kidding."

The light changed to green, but Jack was a nanosecond slow
on the acceleration—a capital offense in Miami. The guy behind
him laid on his horn. Jack ignored him.

"The goal isn't to prove an alibi," said Jack. "We're looking for
an accomplice."

"You think it's her?"

"No, but it wouldn't surprise me if she knows who it is. If
somehow she's back in Miami, I need to talk to her. A last name
would help."

"I'm on it."

Jack ended the call and steered his car into the multistory garage. It was a relief to see that parking was only twelve dollars,
until he read the fine print: FOR THE FIRST FIFTEEN MINUTES.

There goes the rest of the case budget.

Amir Khoury worked on the east side of Brickell Avenue, in
the waterfront office tower directly across the street from the law
firm of Coolidge, Harding & Cash. The South Florida branch
of GC Capital was a lavishly appointed penthouse on the fiftieth floor, which meant that Amir was one of the lucky few who
could literally look down on Duncan Fitz and the two hundred
other lawyers at Cool Cash.

"Elevator number one," the security guard told Jack. It was
an express ride to the penthouse, and in sixty seconds the doors
opened to a cavernous lobby that resembled a glass atrium in
the sky. Views stretched all the way to the Turkey-Point Nu-
clear Generating Station, some thirty miles south, the one potential target that put all of Miami on edge when the terrorist
threat level on the Homeland Security advisory scale inched toward red.

"I'm here to see Amir Khoury," Jack told the receptionist, and he gave her his name.

"Do you have an appointment?"

He'd left a voice mail to say he was coming, albeit a bit vague. You didn't just come out and say, "I need to find out if your son was dating a prostitute," even if the son was a mass murderer. Alleged mass murderer.

"He's expecting me," said Jack, and he waited as she dialed Amir's assistant.

GC Capital was a private equity and credit investment firm that targeted "distressed" companies—high risk, but potentially high reward. Some said GC was a loan-to-own specialist, making its real money not from long-term business strategy but from betting on the borrower's quick default, picking up the pieces in foreclosure, and then selling off the assets at a huge profit. No laws were broken, but it wasn't exactly the "win-win" approach to business.

"Mr. Khoury will see you now," the receptionist said.

With parking at forty-eight bucks an hour, Jack was happy for no wait. An assistant entered the lobby and led him down the hall to a corner office. Amir was behind his desk, pacing as he spoke into his headset on a phone call, and he waved his visitor in. The assistant directed Jack to the armchair and then exited in church-mouse fashion, closing the door on the way out.

"We need to hit the links again soon," Amir said into his headset, about to wrap up his call.

Jack allowed his gaze to wander across the cherry-paneled walls, a quick survey of the trappings of Wall Street success, South Florida–style. Some people found success and favored expensive art. Others built a self-congratulatory shrine. Amir was in the latter camp, the wall behind his desk covered with plaques, awards, and more than a dozen framed photographs. His MBA diploma from the Wharton School. His elbow rubbing with the right politicians. A signed picture of Amir and Molly with Jeff Bezos, himself a product of South Florida, land of the Everglades, before moving to the Pacific Northwest to build his Amazon. And, of course, there was the obligatory display of Lucite cubes across the credenza. Deal toys, they were called. Little desktop mementos that, depending on the nature and size of the transaction, might encase anything from the iconic facade of the New York Stock Exchange to a pair of knights in shining armor jousting over an engraved sum of eight, possibly nine, figures.

Amir ended his phone call and laid his headset atop his desk. It had been a pleasant call, judging from his expression, but the pleasantries faded as he came around to the front of his desk, leaned against the edge, and faced Jack.

"Got your message," said Amir. "I understand you want to know about this Maritza."

This Maritza. Not Jack's words. Obviously, Amir was no fan. "No one told me that Xavier had a girlfriend," said Jack.

"She was *not* his girlfriend. What she is," added Amir, "is a pathological liar."

"What she is and who she is: that's what I came to talk about. I spoke to Imam Hassan."

"Yes, we spoke. He told you what she is. A prostitute."

"I'm curious to know how the imam knows that. Did you tell him?"

"No, *she* told him. Xavier brought her to the mosque as a guest. Imam Hassan has known Xavier since he was born, so naturally he's protective. He asked to speak privately with Maritza, and she agreed."

"She just came right out and told the imam: 'Oh, by the way, I'm a prostitute'?"

"I don't know *how* it came out. I wasn't there. All I cared about was getting Xavier away from her. He was my—he was part of our family."

Jack noted not only his inability to say the word *son*, but also his use of the past tense. "What did you do?"

"Xavier told me where she worked. Apparently, that coffee shop has a reputation for hiring illegals. I didn't know for sure that she was illegal, but I had a hunch. I called ICE to report an illegal, a prostitute, preying on my seventeen-year-old son."

"The manager told me she was deported," said Jack. "Just last week, in fact."

"Okay, I was right. About time, then."

Jack debated whether to mention the "sighting" at the courthouse on Monday. He decided against it. "Do you know Maritza's last name?"

Amir sighed, thinking. "I honestly don't remember. Something Hispanic. Perez, Mendendez, Martinez, Jimenez, Gonzalez, Hernandez, Fernandez, Rodriguez—one of those 'ezzes.'"

"I'm afraid that's not much help," said Jack. It was the Miami equivalent of looking for "stein" in the Long Island phone book.

"You could ask around the coffee shop," said Amir.

"I tried that. No one at the coffee shop will talk to me, now that word is out that Maritza was deported."

"No one wants to be next," said Amir. He checked his watch and reached for his headset, making it clear that Jack's time was up. "I'm sorry, but I have a conference call with a group of Zurich bankers who will be out the door to happy hour if I dial in a minute late."

"Understood," said Jack, rising. "I'm sorry."

"No need to apologize."

Jack wanted to circle back, discreetly, to Amir's use of the past tense—*was* a member of our family. "No, I really am sorry. I can't reveal privileged information, but I should have asked if there is anything you would like to know about Xavier or his case."

Amir's expression ran cold. "No. There's nothing. Absolutely nothing I want to know."

They shook hands, and the strength of Amir's grip only seemed to reaffirm the point: *absolutely nothing.*

"Donna will show you to the elevator," he said, opening the door for Jack.

"I'll find my way."

Jack retraced his steps down the hallway to the lobby. He said good-bye as he breezed past the receptionist and then stopped and did a double take. Theo was seated on the white leather couch taking in the view of Miami Beach.

"What are you doing here?" asked Jack.

Theo smiled as he approached. He was holding a sheet of paper. "Maritza's job application," he said, offering it.

Jack didn't take it. "How'd you get that? And so fast?"

"Me and the manager—we did a little *bizniz.*"

"Doesn't sound like my kind of *business.* Maybe you should get a job working at this place."

Theo dangled it before Jack's eyes, pinching the corner. "Got her name. And her address."

"Let me see that," said Jack, snatching it. He read quickly: Maritza Cruz. Amir's recollection was a little off. At least he'd gotten the *z* right.

"She lives in Uncle Cy's old neighborhood," said Theo. "Ten minutes from here."

Jack double-checked the address. "Let's take a ride," he said.

Andie spent the morning at the field office firing range. She had her Sig Sauer P250, the same 9 mm pistol that she'd used to earn a perfect score on the qualifications course at Quantico— the same pistol that had been locked away in the glove compartment of the family car on the morning of the Riverside school shooting.

The FBI had changed its qualifications course at least twice since Andie's graduation from the National Academy. It wasn't any easier. Agents fired on the target from distances of three, five, seven, fifteen, and twenty-five yards. Each distance posed a different challenge of speed, skill, and accuracy. Draw. Switch hands. From the ready. Standing. Drop to kneeling. Empty-gun reload. Three rounds in two seconds. Six rounds in four seconds. Fifty rounds total, two points for each hit. The target was the QIT silhouette, which looked more like a box-headed robot than a human being. Agents were advised not to distract themselves by personalizing it; no imagining the face of an old boyfriend in the box. From twenty-five yards, Andie jettisoned the warning. In her mind's eye, the target was wearing a camouflage jacket, ski mask, and goggles. He was at one end of the hallway outside the Riverside recreation center. Andie was at the other end. She had twenty seconds.

Go.

Draw and fire four rounds from standing. Drop to kneeling and fire more rounds.

She did it in eleven seconds. Eight out of eight hits. Forty-eight out of fifty overall.

If only she'd had her Sig Sauer with her outside the rec center.

Andie recorded her score in the ledger, cleaned up her station, and put the ear-protection muffs back in her locker.

"Henning, can I speak with you a minute?"

It was the ASAC. She did one more safety check and holstered her sidearm. "Sure."

"In my office," said Schwartz.

The "in my office" part wasn't necessarily a concern. The seriousness of his tone, however, left Andie a little worried. She followed him out of the locker room and down the hall to his office. Schwartz closed the door and went straight to the leather chair behind his desk. "Have a seat, Henning."

It sounded more like an order than an offer. "This is not the part of my job I enjoy," he said.

Andie lowered herself into a chair that was definitely starting to feel like the hot seat. "What's this about?"

He pushed a manila envelope across the desktop toward her. "This letter arrived today."

Andie opened it. The name of the law firm on the letterhead made her stomach churn. "Coolidge, Harding and Cash represents Riverside Day School," she said.

"I know all about the lawsuit," said Schwartz. "I was there when the process server handed you the summons."

"Then what's the problem? The case is ongoing. Nothing has been decided yet."

"It's not just a lawsuit anymore. Duncan Fitz—on behalf of the school—has lodged a formal complaint against you with the Office of Professional Responsibility."

Andie swallowed. "For what?"

"Your conduct during the school shooting."

"I was off duty."

"Agents are responsible for their off-duty conduct."

"Yes. But I did nothing wrong."

He took the letter back from her. "According to Mr. Fitz, you admitted under oath at your deposition that you needlessly put the lives of Riverside students in danger by violating written school policies on active shooter protocols, and by disregarding direct verbal instructions from the head of school in an emergency situation."

"This makes me sick," said Andie. "This is all because the school insists that Jack and I have to pay a full year's tuition to a school that Righley no longer attends."

"It's not about tuition," said Schwartz. "The first wrongful-death action was filed yesterday. One of the science teachers lost his life. His wife wants a million dollars from the school for loss of consortium."

"What does that have to do with me?"

"I'm sure the school knows there will be more lawsuits to come, probably well in excess of their insurance coverage. It seems clear to me that the legal strategy is to prove that the school did everything right by pointing the finger at someone who did something wrong."

It was exactly what Jack, from the get-go, had told her the lawsuit against her was really about: "The school did everything it could, and to the extent that any safety measures failed, it was the fault of people like you who broke the rules."

"I'm the scapegoat."

"I'm afraid so."

Andie sat in silence, absorbing the blow. "Am I suspended?"

"Not by me," said Schwartz. "But the review board has the power to suspend you pending the investigation."

"Do you think they will?"

"I'll recommend against it."

"Thank you."

"But let me be up front about this, Andie. A lot depends on how Duncan Fitz works this in the media. A story about an FBI agent taking matters into her own hands and putting schoolchildren in danger could be very bad for you. And bad for the bureau. Between you, me, and the lamppost, the bureau can be very image conscious. The review board will not want to appear soft on school safety."

Andie didn't need to be reminded of the FBI image. Fidelity. Bravery. Integrity. She'd worked to uphold it her entire career.

"Anything else?" she asked, rising.

"No. But I do hope this all works out. I'll do what I can."

"Thanks," she said, and she left his office.

Jack was in the passenger seat, nonstop busy on his computer, as Theo drove.

They were north of downtown Miami, on Second Avenue between Sixth and Tenth Streets, once a lively stretch that, back
in the day, was known variously as Little Broadway, the Strip,
and the Great Black Way. Once Miami's jazz mecca, the historic village of Overtown bore little resemblance to its former
self. The nightclubs had closed decades earlier, many before Jack
was even born. But he and Theo had heard the stories of Uncle Cy's glory days blowing an old Buescher 400 saxophone at
places like the Cotton Club, the Clover Club, and the Rock-
land Palace Hotel. Theo seemed to enjoy repeating them, playing tour guide.

"Right over there used to be the Knight Beat," said Theo,
"the 'swingingest place in the South.' I'll bet that sly dog Cyrus
Knight impressed a lady or two saying he owned the joint."

Jack was only half listening. He was on the Internet running
searches for "Maritza Cruz." It wasn't exactly an unusual name
in Miami, but it wasn't as common as Maria Cruz. As best Jack
could tell from the photographs associated with the name, the
Maritza Cruz he wanted had no Instagram, no Twitter, and no
Facebook presence. It was the search for deportations, however,
that he found most remarkable.

"Immigration Court docket shows no deportations of anyone
named Maritza Cruz in the last two weeks," said Jack.

"It's that up to date?"

"Good question. She could also be locked up somewhere until
they put her on a plane."

Theo stopped the car. "We're here."

Jack looked up from his computer. "Where?"

"Maritza's address," said Theo, pointing across the street with
a nod of his head. "From her job application."

Jack saw a vacant lot surrounded by a chain-link fence. A faded
billboard promised condominiums "Opening Summer 2015"—a
deadline that could now be met only with the aid of time travel.

There were a few mounds of gravel and deep ruts from truck tires, but the weeds had taken over.

"I think this used to be a joint called the Harlem Square Club," said Theo. "Long gone."

"Yeah," said Jack. "Like Maritza."

CHAPTER 34

Jack didn't like what he heard in Andie's voice. She wasn't suspended, but she'd cashed in a sick day and was calling from home. Andie was not a crier, and the verge-of-tears moment they'd shared that night on their patio, right after she was hit with the lawsuit, was a rarity. But there was something in her voice that Jack had never heard before, something more worrisome: defeat.

"What's happening to me just sucks beyond belief."

"Andie, I don't think you should have left the office."

"You have no idea what a rumor mill that place is, Jack. I had to get out."

He listened in private, through earbuds, as Theo drove them out of Overtown. Andie recounted the whole conversation with the ASAC. Schwartz was a decent guy and, Jack had always thought, a genuine fan of Agent Henning. But they didn't call it the Federal *Bureau* of Investigation because it was immune from bureaucracy, and Schwartz was to some extent a prisoner of his own position. Jack's real beef wasn't with the FBI, anyway. It was with Duncan Fitz.

"He didn't have to involve the bureau in his pissant lawsuit," said Jack. "I know Hannah is your lawyer of record, but I'm not going to stand for this."

"What are you going to do?"

"I can think of a couple things," said Jack. A left hook to Fitz's jaw was high on the fantasy list.

"Please don't do anything while you're angry," she said.

Jack didn't answer.

"Jack, please. *Don't.*"

"I promise on one condition. You need to go back to the office."

"Today?"

"Yes, now. You can't let this beat you. There's no reason for you to feel shame. I'll see you at home tonight. I love you."

The call ended.

"Everything okay?" asked Theo.

"Not really," said Jack. Andie had every right to feel down, but it just wasn't like her to deal with adversity by leaving work early and going home.

Jack's focus turned to the root of the problem. "Drop me off right here," he told Theo.

Theo pulled up to the curb near the side-street entrance to Amir Khoury's office building. Jack's car was still in the parking garage. He got out and watched Theo drive away, but he didn't enter the garage. He walked to the corner and crossed Brickell Avenue—to the offices of Coolidge, Harding & Cash. Not even the pleasant greeting from the young woman at the reception desk could temper his resolve.

"I need to see Duncan Fitz," he told her. "Please tell him it's urgent."

She apparently remembered him from the prior visit. "Right away, Mr. Swyteck."

Jack stood by as she spoke into her headset. He couldn't hear the response, just the receptionist's stream of "Uh-huh, uh-huh, u-huh." Finally, she looked at Jack and relayed the message, straining with concentration to get it exactly right—oddly, the same face Righley made when spelling her name backward.

"Mr. Fitz thanks you very much for stopping by, and he asks that you please leave the check here with me."

"The what?" said Jack, and then his anger surged. Treating him like the courier of the settlement check was beyond insulting. Jack knew the way to Fitz's office, and he started down the hallway.

"Mr. Swyteck!" the receptionist shouted, but Jack had too much of a head start to be chased down by a woman wearing high heels. The door to the senior partner's corner office was open. Jack went straight inside and closed the door behind him, startling Fitz, who was seated at his desk.

"You're lucky you and my father are old friends," said Jack. "Or I might punch you right in the nose."

"Trust me, Jack. There were times when the governor wanted to punch me in the nose, too. Sit, please."

"Don't downplay this. Filing the lawsuit was one thing. Lodging a complaint against my wife with the FBI's Office of Professional Responsibility is crossing the line."

"Easy, Jack. This is not personal. I believe it was Clausewitz who said war is the mere continuation of policy by other means. I think of litigation as the continuation of business by other means."

"This is beneath even you, Duncan."

Fitz rose, but it took longer than it should have. His hip seemed to be bothering him. "My arthritis is acting up," he said, grunting. "Getting old sucks."

It made Jack angry, but in a different way. His intention had been to shred the old man, and Fitz was making it feel like an attack on his own grandfather. Jack half expected him to offer a cherry Life Saver.

"I want you to know that this was not my idea," said Fitz.

"It's your case," said Jack. "If someone on your legal team has a Machiavellian mind, you're responsible."

"No, I meant the idea of lodging a disciplinary complaint did not originate from within this law firm. They asked me to do it."

"You mean your client? The school asked you to do it?"

"No," he said, grimacing as he massaged his hip. "I'm not making myself clear. Sorry. Damn this arthritis. I mean the feds."

Jack wasn't following. "Someone in the federal government asked you to report Andie to the FBI? That's what you're telling me?"

Fitz stood up straight, breathing out the pain. "That's exactly right."

"Who?"

Fitz shook his head. "I can't tell you that, Jack."

"Why did they ask you to do it?"

"I honestly don't know why. But as you know, this law firm has an all-star white-collar criminal defense team. We represent some of the biggest corporations in the world facing billions of dollars in fines for violation of the Foreign Corrupt Practices Act. When the feds ask for a favor, you do it. You never know when you might want to cash in your chips."

"Was it someone in the FBI who asked?"

"I can't say."

"You have to tell me."

He stepped closer and looked Jack in the eye. "All I can tell you is this: you're smack-dab in the middle of something much bigger than you can imagine."

Jack met his stare. "I think you're bullshitting me."

Fitz smiled a little, shaking his head as he returned to his desk. "Then I'll pray for you."

"I thank you for that."

"Oh, and Jack," Fitz said, before Jack reached the door. "Tell the receptionist to validate your parking ticket on the way out. What that garage charges is highway robbery."

"So I've heard."

Jack closed the door on his way out and went straight to the elevator. He wasn't sure what to make of Fitz's claim that someone in the federal government had solicited his complaint against

Andie. But he knew one thing: it wasn't information he should keep to himself. The elevator doors opened to the main lobby. Jack speed-dialed Andie on her cell phone.

"Honey, are you at the office yet?"

"Almost. You don't have to check up on me, Jack. I'm going back to work."

"Sorry, I wasn't checking up. I just met with Duncan Fitz. There's something you need to know."

"What?"

Jack hesitated. Of all the federal agents he'd met over the years, no one was prouder of her work than Andie. She didn't warm easily to conspiracy theories, and neither did Jack.

"This came from Duncan Fitz, so consider the source."

"Jack, I'm walking into the building now. What is it?"

The lobby was more crowded than Jack would have liked, but he found a quieter spot behind a potted palm tree.

And then he gave her the painful news.

CHAPTER 35

Abe Beckham hurried back to his office, late for his meeting with Sylvia Gonzalez. It was his third trip of the day to and from the courthouse. A sentencing hearing before Judge Miller at nine a.m. Back to his office. A guilty plea before Judge Salvador at eleven. Back to his office. Another hearing at two. Back to his office. Thankfully, it was a short walk from the justice center to the Graham Building and its appropriately shaped footprint.

The Boomerang Building.

"Sorry I'm late," he said, as he entered his office and hurried to his desk. Gonzalez was waiting for him.

"Not a problem," she said. "Hopefully you've had time to reconsider our phone conversation."

Gonzalez had called him after her meeting with Swyteck and explained how finding Xavier's accomplice was a "Justice Department priority." To that end, the State Attorney's Office needed to be "flexible" on the death penalty. Beckham had told her no. She'd asked him to think about it, which he'd promised to do. In no way had he encouraged her to fly all the way down from Washington to hear his final answer.

"I'm sorry you made the trip," said Beckham. "If you were under the impression that a face-to-face meeting might make me more amenable to dropping the death penalty, you were mistaken. The state attorney's position is unchanged."

"I'm sorry to hear that. I thought I'd made the DOJ's priorities clear."

"Honestly, I'm not convinced there *was* an accomplice. Maybe someone—his mother, probably—ditched the vest, the ski mask, the goggles, and the rest of his gear as an accessory after the fact. But an accomplice on the front end? No. I see Xavier Khoury the same way history records ninety-nine percent of mass shooters. A lone wolf."

"What if you're wrong about that?"

"Prove me wrong. Show me some evidence."

It was clear from her body language that Gonzalez was reluctant to do so. "I'm not asking you to drop your case, Abe. I shouldn't have to compromise a federal investigation to convince you that it's in the interests of national security to offer Xavier Khoury life without parole in exchange for the name of his accomplice."

"Threatening a man with death unless he names an accomplice is a dangerous game," said Beckham. "Even if you get a name, the accomplice will argue that Khoury just made it up to avoid the death penalty. And you know what? The man may have a point. Everything I see tells me no accomplice."

"Then where did Khoury get the extended magazines?" she asked.

"Really? That's your evidence of an accomplice? It's not illegal to own an extended magazine. Anybody can buy one at a flea market, online, or at countless other places. Unlike a handgun, you don't even have to register them under state or federal law. The important thing is we know exactly where he got the murder weapon."

"The gun with the unidentified fingerprint on it," she said.

"The gun with *Xavier Khoury's* fingerprint on it."

"Aren't you at all concerned that the extraneous print will raise a reasonable doubt in the minds of the jurors?"

"Not in the context of the totality of the evidence. That print could belong to the guy who washes Amir Khoury's car."

"And Swyteck will argue that it could have been *that* guy who shot up Riverside Day School."

"Which the jury will find laughable. It was Xavier Khoury. And I can prove it. He murdered thirteen innocent children, fourteen now with the Abrams girl, and a science teacher—a hero—who died trying to save his students. Khoury deserves to die for what he did."

Gonzalez rose, seeming to realize that Beckham was not about to budge. "I'm very disappointed, Abe."

"Don't be," he said, walking her to the door. "Charge Mr. Khoury under federal terrorism laws as you see fit. But I answer to the people of this community, and fourteen of the youngest and most promising members of that community were murdered in cold blood. The Office of the State Attorney is seeking the death penalty. Period."

Jack was determined to leave his office before five o'clock.

One of the great things about Riverside Day School was its after-care program. Jack and Andie had used it to the fullest extent. With the change of schools, Abuela was filling in at the house from three till seven on school days. But 7 p.m. was practically bedtime—Abuela's, not Righley's. She was in her eighties and too proud to admit that she was slowing down. Max was getting on in years, too, the upside being that he no longer posed a danger of jumping up and knocking Abuela over. But Jack didn't like to push his luck or his grandmother. At a few minutes before five, he headed for the door.

"I have to show you this, Jack," said Hannah.

Two more steps and it would have been a clean getaway. "Can it wait till tomorrow?"

"Five minutes. That's all I need."

She was too excited for Jack to say no. "Two minutes," he said.

She led him to the kitchen, where her laptop was open on the table. On-screen was a frozen frame from what Jack immediately recognized as the surveillance video at Riverside on the morning of the shooting.

"Exactly what am I looking at?" said Jack.

"Xavier Khoury," said Hannah.

Jack looked more closely. The shooter was not in the frame. He saw only high-school-age students running in a hallway.

"I don't see him," said Jack.

Hannah pointed. Jack looked even more closely. It was a boy. Dark hair. About Xavier's build and skin tone. He was wearing the same uniform that all high school students at Riverside wore.

"I don't see it."

Hannah increased the zoom. The resulting pixelation only made the image worse. "Now I really don't see it," said Jack.

"You don't have to. I found a face recognition expert who will say *she* sees it. In her opinion, that is Xavier Khoury running from the gunman, like the rest of the students."

Jack was more than skeptical. To his eye, the zoomed image on the screen was little more than a scattering of magnified dots. "Hannah, there are so many problems with this, not the least of which is how are we going to afford a face recognition expert. How much does she charge?"

"Two thousand dollars."

In the world of expert witnesses, that wasn't much. "That's all? Total?"

"No. Two thousand *an hour.*"

Shades of the parking garage: *For the first fifteen minutes.*

"I don't like this," said Jack. "The jury will see how grainy this image is. Beckham will destroy this expert as a hired gun: 'Pay her enough and she'll say that's Christopher Columbus running down the hallway.'"

"She's highly respected in her field," said Hannah. "She uses an accepted video-pixelation-enhancement technique."

"Let's get real. Do you truly believe that's Xavier caught on video?"

"I believe my expert is qualified to render an opinion that it's him."

Given the day Andie was having, Jack was in no mood to debate the limits of a lawyer's ethical duty to be a "zealous advocate." He wanted to be home when Andie got there.

"We'll talk tomorrow." He said good night to Bonnie on his way out and headed to his car in the driveway. A couple of blue jays had dropped direct hits on his windshield. Jack loved the sprawling limbs of century-old oaks that canopied the front yard, but he wished the birds would find another bathroom. It was such a common occurrence that he kept a spray bottle in the trunk. He was rummaging around for a clean rag behind the spare tire when he heard a footfall in the pea gravel behind him and a voice that was vaguely familiar.

"How is Xavier?"

Jack turned around slowly. He knew he hadn't been seeing things in the courtroom, and one look at her face confirmed it. "Nice to see you, Maritza."

"Is Xavier going to be okay?" she asked.

"I was told you were deported."

"And the best thing is to let everyone keep on thinking it."

She had a black gym bag slung over her shoulder. "What's in the bag?"

"That's not important. A friend from the coffee shop told me you're looking for me. I want you to stop. I'm of no value to you. The alibi was a lie. I was not with Xavier during the shooting."

"I figured that out on my own. I want to know why you lied."

"Because I love him. And because he didn't do it."

Jack was much more interested in the second part of her answer. "How do you know he didn't do it?"

"Xavier got mixed up with some bad people. *I* got him mixed up with bad people."

"The imam told me you're a prostitute."

She paused, and it was apparent to Jack that the word wounded her. "Of course he would say that," she said. "But this is not about me. Xavier is not a murderer. He didn't do this. He's the fall guy."

"Then why doesn't he just deny it?"

"The same reason I want the world to think I've been deported to El Salvador. He's afraid."

"He could get the death penalty if he doesn't deny it."

"He's not afraid for himself. When I say these are bad people, I mean *bad*. They will kill his sister, his brother, his mother. He can't deny it."

"Who are these people?"

"Ask Xavier. I can't tell you."

"I need your help. He won't talk to me. Maybe he'll talk to you. Come visit him with me."

"I can't go anywhere near him! It's risky enough for me to come here and see you."

"Tell me how to break through to him."

"I've told you enough. You don't need me to figure this out. It's all there. Find it. And leave me alone."

"The name you used at the coffee shop was Maritza Cruz. I've run every background check I can legally run. There's nothing to connect 'Maritza Cruz' to anyone who even vaguely resembles you. That's not your real name, is it?"

"What do you think?"

"How do I get in touch with you?"

"You don't. Ever."

"I could tell the FBI we talked. Maybe they know who you are."

Her eyes narrowed. "That would be a very big mistake."

She walked away, and only then did Jack notice the taxi waiting across the street. The driver started the engine. Jack followed her to the end of the driveway, and then, suddenly, she whirled around to face him.

"*Don't* follow me."

Jack froze. Her hand was inside the gym bag, and he couldn't tell if the protrusion from inside was her finger or a gun.

"Please," he said. "Let's talk again."

She backed away slowly, then hurried to the taxi and climbed in the back seat. The door slammed, and as the driver sped away, Jack raised his cell phone, snapped a quick photograph, and enlarged the image on the screen.

"Got it," he said, looking at a clear string of six characters on the rear license plate.

CHAPTER 36

M aritza" caught her breath as the cab pulled away.

"Where to?" asked the driver.

She gave him the address and settled back in the seat.

It had been a bold move, confronting Jack Swyteck. She'd gone back and forth on it, having chickened out at the courthouse, deciding at the last minute not to go through with it. That blunder had left her no choice. He'd obviously recognized her, or thought he had. Why else would he have followed her out of the courtroom, only to have lost her in the crowd? The real danger was not the encounter. The risk was that Swyteck would tell the FBI about it. She was somewhat confident that she'd discouraged him from doing so. Hopefully, he understood that the bulge in the gym bag was no bluff.

"Belt, *por favor*," said the driver.

"Excuse me?"

He apologized for his English, then reverted to his native tongue to ask that she fasten her seat belt. She knew the accent well. Her father, an engineer in the petroleum industry, had moved the family to oil-rich western Venezuela when she was six years old, and they'd lived in Maracaibo almost four years.

"You are from Venezuela, no?" she asked in Spanish.

"*Sí. Caracas. Y usted? De dónde es usted?*" And you? Where are you from?

She smiled back at him but chose not to answer. The driver let the conversation drop. He probably figured that she'd exhausted her knowledge of the Spanish language with one simple sentence that she'd practiced for a visit to Miami. He surely would have been surprised to know that Spanish was only one of four languages she spoke fluently.

It was getting dark outside, and her shadowy reflection appeared in the side window. The cabdriver's question returned to her, but only in her thoughts:

Where are you from?

She didn't answer, and she didn't even want to think about it. But riding in the back seat of a taxi, staring at her ghostly reflection in the window, brought the memories flooding back. She was fourteen years old. The man sitting beside her was probably forty. His name was Abdul. They'd met ten minutes before they'd climbed into the back seat of a taxi near the market in central Baghdad, a place called Kadhimiya, one of Shiite Islam's most important pilgrimage sites. The man driving the taxi said he was a cleric. His title, sayyid, meant that he claimed descent from the prophet Muhammad. Maritza—Rusul—had her doubts.

What is your name, girl?" asked the cleric.

He made eye contact with her in the rearview mirror, as the cab pulled away from the busy market and into early evening traffic.

"Rusul."

She was wearing a black chador, a full-body cloak with a hood that covered all but her face, and beneath it a niqab, a scarf that covered her face below the eyes. The men didn't seem to notice how she was trembling beneath the garments.

"Your uncle tells me you are a virgin," said the cleric.

Rusul had been living with her uncle in Baghdad for almost a year, driven from her home in Mosul by ISIS militants, lucky to have survived the eighty-seven-hour trek on foot. Her father, an American expat, was shot in the face after bribing the wrong man to smuggle his family to Kurd-controlled Ebril in northern Iraq. He'd left Rusul with perfect English and Spanish, but not much hope. Last she'd heard, her mother was trapped in west Mosul with thousands of other civilians—the human shields ISIS used to conquer the city.

"Yes, I am a virgin."

Out of the corner of her eye she saw a smile crease Abdul's lips. She looked out the window at the passing cars, clenching her fists into tight, tense balls.

The driver continued, steering with one hand and smoking a cigarette with the other. "Rusul, be assured that I am licensed to perform the ceremony of marriage by the Iraqi Ministry of Justice. What we are about to do is permitted under religious sharia law. Mut'ah is an ancient custom that allows a man to help a woman in need. By doing so, Abdul is getting closer to God." He took a long drag from his cigarette, then exhaled. "Do you understand?"

"Yes."

"You must never tell anyone about this. Iraqi law is in conflict with religious law. We do not want trouble with the militia, do we, Rusul?"

"No."

Another long drag on his cigarette. The smoke was so thick that Rusul was beginning to feel nauseated. It poured from the cleric's lips as he spoke.

"Rusul, do you agree to the marriage?"

"Yes," she answered in a timid voice.

"A temporary marriage, right?"

"Yes."

"Open your hands and pray with me."

Her fingers ached as she opened her fists, she'd been clenching so tightly.

"Do you, Rusul, give me your consent to do this marriage? Abdul will pay a dowry of one hundred fifty thousand dinars for one day. If you agree, say, 'Yes, I give my consent.'"

She blinked, eyelashes fluttering nervously as she recited the words her uncle had practiced with her. "Yes, Saddir, I give you my consent to marry me."

"Abdul, do you agree to marry Rusul for one day and that you will pay her one hundred fifty thousand dinars? If you agree, say yes."

"Yes."

"Now you are both married and it is halal to be together."

Halal. Holy.

The cab stopped. They were outside an inexpensive hotel. Abdul reached across and opened Rusul's door. She climbed out first and waited on the sidewalk. The driver had final words for Abdul as they settled up the bill, and Rusul was standing close enough to overhear.

"The girl is a virgin, Abdul. You must not penetrate her from the front."

"What about the back?"

"The back is fine."

"What if something happens and she loses her virginity?"

"Then her uncle can come after you and force you to marry her. Then she is your responsibility, not his."

"There is no way to get rid of her?"

"Does her uncle know where you live?"

"No."

The cleric crushed out his cigarette in the ashtray, breathing out one last cloud of smoke. "Then no problem at all."

S eñorita, *estamos aquí,*" said the driver. We're here.

The way he'd said it, as if repeating himself, she must not have heard him the first time. "Sorry."

She paid in cash, which made him more than happy. She had yet to meet a Miami cabdriver who didn't get pissed off by customers with a credit card. Fine by her. Cash was a way of life. No paper trail.

She gathered her bag, climbed out, and stepped onto the sidewalk. The cab pulled away. Rusul slung the strap over her shoulder and started walking along the street. Home.

CHAPTER 37

Jack got in his car but didn't back out of the driveway until the taxi was out of sight. Tailing Maritza home was not his plan. He was no James Bond. Surely she would have noticed and led him to a random place. The only way to find her actual destination was to let her go there and follow up with the driver. He dialed the cab company and gave the dispatcher the license plate number. She put him on hold for several minutes before coming back on the line.

"Sorry, that's not one of our drivers."

Jack had never really paid attention, but apparently the Yellow Cab Company did not have a monopoly over yellow taxis in Miami. Not until the fourth call did he get a match on the license plate, but the dispatcher would not give up the driver's cell-phone number.

"All I can do is ask him to call you," she said. "What's this about?"

Good question. "Tell him it's about his reward. A hundred dollars. I would like to hand it to him personally."

She promised to deliver the message, but Jack suddenly realized that Maritza might still be in the cab and overhear the conversation. "Wait. Tell him not to call me. Only text."

"Our drivers are not allowed to text and drive."

Right. And college students aren't allowed to drink at parties. "Tell him to text me as soon as he can," said Jack, and he gave her his number.

Two minutes later, Jack's cell phone chimed with an incoming text. It was in Spanish. There were times when that C minus in Spanish from Abuela was kind of funny. This was not one of them. Fortunately, this translation was relatively simple:

You say you have money for me?

Jack tried texting back, but he was losing precious time fighting with the autocorrect function on his phone, which kept "correcting" his Spanish with nonsensical English. He finally typed the English words into Google Translate, and then copied and pasted the entire Spanish block into the text bubble.

My friend got in your cab on 9th Court. Tell me where you dropped her and I will Venmo you $100.

He texted back with his Venmo address and a demand: Money first.

Jack wired him fifty dollars from the Venmo app with this message: The other 50 after I get the address.

The address popped up on Jack's screen, along with a little blackmail: Send 200 or I tell her you asked.

Nice guy. For all that driver knew, he was giving up a battered wife or girlfriend, which made Jack worry for the next woman. He sent no more money but texted back: Shame on you if you didn't tell her already.

Jack made a quick call to Theo, who agreed to check out the address. Jack had other plans. Attorney-client visits at the Miami-Dade Detention Center were allowed twenty-four hours a day, seven days a week. Jack called ahead to let them know he was coming, as he drove along the river toward the justice center.

Einstein is credited with defining "insanity" as "doing the same thing over and over again and expecting a different result." Perhaps Jack was insane to think that things would be different this time and Xavier would talk to him. Or maybe he was a little like Max, his ever-optimistic golden retriever, who woke up every morning convinced that "This is it, today is the day Jack is going to make me pancakes for breakfast!" Either way, instinct told him to take Maritza at her word: *"You don't need me to figure this out. I've told you enough. It's all there. Find it."*

Jack parked in the visitor lot, which had plenty of empty spaces. Dusk had turned to darkness. Traffic on the nearby expressway, which Jack never really noticed during daylight, was like the sound of running water at night. Another car pulled up beneath a glowing streetlamp. A car door slammed shut. Then another. Behind Jack, quick footfalls on the pavement became louder and even quicker as two men followed him toward the building. Either they were in a hurry or they were trying to catch up. Jack stopped outside the entrance door and turned to face them.

"I need five minutes of your time, Mr. Swyteck."

The bigger of the two men was doing the talking. Jack didn't recognize the voice or either face. "Who are you?"

He flashed a badge. "Agent Carter. Joint Terrorism Task Force."

Jack looked at it carefully. "Nice shield. How do I know you fellas are for real?"

"We saw you talking with Maritza Cruz in the driveway outside your office," said Carter.

"Did you follow me here?"

"Didn't have to. A corrections officer calls us every time you come here to meet with your client. Go inside and ask her, if you don't believe us."

That didn't seem necessary, and it was more than enough to convince Jack that Carter was the real deal. "What's on your mind?"

"Here's the way it is," said Carter. "Save the 'my client is innocent' bullshit. Your client did it. Somebody helped him. We don't know who it was, but we need to know."

"You're not telling me anything I haven't heard from Sylvia Gonzalez at DOJ."

"This you haven't heard: if we don't get a name, there's going to be another shooting. And another. And another. Riverside Day School was the first of more to come."

It was sobering news. "How do you know that?" asked Jack.

"It's our job to know it."

Jack took a moment to wrap his head around this one. "Let's see if I understand the problem. Here's one situation. If I was sure my client was guilty, and if I knew ten schoolchildren were going to die tomorrow if Xavier didn't give me the name of his accomplice, I'd go upstairs, lock the door to the attorney-client conference room, and beat the living shit out of him until he told me."

"We're not asking you to get disbarred."

"That's good. Because I'm not a hundred percent sure he's guilty."

"We are," said Carter. "But let's get real. Your client is in jail. If we wanted to beat this information out of him, we'd have an operative in there right now shoving his face into a prison toilet until he talks. If our intelligence tells us that the next shooting is imminent, it may come to that—which I will deny having said if you ever repeat it. Just like this meeting never happened."

It was suddenly clear to Jack why this discussion was taking place with two agents in the dark, outside the detention center, rather than in a roomful of higher-ups in Washington, DC. *This meeting never happened.*

"If I hear you correctly, your intelligence isn't telling you that the next shooting is right around the corner."

"On the color code, I'd say we're somewhere between orange and red. But that could change quickly. This is no time to screw around."

"Then exactly what are you asking me to do?"

"We want the name of everyone involved in the Riverside shooting, we want your client to be the star witness against them at their trial, and we want his testimony to be clean enough to get the death penalty for every single one of those bastards. Do all you can, but do it by the book."

"I get it. But I wasn't blowing smoke when I told Sylvia Gonzalez that he doesn't talk to me."

"That's why you need to focus one hundred percent of your energy on your client. Stay away from Maritza. She can't help you make Xavier talk. *You* can make Xavier talk. We got Maritza covered."

Jack wasn't exactly eager to come face-to-face again with a woman who'd just threatened him with a concealed weapon, but any meeting with the government was an exercise in horse trading. "I'm happy to let you cover Maritza, if you're willing to give me your 302s on her."

The Form 302 was the federal agent's written record of a witness interview.

"That's impossible," said Carter.

"It's required, if you're serious about my doing this 'by the book.'"

"That decision is way above my pay grade. I will make sure your request lands on the appropriate desk."

"Thank you."

"One more thing," said Carter. "Tell no one we talked."

"Again, if you're serious about my doing this 'by the book,' I have to tell my client."

"Fine. No one else. Not even your wife."

Not telling Andie about a break in one of his active cases was consistent with the way they'd always done things, but coming from one of her fellow federal agents, it didn't sit well with Jack. "Why not Andie?"

Carter only repeated the directive. "No one."

Jack made no promise. He opened the door and went inside to see his client.

CHAPTER 38

Molly was alone at her kitchen table. Amir didn't seem to notice her or the stack of mail in front of her as he entered from the hallway.

"Then we need a different lender," he said sharply.

His voice startled Molly, but he was holding his smartphone and she noticed the cordless earbuds in each ear. He continued on about the need to get this deal done, speaking not to her but to whoever was on the line, as he grabbed a can of diet soda from the refrigerator. Molly waited for the words that signaled the end of a call from Amir to his subordinates at the office.

"Get it done," he said.

Molly seized the opening. "Can we talk?"

The question snagged him from somewhere deep in his thoughts. "Now?"

"Yes. It's important."

Amir checked his messages on his phone, not even looking at her. "Sure."

"Amir!"

He looked up from his phone and seemed poised to say something about her yelling at him, but the worried expression on her face must have put him in check.

"Who died?" he asked.

"Nobody *died*. I opened the mail today."

"Oh, for God's sake, Molly. I told you not to do that. It's filled with hate."

"I have to open it."

"Why?"

"For Talitha."

"What are you talking about?"

Riverside had not officially expelled Xavier's siblings, but Molly knew they weren't welcome. She'd been homeschooling Talitha and her older brother since the shooting. Talitha missed her friends.

"Most of the parents have cut us off," said Molly. "But Rachel's mother lets her write to Talitha."

"Who's Rachel?"

Rachel had been Talitha's best friend since they were toddlers. "Forget it, all right? This isn't about a letter from Rachel." She pushed an oversized envelope toward the edge of the table. It was opened on one end. "It's about this."

"What?"

"Just look inside. But don't take it out."

Amir stepped toward the table, took the envelope, and squeezed the side seams to enlarge the opening. "What is it?"

"It's a footie."

"A what?"

"You wear it over your shoes so you don't leave footprints. Cleaning people use them. So did the shooter at Riverside."

Molly locked eyes with him, watching as his confusion turned to anger.

"This is how you choose to tell me?" he asked.

"Tell you what?"

"Oh, come on, Molly. The footie worn by the shooter just landed in our mailbox? Is that it?"

"I didn't say it was the actual footie. But it could be."

"Yes! It definitely could be, Molly! Because Xavier still had it with him when you picked him up after the shooting!"

"That's crazy!"

"It's what the police have been saying all along. *Somebody* helped him ditch his stuff after the shooting. Who else but his mother would do it?"

"It wasn't me."

He clutched the envelope. "Then where did you get this?"

"It came in the mail."

"Stop lying!" he shouted, slapping the envelope down on the table. "What did you do with all the other stuff? Burn it? Dump it in the Everglades?"

"I didn't do anything with it!"

"You got rid of all of it, or at least tried to. But like everything else you do, you fucked up. Somehow the footie got separated from all the other stuff. Where'd you find it, Molly? Under the seat in your car? The laundry room? The bottom of your four-thousand-dollar handbag?"

"Why are you saying this?"

"Because it's classic *you*. Brilliant Molly finds the footie and says, 'Hmmm, I'll mail this to myself from some random post office, and then I'll go to the police and say, "See, Detective, I told you my son was innocent. The real killer mailed me his footie!"'"

"Stop it, Amir."

"No, you stop! Your son did this. Do you hear me? He *did it*. This idiotic scheme of yours is just going to get you arrested as an accomplice after the fact and bring me down even further."

"Bring *you* down? Why is this about *you*, Amir?"

"Because I'm the only Muslim in this marriage!"

He grabbed the envelope and stormed out of the kitchen. Molly followed.

"What are you doing?"

Amir continued to the living room and went to the fireplace. "Amir?"

He opened the flue, grabbed some kindling from the tinder-box, and lit it with the starter.

"You can't burn it!" shouted Molly. "That could be evidence."

The kindling burned quickly. Amir tossed the envelope with the footie into the fire. The flames shot up another foot, consuming the package and its contents.

"Not anymore," he said.

CHAPTER 39

Jack's meeting with Xavier entered its second hour of silence.

The opening monologue had taken about twenty minutes. Jack had laid out everything he'd learned about Maritza from their encounter in the driveway and from Agent Carter outside the detention center. Xavier had shown no reaction, except to make momentary eye contact with Jack each time he mentioned the name Maritza. Jack's last question was still pending. He broke an hour of silence by repeating it.

"Do you love Maritza?"

Xavier was slouching in his chair with his shackled wrists crossed in his lap. He cut a glance in Jack's direction, the mention of Maritza's name triggering another reaction. Then he lowered his eyes and retreated into his cocoon.

Jack rose and reached for the ceiling, giving his back muscles a good stretch. "She doesn't want you to die. She risked her own life to come and tell me that tonight."

Xavier didn't reply. Jack returned to his chair.

"I can wait all night for an answer, if I have to," said Jack. "Do you love her?"

It wasn't the most important question on Jack's list, but he was betting that it was the one Xavier was most likely to answer. All Jack needed was a trigger to get him talking. Another minute passed. Then—and Jack almost missed it—Xavier nodded. Just once, and ever so slightly. Jack smiled on the inside.

"Now we're getting somewhere," said Jack. "She clearly loves you."

Xavier made eye contact again. Jack moved to the end of his seat, getting a little closer. "She says you're afraid to deny the shooting."

Xavier looked away. Jack had switched gears to the shooting too quickly. He was losing him again. He tacked back in the other direction.

"Relationships are funny things, aren't they, Xavier?"

His client didn't look at him, but he seemed to reengage.

"Sometimes, when you're in a relationship, you feel like you have no choice. In some cases, that's true. Hell, look at us. I don't have a choice. I can't quit being your lawyer. The judge won't allow it. I'm not complaining. That's just the way it is. But do you understand what that means?"

No answer.

"It means you can tell me anything. You don't have to be afraid when you're with me. Don't be afraid to deny it. Don't be afraid to tell me you did it. Don't be afraid to name the person who helped you do it. I can't tell anyone what you tell me, unless you allow it."

Xavier didn't look at him, but he appeared to be thinking about it.

"It's like a marriage," said Jack, "but it's a weird marriage. You can fire me, but I can't fire you. A marriage where only one person has all the power."

Jack waited, studying his client's reaction. Xavier's lips parted, and he seemed on the verge of saying something. And then he spoke.

"Like Rusul."

Jack could hardly believe that his client had finally spoken. But he didn't understand it. "Like whom?" asked Jack.

No answer.

"Like Russell, did you say? Who's Russell?"

Jack waited and watched. The body language went negative again. No eye contact, no sign of any willingness to speak further. Perhaps Jack should have let the silence linger another hour, if necessary, but he was losing patience.

"Does Russell have something to do with the shooting?"

Xavier sat up in his chair. For an instant, Jack thought he might say something, but he was only getting up to leave.

"Sit your ass down," Jack said harshly.

Xavier seemed taken aback by the tone, and the shackles rattled as he settled back into his chair.

"Like I said, you can fire me. You can walk out of this room right now. But here's what will happen if you do. Tomorrow, maybe the next day, you'll be in the shower. Two guys will grab you, hold you up by your ankles, and shove your head in the toilet until you drown unless you name your accomplice."

Xavier sat motionless.

"I'm not threatening you. I'm not suggesting that I will have anything to do with that. I'm telling you that I can't *stop* it from happening. So here's the choice I'm giving you. Tell me the name of your accomplice. Or sit for a polygraph examination and answer this question: 'Were you the shooter?'"

Jack gave his client a minute to consider it. But only a minute.

"Tell me what it's going to be, Xavier. Before you walk out that door, I want your answer."

Xavier glanced at the door, then back at Jack.

"I'll take the polygraph," he said.

Jack didn't respond immediately. He hadn't expected an answer, and he certainly hadn't expected that one.

"All right, then. I'll line up an examiner."

CHAPTER 40

It was long after dark when Maritza pulled her Toyota Prius into the lot behind the Mount Olive Baptist Church of Fort Lauderdale. Several RVs, a handful of SUVs, and about a dozen other cars had arrived ahead of her. Another Prius was parked in the usual place. Maritza wasn't the type to get to know her neighbors, but the guy in the Prius seemed to think that all Prius owners were members of the same club, so he'd introduced himself one morning. He was a grad student with about four hundred thousand dollars in student debt. The church didn't chase people away at night and had even installed a security light, a bathroom, and a shower for its homeless guests. For Cousin Prius, living in his car was the only affordable option.

Maritza hadn't told him her story.

She parked in her usual spot, not so close to the security lamp behind the church to keep her awake all night, but enough light to hopefully keep away the rapists. She got her blanket and pillow from the trunk and made up her bed in the back seat. Her "neighbor," the grad student, liked to fold down his back seat and sleep with his feet in the trunk, but Maritza wasn't interested in buying a mattress and turning the "Prius Motel" into a way of life. She plugged her phone into the USB charger in the console. An extra-long cord left the phone in reach in an emergency. She put her gym bag on the floor, also within quick reach. The pistol was inside and loaded, just in case. She would never have shot

Jack Swyteck in his driveway, her threat notwithstanding. But that didn't mean she was afraid to use it, if necessary.

Maritza had figured that Swyteck might follow her, so the address she'd given to the cabdriver was a good three blocks away from where she'd parked on the street. When she was sure no one was on her tail, she'd walked to her car, hopped on the expressway, and headed north. The parking lot behind the church was her go-to bridge from one apartment to the next. She moved twice a month. It was a way of life for her—had been, for some time.

Damn, it's hot in here.

It was only her third autumn in South Florida, and like many natives, Maritza had come to hate October in the subtropics. When the rest of the country was enjoying crisp nights, sunny days, and blazing fall foliage, Florida was still stuck in the last vestiges of summer heat, humidity, and even hurricanes. The weather would make a glorious turn any day, bringing millions of snowbirds, some of whom would vie for a spot in the parking lot behind the church. Until then, there was at least one more night of misery on the calendar. She cracked the window open an inch for some air. It didn't help.

She checked the time on her cell phone. 11:28 p.m. The hour was late and she was dead tired, but she could tell that it was going to be another restless night. It had nothing to do with the heat or the fact that the car wasn't wide enough for her to stretch out the full length of her body. Her mind was too active.

The imam said you were a prostitute.

Swyteck's words had been weighing on her all evening, playing over and over again in her head. In hindsight, falling for Xavier had been a mistake—for obvious reasons. But the bigger mistake had been accepting his invitation to go with him to the mosque. Hoping for acceptance and forgiveness had been borderline delusional on her part. She'd trusted the imam for some reason. What she'd told him in private was something she'd told no one since coming to this country.

"Have you been married before?" he'd asked her.

"Yes."

"What was his name?"

"Abdul."

"Abdul what?"

"I don't know. Just Abdul."

It had gone downhill from there. She was a grown woman, but the imam had made her feel like that fourteen-year-old girl in Baghdad who had gone back to the fraud who'd called himself a cleric to tell him that Abdul had taken her virginity and left without paying her the dowry.

"Now that you have chosen this path, you have no choice," the so-called cleric had said to her. "You are a pleasure wife. You will do many pleasure marriages. You will bring many men closer to God."

The tap on the car window made her start. She snapped quickly from her memories and grabbed her gun. The man outside the car took a step back, and she recognized his face in the glow of the security lamp. She put the gun away and lowered the window. He came closer to the car.

"Hello, Rusul," he said in Arabic.

"Hello, Abdul."

CHAPTER 41

Jack got home after midnight. Andie was asleep in their bed. He was too tired to eat, but he went to the kitchen anyway. He checked the trash. No empty wine bottles, which was a relief.

Jack had never known Andie to have a drinking problem, but he'd never known her to drink alone either, until he'd found her nearly passed out on their couch the other night. He knew virtually nothing about Andie's biological mother, except that she was an alcoholic incapable of raising her own child. A doctor had once told Jack that alcoholism was hereditary, but Jack still wasn't sure if it was genetic or "like parent, like child." It bothered him that the fallout from the shooting even had him thinking such things about Andie.

"You hungry?" asked Andie. She'd entered the kitchen so quietly that Jack hadn't even noticed.

"I'm sorry. Did I wake you?"

"It's fine. I was in and out of sleep."

She took a seat at the kitchen table. Jack joined her. Less than twelve hours had passed since she'd called to tell him that she was under disciplinary review. It seemed so much longer.

"I'm glad you went back to work," he said. "I really wanted to be here when you got home, but—"

"There's no need to explain."

"I want to."

"You weren't here, Jack. That's all there is to it."

"Trust me, there's a little more to it."

He didn't go into his meeting with his client, but he told her everything about the meeting with Agent Carter outside the detention center.

"Be careful, Jack," she said.

"Meaning what?"

"Carter looks like a nice guy—kind of like Theo when he's behind his bar at Cy's Place. But if you think Theo has another side, his is nothing compared to Carter's. He's a former Green Beret. His father was from Detroit, but his mother was Libyan. He's fluent in Arabic, so he was at the top of the food chain when US Special Forces started training the Iraqi Special Operations Forces Brigade in counterterrorism."

"Sounds like he should be working in the Pentagon. Why did he leave the military?"

"I only have hearsay," said Andie.

"This isn't a courtroom," said Jack.

"Around two thousand and nine, US advisers were getting ready to transfer counterterrorism efforts to the Iraqis. It was literally called the Iraqi Counter Terrorism Service—CTS. Our exit from Iraq didn't go so smoothly. Troops were leaving, but Carter was one of the US advisers still on the ground conducting side-by-side operations with CTS. That's when things got ugly."

"Ugly for Carter?"

"For CTS. You stopped hearing success stories and started hearing about CTS conducting mass arrests, abusing women, using collective punishment, intimidating entire villages to apprehend a single suspect, and on and on. There was talk of a secret prison and torture."

"Was Carter part of that?"

"I don't know. You asked why he left the army. From what I've heard, it was entirely his decision."

"How'd he get into the FBI?"

"We're talking about the war against terrorism. People as talented as Carter get a second chance. Sometimes a third or a fourth."

"All of what you say fits with the way he handled our meeting. Lots of implied threats. He told me not to tell anyone we even talked."

"Except me?"

"No. Including you."

Andie's expression turned to concern. "Then you shouldn't have told me."

"What?"

"Jack, I'm under disciplinary review. If they ask whether we've talked about the case, I'll have to say that you broke your agreement with the FBI and told me about Agent Carter."

"I didn't break any agreement. I never agreed."

"They won't see it that way."

"I don't care how they see it."

"Well, I do! The FBI is my career, Jack!"

"I didn't mean I don't care—not in that way."

Andie breathed out so hard that it was almost a groan. "I'm so tired of walking this line, Jack. Everything has a footnote."

"What does that mean, 'a footnote'?"

"All you lawyers love your footprints in fine print," she said, and then switched to her "Jack voice," which was about as flattering as any wife's imitation of her husband. "'Andie, I know you don't want me to defend a school shooter—*footnote*—but don't worry about it, because you and I won't talk about the case.'"

"That's not fair. I agreed to take on Xavier only to see if I could convince Abe Beckham to drop the death penalty for life without parole."

Her Jack voice continued. "'I never agreed to take Xavier's case to trial—*footnote*—but now I'm stuck because the judge won't let me out of the case.'"

"It's not a footnote, Andie. It's the law."

"If that's the law, then you should never have said yes to Xavier Khoury."

"I said yes to Nate Abrams, who doesn't want to spend the next ten years of his life attending court hearings, obsessed with whether Xavier Khoury lives or dies."

Andie rested her elbows on the table and massaged between her eyes, as if staving off a massive headache. Slowly, she rose and cinched up her robe.

"Nate Abrams is a good man, and I feel so sorry for him and his wife. But thirteen other families lost a loved one, too. Maybe for those others the death penalty isn't just an obsession, Jack. Maybe it's justice."

Jack watched as she walked away, leaving him alone in their kitchen.

CHAPTER 42

On Monday morning Sylvia Gonzalez left her apartment in Maryland at the usual time, caught the eight a.m. train, and rode the Red Line all the way into the district. Judiciary Square Station was flooded with the morning rush hour when she arrived, thousands of commuters climbing out of a big hole in the ground, robotic slaves to smartphones and electronic devices. On her way to the escalator she noticed a plaque that marked this station as the birthplace of the entire Washington Metro line. No one else seemed to pay it much mind. Sylvia did, but only because her father had operated a rapid transit train for forty-one years. She missed her dad and thought of him often, the proud man who'd put his daughter through Georgetown Law by going back and forth, traveling the same mile, thousands and thousands of times over four decades.

It was actually chillier as she stepped into the city than when she'd left her apartment. A fast-moving cold front was injecting a taste of winter into the middle of autumn. She buttoned her coat and forged ahead three blocks, fighting the wind all the way to her meeting at the J. Edgar Hoover Building. Ned Griffin, chief of Operations Branch I in the Counterterrorism Division of the FBI's National Security Branch, was waiting for her in a secured and windowless conference room in the building's basement.

"Nice hair," he said as she entered.

The cold wind had taken a toll, and the situation was pretty much hopeless.

"Nice gut," she said, referencing the extra ten pounds hanging over his belt.

As one of the top prosecutors in the DOJ's National Security Division, Sylvia had a close enough relationship with Griffin to allow for good-natured kidding. A little humor was good for the soul in this line of work. Operations Branch I was devoted entirely to al-Qaeda, and Griffin was a walking encyclopedia on the organization.

Griffin adjusted the audio on the LCD screen on the wall. Agent Carter was joining them by videoconference from the Miami field office. Carter had an image of sunny South Beach displayed on the green screen behind him. Agents who transferred from Washington to Miami or Los Angeles always seemed to do that for videoconferences, bragging about their balmy new location, until they caught on to the fact that no one at headquarters really gave a shit that they were living in the midst of palm trees and crime.

"What you got for us, Carter?" asked Sylvia.

"Pure gold," he said, the on-screen movement of his lips not quite in sync with his words.

Sylvia had drafted the court filing and coordinated with the US attorney in Miami to get the federal judge to approve electronic surveillance of the Khoury residence. Carter was responsible for monitoring and pulling out the gold nuggets of conversation between husband and wife. There was only audio, so Sylvia closed her eyes and imagined the scene as the entire exchange unfolded, from the argument in the kitchen over the footie that had arrived in the mail, to the shouting match in the living room:

"Because I'm the only Muslim in this marriage!"

Molly Khoury's voice was next, a series of pleas:

"What are you doing?"

"Amir?"

"You can't burn it! That could be evidence."

And finally, Amir: *"Not anymore."*

The audio recording ended. Sylvia opened her eyes.

"Well, what do think?" asked Carter.

"It's complicated," said Sylvia.

"How is this complicated?" asked Carter, incredulous. "It's just like Amir said. The mother managed to ditch everything but the footie on the day of the shooting. It turned up somewhere, and she got a crazy idea about the real shooter sending it to her in the mail. She was probably ready to call Jack Swyteck any second. We've got her, and now we've got her husband for destroying evidence."

"The point is not to build a case for accessory after the fact," said Sylvia. "We want the accomplice on the front end."

"I understand," said Carter. "We bring in mom and dad for questioning. We play the audio, and then I squeeze the shit out of them until they tell us who their son's accomplice was."

"Assuming they know the name of the accomplice," said Sylvia.

Carter scoffed. "Is there anyone on this videoconference who doesn't think *one* of them knows? Get real, Gonzalez. Amir Khoury has to know."

"No, he doesn't *have* to," she said. "You've been eavesdropping since the search team executed the warrant and planted the devices. Almost a month."

"Twenty-six days," said Carter.

"And not a word has been spoken in that house to suggest that either one of them knew anything about the shooting before it happened. This audio doesn't change that. If anything, it makes it sound even more like the parents didn't know."

Griffin seemed eager to get to a decision. "What are you recommending, Sylvia?"

"We can do one of two things," she said. "We can pull the

trigger now, like Carter recommends, and bring them down for questioning. Or we can let this play out and see if we hear what we really want to hear."

"I vote we haul them in now," said Carter. "If they know who helped their son, I'll get it out of them."

"Carter's interrogation skills are second to none," said Griffin.

Sylvia was well aware. Although his multiple tours in Iraq as a US Special Forces adviser to Iraq's Counter Terrorism Service had come to an abrupt end, the bureau had given him a second chance as a legal attaché in the US embassy in Baghdad. The official duty of a "legat" was to serve as a liaison between the FBI and the law enforcement agencies of other nations, but some—as Carter had—functioned as intelligence agents and more.

"I'm not denying his talents," said Sylvia.

"No, you're just chickenshit, and if we blow this opportunity, the next shooting is on you."

Rumor had it that Carter was once in line for Griffin's job as section chief, but his propensity for berating and even sacrificing his colleagues to achieve his objectives—which Sylvia was experiencing firsthand—was the untold story behind his obvious demotion from legat in Baghdad to a mere squad member in the Miami field office.

She kept things professional. "Bringing in the Khourys for questioning now is a risky proposition. At the end of the day, we could be left with nothing but a mother who made a really bad decision *after* the shooting, and a father who burned the evidence of her crime because he's tired of being the Muslim scapegoat."

Griffin glanced at the LCD screen, as if to see if Carter had changed his view.

"You know what I want," Carter said to him.

Griffin looked at the lawyer. "What do you think we should do?"

Sylvia appreciated his respect for her opinion, but the decision was not clear-cut. "What are you hearing on the ground about a possible second shooting?"

"I told Swyteck there's no time to waste," said Carter.

"It's good that he thinks that," said Griffin. "But we have some room to maneuver here."

"*Some,*" said Carter. "Not a lot."

Sylvia's gaze settled on the phony palm trees on the green screen behind Carter. "Let's give the Khourys a little more rope. Smarter people have hanged themselves."

Griffin mulled it over for a moment, then came to his decision. "All right. We wait."

CHAPTER 43

Jack was in the room for the polygraph examination, but he stood in the corner, behind his client and out of view. Xavier was seated in an old wooden chair with an inflatable rubber bladder beneath him and another tucked behind his back. A blood pressure cuff squeezed his right arm. Two fingers on his left hand were wired with electrodes. Pneumographs wrapped his chest and abdomen to measure depth and rate of respiration.

Seated across the table was Ike Sommers, a former FBI agent who, in the estimation of many, was one of the finest private polygraph examiners in the business. He was watching his cardio-amplifier and galvanic skin monitor atop the table. The paper scroll was rolling as the needle inked out a warbling line.

"All set," said Ike. "Are you ready, Xavier?"

He didn't answer. Jack wasn't sure his client was going to keep his promise and go through with the examination. He'd reverted to the silent treatment right after uttering the words *I'll take the polygraph.*

Ike tried again. "Xavier? Are you ready?"

He nodded.

"Good. Let's get started."

Jack had explained the basic process to his client in advance. The examiner's first task was to put him at ease. He started with questions that would make him feel comfortable with him as an interrogator. Do you like chocolate? Did you ever have a dog? Is your hair purple? They seemed innocuous, but with each spoken answer the examiner was monitoring Xavier's physiological response to establish the lower parameters of his blood pressure, respiration, and perspiration. It was almost a game of cat and mouse. The examiner needed to quiet him down, then catch him in a small lie that would serve as a baseline reading for a falsehood. The standard technique was to ask something even a truthful person might lie about.

"Have you ever thought about sex at your mosque?"

Xavier shifted uneasily. "No."

Jack didn't need a polygraph to know he was lying about that one.

The room was silent as the examiner focused on his readings. He appeared satisfied. The trap had worked, and now the examiner knew what it looked like on the polygraph when Xavier lied. It was clear sailing to test his truth telling on the questions that really mattered.

"Is your name Xavier?"

"Yes."

"Do you like ice cream?"

"Yes."

"Are you a medical doctor?"

"No."

"Do you own a gun?"

"No, my dad—"

"Just answer yes or no," said the examiner.

Jack couldn't overlook the irony: his client finally started to talk, and the examiner immediately shut him down.

"Is today Sunday?"

"No?"

"Have you ever climbed Mount Everest?"

"No."

"Did you kill Lindsey Abrams?"

Xavier hesitated. Maybe it was because he didn't know who Lindsey Abrams was. Maybe there was another reason.

"No."

The examiner continued. "Are you sitting down now?"

"Yes."

"Are you a woman?"

"No."

"Are you the Riverside School shooter?"

"No," he said, a little louder than his previous answers.

"Are you deaf?"

"What?"

"Yes or no, please."

"No."

"Are you fluent in Chinese?"

"No."

"Do you know who the Riverside shooter is?"

"No."

"Are you glad this test is over?"

Jack suspected that the last question was Ike's standing joke, a little levity intended to elicit a cathartic smile from the subject. He got nothing from Xavier. He turned off the machine and looked at Jack.

"You want to talk outside?" he asked.

Jack called for the guard, who unlocked the door from the outside, and the two men stepped into the hallway.

"Any initial impressions?" asked Jack.

"I'm a polygraph examiner, not a mind reader," said Ike. "I need to study the data."

"How soon can I have the results?"

Ike checked his watch. "Give me a couple hours."

"Sounds good," said Jack. "Call my cell."

Andie left Abe Beckham's office in the Graham Building with her suspicions confirmed.

Her visit had not been on Jack's behalf. She'd gone on her own account, as an FBI agent facing disciplinary review for her behavior during the Riverside school shooting. She had only one question for the prosecutor.

"Is the state of Florida on board with no death penalty if Xavier Khoury gives up his accomplice to the FBI?"

Beckham's response had come as no surprise. "Absolutely not. And I told Sylvia Gonzalez exactly that."

Ever since Jack had called and told her about his meeting with Duncan Fitz, Andie had been wrestling with the question it had raised: Who in the federal government would ask Fitz to lodge a disciplinary complaint against her? At first, she'd dismissed Fitz's claim as more hot air from a pompous old lawyer who was skilled in the ways of casting confusion to his adversaries. Her meeting with Beckham, however, had vaulted one suspect to the top of the list.

Andie drove straight to the field office, brought her ASAC fully up to speed, and laid her theory on the table.

"I think it was Carter," said Andie.

It nearly knocked Schwartz out of his desk chair. "Whoa."

"I know it's a serious accusation, but it adds up."

"How?"

"Jack and I don't discuss much about his cases, but he told me about his meeting with Carter outside the detention center. Clearly the pressure is being put on Jack to get his client to name his accomplice."

"As it should be."

"Yes, but not at my expense."

"You lost me there," said Schwartz. "How is this at your expense?"

"The original deal was that if Jack's client names his accomplice, he avoids the death penalty."

"Sounds good to me."

"Me, too. But it only works if the State Attorney's Office is on board. They're not. I just talked to Beckham this morning. The death penalty is nonnegotiable for him. Sylvia Gonzalez knows that—which means Carter knows it, too."

"I still don't see what that has to do with you, Andie."

She chose her words carefully, not wanting to sound paranoid. But she was certain she was right. "There's no leverage on Jack if Beckham won't give up the death penalty. Carter and Gonzalez need a new pressure point to make Jack play ball."

Schwartz took a deep breath, seeming to sense where Andie was going with this. "You're saying Carter pushed Fitz to lodge the complaint against you."

"Yes. I think it's Carter's ace in the hole. He's of the badly mistaken view that Jack will give him whatever he wants—betray his own client, if need be—if Carter promises to make my troubles go away."

"Did Jack tell you that Carter put that quid pro quo on the table?"

"No."

"So this is just a theory of yours?"

"It's not *just* a theory," said Andie. "Carter has a history of throwing colleagues under the bus to get his way. That's why he's a squad member on the Miami Joint Task Force instead of the Special Agent in Charge of the Washington, DC, field office."

"How do you know that?"

"The man is grossly overqualified for his current position. Agents talk."

Schwartz leaned back in his chair, eyes cast toward the ceiling, thinking.

"I don't hear you saying I'm wrong," said Andie.

He lowered his gaze, looking straight at Andie. "His undoing was actually the Office of Security Cooperation–Iraq, part of the US embassy in Baghdad. The Iraqi government passed a law that said the Counter Terrorism Service couldn't hit a target without a legal warrant issued by a judge from the Central Criminal Court of Iraq who was independent from CTS. Carter didn't think that was such a good law."

Andie was surprised by the revelation—surprised that Schwartz had shared it, not that Carter had broken the law of a host country.

"But I do know this," said Schwartz. "Not everyone agreed with his demotion, and he still has friends in high places."

"He's using me," said Andie. "I'm an expendable pawn in his big plan to crack the big terrorist plot that will get him back in Washington."

Still no denial from Schwartz, but Andie felt an appeal to reason coming.

"Andie, this complaint against you from Duncan Fitz is bullshit. It won't amount to a hill of beans. Don't take on Agent Carter."

"Really? You want me to stand by and get steamrolled by a disciplinary review?"

"You won't get steamrolled. This complaint against you won't go anywhere. Let it play out, and the disciplinary review committee will see that there was absolutely nothing wrong with your response to the shooting. You don't have to pick a fight with Carter to clear your name."

"I should let it go? That's what you're saying?"

"Yes," he said, his expression very serious. "For your own good, let it go."

Andie rose. "Sorry, boss. Not in my DNA to let it go."

CHAPTER 44

Jack rode with Theo to Miami's Little Havana. It wasn't yet
noon, but Theo had already scouted their lunch spot.

"Pinolandia! Let's do it. I could go for *fritanga*."

A *fritanga* was a restaurant that served a wide assortment and
large quantities of home-style Nicaraguan foods, often sold by
the pound. Little Havana was once known for everything Cuban, but a new wave of immigrants brought new culinary trea-
sures. The carne asada at Pinolandia was so famous that reviewers
wrote poems about it on the tables.

If you like dominatrix, go to Pain-o-landia.
If you like crap jokes, go to Pun-o-landia.
If you love Nic BBQ, go to Pinolandia!

"Work first," said Jack. "Then lunch."

Miami Senior High School's official address was on First
Street, but its grand entrance, hailed upon its opening in 1928 as
"befitting of a Gothic Cathedral," was on Flagler Street, Miami's
east-west equivalent of "Main Street." The main structure had
suffered from years of neglect, but a major twenty-first-century
renovation had restored much of the Mediterranean-style archi-
tectural glory. The first graduates were the children of Miami's
pioneers, all white. By 1984, the student-run newspaper had declared "Spanglish" the official school language. And in another
three decades, the student body of nearly three thousand was
93 percent Hispanic, mostly Cuban, Honduran, Guatemalan, and
Salvadoran.

"Did you know this is where my dad went to high school?" asked Jack, as they pulled into the parking lot.

Former governor Harry Swyteck was one of many famous alumni, including *I Love Lucy* actor Desi Arnaz, an all-star lineup of professional athletes, and the CEO of Apple Computer, Gil Amelio, who was replaced by Steve Jobs after an anonymous party—who turned out to be Jobs—sent the company into free fall by selling off 1.5 million shares of Apple stock in a single day.

"The more important question is, did Maritza Cruz go here," said Theo.

At Jack's first meeting with Maritza at San Lazaro's Café, Maritza had told him that she was a graduate not of Fancy-Pants Day School, as she'd called it, but of Miami Senior High. Over the years, Theo had coached a number of boys from Miami High on his travel basketball team, and he knew the school's principal. She'd agreed to a meeting for eleven a.m. Elena Cantos took them back to her office, and after a few minutes of banter about the top ballers in the school, they got around to the purpose of the meeting.

"I remember Maritza," said Cantos. "Such a sweet girl."

With all the lies he'd gotten from Maritza, Jack tried not to show too much surprise. "You do remember her?"

"Yes." Cantos swiveled in her chair and ran her index finger across the spines of "MiaHi" yearbooks on the bookshelf behind her before pulling one that was five or six years old, guessing from its position on the shelf. She cracked it open and flipped through the pages, a nostalgic smile creasing her lips as she came to the right class portrait.

"This is her," said Cantos, and she handed Jack the open yearbook.

The student body was so large that headshots were about the size of a postage stamp. Jack examined this one closely. It looked a little like the Maritza he knew, but he wasn't sure.

"How old is she in this photograph?"

"Fourteen or fifteen. She was a freshman."

"Do you have any pictures of her as an upperclassman?"

The question seemed to strike her as strange. "Well, no. Of course not."

Jack didn't understand. "Sorry, am I missing something?"

"Maritza was with us only one year. She was killed by a drunk driver the summer before her sophomore year."

Jack caught his breath. "I wasn't aware. So sorry to hear that. Are her parents still in Miami?"

"No. Her father never left El Salvador. Her mother was devastated after the accident. Last I heard, she moved back. I could look up the names of her teachers, if that would help."

Jack was about to accept the offer, then reconsidered. The phony Maritza Cruz was using the name of a deceased teenager who vaguely resembled her. Talking to the real Maritza's teachers, parents, or friends five years after her death seemed pointless.

"That won't be necessary," said Jack. "Thank you for your time."

Cantos walked them across the administrative suite to the exit. Theo reminded her that there was still room on his travel team and asked that she put in a good word with Jose Ramos, a six-foot-eight power forward on the Stingarees' varsity basketball team.

"He's another Udonis Haslem," said Theo. "Just sayin'."

Haslem played his entire NBA career with the Miami Heat, the local kid made good who'd grown up eating as many fish sticks as he could finagle for lunch at Miami Senior High and maybe a red box of raisins for dinner at home. Jack listened and enjoyed it as Theo recounted a half dozen Haslem highlights on the walk back to the car.

Jack's cell phone rang as he climbed into the front seat and got behind the wheel. The results of Xavier's polygraph examination were in. Jack put Ike Sommers on speaker as he backed his car out of the space.

"How'd he do?" asked Jack.

"I'm afraid I don't have great news," said Ike.

Jack stopped the car. "He failed?"

"No. But he didn't pass, either. The results are inconclusive."

"Does that mean he was lying or being truthful?" asked Jack.

"Neither. It means the results are useless."

Jack put the car in gear and continued out of the lot toward Flagler Street. Ike went on for another minute or so explaining the possible reasons for the inconclusive results. Maybe the questions weren't quite right. Maybe Jack's presence in the room, albeit out of sight, had made his client nervous.

"I can do a second test, if you like," said Ike.

Another thousand bucks. "I'll get back to you on that," said Jack, and the call ended.

"Sounds like that was a waste," said Theo.

"Not really," said Jack. "I don't believe in polygraphs. I've seen too many liars pass and too many truth tellers fail."

"White man's logic. Not even gonna try to understand that one."

"It's actually pretty basic. I believe someone's willingness to take the test is more reliable than the results of the test itself."

"Okay, I get it. So the fact that Xavier was willing to take a lie detector tells you he was telling the truth?"

"Not conclusively. But it says more than the test results. On the other hand, back when I first met her, I asked Maritza to sit for a polygraph examination. She freaked out and started screaming at me because I wouldn't take her at her word."

"What does that tell you?"

Jack stopped at the traffic light. "It tells me we shouldn't be surprised to hear that the real Maritza Cruz is dead."

CHAPTER 45

Maritza moved into a furnished efficiency apartment on Tuesday. She'd snagged a bargain on a daily rental in Hollywood through the end of the month. She was by far the youngest tenant in the complex, probably the only one born after Nixon was president, which was a good thing, as people would leave her alone. The rent would triple on November 1, the official transition from hurricane season to snowbird season, but she never stayed anywhere more than two weeks. Her job application was in the manager's hands at five different coffee shops, and surely one of them would bite. She just hoped they didn't call until the afternoon. That morning she would be away from her phone. Abdul had given her strict orders: no electronics on this trip. She left her cell phone on the kitchen counter and headed out.

She was driving to Palm Beach County but nowhere near the millionaires and mansions on the famous island off the coast. Abdul's directions took her west to the farmlands near Lake Okeechobee. Belle Glade was a city of fewer than twenty thousand residents that somehow managed to land near the top of so many lists. Highest rate of HIV infection in the twentieth century. One of the highest crime rates of the twenty-first century. Highest number, per capita, of high school football players to break out and play in the NFL. Maritza had read all those things on the Internet, none of which had anything to do with

her visit. This was about open space. Vacant land. A place to target shoot.

She turned at the gravel road, exactly 1.1 miles east of the
yellow building on Main Street, the one that still had the "temporary" blue tarp on the roof after a hurricane that had cut
across the peninsula four years earlier, and a big sign out front
that said WE BUY GOLD. She followed the road all the way to the
barbed-wire fence at the end, another 1.3 miles. She stopped the
car, turned off the engine—Abdul's instructions had been that
detailed—and got out. The cloud of dust rising up from the road
behind her evaporated. Empty fields stretched before her in every direction. It felt like the middle of nowhere, and she might
have thought she was in the wrong place, but for one thing. Just
as Abdul had promised, an array of paper targets was set up and
standing in the north field. They were set at various distances,
some just a few feet beyond the barbed-wire fence, others a good
thirty yards farther away. Each a human silhouette.

Maritza opened the trunk. Inside was the long, rectangular
plastic carry case Abdul had brought to her in the church parking lot. She opened the case, and for the first time—"Don't
open it till you get there," he'd told her—she saw the weapon of
choice.

It was the AK-47. She recognized it immediately, though she'd
not actually seen one since leaving Baghdad. Not since her last
meeting with Abdul in Iraq. He'd had one just like it when he
took Rusul back to see the cleric.

Another Mut'ah," said Abdul.
He was speaking to the cleric, who was seated behind his
cluttered desk in an office that was barely big enough for the
three of them. They were in Kadhimiya, central Baghdad, and
Rusul could hear the typical noises of the shopping arcade just
outside the office door. Millions visited the holy shrine, and

couples often came to get married there. The certificate from the Iraqi Ministry of Justice that authorized the cleric to perform marriage ceremonies was framed and hanging on the wall behind him.

"For you?" asked the cleric.

"No. A friend."

"Another lonely colleague at CTS?"

Rusul was dressed as before, cloaked in a black chador, but she wondered if the dark blue niqab that covered her face below the eyes had hidden her surprise. She'd heard of the American-trained Iraqi Counter Terrorism Service, but this was the first she'd heard that Abdul was part of it.

"No," said Abdul, smiling. "Not from CTS. At least not directly."

Rusul sat in silence as the two men negotiated the "dowry" that Abdul's friend would pay to her, less the cleric's fee for performing the ceremony and the commission to Abdul as a finder's fee.

"The dowry from your friend is not enough."

"One hundred twenty thousand dinars is more than enough," said Abdul. "She's not fresh."

"She is still young. A beautiful girl. Your friend must pay more."

"He is a good friend. I treat him fair. The dowry is right."

The cleric lit up a cigarette. He and Abdul were locked in the stare down of seasoned negotiators. The cleric inhaled deeply, then spoke.

"For this dowry, one hour."

"It's better for the whole day. A man gets tired."

"Two hours," said the cleric. "Final offer."

"Fine. Two hours."

Abdul opened his wallet, deducted his cut of the dowry, and handed the rest of the cash to the cleric. He counted it, then removed enough bills to cover his fee and locked them in the metal strongbox in his desk. He promised to deliver the rest to Rusul's uncle after the two-hour-long pleasure marriage to Abdul's friend ended. He could not pay the money directly to Rusul. She was, after all, "just a girl."

"Where is your friend?" asked the cleric.

"He is waiting by your taxi," said Abdul.

The first time, for her marriage to Abdul, it had struck Rusul as strange that the cleric performed the ceremony in a taxi. But she had since come to understand. No matter what the cleric told girls about the Mut'ah as an ancient religious custom, it was illegal under Iraqi law. If caught, a cleric risked detention by one of Iraq's feared Shia militias. Better to be in a moving vehicle than trapped in an office in the shopping arcade with no escape.

"Come with me," the cleric said.

The men parted ways outside the office. Rusul went with the cleric, remaining several steps behind him as they wended their way through the crowded arcade, along the cobblestone pedestrian-only walkway. A few minutes later they reached the taxi stand on the busy boulevard. The cleric's cab looked like any other in Baghdad, but she remembered it as "the one" from that ride she'd taken with Abdul as a fourteen-year-old girl. Even the smallest details continued to haunt her. The missing hubcap. The scratch on the right fender. The nauseating smell of tobacco that poured from the back seat as the door opened.

"Get in," said the cleric.

Rusul obeyed. She watched through the windshield as a man approached the cleric on the sidewalk. Abdul hadn't mentioned that his friend was black, and from the bits of conversation Rusul was able to gather through her open window, the cleric apparently had a problem with interracial "marriage," even if for pleasure. The man opened his wallet, handed over more cash, and the matter was resolved. The cleric walked around to the driver's side. The man opened the rear door on the passenger's side. Rusul's heart pounded.

Just then, a black sedan pulled alongside the taxi on the driver's side. The man she was about to "marry" reached across, opened her door, and pushed her out of the taxi. He went with her, and in one fluid motion, the passenger's-side door to the sedan opened, the man pushed Rusul into the back seat, and he got in the sedan with her. The door slammed, and the sedan sped away.

Rusul was certain that she was going to die.

"Don't be afraid," the man said in English.

She could barely speak, overwhelmed by fear and confusion.

"Rest easy," said Carter. "You're safe with me. I'm getting you out of this hellhole."

Rusul caught her breath and forced out the words. "Who are you? How did you know I speak English?"

"I knew your father."

"From the oil company?"

He smiled sadly. "No, Rusul. Your daddy was one of the bravest men I've ever known. He didn't work for no oil company."

Maritza slammed the trunk closed, slung the rifle over her shoulder, and walked to the barbed-wire fence.

A trail of dust rose from the dirt road behind her. She watched as the approaching vehicle and the man behind the wheel came into focus. The car stopped right behind hers. The driver's door opened. Abdul got out. He walked toward her and stopped.

"This will be your only chance to practice," he said in Arabic.

"Do we have a date?"

"Soon. I will tell you the exact date when I know it. Now, let me see how much work we have to do."

Rusul inserted a plug in each ear, raised her rifle, and took aim at the nearest target. One squeeze of the trigger sent a bullet straight to the bull's-eye of target one, followed a second later by another squeeze and another hit, another squeeze, another hit, and another, and another. In less than twenty seconds it was over. Fifteen hits. She removed her earplugs.

"Not bad," said Abdul. "Not bad at all."

CHAPTER 46

Tuesday night was enlightening.

Jack had heard Andie complain about the bureau before, but it had always been the way anyone complained about a job. The boss is an idiot. So-and-so is a brownnoser. Tuesday night was unlike anything Jack had ever heard from his wife.

"Carter is using me," she said. "I'm a pawn."

They were sitting outside on their patio. The overdue turn in the weather had finally arrived, and Andie was covered with a cable-knit blanket. Jack was wearing the UF Gator fleece that he hadn't donned since March. Andie spared no details in laying out a theory that, not too far in the distant past, might have sounded like paranoia. He wondered if Carter would be the one to broach the quid pro quo, or if he was waiting for Jack to be the one to come and say, "I'll give the FBI the name of Xavier's accomplice; just back away from my wife."

Jack was still steaming about it when he left the house on Wednesday morning. Sylvia Gonzalez was in Miami. It was the four-week anniversary of the Riverside shooting, and maybe that explained her visit, knowing how terrorists seemed to love anniversaries. Whatever the reason, Jack seized the opportunity and set up a meeting with her and Agent Carter at the US Attorney's Office in downtown Miami. They listened, along with the US attorney, as Jack explained all that Andie had pieced together. Then he added his own twist.

"This is more than just Agent Carter encouraging Mr. Fitz to lodge a complaint against my wife, though he certainly has a reputation for stepping on anyone and everyone if it helps him achieve his objective. I believe others are in on it," said Jack, and he was looking at Gonzalez as he spoke. "Including you."

Sylvia was too cool to be defensive. She said nothing and showed no reaction at all to the accusation. Jack continued.

"It goes back at least to the DOJ's opposition of my motion to withdraw as counsel for Xavier Khoury. All this BS you fed the court: 'Mr. Swyteck's a known quantity, we can trust him, he has a security clearance going back to his defense of Gitmo detainees.' Very smooth on your part. But let's get real. You wanted to keep me in the case because I'm married to an FBI agent. If push came to shove, you had a pressure point on me like no other defense lawyer."

Jack let the accusation linger. Sylvia and Agent Carter were looking straight at him. The US attorney, per usual, was checking messages on his phone.

"You done?" asked Sylvia.

"No. Not until I get an answer."

"We agreed to this meeting because we thought you were going to give us the name of your client's accomplice. Not to hear this nonsense."

Jack had implied as much when he'd called to arrange the meeting, so he gave her what he had. "Who is Russell?"

"Russell?"

"It's a name my client mentioned."

"Rusul," said the US attorney, looking up from his smartphone.

At once, the FBI agent and the lawyer from Washington shot him a double-barreled look that Jack read as *You're out of the club.*

"Interesting that my work at Gitmo comes back to bite you," said Jack. "Rusul. That's a woman's name. Quite common in Iraq."

Jack got no answer, but the wheels were turning in his head, and one thing after another fell into place.

"Maritza is Rusul, isn't she? She's Iraqi, not Salvadoran. And she's using the name of a dead girl, as I'm certain you're aware."

The US attorney took a shot at damage control. "Hispanics are actually the fastest-growing segment of converts to Islam. At least in South Florida."

Gonzalez shot him another look, this one translating roughly to *Shut the hell up*.

It was almost fun to watch, this living and breathing reminder that the position of US attorney was a political appointment, a highly powerful post that was not always filled with the sharpest tool in the shed. But Jack hadn't forgotten the reason for his visit—or his anger. He started with Carter.

"The FBI literally stood by and did nothing when Maritza ambushed me right outside my office and threatened me with a gun inside her bag. She could have shot me, for all you cared.

"And you," he said, bringing Gonzalez within his crosshairs. "You're standing by, if not helping him screw over my wife. So let me tell you something. I've had enough. Tell me who Rusul is, or I'm going public."

"No!" said Carter.

"Yes. I will."

There was silence in the room.

"Would you excuse us for a minute, Jack?" asked Gonzalez.

"A minute," said Jack. He stepped into the hallway and waited outside the closed office door. A minute later, perhaps a little more, Gonzalez invited him back inside. He returned to the chair, facing them.

"I'm authorized to tell you that Rusul is a trained intelligence gatherer," said Gonzalez.

"Come again?" asked Jack.

"I met her when I was legal attaché at the US embassy in Baghdad," said Carter. "We used every asset at our disposal to fight terrorism in Iraq. Even teenage girls."

Jack wondered if that was "Carter's law" or US policy. "She worked for the American forces?" he asked. "Or for Iraq?"

"She was trained by us. But she worked for the Iraqi Counter Terrorism Service."

"What is she doing in Miami?"

"She's been here quite a while," said Carter.

"Why?"

"That's none of your business, Mr. Swyteck."

"She's working for the FBI?" asked Jack.

Carter was silent. Gonzalez answered: "Technically, yes."

"Technicalities worry me," said Jack.

"That makes two of us," said Gonzalez. "Honestly, we don't know which side she's on anymore. So the sooner your client coughs up the name . . . the sooner we can all feel safe."

CHAPTER 47

Jack went straight from the epicenter of federal prosecutorial power in South Florida to the Miami-Dade Pretrial Detention Center.

Xavier's communication skills had shown no improvement. Every attorney-client communication since Monday's polygraph examination had been a rerun of the Jack Swyteck monologues. Wednesday would be different, Jack resolved. He had leverage.

"Tell me about Rusul. Your Iraqi girlfriend."

Xavier's jaw nearly dropped. Jack had him. Maritza—Rusul—was the one topic his client could not keep quiet about.

"How'd you know where she's from?"

"It was certainly no thanks to you," said Jack. "But I'm not as dumb as I look."

The young man seemed concerned, or at least skeptical. "Did she tell you?"

"No. I heard it from the FBI."

Xavier was now fully engaged, no longer slouched in his chair. He leaned forward, his chest bumping right up against the table between him and Jack.

"Are they watching her because of me?"

"You might say that. She works for them. Or at least she used to."

"That's a lie."

"Did she never tell you she worked for the government?"

"She worked for the coffee shop. San Lazaro's."

Jack flashed the smile of the older and wiser. "Let me tell you something, Xavier. I'm married to a woman who has actually done undercover work for the FBI. She's had a lot of jobs. She may have even been a barista somewhere along the line."

"Undercover? What are you talking about? Rusul loved me. I loved her. I know why she called herself Maritza and pretended to be from someplace she wasn't. She was forced to marry the same man over and over again, every time he wanted pleasure."

Jack assumed the word *marry* was a euphemism. "So, when the imam told me she was a—"

"No! She was not a prostitute!"

"I understand. She was a victim of sex trafficking."

Xavier rose, his wrist shackles rattling as he pushed away angrily from the table. It wasn't news to him, but hearing Jack say it was clearly upsetting. He went to the other side of the room and leaned against the wall. Jack gave him a moment, then continued.

"What was the name of the man she was forced to marry?"

His client didn't answer.

"Xavier? Do you know the man's name?"

"Abdul," he said, muttering.

A man named Abdul from Iraq wasn't much to go on. "What more can you tell me about him?"

"I think he's here."

"Here in Miami?"

Xavier nodded.

Jack couldn't hide his frustration. "Xavier, why has it taken you this long to tell me this?"

No answer.

Jack tried a more understanding tone. "Xavier, I understand you love this girl. But you're looking at the death penalty. If you're trying to protect—"

"I need to talk to her," Xavier said, cutting him off.

"You're free to call anyone you want. But as your lawyer I need to remind you that every call from here is monitored. The police will hear everything."

"Then you need to talk to her for me."

"You want me to call her?"

"No. You can't trust phones. We never trusted phones. No texts, no emails, nothing like that."

No electronic trail was consistent with the evidence in the case so far. "How did you communicate?"

"In person. We had meeting places."

"So you had standing meetings, like every Tuesday at six o'clock in the park?"

"No. In my house it was impossible for the kids to have standing meetings. My mom micromanages everyone's schedule. I had to meet Rusul when an opening popped up."

"How did you arrange meetings if you didn't text or email?"

Jack detected the hint of a smile, the first he'd seen from his client. Xavier seemed proud of his own cleverness.

"Do you know Lincoln Road Mall?"

Interesting, thought Jack, the way teenagers assumed that anyone over the age of forty had never heard of the places young people liked to go on Miami Beach, even though young people had been going to those same places since the 1930s. It was more promenade than mall, a ten-block, pedestrian-only stretch of Lincoln Road running east-west in the heart of Miami Beach. Thousands came every day for the cafés, bars, shops, and galleries in a treasure trove of art deco–style buildings that never seemed dated. The only vehicles were at the cross streets.

"Yes, I know Lincoln Road Mall."

"Something you probably don't know is that at the Pennsylvania Avenue intersection there's a live webcam twenty-four hours a day, seven days a week. It never moves. It's the same camera angle, forever. If you download the EarthCam app, you can see everything as it happens in real time."

"You're right," said Jack. "I had no idea."

"It's cool, right? I never got the app, cuz my parents were always checking my phone. But Maritza opened it every day at four p.m. If I wanted to get together, I would go to the intersection right before four o'clock, and that's how we knew where to meet."

"You met at the intersection where you were on camera?"

"No. In the middle of the intersection there's an oval-shaped island of grass. The island has two palm trees and two lampposts. I would bring a yellow ribbon with me. If I tied it around the nearest tree, we met at the coffee shop across from the candy store on Lincoln Road. The far tree meant our spot on Ocean Drive—the bench by the showers for the beaches. The near lamppost meant the mall at Brickell City Center. The far lamppost, midtown."

On the cuteness scale it was somewhere between teenage crush and puppy love, but Jack couldn't deny its effectiveness.

"What makes you think she still checks the webcam?"

"She's smart. She knows that's the only way I can get a message to her."

Jack was starting to feel a bit like Cyrano de Bergerac. Or Tony Orlando and his hit song about the old oak tree. "So you want me to go to the intersection and tie a yellow ribbon around a palm tree?"

"Yes. Choose the palm tree closest to the camera. In thirty minutes she'll meet you at the coffee shop a block away."

"I know what I want to ask her," said Jack. "What do you want me to ask her?"

Xavier shrugged, and his answer told Jack pretty much all he needed to know about the two of them. "Ask her to stay safe."

CHAPTER 48

At four p.m. Maritza opened the webcam app on her cell phone.

For the first week after Xavier's arrest, she'd checked the Lincoln Road webcam every day at four o'clock without fail. She knew he couldn't call her from police-monitored pay phones in the detention center, and she obviously couldn't visit him. Her only hope of any word from him—even something as simple as "I'm okay"—would have to come through his lawyer at one of their old meeting spots. By the second week, she was checking maybe every other day. That Wednesday, however, she was sure to check. Something told her that if Xavier was going to reach out to her, it would be on the four-week anniversary of the shooting.

"Oh, my God," she said aloud, staring at her phone. The yellow ribbon was on the nearest palm tree.

She gave a minute of thought as to whether it was a trick or trap of some sort. She'd been waiting too long for this signal, and she couldn't ignore it. But she couldn't ignore the risk, either. She packed her gym bag accordingly. The traditional black chador wouldn't conceal her identity, but it would certainly conceal the 9 mm Glock she would carry beneath it. She grabbed her keys, got in her car, and drove to South Beach, speeding down the expressway like Danica Patrick.

The chador was something she hadn't worn since her first and last visit to Xavier's mosque. Agent Carter had given it to her and told her to wear it. Carter had choreographed her every meeting with Xavier, except the ones they'd arranged on their own through the webcam. It had taken him months to get clearance for her to work the assignment, and if her father hadn't been a CIA agent killed in Iraq in service to his country, she never would have been approved. But Carter had pull, not only with the bureau, but with her. She owed him. Carter had reminded her of that when he'd called in the favor from Rusul.

I need you," said Carter.

They were at San Lazaro's Café. Rusul had been working there almost a year as Maritza Cruz. Staying in Iraq as Rusul had not been an option. Not after word got out that it had been Rusul who had helped the American not only put that fraud who called himself a cleric out of business, but put him away for the next fifteen years in an Iraqi prison.

"Just ask," said Maritza.

"There's a family in Coral Gables. Well-to-do. Khoury is the name. They have a seventeen-year-old son named Xavier. We got our eye on him. I'd like you to get to know him."

He showed her a photograph.

"Handsome boy," she said. "But seventeen is a little young for me."

"Not for the role you're going to play it isn't."

"What role is that?"

He hesitated, clearly reluctant. Finally, he said it. "I need you to play a prostitute."

D amn it," said Maritza, still in her car. It was 4:35 p.m. She'd made it to South Beach in record time, but she was wasting precious minutes hunting for a parking space, which was a form of extreme sport on Miami Beach, something that could quickly turn as violent as your average African safari. The trick was to target an unsuspecting gazelle walking along the sidewalk with her car keys in hand, stalk her at a steady and patient 3 mph all the way to her parked car, and then pounce on the opening as she pulled away.

Maritza found her mark and zipped into the opening. Getting dressed in her car was something she'd done on a regular basis when parking overnight behind the church, so slipping on the chador while still in the front seat was a piece of cake. She grabbed her Glock, concealing it beneath the chador, and then jumped out the car, walking as fast as possible to the coffee shop on Lincoln Road Mall.

CHAPTER 49

Jack and Theo waited at a café table beneath the palm trees outside the coffee shop. They were at the geographic heart of Lincoln Road Mall, across the street from Dylan's Candy Bar. The promenade was loaded with places like Dylan's, celebrity-owned shops with lines of tourists out the door, most of whom would buy nothing unless in need of a prop to hold in their store-front selfie.

"You and Andie doin' okay?" asked Theo.

Jack had brought Theo along because the last meeting with Maritza had ended with a gun. Jack didn't think of himself as a risk taker, but this one was worth taking if it meant stopping another school shooting.

"It's getting better," said Jack. "Things were pretty tense for a while."

"What'd you expect, defending a school shooter? You're lucky she didn't up and kick your ass."

"I suppose."

"Because she could, you know. Kick your ass."

"Yes, I'm aware."

"I mean literally. If Jack Swyteck versus Andie Henning was on pay-per-view, Andie would absolutely kick—"

"Theo, I get it."

Jack drank from his tall paper cup. It was decaf at this hour, but the Sumatra bean flavor was still there.

"That has to be her," said Theo, pointing across the street with a nod of his head.

Jack instantly knew whom he meant. He hadn't expected her to show up dressed as if she were still in Baghdad. Nothing was covering her face, however, so if the idea was to conceal her identity, it was beyond ineffective; it seemed counterproductive, more likely to draw attention than deflect it amid a crowd of tourists dressed in shorts.

Then Theo said what Jack was thinking. "I bet money there's a gun under that getup."

"I'm betting you're right," said Jack.

"You scared?"

"No. You?"

"Nope. If she's gonna shoot someone, it'll be you."

Maritza crossed the street and came straight to their small café table. Jack and Theo rose, and then they all took their seats.

"Brought your bodyguard, I see," said Maritza.

"Brought your gun, I'm sure," said Jack.

"Good to know we understand each other," she said.

Jack asked if she wanted coffee. Theo went inside to order it for her, leaving them alone to talk. Jack had not told Theo about his meeting with Agent Carter and Gonzalez in the US Attorney's Office. He told Maritza, right down to the final point.

"Sylvia Gonzalez says she doesn't know which side you're on anymore."

"Makes sense that she would say that. She wants to keep you afraid of meeting with me."

"Should I be afraid?"

"Only if you're afraid of the truth."

"What is the truth?"

She thought for a second. "The truth is I love Xavier."

"I'm guessing that falling in love was not part of your original assignment."

She laughed a little. "No. Not at all."

"What was the original assignment?"

The smile drained away. "Have you heard the myth of the seventy-two virgins?"

Jack had. It was the promise of dark-eyed virgins in paradise that recruiters distorted to induce young men into suicide bombings and other acts of terrorism. Jack first read of it after the attacks of 9/11.

"Yes. I've heard of it."

"Agent Carter didn't think an American boy raised in the Western world of immediate gratification would be quick to act on the promise of what might come in the afterlife. I was to play his real-life virgin. Xavier's reward."

"Reward for what?"

"Martyrdom."

"You mean the shooting," said Jack.

"I didn't know it was a shooting. All I knew from Agent Carter was that Xavier was being groomed for a suicide mission."

"Groomed by whom?"

"Someone with connections with al-Qaeda. The whole point of the assignment was to figure out exactly who that person was."

"Could that be Abdul?"

The very mention of his name seemed to make her cringe. "Did Xavier tell you about Abdul?"

"I'm sorry," said Jack. "I shouldn't have just dropped his name on you like that."

"It's okay. There's a side of Abdul that Xavier doesn't know. Abdul has worked with Carter going back years in Iraq. Way back. They first met when Carter was a Green Beret and an adviser with US Special Forces. Later on, when Carter was the FBI's legal attaché in the embassy, he brought Abdul into the Iraqi Counter Terrorism Service."

"Was it Carter who brought him to Miami?"

"Yes. It's temporary. It was Abdul's job to find the connection between Xavier and al-Qaeda. Offering me up to al-Qaeda as the virgin for Xavier's sacrifice was part of his cover."

"So in this instance, Abdul is actually one of the good guys."

"He's not a good guy," she said firmly. "He's incapable of being good. I told Carter that."

"Told Carter what, exactly?"

"Abdul has gone rogue. He's training *me* for the next shooting."

"Why would he think you are trainable for such a heinous act?"

"He doesn't actually believe I'll go through with it, if you ask me. He's training me because he needs someone to pin it on after it happens."

"He's setting you up?"

"I believe he is," she said.

"The same way he set up Xavier?"

"You said it. Not me."

Jack was skeptical. "It's one thing to think a seventeen-year-old boy can be manipulated. You're savvier than that."

"Not in Abdul's eyes. He thinks I'm still the fourteen-year-old girl under his control—the pleasure bride who will do anything he says, even if she's crying in pain or gagging in disgust."

Jack had researched pleasure marriages and sex trafficking after his talk with Xavier. "You mean the Mut'ah?"

"I don't want to talk about that."

It was clearly a painful subject. "I understand. But help me understand. Why are you going along with this, letting Abdul train you for a shooting?"

"I allow him to *think* he can train me, because I want Carter to see him for who he really is."

"Why doesn't Carter see it?"

"Abdul is a very clever man. Devious with his explanations."

"What's his explanation for training you to be a shooter?"

"He told Carter he's being watched by al-Qaeda, so he's role playing with me, acting like he's really on the al-Qaeda team and planning the next shooting."

"Carter bought that?"

"Apparently. I wouldn't say Carter is naive enough to totally trust Abdul, but Abdul has a proven track record of results for him going back to the Bush Two presidency. Carter's heart is in the right place, but his biggest flaw is that he's willing to cut a deal with the devil if it gives him a clear path to his objective. I guess Carter figures that if he gives Abdul enough latitude, they'll flush out the real al-Qaeda connection."

Jack took a minute to absorb all of it, then framed a question. "Do you know for a fact that Abdul trained Xavier?"

"I don't know for a fact. He probably did."

"Why do you say 'probably'?"

"Why else would Xavier go silent and say nothing in his own defense? He must think Abdul will kill me if he names the shooter."

"Are you saying Abdul was the shooter?"

"I don't know that. You asked me if I thought Abdul trained Xavier, and I gave you my best guess."

Jack didn't respond right away. He gave her words a moment to swirl around her, and he watched her demeanor. It wasn't exactly a lie detector test, but he noted that she didn't feel the need to fill the silence with nervous jabber the way most liars did.

"Let me ask you this, and I want an answer that is based on actual facts known to you and in your head. Was Xavier the shooter?"

"He was targeted and recruited to do it. No question."

"But did he do it?"

Her dark eyes met his, burning with intensity. "No."

"How do you know?"

She looked away, then back at Jack. "Because I wouldn't love him if he did."

Theo returned with Maritza's coffee.

"Theo, can you give us another minute?" asked Jack.

"That's all right," said Maritza, rising. "I have to go. I've said everything I came to say."

Jack believed that much. "We should talk again."

"If Xavier wants," she said. "He knows how to reach me."

Theo gave her the coffee to go, and she thanked him. "See you around, Jack."

"Hope so."

She turned and left, and Jack watched as the only hijab on the promenade disappeared into the early evening crowd of tourists.

CHAPTER 50

J ack and Theo were in no rush to leave their café table. Theo had scheduled himself for bartending duty starting at eight p.m., so he ordered a second espresso to help him power through till closing. Jack was still thinking of his conversation with Maritza. Theo was people watching.

"Why do you think it is that Brazilian women are so freakin' beautiful?" he asked in an almost philosophical voice.

Jack followed his friend's line of sight to the other side of the promenade, through a stand of potted palm trees, to four young women having dinner and cocktails outside a Brazilian steakhouse. They were smiling and cutting glances at the young men at the next table, and it was Jack's quick take that the ladies were trying to decide who among them had the best command of broken English to thank the Americanos for sending a round of drinks. Another case of girl from São Paulo meets boy from Saint Paul. Language was never a barrier on South Beach, but only if you were paying attention.

"I'm sorry. What'd you ask me?"

"Forget it. New question. You gonna spend the rest of your night inside your own head, or you gonna tell me what Maritza said?"

Jack had been too busy processing what he'd learned to waste time repeating it. But he took a minute to give Theo the gist.

"You want to know what I think?" asked Theo.

It had taken him all of thirty seconds to form an opinion. Theo was not the ruminator Jack was. "Okay, I'll bite. What do you think?"

"Your client either did it or knows who did it."

"You could be right," said Jack. "Or you could be wrong."

"If you think I'm wrong, then why'd you ask me what I think?"

"I didn't ask what you think," said Jack. "I think it was you who asked if I wanted to know what you think, and I thought I did—"

Suddenly, that old R.E.M. song that it had taken two days to get out of his head was back again: *I think I thought I saw you . . .*

"Can we drop this?" Jack asked, but there was no dropping it. "The thing is . . ."

"The thing is what?"

The question that had been nagging from somewhere in the back of his mind finally gelled. "Why would someone—Abdul, al-Qaeda, or whoever it was—target Xavier for recruitment and radicalization in the first place?"

Jack's cell phone rang. He checked the incoming number, then told Theo who it was.

"Mike Posten at the *Miami Tribune*."

Jack received at least five calls a day from reporters. He'd stated publicly that the trial of Xavier Khoury was going to take place in the courtroom, not in the media, and he'd meant it. He ignored ninety-nine percent of reporters' calls. Some numbers he'd even blocked. But Posten at the *Tribune* was an old friend, or at least as much of a friend as a criminal defense lawyer who was the son of a former governor could have in the media. Jack answered.

"How goes it, Mr. Posten?"

"I need a quote, Jack."

"Get in line."

"Come on. One sentence. That's all I need."

Jack was about to decline, but an idea struck. "Maybe we can help each other here."

"Wouldn't be the first time."

Posten was the reporter who'd broken the story that the weapon used in the Riverside school shooting was registered in the name of Xavier's father.

"I want to know the date of the first registration of the gun in the name of Amir Khoury," said Jack.

"You do realize that's not public information," said Posten.

"Yes. And even though your story didn't print the date of the *first* registration, I'm guessing you have that information."

"I probably do," the reporter said coyly. "But just so we're clear, you can't just go online or call the Department of Agriculture and get the name of registered gun owners. Florida law prohibits it. That information is exempt from public records laws."

"I understand."

"To put an even finer point on it," said Posten, "if I give you this information, there will be a very usable quote from you."

"Deal."

Jack could almost feel the journalist smiling through the line. "Hold on, Jack."

He waited with the phone pressed to his ear.

"What's this about?" asked Theo.

"I hadn't really thought this was important before. But talking to Maritza got me thinking that maybe I'm focused on the wrong lies and the wrong liars."

"How's that?"

"I keep asking myself the same questions. Did Xavier lie when he said 'I did it'? Was Molly lying when she said she had nothing to do with the disappearance of the clothes, the goggles, and all the other stuff the shooter was wearing? Is Maritza lying about her and Xavier? Then—boom—it hit me. What about Amir?"

"What about him?"

"Amir told me that he bought the gun after nine-eleven."

"So?"

Posten was back on the line. "Got it for you, Jack. The gun was first registered in the name of Amir Khoury on January seventeen, two thousand and one."

It was an easy computation—nine months before the terrorist attacks of September 11, 2001.

"Thanks, Mike."

"Hey, what about my quote?"

Jack said the first thing that popped into his head. "We intend to defend these charges vigorously."

"Bullshit, Swyteck. You're going to have to do a lot better than that."

"Give me twenty-four hours, Mike. This quote will be killer."

CHAPTER 51

Jack's drive from South Beach back to the mainland was against rush-hour traffic. Eastbound lanes on the Julia Tuttle Causeway were three long lines of monotony, but Jack was cruising toward downtown, making a blur of the evening glow from the waterfront homes of entertainment icons, Russian oligarchs, and pharmaceutical billionaires on Star Island. Theo took an Uber back to his bar in the Grove, so Jack had time alone in his car. A phone call was the last thing he wanted, and when his cell rang on Bluetooth, his first inclination was to answer only if it was Andie. He glanced at the number on the console. It was pretty unusual for Bonnie to call from the office after five o'clock. He answered.

"What are you still doing at work?"

"I had some filing to catch up on. Good thing. Molly Khoury came by. She needs to see you."

"Why?"

"She says it's important."

"Can you put her on?"

"She doesn't want to talk on the phone. She's in bad shape, Jack."

"You mean drunk?"

"I mean really bad shape. You need to come."

She was talking as if she couldn't say more. Perhaps Molly was standing nearby, and Bonnie didn't want to be overheard.

Whatever the problem, a call like this from his trusted assistant of almost twenty years wasn't something Jack could ignore.

"Okay. I'll be there in twenty."

He called Andie and let her know he'd be home late, drove past his exit to Key Biscayne, and headed back to his office. He arrived sooner than promised, fifteen minutes later. Molly's Mercedes was in the driveway, but Bonnie's car was not. The door was locked, so he used his key. Molly was alone in the lobby, seated in the armchair.

"Where's Bonnie?"

"The freezer is broken on your refrigerator," said Molly. "She went to get some ice."

"Ice?"

"*For what?*" he was about to add, but then she turned her head, and Jack noticed her eye. The bruising was still fresh, but it was going to be one ugly shiner. Jack went to her, concerned.

"What happened to you?"

"Four-week anniversary of the shooting. A pretty awful day at the Khoury home, as you can imagine. Things got out of hand."

"Did Amir do this to you?"

She hesitated before answering. "I fell."

"You fell," he said in a tone that let her know he wasn't buying it. "Do you want to see a doctor?"

"No. I'm sure this looks a lot worse than it is."

"Has this happened before?"

Another hesitation. "People fall all the time, I guess."

"Molly, you have to be honest with me. You did the right thing by getting out of the house. You probably feel like there are not a lot of people you can turn to, with all that's happened in the last four weeks. But I'm glad you came here. I want to help, and you can trust me."

A tear from her good eye ran down her cheek. The drops pooled in her other eye, trapped by the swelling. Jack went into the kitchen and ran a paper towel under the faucet. Trying to get really cold water from a Florida tap was like the proverbial search for snowballs in hell, but something was better than nothing. He folded up the wet towel and gave it to Molly.

"This'll have to do until Bonnie brings the ice," he said.

Molly thanked him and gently applied it to the swelling.

"Where are you planning to stay tonight?" asked Jack.

"A hotel."

"Which one?"

"The usual."

"So this isn't the first time?"

"Xavier has always been a flash point in our marriage," she said.

"It might sound like a stupid question to ask why," said Jack, "but up until four weeks ago, I would have pegged him for the perfect son. Perfect grades. Accepted to MIT."

"Xavier was perfect. For a long time. Maybe he would have stayed that way if Amir had accepted him."

"Accepted him? In what way?"

She dabbed her eye, then looked at Jack. "Can I tell you a secret?"

"You can tell me anything."

"When Amir and I were engaged, he broke things off six weeks before the wedding."

"Why?"

"If you think he has a temper now, you should have known him then. The 'why' is not important. I was devastated and made a very dumb decision. I got really drunk and went to see my old boyfriend."

"We've all been there," said Jack.

"I suppose. Anyway, Amir and I obviously got back together. A month later, we were married. Eight months later, Xavier was born."

"Oh," was all Jack could say.

"Yeah. Oh."

"I'm guessing Xavier was not the product of make-up sex when you and Amir got back together."

"No. But my old boyfriend looked a lot like Amir. I've never been drawn to WASPy-looking guys. So it was never an issue outside our marriage."

"But inside?"

She lowered her gaze. "Relentless," she said in a soft but sad voice.

"Is that what tonight was about?"

She nodded. "The anniversary of the shooting brought it all to a head. He said Xavier's sin was Allah's punishment for my sin."

"You know that's not true, right?"

Molly didn't answer. Jack didn't know whether to take the conversation in its logical direction, or to let logic wait for her to heal emotionally. But he was running out of time.

"There's something important I need to tell you, Molly."

She looked up. "What?"

"I'm not in a position to share many details, but I can tell you this much. I'm having serious doubts about Xavier's guilt."

A car pulled into the driveway, the sound of tires parting pea gravel alerting Jack.

"That must be Bonnie with the ice," said Molly.

Jack had a completely different thought, knowing how abusers operated, and he went quickly to the door. Through the glass he saw Amir coming up the steps. Before he could turn the deadbolt, Amir charged the entrance and pushed his way inside, the door hitting Jack in the chest as it flew open, knocking Jack backward to the floor. He'd seen Amir's temper before, but nothing like this.

"Molly!" he shouted, in a voice that made his wife shrink.

CHAPTER 52

"Tell me what you said to him!" Amir shouted.

Molly didn't respond, perhaps because she was too afraid to speak, or perhaps because experience had taught her that there was never a right answer.

Jack quickly climbed to his feet and stood firmly between them. "Back off, Amir."

Amir's anger shifted to Jack. "What did she tell you?"

"If you're going to stay, I need you to sit down and shut up. Either way, I'm calling the cops."

"Don't!" Molly shouted, but it wasn't an order. She was begging him. "Please don't do that. If the media gets wind of this, I can't handle it," she said, her voice quaking. "Have you seen my new name on the Internet this week? Machine-Gun Molly, mother of the Riverside School shooter. I just can't handle one more thing, Jack. I just can't."

Jack put his cell phone back in his pocket, then looked at Amir.

"She fell," he said, his tone lacking any hint of believing it. "That's what she told me."

Amir seemed relieved, or at least satisfied enough to take his anger down a notch. He looked past Jack. "I told you not to drink so much," he said, and then he looked at Jack, adding nervous laughter in a lame attempt to wring the awkwardness out of the air. "These women at the country club. They start with a glass of wine at lunch, drink all afternoon, and then come home and fall flat on their face. Literally."

It was a cheap shot, but things were de-escalating, and Jack hoped Molly would let it go. She didn't.

"Jack was just about to tell me what he learned today. He thinks *our* son might be innocent."

She went right for the hot button, choosing not to call Xavier by his name and instead emphasizing *our* son.

"Go on, Jack," she said. "Amir might be curious to hear too."

Jack was in one of the most dangerous places on earth, alone in a room with an abuser and his victim and standing right between them. He wanted nothing more than to help Molly, but she wasn't facilitating it.

"Amir, I think it's best if you leave now," said Jack.

"No!" said Molly. "Amir, you stay. Tell him, Jack. Tell him what you know."

"Yes," said Amir. "Tell me what you know, Jack."

"Molly, it's time for Amir to leave."

She didn't take his lead, and Jack knew it wasn't because she was stupid. Either she felt safer with him standing there, or she'd simply had enough of Amir.

"Just curious," she said. "When did the questions begin in your mind, Jack? Was it the curious lack of evidence that Xavier was radicalized? No social media posts? No suspicious Internet searches? No radical cleric at the local mosque? No crazy uncle visiting from overseas?"

Jack was listening to the voice behind him, but he was watching Amir. Part of his brain told him to call the cops, but the expression on Amir's face told him that he had better not reach for that phone.

"That left only two possibilities," said Molly. "Xavier didn't do it because he was never radicalized. Or he did it because he was radicalized at home."

"This is a very dangerous game you're playing," said Amir.

"I agree," said Jack. "The door is right there, Amir."

The man didn't move.

"Did you know our house has been under surveillance?" asked Molly, her question apparently directed to Jack. "They have listening devices."

"That's not true," said Amir.

"It has to be," said Molly. "I didn't think about this until I was driving over here to see Jack. Apparently, when the FBI or whoever is watching us does surveillance, they have the decency to call the Coral Gables Police when they hear a husband hitting his wife. The cops were at our front door in three minutes. Lucky for you the police can't do anything if the wife doesn't speak up. But who called nine-one-one, Amir? The kids weren't home. It wasn't me."

"I'm leaving now," said Amir. "And you're coming with me."

"No, she's not," said Jack.

"Why would they be watching us?" asked Molly, staying with her own line of questioning. "Unless they thought one of us had something to do with the shooting."

"Maybe they wouldn't be watching us if you hadn't tried to get rid of Xavier's clothes after the shooting," Amir said. "Or if you hadn't mailed the footie to yourself to make it look like someone else was the shooter."

It was the first Jack had heard of the mailing, but he assumed it was a reference to the foot coverings worn by the shooter, which the police never recovered.

"I didn't do either of those things," said Molly. "And you know it."

"We need to go now, Molly."

"No, we need to be honest now!" she said, her voice rising. "Why did they mail you that stupid foot covering? Was that to keep you in line, Amir? Were they afraid you were going to break under the pressure, and they needed to remind you that you were already in too deep?"

"You need to stop right now," said Amir.

"How long has this been going on, Amir? Months? Years? Is this why you wouldn't let me divorce you? The pretty blond wife was your perfect cover?"

Amir charged toward her. Jack pushed him away, knocking him to the floor. Molly hurried to the reception desk and grabbed the telephone. Amir pulled a gun from under his sport coat and fired one shot, which shattered the base of the phone and sent the pieces flying off the reception desk. He then turned the gun on Jack.

"Nobody move!"

Jack froze. Molly was standing at the desk, the receiver still in her hand and the now-detached cord dangling. She didn't move. There was complete silence.

Then, from the driveway, came the sound of a car pulling up.

"Who's that?" asked Amir.

"Bonnie, my assistant. She went to get ice for your wife's eye."

He pointed the gun at Jack, then Molly, then back again, as if not sure who was the bigger problem. The car door shut outside the building.

"We can deal with this," said Jack. "Just put the gun away, Amir."

"Fuck you, Swyteck! Is there a back door to this place?"

"Through the kitchen."

"Let's go."

Jack made one more appeal to reason. "If we go out that door, you go from assault to kidnapping. Twenty-five years to life."

Amir raised his pistol. "If we're not out the back door in ten seconds, you *and* your assistant are looking at a bullet in the head. Now let's move."

They started slowly.

"Move!" said Amir, and they hurried to the kitchen and out the back door. Amir's car was just a few steps away. He had Molly by the collar and his gun aimed at Jack's back.

"You're driving, Swyteck. Molly in front."

At gunpoint, they complied, Jack behind the wheel and Molly in the passenger seat. Amir got in the back seat right behind Jack and pressed the barrel of his pistol up against the base of Jack's skull. The car started with Amir's press of the remote key.

"Drive. And do exactly as I tell you," he said, as he pressed the gun a little harder against the back of Jack's head, "or that is going to be one messy windshield."

Jack had no idea where Amir planned to take them, but for the moment all he could do was obey. The back of the old house faced an alley, and with one streetlamp on the entire block, Jack used his high beams to cut through the darkness. He was turning out of the alley and onto the street when he heard the wail of police sirens.

"Damn it!" said Amir. "I should have taken care of your assistant."

Amir thought Bonnie called the police, but if Molly had managed to punch out 911 before Amir shot the phone off the desk, they had already been dispatched. Jack had done enough criminal defense to know that if you wanted the police to come, dial 911 and talk to the operator; if you wanted the police to come *in a hurry*, dial 911 and hang up. They were trained to assume the worst.

"Go!" said Amir.

"This is not going to turn out well," said Jack.

The gun pulled away suddenly, but it returned with a vengeance, the metal butt striking behind Jack's right ear. The blow stunned him. The car swerved, but Jack fought it off and quickly recovered. Amir jabbed his gun at the side of Jack's skull.

"Do as you're told."

Jack felt blood oozing down the side of his face. It was clear that Amir had no intention of surrendering, but it was even clearer that he had no plan. Just ahead, the traffic light changed from green to amber. Jack noticed a squad car at the cross street, waiting for a green light. On impulse, Jack hit the gas, knowing that he couldn't possibly make the light. The squad car was already in the intersection as Jack sailed past at nearly double the speed limit. Jack's light could not have been redder.

Blue flashing lights swirled behind them as the squad car screeched onto the boulevard and gave chase.

"You did that on purpose!" said Amir. "Outrun him!"

Jack didn't react fast enough.

Amir pushed the gun so hard against the back of Jack's head that his chin hit his chest.

"Floor it, or I'll kill you!"

Jack hit the accelerator, and the car lurched forward. The squad car was a half block behind them and in hot pursuit, siren blaring. The engine growled, and the speedometer rose beyond seventy miles per hour. The squad car was right behind them.

"Faster!"

The streets around Jack's office were short and narrow, harkening back to the days when the neighborhood was purely residential. But at this speed they were quickly out of the old neighborhood.

"Turn here!" said Amir.

They were coming up on LeJeune Road, a major north-south corridor with three lanes in both directions.

"Turn!"

Jack had too much speed. He hit the brake and jerked the steering wheel hard right, which put the car into a skid, forcing a corrective hard left, which put the car into one of those smooth sliding maneuvers that professional drivers do on television commercials. But Jack was no pro. The car was out of control.

Molly screamed, but Jack could barely hear her over the screeching tires, as the car cut across three lanes of oncoming traffic. Horns blasted, vehicles swerved out of the way, and the bright white beams from several pairs of headlamps shot in every direction. The front tires slammed into the curb, and for an instant the car was airborne before coming down hard on an asphalt parking lot, headed straight toward a motor lodge. Jack's childhood flashed before his eyes, memories of those road trips and cheap motels that all looked the same, a string of rooms with outdoor entrances that faced the parking lot, the flimsy front wall consisting of a door, a picture window, and a climate-control unit all in one prefabricated piece. They scored a direct hit on Room 102. It was like driving into a one-car garage without bothering to open the garage door. Both airbags exploded. The car leveled everything in its path, like a high-speed bulldozer, shoving lamps and dressers and two double beds against the back wall of the hotel room. The mountain of debris had acted like a giant cushion, not exactly a soft landing, but better than crashing into a concrete pillar. Jack's door had flown wide open in the crash, but the seat belt and airbag had saved his life.

"Molly, are you okay?" he asked.

She didn't answer, but he heard her crying, so he knew she was alive.

"Molly?"

The room looked as if a bomb had detonated. It was almost completely dark, brightened only by the streetlights that shined through a gaping hole that was once the front of the motel room. The ceiling had partially collapsed into a cloud of dust. Electrical wiring, twisted water pipes, broken furniture, chunks of drywall, and other debris were strewn everywhere. Jack refocused just in time to hear the squad car squealing into the parking lot. The blaring siren drowned out all sounds—except for the gunshots.

Amir was shooting at the cops as he crawled out of the car through the shattered rear window. The officers in the parking lot scrambled for cover and returned the fire. Jack ducked down in the front seat and told Molly to do the same.

There was another exchange of gunfire, and the 9 mm slugs

fired by the police made a popping sound as they hit the interior walls of the demolished hotel room. The wrecked automobile was suddenly bathed in white light. The police had switched on the spotlight that was fastened to the squad car. Another shot rang out, and the light was history. Amir had nailed it with one shot from a distance of at least a hundred feet. The police returned fire.

Molly was able to push open the passenger's-side door and seemed ready to make a run for it. Jack grabbed her before she put herself at risk of getting caught in the cross fire. Another crack of gunfire from somewhere in the demolished hotel room sent an officer falling to the pavement. The other went to his aid. Another shot echoed from somewhere within the mountain of debris, and the second cop went down equally hard. Jack couldn't see Amir, but wherever he was—whoever he really was—he was one crackerjack marksman.

Sirens blared in the distance, signaling that more law enforcement was on the way. Jack spotted a fast-moving shadow on the wall. It was Amir, and the instant Jack realized that, he felt the gun under his chin.

"Move, move!" shouted Amir.

He was pushing Jack over the console and into the passenger seat. It was like the old Chinese fire drills Jack had run with his friends as a teenager—in one door and out the other. Amir pushed until Jack and Molly were all the way out of the car, through the passenger's-side door. Right in front of them was a side door that, Jack surmised, led to an adjoining motel room. With a single shot, Amir destroyed the lock, forced open the door, and shoved his hostages inside. A quick look around confirmed that this room had suffered no damage from the crash. Amir pulled open the drapes on the front window facing the parking lot.

"Molly, stand in the window, hands up! Now!"

He was using his own wife as a human shield.

Molly complied, her arms shaking as she brought them up over her head.

Inside and outside the motel room, all was quiet, but for the sound of their own breathing.

CHAPTER 53

Andie was at home with Righley when the call came.

Righley's kindergarten class was learning all about shapes in school, and Andie was in the middle of a dressing-down from a five-year-old for identifying the little window in their front door as a diamond and not a rhombus. She apologized profusely and stepped into the kitchen to take the call from her ASAC.

"I have some bad news," said Schwartz, in a tone that made the words even more ominous. "It's about Jack."

He told her what he knew, but details were sketchy. He gave her the address. "Hostage negotiation team is on its way."

"So am I," said Andie.

It was a great help having Abuela with them on school nights, but Andie didn't tell her where she was going. "Just don't turn on the news in front of Righley," she said on her way out the door.

Three minutes later she was speeding across the causeway toward a hostage crisis on the mainland. She felt guilty not telling Abuela what was going on, but she couldn't have handled her falling to pieces on the spot. Abuela was the best grandmother anyone could ask for, but she was a Cuban grandmother, which meant that she wailed when Jack caught a cold. Andie couldn't possibly have told her that she had no idea when she and Jack might come home. If Jack came home. The thought was enough to make her crazy. Or cry.

Her phone rang again. It was a number she didn't recognize, but this was not the time to let anything go to voice mail. She answered, and the voice on the line only confused her.

"Please don't hang up."

"Who is this?"

"My name is Maritza Cruz. I know what's going on with your husband. Probably more than you do. Agent Carter told me."

Mention of Agent Carter lent this call instant legitimacy, not to mention the fact that the media had not yet gotten wind of the hostage taking. But she sounded too young to be an agent.

"Are you FBI?"

"I've been helping Agent Carter infiltrate the Khoury family."

Infiltrate? That was news to Andie. "What do you mean by 'infiltrate'?"

"That's a very long story."

"I'm listening."

"The problem is that you're not in the need-to-know universe."

Andie knew what she meant in the strict FBI sense, but she begged to differ. "My husband is a hostage. If there's something you can tell me to help, I *need to know*."

"Just understand: if I tell you, I have to go dark."

She seemed to mean "go dark" in its military parlance, as in breaking off communication from her contact—in this case, Carter.

"If you can live with it, I can live with it."

A few seconds of silence followed. And then Maritza started talking.

CHAPTER 54

M ore, more, more!" said Amir, barking out orders to Jack.

At gunpoint, Jack was turning the motel room into a makeshift fortress. Anyone trying to rescue the hostages by barging through the front door that faced the parking lot, or through the side door to the adjoining room that was now a pile of rubble, would have to get past a mountain of furniture and a hail of bullets. The dressers, the mattresses, the bed frames, the nightstands—the entire room had been cleaned out, except for the television. There was a crack of light at the edge of the wall and along the top of the window. The drapes were so old and worn that, in spots, the lining had lost its blackout quality. The room brightened every few seconds as the intermittent swirl of police lights seeped in from the parking lot.

"Get a blanket over those drapes!"

Jack grabbed the extras from the closet. The room was the typical old-style motel with the climate-control unit below the big picture window. Jack stood on the unit to hang the blankets from the curtain rod. It made the room even darker, but Jack's eyes had adjusted. Amir tried the light switch again. Nothing. They were obviously without electricity. That didn't stop him from pushing the on-off button on the TV every few minutes, determined to get a picture.

"Can't you see that the power's out?" said Molly.

"Shut up!"

The constant blare of sirens over the past twenty minutes told Jack that an army of police had taken up positions outside the motel. He'd heard helicopters as well, though he had no way of knowing if they were part of a tactical team or the media. His guess was that the police were regrouping and tending to the fallen officers. Jack prayed they were alive.

"Too damn quiet out there," Amir said, muttering to himself.

"Gunfight is over," said Jack. "Time to negotiate."

Amir shot him an angry look. Jack hoped this hostage taker would stay calm enough to appreciate that police didn't deal for dead hostages. Amir went to the corner and peeled back the edge of the drapes for a peek at the parking lot.

"What are you going to do?" asked Molly. "Shoot your way out of here?"

"I'll shoot *you* if you don't shut up. I only need one hostage. Remember that. Both of you."

That kind of talk to his own wife spoke volumes, but Jack still had to believe that the lawyer was the more expendable of the two.

Amir looked at the ceiling. "What was that?"

Jack had heard it, too.

"Someone's on the roof," said Amir.

Jack didn't correct him, but it wasn't that kind of sound. Perhaps they were snaking some kind of listening device through the attic. Or, Jack wondered, did law enforcement have the technology to listen through walls remotely and wirelessly these days? Jack wasn't sure. But the very fact that, one way or another, they *were* listening gave him an idea. It was tied to something Molly had said earlier, back at his office, right before Amir had gone apeshit.

"Molly really hit a nerve when she said she was the perfect cover," said Jack. "The perfect cover for what, Amir?"

Amir pointed his pistol at Jack. "Did you not hear what I said? I only need one hostage. And in case you're counting rounds," he said, pulling a second magazine from his coat pocket, "I have more than enough ammunition. Don't mess with me."

Jack had to say something for the benefit of whoever was listening.

"Did you grab that extra magazine from your car, or did you already have it in your pocket when you barged into my office?" asked Jack.

Amir ignored him, but Jack didn't care about the answer. It was all about conveying information to the hostage rescue team. Jack knew they were out there. Somewhere. And it wasn't just about saving Molly and himself. Agent Carter's warning about another school shooting was more pressing than ever.

"How long have you had that gun, Amir?" asked Jack.

"What's it to you?"

"Ah, forget it. You'd probably lie to me anyway. Like you did about the other one. The one used at Riverside."

"I told you why I bought that gun. Do you know what it was like to be a Muslim living in this country on September twelfth, two thousand and one?"

"People were scared, and they made a lot of mistakes. I hear you on that. Problem is, you bought the gun before nine-eleven."

Molly went ashen, as if unable to handle the exposure of one more lie about her husband.

"Is that true, Amir?" she asked.

"So what?" he snapped back. "It's an old gun. Who gives a shit when I bought it?"

"You're right," said Jack. "Why would anyone care? Which raises a better question."

The two men locked eyes, staring at each other in the dark room.

"Why would you lie about it?" asked Jack.

CHAPTER 55

Andie slammed the brakes, and the front bumper nearly kissed the pavement as her car came to an abrupt halt at the police barricade.

LeJeune Road was completely shut down, both north and south, for as far as Andie could see. Eerie was the mood on a normally busy street that was suddenly deserted, particularly at night, with the swirl of police lights coloring the neighborhood. Andie rolled down her window as the Miami-Dade police officer came toward her.

"Agent Henning, FBI," she said, flashing her badge.

Schwartz had made good on his promise to alert perimeter control that she was on her way. She parked at the curb, where another traffic control cop was dealing with media vans with satellite dishes jockeying for position. Andie counted at least three helicopters whirring overhead, their bright white search lamps cutting through the clear night sky to improve the images on television.

Schwartz came out to the barricade to get her.

"Jack's alive and sounds unhurt," were his first words to her. "We snaked a microphone through the attic and heard his voice."

Andie was so happy she could barely speak. "What about Molly?"

"Heard her voice, too. Also got a visual. Amir put her right in the window to make sure we knew he had a hostage. Or to keep us from shooting."

Amir was clearly in contention for worst husband ever.

Schwartz led her down the block toward a fast-food restaurant. Law enforcement was setting up a command post in the parking lot. Its location was strategic—close, but not too close, to the motel—and a ready source of burgers, fries, and coffee didn't hurt. The FBI SWAT van was parked in the drive-through lane. The tactical teams stood idle outside, drinking coffee—decaf, Andie presumed, so as not to get too stimulated. Behind the van was an ambulance at the ready, just in case. Andie hoped Jack wouldn't be the one to need it.

"Well, look who's here," said Schwartz.

A large motor van bearing the blue, green, and black logo of the Miami-Dade Police Department rolled into the parking lot and stopped. The antennae protruding from the roof signified that it was equipped with all the necessary technical gadgets to survey the situation and make contact with the hostage taker. The rear doors to the SWAT vans flew open, and the tactical teams filed out. They were armed with M16 rifles and dressed in black SWAT regalia, including helmets, night-vision goggles, and flak jackets.

"Wait here a sec," said the ASAC, and he started toward the MDPD van.

Almost immediately, Schwartz and the MDPD team leader were in a heated discussion, as if the face-to-face confrontation were a mere continuation of an argument they'd been conducting by telephone or radio. Andie was too far away to overhear, but she knew a turf war when she saw one. A helicopter whirred overhead—low enough for Andie to read the *Action News* logo on the side.

"Too close!" shouted Schwartz, this time speaking in a voice that Andie and everyone else could hear. "Get them to back off—now!"

An officer grabbed a loudspeaker from his patrol car and told the intruding chopper to mind the restricted airspace. It seemed to have no effect.

Schwartz and the MDPD officer continued to haggle for control of the situation. A pair of tactical teams at the ready awaited instructions, doing exactly what many believed to be the true meaning of the SWAT acronym: sit, wait, and talk. Andie's patience was at an end. The FBI's hostage negotiation team had already set up shop in the mobile command center across the street. Andie went alone. Agent Carter stepped out as she arrived.

"You're on the negotiating team?" asked Andie.

"I'm lead negotiator. I did hostage negotiation in Iraq. I speak Arabic. I know how al-Qaeda thinks."

"You're saying Amir is al-Qaeda?"

He didn't answer her question. "I'm sorry, but you can't come inside."

Andie knew that a hostage negotiation mobile command center left little room for visitors. But there was always a secondary negotiator, if only to take notes.

"I can be secondary," said Andie.

"Got one," said Carter. "It's Jones."

This was not the negotiation she'd come for. "I'm going in, Carter. And no one's going to stop me."

"Look, I'm not being petty or sexist or whatever you think I'm being. Last thing I need as lead negotiator is a demand from Amir Khoury to talk to Jack Swyteck's wife."

"Amir doesn't have to know I'm in the van."

Carter looked away, then back, for no apparent reason except that she was annoying him. "It's just not a good idea for you to be at the nerve center of this operation. Aren't you still under disciplinary review?"

It was a shitty thing to say, even from a guy with Carter's reputation for crushing out anyone like a spent cigarette if he or she didn't fit his personal vision of the mission. Andie decided to fight friendly fire with friendly fire.

"Awful lot of media out here," said Andie. "You don't want me talking to them. Not after the earful I just got on the phone from Maritza Cruz."

That got his attention. His gaze drifted toward the mobile command center.

"Sounds like you're in, Agent Henning."

"Good call. But first I have some questions for you. About the fingerprint on Amir's gun."

"Which gun?"

"Don't play stupid. The one used in the school shooting."

"Oh," he said. "That fingerprint."

"Are you going to enlighten me?"

"Here's the only thing I have to say to you, Henning. And this doesn't go beyond you and me."

She didn't commit herself to any of his conditions.

Carter took a half step closer and looked her in the eye. "I've been working this case for almost a year, and I've been watching the Khoury family almost that long. If I have to lose the Riverside School shooter's mother and his lawyer to stop the next school shooting . . ."

He let her draw her own conclusion. It didn't require much brainpower on Andie's part.

"Now, you're welcome to come inside," he said. "But it is what it is."

He turned and disappeared into the van. Andie glanced down the street toward the motel, where Jack was at the mercy of whoever this Amir really was.

CHAPTER 56

Jack's feet were killing him. He and Molly had been walking for so long that, had they not been trapped in a motel room, they probably could have made it all the way to Key Biscayne and back.

"Can we *please* sit down?" asked Molly.

The furniture was piled to block the door and most of the front window, but motel furniture didn't stack up with the precision of a jigsaw puzzle, so there were openings here and there—where the trash can butted up against the desk, the chair against the valet stand, and so on. The double layer of drapes and blankets should have alleviated Amir's concerns about sniper fire through the window, but he was taking no chances. On his order, Jack and Molly had started on opposite sides of the room and were on a loop: walk toward the other wall, pass each other in the middle, continue to the other wall, turn around, and repeat.

"Keep walking," said Amir.

He had the desk chair, the only place to sit in the room, other than the floor. And the floor was looking pretty good to Jack.

"I believe this is a violation of the Geneva Convention," Jack said with sarcasm.

"Shut up, smart-ass. Since when does this country follow the Geneva Convention?"

It wasn't the response Jack had anticipated, but it offered insight as to what he was really up against. Alleged violations of the Geneva Convention had sparked numerous challenges to the treatment of al-Qaeda detainees by US interrogators.

Amir's cell phone rang. He checked the number. It kept ringing.

"Aren't you going to answer it?" asked Molly.

"Just keep walking," he said.

The ringing stopped. The call had probably gone to voice mail. Amir's phone rang again. Jack couldn't be certain, but a call from a hostage negotiator would have made sense.

"They probably want to talk," said Jack, still walking.

Amir silenced the ringer on his phone. "When I want to talk, I'll call them."

Jack was no expert in hostage negotiation, but a hostage taker who didn't want to talk was not a good thing.

A ringtone pierced the silence. Amir had all three cell phones, and Jack knew that Madonna's "Material Girl" was definitely not his ringtone.

Amir jumped up from his chair, clearly agitated. He silenced Molly's phone, and then silenced Jack's.

"Please talk to them," said Molly, pleading.

"Shut up!"

Jack and Molly exchanged looks of concern as they passed each other on their endless loop. Without talk, there was no negotiation. Without negotiation, there was only one ending to this crisis. Jack had to do something. He was betting that the FBI was eavesdropping through some kind of listening device. He had to get Amir talking, if not directly to the FBI, then indirectly—through Jack.

"If you're hungry, you could negotiate for food," said Jack.

Amir didn't say anything. The fact that the suggestion didn't draw the usual vitriol told Jack that maybe he was on to something.

"Just a thought," said Jack. "No telling how long this might last."

Molly picked up Jack's lead. "I'm kind of hungry."

"You can stand to lose a few pounds," said Amir.

The hostages crossed paths on their walk. Jack made eye contact, and they reached a silent agreement to let him do the talking. The mere sound of Molly's voice was enough to set off her husband.

"There's a great little Cuban restaurant not far from here," said Jack. "You could tell the FBI to leave the food outside the door. Arroz con pollo. Plantains. Maybe a little tres leches for dessert. Whatever you want."

Amir didn't answer. He removed the magazine from his pistol and checked the remaining rounds. He was definitely more concerned about ammunition than food.

"You think they'll bring me more bullets?" he asked, clearly facetious.

That was the one thing Jack was certain was off the negotiating table.

Amir shoved the magazine back into the butt of his pistol. Jack hadn't noticed before, but it was a 9 mm semiautomatic, the same type of pistol that had been used in the Riverside shooting, though probably a newer model.

"You like the Glock?" asked Jack. "My wife swears by the Sig Sauer."

Amir studied his weapon, as if actually considering Jack's question.

"Easy to clean, she tells me. I've actually seen her take the whole thing apart and put it back together again in less than a minute."

Jack wasn't just making small talk. Over the past four weeks, he'd spent many hours thinking about the old Glock used in the Riverside shooting. Many of those hours had been spent wracking his brain over the unidentified fingerprint—the lone print that didn't belong to Amir or his son.

"How easy was it to clean that old Glock you owned?" asked Jack.

"What does that have to do with anything?"

"Just curious," said Jack. "You must not have cleaned it very often. Or maybe you didn't do it right."

"Are you some sort of expert marksman?"

"No. But my wife is. I've watched her clean a pistol. You wouldn't find any stray fingerprints on her Sig Sauer. So, when the forensics team examined the murder weapon and found a fingerprint that didn't belong to you or Xavier, my first thought was, didn't they ever clean that thing?"

Jack and Molly passed each other again. She was dragging but pushed on. Jack kept talking.

"Then I saw where the forensics team found the print. It was actually inside the gun, under the slide, a place that would come in contact with a person's fingers only when the gun was completely disassembled."

Jack stopped at the wall, turned, and started back toward the other wall.

"So I asked myself, why would someone disassemble a gun? To clean it, obviously. Or a gun could also be easier to conceal if it's in pieces. Anyway, my conclusion was that the unidentified print belonged to the last person to completely disassemble the gun, whatever the reason. It was on the inside, so it was never smudged or wiped away in normal handling or external cleaning."

"And whose fingerprint do you think it is?"

"I don't know. But I know this, Amir. If that fingerprint belongs to the real shooter, there's a way out of this for you. I've defended clients in much deeper shit than you're in right now. You don't have to go down in a gunfight. Talk to them. Answer the phone and just talk."

A minute passed. Jack had him thinking.

The phone rang. The FBI was definitely listening.

Jack kept walking. The phone kept ringing. Jack tried the most reasoned voice he could muster.

"Pick up, Amir. You have the power in this negotiation. Only you can tell them whose fingerprint is on that gun."

CHAPTER 57

M aritza parked her car on a side street and walked toward LeJeune Road. In the neighborhoods just outside the police perimeter, MDPD officers were going house to house asking residents to stay inside for their own safety. But this was excitement, Miami-style, and onlookers were lined up three deep on the civilian side of the police barricades. Maritza wormed her way to the front and looked all the way down the street, her gaze landing on the old, half-lit sign outside the motel that proclaimed there was ACANCY.

She probably shouldn't have come, but after the phone call to Agent Henning, she found it impossible to stay away. Maritza had done most of the talking, but in each response and follow-up question, Henning's fears and worries for her husband had come through on the phone, no matter how hard she tried sticking to the role of staid FBI agent. There was probably nothing Maritza could do to help resolve a hostage standoff, but she was curious in a way that no other onlooker was curious.

She wondered if Abdul would show up.

If he was there, somewhere in the crowd, Maritza was the only person who knew he alone was rooting for the hostage taker. Carter seemed blind to it. *Indispensable* was the word he'd used to describe Abdul in their Baghdad operations.

Carter had been right about her. Fighting bad guys was in her blood, this daughter of an American CIA agent. Carter had been a Green Beret when he'd met Rusul's father, and though he'd moved on to the FBI and was no longer army when he'd rescued Rusul from that fraud who called himself a cleric, Carter had even more pull at the US embassy in Baghdad as a legal attaché. He put her to work for the Iraqi Counter Terrorism Service, where she was an invaluable set of eyes and ears in the mosques, in the schools, in the markets—anywhere people gathered and talked. He trusted her with the intelligence she brought him from her sources, and she trusted him to keep her out of any mission that might bring her face-to-face with Abdul. It was Carter who'd handpicked Abdul, trained him, and brought him to CTS. He had too much invested in Abdul to get rid of him, even if the man was a pig who married one fourteen-year-old virgin after another. Carter had saved her life, but if Abdul was indispensable in Carter's eyes, she simply had to swallow that pill, no matter how bitter.

But this was Miami, not Baghdad. They were no longer in a war zone, even if they were still "at war" against al-Qaeda. It was mind-boggling to Maritza the way Carter refused to see Abdul for the man he really was three thousand miles from the world in which he'd made himself "indispensable."

Agreeing to be part of Carter's Operation Khoury without first getting the name of her handler had been Rusul's mistake. Naming Abdul as her handler had been Carter's betrayal.

'm not asking you to do *me* a favor," said Abdul. "This is Carter's decision."

They were in the parking lot at San Lazaro's Café in Little Havana. She was five weeks into the Khoury operation, working under the name Maritza Cruz. Carter had placed her there because it was Xavier's regular coffee shop.

"I've done everything Carter asked," she said. "I talk with Xavier almost every morning. Every time he comes in."

"We need to take this to the next level."

"What does that mean?"

"What do you think it means?"

She couldn't find the words to respond. "I need to hear that from Carter himself."

"You know he can't speak to you directly," said Abdul. "He's breaking the FBI's rules by using you. He tried playing it by the book, but the bureau gave him three agents to choose from. The youngest was twenty-five, and not one of them could have pulled off playing a teenager. We're playing this by Carter's rules, and my directions to you are coming straight from Agent Carter. You owe him, wouldn't you agree?"

Rusul had no doubt in her mind that she would have been dead long before her nineteenth birthday had she stayed in Iraq. Still, the irony of Abdul speaking of her rescue—from men like *him*—was more than she could stomach.

"What would he have me do?"

"Carter wants his net to snare as many operatives in this country as possible. That means we have to let Amir and his son play this out to the very last step. Obviously, it's critical that we not push this too far. We need to know when the attack is in motion so we can stop it. We can't be left with egg on our faces and dead victims on the ground."

"How do I help with that?"

"Casual chitchat with a customer at the coffee shop isn't going to get us the information we need."

"You want me to ask him out? Like on a date?"

His expression turned very serious. "We need you to do whatever is necessary."

The words repulsed her, especially coming from him. "I don't believe Carter would ask me to do what I think you're asking."

"You're right. He wouldn't. But that's because he's under the impression that you hated doing what you did for the cleric in Baghdad. I know differently."

"You don't know anything about me, Abdul."

"Do you want this operation to succeed, or don't you?"

"Yes, of course. But—"

"No buts. You're in a position to be our best set of ears in this operation. Xavier's an easy mark. He's being taught to understand that a reward of seventy-two virgins awaits him in the afterlife. Whet his appetite. Be his virgin in this world."

"That's not who I am, Abdul. I am not a prostitute."

"And you're definitely no virgin," he said. "But I play the cards I'm dealt."

A flash of light assaulted her eyes, as a sudden glow from the parking lot outside the motel lit up the night.

LeJeune Road was already alight with permanent streetlamps, but law enforcement had brought in portable trees of vapor lights to bring virtual daylight to the immediate area around the motel. Maritza was in the darkness, but the people on the other side of the street, closer to the motel, were within the outer reaches of the portable glow, bathed in white light.

Rusul's memories burned hotter than vapor lights. Five months into the operation, Carter had finally spoken to her directly to ask what the hell was going on between her and Xavier. She'd confessed that one thing had led to another, and that she'd "developed feelings for Xavier." Carter had gone ballistic and said she was out of line, and when she'd told him that it was Abdul who'd ordered her to cross the line in the first place, her accusation rang hollow.

Across the street, MDPD officers were moving the crowd back, beyond the reach of the vapor lights. Rusul watched, and then she froze, her gaze locking onto the man with the dark beard wearing a baseball cap. It was him.

It was Abdul.

She backed away from the barricade. She had to get to the other side of the street. This would be the night—the night she made it clear to Carter that it was a mistake to trust Abdul more than her.

CHAPTER 58

A ndie waited for the phone to stop ringing, hoping to hear Amir's voice on the line.

She was inside the mobile command center, just a few feet from Carter. It was tight quarters. Carter, as lead negotiator, was seated behind a small table. On it was his coffee mug, a bone mic to communicate with his team leaders in the field, and a telephone within easy reach to speak to the hostage taker. Nearest to him was the secondary negotiator, and next to him, a staff psychologist to evaluate the subject's responses and recommend negotiating strategies. Schwartz was seated next to Andie, facing the team.

"Hello, this is Amir, I'm sorry I can't take your call . . ."

Carter hung up.

"Try Molly's phone," said Andie. "Amir probably has all of them."

Carter didn't seem to appreciate the advice. "Tried that already, as you might have guessed. Let's give him a few minutes."

He put down his headset and breathed in and out.

Andie needed to know more about his approach. His earlier expressed willingness to sacrifice hostages if it would stop the next terrorist attack was weighing on her mind.

"Are you planning to ask Amir about the fingerprint on the gun?" she asked.

"That's not your territory, Henning."

"That's my husband in there. I'm not interfering, but I think I have a right to know if the priority is to gather information or to save the hostages." She was speaking more to her ASAC than to Carter.

"The priority is always to save the hostages," said Carter.

"I told you I spoke with Maritza," said Andie. "She said the fingerprint belongs to a known and confirmed member of al-Qaeda."

Carter was stone-faced.

"That's true, isn't it?" asked Andie, again speaking more to Schwartz.

Carter didn't answer, but she'd apparently gotten through to her ASAC.

"Tell her," said Schwartz.

Carter grumbled, but Schwartz called the shots in this group. "We ran the fingerprint through the dead terrorist data bank. It came up."

"Who?"

"The name wouldn't mean anything to you," said Carter. "He's dead. Been dead for years."

"You're saying that fingerprint does not belong to the Riverside shooter?"

"Only if he rose from the dead," said Carter.

"I'm still not okay with this," she said.

"Not okay with what?"

"You have physical evidence that confirmed a connection between Amir and a known, albeit dead, member of al-Qaeda. And yet you used my husband. You pressured him to get his client to name his accomplice, but you never told him how dangerous this family really was."

"I'm not hearing a problem," said Carter.

"You should have told Jack."

"How do you know I didn't?"

Schwartz leaned forward in his chair, as if to draw the line. "Let's not lie to her, Carter. We didn't tell Jack."

Andie tried to control her anger. "And look where we are now."

"It was your husband who chose to defend Xavier Khoury," said Carter. "Not me."

The phone rang. Carter quickly put on his headset and gave everyone the *quiet* signal. Then he answered.

"So good of you to call back, Amir."

"I want to speak to Swyteck's wife."

Andie was silent. Carter did not so much as glance in her direction.

"I'm afraid that's not possible, Amir. She's not here."

"I don't believe you."

"Let's you and I talk, all right?"

"No, not all right. I think she's sitting right there with you, but she's afraid to talk."

Carter did what a good negotiator was supposed to do, keeping it friendly, no argument.

"Ah, come on, Amir. I'm not lying to you. I promise you, I won't lie to you as long as we keep talking."

"You are so full of shit. I know she's afraid. I read the newspaper article about the lawsuit against her. She ran like a coward. A trained FBI agent ran away from a boy with a pistol, when all she had to do was listen and wait for him to reload—and then overpower him. Her daughter is home safe. The children who followed her the wrong way down the hall, thinking she was leading them to safety, are all dead."

The command center was silent. Not even Carter had a response.

"Nice work, Agent Henning. Now pick up the phone and call me." Amir hung up.

Andie was staring at the floor, stunned.

Schwartz spoke first. "Ignore him, Andie."

Andie took a breath, then looked her ASAC in the eye. "No. I can't ignore him. I want to make the call."

"Not gonna happen," said Carter.

Andie's gaze remained fixed on her ASAC. "I'm asking you, Guy. I want to call him."

J ack wanted to hit him.

He had no idea why Amir wanted to talk to Andie, but he hoped she wouldn't take the bait. He applied the same rule to himself, not taking the bait. The last thing he wanted to discuss with a terrorist was his own family. He turned the conversation back to Amir's.

"Still pinning this on Xavier, are you?"

Jack was doing the loop at the front of the room by himself, walking from one wall to the other, running sniper interference for Amir. Molly was in the bathroom.

"What are you talking about?"

"You said Andie 'ran away from a boy with a pistol.' I assume you meant *your* boy."

"Her boy," said Amir, pointing with a jerk of his head toward the bathroom. And then a look of concern came over him. Molly had been in there an awfully long time.

"Molly, time to get out!" said Amir.

She didn't answer. The thought crossed Jack's mind that she might hurt herself.

Amir went to the door and pounded twice. "Molly!"

"Just a minute, all right?"

Jack was relieved to hear her voice.

The toilet flushed. The bathroom door opened. Molly stepped out tentatively, started across the room, and then stopped.

"I can't walk anymore," she said.

"Didn't you see *American Sniper*?" said Amir. "These guys will shoot through a pinhole if they think there's an opening. Keep walking."

She dragged herself back to the path she and Jack had cut in the carpet. To the far wall, turn. Back to the other wall, turn. Molly was over it.

"I have to sit down, Amir."

"You just spent ten minutes in the bathroom."

"I have cramps, okay?"

"Fine. Take turns. Sit with your back to the wall."

She walked very slowly, her feet shuffling as she passed Jack. Then she whispered to him, "You can hear everything in the bathroom."

Jack kept walking. Molly continued toward the wall and sat with her back to it. Amir apparently hadn't heard what she'd said, and Jack didn't fully understand the point. He continued to the far wall, turned, and started back toward Molly. She cut her eyes, telling him to go. It was his deduction that she had something to say to Amir. Or no—she wanted him to say something to her, and her strategy was that he wasn't likely to say it with Jack in the room.

"I need to use the bathroom," said Jack.

"You got cramps, too?"

"It's been a few hours."

"Go."

Jack walked to the bathroom at the back of the room and closed the door behind him.

"Molly, you have to walk while Swyteck's in there."

Jack heard Amir's voice loud and clear. Molly was right. The walls were like paper. The FBI didn't even need electronic listening devices.

"I'll walk," she said. "But there's something I have to say to you."

"I don't want to hear it."

"Oh, you're going to hear it. Twenty years, Amir. I've had this inside me almost twenty years. You're going to hear it. Whether you want to or not."

CHAPTER 59

A mir took a seat in the armchair, the only stick of furniture that wasn't piled up against the front door and window. He needed a negotiating strategy. He could release one of the hostages. In return for what?

Money? How much?

A plane? To where? Havana was just ninety miles south of Miami. Fidel Castro was dead, but Cuban airspace was still hostile to American interests. US fighter jets couldn't follow him there, unless they wanted to take on Russian-made MiGs. The motel was just a few minutes away from Miami International Airport. This plan could work. But there was an alternative.

A plea. Ratting out . . . who?

He rose and crossed the room to the front barricade. He'd left an opening at the peephole. A sniper's bullet could pierce the door, so there was some risk, but he needed to see what was going on outside. He leaned forward and got a quick fish-eye view of the parking lot. It was brighter than before, thanks to whatever portable lighting the cops had brought in. Obviously, they thought more light was to law enforcement's benefit, but Amir liked it, too. Hard to pull off a sneak attack in virtual daylight. LeJeune Road was quiet. Plenty of flat-roofed buildings across the street for snipers to position themselves on. He counted the cars in the parking lot. Seven. No change since the start of the standoff.

"Are you going to tell them about Ziad?" asked Molly. She was on sniper-fire-intercept duty, walking.

Amir backed away from the door. "Don't say that name."

"Why? Are you afraid the FBI might be listening?"

The thought had crossed his mind. "Just don't say that name."

She stopped. "Ziad Jarrah, Ziad Jarrah, Ziad Jarrah."

He grabbed her by the collar, raised his hand to slap her, and then stopped. What if the cops *were* listening? Beating a hostage and her screaming for help might bring SWAT crashing through the door and charging into the room. At the very least, it might encourage Swyteck to play hero.

"Don't ever say that name again," he said, glaring. He released his grip on her collar.

Molly resumed walking. "The FBI must know by now," she said. "How you two met in Hamburg. How you two reconnected when he came to Florida for his flight training."

"Molly, that's enough."

"It can't possibly take them as long as it took me to figure all this out. Nineteen years. I probably still wouldn't know, if it weren't for Maritza."

Amir froze. From the get-go, he'd suspected that girl was trouble.

"When did you realize you were cooked, Amir?"

She was talking way too much, and Amir was on to her. She was betting that the FBI was listening, and this was her negotiation: let me go, or I bury you. She was overlooking the fact that there was another option.

He opened a music app on his cell phone and played it at full volume. Then he grabbed Molly by the throat, shoved the gun under her chin, and whispered into her ear. "I could strangle you to death, and they wouldn't hear it over the music, even if they are listening. I'm giving you a choice. Fly to Cuba with me. Or go out that door feetfirst on a gurney, and I can fly there with

Swyteck. Like I said, I only need one hostage. It's up to you. Keep your mouth shut, or pay the price."

Her eyes bulged. Her fingers pried at his grip. He released her. She gasped for air. He gave her a moment to recover and then killed the music.

"Keep walking."

She caught her breath, and then put one foot in front of the other.

Amir returned to the armchair, thinking. Molly was right. The FBI must have pieced it all together by now. He'd managed to put Hamburg, Ziad, and al-Qaeda behind him for twenty years and lead a respectable life. Then all of it had come back to haunt him, jeopardizing everything he'd built for himself. He'd thought he could pull it back together, even after the shooting. But Molly had asked the right question. "When did you know you were cooked?" For Amir, that realization had come through a deposition transcript, the moment he'd read the printed collo-quy of Swyteck's examination of the fingerprint expert. When the chief of the MDPD Forensic Bureau's Latent Unit had tes-tified that fingerprints could remain on a gun for ten, twenty, or even forty years. Right about then, the FBI could have stuck a fork in him.

It all went back to his final meeting with Ziad, almost twenty years earlier.

Nice gun," said Ziad, speaking in Arabic.
They were at the kitchen table in Ziad's apartment in Lauderdale-by-the-Sea, just a few blocks away from the South Florida fitness center where Ziad was taking close-quarter-combat training from a master. Amir watched as Ziad disassem-bled Amir's brand-new Glock 9 mm pistol and laid the pieces on the table. It took him even less time to put it all back together.

"Is that how we get the guns on the plane?" asked Amir, also speaking in Arabic. "Take them apart and then put them back together once on board?"

"That was the idea. But that's changed. No guns."

"How do you hijack a plane without a gun?"

"We use these." Ziad opened the kitchen drawer and showed him.

"That's not much of a knife," said Amir.

"It's a box cutter. We can get through airport security with these."

"We need guns. What if the shit hits the fan when the plane lands?"

"The plane isn't going to land."

"What do mean it's not going to land?"

Ziad's expression turned very serious. "I'm flying it into the White House."

"Whoa. *What?* I didn't sign up for a suicide mission."

"We need five, Amir. I don't have time to find another replacement. Mohammed al-Qahtani never made it out of the Orlando airport. You agreed to step in when Immigration sent him back to Saudi Arabia."

"I didn't agree to a suicide mission. I'm no martyr."

"Come on, Amir. There are seventy-two virgins waiting for you."

It was an odd attempt at humor under the circumstances. He knew Ziad wasn't in it for that. He had a girlfriend back in Germany whom he called or emailed almost every day. He was close to his family in Lebanon. He would even go out for a beer every now and then. Amir detected a hint of apprehension in his friend's voice, but he respected his choice.

"Looks like you're in line for a hundred and forty-four virgins, Ziad. I'm out."

Amir's cell phone rang. He answered it immediately. "This better be Agent Henning."

He had a strategy. If anyone inside the FBI would push for his plane to Cuba, it would be Swyteck's wife. But the friendly voice on the line was Carter's.

"Good news, Amir. She's on her way. Ten minutes. Fifteen, tops."

The bathroom door opened and Swyteck stepped into the room. Amir raised his pistol shoulder high and stopped him in his tracks, aiming straight at his chest. Then he spoke into the phone.

"You're on the clock. If she doesn't call me in ten minutes, tell her she's lost the chance to say good-bye."

CHAPTER 60

The mobile command center was silent. Amir's warning had given the FBI plenty to ponder, but Andie was more focused on the separate audio feed from the motel room, which had captured the entire conversation between Amir and his wife, less the part drowned out by music.

"Ziad Jarrah," she said, looking straight at Carter.

It wasn't a question. There wasn't an FBI agent over the age of thirty who didn't know the name of the 9/11 hijacker who took over as pilot of United Flight 93. The fact that no one in the command center was talking about it told her that she was the only one outside the loop.

"You heard right," said Carter. "It took us twenty years. But we finally made the connection."

"How?"

Carter glanced at the ASAC, as if asking for permission not to tell. Permission was denied.

"Tell her," said Schwartz.

"When United Airlines Flight Ninety-Three crashed into an open field in Pennsylvania, there wasn't the complete incineration that occurred with the direct hits on the Twin Towers or the Pentagon. In fact, the passports of two of the Flight Ninety-Three hijackers were recovered in the debris."

Andie wasn't aware of that. "When you say recovered, you mean in good condition?"

"Good enough," said Carter. "The FBI was able to obtain fin-gerprints of those two hijackers. Those are the only fingerprints the US government has for any of the nine-eleven hijackers. Be-fore nine-eleven, fingerprinting wasn't part of routine visa appli-cations under US Immigration laws."

With the mention of fingerprints, it all clicked for Andie. "Are you saying the unidentified fingerprint on Amir Khoury's gun belongs to . . ."

"That's exactly what I'm saying," said Carter. "It belongs to the Lebanese-born pilot of Flight Ninety-Three."

"How did it get there?"

"We don't know. But there's no question about the match. It appears they first met in Germany. Jarrah was a student at Ham-burg University of Applied Sciences when he joined al-Qaeda's Hamburg cell. Amir did a semester abroad in Germany while he was at Wharton. We assume they reconnected when Jarrah came to Florida to take flying lessons."

She was angry at Carter but directed her response to the ASAC. It was one of incredulity.

"You approved this operation, using my husband, without tell-ing me or him about a direct link between Amir and one of the nine-eleven hijackers?"

"Andie," said Schwartz, fumbling for words. "Would it have made a difference if I had told you?"

She took his point. "You're right. Jack would have done it. But maybe he would have finally listened to me and kept a gun in his office to protect himself. I've always told him he's a sitting duck. Maybe this time he would have been in a position to protect himself instead of ending up a hostage."

"Now is not the time for finger-pointing," said Schwartz. "You heard Amir. We're on the clock."

"I can talk to him," said Andie.

"I can't imagine why you would want to do that," said Carter.

It wasn't a question of "want." It had started with the way he'd tormented her with his accusations of cowardice, and it had continued on through the threat against her husband. "I *need* to talk to him," said Andie.

"This could go very badly," said Carter.

"Carter's right," said Schwartz.

The quick decision against her came as a surprise. "You heard Amir," said Andie. "He threatened to kill a hostage—my husband—if I'm not on the line in ten minutes."

"That's one interpretation," said Schwartz.

"You have another one?"

He looked at the tech agent. "Play back that last sentence."

The techie tapped away on the computer, then brought up the audio recording and played it for all to hear.

"If she doesn't call me in ten minutes, tell her she's lost the chance to say good-bye."

The recording ended. Having heard it a second time, Andie understood Schwartz's concern, and she voiced it for both of them.

"He's going to kill him either way," she said.

Schwartz elaborated. "If you don't call, you lose your chance to say good-bye. Either way, you lose Jack."

Carter put a finer point on it. "And the idea that he's gracious enough to let you say good-bye is bullshit. He's a fucking terrorist. He's probably going to blow Jack's brains out while you're on the line, so you can hear it."

"I get the picture," said Andie, meaning that it was hardly necessary for Carter to have painted it so graphically.

"Then we all understand what we have to do?" asked Schwartz.

Andie nodded.

"All right," said Schwartz. "I'm giving SWAT the yellow light. In T minus five it's green."

CHAPTER 61

J ack was pacing more than walking, his mind working furiously to drill down on what exactly Amir had meant by that
last warning: *tell her she's lost the chance to say good-bye.*

As a lawyer, Jack argued constantly as to whether words were
ambiguous. If the language in a statute or agreement was suscep-
tible of more than one meaning, lawyers were allowed to drone
on endlessly about what was really meant. But if the language
was plain on its face, that ended the matter. Judges would shut
down any arguments about the true intent behind the words or
any discussion of what the speaker had really tried to say. The
plain language spoke for itself.

Amir's words were not ambiguous: whether Andie got on the
phone or not, Jack was a dead man. He figured he might as well
take Amir down with him.

"Ever see that movie?" Jack asked. "*Flight 93?*"

Jack had. The true story of how the passengers of United Airlines Flight 93 were able to overcome the hijackers and prevent
them from achieving their terrorist mission was well known. But
he probably wouldn't have recognized the name "Ziad Jarrah" as
that of the pilot if he hadn't seen the film.

"Most of the nine-eleven hijackers were Saudi. Jarrah was Lebanese, as I recall. Aren't you of Lebanese descent?"

"I'm American," said Amir. "Born in this country. Fucked by
this country."

Jack was glad Molly didn't fan the flames with another chip-
on-the-shoulder comment. He wanted to keep this focused. He

talked while he walked, his tone somewhere between the peri-
patetic delivery of a college professor and the cross-examining
technique of a trial lawyer.

"Jarrah was part of the notorious Hamburg cell. You ever spend
any time in Germany, Amir?"

"He was a college student there," said Molly.

Jack moved on quickly, not wanting to make this a three-way
conversation.

"I remember for sure that Mohammed Atta, the pilot of the
first plane to crash into the World Trade Center, took his flight
training in Florida. I don't recall specifically about Jarrah. I'm
guessing he trained in Florida, too. For every disaster, there's
always a Florida connection."

Amir checked the time on his cell phone. "They got seven minutes. Talk all you want, Swyteck. I'm not extending the deadline."

"I remember—not just from the movie, but from everything
I've read—all of the planes hijacked on nine-eleven had five hijackers except for one: United Flight Ninety-Three. There were
only four on that flight, including Ziad Jarrah."

"So?"

"I've never talked to anyone who thinks that having only four
hijackers on Flight Ninety-Three was part of the plan. Either
somebody backed out or didn't get through immigration. There
was some kind of problem with the fifth guy."

"Old news," said Amir. "What's it matter?"

"It matters because, until now, I've never heard anything about
al-Qaeda trying to replace the missing guy."

"Guess he was just lucky. The others are all dead now."

"Yeah," said Jack. "Fifteen on the three planes that hit their
target. Four on the one that didn't get there. All dead. All *nineteen* of them."

Jack stopped walking. He locked eyes with Amir, who stared
right back at him.

"Were you twenty?"

CHAPTER 62

Andie took a sip of water. Her mouth was desert dry. Her stomach was in knots.

Schwartz had made the call. An FBI tactical team armed with M16 rifles and outfitted in black SWAT regalia—helmets, night-vision goggles, and flak jackets—was ready, eager, in fact, to go on a moment's notice. Andie felt anything but ready. Definitely not eager. Negotiation was by far the preferred way to end a hostage crisis. If something went wrong, she'd never forgive herself for standing down and letting her ASAC pull the trigger, so to speak, on the tactical team option.

And the very last thing she needed was to be caught in the middle of a disagreement between Carter and Schwartz.

"I need you to tell SWAT to stand down," said Carter.

"The team is already moving into position," said Schwartz. "We can't change the plan every two minutes."

"I've seen SWAT called back later in the game than this—as late as the breacher's boot in the air, ready to kick the door down."

"With good reason, I presume."

"There's good reason here," said Carter.

"Look, Carter—"

"I want to hear it," said Andie. "If there's good reason to think this is not the best way to get the hostages out alive, I want to know."

"Losing your nerve is not a reason," said Schwartz, a little too harshly, but they were all under stress. He adjusted his tone. "To revisit a decision like this, something in the calculation has to have changed."

"It has," said Carter. "We all just heard it on the audio feed."

"You mean Jack and Amir talking?" asked Andie.

"Yes."

"Mostly what I heard was Jack talking," said Schwartz. "And Amir listening."

"Exactly," said Carter. "Jack essentially accused him of being linked to the worst terrorist attack in history, and Amir didn't shut him down. I think he's ready to talk."

"What I heard," said Andie, "is that the clock is still running no matter how much Jack talks."

Carter directed his response to the ASAC. "We need to keep this dialogue going. Everything we've learned so far tells us that Riverside was job one—the North Tower, if you will. If Amir knows something that could stop the next attack, we lose that the minute SWAT sets foot in the room."

Andie took a deep breath, recalling Carter's warning to her outside the command center: *If I have to lose the Riverside School shooter's mother and his lawyer to stop the next school shooting . . .*

"This is the moment I've been working toward for nearly a year," Carter added.

"You actually had me," said Andie. "Until you made it about you."

Schwartz was of like mind. "What you just said goes double for me, Andie. But Carter's first point still has merit."

Andie couldn't disagree. "We can't just let the deadline pass. We need an extension."

"I can get it," said Carter.

"Or maybe I could," said Andie.

"No," said Carter. "So far, talking to you has been his only demand. Once we put you on the line, there's no leverage to string this out."

For an instant, all Andie could think of was Jack in that motel room, the clock ticking on the five-minute deadline. "What if he shoots him?"

They seemed to understand that it wasn't really a question. Just her fears, out loud.

"You know something?" said Schwartz. "Most people in Jack's position right now would probably be begging for their life. I don't know Jack well, but well enough. He wouldn't have started this dialogue and gone down this road if he wasn't on board with what Carter is proposing."

Those were kind words, and Andie knew her ASAC wasn't just blowing smoke.

"Okay," said Andie, and then Schwartz gave the order.

"Do it, Henning. Get us more time."

Andie did a double take, but it was Carter who put her thoughts into words.

"You said Henning," he pointed out. "You meant me."

"No," said Schwartz. "I definitely meant Andie."

CHAPTER 63

Jack had one eye on the bed frame.

There were two of them in the pile of furniture that was their makeshift barricade, but the one that had caught Jack's attention was broken. It had been broken before Amir had given the order to turn the beds on their sides and shove them up against the front window with the couch, the dresser, and all the other stuff that, throw in a few "angry men," reminded Jack of the battle scene out of *Les Misérables*. The one in good condition had a crossbeam bolted to the frame that kept the full-size mattress from sagging in the middle. The other had lost its crossbeam, probably to children jumping on the bed, or perhaps something more X-rated. The replacement beam was a flat strip of metal; it looked as though the motel's handyman had cut it to order and just shoved it into place, no bolts. *Cut* was the operative word, as it appeared that maintenance had used metal-cutting shears instead of a hacksaw, leaving a jagged end to a six-foot length of metal that was sharp enough to draw blood if applied with enough force. With enough courage. At the right opportunity.

"Why'd you back out, Amir?"

Jack was still walking as he spoke. Molly was seated cross-legged on the floor, her back against the wall. Amir was on the other side of the room. He checked the time on his cell phone, offering no response.

Jack was slowly shifting into cross-examination mode, which was comfortable territory for him, or at least as comfortable as he could be under the circumstances.

"I've heard it said that not all the nine-eleven hijackers knew they were on a suicide mission. Is that true, Amir?"

Amir rose from the armchair. He seemed agitated, but Jack's read was that it was something other than his questions that had the hostage taker so wound up. Time was running out, and maybe Amir didn't know what to do when the deadline inevitably arrived. Or maybe he knew exactly what needed to be done, and he was coming to terms with it. Jack kept talking.

"Some people think the reason Ziad Jarrah failed is that he had only three muscle hijackers to keep the passengers out of the cockpit. If there had been a fourth, who knows what might have happened?"

Amir checked his phone again. Time was ticking.

Jack had exhausted his knowledge of facts and theories about Flight 93. But if he followed his cross-examination instincts and climbed farther out on this limb—if he could tie Amir to Ziad Jarrah's failed mission in a way that would cause Amir to let his guard down for just a moment—maybe Jack's opportunity to draw blood, literally, would present itself.

"The argument could be made that the missing hijacker is what caused the mission to fail," said Jack. "And just imagine if, after all the years of planning and training, someone who'd promised to be the fifth hijacker backed out at the last minute. Wow. *That* would have to piss people off."

Amir returned to the armchair, took a seat, and breathed in and out. He looked mentally exhausted, and not just from the stress of a hostage standoff. Maybe Jack's initial read had been wrong. Maybe his questions were getting to Amir. *Tormented* was the word that came to Jack's mind. Tormented by Jack's words. And the past.

"I didn't go looking for this," said Amir.

Molly bristled. Jack kept walking. He didn't prompt Amir with another question. He just let the man say what he apparently wanted or needed to say. He was looking at his wife.

"Sometimes the past comes back to bite you," said Amir. "Out of nowhere, someone steps into the life you've worked so hard to build for yourself and your family and says, 'You owe us. Pay up. Make this right. Or we ruin you.'"

Molly looked right back at him. "You could have gone to the police."

"Yeah, sure. Like they'd cut a deal with—" He stopped short of saying the twentieth hijacker. "With me."

It wasn't clear what reaction Amir was trying to draw from his wife, but whatever it was—pity, understanding—Jack wasn't feeling it. He did what any trial lawyer would do when cracks appeared in the target. He moved in for the kill.

"You owed them," said Jack, again following his intuition. "So you gave up the one thing that would forever make you and al-Qaeda square. Radicalize your own son."

Amir was still looking at his wife, but slowly his expression changed, as there was not an ounce of pity or understanding coming his way from Molly's direction, either.

"*Her* son."

Jack seized on it. "And Xavier failed, didn't he? The shooter's tactical gear didn't disappear because his mother burned it. It disappeared because the real shooter got away."

Amir checked his ammunition one more time, then shoved the magazine back into place. The stress drained away from his face, as if he were satisfied that he had both the bullets and the nerve to get the job done. "Crazy thing is, if he hadn't met Maritza, they might have actually talked him into doing it."

"Who's they?" asked Jack.

He glanced at Molly. "The same people who put the footie in

our mailbox when they thought the Khoury family might step out of line. A not-so-subtle reminder that they had us by the short hairs."

"Who's *they*?" Jack asked again.

Amir smiled, but only slightly. "Well, if I told you that, then I'd have nothing to negotiate with. That's my ticket to Cuba."

His cell phone rang. He rose, pointed his gun at Jack, and said, "This better be your wife."

Jack hoped it wasn't. Not yet.

Amir starting pacing. "That you, Henning?" he said into the phone.

Jack couldn't hear, but he knew from Amir's reaction that it was indeed Andie on the line.

"Let me put you on speaker," said Amir, a hint of sarcasm in his tone. "This is America. We'll do this democratically. Say it again, Carter."

The agent's voice filled the room. "I'm willing to negotiate. But first I need to talk to Jack."

"I vote no," said Amir. "Swyteck, how do you vote?"

Jack stopped walking. "I vote yes."

"Molly?" said Amir. "It's up to you."

The look of distress on her face was something on the order of what Jack had seen back in his office when the beating from her husband had chased her out of their home. She didn't answer.

"See?" Amir said into the phone. "It doesn't work. This democracy you presume to force on every culture in the entire world—it doesn't even work."

"Come on, Amir," said Andie, her voice carrying over the speaker. "You put in a tall order when you asked the FBI to put me on the line. We gave it to you. All I'm asking in return is to hear Jack's voice on the phone. And then Molly's."

Jack was certain that the FBI had already heard their voices through listening devices. Clearly Andie was just getting the hostage taker in a bargaining frame of mind.

"Sounds like you think my demands are negotiable," said Amir.

"We haven't heard your demands," she said. "What if I get you some food? Or maybe I can get the power turned back on. Is it getting hot in there?"

Jack watched, and Amir seemed to be getting comfortable again, more confident.

"Food and electricity aren't going to cut it."

"Then put something else on the table," said Andie.

Amir stopped pacing and gripped the phone a little tighter. "I want a car with a driver to the airport. I want a plane with a pilot to Havana. And I want room on the plane for me and one hostage. Just one. You can keep the other."

"That's going to be very difficult," said Andie.

"I'm giving you five minutes."

"I need you to work with me on this. It's a big ask. I can't do it in five minutes."

"I'll give you ten. But the next time my phone rings, it better be you calling to tell me the car is here and the plane is on the runway."

"Okay," said Andie.

Amir seemed surprised. "Okay then."

"We're going to get this right," said Andie. "I understand what you want, and we're going to get it right the first time. There are no do-overs."

"You're damn right." Amir hung up and tucked the phone into his pocket.

Jack didn't move. He'd totally understood the message from Andie. That was his favorite expression with Righley as peewee soccer coach: no do-overs. Jack read it to mean, *Take whatever shot you get, Jack. There's not going to be a plane to Cuba.*

He was three feet away from the crossbeam in the broken bed. "Walk," said Amir.

Jack didn't even glance in the direction of what was the weapon of last resort, if not of choice. He turned and started walking, counting down from ten minutes in his head.

CHAPTER 64

Maritza started the walk back to her car.

She'd lost sight of Abdul shortly after crossing to the other side of the street. Had she been allowed to walk straight from point A to point Abdul, all would have been fine. But the MDPD on perimeter patrol had forced her to take the long way, outside the barricades. Before she could reach the spot, Abdul was gone. Maybe it hadn't been him after all. It was petty of her anyway, this urge to spit in his eye and tell him to his face that all his lies were about to catch up with him.

Another thought came to her. Maybe he'd seen her coming. She checked over her shoulder as she crossed back toward her side of the street.

"Keep walking, folks," said the officer at the barricade. "Nothing to see."

The police were doing their best, but with media vans at every barricaded cross street and the *Action News* helicopter whirring overhead, the crowd wasn't buying the "nothing to see" baloney.

"Are they filming a movie?" Maritza overheard someone say.

"Quick, selfie!"

"Move along," said the officer.

An MDPD squad car was parked at the curb, beacons flashing. The driver's-side door was open. A handful of officers were standing near it, talking. From the looks of things, it wasn't just idle chitchat. Something was up. With the door open, the console-mounted computer workstation was in plain view. Maritza glanced at the glaring rectangular screen as she passed, and she did a double take. There were a pair of images on the screen, both the face of the same man. Abdul with facial hair. Abdul clean shaven. She was too far away to read the on-screen message, but she could see the large bold letters directly above the photographs: BOLO. Even the occasional watcher of police dramas knew what that meant.

Be on the lookout—which explained Abdul's sudden disappearance.

Maritza kept walking, exhilarated, wishing Xavier were with her to slap a high five. She couldn't be certain that Xavier had broken his silence. But maybe he'd heard about the hostage standoff on the news and realized that, no matter how many threats Abdul made against his mother, brother, and sister, taking the fall for a crime he didn't commit was no way to protect his family. It was time to hold the real terrorists accountable.

"Don't scream," said Abdul, and suddenly he was walking alongside her, his arm around her shoulder, and his gun pushing up below her rib cage.

They were still a block away from where she'd parked her car, but they were well away from the crowd and commotion on LeJeune Road.

"Just keep walking normally," he said. "We're taking your car."

"There's a BOLO issued for you."

"Yes. It looks like Amir cracked."

Maritza hadn't considered that possibility. Maybe Xavier hadn't broken his silence. "You won't get away."

"I will if I have you with me. They have to give me something for giving up the next school shooter."

"Just like you pinned the first one on Xavier. Except I don't have a family you can threaten to make me take the fall."

"I have ways to make you cooperate."

Maritza was all too aware, and she couldn't deny it, but the voice from behind them made a response unnecessary.

"Police! Stop right there!"

They stopped on command. Abdul whispered in her ear, poking her ribs with the muzzle of his pistol. "Tell him your father is deaf."

She hesitated.

"Do it!" he whispered.

"My father is deaf," she said.

"Then why did he stop when I told him to?" the cop asked.

"Because I stopped," Abdul whispered.

Maritza repeated his answer.

"Okay. Well. Then . . ."

Maritza estimated that the cop was about fifteen feet behind them, and even though she and Abdul were looking down the street in the opposite direction, she could tell the officer was flummoxed.

"Do what you need to do to get your father to put his hands in the air," the cop said.

"I have to sign," Abdul whispered.

Maritza hesitated. She knew Abdul was trying to create a distraction, but he was pressing the gun so hard into her abdomen that her eyes teared.

"I have to sign," she said.

The cop took a moment. "I just want you to raise your hands in the air, and raise his with yours. Nice and slow."

Maritza started to comply, raising both her hands and taking Abdul's left hand with hers. The gun in Abdul's other hand was still poking her in the side as the officer's radio crackled.

"This is Officer Michaels," he said. "Just got off duty and was walking over to the sub shop, and I spotted—"

"He has a gun!" Maritza shouted, but before the cop could say another word, Abdul whirled around and fired two quick shots.

Maritza screamed and saw the officer drop to the sidewalk, as she dove between two parked cars on the street for cover.

Abdul fired one shot in her direction, shattering the taillight just above her head. Then he ran. Maritza hurried to the fallen officer. At least one of Abdul's rounds had hit its mark, and it was an obvious kill shot—a through and through wound, with point of entry to the left of his nose and a deadly exit through the back of his skull. He was probably dead before he'd hit the sidewalk.

"Oh, my God," said Maritza.

She grabbed the radio and told them where they were, what had happened, and who was on the run.

"Stay right there," the dispatcher told her.

She saw no point. The officer was dead. She couldn't help him. Abdul was getting away.

She laid the radio on the sidewalk and made a promise to the dead officer. "I got this," she said. She ran to her car, popped the trunk, and grabbed the AK-47 that Abdul had trained her to use.

Then she ran after him.

CHAPTER 65

A ndie watched the cursor on the computer screen.

The hand-sketched plan as mapped out by the tactical team leader told most of the story. It looked like a play drawn up by a football coach on the blackboard. But this team was already in position, and its SWAT leader had gone silent. So Schwartz filled in the details for the negotiators inside the mobile command center, referencing the on-screen diagram as needed.

"It will be a simultaneous breach from two points of entry," he said.

The cursor moved to the common wall that separated the hostages from the adjacent room. It had been virtually demolished by the crash entry of Amir's car, but SWAT had descended like ghosts to assess the damage and its potential impact on a breach.

"Cameras and on-site inspection confirm that the south wall is seriously compromised," said Schwartz. "There's a section about midpoint that can withstand a blast of explosives needed to create an entry point."

"Explosives?" asked Andie.

"The doors are barricaded," said Schwartz. "We could blast through it, but it could send debris flying and injure the hostages. And we can't have SWAT tripping all over stuff on the way in."

The cursor moved across the screen to the back wall.

"In all these old roadside motels, there's a service corridor that runs right behind the rooms from one end of the building to the other. This motel is so old it's not even close to being up to building-code requirements. SWAT tells me there's only one sheet of drywall on this back wall. The working side, facing the corridor, is exposed studs. And they're thirty inches apart, not the usual sixteen or twenty-four inches. Easy point of breach with enhanced percussion."

Easy. Andie found the word choice interesting. There was nothing easy about breaching the den of a hostage taker.

"Questions?" asked Schwartz.

His cell rang. He checked the number and didn't hesitate to answer, even at such a crucial point. "Keep us apprised," he said into the phone, and the expression on his face made Andie fear the worst.

"Officer down just outside the perimeter. We think it was Abdul."

The words seemed to leave everyone numb. Then Carter spoke. "I guess you were right, Henning. I should have listened to Maritza."

It was probably the first time in his life Carter had eaten crow, but the Pyrrhic victory of an "I told you so" was not what Andie wanted.

Schwartz laid a hand on her shoulder. "You did your job, Henning. I'm confident that Amir is expecting at least one more phone call from us before we breach. SWAT has the element of surprise. And we've done all the talking we can do."

Andie was silent. And then she nodded.

The ASAC put on his headset, adjusted the microphone, and spoke directly to the team in position.

"Green on your ready," he said.

CHAPTER 66

Maritza was running at full speed. Even with a rifle in her hand, she was faster than Abdul. She'd closed the distance between them to about twenty yards, when he stopped, turned, and looked back. Maritza stopped and raised her rifle. She wasn't close enough to hear him or even see his lips move, but everything about his reaction to her weapon screamed *Holy shit!*

He fired a shot in her direction, which missed, and then ran into the alley.

The chase had taken them away from the residential area. Abdul was heading toward the airport. They were in the warehouse district, where every building looked the same and everything shut down after dark. Warehouses were built to zero lot lines, each long and rectangular building separated from the next by a narrow alley. Maritza dialed 911 on her cell phone, still running. She told the dispatcher she was chasing the man in the police BOLO but didn't have an exact address.

"Five blocks east of LeJeune Road," she said, breathing into the phone, "by the hostage standoff."

"Stay on the line, please."

"I can't."

Maritza stopped at the front corner of the warehouse, at the entrance to the alley into which Abdul had disappeared. She put away her phone and caught her breath. With her back against the wall, a rifle in her hand, and the enemy somewhere in the dark alley, it was all eerily reminiscent of another time and her darkest days in Iraq. She poked her head around the corner and peered cautiously down the black alley. The warehouses were much deeper than wide, nearly the length of a football field from front to back. The alley had no streetlamp, or at least not a working one. The moonlight did little more than create confusing shadows in what seemed like an endless black tunnel. She knew he was still in the alley. The run had left her winded, and Abdul had to be in even worse shape. Surely he needed rest.

Maritza could have stayed right there and waited for the police. She chose not to, repeating to herself the words she'd shared with Abdul's latest victim: "I got this."

She entered the alley, keeping close to the wall, her rifle at the ready. Ten feet into the darkness, she stopped, listened, and reassessed. Roll-down steel shutters covered the windows and doors that faced the alley, blocking off escape routes. Corrugated boxes, flattened and stacked one on top of another for disposal, rose in cardboard towers along the wall near the Dumpster. She took another step forward, then stopped. There was a noise. Something—or someone—was behind the Dumpster. She took cover behind a thick stack of flattened boxes and waited. Her heart pounded. The chorus of sirens in the distance grew louder. Police were on the way. It gave her comfort, and yet it heightened the sense of urgency.

Two quick shots rang out, followed by pops in the stacked cardboard that was her cover. Maritza returned fire, squeezing off ten quick shots.

Abdul cried out in the darkness, and then she heard something hit the pavement. It was not at all like the sound of the fallen police officer hitting the sidewalk. It was something inanimate, metallic, like a gun.

Slowly, sliding her back against the wall, Maritza moved deeper into the alley closer to the Dumpster. She heard Abdul groaning on the other side of it. He was definitely wounded. She maneuvered around the Dumpster, leading with her rifle, and saw him. He was down on one knee and clutching his bloody hand. She'd shot the pistol right out of his grip. There was no telling where it had landed, but Abdul was disarmed.

"Don't move," she said.

"You shot me, bitch!"

"Move a muscle and I'll shoot you again." She dug her cell phone out of her pocket to dial 911 again.

No service.

Abdul chuckled through the pain. "Better service in Baghdad, no?"

She put her phone away. "Nothing is better in Baghdad."

"Wrong," he said, grimacing. "Prostitutes are better."

"Shut up."

"You think I wanted the life of pleasure marriages, Rusul?"

The use of her real name was clearly intentional.

"I don't care what you wanted. You're a monster."

Another mirthless chuckle, and then he looked up at her, his expression deadly serious. "Agent Carter used me. His country used me. I gave him everything I had for eight years to fight al-Qaeda. It cost me my wife, my sister, my mother. Everything."

"How could you join a terrorist organization that murdered your family?"

"It wasn't al-Qaeda. They were murdered by ISIS. The Americans left us at their mercy by pulling out before the job was done. Does Carter care? No."

"That wasn't Carter's fault."

"For nine years, I risked my life fighting terrorists for the Americans. Carter owed me more than 'Good-bye and good luck.' Do you know what ISIS did to men like me who helped 'the invaders'?"

She did. She'd witnessed it with her own eyes.

"My wife, my mother, my sister were not enough," said Abdul. "They took my son, my daughter, and all their classmates. They gunned them down like animals."

"At school," she said, purely a reaction.

"Yes. At their school."

"So Riverside was *your idea*. When Carter asked you to help root out Amir Khoury's connection to al-Qaeda, it was you who put the idea of a school shooting in his head."

"Justice. Put down the gun, Rusul. Carter used me. He used you, too."

"No," she said, her voice quaking. "Carter saved me."

"Saved you?" he said, scoffing. "He needed young women to gather intelligence in Iraq."

"And then he brought me to this country, where I would be safe."

"And he paired you with *me* to infiltrate the Khoury family. Saved you," he said, almost spitting out the words. "It's all about the mission, Rusul. He *used* you. The Americans use everyone."

"You're the user, Abdul. You used Xavier. And when he wouldn't do as you asked, you took Amir's pistol and did it yourself. And Amir went along with it. What kind of sick father allows a man like you to pin a school shooting on his own son?"

"Better than letting him fall in love with a whore."

"Shut up, Abdul!"

"Did you kid yourself into thinking you could actually have a boyfriend, Rusul?"

She wanted to pull the trigger.

"Did you think you could undo the thoughts I put into that boy's head? The hatred Amir put into his heart? Did you think the two of you would live happily ever after, Rusul?"

She wanted to pull it so badly.

"Do you honestly believe you can ever be more in this life than a tight virgin for lonely men?"

His words alone might have been enough to push her over the edge, but as he dove to his right, Maritza saw the gun, and she had no choice. She squeezed the trigger, again and again, faster and faster, releasing round after round until the flurry of bullets took Abdul down to the pavement.

The sound of blaring sirens grew louder. The police were near.

Maritza dropped her gun, fell against the Dumpster, and wept until they arrived.

CHAPTER 67

On edge. Stressed out. At the breaking point. From Jack's vantage point, all of the above applied to Amir. The deterioration of his emotional state over the past seven or eight minutes had been precipitous. The darkness was getting to him. Streaks of light seeped through the cracks in the draperies, and his cell phone added a little more. But it wasn't enough.

"Too dark in here," he said for the fifth time in the last five minutes.

"Use my cell phone," said Molly.

"No. I need to save batteries."

"I could peel back a corner of the drapes," said Jack.

"No!"

Amir's worries about a sniper shot had steadily grown to paranoia. Even with the drapes pulled shut, he had both hostages walking from one side of the room to the other as human shields.

"Faster," said Amir. "Both of you. Walk faster."

"A sniper can't see through the drapes," said Molly.

"They have infrared sensors. They can pick up body heat."

Jack had heard of such devices from Andie. They were different from night-vision goggles and actually allowed law enforcement to "see" through solid walls. Maybe Amir wasn't just paranoid.

"I want to sit down," said Molly.

"You can sit when they start taking me serious."

"Serious*ly*," said Molly. "When they start taking you serious*ly*."

He aimed his pistol. "Keep it up, Molly, and you'll be the one who gets the bullet when this deadline passes."

"Nobody needs to die," said Jack, which drew the pistol in his direction.

"Do I hear another volunteer?"

"What I meant is that you're going to get your plane to Cuba," said Jack.

"You'd better hope so. Because either way, the FBI gets one hostage. In ninety seconds we'll know if they want him dead or alive."

Jack glanced at the crossbeam on the bed frame. By his guesstimate, walking at this pace, he'd pass it five or six more times in the next ninety seconds. He was down to his final handful of opportunities.

No do-overs.

"Mix it up a little," said Amir. "Confusion to the enemy. Don't go all the way across the room from wall to wall. Meet in the middle and then turn back."

Molly was on the side Jack wanted. His final handful of opportunities had just slipped through his fingers.

"Andie will get you what you want," said Jack. "Just give her the time she needs."

"I've given them more than enough time."

"What do you think is going to happen when they hear a gun go off in this room? Shooting a hostage is like shooting yourself."

"Not if the other one is still alive."

"My God, Amir," said Molly. "Who *are you*? You talk about killing human beings like we're insects."

"Zip it, Molly."

"How could you—"

"I said, zip it!"

"How could you have anything to do with a school shooting?"

"I didn't know, all right! They gave me a year—one year to

figure out how to make amends for backing out of Flight Ninety-Three, how to make my own mark on the twentieth anniversary of nine-eleven. They never said school shooting! I never said it! Not until Xavier pussied out on blowing himself up in the mall did Abdul—"

Amir stopped. Jack watched as Molly stepped toward her husband, as if confronting the devil himself. "I'm not sure I even believe in hell, but if there is one, you're going there."

"Not today, I'm not."

"Say hello to your friend Ziad Jarrah when you get there."

"Shut up!"

"I'll bet that whole virgin thing didn't work out so well for him."

Amir shoved her the way he'd surely shoved her many times before, knocking her into the barricade. She hit with so much force that the desk stacked on top of the dresser came tumbling down, taking the bed frame with it. The unbolted crossbeam shook loose and landed on the floor. Jack grabbed it and swung it like a baseball bat, hitting Amir squarely on the side of the head. As he staggered into the wall, a gunshot rang out—and then it was suddenly like the Fourth of July, with two quick and even louder explosions to follow the first.

Jack hit the floor. He heard Molly scream, but it was the least of the noises that suddenly filled the room—walls crashing, boots stomping, and men shouting.

"FBI! FBI! FBI!"

Sharp beams of light cut like lasers through smoke and dust. In the confusion, Jack saw Amir on his back, raising his pistol in answer to SWAT's knocking. Jack had an answer of his own, swinging the crossbeam like an axe and bringing it down with all his strength.

It was impossible to discern what he heard next, whether it was the cracking of Amir's skull or the barrage of gunfire from SWAT rifles. It didn't matter.

"Are you hurt?" the SWAT leader asked him.

Jack was looking up at him from the floor. Amir was three feet away, flat on his back, lifeless.

"Sir! Are you hurt?"

Jack could breathe again. "I need to see my wife."

EPILOGUE

The autopsy was inconclusive as to the exact cause of Amir's death, whether it was the blunt trauma to the head or multiple gunshots. That bit of uncertainty didn't change the headlines:

DEATH PENALTY LAWYER EXECUTES TWENTIETH HIJACKER.

Jack was actually okay with it. Andie was more than okay.

"I'm proud of you," she said.

It was mutual. The FBI's Office of Professional Responsibility dismissed Duncan Fitz's disciplinary complaint against Andie. Under subpoena, Fitz testified that Agent Carter had pressured him to lodge the complaint against Andie so that Carter could use it as a quid pro quo, if needed, in his dealings with Jack: "Pressure your client to give me the information I want, and I'll get Fitz to withdraw his complaint against your wife." It wasn't the most outrageous thing Carter had done in his controversial career, but it was enough to get him reassigned to background checks on low-level government hires for the foreseeable future. The very next day, Fitz filed a voluntary dismissal of the school's lawsuit. Andie's good name was restored.

Jack's meeting with the state and federal prosecutors was more of a mixed bag. He paid one last visit to the detention center to give Xavier the bottom line.

"The good news is that the state attorney dropped all charges against you, including homicide."

Xavier didn't jump for joy. His reaction was that of a guy whose head had been held under water for five weeks, and he'd finally been let up for air.

"The other good news is that the US attorney has agreed to bring no charges related to the school shooting."

"*Yesss*," Xavier said, like a tennis player who'd just served an ace. But Jack didn't smile back, which sent the appropriate message.

"The rest of the news is not so good," said Jack.

Xavier's smile faded. "Okay. What's the bad news?"

"There's a catch to the Justice Department's offer. You have to plead guilty to conspiracy in violation of federal antiterrorism laws."

His mouth fell open, but it took a moment for words to follow. "I don't understand. I wasn't the Riverside shooter."

"We know."

"Abdul did it. He used my father's gun to make it look like me."

"I know."

"He said he'd kill Mom, Talitha, and Jamal if I didn't say it was me."

"I get all of that," said Jack.

"Then why do I have to plead guilty?"

Jack had given much thought to what he might say in this meeting, but there was no point in sugarcoating it.

"The FBI was listening to everything that was said in the motel room. They heard Amir say you backed out of a plan to blow yourself up in a shopping mall."

"That's a lie! He is such a liar! We never talked about anything like that. I would never hurt anyone!"

"I'm sure Maritza would completely back you up on that."

"Yes! She knows me! She knows that's not true!"

Jack believed him, if only because it was consistent with Amir's twisted logic to say the school shooting was Xavier's fault because he—*Molly's* son—didn't have the courage to be a suicide bomber.

"There's still a problem," said Jack.

"I didn't *do* anything."

"That's the point, Xavier. You did nothing."

"What was I supposed to do?"

"I can tell you how the Department of Justice sees it. All this could have been avoided if you had done just one simple thing. If you had just told someone."

"Told them *what*?"

"You're not a stupid kid, Xavier. You knew Amir was up to no good. You knew he was putting thoughts in your head, grooming you for something, even if at the end of the day you wanted no part of it."

He didn't deny it. "But I'm eighteen years old."

"There are a lot of eighteen-year-olds in Arlington National Cemetery. Different people make different choices in the war against terrorism."

The frustration was all over Xavier's face, which then turned to worry. "What's going to happen to me?"

"The government's offer is two years, with credit for the time spent in here. Your sentence would be served at a minimum security federal correctional facility, which is a heck of a lot better than Florida State Prison. I recommend you take it."

Xavier was looking at the floor. Jack waited.

"What does my mom think?"

"Why don't you ask her," said Jack. "She'd love to hear from you."

And then there was Maritza.

Everything she'd told Carter about Abdul—and then some—had proven true. It was unusual for a member of the Iraqi Counter Terrorism Service to turn against the US adviser who'd trained him. When Carter asked Abdul to help root out the Khoury family's suspected connection to al-Qaeda, the FBI had no idea how much Abdul had come to hate America.

Five days after Maritza riddled Abdul's body with the bullets he deserved, Jack and Andie visited her at the coffee shop. She still worked there, but no longer under an alias. The story of Abdul, phony clerics, and the abuses of Mut'ah had gone viral. Whether she liked it or not, social media had turned "Rusul" into a household name.

"Get you something?" she asked, as she arrived at their booth.

"Can you sit for a second?" asked Jack.

She shrugged, then slid into the booth beside Andie. "What the heck. So what if they fire me. Today's my last day."

"Where you going?"

"Not sure yet. Far away from here. Maybe the West Coast."

"Of Florida?"

"No. I mean *far away*."

"Seattle's a cool city," said Andie. "And plenty far. That's where I'm from."

"Really? Where did you guys meet?"

"Florida," said Jack.

"Ginnie Springs," Andie added. "Underwater. In a cave."

It was only slightly inaccurate.

"That's a very long story," said Jack.

Andie turned the conversation back to Rusul. "Wherever you land, we wish you well. But I was wondering. Have you thought about law enforcement?"

"You mean as a career?"

"Yes. You speak Arabic. Your father was CIA. I see you more as FBI. It's a long road, but you're still so young."

Rusul smiled, but then shook her head. "I don't think so."

"Why not?"

"I dunno," she said, looking at Jack. "I was thinking maybe I'd be a lawyer."

"Oh, dear God," said Andie.

Jack laughed. "There's hope for the profession."

The manager came by. "You on a break, Maritza?"

"Yes. Permanently." She removed the cap that was part of her uniform and laid it on the table. "And my name is Rusul."

ACKNOWLEDGMENTS

A huge thank-you to my editor, Sarah Stein, and her team at HarperCollins. Richard Pine is the best literary agent in the business, and I am so grateful for all these years together. Janis Koch is so much more than a beta reader. With her wit, love of words, and incredible knowledge of the rules of words, Janis makes me actually look forward to the marked-up galley pages bleeding with good ol' fashioned fountain pen ink.

This book also seems to be the appropriate place to acknowledge the kindness of strangers my wife and I encountered during our 9/11 experience. I was on a book tour of Australia. Tiffany and I mingled with fellow authors at the Melbourne Book Festival, took in *Faust* at the Sydney Opera House, climbed the Sydney Harbour Bridge, snorkeled in the Great Barrier Reef, and simply fell in love with Australia. But after seventeen days, we were more than ready to get back to our children for our son's third birthday—on September 11, 2001. Before leaving the hotel, we got a call from Qantas Airways and turned on the television in time to see the South Tower collapse. All flights were canceled indefinitely.

For days, we and thousands like us followed the same routine: go to airport, get bad news, return to hotel. One morning the line was so long at Sydney Airport that we almost decided to turn around and go back to the hotel without waiting to speak to a ticket agent. We could hear others in line ahead of us getting the same answer: no flights to America. When it was our turn, the ticket agent suddenly did a double take at the screen in front of her and said, "Oh, my God, we're flying." The bad news was that the flight was full and we were last on the waiting list. Then she did the most extraordinary thing. This Australian from Australia's leading airline grabbed the microphone, announced that a flight to Los Angeles was leaving in ninety minutes, and asked if there were any Australians with confirmed reservations who would be willing to give up their seats in favor of Americans who were trying to get home. In a snap, she had a couple of volunteers. Moments later, she had two more. They kept coming.

I don't know how many Australians stepped forward to help stranded Americans get home that day. But even twenty years later, their kindness toward total strangers still brings a lump to my throat. And from the bottom of my heart, I wish to say, "Thanks, mates."

—JG

ABOUT THE AUTHOR

JAMES GRIPPANDO is a *New York Times* bestselling author of suspense and the winner of the Harper Lee Prize for Legal Fiction. *Twenty* is his twenty-ninth novel. He lives in South Florida, where he is a trial lawyer and teaches Law and Literature at the University of Miami School of Law.

The

HEISMAN

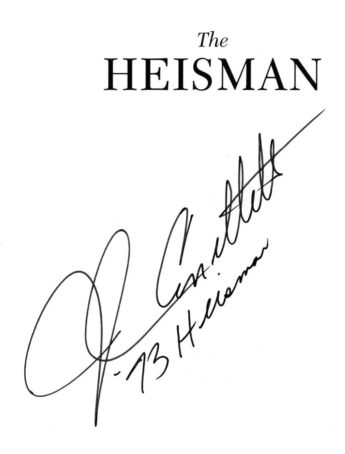

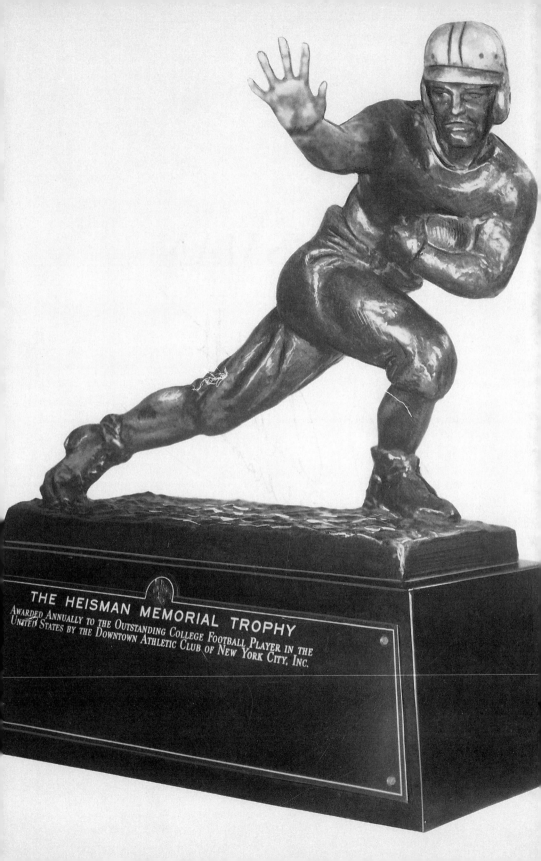

THE HEISMAN MEMORIAL TROPHY

Awarded Annually to the Outstanding College Football Player in the
United States by the Downtown Athletic Club of New York City, Inc.

The
HEISMAN

GREAT AMERICAN STORIES
OF THE MEN WHO WON

Bill Pennington

10 ReganBooks
Celebrating Ten Bestselling Years
An Imprint of HarperCollins*Publishers*

HarperCollins books may be purchased for educational, business, or sales promotional use. For information please write: Special Markets Department, HarperCollins Publishers Inc., 10 East 53rd Street, New York, NY 10022.

FIRST EDITION

Designed by Kris Tobiassen

Printed on acid-free paper

Library of Congress Cataloging-in-Publication Data

Pennington, Bill, 1956–
    The Heisman : great American stories of the men who won / Bill Pennington.—1st ed.
        p. cm.
    Includes index.
    ISBN 0-06-055471-1
    1. Football players—United States—Biography.   2. Heisman Trophy—History.
3. College sports—United States—History—20th century.   I. Title.

GV939.A1P44 2004
796.332'092'2—dc22
[B]
                                                                          2004051011

04 05 06 07 08 WBC/RRD 10 9 8 7 6 5 4 3 2 1

TO JOYCE, ANNE D., ELISE, AND JACK,
*whose love, understanding, and support
breathed life into every word.*

Contents

MIKE GARRETT, HEISMAN WINNER IN 1965

BLANCHARD (35) BEHIND THE ARMY LINE

Acknowledgments

I am indebted to the dozens of Heisman Trophy winners who generously gave their time to tell their stories, to resurrect scenes and situations from years past, and to recreate the tenor of those days. It was my privilege to help document not just their deeds but their thoughts, hopes, and dreams as young men awaiting lives of accomplishment, and later, as mature adults looking back. I also want to thank the family members, teammates, and friends of the winners who provided their observations.

A critical assist in arranging several interviews with Heisman winners came from Mark Panko of the Heisman Winners Association, who not only made personal contacts but kept the Heisman winners aware of this book project—a key contribution.

Also providing information from their files, or arranging help with interview subjects, were the public relations staffs representing the following universities: Texas A&M, Stanford, Iowa, Southern California, Texas, Ohio State, Miami, Syracuse, Nebraska, Notre Dame, Georgia, Penn State, and Michigan. My thanks also to Harvey Greene of the Miami Dolphins, Bill Johnston of the San Diego Chargers, Doug Miller of the New York Jets, Robbie Bohren of the Tennessee Titans, and Pat Hanlon of the New York Giants.

At the *New York Times*, I want to thank my editors Neil Amdur, Tom Jolly, and Alan Finder for their support and for helping me as I managed a writing schedule across the months it took to research and write this book.

At ReganBooks, I was very fortunate to benefit from the artful editing and skilled direction of Aliza Fogelson. Brian Saliba gave the text its first edit and his input focused the narrative at pivotal junctures. Stephen Barbara was also instrumental at this stage.

There were two individuals without whom this book could not have been written. The first is my agent Freya Manston, who dreamed up the idea for a book on the history of the Heisman and tirelessly shepherded that vision from a single introductory meeting to its fruition. Every author should have a friend in the business so willing to walk arm-in-arm through every triumph and travail.

The second person is Rudy Riska, the conscience and caretaker of the Heisman Trophy and its winners. Riska, the longtime executive director of the Downtown Athletic Club, is accorded unwavering respect and admiration throughout the college football community, and with good reason. I showed up in Rudy's office in the fall of 2002 with a good idea and not much more. For the next eighteen months, his counsel and suggestions guided me. His voluminous files and recollections brought to life innumerable stories, and if I was really having trouble getting to speak with someone, Rudy could always open that last door. Rudy Riska is a gift to the Heisman legacy and and tradition.

Finally, a book project is a vast and consuming commitment from many, and without the guidance and reassurance of my wife Joyce, who was also the book's principal researcher, I would have been lost. You cannot be more lucky than to have your best friend and your best editor always at your side. My children were invested in the project as well. I am deeply grateful for their unflinching sacrifice, which could be summed up in a book of their own: *How I Spent My Summer Vacation Chasing Heisman Trophy Winners*. Knowing them, it would be a good read.

Preface

America has always been a land of symbols. In deed and in language, by constitution and institution, Americans have been indoctrinated from our very genesis with the worth and power of symbols endowed with national meaning.

George Washington was not just the first president, but the father of the country. Another national symbol, the flag, begot another symbol, the national anthem. The melting pot society, perhaps the most powerful creation of the New World, is an important notion in the country's consciousness and that intangible but integral society has been given its own symbol, the Statue of Liberty. It is a piece of sculpture, static but flowing, universal and yet holding different meaning for each American.

The landscape of American sport, always among the first cultural entry points for new Americans, is strewn with individual awards. More, in fact, are created every sporting season—MVP awards, Gold Glove awards, the Espys. Some, fortunately, make an effort to recognize achievement, others essentially measure advances in technology or genetics, and others do no more than inelegantly laud celebrity. Few of sport's individual awards have a lasting and creditable history. Even fewer are recognizable to the eye, a vision, image, or outline that is universally identifiable.

Can anyone, for example, describe what the National Football League's Most Valuable Player Award looks like? How many people can close their eyes and conjure the image of baseball's Cy Young Award? Quick, if you win the Indianapolis 500, what do you win? (It is not a car. It is a check and a flower wreath.)

These are prizes, professional accolades for a task well done.

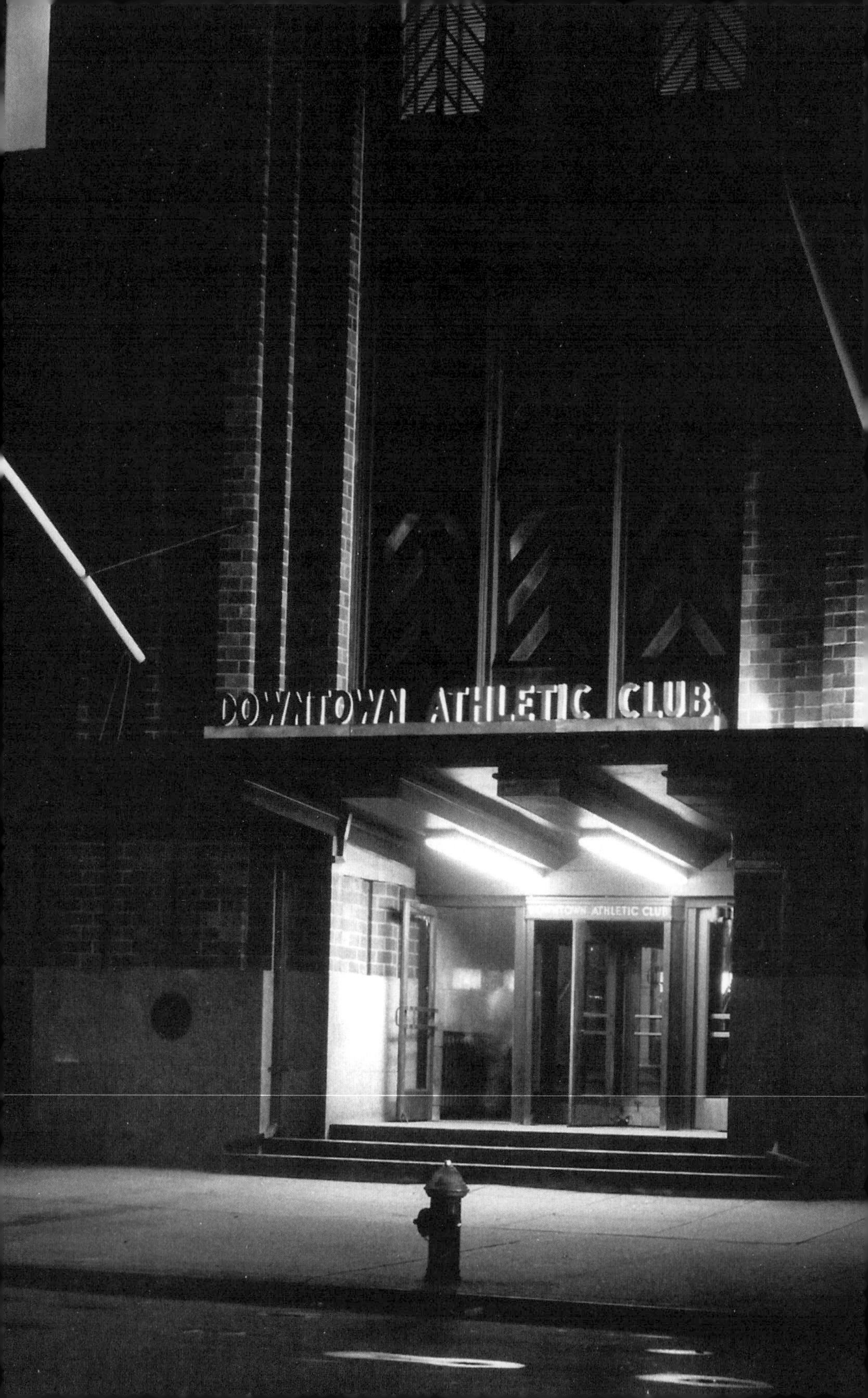
DOWNTOWN ATHLETIC CLUB
DOWNTOWN ATHLETIC CLUB

They are not symbols, and by themselves they hold no mystique. They cannot be seen with eyes closed like the Statue of Liberty. They evoke no special meaning, offer no abstract but undeniable allure. They are not a piece of an American athletic timeline, nor do they connote iconic fame or everlasting fraternity in an exclusive club. The mind's eye cannot see these awards because they do not represent an image of America at its best.

Now close your eyes and picture the Heisman Trophy. The form is easy to conjure, a graceful, fluid pose that is football past and football present in one dignified figure. It is sculpture, peerless in American sport, with a beauty of motion and a sense of the sport it honors.

It is fourteen inches by thirteen and one-half inches of statutory bronze mounted on a seventeen and one-half-inch by five and one-half-inch black onyx base. It is twenty-five polished pounds of grace, power, and majesty. Since it was first awarded in 1935, its strength has been its symbolism.

Pete Dawkins is a former brigadier general, candidate for the United States Senate, Rhodes scholar, and the winner of the 1958 Heisman Trophy. When he has guests at his home for dinner, he sometimes clocks the time from his guests' arrival until they ask an inevitable question. Sometimes, Dawkins breaks the tension by blurting out, "It's in the den."

"Everyone wants to see or touch the trophy," Dawkins says. "That's when you get a sense of the reach of the Heisman."

What one reaches to touch in the Heisman Trophy is the intangible histories of the American twentieth century, of sport, of heroes, of the abstract touchstones of life: achievement, disappointment, tragedy, and triumph. The Heisman Trophy and the lives of its winners tell that story of America.

It is the story of the dauntless, resolute men who created an award founded on idealism. And it is the untold story of the romantic idealist for whom the award is named, John William Heisman.

The story of the Heisman is the story of America since the Great Depression, tracing the country's history from its adolescence as a world power through World War II and its momentous aftermath. It is the story of the expanding American demographic, reflected in the immigrant surnames of the winners, Lujack, Janowicz, Kazmaier, Cassady, and Bellino. It is the story of the turbulent 1960s and unsettled 1970s, when the Heisman was first bequeathed to an African-American, to a Native American and to

HEISMAN WINNERS JAY BERWANGER ('35),
PETE DAWKINS ('58), AND BILLY SIMS ('78)
WITH PRESIDENT RONALD REAGAN

players from all geographic regions. It is the story of an aggrandized, all-consuming phenomenon enveloping the trophy, its place growing larger than ever. It is the story of a changing America, a prospering America, a conflicted America, and a steadfast, confident America.

The setting for this sixty-nine-year cultural narrative is college football and all its Sabbath-like, end-of-the-week congregations in cathedrals draped in ceremonious colors. This is a place of ritualistic fight songs and traditional chants, marches, and slogans, where rivalries are transferred by generations and coaches are treated like tribal chiefs. With spiritual and transcendent connections, college football is like a religion in America. The Heisman Trophy winners are its mythic gods. They are the kings of the richest, most disparate, loyal dominion in American sport.

Handed the Heisman Trophy, they are royalty forever set apart, an eminence that most used to achieve grander accomplishment. Some stumbled and fell, and some stumbled, fell, and got back up.

This book is a sampling of the winners' stories, tales that convey the Heisman heritage in a chronological rendering of time and place, because the Heisman Trophy is meant to mark and honor one football season. The winners profiled in depth in the subsequent pages were chosen for their myriad contributions—historically, socially, culturally—to this timeline. Others certainly might select a different list of winners to recognize; there is no absolute way to qualify any such subjective compilation. But the winners' stories included here are meant as a collection in sum, and it is most important to view them for what they represented as collegians. In the modern sports environment, the common focus is on an athlete's collective worth as a professional, a model sometimes used to judge the merit of Heisman winners. But the measure of a Heisman Trophy winner is his one season and its legacy. It is about what that season meant to his teammates, his fans, and his nation. It is about the possibility that the right combination of leadership, skill, and inspiration can inscribe a name forever in the chronicles of his sport and his time.

The Heisman Trophy, the country's most enduring sports symbol—one treasured and instantly recognized—is an institution. Its story is an American epic. In the rough-hewn features of the fluid, graceful figure on the Heisman Trophy statuette, something deep exists within the piercing shadow of eyes that mysteriously stare back at an adoring public.

"Is It Not Meant to Exemplify the Grandeur of a Thousand Men?"

THE DOWNTOWN ATHLETIC CLUB

AND JOHN W. HEISMAN

In 1926 America, unemployment was virtually nonexistent. The standard of living was at an all-time high. Post–World War I America had the most powerful economy on earth, presaging the still young country's expansion as a world power. In a changing century, America charged forward with rootless abandon. The political and financial leadership of America in 1926 had been raised in a very different country, a primitive place of wide, uncharted open plains. The newspapers of their childhoods had been filled with events like the massacre of General George Armstrong Custer, a seminal episode in American history commemorating its fiftieth anniversary in 1926. But in the industrial society of the day, Custer's demise was treated with a noteworthy detachment, as if it occurred during the American Revolution.

This was an America sprinting so fast into a future of unrestrained hopes and dreams, it placed events like horseback skirmishes in western plains into a bygone era. Time was measured not in the years passed but in the stunning introduction of one technological advance after another: electricity, the automobile, air flight, the motion picture, and the theory of relativity.

Not surprisingly, this exploding America was a sprawling cultural paradox. After years of rallies and national debate, the eighteenth amendment, banning alcohol, had been passed in 1920. Six years later, it was widely ignored. In 1926, the most praised, and notorious, movie was Sergei Eisenstein's *Potemkin*, a communist manifesto. But the most noteworthy literary contribution of the year was F. Scott Fitzgerald's *The Great Gatsby*, an examination of an altogether different society.

In 1926, the country mourned the death of silent film star Rudolph Valentino. In the same year, a Scottish inventor named M. John Baird demonstrated a new machine capable of the wireless transmission of moving pictures. People had taken to calling the device a Baird, but the inventor preferred his own term, the television.

Historically, America of the 1920s is known for its high times of excess: flapper girls, riotous speakeasies, and frivolous twenty-four-hour dance marathons. But it was also a decade of mushrooming interest in athletics. In September 1926, more than 130,000 fans enveloped a Philadelphia boxing ring to see Gene Tunney pummel Jack Dempsey. It was the era of Knute Rockne's "Four Horsemen" in college football, Bobby Jones's golf grand slam, and baseball's rebirth as powered by Babe Ruth.

But what truly intrigued sociologists was an attendant and entirely new American phenomenon in athletics: the pursuit of exercise through sports and games by adult Americans. In a shifting, unsettled society, these Americans gathered in clusters linked by geography, ethnicity, or social status. Suddenly, athletic clubs, sponsored by towns, civic organizations, and churches, were the rage. While much of America was still a land of farmers and agricultural interests, where the work of life was exercise enough, more Americans than ever lived in crowded urban environments.

In these teeming municipalities, leaders began creating parklands, and these civic playgrounds abounded with not only children but, increasingly, adults. More open space was bought up by organized private clubs, which raised money from members to purchase domains dedicated to the unfettered quest of sport—golf, tennis, swimming, bowling, badminton, and other manner of exercise.

These clubs were, in fact, strategic socioeconomic centers, another way to separate and define a man and his position in society.

In 1926, James Kennard and Philip Slinguff, two entrepreneurs who years earlier had helped create another version of the popular men's club—known then as a gentlemen's club—turned their attention to establishing the most majestic men's athletic club ever devised. What intrigued Kennard and Slinguff was that there was no all-purpose place close to Wall Street for successful businessmen to gather for exercise, an activity that frequently led to drinks, dinner, and often a night's stay for the out-of-town industrial magnates.

Kennard and Slinguff decided to form a club that they promised would be "no more than five minutes' walk from Broadway and Wall Street," in the heart of the financial center of post–World War I America, the most commanding, authoritative neighborhood in the world.

They planned a thirty-five-story skyscraper to house their club and began selling lifetime memberships to what they called the Downtown Athletic Club (DAC), memberships that were transferable so that they could be traded like stock.

When the membership roll reached 900, the club confidently decided to take on and finance $3 million in debt to complete building its thirty-five-story athletic and social palace. And what a palace it was to be. The club's china cost $56,000, and a French chef was hired at a lavish salary of $700 a month—at a time when the average annual income was $1,300 a year.

On March 12, 1929, the construction crew broke ground on the DAC building, twenty-five days after the U.S. Federal Reserve, unsettled by months of turbulent ups and downs in the stock market, announced that it favored a permanent curb to stock speculation.

By September 3, the New York Stock Exchange had reached an all-time high, its Dow Jones Index at 381.17, and a month later, a towering new brick building was rising on West Street. On October 24, 1929, the Downtown Athletic Club building was a giant scaffold, through which, depending on your vantage point, you could see Brooklyn or New Jersey. And in its shadow were the front steps of the New York Stock Exchange where investors awaited the day's trading, shaken by a precipitous drop in stock values the previous day.

As the day began, prices continued to drop, and then, between 11:15 A.M. and 12:15 P.M., the trading of shares overcame the floor in a devastating frenzy. As investors dumped their shares, the domino effect was felt nationwide. The Chicago commodities exchange exploded with a near panic of trading. Out West, telegraph and telephone lines were down because of an ill-timed snowstorm, and the lack of communication with New York spurred a vast, unremitting sell-off. Foreign investors reacted similarly, sensing the psychological damage the losses would have on first-generation Americans who had largely known only market prosperity in their new country.

On and on the downward spiral went, with so many trades the stock market ticket fell four hours behind in reporting transactions and prices. By the market's close, nearly 13 million shares had been traded and thousands of fortunes lost. Men wept on the steps of the stock exchange, their pictures published in newspapers the following day as they sat, head in hands, beneath the mammoth statue of George Washington, whose right index finger pointed resolutely forward.

It was in this climate, with its new building literally a shell and its financial arrangement a virtual house of cards, that the Downtown Athletic Club pressed on, borrowing more money to finish its skyscraper club. For decades thereafter, the DAC, the most famous athletic club of its kind and home of the Heisman Trophy, was frequently just one more gloomy auditor's report away from filing for bankruptcy. But the club survived and even thrived decade after decade, always finding ways to maintain its place as a prized destination for either social or athletic congregation. The club always had cachet—it came with its location and with the words on the awning over the door at the club's entrance: Home of the Heisman Trophy. But it would take sixty-six years and a terrorist attack just steps from the club's doorstep to actually force the DAC into a financial reorganization and some manner of dissolution that included losing ownership of its building.

The Downtown Athletic Club, symbolically, rose from the ashes of the Great Depression, an American cataclysm rising from a collapse "no more than five minutes' walk from Broadway and Wall Street." Just as symbolically, the Downtown Athletic Club died a figurative death on September 11, 2001, when the collapse of the World Trade Center buildings shook the 1929 foundation of the DAC building and the entire country.

In between, the Downtown Athletic Club created an American institution, the most heralded sporting award of its kind. It started when the charter members of the Downtown Athletic Club, facing not only the disintegration of their new club but of their way of life, decided to go grander and think bigger.

The American economy was reeling, but the members of the Downtown Athletic Club finished their building, and it was as striking and lavish as planned. The structure included, for example, one oversized floor roughly at midspan to house the revolutionary indoor pool. No pool had ever been erected so far from the ground anywhere in the world. There were also squash courts, a large gymnasium for basketball, floors dedicated to boxing rings and badminton, and more than 130 hotel rooms and suites that rented for as much as $10 a night, a small fortune at the time. It was all part of the DAC image. Finally, such a showplace needed a man of standing for its athletic director. With the club about to open in the summer of 1930, the job of making what would be the most important personnel decision of all fell to Willard B. "Bill" Prince, an executive at the club.

Prince was friends with a retired college football coach, a man who lived a comfortable life that included an apartment on Manhattan's posh Park Avenue. The coach had not been on a football sideline for three years now but Prince sensed that his friend, noted for his mercurial ways—he spent summers as a Shakespearean actor—might be looking for a new challenge. Prince called and set up a lunch and by the end of the day, the Downtown Athletic Club had its first athletic director.

His name was John William Heisman.

It was a quirk of fate that Heisman was in town and available to the Downtown Athletic Club in 1930, one of those consequential happenstances that seem to give history its capricious dynamism. Heisman was not a New Yorker and never had been. He made his fame on the move throughout America's small college towns and its rebuilding cities of the early 1900s, most notably Atlanta.

By the time Heisman came to the Downtown Athletic Club he was 61 years old. The picture distributed of Heisman during his DAC days— which has become something of an official photograph for posterity— shows a man with white hair in small, effete eyeglasses and a crisp, tailored suit. His appearance is decorous and noble; he looks like one of the bank presidents he came to mingle with at the club.

But that photograph depicts a wholly incomplete image. Educated at two Ivy League universities, Heisman was indeed a distinguished, respected man of letters. He was also someone who had still relished at the age of fifty the opportunity to get down in a low stance and bang shoulders with his twenty-year-old linemen in practice.

Like so many of the legendary college football coaches to follow him throughout the century, Heisman was the thinking man's paradox. His greatest love was the stratagem of football, a game he nonetheless knew to be violent, brutish, and dominated by the courageous blast through a snarling pile of opponents.

He always thoroughly embraced the duality of his mission. An accomplished public speaker, one of his favorite opening gambits was to hold aloft a football and ask: "What is this?"

He would then answer himself: "It is a prolate spheroid in which the outer leather casing is drawn tightly over a somewhat smaller rubber tubing."

Pausing for effect, Heisman would add: "Better to have died as a small boy than to fumble this football."

Son of a cooper in northwestern Pennsylvania, John Heisman was an unlikely career football man, since he was small and not particularly fast. But the preteen son of a tradesman in the 1870s worked hand-in-hand with his father, and young John Heisman was no different, making wood barrels by the hundreds. This developed a superb musculature in Heisman's hands, chest, and forearms. Despite his slight frame, he was a fierce, hardnosed, and fearless interior lineman in six years of play at high school and college.

A good student, eighteen-year-old John Heisman traveled to Providence, Rhode Island, in 1887 to attend Brown University and played three seasons of football on the line there. Football was a bizarre enterprise during these years, more of a free-form fistfight than a sport. There were no helmets, pads, or substitutes, and the referees barely had control of the action. Eyes were gouged and ears torn. There could be as much blood on the football as sweat. Little wonder there were frequent calls for the abolition of the sport. But weary of the quiet and pacific nature of his studies at Brown, Heisman relished the aggression and found it an intoxicating respite.

It was not odd for an athlete then, as now, to have a curious attraction to a sport for its excesses while at the same time lamenting them, to regard the bruises, cuts, and soreness the day after a game as both a penalty and a badge. Heisman saw the allure in his beloved sport, even if he knew it would have to change to survive.

After Brown, Heisman pursued his law degree at the University of Pennsylvania, earning it in 1892. He then promptly ignored that achievement by immediately launching his thirty-six-year career as a coach.

By the 1890s, Yale coach Walter Camp, the preeminent coach in the land, had used his influence to implement important new rules, like changes of possession from one team to the other, a system of downs, or attempts, to achieve a first down, and yard markings on the field. These rule modifications established more play schemes, and the necessity to think and plan removed some of the violence from college football. This had an important side effect: Football became more attractive to schools outside the East, and it began spreading rapidly across the Midwest and South.

John Heisman felt the geographic pull, and he left Penn's Philadelphia campus in 1892 and headed west, taking the job of head football coach at Ohio's Oberlin College, where his first team went undefeated. He next coached at Akron, then on to Auburn University in Alabama, where his teams lost just one game in four years. Heisman was building a nationwide reputation, and in 1900 he headed to South Carolina's Clemson University, where he lost only twice in the next four years. One of the teams his Clemson Tigers routed, in 1903, was Georgia Tech, who were shut out, 73–0.

Tired of being on the wrong end of the diminutive Heisman's intangible football genius, in 1904 Georgia Tech offered the son of the Pennsylvania cooper a grand contract, which included the use of a car and a home on the university's Atlanta campus, and the school invented a new position: Chief Football Director.

From a football as well as a publicity standpoint, Georgia Tech got its money's worth. Heisman would stay for sixteen seasons, a period when his teams won nearly 70 percent of their games. From 1915 to 1918, Georgia Tech did not lose a game, a string of twenty-five consecutive victories in which they outscored the opposition 1,129 to 61. Georgia Tech defeated Cumberland College 222–0 in one game and North Carolina State 128–0 in another. The 1917 Georgia Tech team was declared national champions.

Along the way, Heisman did more for football than just win games. He wrote extensively about the game, preparing long treatises that amounted to early textbooks on the game. He invented the center snap—previously, the ball had frequently been rolled back along the ground—and intro-

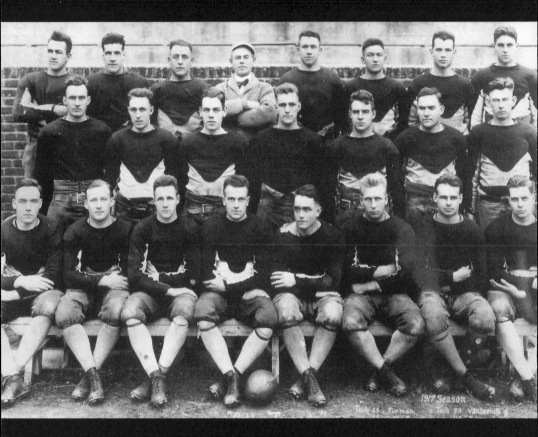

JOHN HEISMAN'S 1917 NATIONAL
CHAMPIONS, GEORGIA TECH. HEISMAN
IS IN THE MIDDLE OF THE TOP ROW.

duced a vocal signal for how the quarterback should summon the snap, a "hut" or "hike" or "hup" sound. Heisman was a friend of the football fan, too. He had the Georgia Tech scoreboard start to list the downs and yardage before each play so fans could more easily follow the game. He also devised the hidden ball trick, wherein after a series of fakes and deceptive handoffs and reverses, a player would conceal the football under his jersey and run off with it. Defenders did not know whom to tackle. If it sounds like a scene from a Marx Brothers movie, that's because it later was, but it scored a lot of touchdowns for Heisman's teams until it was outlawed as simply too tricky or impossible to defend against.

He also contributed to the colorful legacy of football locker-room oration. When Heisman addressed his charges before games or at halftime, he employed a strange stage English: "Thrust your projections into their cavities, grasping them about the knees, and depriving them of their means of propulsion. They must come to earth, location being denied them."

Heisman's greatest contribution to the game was his dogged campaign to legalize the forward pass, which was prohibited by college football's rules until 1906. Players were allowed only to throw or lateral the football backwards. There is no question that football might never have survived as a mainstream sport, let alone have prospered, without this rule change. And while there were other coaches championing the forward pass as essential to the growth of the game, it was Heisman, the eloquent bulldog, who never let up. On this rule and others, he became known as football's nagging voice of conscience.

In 1904, twenty-one players were killed playing college football. Heisman saw the forward pass as a way to minimize the violent collisions. "It will scatter the mob," he said.

Heisman saw something else in the forward pass: a way to furnish every football game with a basic underlying strategy.

If teams on offense could run and pass the football, then teams on defense would have to deploy some of their players farther from the line of scrimmage to prevent a long pass behind their last defender. That would make it easier to run the football. Conversely, moving more players closer to the line of scrimmage would make it easier to pass. This balance is the essence of football strategy nearly 100 years later.

It took several years for all the college football world to see the value of the forward pass that Heisman had seen years earlier. But once embraced, the forward pass led college football to its first golden age, in the 1920s, when long passes thrilled soldout stadium crowds as much as the thunderous rushes of the best runners.

By then Heisman was leaving football, retiring in 1927 after a final few years leading teams for Rice University, Washington and Jefferson College, and Penn. Newspaper accounts of his exit from the game were unequivocal about what the Heisman legacy to college football would be: his successful lobbying for the legalization of the forward pass. Those accounts were wrong.

In time, his name would come to mean so much more to college football, all from the link in the final years of his life to the Downtown Athletic Club. That is something John Heisman would never have seen coming.

Heisman started his new post at the DAC in 1930 with one goal in mind—to give the members plenty of recreation for their dues, and perhaps along the way, to make them more fit.

Heisman quickly organized competitions among the members in basketball, squash, badminton, handball, bowling, swimming, weight-lifting, and volleyball. He set up golf outings, arranged for fencing and boxing instruction, and lured the sons of members into the fold with youth leagues. Heisman became a fixture at the club, barking at members as he cajoled them in their athletic pursuits. Even the most hard-bitten Wall Street financier kowtowed to Heisman's exhortations.

All this activity made the Downtown Athletic Club a busy place. It did not hurt the club's social calendar, either, and parties abounded. Financially, there were still plenty of worries and uncertainties, and the American economy was years from rebounding, but the DAC had more than 3,000 members and that clientele relished the status a DAC member's card held in New York City and beyond. For one thing, it gained them admission through the art deco entrance on West Street (provided they met the jacket-and-tie dress code required to pass through the lobby).

The DAC also had a college football club, and in 1934 William Prince began talking up the idea of the club's sponsoring its own college football award. It would recognize the best or most outstanding player each year, serve as a reason for another banquet celebration, act as a service to the game, and give the club national publicity.

Prince ran the idea by John Heisman, and promptly saw the fierce eyes of the old coach narrow. Heisman disdained the concept of an individual award in football, the ultimate team game in his mind. Ever a coach at heart, Heisman felt the award would be divisive. "Is it not meant to exemplify the grandeur of a thousand men?" one Downtown Athletic Club historian quoted Heisman as asking.

A rhetorical question, and perhaps unintentionally, a window into the elusive mystique of the award.

But in the spring of 1935, Bill Prince had simpler ambitions. Prince saw the majesty of the competition for the award in other terms. It was his idea to have sportswriters and sportscasters make up the panel selecting the winner, because Prince knew it would spawn column after column of newspaper coverage and foster radio coverage as well. There would be arguments over who should win the DAC award and speculation throughout the college football season, a mystery unfolding week upon week, with a surprise announcement at the conclusion of the season.

Serial dramas were highly popular on the radio networks in America during the mid-1930s, and Prince wanted to create his own three-month-long, serial football drama.

While not convinced, Heisman decided there were bigger worries in college football at the time—the influence of gamblers, eligibility issues, renegade colleges recruiting mercenary players—than an award he hardly considered momentous.

Meanwhile, many of the club's members loved the idea. When Prince proposed to name the award after John Heisman, Heisman rejected the idea outright, but he did withdraw his objection to the club's sponsoring an award for the 1935 season.

Bill Prince pushed for the award to be commemorated annually with the commissioning of a trophy rather than a bowl, cup, plaque, or medal, as was common of other sports awards. Later dubbed "the father of the Heisman Trophy," Prince had in mind a memorable figure, part trophy, part sculpture, something that at once represented singular accomplishment but did so as a year-after-year touchstone.

The DAC requested designs for its landmark trophy. A twenty-three-year-old decorated student and recent graduate of the Pratt Institute in Brooklyn, Frank Eliscu was a football fan who decided to give the trophy competition a try. He contacted his former classmate from New York City's George Washington High School football team, Ed Smith, who had

THE ORIGINAL CLAY MODEL OF THE
HEISMAN, CREATED IN 1935. AT RIGHT IS
FORDHAM COACH JIM CROWLEY, ONE OF
NOTRE DAME'S FAMED FOUR HORSEMEN.

gone on to become a star running back for the 1934 New York University team.

Smith struck various poses for Eliscu, who chose one and produced a rough clay model he took to Prince and other DAC members. Prince was immediately taken with the classic nature of the model, a strong, muscular representation of a player with alluring angles created by a side-stepping leg and an extended stiff arm and hand.

The model was brought to Fordham University in the Bronx, where the football team was coached by Jim Crowley, one of Notre Dame's renowned Four Horsemen. Crowley also liked the representation, but his players had some trouble duplicating the pose exactly as it was formed in the sculpture. Eliscu was at Fordham that day as well, and he watched the players in their movements. He took the clay model back to his studio and incorporated some of the dynamics he saw in the Fordham players. Eliscu lengthened the back leg in the model, simulating the action of a player in motion and creating a more forceful, forward stride. The sculpture was fluid and a stop-action grasp of player in mid-stride at the same time.

The final model was finished in a statuary bronze. Although Eliscu would go on to a lengthy career as a sculptor, author, and teacher who created works of art that won many national awards, his first major commission remained his most memorable.

The 1935 DAC Trophy actually recognized the outstanding college football player "east of the Mississippi River." It was the only year the award did not officially cover the entire country. Jay Berwanger of the University of Chicago was named the first recipient of the trophy on December 9, 1935, with the DAC happily at the cynosure of the fanfare the award created. Prince had been right; sportswriters of the day willingly and enthusiastically brought attention to the product of their own voting.

Berwanger was a laudable choice, a gentlemanly, courteous midwestern farm boy raised with a Depression-era work ethic and values. His coach at Chicago, Clark Shaughnessy, gave the 6-foot-1, 200-pound Berwanger number 99 "because that was as close to a perfect 100 as I could get."

A tailback and a threat to run, pass, or kick, Berwanger was called the One Man Gang. He was nimble and tough, as one Michigan player attempt-

ing to tackle Berwanger would attest for the rest of his life. Future President Gerald Ford was an All-American at Michigan when he faced Berwanger, but he failed to bring him down in one collision on the field and instead caught a Berwanger heel on the left cheek of his face, a blow that left a scar.

Said Ford years later when he saw Berwanger at a banquet: "I think of you every morning when I shave."

Although Berwanger played for struggling Chicago teams, he ran for 1,839 yards in his three varsity seasons and scored twenty-two touchdowns. His one-man performances as a senior in Big Ten Conference games against Ohio State and Minnesota featured sideline-to-sideline dashes, spectacular kicking exploits, and punishing tackles as a defender. They filled newspaper sports sections throughout the fall of 1935, and Berwanger won the DAC award that year by a wide margin. Berwanger traveled to New York to receive his trophy in December. He went to Radio City Music Hall and saw a relatively new act, the Rockettes. At a gala DAC dinner that night, he became the first winner to pose with the trophy, grasping it for a series of pictures circulated nationwide.

In 1936, suitably impressed and full of a sense of accomplishment, the DAC's leaders excitedly opened the voting to a nationwide panel, sending ballots throughout the Midwest, to the Southwest and Texas, and to what the DAC then called the Far West. Everything about the award was swiftly becoming more grand. The DAC was thinking big, and it was not alone.

The club was still a few years from something approaching financial solvency, a condition mimicked by the national economy. The minimum wage had been raised to forty cents an hour. The first television for home use was in production and the best-selling book of 1936 was Dale Carnegie's *How to Win Friends and Influence People*. That same year, director Fritz Lang, having recently fled Nazi Germany, gave the American movie audience an unsettling examination of the underbelly of human nature in *Fury*. It showed how demagogues use emotions to turn a society into a mindless mob. It was meant to be, and proved to be, a cautionary tale.

In 1936, Adolf Hitler ignored the demilitarized area mandated by the Treaty of Versailles and reclaimed German lands lost during World War I. When the college football season began that September, the world was

JAY BERWANGER, FIRST RECIPIENT OF THE HEISMAN

thirty-six months away from a shocking loss of innocence. The change on the horizon would be permanent.

And on October 3, 1936, a sunny, crisp Saturday across most of America—a perfect day for a college football game—John Heisman succumbed to bronchial pneumonia. He was sixty-six years old and had been writing a history of college football. The manuscript was never published.

The club quickly named its annual football award The Heisman Memorial Trophy Award. Larry Kelley of Yale won the 1936 award, and Walter L. Conwell, president of the Downtown Athletic Club, delivered a speech before handing the first Heisman Trophy to Kelley. For the first time, the ceremony was broadcast nationally on radio.

"This statuette, fine as it is in artistic conception and flawless as it may be in mechanical construction, is but a poor representation of the idealism that entered into the creation of this trophy," Conwell said. "This award is to recognize the outstanding player of a given season, and outstanding is the one word to describe such a person that we all could agree upon as embraced in our idealism.

"That was last year, and since that time, our idealism, symbolized by this trophy, has become more crystallized. A few months ago, death called John W. Heisman. Football, to John W. Heisman, was not merely a game. He regarded it as a smelter of character, a test which never failed to separate the dross from the gold. Football, to John W. Heisman, was a crucible which exposed the true character worth of the player. We found in this creed of Heisman an expression of our own idealism to the kind of man upon whom we wanted to bestow this trophy and hence we further defined it, gave increased dignity and meaning to it, by renaming it the Heisman Memorial Trophy.

"We award it in the firm belief that it and its winners will exemplify the abilities, character and virtue of the man whose name forevermore represents the trophy and the idealism we attempt to capture with its creation."[1]

[1]The DAC Journal, January 1937.

JAY BERWANGER

"The Football Part Is Incidental"

NILE KINNICK, 1939

In 1939, Joe DiMaggio batted .381, Joe Louis defended his heavyweight crown four times, and Lou Gehrig, baseball's Iron Man, poignantly said goodbye to Yankee Stadium. But when the Associated Press named its sportsman of the year, it chose Nile Kinnick, the small but indomitable leader of the University of Iowa's surprisingly mighty football team.

To a nation bracing for war and sorely in need of heroes, Kinnick arrived like a spirit from the Plains—a dashing streak, part myth, part fable, and full of hope. The Cornbelt Comet, they called him, a meteor that lit up the sky; and everything and everyone looking up to him was brightened by his wake.

Kinnick's athletic feats rose not from traditional wellsprings of physical achievement but from a distinct and astute sense of timing, a gift that seemed shaped by destiny. He moved in and out of every prominent event in his life with precise footprints earmarked for history. This sense of order and chivalry made Kinnick one of the nation's best known pre–World War II personalities.

When he won the 1939 Heisman Trophy, an award that had quickly gained a national reputation, Kinnick delivered the first elegant, heartfelt acceptance speech at the Downtown Athletic Club's Heisman banquet. In a time of budding tumult, as Americans prepared to send yet another generation into a second war to end all wars, Boston journalist Bill Cunningham listened to Kinnick's words and was soothed: "This country is O.K. as long as it produces Nile Kinnicks. The football part is incidental."[2]

Nile Clarke Kinnick was born in Adel, Iowa, on July 9, 1918, two weeks before French, British, and American troops stopped a German advance in the French town of Marne, a pivotal battle that eventually led to the surrender of Austro-Hungarian and German forces on November 11. Aware that news of the war's end had produced dancing in American streets, President Woodrow Wilson immediately declared the day a national holiday, later to be called Armistice Day, an occasion to honor veterans of foreign wars.

Kinnick was the oldest of three sons borne to Nile Sr. and Frances Clarke Kinnick. They were farmers but residents of a certain standing in Adel, where Nile and Frances had graduated first and second in their 1912 high school class. Frances's father, George, had been a one-term governor of Iowa, and Nile Sr. had graduated from Iowa State, where he had been a quarterback and drop-kicking specialist.

The Kinnick house abounded with books, and visitors often came to the parlor for readings of poetry and intellectual exchanges.

According to Kinnick biographer Paul Baender, among the first poems Nile Jr. digested was Henry Wadsworth Longfellow's "Excelsior," a copy of which he received from his maternal grandfather at a young age. The poem's message is one of never-ending perseverance, that the pursuit of personal progress, even to the death, is forever worth the effort. It was a message Nile carried with him throughout his life, quoting from the poem even as an adult.

Nile Kinnick was well read, and though naturally introverted, he was a popular child in school. His parents noted that he offered his help, unsolicited, to classmates, tutoring other students who were failing. He rose early for three months one winter to assist a neighboring family with its morning farm chores when the head of that household was bedridden with pneumonia.

The Kinnick boys, Nile, Ben, and George, played every sport, although Nile, who was naturally ambidextrous, stood out.

Though not physically imposing (he never grew to be more than 5-foot-8 and 175 pounds), Nile managed to be the star of the Adel teams.

[2]*The Boston Globe*, December 7, 1939.

Kinnick had a strong, wiry upper body, and his legs were thick with muscle. He was neither the fastest, quickest, nor strongest member of any of the teams he played for, and yet, as was said about him for the rest of his athletic life, Kinnick always had an innate sense of how to position himself to maximize any athletic situation. People would remark that Nile always found the right place to be at the right time, whether it was to his benefit or a teammate's.

On the basketball court, where his athleticism was first noticed, he had a talent for strategies of the game and an ability to execute them with precise, cunning efficiency. He may not have been noticed before the game began, but by the game's end, everyone knew who had been the best player on the court.

He was a skilled baseball player, too, and in the eighth grade, while playing on a regional American Legion team, he caught the blazing fastball of Bob Feller, another local boy from the town of Van Meter. As a football player, Nile could throw with either arm. He excelled as a punter and as an artist of a now lost skill, the dropkick, which was the manner in which all field goals and extra points were attempted. Nile Sr. had schooled his son in the tricky dropkick and how to punt on the run, a maneuver that could be devastatingly effective in improving field position by pinning an unsuspecting opponent deep in its territory. The "quick kick," as it was known, was routinely employed by teams as often as ten times a game, sometimes executed on second or third down to maximize the surprise factor.

By 1932, when Kinnick was fourteen, the Depression and a severe drought were gripping Iowa's farmbelt. In the previous five years, the mortgages on 25,000 Iowa farms had foreclosed and more than 1,000 banks had dissolved, often with a family's life savings.

Nile Sr. decided to move his family to Omaha, Nebraska, not to farm, but to take an office job in a federal land bank. It was a judicious and timely career decision as farms throughout the Midwest continued to wither, but the move was difficult for the Kinnicks, especially Nile's mother, who considered herself an Iowan by every measure. Nile Jr. sensed the tumult of the times and decided the most prudent response was to devote himself to his studies at his new high school.

That year, he also began keeping a diary, something he did to the end of his life. Forty-eight years after his death, Kinnick's diaries and letters were compiled and arranged by Paul Baender in his splendid book, *A Hero*

Perished,[3] which became a bestseller in Iowa. The earliest letters and entries depict an evolving, sensitive young man, aware that the world of his parents was being dramatically left behind, not just by the Depression but by the new forces of a changing, unstable Europe.

Kinnick wrote frequently of his generation and how much he felt the world would come to expect of it. Walking past the Omaha breadlines as a high school student, watching his penniless neighbors beg for coal to fill empty furnaces, Kinnick wondered if he or America would rise to the challenges.

"Every man's place on earth is important," he wrote. "I fear ours will be most momentous. I cannot see how we will be allowed to fail. So much that we hold dear could fail with us."

Kinnick was an A student at Omaha's Benson High School and was an all-state football and basketball player. After graduation, he returned to his home state, where he was one of 5,000 undergraduates at the university in Iowa City. Kinnick played three sports as a freshman, but quit baseball and basketball as he began his sophomore year. Football was his favorite, and with an eye on postgraduate law school, he also wanted more time to focus on his studies.

"The athlete learns to evaluate," he wrote in his diary. "To evaluate between athletics and studies, between playing for fun and playing as a business, between playing clean and playing dirty, between being conventional and being true to one's convictions. He is facing the identical conditions which will confront him after college—the same dimensions and circumstances. But how many football players realize this?"

The Iowa football program, once a powerhouse, was fairly well in shambles. Iowa football had a roaring '20s stage—undefeated Big Ten Conference champions in 1921 and 1922—and a hollow recession a decade later. The Big Ten was home to many of the biggest universities in the land, and throughout the early 1930s, they saw Iowa as a doormat, the soft spot, the laugher, in everyone's schedule. Iowa would go years without defeating a Big Ten team, even in its 53,000-seat stadium, which was rarely much more than half full.

[3]Baender, Paul, *A Hero Perished: The Diary and Selected Letters of Nile Kinnick* (University of Iowa Press, 1991).

KINNICK IN 1939

In 1938, Kinnick's junior season, Iowa was outscored 135–46 and did not score a touchdown in its final five games. Iowa won one game of eight and that was against the University of Chicago, which summarily resigned from the Big Ten.

Kinnick starred for the downtrodden Iowa teams of 1937–38, building a reputation as a reliable back noted for his throwing accuracy and punting prowess. In 1938, Kinnick was named to the All–Big Ten team, although he likely played most of the season with a broken ankle.

"We never knew for sure because Nile was a Christian Scientist," Iowa teammate Red Frye said in a recent interview. "So he wouldn't let himself be examined. But he limped like it was broken. How he punted with it, I'll never know. We all pushed ourselves then. They were rough times and it was a rough game."

It was about to get rougher for Iowa's football team. Coach Irl Tubbs, who had won two games in the last two seasons, was jettisoned and Iowa reached eastward for a coach with credentials. The College of Holy Cross had unusually gifted football and basketball teams for a small Catholic men's college in central Massachusetts. Its football coach, Dr. Eddie Anderson, was a urologist who, for a while at least, chose to spend his autumns coaching college football. He had been a pupil of Knute Rockne as the captain of Notre Dame's 1921 team and a teammate of George Gipp. Anderson brought his training to Holy Cross and in six seasons lost just seven games. But Anderson was a native of Iowa, and when the University of Iowa came calling, he answered.

Anderson accepted Iowa's lucrative offer of $10,000 a year and on the day he arrived on campus, he assembled everyone who wanted to go out for football and had them run the football stadium steps for an hour without a break. According to Frye, of the sixty players who had showed up, twenty quit that day.

"He used to have us doing push-ups the minute we got to the practice field and then we did fifteen minutes of push-ups before we left," Frye said. "He instructed us to do fifty push-ups every night before we went to bed. And most of us did. He was a vivacious guy, in great shape himself. He believed in conditioning. I believe he thought conditioning could cure anything.

"He really was a good doctor. After he left coaching years later, he became a specialist in heart diseases. But when it came to football you would never know he was a doctor. He was the only doctor I ever met who thought anything could be cured by 'running it off.' From appendicitis to a bloody nose, his medical opinion was the same: 'Run it off.'"

Anderson, an All-American end at Notre Dame, had borrowed two Rockne coaching tenets:

1. Drill the linemen and ends with an unremitting regimen of hard work in practice so they would be fresher at the end of games. This was when Big Ten games were won and lost.
2. Protect and promote the star of your team.

Anderson also brought to Iowa two other former Notre Dame stars as coaches, Frank Carideo, an All-American quarterback and kicking expert, and line coach Jim Harris. The three drove their charges hard, so hard they were left with only a roster of twenty by the start of the 1939 season. It did not matter; Anderson planned to play only the fifteen most fit players anyway. His was a small team physically, as well. Frye was the 185-pound center of a line that averaged only 190 pounds. The 170-pound Kinnick was the focus of Anderson's team, but Anderson also had a crafty quarterback in Al Couppee and a tough, sure-handed end in Erwin Prasse.

No one else thought Anderson could rebuild Iowa in a year, however, and the gaggle of newspapermen covering the Big Ten universally picked Iowa to finish at the bottom again.

But the newspapermen had not been to Iowa City an hour before or an hour after practice when Kinnick would be on the field utilizing an exceptional practice tactic.

"Coach Anderson would have the ends run down and out patterns and at the last minute he would tell Kinnick whether to pass it or punt it," Frye said. "I'm not kidding, Nile was such a perfectionist—always the first one out of the locker room and always the last one in—that he could punt a ball to a spot, drop it right into an end's hands like a pass."

Coach Carideo and Kinnick would also kick footballs back and forth to each other from various spots on the field. "They were so accurate," Couppee told *Sports Illustrated*'s Ron Fimrite in a 1987 article on Kinnick, "it was like watching two guys playing catch."[4]

In his letters home before his senior season in 1939, Kinnick was de-

[4]*Sports Illustrated*, August 31, 1987.

termined to make a bigger impact on the Big Ten that year. He was already certain it would be his last fall of football, and not necessarily because of his intention to attend law school. In somber tones, Kinnick wrote of how he expected America to enter the fray that would become World War II. He used to caution his teammates to pay close attention to developing news from Europe, though they generally ignored him.

Many Americans had a subconscious desire to disregard the developing overseas peril. America in 1939 was finally coming out of the Depression. There was a feel-good attitude, that of a country facing a seemingly endless wealth of new opportunities. Fast trains were shrinking the countryside, swing bands had upped the tempo of the nation, and Hollywood was alive with color—*Gone with the Wind* and *The Wizard of Oz* were each released in 1939. America seemed a more unified, connected place than ever before, in part because of the omnipresent living room radio.

On her traditional Armistice Day radio program, singer Kate Smith introduced a new Irving Berlin song, "God Bless America." Still, as Kinnick's Iowa team prepared for its opening game of the 1939 season, on September 30, Nazi German and Russian forces agreed to a partition of occupied Poland, which Josef Stalin had invaded fifteen days after Hitler's September 1 Blitzkrieg across Polish borders.

"Nile used to talk about the war all the time," Prasse said in a 2003 interview. "We were worried about the season. He always seemed to have one eye on Europe, too. He said we'd be in the war eventually no matter what. We didn't want to believe him. Nile said it was going to be our duty."

Iowa's season began against South Dakota, a team meant to be a tuneup for Eddie Anderson's remade team, which also now operated a highly complicated offense featuring Kinnick. Anderson handpicked South Dakota, wanting to boost his new team's confidence, and he tabbed the right opponent. Iowa battered South Dakota 41–0. Kinnick ran for 110 yards on eight carries—including two touchdowns—passed for two more touchdowns and drop-kicked five extra points after scores.

Next up was Indiana, a team Iowa had not beaten since 1921. Visiting Indiana took a 10–0 halftime lead, but Kinnick, whose quickness stunned the home fans (he no longer had a broken ankle), was at his most dominant on this day. He threw three touchdown passes to Prasse, ran for another score and returned nine punts for 201 yards, an average of 22.3 yards per return. He also never left the game, playing defensive halfback. His quick kicks and punting thwarted a late Indiana comeback. Iowa won a pulsating 32–29 victory.

Word happily spread across the Iowa plains of Anderson's undefeated footballers and their magician of a leader, Kinnick. While Iowa Stadium had been half full for the South Dakota game and two-thirds full for the Indiana visit, no remaining Iowa game in 1939, home or away, was anything less than a sellout.

Kinnick and Michigan's Tom Harmon matched wits and talents the following week in a game at Ann Arbor. For a quarter of play, it was a close game. Kinnick threw an early seventy-one-yards touchdown pass, but Harmon intercepted a Kinnick pass later in the game and ran ninety yards for a touchdown. Harmon, who would later win the 1940 Heisman Trophy, went on to score all of Michigan's points in a 27–7 victory.

At Wisconsin the next week, Iowa came from behind to win, another upset, 19–13. Noting that six Iowa players had played all sixty minutes of Iowa's four games, Anderson told reporters that he was coaching "ironmen." The term stuck. Americans were intrigued by the undersized and resilient Iowa team headed by Nile Kinnick, whose boyish face was a fixture in newspapers nationwide after Iowa improved its record to 4–1 with a 4–0 win over Purdue. Iowa had scored two safeties in the game.

But waiting for Iowa the following weekend was Notre Dame. Surely, more than spunk and ingenuity would be needed against the vaunted Fighting Irish, ranked second in the nation. The national press came to Iowa City for the game, expecting to chronicle the extinguishing of the Cornbelt Comet.

But Iowa's Ironmen were a surprising match for Notre Dame's bigger, more seasoned lineup. Anderson had schooled his charges well in Notre Dame's tendencies. Iowa was also better defensively than Notre Dame expected with Kinnick cleverly patrolling the defensive backfield and Prasse pressuring the Notre Dame backs.

A tense struggle set in, one featuring gnarly pile-ups and jarring collisions as neither team could get its speediest backs free for dashes around the end. Punting became a necessary, game-saving maneuver. The first break in the game came late in the first half when Notre Dame fumbled a Kinnick punt on its four-yard line. Two plays later, Iowa had not advanced the ball even an inch.

Now, with just forty seconds remaining in the half, Couppee entered the huddle and announced that he wanted to switch Kinnick from left to right halfback on the upcoming third-down play. Watching the grainy game film of the play more than sixty years later, the switch, a jumping of players from left to right and right to left, is apparent an instant before the ball is snapped directly to Kinnick.

Tucking the football beneath his left arm, Kinnick ran left behind a corridor of blockers. But at the goal line, he was confronted by a last Notre Dame defender.

Kinnick lowered his right shoulder and delivered a crunching blow, then bounced off the would-be tackler and into the end zone. A photographer snapped a shot of the determined Kinnick just before his dramatic collision and touchdown, a picture that ran in thousands of newspapers the next day. It was framed and displayed in homes throughout Iowa for several years to come, and the image graces the athletic offices of the University of Iowa to this day.

Following the score, Kinnick also drop-kicked the extra point for a 7–0 Iowa lead.

Notre Dame came back in the third quarter to score its own touchdown, but the extra point was missed, leaving Iowa with a 7–6 lead. Notre Dame's defense spent the remaining portion of the second half furiously pursuing Kinnick while the Irish offense charged up the field toward the Iowa goal line. But Kinnick and Iowa's Ironmen repulsed Notre Dame's every advance. The game came down to the final minutes with Iowa facing a fourth down at its own 34-yard line.

The day was growing cold. As the sun set behind the University of Iowa stadium grandstand, the field, soft at midday, took on a hardened, slippery glaze. A punt deep into Notre Dame's territory could seal the victory for Iowa but it was a risky play given the field conditions. Besides, Notre Dame's defense would attack Kinnick in punt formation with renewed zeal, knowing a blocked kick—or even one rushed and poorly executed—would give Notre Dame the advantageous field position they sought.

In the midst of a charging Notre Dame line, Kinnick delivered a sixty-three-yard punt that rolled out of bounds at the Notre Dame 6-yard line. "You could see the punt bounce right on the chalk at the 6-yard line," Prasse said in 2003. "I can see it still. One of the greatest clutch plays I've ever seen on a football field."

It was Kinnick's 16th punt of the day.

Notre Dame's star safety, Steve Sitko, watched Kinnick's punt go out of bounds, then ripped his helmet off and slammed it to the ground. Sitko knew Notre Dame's chances at victory had sailed out of bounds with Kinnick's kick.

When Iowa's 7–6 victory—the greatest upset of the 1939 college football season—was complete, Kinnick's teammates hoisted him on their shoulders and carried him to the locker room. It was Kinnick's signature performance: a run for a touchdown, the game-winning extra point, defensive brilliance, and a game-saving punt. Later that day, November 11, 1939, all the players attended an Armistice Day parade honoring the World War I veterans.

The legend of the indestructible, resourceful Kinnick grew with the unexpected Notre Dame victory. Viewing newsreels of Kinnick's exploits in darkened movie theatres across the nation the following weekend, audiences stood and applauded the vision of the plucky Kinnick racing into the end zone against Notre Dame.

"I know every kid in Iowa went to his mother the next week and asked her to sew a number 24 on his shirt so he could pretend to be Nile Kinnick," Dr. Jerry Anderson, son of coach Eddie Anderson, told ESPN Classic in 2000 during an interview for a retrospective on Kinnick's life. "They may have been doing the same thing across the country."

The focus remained in Iowa for the next week's opponent, Minnesota, winners of three national championships in the 1930s. Guided by their stone-faced, hard-nosed coach Bernie Bierman, a Vince Lombardi–like figure in that era of college football, Bierman had scouted Kinnick as a Nebraska high school star and told Kinnick's family that their son was too small and too slow for Minnesota's powerhouse program.

Bierman might have felt his judgment was vindicated midway through the fourth quarter when his team, which had dominated Iowa in every phase, held a 9–0 lead. Kinnick, stung by Bierman's assessment four years earlier and tutored in the power of perseverance since his first reading of Longfellow's "Excelsior," implored his teammates to continue to pursue the victory despite Minnesota's apparent advantage.

"It was a pass play to me in the far corner of the left end zone," Prasse said. "Nile, running to his right, threw the football all the way across the field, just over a Minnesota player, and right into my hands."

It was a forty-five-yard touchdown pass. Five minutes later, Kinnick connected with Bill Green for a twenty-eight-yard touchdown pass, an option fake that again had Kinnick throwing on the run. Green caught the football over his shoulder as he fell into the end zone, which had been surrounded by Iowa fans.

Twenty thousand fans stormed the field following Iowa's 13–9 victory, a third successive shocker.

After playing every minute in seven games, Kinnick separated his shoulder in the season finale against Northwestern and sat out most of the game, a dispiriting 7–7 tie. Still, Iowa, winners of just one game a year earlier, had finished their season 6–1–1, and a country searching for something to feel good about had its hero: Nile Kinnick.

In late November, Kinnick was awarded the 1939 Heisman Trophy, defeating Harmon by 246 votes (of the 1,740 cast). Summoned to the Downtown Athletic Club, Kinnick prepared a memorable acceptance speech. His comments were the starting point in a long line of addresses by Heisman winners that have become part of the trophy's considerable folklore.

At the microphone of a national radio audience Kinnick thanked God he was "born to the gridirons of the Middle West and not to the battlefields of Europe." He added: "I can say confidently and positively that the football players of this country would much rather fight for the Heisman award than for the Croix de Guerre."

Senior class president at Iowa and a Phi Beta Kappa, Kinnick spurned an offer of $10,000 to play in the National Football League, so he could enroll in law school. Kinnick's last football game was with a college all-star team in an exhibition against the 1939 NFL champion Green Bay Packers. Featured on the front of the game program, Kinnick passed for two touchdowns and kicked four extra points. He took the train back to Iowa City with his teammate Erwin Prasse.

"He said: 'Erwin, my football career is over,'" Prasse said. "Later, I looked up and he wasn't in our train car. I went looking for him. There was a car full of deaf students and Nile was back there talking with them in sign language. I said, 'Nile, when did you learn sign language?' And he said: 'I memorized the finger movements in a book I read last year.'

"I tell you, the guy was unbelievable."

Kinnick threw himself into his law studies and prepared for a political career, studying the prominent national candidates in the 1940 election. When Republican presidential candidate Wendell Wilkie came to Iowa,

Kinnick was invited to introduce Wilkie at an Iowa City rally. Kinnick gave a brief but moving speech, one so effective that Wilkie tried to convince Kinnick to accompany him on the next month of the campaign so Kinnick could repeat his introduction elsewhere. Kinnick demurred, but his friends said the episode helped convince him that he had an affinity for public speaking and no shortage of ideas on what ailed the country and American society. Kinnick began talking about running for the United States Senate from Iowa.

First, however, Kinnick knew the United States would soon be drawn to the battlefronts in Europe and the Pacific. On December 4, 1941, he enlisted in the Navy Air Corps. He could have continued his law studies, especially since there was as yet no conscription of American men.

He wrote to his brother George, "I would be lacking in appreciation for all America has done for me if I did not offer what little I had to her."

In his diary, Kinnick wrote: "Every man who I have admired in history has willingly and courageously served in his country's armed forces in times of danger."

The Kinnick diaries are archived at the University of Iowa and the pen-and-ink writings on the notebook-like, lined pages depict an earnest and thoughtful young man with a great sense of responsibility to a world that, in his mind, reached far beyond the Iowa campus and cornfields. Preparing for his first military assignments in 1941, he wrote:

"It is not only a duty but an honor . . . May God give me the courage and ability to so conduct myself in every situation that my country, my family and my friends will be proud of me."

Trained as a fighter pilot, it took Kinnick two years to achieve the status of squadron leader aboard the aircraft carrier U.S.S. *Lexington*. In 1943, Kinnick's squadron was in the final stages of training in the Caribbean before they would be assigned to fly and fight over the Pacific Ocean.

On a clear, cloudless day, June 2, 1943, Kinnick and several other pilots took off from the *Lexington* for a morning training mission. Ninety minutes into the exercise, Kinnick was in his Grumman F4F Wildcat Navy fighter plane when another pilot flying alongside him, Ensign Bill Reiter, noticed that Kinnick's plane was leaking oil. Soon, the fuselage of Kinnick's aircraft was streaked with the oil hemorrhaging from the engine. Complete engine failure was an immediate certainty. Kinnick was four miles from the aircraft carrier and could probably have made a dash to safety. But Kinnick and his squadron had not been scheduled to return for hours and the carrier deck was crowded with planes and crews waiting to take off.

Kinnick understood an emergency landing with a disabled plane could turn the deck of the *Lexington* into a fireball, endangering crew and a dozen planes. Without apparent deliberation, Kinnick radioed that he would ditch his plane in the sea. He signaled to Reiter that he would attempt a landing in the Gulf of Paria, off the coast of Venezuela. And then, as calmly as he seemed to do everything else in his life, Kinnick made a textbook-perfect water landing.

Reiter saw that Kinnick's airplane had remained intact, floating in the water. Reiter later said he was not surprised when he saw Kinnick climb from the pilot cabin. Kinnick waved from the water, but Reiter did think that Kinnick appeared dazed bobbing alongside the plane. Reiter radioed for help, noting Kinnick's location, then turned back toward the carrier so he could direct the rescue vessel to Kinnick. In minutes the rescue craft and Reiter returned.

The search over calm seas lasted two hours. There was no sign of the plane or Kinnick.

Kinnick, weeks short of his twenty-fifth birthday, was gone.

"When I heard the news, I was in naval fighter pilot training, too," Red Frye, an Iowa teammate in 1939, said in a conversation sixty years after Kinnick's death. "I knew Nile couldn't have made a mistake. He didn't make mistakes. I couldn't have imagined what happened. Where did he go? Lost at sea, they said."

All these years later, Frye disputed the concept.

"Lost at sea?" the eighty-four-year-old Frye said. "Nile Kinnick? How does somebody like that just vanish?"

Nile Sr. wrote a letter to his son, Ben, an Army bomber pilot, after Nile's death: "Benjamin, tonight, the stars will not shine as brightly as they did before, but they will shine."

Fifteen months later, Benjamin Kinnick was shot down and killed in a bombing mission in the Pacific.

For decades, the Kinnick family resisted all efforts to commemorate the lives of their two sons in Iowa, believing they should not be singled out from the more than 400,000 Americans who lost their lives in World War II. In 1972, they did permit the University of Iowa to rename its football stadium Kinnick Stadium. The Big Ten Conference, to this day,

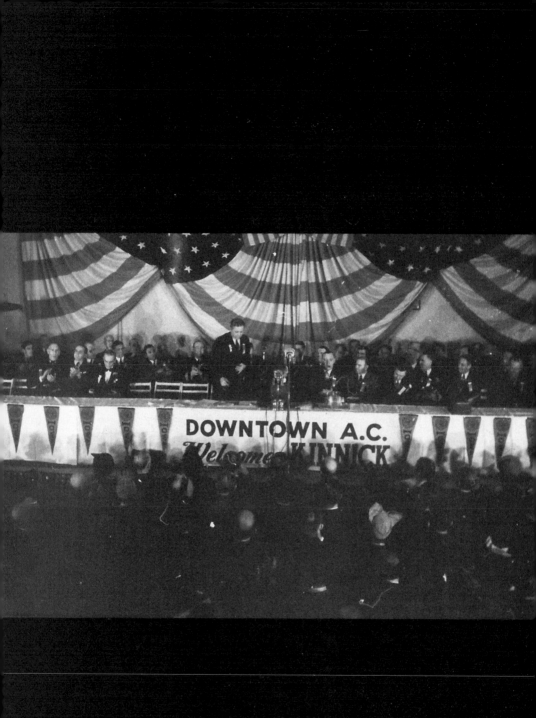

KINNICK'S HEISMAN AWARD CEREMONY
IN 1939

uses a coin bearing the likeness of Nile Kinnick for the coin flip before each game.

In 1996, after the remains of Kinnick's plane were discovered in the Gulf of Paria, the surviving members of the Iowa Ironmen—still celebrities in Iowa—raised several thousand dollars to pay for a recovery of the plane. They wanted to bring it back to Iowa City and place it next to Kinnick Stadium as a monument to their former teammate.

Some voices in Iowa, including Kinnick family members, discouraged the project, and the recovery effort was quietly halted.

The gift of Kinnick's time on earth could not be memorialized in structure or form. It was a gift as hard to grasp as a gentle breeze or an illuminating sun. It was better to leave the presence of Nile Kinnick in the collective consciousness, as if he had been an apparition.

Kinnick no doubt grasped gifts of such ethereal quality.

Writing a friend who was visiting the Iowa campus in 1943, Kinnick said: "It is like home and how do you define home? I hope you strolled across the campus just at twilight and felt the peace and quiet of an Iowa evening, just as I used to do."

3.

Under a Hero's Light

TOM HARMON, 1940

Tom Harmon was America's first mass media sports hero, a mid-century renaissance man with one foot in 1930 and the other in 1990. He was the perfectly cast man of his times—all of them.

All-American football player, magazine cover boy, newsreel idol, Heisman Trophy winner, war hero, author, broadcaster, movie star, and husband of a movie starlet, Harmon did nothing without precision, proficiency, and panache. His life was among the first in American sports played out entirely before the fast-moving, all-seeing cameras of a developing electronic entertainment industry.

He was introduced to America as "Harmon of Michigan," which later became the title of a Hollywood movie about his life. The University of Michigan star played himself, as no one else could have. In the last year before war enveloped the nation, Harmon was an action hero with a football under his arm, dauntless and gallant. He was "Old 98," an allusion to his uniform number that aptly made him sound like a train engine. His career unfolded in newsreel footage flickering in movie houses across America. There was Harmon eluding eight or ten tackles to score from sixty yards, his ripped jersey flapping behind him. There was Harmon scoring from eighty-two yards after losing a shoe. There was Harmon leaping over three defenders, soaring over the goal line like Superman.

In time, it was not just the dazzling exploits on the football field—end-to-end dashes that seemed an impossible mix of speed and strength—that made Harmon legend. It was poise and courage in war. It was Middle American modesty and rugged good looks. His place and standing with average Americans was cast early and never wavered.

Harmon's son, the actor Mark Harmon, tells a story of when he was eight years old and accompanied his father on a trip back to the Michigan campus. It was the late 1950s and Harmon was nearly twenty years past his last football game for the Wolverines. Nonetheless, when his rental car came to a stop at an intersection, Harmon was instantly recognized.

"They surrounded my dad's car," Mark Harmon said. "They stopped traffic. They were leaning inside the car, asking for his autograph, taking pictures. They encircled the car. I was sitting in the passenger seat, my face barely above the dashboard, but I looked over at him and thought: 'Just who are you?'"

Harmon believed in the power, merit, and worth of heroes and welcomed the notion that his entire adult life had been held under a spotlight.

"Every Heisman Trophy winner walks under a hero's light; that is our responsibility and we are honored to have it," Harmon wrote in 1985. "It is vital to American society that it be that way. This country of ours should never do away with its pursuit of heroes."

What Harmon recognized was a most unique American tradition. Other countries deify royalty; Americans, beginning with George Washington's prescient decision to decline a third presidential term, have spurned the concept of a ruling family. That does not produce a leaderless society. Instead, in every walk of life, the uniquely American phenomenon is to find the everyday hero. And we enjoy finding them everywhere.

Born in 1919, the son of a Gary, Indiana, policeman, Harmon was the youngest of four brothers. Many Heisman winners are, interestingly enough, either the oldest or youngest in their family. In Harmon's case, being the youngest meant learning virtually every sport at the knee of his athletically gifted brothers, including Lou and Harold, who each went on to star in college athletics.

But Tom Harmon was blessed with a peerless medley of athletic skills. Although not broad-shouldered in the classic football tradition, he was extraordinarily strong below the waist with thick hip, thigh, and calf muscles, a characteristic that would serve him well in the football and wartime challenges that lay ahead. Harmon earned fourteen varsity letters at Horace

Mann High School, and it was this vast range of physical abilities that left college recruiters marveling. He was a bruising power forward on the basketball court, and on the track he was timed in the 100-yard dash at 9.9— only a few tenths of a second off the times of Olympic level sprinters of the late 1930s. He was agile, too, and a state champion in the high hurdles. A licensed lifeguard, he always won the annual Lake Michigan swimming races.

Harmon had offers to attend fifty-four institutions but chose Michigan, sensing, as others did, that it was a budding Big Ten power. He was not given a scholarship, only limited aid that covered part of his tuition. All the Michigan players were in the same boat financially.

"I remember that practice had to end by 5:30 every day because we all had jobs in the evening," said Forest Evashevski, a Michigan teammate who became Harmon's longtime friend. "It is how we paid for books, meals, and clothes."

Harmon washed breakfast dishes in the student cafeteria before his morning classes and folded shirts as a clerk in the campus store by night. Over the summers, he worked in the Gary steel mills.

Harmon was a sensation almost from his arrival at Michigan. Although freshmen were not allowed to play varsity, Harmon still dazzled head coach Fritz Crisler, who made frequent trips over to the freshman games to see how his prized catch was doing. By his junior year, Harmon was Michigan's only All-American on a strong team with a 6–2 record. He punted, ran the football, passed the football, played tenacious defense, and kicked all the field goals and extra points.

By Harmon's senior season in 1940, college football was in the last days of its leather helmet era, and Harmon's performance during this period of transition had a certain karma to it. The season began with a memorable cross-country hike to play the University of California in Berkeley.

"We took off in three DC3s," said Evashevski. "Everybody on the plane except Tom and two other guys got airsick because none of us had flown. I don't think Tom had flown either, but being Tom, he didn't get sick."

The planes stopped over in Denver for the night to refuel. That afternoon, Michigan held a practice in the Mile High City, drawing a curious crowd of ranchers and farmers from the adjacent hills and plains. The Wolverines were like a traveling football circus, and everyone came to see the great Tom Harmon of Michigan.

In Berkeley that Saturday, September 28, the game was played before a sun-splashed prewar crowd that included several thousand sailors and Navy officers stationed near San Francisco. In a little more than a year's time, they would be embarking for the Pacific Theatre. Among those at the game was a skinny future captain of a U.S. Navy PT boat, John F. Kennedy.

Evashevski, co-captain along with Harmon, got his teammates together before the game for a pep talk.

"It's Tom's twenty-first birthday—let's show the world what we think of him," Evashevski said.

Harmon caught the opening kickoff on the 5-yard line, and with superb blocking clearing his way, dashed upfield, outrunning every Cal player until he trotted into the end zone untouched on the play. Harmon would score twice more in the first half, displaying his remarkable cutback ability on a seventy-five-yard touchdown run. Harmon was a skilled practioner of what has come to be known in football parlance as "shooting the rapids," a tactic that has the runner slicing back to the opposite side of the field in mid-run. It sends the ball carrier directly into the face of an advancing onslaught of defenders. As a surprise move, going against the grain has its advantages, provided the ball carrier accurately times his cutback. If he does not, the consequences can be perilous. It not only takes timing but also courage. And no one in the 1940s, or perhaps for decades after, was better at "shooting the rapids" than Harmon.

In the first half of the game at Cal, Harmon scored the game's first three touchdowns, threw for another score, kicked all the extra points, and added a field goal as well.

Late in the second half, Harmon's dominance of Cal spawned one of the most memorable plays of the prewar days of college football. Back then, the games were attended by fans in porkpie hats and raccoon coats, which were convenient for storing another common commodity of the times—a hip flask. With time running out in the game and Michigan ahead by 34 points, Harmon took the ball at his own 14-yard line and ran around the left end. He cut back against the flow of tacklers once, then again, and once more again at midfield. He was running free, a full ten yards ahead of any Cal tackler.

At that moment, Bud Brennan, a Cal grad who may have been a bit overserved from someone's hip flask, started to run down the aisle from his 34th row seat behind the Cal end zone. Brennan jumped the low railing—there was little security back then and little need for it—and sprinted toward the field.

Five yards from the end zone, Harmon slowed to look over his shoulder. When he turned back, there was Brennan, attempting to make a tackle at the 1-yard line.

"I dove for him," Brennan said during a television broadcast, hosted by Bing Crosby, that celebrated the twenty-fifth anniversary of Harmon's Heisman Trophy season. "He stiff-armed me and gave me a loose left leg that I missed. The next thing I saw he was in the end zone."

Brennan was led gingerly from the field by the game referee. Interestingly, Brennan later apologized to Harmon in a letter that began a lifelong correspondence between the two men.

Michigan's 41–0 victory over California was featured in the next edition of *Life* magazine and his brilliant, powerful runs through California's defense, before the gleaming Cal stadium and despite a bizarre tackle attempt from the grandstand, became the first newsreel images flashed through movie houses the next weekend. America was smitten with Old 98.

"If I counted the number of people who said they had been in the stands for that game in Berkeley," Harmon would say years later, "it would have to be three million, easy. If I counted the number of people who said they saw it in their local theatre, it would be twenty million."

The victories for Michigan rolled on, a shutout cavalcade—26–0 over Harvard, 14–0 over Penn and 28–0 over Illinois, a victory that avenged one of two losses by the 1939 Michigan team.

The other loss in that 1939 season had been to Minnesota, the most feared of all Big Ten football teams, led by a clever, sharp-tongued, and resourceful coach, Bernie Bierman. The 1940 Minnesota–Michigan game was played in Minneapolis just after a heavy rainstorm had moved up the Mississippi River. Though his university usually made attempts to shield its field and keep it dry, on this occasion, Bierman had decided to leave the field exposed to the heavy downpour.

Bierman knew that Michigan's running attack, its bread and butter, was based on a diagonal, cross-blocking style from the linemen, and the slashing, lightning quick cutback style of Harmon.

By game time, the field was a quagmire. "Your cleats would be full of mud after two steps," Harmon later said.

Michigan nearly doubled Minnesota's yardage total and had eighteen first downs in the game to Minnesota's three. But it was the field conditions that were the story of the day to Michigan's followers. Each team scored one touchdown, but Harmon, stunningly, slipped and missed the extra point kick after Michigan's score and Minnesota won the game, 7–6. Minnesota went on to win the national championship, its fourth in nine years, while Michigan finished second.

In an interview sixty-three years later, Evashevski lamented the lost opportunity.

"You know, we were a cutback running team and Minnesota was a straight ahead team," he said. "I had their end pushed out twice and there were gaping holes for Tom. He would have scored easily—you can see it on the films, I tell you! We should have won easily. But both times, Tom fell down trying to cut in the mud. It was a shame."

Harmon and Evashevski talked about the Minnesota game for decades. "Every time we got together," Evashevski said. "Isn't that crazy? We won seven games that year and lost one, and it's the one we lost we talked about. I guess that's just the way it is."

Still, despite the setback in Minneapolis, Michigan rolled on, past Michigan State and Iowa until the final game against Ohio State.

As a freshman and unable to play for the varsity, Harmon had watched from the Ohio State stands as the home team humbled Michigan. He vowed revenge, and while Harmon's 1939 team had defeated Ohio State in Ann Arbor, Michigan, the 1940 game was Harmon's last college game and Harmon had saved a magical conclusion to a magical season.

The game between these two pitched and bitter rivals was expected to be a close, tense affair, but Harmon soon took over before a sellout crowd at Ohio State's immense, concrete, horseshoe-shaped stadium. Harmon quickly ran for one touchdown—the first of two— and then passed for two touchdowns. He would finish with 139 yards rushing and 151 yards passing, completing eleven of twelve passes. He intercepted three passes, returning one for a touchdown; kicked four extra points; and averaged fifty yards on three punts. He also knocked down several other Ohio State passes from his defensive back's position.

It was Harmon at his best, his old jersey number 98 ripped from his back as he broke tackles and spun from the grasp of defenders. The Ohio State defense mounted charge after charge at Michigan's backfield ace, but Harmon, knowing how to fashion an exit, was undeterred. Michigan won the game, 40–0.

As the game ended, Harmon, his jersey in tatters, walked off the Ohio State field to a standing ovation from a crowd of 73,000 that had come to cheer against him. It was one of those singular moments in athletics when fans and competitors come together to recognize an occasion beyond the rudiments of score and statistics. Tom Harmon, one of the great college football players ever, was exiting the game. Professional football had little prestige in those days, and so Harmon was leaving the stage, in most eyes, for a final time.

"It was moving," Evashevski said of the ovation from the Ohio State fans. "On the one hand, we were all dirty and tired. But there was this feeling that we had all been a part of something special. The last day of a remarkable college career."

Harmon concluded his Michigan career with 237 points scored, 2,134 yards rushing on 398 attempts, a 5.4 yards-per-carry average, and 1,399 yards passing. In the Ohio State victory, Harmon had increased his career touchdown total from thirty to thirty-three, which moved him past the record thirty-one touchdowns scored by Illinois's Red Grange in the mid-1920s, a mark many thought unattainable.

Years later, Harmon's son Mark said he still watches a videotape given to him of his father's thirty-three touchdowns scored.

"I've watched that tape until I know each run by heart," Mark said. "I knew them by heart in my childhood. In fact, until I was ten years old, I thought my father had never been tackled in a football game. All I had watched was that tape, and every time he scored. There are some amazing runs. He could run away from you and he could run over you."

After the Ohio State game, Harmon was an easy choice for the 1940 Heisman Trophy. "When I got the call from the Downtown Athletic Club that I had won," Harmon wrote years later, "I cried with tears of happiness. It was the dream of a lifetime."

He attended the ceremony awarding him the trophy with his college coach and his parents.

"My parents were busting with pride," Harmon said of the occasion. "They had made sacrifices and I had made sacrifices for ten years of football. I thanked Coach Crisler and all my teammates. We were all in it to-gether."

Just before the holiday season in 1940, Harmon made the rounds of all-star games and All-America banquets. At one such gathering, when Harmon was in Los Angeles for the East–West college all-star game, he was invited to appear on Bing Crosby's radio show. Also on the show that day was Elyse Knox, a Hollywood actress who had recently relocated from Hartford, Connecticut, to California. Harmon and Knox began dating, al-though their romance was interrupted by Harmon's enlistment in the Army Air Corps.

Harmon became a bomber pilot and by early 1943 was making training runs over inland areas of western South America not far from the ocean. On one mission, he was caught in a tropical storm. Lightning hit the left wing of his B-25, shearing it off and sending the plane into a death spiral.

Harmon immediately ordered the crew to parachute from the doomed plane as he and his copilot attempted to forestall the plane's descent. But in the midst of the storm, there was little that could be done to a large bomber with only one wing. That day eight of the fourteen planes in Har-mon's formation would crash in the jungles of South America. Harmon and his copilot jumped from their plane at 1,200 feet, but it was not a high enough altitude to effectively open a parachute. Harmon slammed into a jungle palm tree with such force that it ripped off the soles of his shoes, and he found himself suspended above the ground by his parachute.

Miraculously, Harmon was not seriously hurt. Dazed and shaken, he was alone in the heart of a swampy, dense jungle with only a compass and a machete on him.

The jungle was so thick he could not see the sky above him as he hacked a meager path in the overgrown foliage. He would come upon mas-sive swamps that took all day to cross. Without food or liquid, he was afraid to drink from the tepid springs of water he came upon, fearful that they might make him ill.

"I figured I could be in this jungle for a while," Harmon later wrote. "I believed in my stamina. I believed in my football legs. I thought sickness might kill me before my football legs ran out. I wanted to give it that chance."

Harmon had other grim reminders that a long, solitary struggle in the jungle might lie ahead. He came upon some of the crew of his bomber, all of them dead and several impaled by trees that awkwardly broke their fall or snapped their necks. No one from Harmon's crashed plane would survive except the pilot.

And in the first day and a half after the crash, even Harmon was far from certain that he would make it out of the jungle. At one point, he came upon a swamp so deep and ominous, with any manner of hidden underwater threats to his well-being, that he felt sure he would never cross it alive. So he reversed his field and headed north, cutting his way through the jungle for another two days. He still had not had anything to drink since the crash.

"I felt I had the strength to get through anything," Harmon later said. "I was scared and praying for help, but it was like a fourth quarter march and I was determined to try to win. I'm not saying it was easy but you either strive or you give up."

Four days and fifty miles later, Harmon came upon a bottle in the jungle. He felt certain that he was near some kind of village or outpost of civilization. And soon, Harmon walked into a native village in Dutch Guyana. The villagers then led him out of the jungle.

"He survived but the death of all of his crew was a great burden to him," Mark said. "It was a large part of his motivation to ask for a transfer to single-pilot fighter planes. He did not want anything he did to in any way lead to other lives lost."

After recovering from his ordeal in the jungle, Harmon was reassigned to the Pacific Theatre of the war where he became a superb fighter pilot, downing several Japanese Zero planes in combat. Before long, the enemy knew of Harmon of Michigan, the Heisman Trophy winner. They knew him so well that there was a price placed on the head of the American football hero and a reward offered to the Japanese pilot who shot down his plane.

There is no evidence that the bounty played a factor in the dogfight Harmon found himself in, late in 1943, when his squadron engaged a squadron of Japanese Zeros over mainland China. Shortly after downing two Japanese planes, he doubled back to offer his help elsewhere. Suddenly, he felt bullets striking the metal behind his back. It was gunfire from another Zero's machine guns and it began to rake across Harmon's aircraft, piercing the entire pilot's cabin. The hail of bullets came up directly between Harmon's legs as he sat in the cramped pilot's confines and then several struck the control panel inches from his face.

The control panel exploded and flames quickly began to envelop Harmon. He tried to put the blaze out with his hands, slapping at the flames, but realized he would soon be overcome by the heat of the blaze that had spread to his clothing.

Remembering his last crash when he had bailed out too late, Harmon turned his plane over and ejected several thousand feet above China. This time, his parachute opened and billowed, but he was far from safe. Harmon was parachuting directly through a still raging dogfight. Enemy planes fired continually at him on his descent, strafing his parachute and the cords that suspended him beneath the easy-to-spot white canopy. Understanding he was an easy target, but that the enemy planes had other pressing worries as well, Harmon played dead, doing his best to hang lifelessly from his parachute.

Unable to steer his parachute, Harmon once again could only land where the winds and gravity took him. And once again, that was in a tree, suspended by his parachute above a large pond. This time he was not hanging above a neutral jungle, but above Japanese-occupied China. Harmon continued to play dead, but he spotted a Japanese soldier standing below him. The soldier began to unholster his pistol, readying a shot at the American aviator.

As the Japanese soldier moved his pistol into position, gunfire rang out and the Japanese soldier crumpled to the ground. From the water, and out of the low-lying bushes—from two dozens spots beneath Harmon—members of an underground Chinese guerrilla unit suddenly emerged. They scurried up the tree, cut Harmon down, and realizing that Harmon was badly burned, gently placed him in a small sam pan in the pond.

There were a number of small boats nearby. Later, telling the story, Harmon said his rescuers were aware, or concerned, that the Japanese pilots or their fellow soldiers on higher ground might have been watching their efforts to save the American pilot. So they covered him with large native leaves in his boat and did the same to the other boats, disguising which boat actually bore Harmon. Then, the handful of boats scattered in different directions. That way, if anyone had been watching from above, they would not know definitively which course Harmon's rescuers had taken to bring him to safety.

"My dad told me that not long after that he was transferred to another boat and in it was a small handheld mirror," Mark Harmon said. "He looked at his face and the skin was hanging off his chin. He felt he had lost his face."

In the wake of this crash, Tom Harmon could not machete his way to a welcoming village. He could not walk with burns over much of his body. His Chinese rescuers placed him in a bamboo litter and conveyed him across rivers and other estuaries in the bottom of shallow boats. They began a long trek toward an American base on a desolate Pacific island, and as they went from secure outpost to secure outpost, it was related to Harmon that the news reports of his downing had made their way to the Japanese.

"He was told the enemy knew who it was that had been shot down," Mark Harmon said. "The price was still on his head. They knew about Harmon the Heisman Trophy winner and it meant something to find him."

But the Japanese did not find him. For twenty-nine days Harmon was carried through the jungle and paddled across waterways. "Then they walked him into an American base," Mark Harmon said.

Reported missing in action for a second time, Harmon had instead persevered again. Back home, after two years of troubling news from the warfront, the tale of another near miraculous escape by Harmon buoyed American spirits. To them, Harmon represented a time of innocence that the country was unsure it would ever recapture. He had been the winsome, smiling star of those carefree Saturday afternoon and evening movie house newsreels before the second war to end all wars, before every newspaper carried the daily roll call of dead from farflung battlefronts. That was before a star was something placed on the front door of American homes that had lost a son in battle.

It was in this atmosphere that Harmon returned to a hero's welcome. Awarded the Silver Star and Purple Heart, Harmon wrote a book, *Pilots Also Pray*, that sold out seven printings. He settled in southern California to be near Elyse Knox, and began the extensive recovery from his burns and wounds. Around him, a cultural America was emerging from the wartime cloud ever so slightly. Humphrey Bogart and Ingrid Bergman were starring in *Casablanca*, and Jane Russell was winning fans—many of them servicemen—in *The Outlaw*.

On November 28, 1943, President Roosevelt, Joseph Stalin, and Winston Churchill met for the first time in Tehran, Iran, to plot the reconstruction of central Europe in the wake of a war the allies felt sure they would win. Dwight Eisenhower was named to lead the invasion of Europe the day before Christmas 1943.

Harmon's rehabilitation was arduous and included plastic surgery for his burns. He did not return to combat duty. On August 26, 1944, he went back to the University of Michigan campus, to St. Mary's chapel, where he had worshipped as a student. Accompanying him on the trip was his bride-to-be, Elyse Knox, who wore white silk and white cords in her wedding gown taken from the parachute that bore Harmon through the thick of the dogfight over China.

Harmon limped slightly as he escorted Elyse up the aisle at St. Mary's, though in a picture of the day you cannot see a hint of how the last four years had changed either of them. Their eyes shine brightly out the door of the chapel, to a future of new and different accomplishments.

The war in Europe would be over in less than a year, the war with Japan a few months thereafter.

Though Harmon was ready to start his broadcasting career, he had no more experience than his college radio show and he was not exactly besieged with high-salary offers. Harmon was unsure where to turn. Elyse was pregnant with the couple's first child.

In 1946, the Los Angeles Rams of the NFL offered Harmon a two-year, $40,000 contract. The team's ownership knew the Harmon name was gold, even if he had not carried a football in six years. Harmon signed with the Rams and became an accomplished pro player who showed flashes of his old form, but not with any consistency. Harmon was troubled by the days he felt no more than average and recognized that his wartime injuries had stolen some of the speed and drive in his legs that broke a thousand tackles from Gary to Ann Arbor. The Rams offered Harmon another contract at the end of the 1947 season, but he gamely decided it was time to start the next chapter in his life.

"As much as I loved football," Harmon said. "I had prepared all my life for a life after football."

Harmon went back to Michigan, using his fame in the state to land a job as a television sports anchor at Detroit's WJR radio and television. He quickly learned to be a smooth, glib, and organized professional broadcaster.

"My Dad was from a blue-collar family all the way," Mark Harmon said. "And all he knew was to work and prepare. He worked at his broadcasting very hard, just as hard as he did his football, which he sometimes liked to call his previous life."

Large syndicated networks often produced broadcast programming for the national television and radio networks in those days, and soon Harmon signed on as sports director of the Columbia Pacific Network doing daily radio and television shows. It was the beginning of a whirlwind tour of the world that led to a post with the bigger and more prestigious Hughes Television Network. Harmon not only did football, but he was also a regular golf commentator, which gave him the opportunity to work on his golf game. Naturally, he became an expert golfer, playing like a pro.

Harmon was a fixture as a broadcaster at several Olympic Games. He continued to regularly host radio and television shows. He showed up everywhere, trying every career twist or athletic challenge. Uniquely, Tom Harmon could do anything and do it well.

"Tom Harmon insisted he do well in everything he did," Jim Murray, the Pulitzer Prize winning sports columnist of the *Los Angeles Times*, once wrote of his friend. "He never got more than a few pounds over his playing weight, his dress was impeccable, his habits beyond reproach. He radiated dignity and reserve. The phrase All-American was invented for guys such as Tom Harmon."[5]

Murray related a story from when he was playing golf with Harmon one day. A younger member of their foursome whom Murray did not identify, other than to call him "a prominent ex-athlete," started to rib Harmon about his fame as a Heisman Trophy winner, about his celebrity summed up in "Harmon of Michigan."

"The guy wanted to know what the big deal was," Murray said. "He said, 'I bet you I can beat you in a footrace.' Tom wanted to know when and where. The guy said 'Right now,' and Tom said, 'Let's go.'

"As they lined up for the start, the fellow looked nervously at Tom. 'Aren't you going to take your coat off?' he asked. Said Tom: 'Why, we're

[5]*The Los Angeles Times*, March 18, 1990.

only going to run. We're not going to fight or anything, right?' Well, they ran sixty yards and Tom beat the kid by ten yards."

Even the children of Elyse and Tom Harmon seemed extraordinary. One daughter, Kristin, married teen idol and former television star Ricky Nelson. Kelly became a noted actress and model. Mark Harmon played quarterback on two successful UCLA teams and went on to be a star in television dramas and movies.

On March 16, 1990, Tom Harmon won a golf tournament at Bel Air Country Club near Los Angeles. He showered, posed for pictures with his newest trophy, and headed to a travel agency to pick up airline tickets for another charity golf tournament that June in Ohio. Spring was Harmon's intense golf season. Fall and winter were still reserved for work, when he broadcast the games of the NFL's Los Angeles Raiders.

At the travel agency that day, Harmon said he began to feel ill and asked workers at the agency to call his doctor. Shortly after, he collapsed. Roughly an hour later, Tom Harmon was pronounced dead on arrival at the UCLA Medical Center emergency room. The cause was a heart attack.

Harmon's death was one of many for a generation of World War II veterans during the 1990s, a roll call that struck hard at a core of Americans honed by a great depression and scarred by unprecedented worldwide conflict. They had persevered to construct the major world power of the twentieth century. Harmon's death had a strong impact in particular because as a dashing, famous football star he had exemplified all the fresh-faced, brave young American men who dropped their successful pursuits in one field and enthusiastically devoted their lives to a struggling war effort. And they did not rest when they came home from war. They built a better America than they had left in 1941.

The days before the war, however, had bestowed upon Harmon something that lived on after his death.

"I have always been introduced as 'Heisman Trophy winner Tom Harmon,'" Harmon wrote in the 1985 *Heisman Journal* celebrating the fiftieth anniversary of the award. "Someday I will pass away and I will be proud to be referred to as 'Heisman Trophy winner Tom Harmon.' I have always known what that trophy means. It has always rested in the center of my desk since the day I won it, and I saw what it means in the eyes of youngsters who came to my home.

"They would come to my den and say, 'Hey, there's the Heisman.' They would walk to the trophy and feel its outline, like it had a power they could touch."

Mark Harmon was once one of those youngsters touching the trophy.

"You know, as a kid I always thought the guy on the Heisman Trophy was my father," Mark Harmon said. "The sons of all Heisman Trophy winners, at least from that era, probably think that. And I know the truth about how and when the trophy was designed. But in my mind, I will never think otherwise.

"Look at his whole life. That trophy was my dad, let's face it."

BLANCHARD (LEFT) AND DAVIS WITH
COACH RED BLAIK

More Than a Game

GLENN DAVIS, 1945;

AND DOC BLANCHARD, 1946

It was December 2, 1944, but somehow, far from just another Saturday in the United States of America. Nearly six months had passed since D-Day, June 6, the single most pivotal moment in World War II. Roughly three years had gone by since the bombing of Pearl Harbor, a turning point in the modern history of the world.

For years, until it almost seemed normal, Americans had rationed food, clothing, and gasoline, endured blackouts, held scrap metal drives, and learned to scour newspapers for every account from battlefields in villages and on islands no American grammar school map had ever charted. Details of slaughterhouse combat scenes, like something out of a Civil War textbook, had shaken a culture that had once felt removed from cataclysmic international turmoil. Hardly a neighborhood in the country had not been hardened by tragedy that arrived on the doorstep in the form of a plain government car, a uniformed soldier, and a telegram bearing the most feared news of all.

On December 2, for all the gains in the war on both the European and Pacific Ocean fronts, the country was gripped by disconcerting news from the Belgian town of Bastogne, where the confusing strategic maneuvers of

Nazi troops presaged a counterattack. There was an uneasiness as Allied forces advanced on German borders.

By 1944, more than 300 American colleges had stopped playing football, since most young men were serving in the armed forces. Many major institutions, like the University of Southern California, Michigan, Notre Dame, and North Carolina, had converted classrooms into Navy flight training schools, which made it easier for them to field football teams. And the two national military academies, at West Point, New York, and Annapolis, Maryland, continued to educate and prepare officers, which allowed those institutions to continue to play football. Graduates of those academies, including many ex–football players, were the backbone of the current Allied command.

So it was on December 2, 1944, days before the start of the Battle of the Bulge, that there was one meaningful regular season college football game left to be played, and not surprisingly it featured Army, the nation's top-ranked team, and Navy, ranked second. If there was ever an event that signified the times, on several levels, it was this symbolic meeting of representatives of the Army and the Navy. And if there were ever two men who came to embody America's final flourish in the war years—the rising, inspirational belief that America was going to succeed and prevail in the war—they were Felix "Doc" Blanchard and Glenn Davis, the stars of the 1944 Army–Navy game.

"We came into that game and it seemed like the whole country was either in the Army or Navy or knew and cared about someone who was," Doc Blanchard said nearly sixty years later. "It was one of those times when a game just felt like more than a game."

Weeks before, President Franklin Delano Roosevelt, recently elected to a fourth term, had ordered the game moved to Baltimore's 65,000-seat Municipal Stadium, and then made it a requirement of admission that every fan purchase a war bond with a game ticket.

The sellout at Municipal Stadium raised more than $60 million, the highest total of any war bond event during World War II.

To reach Baltimore for the game, the 2,200 members of the Army Corps of Cadets assembled on the dock at the United States Military Academy on the west bank of the Hudson River. The Navy sent a troop ship for transportation of the cadets down the Hudson River into the Atlantic Ocean and on to Maryland's Chesapeake Bay and the port of Baltimore.

Since German U-boats still lurked within the Atlantic waters, the Navy dispatched warships, submarine-hunting planes, and blimps to accompany the convoy.

The plan was daring, but it was, like most everything else, a by-product of the war effort. The cadets traveled by ship to abide by a federal government mandate keeping the railways clear for the shipment of goods and munitions for the armed forces.

Soldiers, seamen, and fans filled the Baltimore stadium on a beautiful, crisp day for football, and the game proved to be thrilling and tense, a needed and welcome respite from the war effort. Army led 9–7 entering the final quarter.

Sophomores Blanchard and Davis, in their first season on the varsity, had led Army to eight previous victories in 1944, including an astounding 59–0 whitewash of Notre Dame. But their final fifteen minutes of football on this day would spawn their linked legend, a perfect mix of timing and theater, attributes the duo would display throughout their three undefeated seasons together.

Davis, who may be the most athletically gifted cadet ever to walk through the massive stone gate at West Point, intercepted a pass to open the fourth quarter just as Navy had crossed into Army territory. Blanchard, the most physically imposing running back of his era, then took over, stampeding through the middle of the field on six successive carries, battering defenders with his shoulders in charges that were halted only when the heap of bodies before him grew too thick to continue.

Finally, from the 10-yard line, Blanchard bolted through a thunderstruck Navy defense, carrying a Navy safety on his back into the end zone, where Blanchard, still on his feet, handed the football to an official.

The California-born Davis provided the finishing touch, a fifty-yard touchdown on a play designed for him, called the California Special. Davis took the handoff at midfield and hurtled down the sideline untouched, his pace quickening, the yard markers disappearing beneath his feet like rail ties beneath a locomotive.

Together, it was a fine demonstration of the skills that engendered their indelible nicknames, created by *New York Sun* sportswriter George Trevor in 1944:Mr. Inside and Mr. Outside. Army's 23–7 victory was its first over Navy in five years, a period when Navy had also held Army scoreless.

On his way back to West Point, Army Coach Colonel Earl "Red" Blaik,

himself a West Point grad, received a telegram from General Douglas MacArthur, who had been the manager for the 1902 Army football team. Officers and troops in the Philippines, where MacArthur had just made his triumphant return, had listened to the Armed Forces Radio broadcast of the game into the early morning hours of Sunday, December 3.

"The greatest of all Army teams," MacArthur wired to Blaik. "We have stopped the war to celebrate your magnificent success."

Supreme Commander of the Allied Forces Dwight Eisenhower, a West Point back until a knee injury curtailed his career, also sent his congratulations to Blaik. Eisenhower's communiqué included regards from General Omar Bradley, the center on Army's unbeaten 1914 team, who was now in command of the European ground forces.

Blanchard and Davis soon became landmark names in Army circles. After the Germans mounted their December 16 offensive in the Ardennes, the first act of a prolonged but last gasp counterattack to protect their borders, several divisions of U.S. Army troops began using verbal signals in dark and dangerous frontline encounters. One GI would whisper, "Blanchard," knowing he was among friends if he heard the response "Davis."

And when German forces infiltrated American forces by sending English-speaking soldiers behind the lines in American uniforms, one of the ploys to uncover these spies was the question: What was the score of Army's game with Notre Dame this year?

"Fifty-nine to nothing," was the only appropriate answer.

In a wartorn country, these were the seeds of an embrace that several generations of Americans have yet to relinquish on Doc Blanchard and Glenn Davis. In Army football uniforms, Blanchard and Davis were the home soil incarnation of the might, ingenuity, and determination Americans saw in the men fighting battles a hemisphere away. Hollywood made movies hoping to boost morale. Blanchard and Davis could deliver the goods with newsreel football highlights playing to the same movie houses.

Neither man, when asked in recent interviews, warmed to the subject of playing a figurative role in the war effort, but when pressed, they humbly acknowledged it.

"We knew the guys overseas felt a closeness to us," said Davis, who lives quietly in the Philadelphia area and on the New Jersey shore. "Yes, I

GLENN DAVIS

think we knew that. Many of them had been sitting the same classrooms as us just a year or two before. And the others, many of them had been football players, high school, college, whatever. Now we were all in the Army. How could we not feel part of their thoughts?"

Said Blanchard, who leads a semireclusive life in the home of his daughter outside San Antonio: "We had to represent them well. To let them down at that time, when guys are giving their lives, would have been disrespectful. But I think the whole country felt that way, too, not just us."

Defining the enduring popularity of Blanchard and Davis, however, is more than an examination of their symbolically important roles in the war years. For one, at a time when college football was the major national sport, rivaled only by horse racing or boxing, Blanchard and Davis were simply fabulous football players. They were a two-man powerhouse, certainly the greatest backfield combination in the history of college football.

In three seasons together, they never lost a game. They played in one of the most historic games in college football history, the 0–0 tie with Notre Dame in 1946. Each won a Heisman Trophy, the only backfield duo to do so. They had songs written about them, graced the cover of *Time*, *Life, the Saturday Evening Post*, and dozens of other newsmagazines.

Opposing coaches ran out of the usual superlatives after facing the Army teams, as Notre Dame's Ed McKeever proved in his cable back to the Irish's South Bend campus after the 1944 loss: "Have just seen Superman in the flesh. He wears No. 35 and his name is Blanchard."

Writers of the day struggled to depict what they saw, turning to rhyme:

Ashes to ashes, dust to dust;
If Blanchard don't get you, then Davis must.

Off the field, they were larger than life, treated like movie stars, which wasn't much of a stretch since they starred in a movie that was made of their Army careers, *The Spirit of West Point*. In addition, the dashing Davis was briefly engaged to actress Elizabeth Taylor, and all of the couple's comings and goings were profiled as if the two were American royalty. Their romance was brief, but Davis went on to marry another movie star, Terry Moore.

Blanchard, the son of a Mississippi doctor and always more of a coun-

DOC BLANCHARD

try boy who avoided the limelight, went on to fly more than 100 combat missions in the Army Air Corps and the Air Force during the Korean and Vietnam wars, where his bravery and coolness under pressure are well documented. Blanchard in turn achieved a John Wayne–like status in America. He was a real-life American football icon turned war hero.

They came together from wholly different backgrounds and remained dissimilar throughout their association, something that continues today. Their union, in fact, was complete happenstance.

Davis was the son of a bank manager in Claremont, California. He grew up in the closest thing to a suburban lifestyle during the 1930s, as his family owned an orange and a lemon grove behind their house. Davis had wide-open spaces to roam with his twin brother Ralph, and the two played every kind of sport. But Glenn excelled in a way that was unparalleled by any other athlete ever to come out of Southern California at the time. At Bonita High School, Glenn played on two state championship high school teams, in football and baseball. A 5-foot-9, 170-pounder, he could run the 100-yard dash in 9.7 seconds, a world-class time on an unforgiving cinder track. In nine games of his senior high school football season, Davis averaged more than twenty six points per game.

In 1943, Glenn and Ralph considered attending Southern Cal together, but in choosing schools they figured that if they were going to be in the military, they might as well go in as officers. Army was their choice, in part because of the impeccable reputation of the West Point coach, Red Blaik, who impressed the twins' mother Ina during a personal visit to the Davis home.

Glenn and Ralph earned their admission to West Point on an appointment from California Congressman Jerry Voorhis, who would later lose his seat to Richard Nixon, a young lawyer building a name in the postwar years because of his fervent anti-communism stance.

In the late spring of August 1943, Ina Davis packed fried chicken for her sons, who left the station in San Bernardino for the four-day trip to New York. Ina Davis would not see her sons for a year, as freshman at West Point were not allowed to leave campus.

On arrival, Davis was required to take a physical that included a variety of fitness-measuring drills and exercises. There was a timed 300-yard run, a bar vault, the standing long jump, and the vertical jump. There was a rope climb, a softball throw, and a measure of how many chin-ups, sit-ups, and pull-ups one could do in a minute.

A perfect score, based on a weighted performance scale, was 1,000. No one in the history of West Point had exceeded 901 points and the average for all cadets was 550.

Davis's score was 962.5.

"I could do all those things," Davis said. "From the time I was a little boy, sports and athletics was my whole life. I ran and threw and jumped from morning to night and couldn't get enough of it."

But Davis concedes he was ill-prepared for the academic rigors of his freshman year at West Point. "I had five classes, and they were tough for just about anybody," Davis said. "I would get out of class, go practice football with the freshman team, come in late to the mess hall, and eat a big dinner. I'd get back to my room where I was supposed to study, but too often, I would fall asleep and suddenly wake up for the morning march without having really prepared for that day's classes."

He flunked mathematics that spring and was sent home, where he went to summer school, passed his math class, and qualified for readmission to the academy in the fall of 1944.

Glenn and Ralph were on the train heading east that summer when they noticed that a man seated near them appeared unusually interested in their discussions about the upcoming Army football team. Striking up a conversation, the Davises learned that the man was Clark Shaughnessy, the former football coach at Stanford now on his way to take over at the University of Pittsburgh.

Shaughnessy, who had coached Felix Anthony Blanchard Sr. at Tulane University in New Orleans in 1920, told the Davises that he had recently recommended a fine young fullback, the son of a former player of his, to Colonel Blaik. Shaughnessy explained that the player, a doctor's son, used to be called "Little Doc," until he grew to six feet and 210 pounds.

"Now they just call him Doc Blanchard," Shaughnessy said. "Remember the name."

Davis made a note of it. Several weeks later, he got a glimpse of "Little Doc."

"I don't remember anything about the first day, but pretty quickly I saw that he was more than anybody on our Army team could handle one-on-one," Davis said. "And we had some pretty feisty and proud players. But Doc was so strong and agile."

"He also played linebacker since we all played both ways. He just

creamed people. He might have been a better linebacker than running back, and he was a great, great running back."

Blanchard was born in South Carolina, where his father had started a medical practice. Little Doc learned football from Big Doc, who taught him to punt, placekick, and perform all the other rudiments of the game. When Little Doc was thirteen, he was sent to the St. Stanislaus prep school in Bay St. Louis, Mississippi, where just about everyone in the Blanchard clan, including Big Doc, had matriculated.

"When I started, I was a little thirteen-year-old scared to death out there on that football field," Blanchard said in a recent interview. With a booming voice full of both emotion and his southern upbringing, Blanchard added: "Then I grew to 200 pounds and was scaring them to death out there."

He chose to attend the University of North Carolina, partly because the head coach was his mother's cousin. But after his freshman season, he was drafted into the Army. On Coach Shaughnessy's suggestion, Colonel Blaik intervened in Blanchard's behalf, helping him get an appointment from his congressman for admission to West Point.

Blanchard and Davis quickly became the new starting tandem, and for the next three years, one was rarely mentioned without the other. Blaik encouraged that, refusing, for example, to let them be interviewed separately by reporters visiting West Point.

They may have been forever together, in practice and in lore, but they were not close friends. They were casual friends, Davis said—friendly but with decidedly different personalities.

Davis, careful not to fail again, was serious about his studies and his football. Pictures of him at West Point rarely show him smiling, unlike those taken years later when he had a Hollywood starlet on his arm. But during his playing career, he concedes he was something of a worrier.

At West Point, Blanchard was fun-loving and jovial with an easy smile. He was not a great student, but he was sure he would get by because he had already adapted to the military school/boarding school regimen at St. Stanislaus. At the first practice in 1944, Blaik asked Blanchard and Davis if they drank alcohol. Davis was mortified and said no. Blanchard replied: "Oh, sure."

On the field, however, they were the perfect complement to each

DAVIS

other. They were also far more multidimensional than their eternal nickname suggests. Blanchard had the speed to get outside and Davis knew how to pick his way through the pileup at the line of scrimmage.

And though they are always referred to as one entity, they could succeed quite well without one another. Army assistant coach Herman Hickman said of Blanchard that he is "the only man who runs his own interference."

Davis, at heart, was more of a deft, fleet runner. And why not? He could accelerate like few others anywhere in America in the mid-1940s. *Time* magazine wrote of Davis in 1945: "He has a special kind of speed that is all his own. After a brief show of hippiness, enough to get around the end, he simply leans forward and sprouts wings."[6]

The duo was also blessed to be coached by Blaik, one of the great football minds of the middle of the century, or in any recounting of college football history. An offensive genius, Blaik shaped a strong, gifted team around his two stars—fourteen All-Americans in their three varsity seasons—and a powerful line that opened gaping holes.

Blaik, like the former soldier he was, drilled his teams relentlessly and with precision. He had a regal carriage, dressed in fine clothes, and with the help of an admiring clan of New York sportswriters, whom Blaik assiduously courted, he was known nationwide as a sort of imperial wizard of West Point. Blaik used that pedigree to recruit one of the most talented assistant coaching staffs anywhere in the land. Blaik's assistants went on to become head coaches at more than three dozen major university football programs. Another assistant, Vince Lombardi, left to become the offensive coordinator for the New York Giants and then head coach of the dynastic Green Bay Packers.

What made Blaik and his coaches so good was their limitless devotion to preparation. Blaik always scheduled the first coaches' meeting of a new season on New Year's Day, so no other football program anywhere in the nation could say they started preparing for their season even a day earlier.

Blaik was also among the first college football coaches to begin filming practice. He and his coaches would congregate following the post-practice dinner to go over that day's practice films. They would also watch

[6]*Time Magazine*, November 16, 1946.

BLANCHARD

films of that week's opponent and prepare the plan for that week's game. Blaik, a stern, stoic son of a Presbyterian Scotsman from Dayton, Ohio, was obsessed with the notion that film preparation could avoid all surprises in a game.

Blaik craved control and he exhibited it in every way. He dressed the same for nearly every practice: Army hat, sweatshirt, pleated trousers, wool socks. None of his players ever heard him curse, no matter how unruly the team practiced.

"If somebody did something wrong, he would call the player over to the side, where he always stood," Davis said. "The assistants got close to things, he watched more from afar. He would never show anyone up, but he would in plain English tell you what you were doing wrong."

Said Blanchard: "Yeah, but you better do it right after the Old Man showed you how to do it. If you didn't, he'd bomb you—you would be out of there. He didn't waste his words for show. You learned or he cut you."

Blaik played football at Army during General MacArthur's term as West Point superintendent from 1919 to 1922, and grew familiar with MacArthur, who liked to attend practices standing alongside the coaches with a riding crop under his arm. The two developed a lasting relationship and corresponded with each other for decades thereafter.

It is MacArthur whose thoughts on sport and war are carved in stone near the West Point gymnasium:

UPON THE FIELD OF FRIENDLY STRIFE
ARE SOWN THE SEEDS THAT
UPON OTHER FIELDS, ON OTHER DAYS
WILL BEAR THE FRUITS OF VICTORY

Blaik had several football axioms, some clearly borrowed from MacArthur's writings and speeches. Among them was "There is a vast difference between a good sport and a good loser." But he was most fond of quoting MacArthur's motto: "There is no substitute for victory."

Many believe Blaik's frequent recitation of those six words was the genesis for Vince Lombardi's oft-quoted "Winning isn't everything, it's the only thing."

The 1945 Army football season began just days after MacArthur had accepted the unconditional surrender of a Japanese delegation aboard the USS *Missouri* in Tokyo Bay.

By season's end, Army had secured a second consecutive national championship and Blanchard had become the U.S. Military Academy's first Heisman Trophy winner.

In the fall of 1945, Army hosted Michigan and Notre Dame at Yankee Stadium. Both games were watched by more than 70,000 spectators. Michigan introduced a new concept to major college football: two-platoon football, separate offensive and defensive players.

Blanchard and Davis were too much, even for the rested. Michigan fell, 28–7.

Against Notre Dame, Davis scored three times, including a twenty-six-yard run on the game's third play. Blanchard added his own rushing touchdown and returned an interception for another score, the first of three defensive TDs he scored that season.

As was common throughout most of the 1945 and 1946 seasons, Blaik pulled Blanchard and Davis out of the game by the third quarter in what became a 48–0 victory over Notre Dame. Blaik did the same thing in a 61–0 rout of nationally ranked and once-beaten Penn the following week.

As well as Davis was playing, it was shaping up as Blanchard's year to shine. He averaged seven yards per rushing carry on the season, and though he caught just four passes, he averaged 41.5 yards per reception.

On the first weekend of December 1945, Army faced the undefeated and second-ranked Navy Midshipmen at Philadelphia's 102,000-seat Municipal Stadium, a low-slung bowl that was aging even then. President Harry Truman attended the game, the first chief executive to do so since Calvin Coolidge.

"You can't beat the feeling of running out before 100,000 people and the whole corps of cadets and the President of the United States, who was sitting next to my parents," Davis said. "It was a pretty big deal."

With Blanchard leading the way with his blocking, Davis scored two touchdowns. Blanchard intercepted a Navy pass and returned it forty-six yards for his team-leading nineteenth touchdown of the season. A 32–13 victory sealed Army's second national championship season. The Cadets had not lost a game in either season.

Several days later, a telegram to Blaik informed him that Felix "Doc"

BLANCHARD RECEIVING THE HEISMAN
IN 1945

Blanchard had won the 1945 Heisman. As he had in 1944 when Ohio State's Les Horvath won the trophy, Davis came in second.

"They took me down to New York, gave me the trophy in a little room off the entrance," Blanchard said. "I signed some autographs, did some interviews, posed for some pictures, and had something to eat. Then we came home. That was it. I had class the next day.

"I was excited but when I think of all the times people have talked to me about my Heisman, or come to my house just to see it or rub it like it's a genie or something, well, it makes me try to remember more about that day. But I'm too old now, I can't. It changed my life. I just didn't know it."

Football historians occasionally like to try to temper the accomplishments of Blanchard and Davis in 1944 and 1945 because so many other collegiate teams had rosters depleted by the war. But in 1946, scores of veterans, now grown, mature men toughened by the harshest circumstances of war, were returning to play the game with new might and fortitude. Army's football team, meanwhile, had actually lost most of its starters. But it is a measure of the resolve of Blanchard and particularly the versatility of Davis that Army did not lose a game in 1946 either.

In the season-opening game with Villanova, Blanchard sustained a serious knee injury, tearing his anterior cruciate ligament.

"Nowadays, you would have surgery and come back next year after a lot of rehabilitation," Blanchard said. "In my case, I missed two games, then sat out a lot in practice. They taped it and I did the best I could from then on. But I didn't think I was much good in 1946, to tell you the truth.

"Frankly, I was planning to win the Heisman again. I was going to be the first Archie Griffin. But not after that knee injury. It was Glenn's turn."

In fact, Blanchard came back as a very capable player. Blaik estimated that Blanchard was 60 percent of himself, adding that 60 percent of the old Doc was "still a heckuva player."

Davis became the focus of the offense, and he assumed the kicking duties from the injured Blanchard. Then, quarterback Arnold Tucker hurt his shoulder, and Davis took over the throwing assignments for any pass that figured to be more than fifteen yards.

Late in a tied game against a favored Michigan team, Davis, who had

BLANCHARD (35) AND DAVIS (41)
PREPARING TO LAUNCH A TRADEMARK
SWEEP

already rushed for 105 yards and completed six of seven passes, rifled a long pass to Blanchard down to the Michigan 7-yard line. Blanchard took over from there to score on another classic run, a blood-and-guts charge as he stomped into the end zone with a Wolverine defender along for the ride during the final three yards.

Two weeks later, on November 9, undefeated Notre Dame, ranked number two in the nation but outscored by 107–0 in its last two encounters with Blanchard and Davis, came to Yankee Stadium for yet another shot at number one Army.

Just a week earlier, the federal government had repealed war act order L85, which prohibited the making of or purchase of many luxury items, most specifically women's fashions, like stockings and dress shoes. The country was officially coming out from under its wartime blues. The most popular movie nationwide starred Myrna Loy who comforted a returning soldier (Fredric March) in *The Best Years of Our Lives*.

America was ready to get wildly excited about something frivolous, and in early November, it was the final meeting of the famed Blanchard and Davis and Notre Dame's once and future All-Americans: quarterback Johnny Lujack, end Leon Hart, and lineman George Connor.

Four Heisman Trophy winners would play in the game: Blanchard (1945), Davis (1946), Lujack (1947), and Hart (1949). Connor would win the Outland Trophy, given every year to the outstanding interior lineman.

What stirred the imagination most was the speculation that the great Blanchard and Davis would finally meet their equals in the powerhouse postwar players of Notre Dame's 1946 team. The Fighting Irish were still the most celebrated college football program in the land, and they were looking for revenge. Despite being ranked second, Notre Dame was favored and they had the overwhelming support of the 76,000 fans at Yankee Stadium, the ancestral reunion lodge of Notre Dame football's subway alumni.

Sportswriters more than a bit presumptuously billed it "The Game of the Century." It might have been a lesson in how too much hype can spoil a good matchup. Twenty years and two months before the first Super Bowl, Army and Notre Dame came into a game of high anticipation playing tentative, flat, conservative football. The players on both sides were a little jumpy, too, creating eleven turnovers.

Blanchard, fifty-seven years afterward, called it "the most boring game I ever played in."

Blaik and Notre Dame Coach Frank Leahy, two celebrated tacticians, overthought their strategies, with each waiting for the other to cut loose so they could counterpunch. Instead, both teams ran series after series of routine running plays. And since each team had skilled, two-way players, the defenses controlled the action.

"They treated it the same way we did—no one took any chances," Davis said. "Notre Dame did try to pass a little in the second half, but we intercepted two of their passes and that was that."

Blanchard is particularly perturbed that Army was not more aggressive. "Everybody was worrying about who was going to lose," he said. "That's no way to play a game."

The game was not without its moments of drama. In the second quarter, Notre Dame got to the Army 4-yard line but was stopped on a failed fourth down end around play. Army advanced inside the Irish's 30-yard line six times. Neither team tried a field goal, which was somewhat standard policy at the time in college football. Most powerful teams lived by a kind of spurn-the-kick machismo.

The single most memorable play of the game came late in the third quarter with Blanchard running free, about forty yards from the Notre Dame end zone. Lujack, Notre Dame's safety, waited in his path.

"Well, John did a good job," Blanchard said of Lujack. "He chased me toward the sideline, grabbed my legs, and held on for the tackle."

But Blanchard, with a cackle, has a final thought: "Before my knee injury, I wouldn't have been running toward the sideline. I would have just run him over."

The tie did not satisfy either squad but it added considerably to the legend of each of the teams. It is hard to find another pivotal, championship-quality meeting of top teams in any American sport that ended with a 0–0 score. It has a certain timelessness, as something that can no longer happen in any of the biggest games of our major sports now. Games of that import go to sudden death, or overtime, or several overtimes.

"Well, it's certainly the most talked-about game I played in," Davis said, "which is funny because I feel like I didn't do all that much."

Army went on to defeat Oklahoma and Penn, while Notre Dame also cruised through its schedule. Army's final game was again at a soldout

Philadelphia Municipal Stadium, where it was to meet a woeful Navy team that had been hit hard by graduation. Army was a three-touchdown favorite and took a 21–6 halftime lead.

"We were waiting for the game to end," Blanchard said. "We were sitting around relaxing."

In the locker room at intermission, Davis said there was talk of scoring fifty points, going out in a flurry of touchdowns. Unbeknownst to anyone, the great Blanchard–Davis tandem had already scored the last of its ninety-seven touchdowns.

In the second half, Navy stormed back, scoring two touchdowns to trail 21–18 (Navy had missed all three extra points). With the game winding down, the Navy offense surged across the field again, reaching the Army 3-yard line with ninety seconds remaining. On first down, Navy's run up the middle was stopped by a swarm of Army players. Blanchard stopped the second Navy running attempt for no gain. Navy, which was out of timeouts, tried to call one anyway and was assessed a five-yard penalty to the 8-yard line.

There was time for one more play.

Davis then did something he said he had never done before on a football field. He talked in the huddle.

"It just struck me that everything we had worked for in three years was about to go down the drain if we didn't stop them on this one play," Davis said. "I was excited and just blurted all that out in the huddle. I said: 'We've got to stop them or we've lost it all.'"

On the final play, Navy halfback Pete Williams took a pitch and sprinted for the corner of the end zone. He was tackled short of the goal line by several players, Blanchard included. Army's three-point victory meant the Blanchard–Davis era ended with a 27–0–1 record across three seasons.

"I looked up in the stands at my parents as I walked off the field," Davis said. "I smiled. A minute earlier, I was afraid I wasn't going to be able to look anyone in the eye."

But the wobbly victory came with a cost. Because Army had also lost to what was widely considered an inferior opponent, most of the final national polls ranked undefeated and once-tied Notre Dame ahead of undefeated and once-tied Army.

It did not stop Davis from winning the Heisman Trophy ten days later. Although he had not had his best season at Army, with just seven touch-

DAVIS, SECOND FROM RIGHT, ON THE
NIGHT OF THE CEREMONY

downs and 712 rushing yards, he had done a great many others things to keep his team unbeaten, including playing a dominating defensive safety and completing seventeen passes for 396 yards and four touchdowns. He was the obvious choice.

In addition, after three remarkable seasons, Davis was leaving college with a cache of records, including an average of 8.26 yards per rushing attempt, a record that stands to this day. He had scored fifty-nine touchdowns, run for 2,957 yards, thrown for 855 yards and run back two punts for touchdowns. And he had never lost a game.

"For one of us to win a second Heisman just seemed like the perfect ending to our football times," Davis said. "You know they called us the Touchdown Twins and now we each had a Heisman. I remember going to the theater to see a movie that winter at Christmastime and there I was in the Movietone News newsreel. It was in all the theaters. It was a pretty Cinderella-type story."

And then, from a football standpoint, just like that, it was over.

There was some talk of letting Blanchard and Davis free of their military commitments because they had plenty of professional football offers, but the War Department knew what kind of message that would send. Davis would soon be on his way to Korea, Blanchard to flight training in the Army Air Corps.

First, there was a month-and-a-half stint in Los Angeles to film *The Spirit of West Point*. The movie was hokey, but Blanchard had fun hanging out with the celebrities. Davis met his first starlets.

"After living in barracks for four years, spending forty-five days in a Los Angeles hotel was pretty good duty," Blanchard said. "I was self-conscious and not a very good actor, but I was enjoying myself."

During filming at UCLA's practice field one day, Davis was told to catch a punt and run upfield.

"I was there and Glenn's knee just collapsed for no apparent reason," Blanchard said. "He wasn't even doing anything."

Now the Touchdown Twins had twin ligament tears in their knees.

"That was the end of me," Davis said. "I never could cut on that knee again."

They finished the film and went their separate ways. Davis completed his three-year obligation, a pawn in a prickly Cold War standoff at the

DAVIS AND COACH RED BLAIK (CENTER)
WITH WILFRED WOOTRICH, THE
DOWNTOWN ATHLETIC CLUB PRESIDENT,
IN 1946

thirty-eighth parallel in Korea. Davis left before North Korean forces attacked to draw America into another war.

He played two seasons for the Los Angeles Rams, who lost in the NFL championship game in 1950, then won the title in 1951. A valuable contributor, Davis led the ream in rushing in 1950, but his knee grew worse in 1951 and he retired rather than endure what would have been experimental knee surgery.

With football officially behind him, he worked for more than thirty-five years in public relations and promotions for the *Los Angeles Times*.

But the most fascinating twist of Glenn Davis's post-football life came in 1995, when Davis, a widower at the time, attended a Heisman Family Night banquet in New York City. There, he met Yvonne Ameche, whose husband Alan, the 1954 Heisman Trophy winner, had died during heart surgery in 1988. The two fell in love and a year later, Glenn and Yvonne married.

The Heisman plot thickens. The Ameches had settled in the Philadelphia area where Alan and his Baltimore Colts teammate Gino Marchetti founded the fast-food chain Gino's in the early 1960s. One of their children, Cathy Ameche, married Michael Cappelletti, the brother of 1973 Heisman Trophy winner John Cappelletti.

"Around here," Davis's wife Yvonne likes to say. "If someone mentions the Heisman Trophy, you have to ask which one. Pretty amazing considering how few there have been."

Recently, when his high school named its football stadium for him, Davis donated his Heisman Trophy to the school. He admits that when someone calls and wants him to pose with his Heisman, he sometimes goes upstairs and gets Alan Ameche's Heisman as a substitute.

Blanchard never played pro football and only stepped on the gridiron twice after the 1946 Navy game for two exhibitions in 1947. "I was ready to get on with the rest of my life," he said. "The military was very good to me."

He became a pilot, the beginning of a military career that ended with his 1971 retirement as a brigadier general.

Active during the Korean War, Blanchard gained more fame for a crash landing he made while stationed in England in 1959. He was flying over the busy English village of Finchingfield when he noticed his oil pressure was low.

"Then, in an instant, there were these big red letters on the instrument panel, FIRE!" Blanchard recounted. "I looked in my rearview mirror and saw smoke and flames. According to procedures, I was supposed to ditch the plane, eject with a parachute. But I saw that village straight ahead; I would have sent a burning plane into a heavily populated area."

Blanchard decided to try to land at the air force base a few miles away.

"I guess it only took about five minutes to get there," Blanchard said. "But it felt like forever."

Roughly a decade later, as a bomber pilot over Vietnam and Thailand, Blanchard flew 113 missions in a year's duty.

When asked about the inherent danger of such an assignment, Doc Blanchard chuckled heartily.

"It's only dangerous if you mind people shooting at you," he said.

Didn't he mind people shooting at him?

"You're damn right I did," he answered. "It scared me every day I went up. They're all shooting at you. But really, you do find a way to get through it with your sanity intact.

"There is a connection to something like that and playing a sport. The more often you're under pressure, the better and better you get at handling it. You get nervous in games and learn to adjust and perform your job. You get terrified in war, but learn to perform your job. One is about finding the confidence to win, the other one is about finding the confidence to stay alive."

In one, it was suggested to Blanchard, you lead your team to victory. "In the other," Blanchard said, finishing the thought, "you keep your crew alive."

Following his retirement, Blanchard eventually settled in the Austin, Texas, area with his wife Jody, whom he met and married in 1948 while stationed in Texas.

When Jody died in 1993, he moved in with his daughter, Resa, in Bulverde, Texas.

"I don't get around as much," Blanchard said. "I watch my football on television."

He does converse regularly with Davis. One of their favorite topics: their mutual disgust over modern players celebrating their touchdowns with end zone histrionics.

"What's that they call it now?" Blanchard said. "The 'Me Generation.' Well, that's it. 'Look at me.'"

Said Davis: "I just hate it. I can only imagine the look on Colonel Blaik's face if we had done that."

Blanchard and Davis, two very different men still separated by distance and lifestyle, have had time to consider the lasting significance, culturally or historically, of their contributions, the era they played in, and their association, which will be eternal.

"I guess it was just meant to be," Davis said. "Maybe the nation needed heroes. Surely, I don't think of myself as a hero, but maybe we made people feel better at just the right time."

Blanchard, a man of few hidden emotions, almost growls when asked to respond to a question about his legacy.

"Look, I don't know," he said. "Come on, it's so long ago. They were rough times in America. We were just playing football and going to school. But we were not just in any school. We were in the country's military academy. And we were going to represent it properly."

Three weeks after Blanchard and Davis's final football game at Army, Frank Capra's *It's a Wonderful Life* opened, starring Donna Reed and Jimmy Stewart. On December 31, 1946, sixteen months after Japan's surrender, President Truman, as a New Year's Eve gift to the nation, formally announced the end of World War II.

The country was moving on.

"I've been running into people all my life who tell me about something I did that they remember," Blanchard said, unable to let go of the question of his and Davis's legacy without a final thought. "I don't even remember these things in these games. It's amazing to me.

"But they'll say, 'I was stationed in Guam, or New Guinea, or France listening to you and Glenn do this or that.' Or they'll say, 'Oh, I remember going to the movie house with my mother. Oh, we watched you in those newsreels.'

"And they all have these big smiles. It definitely means something. Look, I don't live in the past much. I was just a football player. But I've seen it in those faces. I have. People just kind of look at you like you did something special for them."

The Melting Pot Dynasty

ROCKNE'S LEGACY AND LEAHY'S LADS: ANGELO BERTELLI, 1946; JOHN LUJACK, 1947; LEON HART, 1949; AND JOHN LATTNER, 1953

Frank Leahy's parents emigrated to America from Ireland's County Westmeath in the last days of the nineteenth century, arriving at Ellis Island in New York harbor just a few hundred yards from the buildings and bustle of lower Manhattan. Visible from the red brick edifice of Ellis Island, across the grand New York port, was the West Side city block that would, roughly twenty-five years later, house the Downtown Athletic Club.

New York in the late 1800s, enveloped by the hum of boat engines and the buzz of electric powered trolleys, lured hundreds of thousands of Irish to its shores, where many would stay. But the Leahys would not be among them. The Leahys were from the very heart of Ireland, a Spartan place of

COACH FRANK LEAHY WITH ANGELO BERTELLI, WINNER OF THE HEISMAN IN 1943 flat land, peat bogs, and waterways. Other County Westmeath émigrés in decades past had quickly headed west, looking for land that reminded them of home. As early as 1859, these Irish families had settled in what is now southeastern South Dakota, next to the Missouri River and rich farmlands that extended into what was then the Nebraska Territory. The Leahys, cleared by authorities and dispatched from Ellis Island, journeyed westward as well. Shortly after 1908, when their son Frank was born, they linked with dozens of other Irish immigrants in South Dakota, moving to an aptly named town in the south-central part of the state: Winner.

Frank was a multisport star in high school at Winner, where his coach was Earl Walsh, a former lineman for Coach Knute Rockne at the University of Notre Dame. Leahy was also a successful amateur boxer, a skill he learned from his father, a foreman in the rough-and-tumble world of railroad freight handling. Through Walsh, news of Leahy's athletic exploits reached Rockne, who saw something of himself in the young Leahy. A Norwegian immigrant, Rockne had been raised in a predominantly Irish neighborhood in Chicago, where he, too, had been an amateur boxer. Rockne liked fighters.

Rockne frequently traveled far and wide for feisty players, attracting 300 a year to Notre Dame. He left no recruiting outpost untapped, venturing from the rural upper Midwest to the Southeast, to the crowded urban areas of Chicago, New York, Boston, and Philadelphia.

In the pursuit of football talent, Rockne, in a very symbolic way, was establishing a pipeline foundation for a new kind of American university. Rockne's winning football teams at Notre Dame, with players named O'Donnell, Kieran, Cardideo, and Niezgodski, epitomized the majestic dreams of first-generation Americans of European descent across the land, especially those who were Roman Catholic. Notre Dame's football successes fostered the notion that there was a place, a college, for these Americans, too. Who can doubt that "The Fighting Irish" moniker, at least figuratively, was born as a decades-after-the-fact response to a common nineteenth-century sign in urban America: "No Irish Need Apply"?

In this way, Notre Dame became a powerful icon in American culture. Even today, millions of American sports fans root for Notre Dame football even though they did not attend the school; indeed, the vast majority have never stepped foot on the campus. They cheer for what was once an obscure college in a barren Indiana town because their parents did or their grandparents did. And what Notre Dame represented to these people, in its games against the established, well-heeled college football powers of the early and middle part of the twentieth century, was hope for a burgeoning immigrant population. If this unheard-of school could succeed against the best college football teams in the land, why then, couldn't any newcomer to the country make his mark, too?

This is what Rockne preached to the parents of athletic children across the land—the concept of a university meant for their benefit. It was not the university of old money, certainly not an Ivy League school and not a large state university of the farm belt, the South, or the Great Lakes. It was a school for the next emerging power in America—the sons of America's immigrants. It was also a school with theological principles, a school modeled after the great European learning institutions.

This is what Rockne provided to an America he knew and well understood, along with a remarkable football mind, the tenacious spirit of an amateur boxer, and the promotional skill of a carnival barker. From the beginning, Rockne and later his disciple Frank Leahy created the emblematic Notre Dame football program.

Rockne teams won 105 games and lost just twelve over the course of thirteen seasons. He had five undefeated teams and coached three national champions. Leahy had six undefeated teams and five national champions in eleven seasons at Notre Dame.

Rockne first came to Notre Dame in 1910 when the campus had just five student halls. A small, 145-pound end, in three years' time he would nonetheless be witness to, and play a pivotal role in, Notre Dame's unforeseen gallop to national prominence. In 1913, Notre Dame coach Jesse Harper, almost on a lark, wrote a letter to West Point officials asking for a game. Army, a power of the day, indeed had an opening on its 1913 schedule because Yale had backed out of a scheduled meeting. Knowing little about Notre Dame and expecting an easy game, Army struck a deal and agreed to pay the Fighting Irish $1,000 to come eastward.

And so, in late October, eighteen players from the little-known tank town of South Bend, Indiana, gathered several dozen bag lunches of sandwiches and fruit prepared by the kitchen ladies at Notre Dame's refectory and began a two-day train trip to Army's garrison campus on the Hudson River.

Few in New York knew much about Notre Dame. The *New York Times* wrote that the university was based in South Bend, Illinois, not Indiana. But Coach Harper knew something Army did not. His quarterback Gus Dorais and his diminutive end Rockne had spent the previous summer as life-guards at Cedar Point, Ohio, on Lake Erie. Harper had given them a foot-ball, and the two players had spent hours perfecting a new art: passing the football.

While the forward pass had been legal since 1906, few teams em-ployed it, and when they did, their quarterbacks would almost always throw the football underhand. But Dorais, a talented baseball player, de-cided to throw the ball overhand like a pitcher. He discovered that he could fire the football accurately and as far as forty yards if he needed to, and Rockne discovered he could run under it and catch it. Entering their senior seasons, over time the two developed a symbiotic relationship based on this new skill.

On November 1, 1913, when Notre Dame sprung its surprise offense on the West Point Cadets, the home side had no defense for it. The New York newspapers the following day described Notre Dame's "wide open" and "newfangled" offense, which included seventeen forward passes (thir-teen of them completed) for a shocking 243 passing yards. Notre Dame stunned the college football world with a 35–13 victory. A legend was born.

That legend was solidified fifteen years later, again against Army, and this time Rockne was the Notre Dame coach. Among the players awaiting Rockne at intermission of a sold-out game at Yankee Stadium was lineman Frank Leahy. The score of the game was 0–0.

In 1920, George Gipp, an enigmatic but wildly popular star for Notre Dame football, had died suddenly of a virulent chest infection. Roughly two weeks before his death, Gipp, Notre Dame's first player to make Wal-ter Camp's All-America first team, had led a victory over Northwestern. Within days of that game, Gipp was bedridden. He died at South Bend's St. Joseph Hospital. Notre Dame lore had it that Rockne was at Gipp's side.

So in December 1928, Leahy sat with his teammates inside a locker room beneath the teeming grandstands of Yankee Stadium as Rockne asked for quiet and began to speak in a slow, measured voice.

Rockne, with tears welling in his eyes, described the scene in Gipp's hospital room and added: "Before he died, Gipp said to me: 'I've got to go, Rock. It's all right. I'm not afraid. Sometime, when things are going wrong, when the breaks are beating the boys, tell them to go out and win one for the Gipper. I don't know where I'll be then, Rock. But I'll know about it and I'll be happy.'"

With that, Rockne turned and walked out of the room. There was a moment of quiet, and then Leahy and the rest of the players—wiping their eyes—stormed from the room.

Notre Dame won the game, 12–6. After scoring the decisive touchdown, running back Jack Chevigny stood in the end zone and shouted: "That's one for the Gipper."

It was scenes and feats like these that shaped Leahy's coaching pedigree. In his career, Leahy never matched the melodramatic oratory of Rockne, who died in a small plane crash in 1931, but he did not have to. Leahy won games with ceaseless preparation molded from the technical genius of his mentor. When Leahy's Notre Dame playing career was cut short with a severe knee injury in 1930, he became an assistant coach, and later that year, as Rockne recovered from a bout of phlebitis at the Mayo Clinic in Minnesota, it was Leahy who accompanied him. The two men spent three days talking over the fine points of offensive and defensive football, turning a hospital room into a football laboratory.

Leahy's career coaching statistics nearly matched his mentor, and he coached four Heisman Trophy winners: Angelo Bertelli, John Lujack, Leon Hart, and John Lattner.

Moreover, Leahy extended the cultural pipeline fashioned by Rockne, making Notre Dame the college of choice for thousands of urban, ethnic athletes and non-athletes who viewed attending Notre Dame as a seminal moment for the upwardly mobile in a melting pot society.

Leahy's first coaching job after he left Notre Dame in 1932 was at Georgetown University in Washington, D.C. Then he went to Fordham University in New York City, where he served as the line coach of the famous Fordham "Seven Blocks of Granite," a group of linemen that included a future coach of some note, Vince Lombardi.

Leahy then coached several successful teams at Boston College before returning to Notre Dame as head coach in 1941. For the next fourteen seasons, Leahy used his ties not only in the traditional Notre Dame Midwestern outposts like Chicago and St. Louis to lure football talent to South Bend; he also worked the network of football coaches he established during his time in Washington, New York, and Boston. And he could do it as one who understood the inherent contract between Notre Dame and its

following because he was a part and a by-product of it. He was the immigrant's son who flocked to Notre Dame, who was made better for it and who considered himself a living model of a Notre Dame education.

Those who came to play for him were known as Leahy's Lads, which also became the title of a landmark 1994 book written one of Leahy's players, Jack Connor. It is a reference to a Leahy predilection for calling his players "lads," but it might as well have described the ongoing relationship of an institution and its constituency.

As Rockne had before him, Leahy quickly revolutionized Notre Dame's approach to the game, installing the T formation, an innovation he had studied at a coaching clinic. It made the most of the fleet and versatile players Leahy had been ferreting out of dynamic and fiercely competitive city neighborhoods nationwide. In 1943, behind Leahy's hybrid of the T formation, Notre Dame soon won its first national championship since the Rockne era, and Bertelli also became the first Notre Dame player to win the Heisman Trophy.

Bertelli, who started the first six games of the 1943 season, was a skilled passer for a Notre Dame team that outscored its opponents 261–31. He had been raised near the central Massachusetts city of Springfield, situated on the Connecticut River, a haven for the arms factories that were fueling the American war drive on two fronts. It was a sign of the times, an acknowledgment of his surroundings and a tribute to Bertelli's throwing arm, that he was nicknamed "The Springfield Rifle." Bertelli was not a pure runner in the mold of many prewar, single wingbacks. As one writer said critically of Bertelli: "All he can do is pass." To which Boston sportswriter Bill Egan wrote back, "And all Rembrandt could do was paint."

Bertelli was a new and dangerous kind of weapon in Leahy's multifaceted T formation. In the six games he played in 1943, he completed seventy-two passes for ten touchdowns—this in an era when teams sent no more than two ends out to receive potential passes.

On defense, Bertelli was cagey and not to be underestimated. He set a Notre Dame record as a safety with eight interceptions in one season, and

NOTRE DAME'S HEISMAN WINNERS: LUJACK (FAR LEFT), BERTELLI (SECOND FROM LEFT), HART (THIRD FROM LEFT), BROWN (FIFTH FROM RIGHT), PAUL HORNUNG (THIRD FROM RIGHT), HUARTE (SECOND FROM RIGHT), LATTNER (FAR RIGHT)

on the eve of the 1943 season, it was Bertelli's overall abilities that convinced Leahy to switch to the revolutionary T formation. "Accurate Angelo," as he also came to be known, made the transition work.

Notre Dame won each of the six games Bertelli started in 1943, the last a 33–6 upset of third-ranked Navy before 77,900 fans in Cleveland's Municipal Stadium. The day after that victory, Allied forces in Italy were halted by a large German force occupying a Benedictine monastery in the town of Monte Cassino. The same day, Bertelli was called to service in the U.S. Marines.

The tide of war had turned in favor of the Allies, but President Roosevelt called for more troops in Europe to aid an invasion soon to be launched behind German lines at the Italian town of Anzio. More men were needed in the Pacific Theater as well, where General Douglas MacArthur was set to begin his drive from Australia to the Philippines.

In this climate, Bertelli's call to active duty, hours after a stirring football triumph, spawned no public controversy. In the newspapers of the day, there was not the slightest inference that the star quarterback of undefeated Notre Dame might have been allowed to finish the college football season. The newspapers were too full of the details of thousands of conscription notices and expanded obituary pages, which often spanned two broad sheets in the large metropolitan dailies. The extra space was needed to record the dire details of fatal battlefield news: a numbing drumbeat of tragic score-keeping.

When called, Angelo Bertelli reported to the Marine Corps Recruit Depot at Parris Island off the coast of South Carolina, as ordered. Lujack finished out the final four games as Notre Dame concluded its season with a 9–1 record. In December, while in his barracks at Parris Island, Bertelli learned via telegram that he had won the Heisman Trophy. For the first time, however, the ceremony was delayed until January 12, 1944, because that was the first weekend that Private Bertelli could get a two-day leave to travel to New York. He accepted the Heisman Trophy in his Marine uniform in a ceremony emceed by sportswriter Grantland Rice and broadcast on Bill Stern's national radio program.

Bertelli did not get to display his football trophy for long. Thirty-four days after he received his Heisman, American bombers ended the standoff at the Italian monastery fortress in Monte Cassino, leveling buildings that had stood for more than 1,400 years in a four-hour raid. Six days later 2,000 American planes obliterated the bulk of the German aircraft factories, and afterward, the Allies turned a determined eye toward Japan's stubborn island defense. Among the thousands of troops dispatched to the Pacific was a recent graduate of officer training, Marine Lieutenant Bertelli.

Bertelli saw action at Guam and Iwo Jima, where as a lieutenant in the 21st Marines, he was one of the 70,000 American soldiers caught in a slaughterhouse of a conflict spread across an island of volcanic rock. Bertelli was on Iwo Jima for seventeen days, assuming command of three rifle platoons as other officers—some of the 25,000 Americans casualties on Iwo Jima—were killed or wounded. Bertelli was wounded, too, receiving the Purple Heart and Bronze Star for his valor. He twice narrowly escaped death as his platoon attacked well-fortified Japanese hillside bunkers, and his wartime exploits made headlines back home where news of a Notre Dame All-American risking his life had a certain resonance. Sadly, so did the story of Jack Chevigny, the dramatic Notre Dame star of the 1928 "Win One for the Gipper" victory over Army. Chevigny died in the Marine invasion of Iwo Jima on February 19, 1945.

After the war, now recovered from the mortar shrapnel that tore apart his left shoulder, Bertelli played professional football briefly, though he was hardly the same player. A 165-pound quarterback needed speed and quick reflexes, attributes diminished by the ground fighting at Iwo Jima. Bertelli, Leahy's handpicked first T formation quarterback, retired from the game in the late 1940s, settling in New Jersey where he eventually owned a chain of liquor stores (with Frank Tripucka, another Notre Dame quarterback of the 1940s).

Bertelli was famed in New Jersey for his zeal in promoting local athletics, speaking at hundreds of functions and sponsoring a myriad of amateur teams. He was also a fixture at Notre Dame football activities for nearly fifty years. In 1991, a veteran group of Iwo Jima survivors honored Bertelli in a ceremony at Parris Island. Bertelli brought the Heisman Trophy he won in 1943, a full-circle moment as the award came to the place where, as a young man facing an uncertain future, he had first learned of his selection into the Heisman fraternity. On this day in 1991, an honor platoon of

BERTELLI

young Marines saluted Bertelli as his wartime record was read. Bertelli was handed a leather-bound commendation and a replica of another iconic sculpture, the Iwo Jima Memorial monument. And with tears in his eyes, Bertelli stood at attention as the Parris Island band played the Marine Hymn followed by the Notre Dame Victory March.

Bertelli died in 1999 at the age of seventy-eight.

"Angelo Bertelli represented the university with class and distinction on hundreds of occasions," the Reverend E. William Beauchamp, Notre Dame's executive vice president, said at the time of Bertelli's death. "When you talk about the history and tradition of Notre Dame football, one of the central figures always has been Angelo Bertelli."

Bertelli represented Notre Dame's connection with Italian-Americans in New England; similarly, Johnny Lujack represented the school's relationship with the Polish and German families in western Pennsylvania. Notre Dame's football success and growing academic reputation were attracting unprecedented numbers of lower- and middle-income students, and the allure was not confined to Catholics. Just as Rockne had been before him, Leahy was often teased by his coaching brethren for the decidedly non-Catholic names on his roster of Fighting Irish, names like Schwartz and Mergenthal.

The best athlete in little Connelsville, Pennsylvania, in the early 1940s, Lujack starred in several sports. Local officials lobbied their congressional delegates to get Lujack an appointment to West Point, which Lujack considered an honor. But he also informed everyone in Connelsville that it had been his dream since he was a boy to play football for Notre Dame. By then, Notre Dame had built a far-reaching radio network. Johnny Lujack was another impressionable adolescent smitten with the Notre Dame aura.

"A lot of people in town called my Dad to tell him what a terrible mistake I was making turning down West Point," Lujack says now. "But my Dad trusted me with athletics and what it might be able to do for me in the long run."

In 1943, at the age of eighteen, Lujack became the youngest player to have called signals as the quarterback at Notre Dame. Before the 1944 season, he, too, was off to war, spending three years patrolling the English Chan-

JOHN LUJACK

nel in a navy sub-chasing vessel. (He later joked that the blast of exploding depth charges deafened his ears to the jeers and boos of opposing fans in away football games after the war.)

In 1946, when Lujack returned to the Notre Dame campus, he was one of a record two and one-half million students enrolled in American colleges. Nearly half of those students were ex-veterans taking advantage of the GI bill.

Notre Dame's team was especially stocked with ex-soldiers who had the talent and brawn for college football. As with everything else that happened under the watch of Frank Leahy, that was no accident. Leahy's wartime job was to organize recreational and athletic activities for servicemen stationed in the Pacific Theater. Leahy used this assignment to survey, assess, and recruit future players. He set up shop at Pearl Harbor in 1945 and cataloged the addresses of his recruits. Over time, Leahy talked a host of large, agile, and fit young men into making Notre Dame their next stop in postwar America. These were not the teenagers he had been bringing to Notre Dame before the war, but men in their early twenties, physically mature and mentally tough athletes hardened by combat.

In 1946, they arrived in droves at South Bend, full of so much talent that several players who were not starters later went on to have lengthy professional football careers. Forty-three players from Leahy's 1946 and 1947 teams eventually played in the pros, at a time when there were only eighteen professional teams in two leagues, the National Football League and the All-America Football Conference.

Lujack was the top quarterback in part because of his versatility. He would become just the third athlete at Notre Dame to win varsity letters (at Notre Dame they are called monograms) in four different sports in one year: football, baseball, track, and basketball. Lujack would play in a baseball game and then run over to compete in a track meet, leaping over the high-jump bar still wearing his baseball pants. Later in the same week, he would be at spring football practice.

"In those postwar years, many of us were just happy to be back and not be injured from the war," Lujack says. "I reveled in everything about being at Notre Dame. It was a very happy time in America."

War had changed the nation, somehow draining it and revitalizing it at once. In 1946 and 1947, with great haste and a newfound appreciation of life's graces, the world was moving on. At the Bell Laboratories in the United States, the transistor was invented and perfected, a key step in bringing the typical American living room alive with television. Horizons were expanding in all directions. Recently married couples were spawning the Baby Boom and Dr. Spock wrote his first book, *Baby and Child Care.*

The years 1946 and 1947 were also a great time to be a football player at Notre Dame, a period when the Fighting Irish never lost. The 1946 team did tie Army 0–0 and the pivotal sequence of the game matched the 1945 Heisman Trophy winner, Army's Doc Blanchard, against Lujack, who went on to win the 1947 Heisman. The 230-pound Blanchard broke free on a run off the left tackle and sprinted toward the Notre Dame end zone with only the 190-pound Lujack, a defensive back, in his way.

But Lujack chased Blanchard to the sideline, threw himself at Blanchard's legs and held on, wrapping his arms around Blanchard's ankles as Leahy watched from a few feet away. "At the time, I thought of it as a routine tackle," Lujack says. "But since everyone says it saved the game, and since I've been hearing about it for almost sixty years now, I guess it was a pretty big tackle."

It is, indisputably, one of the most famed clutch tackles in college football history. The 1946 game between undefeated Notre Dame, national champions three years earlier, and Army, undefeated for three seasons and national champions in 1944 and 1945, was surely the most hyped and anticipated game of any that preceded it in college football history. More than 76,000 fans filled Yankee Stadium, with tickets going for $200 a seat, an astounding sum in 1946 America when many laborers were making $1 an hour.

Army had routed Notre Dame in the two previous seasons, but when No. 1 Army took the field at Yankee Stadium that day they were surprised to find that Notre Dame's subway alumni had filled a vast majority of the seats.

"We were only just up the Hudson River at West Point and we thought we should be the home team," says Army's Glenn Davis, recalling the game. "But all we had was about 2,000 voices in the Corps of Cadets. The rest of the fans were letting us have it."

Participants on both sides of the ball agree that Leahy and Army Coach Red Blaik played the game conservatively. Both teams had chances to kick field goals, but neither attempted one. Of Leahy's choice to eschew the field goal, Lujack said: "It would have been an admission of defeat for Leahy and he would never do that."

As good as the 1946 Notre Dame team was, most consider the 1947 team superior and some say the 1947 squad was the most dominant team ever. The toughest test the Notre Dame starters may have faced that season were the Notre Dame reserves in practice. The 1947 Fighting Irish blitzed through nine opponents unbeaten and untied—the first Notre Dame team to have an unblemished record since Rockne's last team, in 1930.

The 1947 Irish never trailed for a single second in its nine-game season, all easy victories. Notre Dame, on average, outscored opponents 32–6. Lujack completed 61 of 109 passes for 791 yards and nine touchdowns. He averaged 11.6 yards each time he ran the football and continued to excel in the defensive secondary. At the end of the season, in the visiting locker room at the Los Angeles Coliseum, minutes after Notre Dame had crushed third-ranked Southern California 38–7, Lujack was informed he had won the Heisman Trophy.

He was stunned that the Downtown Athletic Club was going to pay his way to fly across the country to New York and stupefied to see his parents and oldest brother waiting for him outside the club's ornate West Street entrance when he arrived. Lujack's father had seen just one of his college games.

"It was great that we got to celebrate together," Lujack said. "We saw all of New York in that trip."

It was a different New York than any previous Heisman Trophy winner had experienced. That year, the last streetcar trolley in the city made its last pass up Broadway. At the end of World War I, 25,000 miles of trolley tracks had criss-crossed U.S. cities, and retail shops fought to claim locations nearest the tracks. A few years after the surrenders that ended World War II, trolleys were phased out in most cities, the better to make room for passing automobiles. Being near available parking, or better yet, highway exits, would soon be the target for retail businesses.

Lujack, a man of the times, at least subconsciously absorbed this lesson. After four successful seasons for the Chicago Bears—he made the Pro Bowl three times—and after two seasons coaching under Leahy, John Lujack opened an automobile dealership in Davenport, Iowa, which became a local institution until he sold it to his son-in-law in 1988.

Lujack credited Leahy with teaching him how to succeed in any endeavor. "He was a magnificent leader," Lujack said. "Quiet and dignified but effective, and everyone who played for him loved him. Although he could be a tough son of a gun, I never in my life met anyone just like him again."

The stories of Leahy's peculiarities abound from the lips of those who played for him. Nearly every Notre Dame player of the Leahy's Lads era could do an impression of the fabled coach, including the affected, almost prissy speaking manner. Proper and regal, Leahy had their respect, but they all knew they were bearing witness to an odd genius. It seemed that every Notre Dame player or assistant coach had at least one notable, idiosyncratic exchange with the great coach that they spent the rest of their life retelling.

Ed "Moose" Krause was a coach for Leahy and later became Notre Dame's longtime athletic director. In 1980, he told Dave Anderson of the *New York Times* of a Leahy-led practice in 1947:

> "Lujack had cursed one of his halfbacks, Bob Livingston, for missing a block," Krause told Anderson. "And Leahy heard him. He stopped practice and chewed out Lujack for using profanity as only Leahy could, saying, 'You might well remember, Mister Lujack, that when I recruited you, I promised your parents that you would have a splendid Catholic upbringing.' Lujack hung his head. On the next play, Livingston missed another block. Lujack didn't say a word, but Leahy turned toward the bench and said, 'Gentlemen, I fear that Mister Lujack is right about Mister Livingston.'"[7]

Frank Tripucka was Lujack's understudy at quarterback and took over in 1948. In one game that year, Tripucka called a fourth-down run during a pivotal stretch of a game. As Tripucka, who like Lujack was also the team's punter, approached the center standing close at the line of scrimmage, Leahy realized Tripucka was going to run a play and not punt the football.

"Oh, no," Leahy said loud enough for Tripucka to hear. "Francis, no."

As Tripucka told the story for years thereafter, he ran the play he called anyway, which resulted in a fumble. When Tripucka reached the sideline, Leahy did not scream, rant, or rave. "That was never his way," Tripucka said. "It was always more like talking to God."

[7]*New York Times*, December 30, 1980.

Leahy nevertheless had a missive to deliver.

"You hate me," Leahy said, pausing for effect.

Then he said: "You hate your teammates."

Finally, after a longer pause, he added: "You hate the Lady on the Dome."

Leahy walked away. Tripucka went to the bench, where he remained for the rest of the game.

No one, it seemed, escaped Leahy's singular motivational methods and odd verbal directives. A star of the 1948 and 1949 teams was mammoth end Leon Hart. The 1948 team went undefeated with one tie, which left them ranked second nationally to Michigan. Entering the 1949 season, Hart had already been hailed as one of the biggest, most effective two-way ends in college football history. He was a popular, highly publicized leader and had been a regular contributor at Notre Dame since he was a freshman. He had never played in a game that ended in defeat, but even Hart did not escape the mercurial teaching technique of Coach Leahy.

Hart would tell this story for years:

At the end of a difficult practice one day in 1949, Leahy approached Hart and asked him how he felt.

"Tough practice, Coach," Hart answered. "I'm a little tired."

"Oh, Leon, you must not be in proper shape, take ten laps around the field," Leahy said.

At the end of the next practice, Leahy waited for Hart again.

"Leon, how do you feel?

Hart hoped to outsmart his coach and responded by saying: "I feel great, Coach."

"If you feel so good, Leon," Leahy said, "you must not have had a strong enough workout. Take ten laps."

On the third day, Leahy again found Hart on the walk off the practice field.

"Leon, how do you feel?"

Said Hart: "How do you want me to feel, Coach?"

And even Leahy let down, giving Hart the rest of the day off.

Hart became one of Leahy's favorites, and his third Heisman Trophy winner. Moreover, Hart was only the second lineman to win the

LEON HART

award. Yale's Larry Kelley won in 1936. No lineman has won the award since.

Hart was technically an end but in the 1940s that hardly meant what it does now. At 6-foot-5 and 265 pounds, Hart was an intimidating presence. He was first and foremost a devastating blocker and punishing tackler on defense. He did run frequent end-around plays and lined up at fullback where he could block and carry the football as well. Opponents thought the best strategy might be to try to fake him out of position, but the big end, who would earn an engineering degree from Notre Dame, was not easily fooled.

Hart, who also hailed from western Pennsylvania, was an athletic phenomenon in 1949, when he was voted the Associated Press's male athlete of the year, no small feat when the second-and third-place finishers were Jackie Robinson and golfer Sam Snead.

By the end of the 1949 season, the whole country knew that Hart had played in thirty-seven successive games at Notre Dame without a loss. It heightened the tension on the eve of the season finale as the Fighting Irish traveled to Dallas to face Southern Methodist University. SMU's 1948 Heisman Trophy winner Doak Walker was injured and out of the game, but his replacement, Kyle Rote, scored three touchdowns and the game was tied 20–20 in the fourth period.

Notre Dame regained the lead with the help of several up-the-middle charges by Hart at fullback, but Rote, who would have a lengthy professional career with the New York Giants, led SMU back to the Notre Dame 5-yard line with just seconds to play. On the next play, Hart leveled Rote on a sweep to the left, knocking Rote from the game. SMU did not score, Notre Dame won 27–20, and Notre Dame had its fourth successive undefeated season.

Hart was announced as the Heisman Trophy winner a week later. Hart would play eight seasons for the NFL's Detroit Lions, helping the team to three NFL titles while winning All-Pro honors on offense and defense. He established a series of successful businesses in Michigan.

"There were not many of us who played for Leahy who did not take a certain work ethic to everything we did after we left him and Notre Dame," Hart said in an interview months before his death in 2003 at the age of seventy-three. "The man worked us in three-a-day practices, but we all knew he went back to his office after those workouts and worked himself for another few hours, trying to make sure we were prepared.

"It wasn't just the physical part. He drilled our minds to react superbly. He was a football coach, but like they said, he was really a teacher of men."

Leahy's teams worked year-round, taking only the Catholic holidays off. This was years before the National Collegiate Athletic Association set restrictions on the number and length of off-season practice schedules. Leahy devised his own regimen and drilled his players, even in the summer. He did hold some formal practices, but often he got players jobs working on painting or construction projects at Notre Dame's football stadium. And if that made it easier for those players to run stadium steps twice or three times a day, or to throw the football around, well, then, lads will be lads.

John Lattner, the last of Leahy's Lads to win the Heisman Trophy, was a bit more of a free spirit than some of the others who preceded him at Notre Dame. This came, no doubt, from his mother, Mae, the kind of Irish woman who adored Frank Leahy. Mae Lattner knew how to have a good time and may have contributed the most prized story of a pre-Heisman ceremony outing in New York when her son won in 1953.

"Well, my father died in my freshman year at Notre Dame and never really got to see me play but I took my mother with me to New York for the Heisman ceremony," Lattner recounted in 2003. "And the night before the award ceremonies I asked my mom what she wanted to see in the city. The Downtown Athletic Club provided a limo and we went and saw the Queen Mary, which was in port on the West Side. And we went to dinner at Mama Leone's. And then we went to Toots Shor's bar and another bar. And I know we went to the Stork Club, too. My mom liked martinis and she was a pretty good drinker.

"So at around 2:00 A.M., now we're at the Copacabana and Ray Tierney, the Downtown Athletic Club member who was showing us around says to me, 'John, you know, we're going to have a full day tomorrow with press conferences and the big awards ceremony.' He was saying we might want to get to bed. So I said I would talk to my mom.

"I told Mom that Mr. Tierney said tomorrow might be a rough day and all that. And my mom says: 'All right, John. I understand. Get me a Miller High Life instead.'"

Lattner played on Leahy's last team, which won every game except for a controversial tie at Iowa. Still, the Irish were named the national champions by a majority of the polls of the day.

JOHN LATTNER

Like most of Leahy's backs, Lattner was versatile. He was a slashing runner who also caught passes, returned punts and kickoffs, and played cornerback where his timing and ability to intercept passes preserved several Notre Dame victories.

Leahy was not always sold on Lattner, who as a junior committed a key fumble in a close game. In response, Leahy had a football taped to Lattner's arm and ordered that the football stay there. Lattner slept with it, studied with it, and ate with it taped to his arm until the next game.

"It was just Coach's way," Lattner said. "I didn't complain."

By the 1950s, with air travel and increasing electronic media attention broadening the national scope of most of the major college football powers, Notre Dame was at the forefront of teams playing a coast-to-coast schedule. Lattner, as Notre Dame's star two-way back, was at the center of two memorable, crucial games.

In 1952, Oklahoma, which was on its way to building a football dynasty under Coach Bud Wilkinson, played Notre Dame for the first time in South Bend. Lattner intercepted a third-quarter pass and recovered a fourth-quarter fumble by the 1952 Heisman Trophy winner, Billy Vessels, and the Irish won in an upset, 27–21.

The Irish came into the following year's rematch ranked number one in the country. But since the game was in Norman, Oklahoma, where the Sooners rarely lost, Oklahoma was considered the favorite. Leahy and Wilkinson were friends, devoted disciples of the nuances and advantages of the T formation, but Leahy also knew that Wilkinson, who had a big and imposing team, believed they should have won the year before in South Bend.

"Coach Leahy was a master at psyching the other teams out," Lattner said. "So first of all, he spent the entire week telling the press that we would be lucky to score a point against Oklahoma. Then, he sent us out for pregame warm-ups without any shoulder pads or helmets.

"One reason he did that was because it was about 103 degrees that day in Oklahoma. But those Oklahoma boys looked at us from across the field and just thought we looked so small. They were definitely overconfident."

It was an attitude that seemed justified when Lattner fumbled the opening kickoff and Oklahoma turned the mistake into a 7–0 lead.

"I found out later that Coach Leahy turned to the backfield coach, Bill

Earley, after my fumble and said: 'There's your All-American,'" Lattner said. "Then he added: 'How long do I have to tape the football to his arm this time?'"

But in a close game, Leahy's players were still the masters of the T formation and took a 28–14 lead that went unthreatened until Oklahoma returned a Lattner punt for a touchdown in the fourth quarter. "I had the last shot at the guy, too, and he faked my jockstrap into the stands," Lattner said.

Oklahoma was driving for the potential tying or winning score late in the game when an errant pass came right to Lattner on defense. The interception preserved a 28–21 Notre Dame victory.

"If I had dropped that interception, they would have kicked me out of school," Lattner said fifty years after the fact.

Oklahoma did not lose again for more than four years, winning forty-seven consecutive games.

Lattner was also on the field at South Bend against Iowa in 1953, when, taking advantage of the rules of the day, Notre Dame players faked injuries at the end of each half.

"Coach Leahy actually had us practice faking injuries," Lattner said. "If we were out of time-outs, Leahy would signal from the sideline and the right tackle, Frank Varrichione, was supposed to go down and fake a back injury. The officials would be forced to call an official's time-out. And Leahy would drill us in how to be ready to snap the football as soon as the officials restarted the clock. So at Iowa, we were on their 12-yard line and trailing 7–0 right at the end of the half. After they helped Varrichione off the field, we scored to tie the game."

For Iowa, it got worse. With six seconds remaining in the game and Iowa leading 14–7, Notre Dame was out of time-outs when a host of Notre Dame players went down. Notre Dame came out of the official's time-out and scored again. The game ended in a 14–14 tie.

"Oh, geez, there must have been five guys falling down and rolling around," Lattner said.

Forest Evashevski, Heisman Trophy winner Tom Harmon's co-captain on the 1940 Michigan team, was the Iowa head football coach in 1953. "Evashevski stormed across the field at Coach Leahy after the game," Lattner said. "I thought he was going to kill Leahy. But you know, with a straight face, Coach said: 'Forest, that was a well-played game by your lads.'"

The newspaper headlines the next day read: "Fainting Irish tie Iowa."

Weeks later, Evashevski, borrowing from the famous phrase penned by sportswriter Grantland Rice, wrote a brief poem of his own about the experience at South Bend:

When that one great scorer comes to write against your name,
He writes not that you won or lost,
But how come we got gypped at Notre Dame.

Lattner had a brief NFL career, winning the rookie of the year award for the Pittsburgh Steelers before a knee injury forced him from the game. He ran Lattner's Steak House in Chicago for several years, where his Heisman Trophy was always on display behind the bar, and he somehow stayed in the news.

Returning home from the restaurant late one night in 1962, Lattner and his wife Margaret smelled smoke.

"And we heard a crackling noise," Lattner said. "Three houses down from us the whole back of the apartment building was going up in flames."

John and Margaret rushed into the building, banging on doors and kicking open exit doors at the end of every hallway.

"We got to the third floor where the fire had started in somebody's kitchen," Lattner said. "And we closed a bunch of doors all around there that restricted the flames a bit until the firemen came, although the building was still engulfed eventually."

The Lattners rescued thirty-five people from the flames, including eight survivors who had been rendered unconscious, overcome by smoke.

Back in 1953, Lattner and his band of plucky, ingenious teammates had no idea they would be Leahy's last squad at Notre Dame. But Leahy would become among the first public coaching examples of a latter-day affliction: burnout. For all of Leahy's attributes as a coach, as his tenure at South Bend went on, he began to obsess over every game, working longer and longer hours. It was said that Leahy could do everything but relax. As each season unfolded from September to November, he would eat less and less until he was actually sitting down to dinner no more than twice a week. On game days, he would be so wound up it drove him to total distraction. At the end of games, his assistants had to make many of the decisions.

"He had the most able mind of any football coach I ever saw during practice," Lattner said. "It was all perfect fundamentals and repetition. But on the day of a game, he was not of sound mind."

Against Georgia Tech, the fourth game of the 1953 season, Leahy collapsed at halftime and was even given the last rites of the Catholic Church. Diagnosed with a stomach disorder, Leahy recovered and coached the rest of the season without another serious episode, but in January of 1954, Leahy resigned at the age of forty-five.

Leahy's stomach problems were not life-threatening, but he never coached again. He flirted with the idea of taking over at Texas A&M in 1958—not long after Bear Bryant had left the school—but simply contemplating a return to coaching brought out some of his old ailments: stomach problems and high blood pressure.

He remained in touch with Notre Dame and his lads and traveled extensively. Still in demand as a football strategist, he could turn a one-hour coaching clinic into a day-long symposium. Few coaches got up to leave until Leahy was done explaining his football theories.

Though he had retired at a young age, Leahy's place as an innovator in the game was never overlooked. He had, after all, brought the zone pass defense, the erect stance, the open huddle, and the line of scrimmage audible to college football. Schooled as a lineman by Rockne, he had come up with another groundbreaking advance for line play: optional blocking assignments for linemen on the same running play. Usually led by the center, who would read the defense and make a call, the linemen could adjust their blocking schemes in unison based on the formation the defense presented just before the ball was snapped.

In the late 1960s, Leahy was diagnosed with leukemia, a disease that took his life in 1973.

Following the 1994 publication of Jack Connor's *Leahy's Lads*, a collection of Leahy's players started a Frank Leahy Memorial scholarship fund at Notre Dame and then commissioned a 10-foot statue of their coach, which was placed outside the eastern walls of the football stadium at Notre Dame in 1997.

The statue depicts Leahy kneeling with a football grasped in both hands, a pose he frequently took to address his players at the end of practices. Leahy's broad face smiles and seems to stare directly across Juniper Street into the windows of the office of the head coach of Notre Dame.

The statue calls attention to Leahy's great teams of the 1940s and early

1950s when the players had names like Bucky O'Connor, Terry Brennan, Emil Sitko, Ziggie Czarobski, Lujack, Tripucka, and Bertelli—a roll call that is as much Leahy's legacy as his distinguished coaching record.

When Leahy left Notre Dame in 1953, the first-generation sons and daughters of immigrant parents were charging through a decade that would thrust them headlong into mainstream America. In 1953, Rocky Marciano was heavyweight champion. Lucille Ball, born to Irish and Scottish parents, and her Cuban-born husband Desi Arnaz, had launched *I Love Lucy*, a television show that would become a cultural artifact. And in that bastion of the American aristocracy—Newport, Rhode Island—Senator John F. Kennedy, grandson of a hardscrabble Boston Irish politician, had wed Jacqueline Lee Bouvier, a scion of an old-money wealthy American family.

Notre Dame had played a prominent role in the socioeconomic ascent of the immigrant population, providing a lifeline—even if just by football newsreel—to multitudes trying to carve their place in an adopted home. What dawned at Notre Dame in the 1940s was one of the greatest dynasties in the history of American sport, but there was a method to the magic so often attributed to those victorious Notre Dame teams. It was the melting pot football team winning at the dawn of the melting pot society.

Frank Leahy's parents arrived across the harbor from the site of the club that would make the Heisman Trophy famous in the final days of the nineteenth century. The Leahys headed west, and forty-something years later, their son sent his best back east, within a football field or two of the same shores that had greeted his parents. No one coached more players who walked through the doors of the Downtown Athletic Club to claim the Heisman Trophy. Each was a symbolic accomplishment. A changing America happily took notice.

Frank Leahy might have personally coached roughly a thousand players at Notre Dame. But his lads were everywhere in America.

6.

The Last Ivy Leaguer

DICK KAZMAIER, 1951

Princeton University's Dick Kazmaier was a brilliant player, a running back acclaimed for poise under pressure and popular enough to have graced the cover of *Time* magazine in 1951. But it is likely that Kazmaier's place in college football will forever be framed by his designation as the last Ivy Leaguer to win the Heisman. In 1936, Larry Kelley of Yale had won the second Heisman Trophy and his teammate Clint Frank won the award a year later.

The last Ivy League player to come close to winning the trophy was Cornell running back Ed Marinaro, who finished a controversial second, in some quarters, to Auburn quarterback Pat Sullivan in 1971.

But Ivy League football's legacy in college football cannot be understated, for it goes to the heart of the game. In 1869, Princeton played in the first recorded American football game, against Rutgers.

For the next half century, college football's cultivating grounds were campuses along the eastern seaboard, such as Princeton, Yale, and Harvard. Walter Camp, considered the father of American football, played football at Yale and later became a groundbreaking coach. In 1880, it was Camp who broke up the mob scenes common on football fields, limiting teams to eleven men per side. Camp introduced the concept of possession of the football to one team at a time for a series of downs, or trials—the central difference between rugby and football. Camp put the chalk lines on the field to mark the progress of these downs, hence the term *gridiron.*

Notre Dame's sage, Knute Rockne, was once asked where his maneuverable shifts and formations came from and Rockne answered: "Yale. All football comes from Yale."

For decades before and after the turn of the century, as college football was gaining a footing in America, either Yale, Harvard, or Princeton won the mythical Eastern or national championship, which were often the same thing, virtually every year. At the same time, Ivy Leaguers, like John Heisman (Brown and Penn), Yale's Amos Alonzo Stagg, and Cornell's Glenn Scobey "Pop" Warner began carrying the game to all parts of the country.

The venues for Ivy League football even played a role in the game's development. Harvard Stadium, a classic concrete horseshoe, was one of the signature meeting places for college football in the early part of the twentieth century. At one point in that period, there was much support for a proposal to widen the measurement of the football field beyond 52 and one-half yards, the standard width for several years. All the important powers of the day agreed an extra ten yards might produce a more free-flowing game.

The proposal had a good chance of being adopted—until someone measured the immovable grandstand walls along the field inside Harvard Stadium. The stadium would not have been able to accommodate another ten yards. That killed the proposal. Football fields, in the United States at least, remain at fifty-two and one-half yards to this day.

In 1914, football had become so meaningful to Yale, it erected the largest football stadium anyone in America had ever seen. On November 21 that year, 70,874 spectators filled the Yale Bowl, the biggest crowd to ever watch a football game.

Ivy League football remained the vanguard of the game for several years. Yale and Harvard, in particular, had standout teams that competed with the burgeoning national powers well into the 1940s.

By 1950, however, the schools in the Midwest, South, and West were putting together teams that featured not only talent, but depth, with rosters of skilled—and big—players that often numbered 200. They also did something that the Ivy League teams, at least officially, did not—award athletic scholarships. Still, in the Ivy League of the early 1950s, football was a popular enterprise, with games often on television and played before soldout stadiums. But the league was slowly drifting out of its glory years as an association of schools with a national football presence.

Princeton, for example, despite successive undefeated seasons in 1950 and 1951, was ranked sixth nationally at the end of each of those seasons. Few in the East disagreed with the outcome of those polls. By 1954, the Ivy League presidents came to an agreement that has been called the official deemphasis of Ivy League football: fewer coaches allowed, no postseason play, limited recruiting.

As many of the major institutions in American higher education were aggressively pursuing a big-time football agenda, the Ivies were heading in the other direction. They hoped they were starting a counter reaffirmation. They were not.

"I don't think the Ivies changed," Kazmaier said. "They stayed the same and everyone else changed—more scholarships, more sponsorships, more television money."

It is an argument that would seem contemporary even now. But the Ivies did something in 1956 that sealed their place as outsiders to the top level of the game by adopting a policy of isolationism. The Ivy group settled on eight official members and created a round-robin schedule. Since the league prohibited any team playing more than nine games, there was little opportunity for Ivy League schools to play outside of the Ivy League.

There would be no more visits eastward by Michigan or California to the old, famous Ivy League stadiums, birthplaces to once-celebrated regional rivalries. For the next twenty-five years, an Ivy League team would still play Army, Navy, or Air Force. Then, in the early 1980s, shortly after the 1981 Yale team had defeated Navy and Air Force in the same season and nearly cracked the final Associated Press top 20 poll, the Ivy League presidents—uncomfortable with Yale's attention-grabbing success—shackled their football programs anew. There were sweeping restrictions on recruiting and cutbacks on staff and funding.

Since then, the Ivies have drifted, by intent, to a level of play well outside the spotlight of the nation's top 100 teams.

And so, Kazmaier concedes it is improbable he will ever lose the tag "last Ivy League winner of the Heisman." But in 1951, he was an easy choice as the best football player in the land, a mesmerizing back in the

last days of the single wing, where the center snap might go to one of several players, who would then shift and fake—sometimes making two handoffs and two laterals—before moving upfield. Or the back with the ball might settle into the pocket and throw a pass. That was frequently Kazmaier's role.

Kazmaier became a starter at Princeton as a 155-pound sophomore after he scored two touchdowns in one quarter early in the season. By his junior year, Kazmaier, who was also a good kicker and punter, was a top attraction with sportswriters of the era, who flocked to Princeton's Palmer Stadium to see "Kaz." He was fun to watch, and like many great runners, had fluid, shifty hips, which made it seem like he was running in one direction while actually cutting to reverse field and elude tacklers.

His place in the game, and his position atop the Heisman balloting, was assured on October 27, 1951, when Kazmaier's unbeaten Princeton team played undefeated Cornell. A national television audience watched Kaz throw three touchdowns and run for two more to lead Princeton to a 52–15 victory. Kazmaier completed fifteen of his seventeen passes for 236 passing yards and ran for another 124 yards.

"One of those days when everything went right," Kazmaier said.

In the lopsided Heisman vote, Kazmaier outpointed, among others, Frank Gifford of Southern California. Kazmaier accepted his Heisman on a Saturday and returned to the Princeton campus in time to perform his usual weekend job, which he needed to defray his tuition costs. Kazmaier delivered dry cleaning to the dorm rooms of other Princeton students.

Like the 1935 Heisman Trophy winner Jay Berwanger, Kazmaier received a contract offer from Chicago Bears owner George "Papa Bear" Halas, and, like Berwanger, Kazmaier thanked Halas but said he wanted to go into the business world.

"When I came out of college, to win the Heisman was everything," Kazmaier said. "You couldn't do better. Why not go out on top?"

Kazmaier headed to Harvard Business School, then served in the Navy for three years before starting his own business. Kazmaier Associates, a marketing and investment company with interests in the sports and leisure industry, now employs more than 1,200.

In 1990, Kazmaier used his Heisman experience to make something positive of a personal family tragedy. Kazmaier's daughter, Patty, had been a pioneering women's college ice hockey player at Princeton at a time when there were few women's college ice hockey teams playing anywhere in the United States. After college she had married and was pregnant with her first child when she sustained a series of strokes. With Patty near death, the baby was taken from her prematurely and survived. Several months later, Patty had another stroke. She was diagnosed with a rare blood disorder, thrombotic thrombocytopenic purpura, which often brings about a lethal combination of bleeding and clotting.

Patty died in 1990 at the age of twenty-eight.

In the wake of Patty's death, Dick and his wife Patricia searched for ways to establish some kind of everlasting recognition for their daughter. With the help of an endowment established by the Kazmaiers, in 1998 USA Hockey instituted the Patty Kazmaier Memorial Award, given annually to the outstanding female college ice hockey player as selected by a national panel.

Dick Kazmaier speaks at the awards ceremony every year.

"I tell those at the ceremony, most of them very accomplished young women, that I have some appreciation for how these awards grow and develop a stature over time," Kazmaier said. "Most people probably don't know much about John Heisman anymore. But I do. He was quite a man.

"But the reason everyone knows about the award named for him is because of the people who have won it. They have given the award an identity and an image with their actions and contributions. One winner's accomplishments follow another and the legacy of the trophy compounds. Players come along with different backgrounds, different skills and different personalities and they all add something. The trophy becomes self-sustaining.

"That's what will happen with the Patty Kazmaier Award. There will be a mystique and the trophy will take on a life of its own. I tell them at the awards ceremony that this will be the gift to the sport and the game. There is power in an award. I tell them: 'Trust me, I know.'"

Serena, the baby girl born to Patty Kazmaier in the wake of her first, telling medical setback, is now fourteen years old.

"And a thriving, happy fourteen-year-old," Kazmaier said of his grandchild. "So a part of Patty is always still with us."

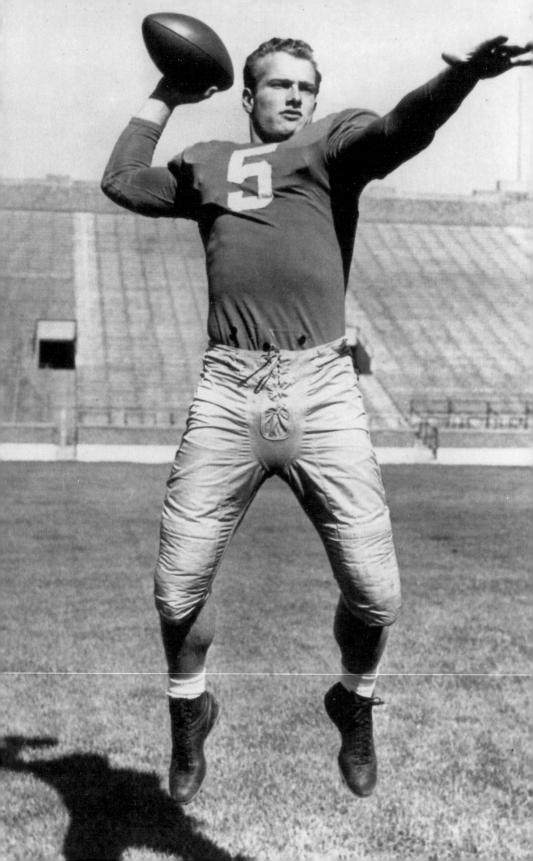

Everybody's Golden Boy

PAUL HORNUNG, 1956

On Sunday night, September 9, 1956, Elvis Presley made his first appearance on Ed Sullivan's television show, *Toast of the Town*. It was one of those pure moments of cultural revelation. Fifty-four million people—roughly 82 percent of all those who owned a television in America—watched.

Shoulder-shaking, hip-bucking, arm-flailing, lip-curling Elvis was irresistible. There, shimmying across the stage, was the dynamism of a new generation. This was an America rising from years of war, including the latest on the Korean Peninsula, which had cost the country nearly 25,000 lives. It was an America looking forward, an America hurtling toward the Space Age and a mushrooming technological era that seemed far more than six years past the midpoint of the twentieth century.

It was also an America with something it had never truly possessed before: a self-reliance, a swagger, a buoyancy, something that forty years later people would call an attitude. Elvis had it, and he was not alone. Marlon Brando had it. James Dean had it.

It was an America sizing up the future with a sly smile. It was called the Feel-Good Fifties, and if it had a face, it was Elvis Presley's that night on Ed Sullivan's show. Did he not look like he was feeling good?

On the Saturday afternoon before Elvis sang his two songs on *Toast of the Town*, Paul Vernon Hornung played the first game of his senior season for the University of Notre Dame. By the end of the year, when he would win the Heisman Trophy, Hornung would be another new dominant personality of 1956. There may never have been a sports figure in his prime so suited to his times.

Cary Grant was romancing Sophia Loren on and off the movie set of *The Pride and the Passion*. Hugh Hefner had started a landmark magazine in a small office in Chicago. And Paul Hornung was running at top speed through defenders and life at the same time.

Years later, when Vince Lombardi caught Hornung coming into the Green Bay Packers' training camp dormitory far past curfew, the coach barked: "Paul, do you want to be a football player or a playboy?"

Answered Hornung: "A playboy."

In a 2003 interview, Hornung offered this explanation of that remark:

"What I meant to say was, 'Both,'" Hornung said, laughing. "It was a time when it was becoming okay to be both. I just said 'playboy,' in the spirit of a playboy."

If Elvis was irresistible, Paul Hornung, dubbed "The Golden Boy," was irrepressible. With his wavy, curly blond hair, dimples, and an impish grin to fit the times, Hornung was far more than a wise-cracking football star. He appealed to a cross-section of football fans—men, women, and children. Dozens of Paul Hornung fan clubs sprung up around the country after color pictures of the handsome Notre Dame star ran in all the top weekly newsmagazines. He played quarterback under the Golden Dome at Notre Dame and had his own agent, who lent him a fancy car and set up speaking engagements. He was living life on one of the fullest scholarships.

It was a heady time for Hornung, who for all his swagger knew what others did not: In his heart he was a mama's boy.

Until her death in the late 1980s, Hornung took his mother Loretta out to dinner every Wednesday that he could. He lived with her in his hometown of Louisville until he was thirty. When he was in college and later at Green Bay, he missed many of the Wednesday night dinners, but never more than three weeks went by without Hornung hitchhiking from Notre Dame or flying home from Green Bay to take his mother out to dinner again.

Loretta Hornung had grown up in Louisville on Portland Street, in a neighborhood populated by what came to be called the Portland Irish.

"The Irish had to stick together in Louisville because no one else would talk to them," Paul said. "There weren't a lot of Catholics around then either. There was a lot of bias."

The year the first Heisman Trophy was awarded, 1935, Loretta Hornung was pregnant with her only son when she separated from her husband, Paul Sr., a New York insurance executive. The Hornungs had been living on Long Island, but as Paul Jr. said: "My Dad got mixed up with a tough crowd and got to drinking. He became an alcoholic. My Mom went back to Louisville where her parents were, and my parents were officially divorced a few years later."

In 1937, the Ohio River jumped its banks and flooded Portland Street. Loretta grabbed Paul and clambered to the top of her parents' house, where they were living. After several tense minutes, a man in a rowboat came by and rescued Loretta and her toddler. The man in the rowboat was Henry Hofmann, a Louisville real estate developer with holdings throughout the city. Henry Hofmann rescued Paul Hornung in a host of ways that day.

"He was the most influential man in my life," Hornung said. "I called him Uncle Henry from then on. He advised me, watched out for me. When I was in college, he helped me with money. When I made any money, I would send it to Henry and he would invest it for me, usually in the Louisville real estate market. He would turn $1,500 into $15,000 and over time he would turn that $15,000 into $50,000.

"He introduced me to my future business partner, Frank Metts. He was a great, honest, giving man."

When Paul was nine, his grandmother in Louisville died and he and Loretta were suddenly on their own. "My Mom said, 'Paul, you've got to be the man of the house now,'" Hornung said. For a while, they slept on two Army cots in the front room of someone else's house.

"I remember that very well, but you know, I didn't know it was supposed to be a hardship," Hornung said. "I had a very enjoyable childhood. My Mom was all I had and I was all she had. She worked real hard to keep it together for both of us. But we had food. We were fine. She would give me a football to play with in football season, and she could afford a basketball in basketball season and a serviceable baseball glove in baseball season."

Paul got jobs at the nearby Churchill Downs race track. In summers, he lied about his age to get the better-paying construction jobs building new grandstands.

"Eventually, we got our own apartment," Hornung said. "Still on the west side, but the best part was it was across the street from a Marine Hospital."

The front lawn of the hospital was a wide, open swath of grass, bigger than a football field.

"I would come home and cross the street and play football all day," Hornung remembered. "I would come home from high school football practice and go play more football."

At Flaget High School, Hornung was the star quarterback, placekicker, punter, and safety. He was the most highly recruited high school football player in Kentucky history, wooed by Paul "Bear" Bryant, the University of Kentucky coach who would soon take a job at Texas A&M, and Frank Leahy, just before his resignation from Notre Dame.

"But when it came to college, I was going to do whatever my mom said," Paul recalled. "And she said: 'If you want to go to Kentucky, you can. If you want to go to Oklahoma, you can.' But she was Irish and she was Catholic, and she looked at me and said, 'But you had better go Notre Dame.'"

Unfortunately for Notre Dame and Hornung, Leahy was not easily replaced and the Fighting Irish struggled under new coach Terry Brennan in the mid-1950s. Though more of a running quarterback than a throwing one, Hornung still found a way to stand out. At 215 pounds, he was a devastating defensive player and a highly accomplished placekicker. He ran back kickoffs and punts, and soon games with 350 yards of total offense were common for Hornung. Late in a game against Iowa during his junior season, Hornung passed for a tying touchdown, kicked the extra point, then kicked off deep into Iowa territory and made the tackle. After helping to force a punt with several defensive plays as a linebacker and a safety, the Irish got the football back in time for Hornung to drive Notre Dame into position for a Hornung field goal to win the game.

Performances like that made Hornung the Heisman Trophy favorite entering his senior season despite a strong class of seniors at other schools, most notably Jim Brown of Syracuse, Johnny Majors at Tennessee, and Oklahoma's Tommy McDonald. Sportswriters of the time expected Notre Dame to rebound under Hornung, in part because they believed whatever Notre Dame's respected publicity guru Charlie Callahan said, and Callahan told them Hornung was the best in the land.

So, when the 1956 Notre Dame football team stumbled to a disappointing 2–8 record, a nation of sportswriters—many of them Heisman voters—still managed to notice Hornung's remarkable statistics. Even playing for a team that lost eight of ten games, Hornung was second in the nation in total offense and his accomplishments didn't escape Heisman voters. In his final game at Notre Dame, a 21–13 victory over North Carolina, Hornung scored every point for the Irish.

In December 1956, Hornung was in a physics class—since high school he had always been a solid student—when he was summoned to Callahan's office. He walked through the door and Callahan began dialing a number on his black desk telephone.

"Here," Callahan said, handing Hornung the phone, "tell your mother you won the Heisman Trophy."

Hornung is the only player ever to win the Heisman while playing for a losing team.

"It's one of those things that always comes up because I'm the only one," Hornung said. "But you've got to remember, these were the days of one-platoon football. I kicked and punted. I did a lot of things."

Paul took his mother to New York City for the Heisman ceremony, where the trophy was presented to him by Ed Sullivan.

"I also went on the Jackie Gleason show and after it, Gleason took me to Toots Shor's bar," Hornung said. "He introduced me to Toots and I'll tell you, we became famous friends. Toots was one of the great drinking buddies of all time. We had a great time that weekend."

The lowly Green Bay Packers of the NFL were given the first of the 1957 college draft and they took Hornung. In two desultory seasons for two miserable Packers teams, Hornung played quarterback in some games, halfback in others, and fullback in another. And he still played defense, too. Hornung was not happy.

"I was ready to give it up after the 1958 season," Hornung said. "There was such uncertainty on that team and a lot of selfishness. My Uncle Henry had made some good investments; I went home to Louisville after the '58 season and I thought to myself, 'I could stay right here and develop this real estate business. I could make more than I'm making in football.' There was no big money in pro football then."

But the 1958 National Football League season concluded with a seminal event in the history of televised sports programming and professional sports. The Baltimore Colts, led by the magnetic Johnny Unitas, faced the New York Giants, titans of the league, for the league championship. The game was televised nationally, on a chilly Sunday three days after Christmas Day, live from a Yankee Stadium crammed to capacity. The game was full of celebrated players, like Frank Gifford, Kyle Rote, and Charlie Conerly of the Giants, while Baltimore had Raymond Berry and the 1954 Heisman Trophy winner, Alan Ameche.

It was more than a game; it was perfectly timed drama. Played out across the twilight of a Sunday caught equidistant between two holidays, some 15 million people found themselves lured into the scene from the light and shadows of Yankee Stadium. The slump-shouldered Unitas built an early lead, then the gilded, glamorous Giants made their comeback. The Colts fought back once more, aided by a controversial referee's decision which led to a late, tying field goal. There followed a sudden-death overtime—the first of its kind—and a clinching score for the Colts on a thunderous run by Ameche, nicknamed "The Horse."

Sports Illustrated called it the best football game ever played, which was most probably a stretch, but it did not matter.

It was the best football game ever seen on television. It was the best football game, perhaps the best sporting event, ever seen by 15 million people. It was the game that made television sports seem more intimate. For years, only boxing seemed a natural for television. People enjoyed watching televised baseball, but it was years before the camera work caught up with the action, years before cameras with grand zoom lenses positioned in center field accurately captured every ball and strike.

But in 1958, and not entirely by accident, the NFL had put on a Sunday afternoon show, and it was set in a confined rectangular field, an outdoor sports studio. The NFL had found its ticket to a prosperous future.

The offensive coordinator of those 1958 Giants was Vince Lombardi, and within days of the championship game defeat, he was named the new head coach of the Packers. Together with Golden Boy Paul Hornung, they would ride the Packers and the NFL into its Golden Age. The Packers became NFL royalty and Hornung was their prince.

But first, new coach and star player had to come to terms.

As Hornung told Beano Cook in an interview for the ESPN Classic network:

"I got a phone call from Coach Lombardi in 1959 and he says to me, 'Paul, I'm going to kick you in the butt and I'm going to stay on your butt.'

HORNUNG AS A GREEN BAY PACKER

And I said, 'Excuse me?' And then he says he's going to be tough on me and he's going to be tough on everybody. And then, he says, 'And don't bother coming to camp unless you're ready to play left halfback and nothing but left halfback,' and I said: 'Pardon me?'

"Well, the fact is I wasn't going to be successful in the NFL as a quarterback, but Coach Lombardi just made it so plain. He told me I'd be a better football player for it. Lombardi saved my life in pro football."

Hornung was a brilliant left halfback, running behind Lombardi's signature play, the sweep, when he would outrace linebackers to the corner, or if overpursued, cut back and outmaneuver them to the inside of the field. Because he had been a quarterback, he was also a constant threat on runs to the right to execute the halfback option pass. There were Green Bay offensive possessions where Lombardi would call Hornung's halfback option seven or eight plays in a row.

Sometimes Hornung would pass, sometimes run. Either way, he gained yards.

"It's still the most underutilized play in football," Hornung said of the halfback option. "People think it's a gimmick. It's not a gimmick, it's a great optional run/pass play, if run with the right amount of deceit."

But the option pass was only one way Hornung displayed his versatility. He was the best offensive triple-threat weapon in pro football history and its most prolific scorer given the number of games he played (the NFL had a twelve-game regular season then). Hornung led the NFL in scoring for three seasons and was the league's Most Valuable Player in 1960 and 1961 despite injuries and military obligations that kept him from practicing for weeks at a time, especially when stationed at an Army base in North Dakota from Monday to Friday. In the twelve games of the 1960 season, Hornung kicked fifteen field goals and forty-one extra points, and scored fifteen touchdowns for 176 points.

In a single game against the Colts in 1961, he scored thirty-three points (four touchdowns, six extra points, and a field goal) in only three quarters of play. "Coach Lombardi came over to me later that day and says he didn't know the record for points in a game by one player was forty or he would have left me in," Hornung said. "I told him not to worry about it. I didn't care."

In the conference championship in 1965, he scored five touchdowns against the Colts, rushes that alternatively showed Hornung's speed, determination, and guile. In the 1965 NFL championship game against the

Cleveland Browns—when the great Packers were being called over the hill—Hornung made one last great charge, scoring the decisive touchdown in a 23–12 victory. Lombardi, who used to say that Hornung was an ordinary player at midfield but the best in the game near the goal line, left the field with his left arm draped across Hornung's shoulder pads.

Hornung was not only productive, he did it with flair. In a time when players rarely, if ever, showed emotion on the field, Hornung exhibited one of the first known end zone celebrations. After scoring a touchdown in Chicago's Wrigley Field against the Packers' arch-rival Chicago Bears, Hornung flung the ball high into the stands.

"You'll pay for that, young man," Bears Coach George Halas barked.

"No you won't," Lombardi answered. "I'll take care of it."

Hornung was well liked by teammates and by Madison Avenue. Although playing in the smallest outpost of any in professional sports, Hornung still was considered the model pitchman for national advertisers. At one point in the 1960s, he had twenty-one promotional contracts, for everything from Marlboro to Aqua Velva. He pitched chili, chewing tobacco, and Chevrolets. Everybody smiled when the Golden Boy smiled.

Admired as the wink-of-the-eye embodiment of mischief, he never seemed to be resented for it. He played, for example, seven years for the very embodiment of American sporting discipline, Vince Lombardi. But everyone from those teams insists that Hornung was far and away Lombardi's favorite player.

They might have seemed like football's ultimate odd couple, but Lombardi privately laughed when he read some of the quotes that would be attributed to his left halfback, for example, Hornung's comment about his carousing teammate Max McGee: "Max was my roommate, and one year at Packers training camp he was out every night. I know, because sometimes I had to wake him to come with me."

But Lombardi also knew that Hornung was a tough, reliable football player, and far from a prima donna. Lombardi intentionally rode Hornung harder in practice than any other player, routinely singling him out for criticism in practices, rebuking him in a way that he would not rebuke, say, the team's quiet, self-conscious quarterback, Bart Starr.

"Vince came to me and said, 'Paul, you make more money because of the endorsements and everyone knows you're the star, so I'm going to make an example of you,'" Hornung said. "He said, 'I know you won't take it personally. But to the other guys, it will mean a lot.' And I do think the guys thought, 'Wow, if he goes after Paul like that, he's not playing favorites. I better put my nose to the grindstone or the Old Man will come after me.'"

Even Hornung's most public and embarrassing blunder did not permanently taint his image, probably because Hornung had an authenticity about him that people accepted. When he and Detroit tackle Alex Karras were suspended by NFL Commissioner Pete Rozelle for gambling in 1963—Hornung had placed bets on the Packers to win, none more than $500—it was understood that Hornung, a bona fide star, and Karras, also a Pro Bowler, were taking the fall for players all over the league who gambled on their own teams from time to time. Federal officials had considered a grand jury investigation, and in that light, Hornung readily acknowledged that Rozelle had wisely preempted Washington officials. As Hornung said, "If Pete hadn't done that, there would have been a lot more people than Hornung and Karras parading to Washington."

Nonetheless, it was a startling controversy. *Sports Illustrated* put Hornung's face on its cover next to the headline: The Moral Crisis in Sport. Hornung accepted the consequences like a fusillade of Lombardi practice taunts and insults and never protested his one-year suspension. For nearly forty years, reporters and fans have approached Hornung asking if he thought Rozelle overreacted, and always, Hornung has insisted that Rozelle did the right thing, that he, Hornung, had broken a rule and should have known better.

"My mom always said a good person knows right from wrong," Hornung said. "You're going to make mistakes. One of the important things is to know when you make one."

Hornung paid for his mistake. He waited unusually long to be inducted into the Pro Football Hall of Fame and he once had to sue the National Collegiate Athletic Association, which attempted to bar him from broadcasting some of its games because of his gambling suspension (Hornung won the suit). In the court of public opinion it seems clear Hornung has been forgiven, maybe because there is a vulnerability to him, and it was on display from the moment he quietly accepted his one-year absence from football and came back without resentment.

He played three more seasons for the Packers and one for the New Orleans Saints, then launched a successful broadcasting career. Hornung later threw himself into his real estate business, buying up buildings and businesses in Louisville and developing a highly popular shopping mall with a former teammate, Lenny Lyles. He also owns a soybean refinery and other interests.

"It's a nice little company," Hornung said in 2003, a year after that nice little company took in $275 million in sales.

He stills lives in Louisville and has never called anywhere else his permanent, official residence. He has been married for decades to his wife, Angela, whom Paul calls "the attractive spouse in my house."

"But I am the trophy husband," he says.

For decades, Hornung has provided radio color commentary for Notre Dame games. In 2003, at the age of sixty-seven, he was asked if he planned to retire and Hornung replied: "Retire from what? I've never had a job in my life. Playing football isn't a job. Broadcasting football isn't a job. Making little business deals here and there isn't really a job. Not like hard work that other people do. That's a job."

The Golden Boy's hair is a wavy gray now and he is well past his playing weight. Nights end much sooner for Paul Hornung. He sleeps far more hours than he did when he was in his twenties.

But there is still a sparkle in his eye and the smile that comes easily. Paul Hornung can make a joke, usually at his own expense, then add a playful wink, and in that moment, convey the entire experience of the Feel-Good Fifties. For an instant, it is 1956 again and Paul Hornung is dashing through defenders and life at the same pace: young, happy, daring, and ready to rock the world—the Elvis Presley of football.

He has not lost that passion, the zest for life's game and his place in it.

In the late 1990s, NFL Films was interviewing Hornung for a series on the game's greatest players. They asked Hornung a hypothetical question: If he were starting a football team and he could take anyone dead or alive throughout history—except himself—whom would he take?

"I would take me," Hornung responded.

"No, you can't . . ." the ESPN interviewer said.

"What do you mean?" Hornung said. "Why, I could run, I could pass, I could kick. I could return kicks. Of course, I would take me. Look at some of my games. . . ."

"No, you can't take yourself," the interviewer finally interjected. "Other than you, who would you take first?"

"Oh," Hornung said. "Well, I guess there is somebody else I could take. Sure, there would be a lot of guys. But, you know, somebody else would take me next."

A HEISMAN AWARD DINNER IN THE 1950s

JOHN DAVID CROW WITH HIS PARENTS,
VELMA AND HARRY CROW

If There Was a Job Worth Doing, It Was Worth Doing It Right

JOHN DAVID CROW, 1957

John David Crow was raised in Springhill, Louisiana, a collection of wooden cabins and cottages so deep in the forests of northwestern Louisiana that Crow used to say, "They had to pipe in the sunshine."

John David's father, Harry, was a tall, broad, no-nonsense man who considered football a distraction from the essence of life, which was hard work in preparation for the next Great Depression. Harry Crow's roots were in the poor South of the 1930s, and he filled his youngest son John David with stories of dry, dying crops and windstorms so fierce they would pierce the walls and floorboards at night and cover Harry's blanket with half an inch of dust. A hero to Harry Crow was someone who put food on his family's table.

In the early 1950s, Harry felt lucky to work ten hours a day in a paper mill in northwestern Louisiana. Everyone for miles around, as far as away as central Arkansas, pursued a job at the same Spinghill mill, lured through the thick woods to the unending noise because of what it represented: steady work.

Harry left school at the age of twelve to find his job in Springhill, where tethered to a mule he hauled cross-ties used for railroad tracks from the most densely wooded sections. He moved up to a job hoisting 100-pound pine logs to his shoulders, then unloading them from a boxcar.

At the end of each workday, Harry Crow went home nearly deaf, his ears ringing from the ceaseless, high-pitched screech of the company wood-chippers and the roaring engines used to heat the pulp-making cook-eries. Harry worked there for forty-four years.

John David was the third and youngest child of Harry and Velma Crow, born in northwest Louisiana's Union Parish. During the delivery, the attending midwife saw that the umbilical cord was draped around the baby's neck and forehead. She quickly unraveled the cord, saving John David's life, but a cluster of small developing nerves in the neck had been damaged. The injury affected the muscles on the left side of John David's face, causing a slight sag to half his face, a sleepy eye, and a lip that drooped to one side, making for a permanently crooked grin.

John David's health problems continued into his childhood, and he nearly died from pneumonia at the age of two. In time, he grew muscular and strong like his father. But in the little town of Springhill, he was still teased by classmates over his facial features.

"You know how kids will pick on anything, and having a crooked mouth is an easy thing to spot," said Crow. "It was one of those things that maybe is a hidden blessing, because their teasing made me work harder to show them I wasn't different or deformed. It's only human nature. But I worked pretty hard to shut some people up."

Velma Crow worked at the grocery store in town, a mile and a half from home. On weekends and summer days, John David as a young teen would run to town to see his mother, sometimes twice a day. But he wouldn't take the asphalt and dirt road. John David ran along the railroad tracks, and not in between them.

"I would hop from side to side, from rail to rail, left foot to right foot, pushing off and balancing on the rails as I went," Crow said. "Every other cross-tie, I would cross over from rail to rail. I was just bored and making a trek into a game, but that's a football drill. What I was doing was building my ankle strength and agility. I did that for days and days, hours and hours."

When he got a little older, he was off to the wood yard and paper mill with his father. "Challenging, tough work that will test your insides," John

David said. There were other lessons learned inside the wood yard at the side of Harry Crow.

"Father never taught school stuff—I don't know how much schooling he had himself," said Crow, who sixty years later refers to his parents as Father and Mother, but never "my father" or "my mother."

"Father taught his life rules. And one big rule was that if you start a job, no matter what it is or what happens, you finish the job. And the other thing he demanded is that if there was a job worth doing, it was worth doing it right."

Harry Crow did not consider athletics important. They didn't fit into his model of hard work and providing for a family. But his eldest son, Raymond, was a high school football player and earned an athletic scholarship to Southern State just across the state line in Arkansas. When John David reached high school, he was 6-foot-2 and 195 pounds, and already a better prospect than his brother.

John David ran the 100-yard dash on Springhill's dusty cinder track in 9.9 seconds and he was a good basketball player. He was an even better athlete in the one sport that mattered most in the South: football. But there was no money in the Springhill schools and their teams rarely stood out.

"My first football cleats were literally two left feet," said Crow, who was a running back and linebacker. "I'm not kidding, that is all that they had for me. And they were two sizes too big as well. We learned to improvise quite a bit in that town."

By a quirk of fate, his brother Raymond's college coach, Elmer Smith, took a job as an assistant to Coach Paul "Bear" Bryant, the new coach at Texas A&M. Bryant had left the University of Kentucky after eight successful, if stormy, years, quitting in a snit when he realized he would never get Kentucky football funded and pampered like the basketball program.

Smith knew the little roads and small schools in Louisiana, and when he saw Crow play he quickly got Bryant interested. The more Bryant learned about Crow's upbringing, the more he wanted him on his team.

Crow had an offer from Louisiana State and interest from Oklahoma University but he saw in Bryant the same no-nonsense, penetrating gaze he had come to recognize in his father's eyes, and that was a comfort for a country boy leaving home.

"I remember Coach Bryant asking me if my father had ever taken the strap to me," Crow said. "I answered: 'Several times, sir.' And Coach Bryant smiled."

Bryant, the eleventh of twelve children raised in a south Arkansas shack with no plumbing or electricity, had grown up fast, too. His first job paid fifty cents a day for a fourteen-hour shift picking cotton. In 1954, Bryant was just beginning a journey that made him one of the century's iconic figures. He would coach in five decades of college football, win six national championships and 323 games, but he would coach only one Heisman Trophy winner—Harry Crow's son from the dark woods of Springhill.

Crow agreed to come to Texas A&M's College Station campus, which at the time was an all-male military institution in the flat, indistinct landscape of central Texas. It was a place not affectionately called Old Army.

Crow was the showcase freshman in Bryant's first Texas A&M recruiting class, which coincidentally made him a footnote to the most documented moment of that first Bryant season at A&M. As a freshman, Crow could not play varsity games and therefore did not attend the legendary 1954 training camp made famous by the book and television movie *The Junction Boys*. The sleepy town of Junction, Texas, was situated in a drought-ridden prairie, a setting that tested and occasionally tortured the players. Before Bryant's arrival, Texas A&M's teams were notoriously padded with soft players. The new coach's exhausting practices in Junction were a purposeful attempt to toughen the committed players while ferreting out those who could not play college football with the fury Bryant demanded.

So, in the late summer of 1954, a glum-faced Crow waved goodbye to two buses containing 111 Texas Aggies departing from campus for training camp. Eleven days later, Crow waited in the same spot as a single, half-empty bus of thirty-five Junction survivors returned to College Station. Only twenty-three would actually be fit enough to play that year.

Asked Crow, in a now famous question: "Hey, guys, where the hell did everybody go?"

What was left of the 1954 Aggies won just one of ten games, but it was a tough-minded if overmatched team that may have lacked depth but not diligence. Talented players were few, but perseverance was abundant. Bryant had made his point. He had hardened a nucleus that he would surround with fresh talent like Crow and another freshman running back of greater renown, Ken Hall from Sugar Land, Texas. Hall was known as the

Sugar Land Express after he rushed for more than 11,000 yards in high school—a national record.

The Aggies had a 7–2–1 record during the 1955 season, Crow's first with the varsity. Avenging the 1–9 season from a year before, Bryant had gotten the attention of the Southwest Conference with a rugged team and a budding leader in Crow. He was a punishing runner and tackler, an important combination in the one-platoon football of the day. And Crow was something else that Bryant admired greatly. He was durable, shaking off any number of injuries to remain in games.

As a player at Alabama, Bryant once played an entire game against rival Tennessee despite a broken leg. Crow, as a player for Bryant, would do the same at the end of the 1956 season.

Play in the Southwest Conference in the mid-1950s was a war every weekend, football brawls for bragging rights among Texas universities with prideful constituencies and historical grudges. Clashes between Rice, Baylor, Houston, Texas A&M, Texas Christian, Texas Tech, Southern Methodist, and the University of Texas were arousing and arresting. The buses of visiting teams approaching the pastoral grounds of Baylor University in Waco, Texas, were often greeted on the outskirts of town by jeering fans who pelted the buses with soda bottles and rocks. Baylor was a Southern Baptist college, a place where church attendance was mandatory for students in the 1950s, but the Bible didn't define how one should behave during epic football clashes with one's hated, in-state rivals. Baylor, like their Texas brethren, made up their own rules.

The 1956 Texas A&M team was deep and talented, with fullback/linebacker Jack Pardee a bruising complement to Crow. That season, the Aggies were breezing through the Southwest Conference behind Crow and Pardee, who were unstoppable forces in Bryant's grind-it-out offense. Bryant had even allowed his quarterback to throw a few touchdown passes to Crow, who was a dangerously elusive downfield threat.

But when the Aggies went to Baylor that fall, they met another undefeated team with its own stars, including the future New York Giants star end Del Shofner. The shoving, grabbing, and after-the-whistle punches at the bottom of pile-ups began on the game's first play. By the third quarter, when Crow was knocked out of bounds near midfield directly in front of the home bench, he disappeared beneath a sea of Baylor jerseys.

"I was lying on my back when I started to see all these feet coming at me," Crow said. "They were trying to kick me in the face, and all I had was that one little bar for a facemask. I turned my head, but I still got an awful lickin'."

Two Baylor players were ejected from the game, but not before they bloodied Crow's nose and bruised his ribs and stomach. Still, Crow did not leave the game even for one play since substitution rules of the time would have kept him out until the fourth quarter. Crow inspected his chest several plays later, lifting his jersey to uncover numerous purple and blue welts, a scene that enraged his teammates.

Late in the game, with Baylor leading 13–12, the Aggies faced a fourth down on the Baylor 2-yard line. Coach Bryant was not going to kick a field goal; he believed that if his team couldn't get two yards, they didn't deserve to win the game. Forgoing field goal attempts would eventually cost Bryant two important games at Texas A&M. But on this day, with the other Aggies looking toward Bryant for direction, it was a vengeful Crow who demanded the football in the team huddle. Crow slammed into the line and emerged on the other side, falling into the end zone, the last of his eighty-four yards rushing in the game.

Two games later, on November 23, Crow broke his right foot in a victory against Rice. After the game, the foot ballooned with swelling and team doctors knew he needed a cast. But A&M was playing the University of Texas in Austin in five days. Crow wouldn't even let doctors x-ray the foot.

"I was going to play anyway," Crow said. "What difference would an x-ray make?"

Although the 7–0–1 Aggies were ranked third in the nation by the Associated Press, in many minds they were the underdogs going into the season finale against Texas, the university of the state's more well-to-do families. In every way, Texas lorded over the Aggies, who had not won a football game in Austin in thirty-three years.

On the first drive of the game, which was the first Southwest Conference game ever televised live, Crow gave the Aggies a 7–0 lead with a twenty-seven-yard touchdown run. The Aggies followed Crow's lead, and after some anxious moments, held on for a thirteen-point victory. Bryant and Crow had brought the downtrodden Aggies from perennial doormat to the doorstep of a national championship. And surely they could rectify that in 1957, Crow's senior season.

That year, Bryant began to refer to his star running back as "John David," and it caused a stir among the Texas writers. Bryant never referred to any of his players by their first names. While there were a lot of players in the Southwest Conference of the 1950s who used their middle names, there was something about Bryant's slow Southern baritone voice intoning "John David" after games that carried an almost biblical connotation. It got the college football world to pay attention.

When asked about Crow's rushing statistics—he had gained a respectable but not spectacular 561 rushing yards as a junior—Bryant would glare at his questioner and say: "Don't count the yards. Count the people he's run over."

In 1957, with Crow still running over people on his way to compiling a nearly identical rushing total (562 yards), the Aggies were 8–0 and ranked number one in the nation when they traveled to Rice on November 16. Surprisingly out of sync, the Aggies trailed 7–6 late in the game as they moved the football to the Rice 13-yard line. On fourth down, again, Bryant eschewed the field goal even though his kicker, Bobby Joe Conrad, had an accurate and strong leg. The Aggies did not advance the football on fourth down and suffered a crushing loss. Texas A&M's chances at a national championship vanished. The title eventually went to Ohio State.

As bad as the defeat was, rumors that Bryant was going to leave Texas A&M to return to Alabama cast a larger pall over the College Station campus. Soon, Bryant would be on his way to Alabama, announcing in his farewell speech that "Mama called, and I'm going home."

Before he left, however, Bryant gave parting advice to those preparing their Heisman Trophy ballots. Crow, across three seasons, had been one of the most reliable, productive running backs and defensive players in the nation for Texas A&M teams that had lost just three games in three years. "If he doesn't win the Heisman," Bryant said at the time, "they ought to stop giving it out."

Heisman voters were apparently swayed by that argument. Crow won the 1957 Heisman balloting by a wide margin over Alex Karras, the defensive lineman from Iowa.

A whirlwind month followed for Crow. Whisked to New York City a week before the Heisman ceremony to appear on Ed Sullivan's show, *Toast of the Town*, he took the stage minutes before another guest flown in from Texas: rock-and-roller Buddy Holly of Lubbock. The next night, Crow and teammate Charlie Krueger, who had also been invited to appear on Ed Sullivan's show, were given tickets to the Broadway show *My Fair Lady*.

"Well, going to a play wasn't what we had in mind," Crow said. "We were two young guys from Texas in New York for the first time and we wanted to go see the town. We made a plan to slip out of the play at intermission. Well, the show had Julie Andrews and Rex Harrison and we were spellbound. We didn't leave our seats at intermission even to go to the bathroom. We were mesmerized."

Crow graduated in 1958 and enjoyed a successful eleven-year playing career in the NFL, making the Pro Bowl four times. He became a coach for Bryant at Alabama and later the athletic director at his alma mater. The lasting legacy of his term as athletic director was his drive to greatly enhance Texas A&M's women's sports programs. Under Crow's direction, the university spent millions on facilities and coaching to upgrade the existing women's programs and to create new ones.

"I had two daughters," Crow said. "I don't know, maybe it was my upbringing, which preached basic fairness. But it seemed like high time to show a little respect to women athletes who were trying just as hard as the men."

Through the decades, Crow was forever linked with Coach Bear Bryant, who never did call another player by his first name. Eulogizing Bryant at his funeral in 1983, Crow recalled a day during his time as Bryant's most trusted assistant that the two men were walking silently off the practice field when Bryant suddenly blurted: "God dang it, John David, how did we not win a national championship at A&M?"

To which Crow responded, "Well, if you had let us kick two field goals, we would have." Retelling the story, Crow added: "And then I took off running as fast as I could. I ran straight home. I wasn't going to face him. But you know, that's just the way he was. He thought if you were good enough to run it into the end zone, you were good enough to win. And if not, then you weren't good enough."

In his eulogy, Crow also called Bryant a father to him. And it has always been the father–son relationships that have marked the major junctures and defining moments of Crow's life.

Asked to summarize the meaning of winning the Heisman Trophy in his life, John David Crow again returned to the Springhill wood yard and Harry Crow.

Late in 1957, it was Velma Crow who first received the news, by telephone, that her son had won the Heisman Trophy. "It must be some nice award," she told John David, who was home in Springhill on break. "They plan to fly all of us to New York City."

Velma Crow decided it might be worth telling the news to her husband, who was at work at the wood yard.

"So we went down there," John David said. "And there was Father covered in a kind of wood dust. I didn't think he would know what the Heisman Trophy was or what it meant. But when Mother told him, he kind of smiled then put his head down.

"I had never seen Father show a great deal of emotion. But when he looked back up at me, I could see the tears in his eyes. For all my life, for as long as I live, that will mean more to me than anything else. To stand there in the wood yard and to see the tears in his eyes. It never goes away."

Fundamental Principles

PETE DAWKINS, 1958

Five years removed from the last gallant days of Doc Blanchard and Glenn Davis, when the West Point Corps of Cadets had brought ceremony and nobility to college football in annual marches before sold-out Yankee Stadium crowds, the United States Military Academy was rocked by the worst kind of scandal for an institution built on the motto "Duty, Honor, Country."

In 1951, nearly ninety cadets, more than half of them varsity football players, were expelled for violating the academy honor code. An investigation had determined that certain cadets had formed a covert ring to unearth and dispense questions and answers to upcoming tests and quizzes. Some of the discharged cadets were accused not of cheating but of knowing about the ring and not informing officials of it. But that, too, was a violation of the academy honor code, which reads:

> A cadet does not lie, cheat, or steal. A cadet who knows about someone who has lied, cheated, or stolen must report him for violating the code.

With yet another war unfolding, this one on the Korean Peninsula, the effect of the cheating scandal on the country was as pronounced as it was on the grounds of the academy. Army cadets were viewed as fabled leaders in American society, their honesty and valor celebrated frequently in film and literature. The garrison campus on the Hudson River was a place of myth and moral order. Americans sent their best and brightest there, and their tax dollars, to mold leaders for the darkest times the nation might face. That nearly a hundred cadets were operating outside a simple, time-honored code of conduct brought a deep sense of betrayal.

The fact that so many Army football players were implicated, most of them upperclassmen, brought a public face to the scandal. In 1951, Army was still the vanguard of Eastern football. In the previous six years, Coach Colonel Earl "Red" Blaik's teams had won two national championships and five Eastern titles and had compiled a 57–3–4 record.

Moreover, several former Army football players had helped carry the nation through World War II. Generals Eisenhower, Bradley, and MacArthur were all connected to the Army football program. It was a symbolic and powerful connection exemplified in a quote from General George C. Marshall, Army chief of staff, who at the height of World War II said: "I have a secret and dangerous mission. Send me an Army football player."

If the aura enveloping Army football was more lore than reality, it did not much matter when forty-five Army football players, including the starting quarterback and son of Colonel Blaik, were dismissed for cheating or failing to turn in the cheaters. Bobby Blaik, a good student, confided to his father that he had violated the honor code because he had known about the cribbing of exam questions and answers but did not report it.

"My God!" said Colonel Blaik. "How could you? How could you?"

Dishonor at West Point was more bad news in a rough year for sport in 1951. Around the country, Americans watched uneasily as the sheen of innocent amateurism wore thin on the games collegians played. A month before the Army cheating scandal broke, fourteen former basketball players from New York City's most successful basketball-playing universities and colleges pleaded guilty to taking money from gamblers to fix games. Later that summer, three more players from Illinois's Bradley University, another college basketball powerhouse, admitted to similarly fixing games.

The effect on Army football was immediate. In addition to suffering a loss of prestige and standing, the highly touted 1951 team won just two of nine games. With half the team expelled, Army was forced to play mostly sophomores and stragglers from the campus intramural football program. Blaik fell into a deep, dispirited funk, and although Army football would have better seasons over the next several years, the charm and mystique that had once swathed the Army football program was gone.

By 1958, no one expected Army to field a football team that would craft a magical season and restore the magnetism and allure of the program as a sporting institution. Blaik was approaching the end of his coaching career, and across the land, the focus of college football was increasingly shifting to the South and Midwest.

But the 1958 Army team proved to be a team of rebirth and revival, and the impetus for change was a little-known player entering his senior season, a player whom Colonel Blaik had tried to cut from the team just two years earlier because he considered him, as Blaik said, "hopeless."

In 1956, Pete Dawkins was a smallish, left-handed Army quarterback from the Detroit suburbs whose primary skill was running the football. Blaik wanted his quarterbacks to be passers, first and foremost, and after Dawkins's first few varsity practices, Blaik had seen enough.

"He summoned me and very unceremoniously said, 'Look, we've got seven quarterbacks and we can only keep five. You're seventh. You're fired,'" Dawkins said, recalling the scene nearly fifty years later. "He said it just like that. I was absolutely, totally devastated. Football was the centerpiece of my life, and suddenly, it was demolished in about twenty seconds of conversation."

Dawkins stood at attention in Blaik's office but could not hide his utter dejection.

"Finally, he looked at me and said if I wanted to, I could remain as a scrub back," Dawkins said. "That is someone who practices against the varsity, only as a way to help them prepare, but not really with the varsity.

"Later he said he only did it as a courtesy. He took pity on me."

Dawkins, who at the time was 180 pounds, began by returning punts against the first-string punt team. He was the slender target for a legion of hungry young cadet football players looking to make their mark as special teams' aces. They called these players chasing down the field after the football—and after the poor soul about to catch it—gunners.

Play after play in practice, Dawkins caught punts and was repeatedly flattened by bigger, hard-charging teammates. The collisions were almost comical in their one-sidedness. Blaik always filmed his practices, and he and his assistant coaches would analyze what they saw late into the night. At the end of these exhausting sessions, as a way of lightening the mood, the coaches would watch the lopsided takedowns of poor Pete Dawkins, Army's moving tackling dummy.

"I was really getting creamed," Dawkins said.

If the Army coaches were amused by Dawkins's efforts, he was still deadly serious about his part in the game. Dawkins was hardly dejected by his rugged, thankless assignment. He had been through worse in pursuit of his football dreams.

Born March 8, 1938, in Royal Oak, Michigan, Dawkins was stricken with polio as a child. At the age of eleven, Dawkins developed scoliosis, a debilitating, degenerative back condition. The family doctor prescribed the standard treatment of the day: a back brace.

Dawkins was told he would never play sports, especially football, again. At that point, Pete's parents and his doctors saw an earlier version of the disconsolate football player standing in Colonel Blaik's office.

"I loved football and I said I wasn't going to stop," he said. "I didn't throw a tantrum exactly but I made it plain where I stood on the topic."

Pete's father, Henry, was a dentist and had heard of a nearby clinic that was perfecting a then-experimental treatment for his son's ailment. It included very aggressive physiotherapy to help correct the spine curvature. Exercise and strength were considered cornerstones to the cure at this clinic, and Henry Dawkins brought his son there. Encouraged to develop a training regimen, the 115-pound Pete Dawkins wrote away for a Charles Atlas weight-lifting program, fashioning his first set of barbells from two five-pound coffee cans filled with concrete and attached to the ends of a lead pipe.

Six years later, Dawkins was a 180-pound star quarterback at a Michigan prep school. He shunned an offer from Yale University to pursue a more high-profile football career at West Point.

"To me, it was such a place of honor and tradition, and that included football tradition," Dawkins said. "We were all very aware of the cheating scandal. When I got there everyone was conscious of it; it was still all around on the grounds.

"Bobby Blaik had gone off to Colorado and graduated from college. He was back living with his family, and I used to play hockey with him in pick-up games at West Point. I knew Bobby. So the cheating scandal was hardly deep history. We still lived it. We knew that Army's football fortunes had sagged. There was a desire to do something about that, although when I got there, I had a lot of other things to worry about."

Among those "other things" were his dismissal as a quarterback and the assignment that followed: getting mauled daily in practice as a punt returner. But one day, Dawkins eluded all the tacklers sizing him up for another late-night film session highlight and ran the punt back for a touchdown. His coaches weren't impressed—they were enraged at the coverage team. The next day Dawkins returned another punt for a touchdown. Two days later, he did it again.

Watching film of Dawkins at night, the coaches began to wonder if they had a hidden gem in their midst. Instead of a quarterback, Blaik thought, maybe Dawkins could be a running back. Pete started at his new position on the third string.

"Eight-hundred eighty-four days later," Dawkins likes to say, "I won the Heisman Trophy. Sometimes the things you think are the most awful disappointments turn out to be the most important opportunities you ever had."

Not so fast. Dawkins was still lucky to be on the third-string and still too small. As he had in his battle with polio, Dawkins turned to weight training.

"Back then, coaches thought weight lifting was bad for athletes," Dawkins said. "They thought it made you clumsy. Lifting weights, in fact, was prohibited. But I had my parents bring me a set of weights from Michigan. I hid the metal plates under the spring in my mattress and I took two belts and hooked them around the bar and hung it behind the back rung of my bed so they wouldn't see it during inspections.

"Then, after 'Taps' when the lights went out, I would take the weights out and lift in the dark. I did that for my four years at West Point. By the time I was a senior, I was 220 pounds, pretty big for a running back in 1958."

Dawkins didn't play much as a sophomore or as a junior, but in 1958 Dawkins, the one-time scrub running back, was poised to unleash the fruits of years of hard work.

Dawkins was only one of several surprises Blaik had for the world of college football. The 1958 season would prove to be Blaik's last, but as a final gift to the game to which he had dedicated much of his life, he came up with an innovation that may have been more noteworthy than any introduced since the advent of the forward pass in 1913. Blaik was always tinkering with his offensive systems, and now, several years removed from the cheating scandal, his mind was busy with the geometry of plays, specifically, how he could get defenses to concentrate fewer players in the traditional positions near the middle of the field. As players had grown bigger physically, there was even less room in the center of the field, where most plays were run. The game was slowing down, with too many of its wide open spaces ignored.

The idea came to Blaik that he could have one of his ends line up far from the rest of the formation, fifteen yards from the tackle and maybe ten yards from the sideline. The defense, Blaik theorized correctly, would have to dedicate a man to this player, who came to be known as "The Lonely End" or, in some cases, "The Lonesome End."

When Bill Carpenter, who took on this role in 1958, proved to be fast and hard to cover—too much for one man—teams began dedicating a cornerback and another player in his direction.

This completely opened up the middle of the field for Army's running backs. And then, realizing that he had the defenses guessing, Blaik installed a host of run/pass option plays that took additional advantage of overtaxed defenses. Army, not by coincidence, had the perfect running back to run those option plays, the left-handed running back Dawkins, a former quarterback. Dawkins might not have been the best passer on the team, but he was accurate enough to hit a receiver left wide open by a perplexed defense.

There was more, and it was the most cunning aspect of Blaik's mastermind project. As a last bit of psychological genius, Blaik had his Lonely End never come back to the team huddle after plays. Carpenter remained at his post near the sideline, some fifteen yards away from all his teammates as plays were called in the huddle. Then, somehow, as Army came to the line of scrimmage and snapped the football, Carpenter would execute his part of the play as if he had been in the huddle. Often, the pass would be to him and defenses were left wondering how he knew where to go and what to do.

Nowadays it is common for quarterbacks to call verbal signals or audible at the line of scrimmage before the ball is snapped. But this system of communication was not widespread in 1958 and Army quarterback Joe

Caldwell made no effort to verbally signal Carpenter. In fact, there was no outward, obvious communication at all with Carpenter.

Army's lightly regarded 1958 team unveiled its revolutionary formation in a September home game against the University of South Carolina and future NFL Pro Bowler Alex Hawkins, who entered the 1958 season a top Heisman Trophy candidate.

As Dawkins described the game in a 2003 interview: "South Carolina was utterly befuddled. They had no idea what was going on. What was that guy doing out by the sideline, and how are we supposed to cover him? And how did he know the plays anyway? It was amazing watching the chaos the formation caused. It was football genius."

Dawkins scored four touchdowns in the game, a 45–8 rout. Since the contest featured the Heisman Trophy candidate Hawkins and was a regional clash, most of the top sportswriters from throughout the Eastern seaboard had come to West Point to see it. They did not expect to come across the sensation of the 1958 college football season.

The Lonely End formation won the game, introduced a new Heisman Trophy candidate in Dawkins, and roused a clamorous stir as the writers besieged Army players and coaches with questions about how Carpenter got word of the plays called.

But the writers were, in effect, asking for military secrets, and the Army players and coaches gave them nothing more than the equivalent of name, rank, and serial number. It turned out that Blaik's friend General Douglas MacArthur himself had helped devise the surreptitious signaling to Carpenter. No one associated with Army was going to rat out the general.

Of course, having no answer to the Lonely End mystery only made it that much more compelling. The country was agog over Army's furtive formation, especially after Army shut out Penn State, 26–0, and then made a rare journey to Notre Dame, where the Cadets won 14–2, with Dawkins scoring the clinching touchdown. Virginia fell next (35–6), as did Colgate, 68–6.

Though he saw the football far less often than Dawkins, Carpenter was having a stellar season as well. The Lonely End's biggest contribution was causing trouble for opposing defenses.

"Every team we played had to put in a whole new set of defenses to face us," Dawkins said. "And they only had a few days between games to do it. It really was a cruel thing to do to a football team. And when I would run into guys we played against, some thirty or forty years later, they would tell me how many hours they spent thinking and trying to figure out how Bill Carpenter got his signals.

"Which has nothing to do with playing the game against us. The psychological warfare of Blaik's Lonely End couldn't be underestimated. It was a brilliant strategy."

As Blaik explained after the season to reporters, Carpenter picked up the plays initially by watching quarterback Joe Caldwell's feet in the huddle. If Caldwell stood with his feet side by side and square, it was a run. If Caldwell advanced one foot in front of the other, it was a pass.

Dawkins was in on the subterfuge, too. He was always positioned in the huddle nearest to the side Carpenter on which was aligned. As Army broke from its huddle, Dawkins used subtle hand, arm, and body signals to identify which of five predesigned routes Carpenter was to run on the called play. If it was a run, Carpenter would execute the same route but block downfield. If it was a pass, he would run the route in an effort to get open as a receiver.

Dawkins was the greatest beneficiary of the Lonely End as his running and passing abilities blossomed in the open spaces created. And as he racked up yards and points every week, the nation's sportswriters inevitably gravitated to him and found Dawkins to be bright and insightful. Since the sports world could not get enough of the intriguing Lonely End saga, writers of all the top New York City newspapers and the top weekly magazines—also based in New York—made treks to nearby West Point to profile Dawkins. So did the powerful radio networks and a burgeoning television industry.

They flocked to the well-spoken, photogenic Dawkins. When they did, out came the stories, not only of his childhood polio and Blaik's attempts to cut Dawkins from the team two years earlier, but of Dawkins's responsibilities as a cadet at West Point.

Dawkins was the brigade captain of the Corps of Cadets, the highest honor a cadet can hold. As such, he ruled on and enforced all disciplinary matters pertaining to the 2,500 other cadets. Furthermore, Dawkins was senior class president, ranked in the top 5 percent of his class, making him a "star man," and was the captain of the football team. In the history of the

DAWKINS (WITH FOOTBALL)

U.S. military academy, Dawkins is the only cadet to be the brigade captain of the corps, the class president, a star man, and a football captain.

If such a multifaceted, winsome story needed a last bit of polish, Dawkins was, and is, an engaging interview subject. After games and after practices in 1958, Dawkins spoke with wit and wisdom about his team and about Army football's place in American society. If asked, he would talk with passion about art, music, food, and film. The national press were charmed.

In a matter of weeks, the Lonely End created a national buzz and put the Army football program at the epicenter of the hubbub. The spirit of the Corps of Cadets was revived, too. Friday nights that fall at West Point meant a spontaneous post-dinner pep rally after which every single player would be hoisted onto the shoulders of eight or ten of his fellow students and carried back to his room. And with each Army victory, the Army cheating scandal was receding.

In November, Army defeated Rice, 14–7, with Dawkins scoring the winning touchdown on a sixty-four-yard touchdown pass in the final minute. Adding to the budding legend of his season, Dawkins had discerned a weakness in the Rice defense and devised a new pass play on the fly in the Army huddle. Quarterback Joe Caldwell threw the football as instructed and Dawkins hauled it in and outran the Rice team to the end zone.

Against Villanova the next week, Dawkins returned a punt eighty yards, caught a forty-six-yard touchdown pass and set up a final touchdown with another long reception in a 26–0 victory.

Entering Army's final game of the season, against Navy in Philadelphia, the Cadets were 7–0–1. The lone blemish had been a rainy day 14–14 tie at the University of Pittsburgh when Dawkins had sat out most of the game with an injured leg.

The Army–Navy game was nationally televised, and many fans would be getting their first look at the Lonely End that they had read and heard so much about. Navy stole some of Army's thunder with an early 6–0 lead— earned when Dawkins fumbled the opening kickoff—but despite their academy training, Navy was no better at decoding the Lonely End chicanery than any of Army's other opponents. Thanks to distractions by Carpenter, who was frequently used as a decoy, Army slowly built a commanding lead.

Dawkins's last contribution on a football field was his successful pass to backfield mate Bob Anderson for a two-point conversion in Army's 22–6 victory.

Dawkins won a close vote for the 1958 Heisman Trophy, defeating Iowa quarterback Randy Duncan and Louisiana State halfback Billy Cannon, who would win the trophy in 1959. At the Heisman celebratory dinner in New York, Dawkins's moving acceptance speech, broadcast live nationally on radio, thanked Blaik, his teammates, and the academy at West Point for four years' worth of lessons.

Blaik, whose football career began as a West Point plebe in 1919 shortly after the end of World War I, retired two weeks later. To date, his last team is the last in Army football history to complete a season undefeated.

Dawkins left West Point, but not the spotlight. He quickly began three years as a Rhodes scholar at England's Oxford University, studying philosophy, politics, and economics. Not surprisingly, Dawkins decided to try his hand at some new sports, cricket and rugby. In rugby, he was not only an elite player competing on the international level, he also brought a little Lonely End innovation with him. For as long as people had been playing rugby, the standard way to throw the ball back into play from the sideline after a stoppage in play was an underhand toss of five to ten yards.

Given the chance, Dawkins picked the ball up and heaved it overhand thirty or forty yards down the field to a teammate, a stunning, and legal, adaptation that had British sportswriters nearly as frenzied as their American counterparts had been with the Lonely End. It became known as the "Yank's torpedo pass," and was soon widely emulated.

By 1966, Dawkins had returned to the United States, married his girlfriend Judi, and begun a career in the military that would span the next twenty-four years. He finished infantry, parachute, and Ranger training; learned to speak Vietnamese in a California language training school; and became a company commander in the 82nd Airborne Division. But America had changed since he left West Point in 1958.

By the earliest days of 1966, what had been called the conflict in Vietnam had become America's first undeclared war. President Lyndon B. Johnson had dispatched 154,000 American soldiers to Vietnam, with more to follow.

The war was creating a chasm in America, a breach that would spawn a groundswell peace movement and lead to the most tumultuous, ongoing civil disturbances America had seen since the end of the Civil War a century earlier. The country seemed split in a myriad of confusing ways. On the one hand, Americans, in record numbers, were happily tuning in to

watch a talking horse, Mr. Ed, in the new top-rated television show. Fashion designers had introduced the miniskirt to great fanfare, and Hollywood was engrossed in gossip over a five-minute ceremony in Las Vegas that wed fifty-year-old star Frank Sinatra to twenty-year-old actress Mia Farrow.

At the same time, other sectors in America were grim-faced and troubled. They were not laughing along with Mr. Ed. They were far more likely to be listening to Bob Dylan's hit "The Times They Are A-Changin'" than Nancy Sinatra's "These Boots Are Made for Walking." In rallies across the country, young men burned their draft cards in defiance of war. By the thousands, others fled to Canada to evade the draft. Hippies, peaceniks, and doves became new and vocal threads in the fabric of a charged culture on edge. On April 26, the weekly total of American dead in Vietnam, presented on the evening news with a scoreboard-like graphic as if it were a football game—America 95, Vietnam 67—revealed that for the first time more Americans were dying in the war than Vietnamese. Soon after, there was a march of 10,000 demonstrators to the lawn of the White House. Students at the University of Chicago and City College in New York took over school administration offices to protest their institution's cooperation with the national selective service, the Army draft.

More than 20,000 war protesters marched down New York's Fifth Avenue in the largest demonstration against the war yet. When the march reached Eighty-Sixth Street, it was met by angry war veterans in a counterprotest. A melee ensued that had to be quelled by riot police.

"Anyone in the military then, anyone in the military for the next twenty years, was well aware of how difficult a time it was," Dawkins said. "There was no blindness to it. But we had our assignments with a lot of young soldiers counting on them."

In early 1966, Dawkins, then a captain, was stationed as a senior advisor to South Vietnamese airborne troops when he was suddenly dropped into the middle of a menacing, life-and-death combat zone.

"It was a helicopter assault and we were supposed to be landing on a highly decorated South Vietnamese battalion," Dawkins, recounted. "Turns out we were landing on a North Vietnamese regiment. This was the beginning of the North Vietnamese advance in the country. We got some troops on the ground and then the North Vietnamese started shooting our helicopters out of the sky. I had a rifle company of U.S. Marines and a limited number of South Vietnamese troops but we were getting shellacked. They were beating the devil out of us.

"We were in tremendous trouble—surrounded, outnumbered, no way to get reinforcements—and we were at the bottom of a hill while the North Vietnamese were on top of the hill flinging grenades down at us. Then, the officer in command of the South Vietnamese troops took off, dug a hole, and got in it. He exited the battle. I was like, 'What now?'"

Dawkins had access to air and artillery support and began radioing for help. He directed the South Vietnamese officers in their own language to establish layered defense positions to hold back the enemy. He instructed the Marine rifle company similarly, imploring them to shift and move, both for safety and to confuse the enemy.

Switching frequencies on the radio channels used by the South Vietnamese and a different channel used by the U.S. Marines, Dawkins coordinated the air and artillery support to direct the shelling to the greatest concentrations of North Vietnamese forces.

"We were staying alive, but only because of that support, and then the weather turned bad and the air support had to turn back," Dawkins said.

After a few tense hours, Dawkins was told that the artillery support was slated to end as well, at midnight. Because the battle had been unexpected, the Marine artillery was not adequately supplied. The only way to get more ammunition was to traverse an unsecured road, and the rules of the company forbade resupply runs across that road in darkness. Ambushes were common.

Sitting comfortably in his lavish midtown Manhattan office in 2003, Dawkins recalled the radio communication that night thirty-seven years ago. "I said without any particular emotion that we wouldn't be there in the morning. I said: 'We won't make it. By the time you resupply, we'll be dead or prisoners without that artillery.'"

Unbeknownst to Dawkins, Marine Brigadier General Joe Platt was listening to the radio transmission. "He had been fighting since World War II," Dawkins said. "He had his own idea on some of these rules." General Platt ordered a middle-of-the-night resupply mission across the unsecured road.

DAWKINS AT OXFORD

"Just before dawn, after a long night, the North Vietnamese attacked, thinking we were sitting ducks," Dawkins said. "And with fresh ammo, the Marine batteries cut them to pieces. We got out of there not long after. They saved our lives."

Dawkins told the story as do many war veterans, with a matter-of-factness to his voice that made it seem like an ordinary day's work.

Dawkins remained in Vietnam, serving as a captain in both the U.S. Army and the South Vietnamese Army. He left as a much decorated officer, receiving two Bronze Stars with oak leaf clusters. His immediate successor at his Vietnam post was the former Lonely End, Bill Carpenter, who would one day be recommended for the Congressional Medal of Honor for his valor in combat.

After serving in various high-ranking military posts, Dawkins ended his army career in 1983 to begin a career in finance and backing. He left knowing his military life had spanned a historic and turbulent period in American history.

"It was a very difficult time," he said. "A wonderful institution, the United States military, was battered by Vietnam, dismembered in many ways. The place of the military in a free country is dependent on the support of and confidence of the people, and that was lost. The institution had lost confidence in itself. Many of us who lived through that period, particularly those of us who were young battalion commanders in the late 1960s and 1970s—as I was and Colin Powell was—really felt a responsibility to build back and restore the institution.

"We had a lot of problems, but over time, and while adjusting to a volunteer army, a lot of people accomplished some vitally important work. There are some of us who take a quiet sort of pride in putting the institution back on a path to where now it is the unchallengeable military organization on the face of the earth and has a kind of stature and standing with the American public again."

In 1988, as the Republican Party candidate, Dawkins made an unsuccessful attempt to win election to the United States Senate in New Jersey. These days, in his Manhattan office at Citicorp, there are a few reminders of his football career, including a replica of the helmet he wore in 1958, with a single gray facemask bar. His Heisman Trophy is at home, in his den, where sooner or later virtually every visitor to the Dawkins household ends up gazing at it.

"The thing is just a magnet," Dawkins said of his Heisman Trophy. "Symbolically, it's a giant in people's minds."

Like his brethren in the Heisman winners fraternity, Dawkins has contemplated the award's meaning and believes he has at least a partial answer. His deliberations begin on the value of athletics in general.

"I sincerely believe that athletics teaches important fundamental principles," Dawkins said. "For example, you have to develop real competencies. You can't fake it. You have to learn to be good at something by working at it and studying it until you know you can do it and can prove it.

"Secondly, teamwork is a real concept. A group of people, like-minded and committed, can achieve remarkable things. Third, accountability is real. When you fumble the ball in football, you are accountable. You take responsibility. A fourth thing is that athletics teaches you that you cannot give up when things are not going your way. You must keep trying. That is real, too.

"So there are all these basic, fundamental elements of life that you can't learn by talking about them; they are experiential. You learn by doing them. Athletics is not the only way to learn them but it is proven to be a very good way to learn them. Now, Americans have learned to love sports in part because it imparts all these lessons. We love the notion of excelling and achieving. We want to feel good about others. Our football team in 1958 did not set out to restore some of the luster to Army football but as the season was going on, we knew it was happening. And we all saw the benefits."

And where does the Heisman come in?

"People have difficulty coming to grips with abstractions," Dawkins said, smiling. "Maybe these notions of excelling and victory need to be embodied in a person before we can identify with them. My belief is that people like symbols of success and achievement, not only in football but in America, and here is this thing—the Heisman Trophy—and somehow it distills all these abstract notions into a person who does things that give success a texture and understandability."

Dawkins let his theory hover in the air for a minute, then summoned a final thought.

"People sometimes ask me if I regret having never played professional football," Dawkins said. "And I answer by asking them to picture my last act as a football player, which was to walk out of the Downtown Athletic Club with the Heisman Trophy under my arm. I don't usually have to say anything else."

"The Perfect Kid"

ERNIE DAVIS, 1961

Hanging in the old Heisman Room of the Downtown Athletic Club, before it was shuttered in 2002, the oil paintings of each of the Heisman winners gave the space an imposing panoramic aura. Arranged chronologically, to view these tableaus one by one was a trip in time for any visitor.

Going down the line, to come upon Davis's smiling face is a touchstone moment, and not just because one must scan twenty-six paintings to find the face of a black man. There is an assured, happy pride in the portrait of Davis that enlivens the room. Here is the likeness of a man in his moment, fully understanding its meaning. Sadly, this is also the portrait of a man looking toward a bright future, unaware he would never see his twenty-fourth birthday.

To this day, the portrait carries the light of Davis's special countenance, even an air of the nobility that has made him a sporting immortal. At home in Elmira, New York, the entire inscription on the thirty-inch-high tombstone of Ernie Davis is a simple acknowledgment: Ernie Davis, Heisman Trophy 1961. It defines the accomplishments of the perfect man for an imperfect world.

Race was not a factor in the balloting for the Heisman Trophy for most of the early years of the award. Few African-Americans played college football; fewer still were given prominent, contributing roles at featured universities. That began to change in the 1950s, but college football moved very slowly to change with it.

Jackie Robinson broke the color barrier in Major League Baseball in 1947, but nine years later, Jim Brown, a black running back at Syracuse University who was considered by many to be one of the best football players ever, finished fifth in the Heisman balloting. Paul Hornung, among the most versatile, gifted football players of the 1950s, was undoubtedly a worthy winner of the 1956 trophy, but it was the breakdown of the voting that year that revealed the racial divisions still existing in America. Brown received the most votes on ballots cast in the East. In the South, he was fifth. And in the Midwest, Southwest, and Far West, Brown did not even crack the top five, a voting anomaly that has occurred only four other times in the sixty-eight years of the award.

The dynamic of a Heisman election is routinely laden by the subjective, which in the best of cases is an intellectual labyrinth meant to separate opinion from bias. But in 1956, any understanding of the times would say race played a dominant role in the vote's outcome. It was in this climate, albeit two years later, that Ernie Davis enrolled at Syracuse.

Born on December 14, 1939, Davis was raised in Uniontown, outside Pittsburgh, by his grandparents, Willie and Elizabeth Davis. Ernie's father, a Pennsylvania coal miner, perished in an accident while his mother Marie was pregnant with Ernie. Young and jobless, Marie felt ill-prepared to care for a baby, so she sent Ernie to live with her parents. Willie Davis was another six-day-a-week coal miner with twelve children of his own, and Ernie blended in. Virtually everyone in Uniontown thought Ernie was just another Davis sibling.

Neighbors found the Davis household fascinating. Willie Davis had strict time schedules for his children, a set of written rules and various canons that stressed deep religious faith and obligated everyone in the family to devote regular hours to charity services in the community. Willie Davis also liked to engage his children and Ernie in current events discussions at the dinner table nightly, an occasion when everyone was expected to dress neatly. Willie would usually name the topic, often based on something he had read or heard that day. Everyone in the room was expected to participate.

Ernie was considered more of a listener who waited until the end of the discussion to make brief, cogent remarks. Though he was known to

speak his mind, Ernie often stuttered, especially if nervous. Although he was shy and quiet, people in the Uniontown community noticed that Ernie made friends easily, that even among rival groups or school cliques, Ernie was welcome in any circle.

In 1952, when he was twelve, Ernie's mother, then newly remarried and living in Elmira, New York sent for him. "I think she needs me," Ernie told one of his uncles, "and I need to know her."

"It was time," said Marie Davis Fleming. "We were good for each other."

Ernie was big for a twelve-year-old and he was quickly recruited into Elmira's omnipresent sports culture. Like most northern cities in the 1950s, African-Americans mostly lived in their own sections of town, frequenting their own restaurants and shops. Athletics in town, however, were a mix, especially if you were the best athlete for miles around.

As he had demonstrated in Pennsylvania, Davis had a way of putting people at ease. Despite his size, he did not bully or thrash his overwhelmed opponents in peewee football games, preferring to just stop their progress on defense, literally holding them off the ground until the whistle blew.

At the Elmira Free Academy, Davis starred in football and basketball, where the team won the last fifty-two games Ernie played. In football, he was unstoppable, dubbed the Elmira Express, averaging 7.4 yards per carry in his high school career. Davis was immensely popular with Elmira's youth, and a routine trip by Davis to a local park could draw a crowd of twenty-five small children tugging and climbing on his strong arms and legs. He was as well received by the Elmira elders, who welcomed the gentle peacemaker at a time when unrest between the white and black factions in the city was brewing.

Ernie Davis was an equal opportunity mediator, defusing some disputes in Elmira with no more than his presence on a mixed playground of whites and blacks or, on at least one occasion, with his fists when one of his black friends had picked on a white teammate.

William Nack, who wrote a moving story on Davis's life for *Sports Illustrated*, interviewed Davis's high school coach, Jim Flynn, in 1989. Flynn told a story about a young white boy who came out to play football for the first time and inadvertently put his shoulder pads on backwards. The boy was being teased and ridiculed.

Davis, a junior and already a star, hurried across the room, lifted the shoulder pads from the boy and said: "Let me help you. These things can be confusing. Don't be embarrassed, I did the same thing on my first day here." Davis settled the shoulder pads in their proper place, stared around the room at his teammates, and laced them up.

Davis was among the best-known high school football players in the nation, but many colleges were not ready for a star black player, and they ignored the Elmira Express. Syracuse, however, sent Jim Brown to help recruit Davis. While Davis would gladly follow in Brown's footsteps, even at Syracuse, he was still entering an environment rife with racial tension. And it centered around the black athletes on campus.

It was only a few years earlier that another black football player at Syracuse, Avatus Stone, had brought scandal to the school by dating a blonde, white majorette who performed with the school band. This spawned a tense campus firestorm. In 1958 America, when Davis began his college education, placing black and white grammar school children in the same classroom was controversial. Arkansas Governor Orval Faubus had recently shut down the Little Rock high schools in opposition to new federal desegregation laws, and the local courts backed the governor.

So even in the middle of upstate New York, at a private university attended by thousands of historically liberal-thinking upper middle class students from metropolitan New York City, Davis, like Brown before him, had clear marching orders: Be careful in everything you do, especially around the white students. Brown has often spoken of how his every move was examined, though he too persevered in his time at Syracuse to become a standard-bearer himself, and an All-American in both football and lacrosse.

But Brown always felt Davis took the path he blazed and broadened it, making it more accessible to more black players and less threatening to whites. As Brown told Nack: "The greatest thing about Ernie Davis is that white people liked him and black people liked him. And I liked him, too, because I never thought of him as an Uncle Tom. I thought of him as a certain kind of spiritual individual, a true kind of spirit who had the ability to rise above things and deal more with the universe, so that white people would forget their racism with him and black people would never think he was acquiescing to white people. Usually, you either line up on one side or the other. So Ernie Davis transcended racism. That was his essence. That was his greatness."

Davis did not smoke, drink, or swear. Every night before he went to sleep, he knelt on the floor, and with his elbows on his bed, prayed as his grandfather had taught him to do. His roommate, John Mackey, the future Pro Bowl tight end for the Baltimore Colts, learned to pray with him. Mackey, a big, strapping high school star, had come to Syracuse expecting to compete with Davis for the starting running back job. He had switched to tight end a few days after watching with admiration as Davis tore through the Syracuse practices with his powerful, fleet running style. It was not the only way Davis influenced Mackey's life. Ernie later introduced Mackey to his future wife, insisting that Mackey go out with her.

Davis was also revered by his coaches. The late Syracuse Coach Ben Schwartzwalder once said of Davis that although he knew he was getting a gifted player, he did not know he was getting the greatest gift of his coaching career. "The perfect kid," Schwartzwalder said. "The kind of person who dominated a game—he would run over guys in his way—and then spend all the time after the play complimenting the other players. When somebody brought him down he would say 'Good tackle' as he picked the guy up and patted him on the back. He was so thoughtful and polite that opponents would come into the dressing room after games to see him."

Not everyone Davis played against treated him with respect. Some white players on opposing teams would scratch and gouge at Davis's arms or sucker punch him in the stomach or kidneys on the bottom of pile-ups. Davis, as instructed, never responded verbally or physically. Like Jackie Robinson, he had to avoid any incident that would ruin the greater cause. But his teammates became his allies in the effort, a bond that blossomed in Davis's very first season with the varsity as a sophomore. Syracuse won the national title that year, but the meaning of that accomplishment—with Davis as the protagonist—was delivered during the final game that season at the Cotton Bowl.

Syracuse was a balanced, well-coached, and seasoned team in 1959. Davis led the way with ten touchdowns, an average of seven yards per rushing carry, and superlative defensive back play. He was a big running back, gutty and graceful, who rarely went down on the first hit and frequently turned three-yard gains up the middle into long, sweeping dashes down the sideline.

"He could just glide," said John Brown, Davis's teammate and longtime friend.

Syracuse streaked through the 1959 regular season undefeated in its ten games. At that time in college football, national champions were voted on by the major wire service and coaching polls before the New Year's Day bowl games, and Syracuse was everyone's number one team. The Orangemen headed to the Cotton Bowl to face Texas, the storied powerhouse of the Southwest. They knew a loss would, at least figuratively, cancel their selection as national champion.

Brown, one of Davis's few black teammates, describes the atmosphere for the Cotton Bowl in Dallas as troublesome from the very beginning.

"We arrived at the Melrose Hotel in the city and Ernie and I were immediately escorted around the lobby to a room with two cots behind the kitchen," Brown said in a 2003 interview. "That is where we were to sleep. They also said they knew we were going to have team meetings in the upper floors of the hotel where the rest of the team was staying, but we were told to stay off the elevators so we wouldn't offend any of the white guests. And you know, I tell you honestly, we understood that. That's the way it was down there back then."

The days leading up to the New Year's Day game left the black Syracuse players feeling more and more isolated and offended. On the day of the game, as they stood on the Cotton Bowl field awaiting the opening kickoff, according to Brown, some of his teammates, and newspaper accounts of the game, several members of Texas's all-white team taunted Davis and Brown. Later, Brown said, he was ridiculed with a racial slur. Texas players, meanwhile, would claim that the Syracuse players were the ones initiating the verbal war.

Davis appeared unfazed, although not necessarily unperturbed. He responded the best way he knew how. On Syracuse's second play from scrimmage, he caught a short pass over the middle and raced eighty-seven yards through the entire Texas defense, limping slightly from a pulled hamstring sustained before the game but still too swift and strong to be caught or stopped. It was the longest reception in a major college bowl game at the time.

But Davis was not done. He would score another touchdown and intercept a pass that set up a third touchdown. He also scored both two-point conversions Syracuse attempted that day in a thorough 23–14 rout of Texas.

The game was marred by a brawl just before halftime, ignited in part by John Brown, who said he took offense at a remark made to him by one of the Texas players. "I was nineteen years old and I had been down there for two weeks, subjected to their brand of hospitality," Brown, a tackle, said. "I watched them taunting us. And when somebody said something to me, finally, I couldn't take it. I wasn't as good at that as Ernie. Nobody was."

Players from both teams spilled off the sidelines in the tussle, which never got completely out of hand, but there were punches thrown and a lot of grabbing and shoving. Texas newspapers the following day called it a "gang-like rhubarb." The specifics of who did what, or what exactly was said, were never verified by any independent sources, even after Texas Coach Darrell Royal called a postgame meeting and asked his players to raise a hand if they heard or if they made any racial slurs (no hands were raised).

"It was a lot of emotion," Brown said. "I have to say I went back to Dallas several years ago because they were honoring Ernie at the Cotton Bowl. I met Darrell Royal, a magnificent man. He shook my hand and apologized. He said he did not know that anything was being said. He was very gracious. It was the times, but I don't fault anybody."

Davis, although just a sophomore, was the unquestioned star of the 1959 Cotton Bowl and was named the game's MVP. He was informed by Cotton Bowl officials that there was a dinner and awards ceremony that evening where he would be presented his MVP trophy. The officials also told Davis he could show up for the awards ceremony but could not remain for any of the festivities that would follow.

"And that's what we did," Brown said. "We went to their little show and then we had to leave."

For years afterward, Davis always declined to acknowledge any of the harassment he received for being a black player in a mostly white sport. He behaved, to his friends and family, as if it had never happened. Except for his Cotton Bowl experience. That rankled him forever.

"He never talked about anything he went through," Ernie's mother, Marie Davis Fleming, said in an interview for a superb 1999 documentary on Davis's life produced by ESPN Classic. "But he did after that game. He was on the telephone and he was stuttering. I hadn't heard Ernie stutter for years. But he was stuttering that night. He was that upset. But in a few weeks, he was ready to put the Cotton Bowl experience behind him."

Davis pressed on and was named an All-American in each of his next two college seasons. He assimilated into the culture of the Syracuse campus, where he was popular, even if he was still viewed as someone apart from the rest of the student body. But by his senior season, in a landmark event of some measure, Davis was invited to join an all-white Jewish fraternity on campus. The vote of his future fraternity brothers was far from unanimous, but Davis was admitted. A devout Christian, Davis used to laugh that he had hurdled another barrier, even if it was an ecumenical one.

As a junior, he received some votes for the Heisman, although he did not finish in the top ten in the balloting. By the end of his senior season, however, Davis was clearly the best running back in the nation. In three seasons, he had broken all of Jim Brown's records, including rushing yards (2,386 to 2,091), yards per carry (6.6 to 5.8), touchdowns (35 to 25), and points scored (220 to 187).

When it came time for the voting for the 1961 Heisman, Davis was completing a stellar year but, in a sense, his selection for the award may have been more of a tribute to three successive seasons of excellence. At the time, Davis had taken his place among the best running backs in college football history.

Davis became the first African-American Heisman Trophy winner, while wearing Jim Brown's jersey number 44 in tribute. The 1961 vote was the second closest ever—Bob Ferguson of Ohio State was second—and Davis won only one region (the East), but he did place among the top five in the voting from each of the other four regions.

"Still, he was surprised when he won," John Brown said. "Because we both thought that if the great Jim Brown couldn't win the Heisman, what chance did Ernie have? But you know, as great as Jim Brown was, Ernie probably was better."

The grandest, most carefree days in the brief adult life of Ernie Davis probably occurred in the few days when Davis went to the Downtown Athletic Club to accept his Heisman Trophy. As usual, the club rolled out the red carpet for the winner and his family. Davis saw the town and was feted on radio, on Broadway (where he received an ovation at intermission of the play he attended), and in the pages of the city's eminent newspapers. All the big-time sports columnists, who had seen Davis play football, were now smitten by Davis's humble, sincere comportment, something he maintained even in the brightest spotlights.

President John F. Kennedy was in Manhattan during the Heisman weekend, attending a United Nations conference on what to do about an August 1961 construction project, the most famous cinder block structure ever—the Berlin Wall. Kennedy read the glowing coverage of Davis and asked to meet him. Davis was spirited by limousine to the Waldorf-Astoria, where he and Kennedy talked briefly. Photographs were taken of the two shaking hands, and Davis kept a copy of the picture with him for the rest of his life.

Davis left his meeting with Kennedy and soon saw Coach Schwartzwalder. "Put 'er there, Coach," Davis said. "Shake the hand that shook the hand of President Kennedy." He repeated the same greeting with friends for days afterward.

"He was like a kid," John Brown said. "I don't think he washed that hand for days either. He was on top of the world. Those were great times for Ernie."

But not everything about the times was great for Ernie Davis or for other blacks like him. Brown also tells the story of their trip to York, Pennsylvania, in the spring of 1962. Late at night, just outside the city limits, they stopped at a roadside diner. They were refused service. Only the counter was open, and blacks were not allowed at the counter.

"Ernie and I looked at each other like 'What? Where are we?'" Brown said. "We just got back in the car and kept driving. But you think about things like that. Here was Ernie shaking hands with the President of the United States one day and a few months later, not that far from Washington, D.C., we couldn't get a bacon and egg sandwich. You just shake your head. I still shake my head at the thought."

There was a movement afoot to protest such discrimination. Organized sit-in demonstrations at white-only restaurants were cropping up across America. They led to arrests and jail sentences, but just five days after Davis accepted his Heisman Trophy at the gala dinner in New York, the U.S. Supreme Court voided the first of those integration sit-in convictions, a significant precedent-setting ruling.

Elsewhere in Washington, D.C., Ernie Davis was everyone's choice as the top pick in the NFL draft, held by the Washington Redskins, who, coincidentally, were the last remaining team in the league without a black player. Pressure had been mounting on Redskins owner George Preston Marshall to end what appeared to be a boycott of black players, but the mercurial Marshall had stubbornly resisted. In a strange twist, Marshall did not welcome Davis as his new star and franchise player. Instead, he traded the first overall pick to the Cleveland Browns for running backs Bobby Mitchell and Leroy Jackson, two other black players.

Browns owner Art Modell was ecstatic to capitalize on Marshall's bizarre choice. Modell already had Jim Brown in his backfield—imagine adding Davis to the mix! Davis was thrilled at the prospect of playing with his one-time idol, the man who had blazed the trail for him at Syracuse.

In his first post-college football game, an exhibition of college all-stars in Buffalo, Davis looked uncharacteristically listless. Davis remarked that he felt exhausted, but it was a hot night and no one made much of it. Many players were weary in the heat. Besides, in the days before the game, Davis was having trouble with his teeth, frequently complaining of canker sores and tender, bleeding gums.

"I should have known something right then," Brown said. "Ernie never complained."

In late July, Davis was in Chicago, where every year a team of the top graduating college players from the previous season played a much bally-hooed game against the defending NFL champions at Soldier Field. The game included a week of practices, after which most of the former college players would join their pro teams. Otto Graham, the NFL Hall of Fame quarterback, was coaching the college team. He had never before seen Davis perform in person.

"We all just looked at each other and someone said, 'He's an All-American?'" Graham said in a 1989 interview, recalling the first day of practice. "He had no pep. He wasn't showing us anything."

Davis was still bothered by mouth problems and had two wisdom teeth removed. It took a day to stop the bleeding. The next day, when Davis complained of swelling in his neck, he was admitted to Evanston Hospital, not far from the college all-stars practice site at Northwestern University. Given Davis's fatigue, the doctors' first thought was that he had mononucleosis or perhaps mumps.

But further tests revealed a devastating diagnosis: acute monocytic leukemia, the most deadly form of leukemia. Modell was the first to receive the news and refused to believe the Chicago doctors. "Don't touch him," Modell said over the phone when he received the call from Evanston Hospital. "I'm taking him to other doctors."

Modell went on a crusade to help Davis. Modell had come to know

Ernie over the previous few months, and he, like many authority figures in Davis's life, was drawn to him in a very personal way. Though he never knew his own father, throughout his life Davis was surrounded by men who adopted him in a paternalistic way. Coaches, mentors, and club owners all willingly became father figures. To be sure, Modell had a financial interest in Davis's well-being, but even four decades later, Modell makes it clear how fervent and passionate he was in his desire to make Ernie's plight somehow better.

But Modell's handpicked doctors had the same diagnosis; indeed, they confirmed it irrefutably. The usual treatment course was chemotherapy, but few patients lived for more than a year. Davis was told he had a blood disorder, even if the severity of his condition was not made plain. Ernie checked into a Cleveland area hospital for treatment, was scratched from the Chicago all-star game, and not permitted to practice with the Browns. Modell at first told reporters that Davis had a disorder that required rest and hospital treatment and said nothing more. Eventually, in another remarkable representation of how different 1962 was from the current media culture, Modell assembled the reporters covering the Browns in his office and informed them, off the record, that Davis had a potentially fatal disease but he did not want it written. The grievousness of Davis's condition never made its way into print that summer.

"Ernie did everything they asked of him, and he believed he would beat it," said John Brown, who lived with Davis in Cleveland and was beginning a long professional career as a player in Cleveland and Pittsburgh. "I believed it, too. You could easily believe those kind of things about Ernie."

By the fall, Davis's condition did improve when his leukemia appeared to be temporarily in remission. It was then that Ernie's doctors told him of the extent of his condition, that there was hope and treatment, but no known cure. The team made a vague announcement to reporters that Davis had a form of leukemia but provided no specifics. Davis's spirits were buoyed when his doctors said that with his condition stabilized, he could resume playing football.

But Cleveland Coach Paul Brown, a pro football icon for whom the team was named, had been consulting his own doctors on Davis's condition. Brown's doctors told him it was too risky to allow Davis to play. John

Brown said he felt Paul Brown thought Ernie's playing would be a distraction to the team. Modell pleaded with his coach to reconsider and the confrontation that arose was the beginning of a rift that ended with Paul Brown leaving Cleveland after the 1962 season.

Davis remained out of the quarrel. He had been stoic throughout his ordeal that summer and fall, never showing any distress, worry, or self-pity. During his treatment, Davis had told the Browns front office he had a lot of time on hands since he wasn't playing, and he asked if they needed any community service or charity work to be done. Davis was everywhere in the community thereafter, becoming one of the best-known and popular Browns, even without a uniform.

In October, after another failed attempt to convince Paul Brown to allow Davis to suit up for just one play, or maybe a kickoff return, Modell decided he would at least give Davis a moment to celebrate at Cleveland's mammoth Municipal Stadium. Davis was introduced with the team before their next home game, walking onto the field and then jogging past the goalposts where he was enveloped by his teammates.

Said Modell: "There wasn't a dry eye in the house."

By March 1963, Davis's leukemia was once again causing a myriad of physical problems. Those around Ernie learned to avert their eyes as Ernie stuffed cotton up his nose to stem sudden nosebleeds. The disease inhibited his blood's ability to clot, so while Ernie was eating dinner at restaurants or attending public charity functions, he kept a stash of handkerchiefs or other tissues so that he could quietly retire to the men's room and surreptitiously minimize another episode. At their rented apartment, John Brown frequently found bloody bandages in the garbage. Davis made regular visits to the hospital, getting treatments and blood transfusions.

"He would never let anyone know what was going on," Brown said. "When he was in the hospital, he always said I should tell anyone who asked that he was out of town. He didn't want anyone feeling sorry for him."

Modell flew into action again, conferring with doctors nationwide. He weighed experimental theories, brought in a host of specialists to examine Davis, and paid for radical testing and research. At home in Elmira and back in Syracuse, Ernie's family and friends knew how sick he had become, but Ernie would not discuss it or how badly he felt. He would talk about what he was going to do to get better.

On a Thursday in mid-May 1963, John Brown came home and found bloody towels by the sink in the bathroom. He also discovered a note, written on yellow lined paper, from Ernie: "Going to the hospital for a few days. Don't tell anybody. See you around."

Davis actually first went to Modell's office in downtown Cleveland. He arrived unannounced, which surprised Modell. Ernie usually called before coming to see him.

"He had gone into the hospital in the past for blood transfusions and treatments but he had never come down to see me for that," Modell said. "And I told him, 'You didn't have to come down here to tell me that.' I told him I would see him when he got out, that I wanted him to start lifting weights and working out.

"He just kind of looked at me and didn't say anything. And he thanked me for everything. I thanked him."

The two shook hands before Davis left.

A day later, Davis lapsed into a coma. He died the following morning, May 18.

"What I thought at the time and what I will always remember," Modell said forty years later, "is that Ernie took the time to come down and say goodbye. I will never forget that."

Ernie Davis's wake lasted for two days in Elmira and the line to stand or kneel beside his coffin stretched two city blocks. Thousands waited. "It was like the whole world, even those who never met Ernie, knew we had all lost someone special," said John Brown, who nine years later named his son Ernie Davis Brown. "It was very sad. You could sense the mourning everywhere."

During the funeral, people stood three deep to catch a glimpse of the Davis hearse on downtown streets. Modell chartered two planes for Browns players, scouts, coaches, and team employees to attend the funeral. Crowds surged to the Woodlawn Cemetery.

They came to pay homage to the Jackie Robinson of college football, a groundbreaking player who was not only athletically gifted on the field, but also had to be exemplary in every way off the field. Like Robinson, because he accepted this unsolicited assignment with unflappable courage and dignity, he became the standard bearer for the burgeoning number of black college players nationwide.

The triumph of Ernie Davis's 1961 Heisman Trophy victory is the story of a bridge builder. In a time when the country's gaps were being highlighted at every cultural and societal turn, Davis was a beacon of unity. At the dawning of a new decade that would bear witness to revolutionary change in nearly all walks of American life, Davis was the force in college football that thrust the game out of its darkest, most narrow-minded prejudices.

In Elmira today, the high school from which Ernie graduated is named for him. At Syracuse, they did not retire his jersey number 44; instead, it was worn by another great black running back, Floyd Little, who came to the school because he had been encouraged to do so by Ernie Davis. Little did not win the Heisman Trophy, but in 1965 he finished fifth, and another African-American running back from the University of Southern California, Mike Garrett, won the award.

In less than a decade, the presence of African-American players in college football programs throughout the country became so universal, the Heisman Trophy was awarded to an African-American for ten successive seasons, from 1974 to 1983.

Ernie Davis, son of a Pennsylvania coal miner, raised by his grandparents, schooled in a gritty factory town and further educated in a New York snowbelt university city, never figured his life would someday be fabled. His way, in fact, was to avoid drawing attention to himself.

He has been dead more years now than he lived, yet the effects of his life remain. The gift of Ernie Davis, as with other pioneers, was his ability to make people change without knowing they were being changed. In his way, with humility, courage, dignity, and quiet perseverance, he emboldened some who were weighing their positions in the midst of a stormy civil rights era, while he unintentionally embarrassed others, who in his presence must have felt shamed by prejudices long held and defended.

Ernie Davis was a football player who changed America with every step off the field. He left too soon but he left behind a better America. Ernie Davis was not only the first African-American Heisman Trophy winner in 1961; he was also, in 1961 and for years before, the perfect choice at a time when his country, and all its people, most needed him.

America's Quarterback

ROGER STAUBACH, 1963

It was 1961 and Roger Staubach waited nervously in line with two dozen other Naval Academy applicants beside a small medical examination office in Denver. Passing the physical exam required for entry into the academy did not worry Staubach. But this was an eye exam for color blindness and that made him jumpy.

Though Staubach had 20/10 vision and could see colors well enough to match his clothes, he had never passed a test for color blindness in his life. Staubach knew that the Naval Academy would not admit future pilots, future artillery officers or future ship captains if they lacked the ability to perfectly distinguish all the gradations of a rainbow. No color blindness waiver into the U.S. Naval Academy existed—only an automatic rejection slip, coded, as it happened, in three-color triplicate.

"I went in pretty sure I could see the colors well enough," Staubach said, "but standing there in line I was beginning to think I was wrong."

Here, awaiting a tiresome eye test on a sleepy summer Saturday morning, was nineteen-year-old Roger Staubach scrambling to keep another broken, busted play alive. As he would later do countless times on the football field, Staubach found the uncommon ability to improvise under pressure.

Fortunately for Staubach, it was clear to everyone approaching the examination room that the Navy seaman administering this academy test was bored or distracted, his feet propped on the desk in front of him. He was showing only scant interest in the answers given. Everyone was passing. When Staubach's turn came, he misidentified some of the colored numbers within the colored shading.

The seaman was jolted into paying attention. He wasn't sure what he heard. Staubach adjusted and, looking closely, tried a different answer.

"I wasn't cheating," Staubach would say decades later. "I was sure I could do it, but I don't know, I was getting some wrong. I was trying very hard to find a way through the test. I did get most of them right."

But not enough to actually pass. "No, but it wasn't a conspiracy to get me in," Staubach said. "The seaman really wasn't paying attention. He was going, 'Wait a minute. What was that answer again?'"

There was also an applicant in line behind Staubach offering his help. Listening to Staubach he would say: "That last answer was wrong," and Staubach would scramble and recover again.

The seaman was more confused than ever. Staubach had gotten some right and some wrong. He had even gotten some right, it seemed, after he got them wrong. Staubach made small talk.

The seaman looked up, smiled, and looked back down.

"Oh, I guess you got enough right," he said and checked Staubach off as having passed the test.

A little more than a year later, while taking a physical examination before entering his second year at the Naval Academy, Staubach was required to take the eye test again. He gazed at the little round dots of red and green, tried to make out the forms, and gave his answers. This time, an academy physician was scrutinizing his responses. Listening to Staubach's answers on the color blindness test, the doctor finally put down Staubach's chart and medical file, turned, and said: "Son, how did you get in here?"

Five years later, Navy officials were asking Roger Staubach a slightly different question: How did you get out of here?

Staubach was participating in a mock prisoner of war camp on a desolate island off the state of Washington, an intensive and harrowing assignment designed to prepare American soldiers, sailors, and officers for active duty in the Vietnam War. It was Staubach's first assignment during his four years of service following his graduation from the Naval Academy.

Officers designed the camp as realistically as possible, based on interviews with prisoners of war from the Korean War and Vietnam. "They were doing all kinds of stuff to you, physically manhandling you, slapping you in the face and all that stuff," Staubach said. "It was pretty realistic and I have such respect for POWs. It broke a lot of wills.

"They put a hood over your head for hours and berated you. You had the hood on even as they took you from place to place."

But if there was a hole in any scheme, Staubach could always find it. In this case, Staubach maneuvered the hood on his head until he could faintly see through it. As he was marched between buildings, Staubach saw a six-foot barbed wire fence to his left. When nightfall came, although still wearing the hood, he suddenly dashed from his mock captors. At the fence, he tore off his jacket and threw it over the barbed wire, using it as a shield against the jagged ends of metal as he scrambled over the barrier in the dark.

By the time anyone had reached the fence, Staubach was on the other side and had disappeared into the dense woods. It took the camp officials half an hour to catch up with him, and he gave up his position in the woods only after they complimented him for his "good, successful escape."

There is nothing in either story—somehow beating a test he was doomed to fail or finding a way out of a situation that had stopped every-one else—that would surprise anyone who watched Staubach play football. Such ingenuity and resourcefulness were Staubach hallmarks and would serve him well as he revolutionized the quarterback position in college and later in the professional ranks as well.

Staubach is an American phenomenon, someone out of a Hardy Boys book, whose clean-cut good looks brought him a glut of magazine cover pho-tos in his Heisman Trophy–winning season of 1963, and whose unpre-dictable, abrupt scrambling style nurtured not one, but two nicknames: "Roger the Dodger" and "Jolly Roger." But Staubach grew beyond the bound-aries of a good, popular story. He was a dominant American personality, a Heisman winner who within months of accepting the trophy began a one-year combat stint in a new and different kind of American war, in Vietnam.

Staubach, to date at least, is the last service academy winner of the Heisman Trophy, a watershed mark for the military's role in the country and in college football. Although others who attended service academies after him frequently found ways to get their military commitment short-ened to pursue an NFL career, Staubach served his four-year obligation willingly.

"I could have left after my junior year at Navy; heck, I was drafted by the pros as a junior," Staubach said. "People talked to me about leaving but I said no. I really felt that if I tried to get out of something then I would be doing that the rest of my life. And that didn't fit with how I was brought up or how I wanted to live."

Bob and Betty Staubach raised their only child, Roger, in a mixed, middle-class neighborhood on the outskirts of Cincinnati. It was Betty Staubach who was the competitive one. She encouraged her son to try to be the best at everything he did. And he was a good student, a good Boy Scout, a good paperboy. But from the beginning, he was an outstanding athlete.

"I can remember, even as an eight- or nine-year-old, when I had the football in the playground, I was the hardest to tackle," Staubach said. "I'm not sure where that came from. My mom was encouraging and driven to succeed but I didn't have an older brother to make me want to win. But I always wanted to win. I didn't get it from my dad. He was a great guy who would give you the shirt off his back and he worked hard. But no one called him an overachiever."

Bob Staubach did instill one important concept in his son. On one of Staubach's early baseball teams—he was much more of a baseball star than a football star—Roger had asked to play first base or outfield. The coach, however, wanted him to be the team's catcher, the toughest, most demanding position on the field, which required leadership.

Roger complained to his father, asking if he had to play catcher. Bob Staubach told Roger that not everyone could be a leader, explaining that the coach needed him at catcher for the betterment of the team. Bob Staubach said Roger should honor the request by being the best catcher he could be.

Roger became the area's all-star catcher.

"I never liked playing catcher," Roger said. "But I understood how important it was."

Roger also developed an affinity for pressure situations.

"My father used to joke that even in Little League I would be rooting for the game to be close so I could come up with us down by a run in the last inning with runners on second and third," Staubach said. "He may be right. I had these juices inside of me.

"Some kids don't like pressure, but the thing is, you have to understand that you're not always going to succeed under pressure. But you can't let that failure intimidate you. Use it to make you stronger."

Staubach progressed as a top three-sport athlete, and when he entered high school went out for the football team, hoping to be a running back. His coach saw a natural quarterback. Injuries kept the young Staubach off the field for long stretches, however, and when he returned the only open spots were on defense. It wasn't until his senior year that he earned the starting quarterback's job and Staubach treated his new position as an equal opportunity to run or pass. From the beginning, he won games, including the 1959 Cincinnati city championship.

During his senior year, all the Big Ten universities came calling at the Staubach doorstep, and none wanted him more than Woody Hayes of Ohio State. Staubach wasn't sure where he wanted to go, though at one point, he verbally committed to Purdue University in Indiana.

Things were changing all around Staubach, as they were all around America. In the Staubachs' once all-white neighborhood, several black families had moved in, causing strife and anger among a close-knit community. Staubach, who as an only child treated his neighborhood buddies and their families as an extension of his family, saw what he knew was discrimination against his new neighbors, but he wasn't sure what to make of it at first. He got an early clue from his mother.

"There was a neighborhood gathering right in our living room," Staubach said. "And my mother called a bunch of the neighbors—her friends for years—hypocrites right to their faces. My mom was very aware of her surroundings and active. She had gone back to work when I was nine years old and become the secretary for a large division at the General Motors Company. She was a lone voice on this, but she wasn't going to let people discriminate in her neighborhood. She thought we had to respect everyone.

"And I think she pulled some people together. Years later, I think I learned a lot about treating people with respect from watching her. Later, it helped me a lot as a quarterback trying to lead a team of guys from very different backgrounds."

The Naval Academy was not on Staubach's radar as a potential next step in life until he visited the campus in Annapolis, Maryland. In visits to other schools, Staubach had sensed he would be more of a football player

JOE BELLINO, HEISMAN WINNER IN 1960 AND FRESHMAN COACH AT NAVY WHO RECOMMENDED THAT STAUBACK NOT BE MOVED TO RUNNING BACK

with a chance to get a good education. At Navy, he saw that the Midshipmen were students first, tutored and driven to learn.

"I actually thought my study habits were weak," Staubach said. "I felt smart enough but I felt like I needed help."

So even as Notre Dame was making a late, last effort to sign him, Staubach agreed to go to Navy. And Navy's first suggestion was that he attend the New Mexico Military Institute, a junior college where Navy placed upwards of twenty recruits a year to season them for college football and college academics.

In New Mexico, Staubach continued to be a dual-threat quarterback and was named a junior college All-American. He also learned the balance of a military school life, with its drills, formations, and jam-packed schedule.

At the Naval Academy, Staubach could not play varsity as a freshman, but he earned the admiration of one of the freshman coaches, Joe Bellino, Navy's first Heisman Trophy winner from 1960.

Bellino's impressions of Staubach proved important a year later when Navy Coach Wayne Hardin, after assigning Staubach the number five quarterback slot, talked about moving Staubach to defensive back or running back. Bellino not only disagreed, he insisted it would be Hardin's biggest mistake as a coach.

"I knew my place but I was vehement about telling them Roger had to be their quarterback," Bellino said. "I talked until I was blue in the face. At the time, Roger as a passer didn't throw a pretty ball. It wasn't a perfect spiral. But it always got to where it should be. And I told them the most important thing was that Roger was a winner.

"All you had to do to know that was watch him for a while. Of course, I also joked that I didn't want Roger to break my rushing records. But I was joking. Roger was made to be a quarterback."

Hardin relented but when the 1962 season began, he still had Staubach well down the list of starters. Navy lost two of its first three games, and two other quarterbacks to injuries as well, which moved Staubach up the depth chart. Trailing Cornell in the first quarter of the fourth game of the season, Navy's top quarterback got hurt. Hoping to jump-start his team with his most charismatic back-up quarterback, Hardin sent Staubach into the game.

What followed was one of those moments in sport when a little-known player is thrust into the perfect role on the perfect stage to launch what becomes an unforgettable career. Staubach led Navy on six touchdown drives that day, throwing for ninety-nine yards and running for another eighty-nine. He had two touchdown passes and ran for another, a crazy-legged dash through half a dozen Cornell defenders when he reversed field twice and scored from sixty-eight yards away. The play called had been a simple short pass.

With Staubach at the helm, the Midshipmen then defeated Boston College and Pittsburgh. Next came a narrow loss to eventual national champion Southern California. In the final game of the season against Army, Staubach made his first national television appearance before a sellout crowd of 102,000 fans at Philadelphia's Municipal Stadium. President Kennedy, who thirty-three days earlier had negotiated an end to the Cuban Missile Crisis with Soviet premier Nikita Khrushchev, walked onto the field to flip the coin before kickoff. Staubach led Navy to a 34–14 upset of Army with two touchdown runs and a touchdown pass. He dazzled everyone in attendance with several implausible escapes from the pocket as Army players clawed at his feet and at his shoulders, sequences when Staubach turned certain losses into long, entertaining gains. On one astounding twenty-one-yard touchdown run, Staubach evaded, at one time or another, the grasp of every Army player on the field.

"President Kennedy came to shake my hand and say a few words afterward," Staubach said, "but I was such a nervous wreck I don't remember anything he said or did."

Preparing for the 1963 season, Navy knew it had a star in its junior quarterback from Ohio. Navy sports information director Budd Thalman also knew that the country had entered a new era of mass media. Gone was the time that college football stars earned their legend in movie house newsreels. With the advent of reliable commercial air travel, more writers were able to see more games in different parts of the nation. A new television technology, called instant replay, would make its debut in the telecast of the 1963 Army–Navy game, making the viewing of twenty-two jumbled bodies on a football field more enjoyable on TV. Instant replay would also bring about the notion of highlight reels and highlight sports footage for evening television news programs.

Things were moving fast in America. Thalman sized up this changing America and invented a new way of doing business in college athletic departments. He invented the first preseason campaign to promote a player for the Heisman Trophy. Nowadays, these campaigns are highly orchestrated, professional operations run by firms outside universities. Millions are spent promoting as many as 100 top players for the Heisman. In 2001, the University of Oregon paid to have a ten-story image of quarterback Joey Harrington painted on a Manhattan skyscraper to promote his Heisman worthiness.

In 1963, Thalman wrote a short pamphlet titled "Meet Roger Staubach," a modest introduction to a modest young man, and sent it to thousands of sportswriters. It was a small act, but it got the attention of a nation of writers. It also got the attention of Staubach's teammates. In a place like a service academy where every effort is made to improve the whole corps, Staubach was teased, but he was also too well liked for it to cause resentment.

"Roger tried so hard he never had to ask for respect," said teammate Tom Lynch, the team captain who would become superintendent of the academy years later. "As blockers, for example, everyone learned pretty quick that blocking your one man wasn't going to be good enough. Roger would be back there running around for several seconds and frequently something good happened. Everyone knew that you had better block your first guy and then look for two or three more."

Hardin redesigned his offense to maximize the strategic advantage Staubach brought to the line of scrimmage on every play. Deception and improvisation at the quarterback position, with option roll-out plays, became a staple of the Navy offense.

With Staubach's craftiness and backfield magic a constant distraction to opposing defenses, Navy began the 1963 season with easy victories over West Virginia and William & Mary. Staubach racked up impressive rushing and passing totals in each win. In the third game, against Michigan, Staubach completed fourteen of sixteen passes for 237 yards, a huge sum for so few passes attempted (and almost seventeen yards per completion). Moreover, Staubach was becoming a regular in the burgeoning highlight reel industry with wild, inspiring scrambles—sometimes running backward twenty yards behind the line of scrimmage before flinging the football downfield beyond an exhausted defense.

The Michigan game had a couple of classic Staubach moments, sequences that foreshadowed his legend as a player of incredible instincts. In a single six-yard touchdown run, Roger dodged six defenders in close quarters, darting and juking until he was in the end zone—upright, unharmed, and apparently unfazed as he flipped the football to an official. Earlier in the game, with a few seconds remaining in the first half, Navy appeared ready to run out the clock as Staubach turned to make a handoff in the backfield. Instead, it was a fake and Staubach suddenly wheeled to his right, firing the football down the field. With time expired in the half, Staubach trotted toward the Navy locker room as Michigan's players, frozen at the line of scrimmage by the fake, watched the football sail into the end zone where Staubach's teammate, Johnny Sai, caught it for a fifty-four yard touchdown.

Navy won the game, 26–13.

In their fourth game, the Midshipmen lost for the only time in the 1963 regular season, falling to Southern Methodist University, 32–28. Staubach missed several key plays with an injured shoulder, but the game became a Staubach classic nonetheless. In the fourth quarter, he reentered the game with his shoulder taped and led a comeback that fell short on the game's final play, as Staubach nearly completed what would have been the game-winning touchdown pass.

Navy went on to rout the Virginia Military Institute and upset Pittsburgh, which cemented Navy's standing as the East's top college football team. Next up for Navy was a trip to Notre Dame, a challenge for any team, let alone one from a service academy with a long history of dueling with the Fighting Irish. Notre Dame's players were drilled all week in containing the elusive Staubach, already the runaway favorite to win the Heisman Trophy.

Notre Dame, however, considered itself the de facto home of the Heisman. Five of its players had already won the trophy, more than any other college. The road to the Heisman, in the eyes of Notre Dame's players and quite a few Heisman voters, went through South Bend, Indiana.

At the game's midpoint, the teams were tied 7–7. Staubach was effectively sealed off, frustrated by a persistent Notre Dame rush and a Notre Dame offense that was systematically controlling play and keeping Staubach off the field.

In the visiting locker room between halves, Hardin asked Staubach to leave the room. He then regaled his players with what amounted to his own "Win One for Roger" speech, telling those in the room that they owed it to the popular Staubach to find a way to let him win the game and the Heisman Trophy.

"Just give him some time out there," Hardin said. "He'll do the rest. Doesn't he deserve that from you?"

Navy players later said Notre Dame didn't stand a chance once Hardin was through with his speech.

Staubach threw three touchdown passes in the second half and Navy ran away with a 35–14 victory, its last win over Notre Dame to date.

The Notre Dame victory vaulted Navy to number two in the national polls behind the University of Texas, which was in the midst of another one of its powerhouse seasons.

Thalman's Heisman campaign was virtually assured of success. Soon, writers from *Time, Life, Sports Illustrated,* and *Boy's Life* magazines were making pilgrimages to the academy's Annapolis, Maryland, campus to prepare cover stories on Staubach. Staubach was also receiving a deluge of fan mail, often with requests for his autograph. For the next few weeks, Staubach would amble by Thalman's office asking for a few copies of his Navy football publicity shot. Finally, Thalman realized Staubach was answering all his fan mail himself, dutifully writing people back and paying for the postage, too. Thalman took the boxes of letters from Staubach and arranged for his staff to help him.

Navy won its next two games, setting up the match-up with Army scheduled for November 30, 1963. Army had a good team, and the winner of the game would go on to play Texas in the Cotton Bowl, the historic oval a few miles south of downtown Dallas's Dealey Plaza.

On November 22, 1963, Staubach did not know President Kennedy had traveled to Dallas for a couple of speeches and what was supposed to be some political fence mending. He had seen the president at a recent football practice, although they had not spoken on that occasion. His last conversation with Kennedy had been during the Navy's preseason training camp at Quonset Point Naval Air Station in Rhode Island.

"He would come by all the time then and just visit with us," Staubach said. "He would use the Quonset Point base as a place to land Air Force One from Washington or wherever and then he would transfer on a helicopter to go to his home in Hyannisport on Cape Cod. He was a Navy guy and he liked being around us. I know some in his family liked to play football and he just seemed relaxed. He reminded me of a lot of the other World War II naval officers, which he was, who seemed eager to connect with the next generation of navy officers."

Staubach got the news of Kennedy's assassination in his dormitory room as he prepared for a class in thermodynamics.

"Everyone was in shock, and the professors dismissed us from classes," Staubach said. "It was an awful feeling, as anyone who was alive then can remember. We went down to the athletic complex but no one even opened a locker. We all felt like we lost a president and a friend. Coach Hardin came in and we prayed. They canceled the Army game and then later said they would play in two weeks.

"*Life* magazine printed a bunch of issues due out that day that had my picture on it. Then they pulled it from the shelf and replaced it with one with the President's face on it. Everyone was in mourning for days. The next two weeks were difficult and weird. We were playing Army but there were none of the usual celebrations. No bonfires. No pep rallies. No banners hanging from the dormitory windows."

On November 26, the Downtown Athletic Club announced that Staubach had won the Heisman Trophy.

"Guys were happy for me, but there was no party either," Staubach said. "It was still too raw." Staubach did stand in the locker room and say he wished he could cut the trophy in forty-four pieces to distribute it to each deserving teammate.

Finally, on December 7, Pearl Harbor Day, the players took the field for the 1963 Army–Navy game. "We played the game as a tribute, they said, and I can tell you that it was like a release because both teams really let it all go that day," Staubach said.

Army employed a ball-control offense to keep the prolific Staubach off the field, and while the Navy offense had just five possessions in the game, Staubach managed to guide his team to a 21–7 fourth-quarter lead. Army closed the gap to 21–15 and reached the Navy 2-yard line with twenty seconds remaining. Army's upset bid was undone, however, in a mix-up between the Cadets quarterback and the game referee. Army did not have any time-outs on its last drive into Navy territory, but the referee had stopped the clock whenever the crowd noise made Army's signal calling impossible. At the 2-yard line, Army thought the referee had once again stopped the clock because of crowd noise. He had not, and with a confused Army team moving in and out of its huddle, the game clock ran out without Army running another play.

Within days, Staubach was in New York City for a whirlwind week of dinners and appearances as the Heisman Trophy winner. He appeared on *The Ed Sullivan Show* and attended a Broadway play.

Standing outside the lobby in his Naval Academy uniform, theater patrons mistook Staubach for an usher and handed him their tickets. The next night, he and Tom Lynch, who accompanied Staubach to New York, decided to go out on the town, but Staubach did not have any civilian clothes. Thalman loaned Staubach a shirt and suit.

"But the pants were at least three inches too short," Staubach said. "We went to the Playboy Club, but you needed a key to get in. Lynch was standing outside trying to convince people showing up with their Playboy Club keys to let us in. He would point to me and say: 'Hey, that's Roger Staubach, he just won the Heisman Trophy.' And the people would look over at me with my short pants and go, 'You've got to be kidding me.'"

Remember, this is the college kid of whom Los Angeles newspaper columnist Jim Murray wrote: "He would make Pat Boone look kinky."

Staubach and Lynch's big night on the town became a stint at the Howard Johnson's Diner countertop in Times Square. "When I got back to Annapolis," Staubach said, "they said to me, 'I hope you're humbled now.'"

Although Staubach played well and set passing records in the Cotton Bowl game that season, Navy was outmatched by Texas, losing 28–6. Going into his senior season, Staubach was a heavy favorite to win a second Heisman Trophy, but he sustained a severe ankle injury in the first game of the 1964 season. He did not start the next game and played the rest of the year hobbled, his noted pocket mobility lost in the pain and swelling of an ankle that did not heal for months. Still, when Staubach concluded his college football career, he had set a record for total offense with 4,253 yards gained. The Naval Academy retired his number 12 jersey during the ceremony celebrating his class graduation.

The world awaiting the newly commissioned officer, Lieutenant Roger Staubach, in the spring of 1965 was very different than the world Roger Staubach had known when he was fortuitously passing an eye exam to gain admittance to an armed service academy. At the end of 1964, Pentagon officials announced that 136 Americans had died in action during the previous twelve months of the Vietnam War. A little more than a year later, 144 Americans died in a single week of combat in Vietnam.

In 1965, Martin Luther King Jr. led his freedom march from Selma, Alabama, to the state capitol in Montgomery. Malcolm X was murdered. Two days after American bombers first used napalm to strafe suspected Vietcong strongholds, 15,000 antiwar protesters, mostly students, picketed outside the White House. Race riots in the Watts section of Los Angeles brought out 20,000 National Guard forces. In the same week, President Lyndon Johnson held a nationally televised news conference to announce he was sending 50,000 additional men to Vietnam and more than doubling the monthly draft calls from 17,000 American men to 35,000.

Staubach could have requested an assignment that kept him far from the war. There were a number of competitive service football teams at the large American naval bases in Florida and California that would have lavishly welcomed Staubach. Staubach chose to serve in the Vietnam supply corps.

"Staying home was an option," Staubach said. "But I didn't think it was the right thing to do. So many guys were making the sacrifice. I believed we were doing the right thing. I believed it when I was told it was a necessary fight to stop the spread of communism. Later, I had some questions. There was much more of a gray area to the whole thing, but at the time, I felt I had a duty."

Staubach volunteered for a one-year term in Vietnam, a time he would later call the longest year of his life. "And I wasn't on the front lines, although the guy I replaced did get wounded so I wasn't out of danger either," Staubach said. "No one in that war was ever out of danger. I'm proud of my service and it changed me. I not only have so much respect for all veterans but for the freedoms we have, to do whatever we choose. I came back understanding how lucky we are."

Leaving Vietnam in 1967, Staubach also came to understand the deep bitterness over the war back in America, a groundswell reflected not just on college campuses.

"I took in the controversy," he said. "I saw how different people felt, though I naturally had the perspective of a military person, knowing how the war was being waged, and I had some serious questions about that. But mostly, no matter what, I wanted people to feel for the guys who went over there. Because they were fighting for their country, and you know what, some of them did it even though they didn't support the war either. But they put their life on the line. I just wish we supported them more, that's all."

Over the years, Staubach has used a football reference to summarize his thoughts on the war policy: "It was like playing for a tie."

Staubach completed his four-year Navy commitment in stateside bases, playing service football to keep his skills relatively sharp. After eight years in the Naval Academy and the Navy, he resigned his commission in July 1969, just in time to join the Dallas Cowboys at their summer training camp.

Staubach was far from an immediate success as a pro. Football experts said his scrambling, improvisational style would never work in the NFL, which was entering the first of many periods of regimented overorganiz- ation. Football coaches had discovered computers and their ability to cite tendencies. That caused the offensive systems of most teams to emphasize predictable attacks to what they saw as predictable defenses. Freelancing was frowned upon. As it happened, Staubach had settled with perhaps the most orderly, systematic football organization of them all, led by a coach with a famously stoic countenance, Tom Landry.

But Landry's appearance could be deceiving. A former World War II fighter pilot, Landry's calm belied an imaginative, resourceful mind that was a winning complement to Staubach. Though he wore the same style hat on the sidelines for three decades, Landry knew how to freelance, too. Late in his life, flying a four-seat Cessna across Texas to make an appear- ance, Landry's plane experienced engine failure. Landry confidently scanned the countryside and glided his plane to an emergency landing in a barren, flat field. He even chose a landing spot close to a major highway, making it easier to get help and retrieve his stricken aircraft.

Though it took a while—and Landry tried to caution Staubach to run less (Staubach listened but ignored him)—Staubach and Landry became a good team. They devised an innovative offense that utilized Staubach's many gifts. The two were always tinkering and in one case brought back a formation not utilized in decades—the shotgun formation, where in obvi- ous passing situations, Staubach would line up six yards behind the line of scrimmage to receive a direct snap from the center. For the previous twenty-five years, quarterbacks had taken every snap directly behind the center and wasted time retreating into the pocket.

Football teams in the 1930s and 1940s had used the shotgun formation but modern teams considered it archaic. Not Landry, and in Staubach, he had the perfect player to implement it. Twenty years after Dallas reintroduced it to football, the shotgun formation is a pivotal part of every team's offense, from high school to the NFL.

Staubach led the Cowboys to four Super Bowls and won two of them. Dallas was more than a winning team, though. In Staubach's pro football prime during the 1970s, the Cowboys frequently played the late game on Sunday afternoons, which started at 4:00 P.M. in the Eastern time zone. It was the last game of the day all over the country, and unlike the regional games that were played in the early afternoon, it was a national broadcast, sent to every American home with a television. Staubach's wild dashes around the field and his uncanny ability to lead the Cowboys on striking rallies in the waning seconds of close games built a legend. Scores of young fans who knew nothing of Staubach's playing days at the Naval Academy tuned in to see what Roger the Dodger would do that week. His late game exploits became something like an action-thriller TV show, an American tradition on every fall or winter Sunday afternoon.

Meanwhile, older fans, those who remembered the 1963 Heisman Trophy–winning season, tuned in with fond reminiscence and perhaps a certain pride by association. Here was an athlete who once represented a different, gentler America, a man who had then helped fight a divisive war, survived a changed America, and had found a way to adapt and succeed nearly twenty years later.

Not insignificantly, in this period Staubach and the Cowboys lifted Dallas above its parochial reputation and helped rid the city of the stigma cast by the 1963 assassination of President Kennedy. In the city where the dream of a new generation of Americans exploded with the irrevocable tightening of a sniper's trigger finger, Staubach, college star from 1963, led a renaissance from the nightmare. The Cowboys became "America's Team."

These days, Staubach's workplace is a real estate office in North Dallas that overlooks a sprawling complex of offices, cafes, and retail outlets owned by The Staubach Companies, which employs 1,100 worldwide in nine countries. Staubach said he has utilized the same management lessons he used in football at his global real estate firm.

"Leadership in any sport or business is the ability to convey your confidence to a team of people," Staubach said. "You can't force your confidence on other people but they can see your confidence under pressure. Show them that you're not going to give up—and show that you really believe you still have a chance to win. The drive to win gets a bad rap. I was never a sore loser, and that's important, but I wanted to win and it bothered me if I didn't and that's okay, too."

If Staubach has a complaint about the football he watches today, it's that losing doesn't seem to bother some of the athletes the way it used to bother him.

"It drives me crazy to watch these quarterbacks throw an interception, then go to the sideline, put on a baseball cap, and stand there like nothing bad happened," Staubach said. "The other thing that drives me crazy is the guys who, after they've lost, go find their opponents on the field and give them a hug after the game. I couldn't do that. You shouldn't do that. You just lost, you should feel pain and you should be mad for a while. It helps you appreciate winning.

"I notice that Tiger Woods doesn't smile and hug everyone after he loses. Did Michael Jordan smile after he lost? People say the athletes are different today because of all the money they make. Money didn't ruin the desire to win in Michael Jordan or Tiger Woods. The great athlete is the one who knows that winning is the priority. The money will follow. Without the will to win you have no point being out there."

Staubach keeps his Heisman Trophy in his den, arranged in a place of prominence by his wife Marianne, who knew it was important to give visitors to the Staubach home easy access to the statuette.

"We just expanded our dining room because we entertain a lot," Staubach said. "I've heard other Heisman winners say the same thing but it's true, the first thing people say when they come over is, 'Can I see the Heisman?' People don't ask to see the 1973 passing award I won or the Walter Camp award or the Bert Bell trophy I won. And they are nice-looking awards.

"The Heisman is the draw. All these years later, after all the awards and Super Bowls I've won, if I am introduced at a dinner or a function, I am introduced as 'Heisman Trophy winner Roger Staubach.' I like that."

To Staubach, a glimpse of the Heisman Trophy in his den can take him back to the eye examiner's office in Denver, to the Naval Academy, to his boyhood in Cincinnati, all in a glance. Staubach can look at the trophy and see the glow in the face of his parents at the dinner recognizing him as the 1963 Heisman winner.

"My dad got up to speak at the Heisman dinner," Staubach said quietly as he stood outside his office on a warm fall day in 2002. "He was diabetic and really suffering at that time, but he got up at the Heisman dinner. He was not a guy who said much in public but he chose this occasion because he knew it mattered. He went to the microphone and he said: 'We only had one child but we had a good one.'

"That is what I'll always remember."

(TOP) GARY BEBAN AND (BOTTOM)
O. J. SIMPSON (CENTER)

"He Hasn't Been Asked to Join. And He Hasn't Asked to Join."

GARY BEBAN, 1967;

AND O. J. SIMPSON, 1968

In the mid-1960s, astride a decade when expanding Los Angeles would surpass Chicago as America's second most populous city, two Los Angeles college campuses made the city a mid-century Athens of athletics. In thought, culture, diversity, and production, at the University of California at Los Angeles and the University of Southern California, sport evolved and progressed in ways that forevermore reshaped the landscape of college athletics.

Lew Alcindor, the most dominant college basketball player the game had ever seen, was helping to launch Coach John Wooden's UCLA dynasty. Arthur Ashe was the Bruins' All-American tennis player, soon to be followed by a young freshman tennis phenom from Indiana, Jimmy Connors. Rafer Johnson had just left the UCLA campus, traveling to Tokyo to win the Olympic gold medal in the decathlon.

At USC, pitcher Tom Seaver had recently taken his considerable talent and charm to New York where he would engineer a charismatic revival of the Mets. On the track, USC's sprint relay team was, in effect, the United States Olympic sprint relay team. The top pole vaulter in the world was

USC's Bob Seagren, and his classmate, Stan Smith, was about to become the world's number one–ranked tennis player. In 1965, Southern Cal's Mike Garrett became the first Heisman Trophy winner from a California university and the second African-American to win the award.

And then, there was UCLA quarterback Gary Beban, known simply as "The Great One." And if that title was later bestowed, more lastingly, to hockey's Wayne Gretzky in Los Angeles during the mid-1960s, the designation fell naturally to Beban, one of the most accomplished, underrated college football quarterbacks ever. Beban set numerous passing and rushing records and compiled an astounding 24–4–2 record as a starter for UCLA. For that, he won the 1967 Heisman Trophy.

At the same time, at USC, there was a star running back who became one of the first sports stars to simply go by his initials, a trademark moniker more common, then and now, to movie or music stars. Sure, there had been athletes known as Joe D., or Johnny U., but this running back at USC was different, and always would be. At USC, and soon throughout the rest of the country, there was only one O.J., the winner of the 1968 Heisman Trophy.

For several years after their college careers ended, Beban and O.J., back-to-back winners of the grandest individual sports award in the nation, would sit side by side at charity dinners and football functions. It was an association that kept them shoulder to shoulder during a myriad of occasions.

But in time it would seem as if they were reverse sides of a coin minted at the Downtown Athletic Club in the mid-1960s. Beban faded from public view, with no pro football career to speak of, and built a billion-dollar real estate enterprise as he raised a family. Simpson's fame only grew, first as a professional football player, broadcaster, and Hollywood personality. Later, his life scandalously troubled, he became a figure of iconic notoriety, an international poster boy for any number of thorny societal issues, from judicial system inadequacies to the chasm in American race relations.

And yet today, the lives of The Great One and O.J. remain poignantly and curiously intertwined, as the link that once brought them together, the Heisman Trophy, evolved into the connection that led to a noteworthy, figurative separation. There had always been ties between The Great One and O.J., a parallel if dissimilar development that began with their upbringing in different parts of the San Francisco area. The son of Italian immigrants, Beban's first language had been Italian. Beban was raised in a two-income family before that was common in America, with his mother working in an office and his father a Teamster at the San Francisco docks.

"I was encouraged to play sports, but the rule always was 'No grades, no play,' and they exercised that rule once," Beban said. "But it was my father who first made me aware that I might get an athletic scholarship. I never dreamed of that. But I knew it was the only way I was going to a major college. We couldn't have afforded it otherwise."

As a high school quarterback, Beban also got some extra tutoring from a local coach, Dick Vermeil, who was then guiding the team at the College of San Mateo. Vermeil became the head coach at UCLA a decade later, and after that, guided three successful NFL teams.

Vermeil had first seen Beban play when his high school faced Beban's. "He said he saw something in me," Beban said of Vermeil. "And he worked with me even though he didn't have to. It was a great benefit. When I think back, I wonder how I got from one place to another. Because my beginnings were very humble, maybe more humble than I realized growing up."

Years later, on a trip to New York, Beban went to Ellis Island, through which his mother had passed before settling in San Francisco's North Beach. At Ellis Island, he researched the files and uncovered the ship manifest bearing the name of his mother emigrating from Italy. "It's wonderful, it lists every little thing she brought with her," Beban said. "And it wasn't much. It makes you understand just where you came from."

O. J. Simpson grew up across the city from Beban, in one of San Francisco's roughest districts. His parents separated when he was four years old. He had rickets as a young boy, which kept him out of school for months, slightly bowed his legs, and brought ridicule from classmates. In interviews over the years, Simpson conceded that he began hanging with a tough crowd, including street gangs. Arrested three times as a teen, he was a poor student even as he grew into a sports star at Galileo High School.

"There might have been more arrests for me," Simpson said in an ESPN Classic documentary of his life. "But when things would happen and the cops would come to our block and jump out of their cars, I was the fastest kid around. They caught the slow guys. The fastest guy got away."

His local coaches and a cadre of community leaders who sensed Simpson's potential got together one evening hoping to figure out a way to redirect the wayward O.J. They decided to reach out to a local sports star, asking him to counsel their young prodigy. At the time, there was no bigger Bay Area sports figure than Willie Mays, center fielder for the San Francisco Giants.

Mays agreed to take O.J. to dinner and in that meeting sternly told O.J. that he could be anything he wanted if he just used his sports skills "and let that other junk go," according to Mays.

"I said, 'You can be me and much more,'" Mays told ESPN Classic. "I said: 'I was held down when I was coming up but that's all changing.' I told him that America was waiting to accept a black athlete as a big star."

Mays's words were prescient, even if there would continue to be various levels of cultural acceptance. What is unquestioned is that black athletes, especially in professional sports centered in America's largest cities, were changing the pace, and the face, of the games Americans played. Whether it was Maury Wills remaking baseball's stolen base records for the Los Angeles Dodgers, Philadelphia's Wilt Chamberlain rewriting basketball's scoring marks, or "Bullet Bob" Hayes, the Olympic sprint champion who scored an eighty-two-yard touchdown the second time he touched the football for the Dallas Cowboys, there was a speed, spirit, and style altering the games forever.

There was no ignoring the impact as more schools nationwide desegregated, permitting more black athletes to play sports on local teams that got them noticed by college recruiters and pro scouts. A prime example had been Mike Garrett, a native of Los Angeles's Maravilla government housing projects, who became the prototype for a swarm of power-I formation U.S.C. tailbacks to succeed him, including the Heisman winners, Simpson, Charles White (1979), and Marcus Allen (1981).

After his dinner with Mays, O.J. was a few years from following in Garrett's footsteps. As Mays had suggested, he stayed far enough from the troubled streets of his neighborhood to improve his standing with school officials, and in turn, they recommended him to college recruiters. There was plenty of interest, but O.J.'s grades were still subpar. If he wanted to attend any of the top California football schools, he would have to first raise his academic credentials with two years at a junior college.

Simpson thrived during his time at junior college and then considered attending UCLA and USC. He chose Southern Cal, in part because the Trojans had lost their most recent meetings with UCLA and O.J. liked the idea of leading an underdog cause. He was coming to the right place at the right time. USC would spend the next fifteen years establishing itself as the ultimate running back university.

When O.J. enrolled at Southern Cal in the fall of 1967, it put him on a course to meet Beban in one of the most consequential and influential games in college football history. It was a game that decided a national championship and the balloting for the Heisman Trophy. In the development of college football, it was also a signature game, a sea change moment.

The only football showdown of O.J. and The Great One, the 1967 UCLA–USC game signaled the shifting of college football to a faster-paced, higher-scoring mold—in part a reflection of a cultural revolution evident for years to come. One season earlier in college football, a national championship hung in the balance of a taut, defensive-minded matchup between first-ranked Notre Dame and second-ranked Michigan State. Symbolically, that game ended with Notre Dame playing for a stalemate, running out the clock to assure a 10–10 tie that kept the Irish's hold on the top rung of the national championship balloting.

These Midwestern football giants could have just as easily been battling for the national championship in 1926 as 1966. And they played a game that might have been recognizable in 1926—lots of running plays up the middle, a close-to-the-vest offense suited to the often inhospitable Midwest weather in late fall.

When number one UCLA and number three USC met for the national title just a year later in sunny LA, the chains were off. College football was in its liberation mode. Players then were influenced by the growing number of campus rallies and sit-ins and, like other students, questioned everything. Some coaches responded well to the players' new desire for input in the game plan, while others did not. Among those with an open mind was UCLA's Tommy Prothro. He was a slow-drawling Tennessean who may have given the appearance of a county sheriff. In fact, Prothro was a free-thinker who encouraged his players to participate in other extracurricular campus activities, even if that included student protests.

"Tommy used to say that college was supposed to be the times of our lives," Beban said. "He said to go and see it. See the times of our life."

The times were turbulent and chaotic. The United States had begun its biggest assault of the Vietnam War in February. Muhammad Ali had been stripped of his heavyweight title for refusing to be inducted into military service. In the same month that Elvis Presley married Priscilla Beaulieu,

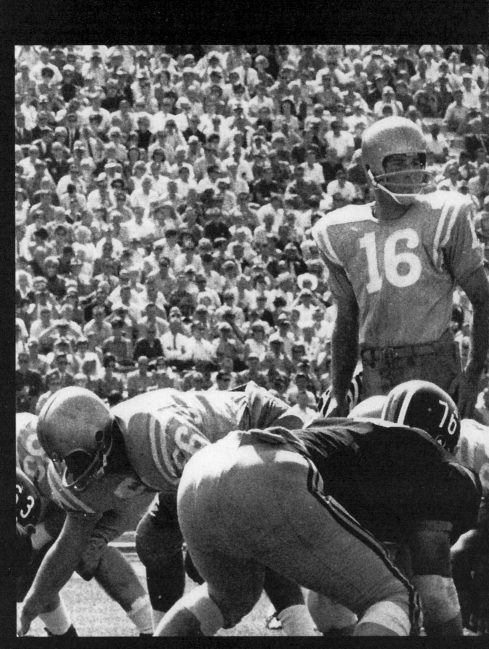

BEBAN (STANDING)

the Beatles released *Sgt. Pepper's Lonely Hearts Club Band*. The spoof series *Batman* was television's highest-rated show in the same year that the Academy Award for best picture went to *In the Heat of the Night*, a story of a black detective forced by circumstances to help solve a murder in a rural Southern town.

In Los Angeles, the city was still reeling from the most devastating racial riots of the 1960s. Watts, the poorest city ghetto, had been a ravaged war zone with thirty killed in a matter of days and 2,500 arrested.

"It was a stunning time for all," Beban said. "We lived and experienced it all. We didn't have athletic dorms like they do now, and most of the athletes were very active parts of the student body. I remember Tommy Prothro saying he only needed us between 1:00 and 3:00 in the afternoon. He said to go be college students."

Prothro's broadmindedness extended to his football philosophy, something that was becoming increasingly necessary as the power bases in college football widened to include more far-flung outposts. Many of the traditional powerhouses in the game were still holding sway: Alabama, Notre Dame, Oklahoma, and Michigan had hardly gone away. But it was significant that in 1967, two of the top three teams in the country at season's end were from Los Angeles, the new land of plenty in America.

So it was on November 18, 1967, when two flashy powers from sunny Southern California played before 90,000 short-sleeve-wearing fans in the Los Angeles Coliseum and a national television audience. In this game, the coaches called reverses, flea flickers, option passes, and dangerous safety blitzes, and tried numerous field goals from the foot of a new breed of kicker, the soccer-style specialist.

Innovation was part of the football crescendo building on the West Coast, led by its most prominent conference, the Pac-8. The 1967 game between UCLA and USC became the thunderclap that forced the college football nation to force its glance westward, to think of the Pac-8 teams as something more than just the West Coast representative in the annual Rose Bowl game. They were demanding to be noticed, with some of the best players in the country and a fast-tempo brand of offense that stressed burning, blinding speed.

College football was emerging from the single-wing era of offensive strategy, where quarterbacks ran more than they passed. Multiple-formation football, with men in motion and more plays that took the football out of the quarterback's hands, was the new trend.

While quarterbacks would win five of the six Heisman trophies awarded from 1962 to 1967, concluding with Beban's Heisman, Simpson and Oklahoma's running back Steve Owens would win the next two. A different kind of quarterback, one who passed more than he ran, Jim Plunkett and Pat Sullivan were winners in the early 1970s. When Penn State's John Cappelletti won the 1973 Heisman Trophy, it marked the first of eleven successive years the award went to a running back. The last ten times in that span, the Heisman went to an African-American running back, twice from USC.

The game was changing. In many ways, it began with a single game in the Los Angeles Coliseum in 1967.

As Simpson had observed, Beban and UCLA had the stamp of superiority in their rivalry with USC. Beban had seen to that by tossing a forty-eight-yard touchdown pass to win the game against Garrett's heavily favored Southern Cal Trojans in 1965. Then Beban, just a sophomore, led the UCLA Bruins to a second shocker that season, defeating an even bigger favorite, Michigan State, 14–12, in the Rose Bowl on New Year's Day 1996.

As a junior, Beban led a balanced UCLA team to a second successful season that included another upset of USC, a game Simpson attended.

"I remember the party after the game," Simpson told the *Riverside Press-Enterprise* newspaper in California during a 1992 interview. "The UCLA guys were talking big. I just wanted to be on the other side, turning the tables. I remembered thinking: 'You just wait until next year.'"[8]

UCLA was 7–0–1 entering the 1967 game, the only blemish having occurred at Washington. USC had lost in a downpour at Oregon State the week earlier, dropping its record to 8–1. Still, the Trojans were three-point favorites against UCLA, largely on the strength of Simpson, a sprinter on the USC track team who would line up seven yards behind a mammoth line of blockers in USC's power-I formation—which was fast becoming the most feared running formation in the land. Simpson dared the defense to stop him. Opposing teams knew Simpson was getting the football, but they also knew that with a seven-yard head start, O.J. would be at top speed by

[8]*The Press Enterprise* (Riverside California) November 17, 1992.

the time he got to the line of scrimmage. And on most days, no one in uniform had the speed to catch him.

They did gang tackle him when given the chance, taking extra shots after the whistle, hoping to either provoke O.J. or simply wear him out. They could, and did, try other tactics: If USC was the visiting team, it was common for the home side to grow its stadium grass long, even douse it with the water hose to make it muddy, all in an attempt to slow down college football's fastest running back.

But it was largely fruitless as Simpson was a modern marvel, perhaps as good as any running back in the history of the game—as fast as Glenn Davis, Army's Mr. Outside, and as big (225 pounds) and as hard to tackle as Doc Blanchard, Mr. Inside.

He ran through defenders, he ran over defenders (hurdling tacklers was a favorite move of his), and he ran away from defenders. USC coach John McKay, irreverent and quick-witted, used to say he had only five plays in his playbook, four of them runs to his halfback. Asked if his backs got tired, McKay quipped: "Why would they? That football isn't that heavy." Consider that against UCLA in 1967, USC threw just six passes.

Beban, meanwhile, had made his fame with his throwing ability, unleashing long passes with uncanny accuracy that devastated opposing secondaries, which then were largely made up of just three players: two cornerbacks and a single safety. It was a defensive alignment soon to change, with an added safety dropping back in the formation to guard against quarterbacks like Beban. Beban's passing statistics, twenty-three career touchdown passes, may seem unimpressive by today's standards, but not if they are time-adjusted. Beban still had to run the football, and many of his best plays were designed runs for him, which led to thirty-five career touchdowns. But what defined The Great One was his leadership and his poise under pressure.

"Late in a game, watching Gary Beban in the huddle is like watching a great ship captain in a stormy sea," Prothro said. "He'll get you through it."

When the teams finally met for their pivotal clash in 1967, the build-up had created a frenzy. Beban remembers arriving at the Los Angeles Coliseum three hours before the game and seeing a swelling mass of people on the streets outside the vast bowl, the site for the 1932 and 1984 Summer Olympic Games. When Beban jogged onto the field forty-five minutes later, he saw that fans had already filled two thirds of the seats. By kickoff, a crowd of 90,772, roughly 5,000 short of the capacity then, had arrived to watch the game.

By contrast, the first Super Bowl had been played in the same Coliseum ten months earlier in front of less than 60,000 fans. UCLA–USC was the Super Bowl of 1967 as far as America was concerned.

UCLA scored first, as Beban turned a poor USC punt into a quick touchdown drive and a 7–0 lead. Simpson struggled early as the Bruins stacked the line, knowing USC's aversion to the pass. But late in the first quarter, near midfield, Prothro gambled on a trick play that called for Beban to fake a handoff to running back Greg Jones, who would continue to run to his left. Beban would look downfield to his right and at the last moment, throw back to Jones in the left flat, who would presumably be ignored by the defense.

But USC defensive back Pat Cashman was waiting for the pass and stepped in front of Jones to stun Beban, who saw his trick pass intercepted and run back for a touchdown.

"I honestly think SC had spied on our practices and knew the play was coming," Beban said. "The practices were closed, but when it comes to USC–UCLA, everybody has done a lot of wild things. There have been guys in trees with binoculars. I give him credit, but Pat Cashman acted like he knew the design of the play."

As the game went on, it was USC's turn to unveil the chicanery waiting in its playbook. Simpson was not the only world-class sprinter in the Trojans' distinctive scarlet and yellow uniforms. Earl McCullouch, who would one day be an Olympic gold medal–winning sprinter, took a reverse for 52 yards to the UCLA 13-yard line. Simpson scored from there, on a run during which ten different UCLA defenders had a chance to tackle him.

"Without question, one of the best touchdown runs I've seen in person," Beban said. "Of course, his other one that day wasn't too bad either."

Beban, despite torn cartilage in his ribs, quickly led UCLA back into USC territory. But UCLA had one glaring weakness even The Great One could not overcome. Placekicker Zenon Audrusyshyn, an immigrant from the Soviet Union, was one of a score of new kickers in the game who had come to college football from the world of soccer.

Unlike most placekickers of the 1980s and beyond, who were generally

American suburbanites who might have grown up playing soccer but quickly learned in placekicking manuals or summer kicking camps that kicking a football requires a different technique than kicking a soccer ball, Audrusyshyn represented the first wave of soccer-style kickers. Many of these new kicking specialists, with no advice on how to adjust to their new craft, kicked the football like a soccer ball, which produced an unpredictable ball flight that was frequently too low as well.

Inside the Los Angeles Coliseum that day, Audrusyshyn missed two field goals—both too low and wide.

In the third quarter, after Beban hurled a rousing fifty-three-yard touchdown pass to end George Farmer to cut USC's lead to 14–13, Andrusyshyn also missed the extra point kick after the score. Still, Beban, fighting through the stinging pain in his ribs, threw another third-quarter touchdown pass, for twenty yards, and Andrusyshyn managed that extra point through the goal posts. UCLA had a 20–14 lead.

"The Coliseum was just throbbing with noise," said Simpson in his 1992 interview with the *Press-Enterprise*. "I could hear it but I was too exhausted to even pick up my head to look around."

With ten minutes and thirty-eight seconds remaining in the game, USC faced a third-and-seven at its own 36-yard line. In the huddle, the Trojans called for a rare pass play to the tight end. Simpson remembered feeling relieved—he could not run another play at that juncture.

But at the line of scrimmage, USC quarterback Toby Page saw that the tight end was being double-teamed. He changed the play at the line, barking out an audible that called for another play: 23 Blast. That was an O.J. play, a run to the left.

Simpson later said he shook his head trying to get his quarterback's attention in the backfield. He said he even considered going into motion on his own, which would have obligated Page to either change the play again or call time-out.

"But then the ball was snapped and it was all instinct," Simpson told reporters after the game.

In Southern California for the next several years, what transpired was simply known as The Run. Easily the most memorable play in the history of the UCLA–USC rivalry, it is one of the most celebrated runs in the history of college football.

Simpson took off to his left accompanied by three blockers. At the line of scrimmage, he cut to his right, and then fifteen yards later, across to his left, evading four UCLA defenders, who alternatively grasped at his legs and shoulder pads. Running down the left sideline, Simpson made a practiced cutback to the middle of the field and saw nothing in his way to the end zone. The man who would one day run a leg on a USC sprint relay team that set a world record was not about to be caught from behind, fatigued or not.

USC's Rikki Aldredge, a conventional, straight-on kicker, made the extra point attempt for a 21–20 lead.

"But there were still ten minutes left in the game," Beban said. "It has always bothered me that we couldn't, I couldn't, get the ball into the end zone anyway. That was a great run by O.J. I wish we could have come back one more time. It is a game that never goes away really."

Simpson finished with 177 rushing yards. Beban threw for 301 passing yards, a performance that, even in defeat, earned him the Heisman Trophy two weeks later. Simpson, at the time and for years thereafter, agreed with the 1967 Heisman balloting.

Beban said he was still stunned and disheartened by the loss to USC when he went to New York City for the Heisman Trophy presentation. "But it was a great, dramatic weekend that lifted my spirits," Beban said. "I remember that my dad got to wear a tuxedo for the first time in his life. He had been married in his army uniform. That trip was a bonding time for us."

Simpson would win his Heisman the next season, when he ran for what was then a record 1,709 yards. He enjoyed a Hall of Fame career in the National Football League, where he also set the single-season rushing record. More telling, he signed a quarter of a million dollar contract with Chevrolet before he had played a pro game. He had made his first guest appearance in a television drama before his first NFL game. As good a football player as he was—and in his prime he may have been as good as any running back in the history of the pro game—Simpson was always better known throughout the country for his presence as a personality and marketer of goods and services.

It continued that way, largely unabated, until the 1994 murders of his ex-wife, Nicole Simpson, and Ronald Goldman.

Simpson, whose agent and other representatives rejected requests for an interview to be a part of this book, was found not guilty in those mur-

ders, but he lost a multimillion-dollar civil suit that forced him to liquidate many of his assets, including his Heisman Trophy.

While Simpson enjoyed a long and productive pro career, Beban's lasted just two seasons. With the Washington Redskins, who were then coached by Vince Lombardi, Beban never attempted a single pass and was converted into a wide receiver. It was an experiment that failed, and in 1969, Beban retired quickly, with few regrets, he said. Within a few weeks he happened to sign on with a company that later became CB Richard Ellis, a billion-dollar worldwide commercial real estate service organization. Beban was the company president for several years and is now its senior executive managing director responsible for a portfolio of large global clients.

Along the way, Beban also helped create the only official organization of Heisman Trophy winners, the Heisman Winners Association. Beban gave it shape and helped establish an executive board. In yet another ignominious circumstance in a life of growing infamy, Simpson's standing as a worthy member of the Heisman Winners Association came to a vote before the membership several years ago.

The group overwhelmingly decided to exclude Simpson from the Heisman Winners Association. Simpson is the only Heisman Trophy winner who is not a part of the organization. Even the heirs, or the estates, of Heisman winners have some measure of membership. But not O. J.

"The vote was 75 percent against him," Beban said. "He is not included. It was a by-product of a series of very well documented events in O. J.'s life. Unfortunately, that is part of his life that he has to live with forever. But O. J. was a great football player."

From his Chicago area home, Beban has watched Simpson's life saga— the two trials related to the unsolved murders, allegations of spousal abuse, and the dissolution of most of Simpson's assets—play out with growing distress and disenchantment.

"It has been a little more personal for me because we have always been connected and still are," Beban said. "People think of us together because of where we played, because of the 1967 game and the Heisman. So that brought it much closer. It brought it closer to all of us who were Heisman Trophy winners, frankly. Maybe it troubled us more."

O. J. SIMPSON RECEIVING THE HEISMAN IN 1968

To many winners, including Beban, the Heisman Trophy is both an award and a duty. A college football player covets the former and inherits the latter. Most Heisman winners grasp the complexity of that subtle contract, even if that realization may take days, months, or even years. Often, the lesson is delivered in the way others act toward the trophy itself.

Beban, for example, keeps his Heisman Trophy in his den. It is visible from the street outside his home, and he occasionally sees people walking past his house craning their necks or standing on their toes just to catch a glimpse of the Heisman Trophy awarded to the most outstanding football player in the land in 1967. If Beban himself stands outside his house, it does not cause a stir. But people will cross the street to try and see Beban's trophy.

Not long ago, when Beban was having his house painted, he walked into his den to see one of the workers pulling an Instamatic camera from his pocket. The worker wanted a picture of the trophy to prove what he had been bragging about back in his neighborhood—that he was painting the house of a Heisman Trophy winner.

So there is symbolism in a Heisman Trophy winner's being ordered to sell his trophy at auction, as O. J. was.

"You cannot tell the history of the Heisman Trophy, or college football, without O. J. Simpson," Beban said. "But the fact is the award comes with a responsibility. Too many people look up to the trophy and what it means.

"All of us from my era, we got to know the winners before us, men like Jay Berwanger, Clint Frank, and Leon Hart. Men like Pete Dawkins and Alan Ameche. They influenced my values. It affected my life choices. Because I won the Heisman Trophy, I did things differently. And I'm sure many other Heisman Trophy winners did, too.

"O.J. has made certain choices. He has to live with that part of his life."

It is clear, after interviews with dozens of Heisman Trophy winners, that Simpson's exclusion from the Heisman Winners Association is not a frequent topic of conversation within the membership. The chief of the Heisman Winners Association executive committee, Archie Griffin, the only two-time winner of the trophy, declined to discuss Simpson's status in any specifics.

It was left to Beban, The Great One all those years ago, who emerged from the historic game at the Los Angeles Coliseum forevermore linked to

O. J. Simpson. He accepts that connection without apparent unease, but more than thirty-five years later, they are still standing on opposite side-lines.

Asked if the Heisman Winners Association holds annual votes on whether to invite Simpson into the fold, Beban answered:

"He hasn't been asked to join. And he hasn't asked to join."

"It's All in Your Hands"

JIM PLUNKETT, 1970

Jim Plunkett's earliest memories are of his mother cooking in the kitchen of their home. Carmen Plunkett would move around the room with practiced efficacy, pulling a wooden soup spoon from a drawer to taste the bubbling soup before retreating to the pantry for additional spices and ingredients. She would cut vegetables, peel potatoes, and knead the dough for bread. She would bake, can fruits, and carve apart whole chickens.

But Jim would look most closely when his mother would ignite the gas stovetop burner and position a frying pan. Carmen would wait by the stove, then touch her fingertips to the pan—once, twice, three times—testing to see if it was hot enough to begin the frying.

"She would touch it until she burnt her fingers," Jim Plunkett says. "Because she had done it so many times, they had grown calloused and she was losing her sense of touch."

Carmen Plunkett was blind from birth.

"She cleaned, ironed, sewed, shopped, nothing stopped her," Jim says of his mother. "Totally amazing."

Her husband William, Jim's father, often helped. And he, too, was blind.

"Between my wife and myself, we have four good eyes and we have our hands full raising two kids," Jim Plunkett says today. "How my parents raised myself and my two sisters without one good eye is beyond me. And maybe the most incredible thing is that growing up in my house, it was no big deal. We never even talked about it.

"We certainly never called it a handicap. I still don't use that word. What they had to do was cope with not being able to see."

William Plunkett grew up with some sight and developed a progressive blindness that made him legally blind, although he could make out some shadowy figures. That allowed him, in some small but significant ways, to be the eyes for his wife.

"My parents had a wonderful romance," Jim says of Carmen and William, who met in their native New Mexico at a school for the blind. "What was neat was when my dad would take my mom in the backyard for a walk. She would ask him to describe the birds she heard or the brightness of the sun she felt on her face. He would find all the details to bring it to life. Then, he would have her reach down and touch the flowers in the garden and he would tell her what they looked like, and how beautiful they were. It was great to watch."

Little wonder, then, that Jim Plunkett grew up with a resolve to find ways around life's tangible, and less tangible, obstacles.

"For one, I let very few things bother or distract me," Plunkett says. "Not after what I saw my parents endure. And two, after all the work they did to create a life for me, wherever I was going in this life, I wasn't going to let them down."

It was unlikely, however, that determination alone would fix things for Jim Plunkett. The path outside the door of the Plunkett household in San Jose, California, was hardly strewn with rose petals.

"All around us was a place of little hope," Plunkett says. "It was a desperate place. You could see it. You could feel it. It was a place with no sidewalks, rotting garbage in the alleys, and people just going to pieces on the street corner. It may not have been a ghetto, I didn't know that term then, but it was certainly the lowest end of the totem pole."

Most called the neighborhood San Jose's barrio. William and Carmen Plunkett were each of Mexican descent, with William part German and Carmen part Native American. William moved his family to California to work on the Bay Area docks during World War II, but those jobs dried up, especially for William, whose declining eyesight made such work increasingly dangerous. Thereafter, the family subsisted on a weekly welfare check, and to earn it, William worked in a state-sponsored job at a news-stand in the welfare office.

"We never had much money," Plunkett says. "Obviously, we never had a car. Not many people who lived on that neighborhood block ever got out. Some turned to crime, some to drugs, others went to Vietnam and died or came home shattered. A lot of guys I played sports with just lost it. They are still on that block. And it is still not a good place to be."

Jim Plunkett insists he knows how he made it out.

"I had the example for hard work and perseverance before me every day in my parents," he says. "I owed it to them and to myself to do the same. I'm not saying it was easy. It's damn hard to get out of those situations.

"But I said to myself, 'I'm going to get good grades in school.' And then later, since I loved sports, I said: 'I want to be a good enough athlete to get out of here.' One way or the other, I wasn't going to stay in that place."

From his childhood, Plunkett was a good, although not great, athlete. Asked if anyone in his extended family in New Mexico played sports—parents, grandparents, uncles, aunts, cousins—Plunkett says, "Nope. Nobody."

"But I liked to play and I liked to practice. Other than studying, it was what I did. There wasn't anything else for me to do. I remember that the pinball machine at the corner store was ten cents. Well, I didn't have ten cents. I stayed at the school playground and practiced. I wasn't the best athlete on my block, but if one summer somebody was better than me at something, I kept working at it and by the next summer, he wasn't better than me anymore."

By the time Jim was in junior high school, his coaches had taken him under their wing. "I was lucky; they became like surrogate parents," he says. "They saw something in me and helped me perfect it. I had good grades; they knew I might be able to go someplace."

By his high school years, he was a leading quarterback prospect in a talent-rich area that had recently produced Heisman winner Gary Beban. At 6-foot-2 and 210 pounds, he was fairly big for a quarterback in those days. But Plunkett, unlike Beban in high school, was primarily a passing quarterback. And as early as the 1950s, Stanford University had been a passing team. It had fielded a great quarterback before Plunkett in John Brodie and would nurture another one after Plunkett in John Elway.

Given Stanford's proximity to San Jose, it was an easy decision, and when he chose Stanford, Plunkett became the first, and only, member of his family to attend college. Jim recalls attending a National Football Foundation dinner in San Francisco just before his high school graduation. He was to be honored as a scholar-athlete and accompanying him was his father William.

"I remember we were waiting for my coach and principal to pick us up and drive us into downtown San Francisco," Plunkett says. "We were outside the house and my dad was sitting with me, wearing a tie for one of the few times in his life. My dad was a quiet guy; he didn't talk a lot. But as we were waiting, he reached over and held my hand, and said: 'I'm proud of you, son.'

"He couldn't see the tears welling in my eyes. But then, he probably knew."

It was a moment to remember two years later when William Plunkett died of a heart attack at the age of fifty-six.

"That was devastating to my mother," Jim says. "He was so wonderful to her. She lived with my sister but she missed my dad. I did, too. I wished he had been around for my success in college."

After his freshman season when he was not eligible for the varsity, Plunkett was red-shirted at Stanford in 1967, an added delay that frustrated him.

"I was sure I was ready to play then," he says. "I was a little angry and upset that I had to sit around and wait."

But like many things in the circuitous, knotty athletic path Plunkett would follow, it may have had hidden benefit. The delay served as motivation. When Plunkett did make his varsity debut, he called his performance no surprise at all. To the rest of the country, it was shocking.

On September 21, 1968, the college football community got its first glimpse of Stanford's new sophomore quarterback, who threw four touchdown passes in a 68–20 rout of San Jose State.

By the end of the season, Jim Plunkett had thrown for more yards (2,156) than any quarterback in Pac-8 Conference history. In his junior year, Plunkett broke his own record and one for touchdown passes, too, a stunning encore as he threw for 2,673 yards and twenty touchdowns in eleven games. Plunkett was among the top quarterbacks in the game, and a hot story, too, celebrated as one of the first major college football stars who was of Mexican descent.

Plunkett was smart, well-spoken, acclaimed by his teammates, and because he had been red-shirted, eligible for the National Football League. He had already earned his degree in international relations. In the spring of 1970, many believed Plunkett would enter the NFL college draft, where he was likely to be a top pick.

Pro scouts liked Plunkett's passing style, a model of over-the-top throwing efficiency. He was a pocket passer with exceptional field vision and a steady field countenance. He threw crisp, short passes and long, lofty spirals deep downfield that exhibited not just his arm strength but his sense of touch and accuracy. It was said he had to be accurate, since his favorite receiver at Stanford, the overachieving and indomitable Randy Vataha, was not a big target. Plunkett had a calm, quiet manner on the field, something the pros expected to be an important asset in the frenzied, rough-and-tumble world of the NFL.

"But in my first year on the Stanford varsity, all the guys on the team had made a commitment that we'd get to the Rose Bowl before we left," Plunkett says. "Well, we hadn't made it to the Rose Bowl yet. We had been so close, but it was hard getting past Southern Cal back then. So I told the pros to wait and I stayed at Stanford, and others stayed, to fulfill the commitment."

The 1970 Stanford team coached by John Ralston was a diverse mix of athletes: rich, white suburban kids; California inner-city blacks; the Latino Plunkett; and a few players from rural locales, like Montana and Nevada. The group liked to say it was a team of rednecks, peaceniks, and revolutionaries, but its real passion was getting to the Rose Bowl.

The first magical moment of Stanford's storybook season was at Arkansas when the Cardinals upset the third-ranked Razorbacks, 34–28. A 34–3 victory over San Jose State was next, and a 33–10 win at Oregon got Stanford noticed nationally.

But Ralston was most fond of telling his players that "the road to the Rose Bowl goes through Southern Cal."

Facing USC that season, Plunkett threw for 275 yards in a pivotal 24–14 victory that had the characteristically anti-sport hippies on the Stanford campus celebrating into the night. Their administrators, emblematic adversaries of the students in 1970, rejoiced side by side with them. When Plunkett passed for four touchdowns in a 29–22 win against Washington, Stanford had earned its first Rose Bowl berth in nineteen years. Parties on the floral Stanford campus abounded.

Stanford lost its last two regular season games to complete the regular season with an 8–3 record, a disappointment that would set up a month of hard practices for the Stanford players as they prepared for the Rose Bowl under an infuriated Ralston.

But first came several weeks of recognition for Plunkett, who had nonetheless finished the season with strong performances. He completed his senior season with 2,715 passing yards and set several career NCAA records, most notably in net yards (7,544) and total offense (7,887). He established a host of Stanford records, including most touchdown passes (52).

Plunkett won the Heisman Trophy balloting, no small feat in 1970 because his competition for the award was without question better organized. The marketing of Heisman Trophy candidates, commonplace by the 1980s, was just gearing up in 1970.

At Notre Dame that season, the quarterback was Joe Theismann, whose family had always pronounced the surname "Thees-man." At Notre Dame, Theismann was encouraged to change the pronunciation to "Thighs-man" so it would rhyme with Heisman. As Notre Dame's systematic marketing campaign for their quarterback in 1970 proclaimed: "It's Theismann, as in Heisman."

In the same season, there was also the University of Mississippi's dynamic one-man show, Archie Manning. He had an almost mystical presence, a throwback to the halcyon days of college football in the deep South. Constantly on the run, Manning simply willed Ole Miss to victories against deeper, more talented teams.

Ohio State, meanwhile, had one of its best teams in a decade, a powerhouse that stormed through the Big Ten behind senior quarterback Rex Kern.

And then there was Plunkett. Stanford made sure they marketed his Heisman candidacy, too. As Plunkett said years later, "They spent $139 on one-page flyers."

A lack of mass marketing notwithstanding, it was becoming clear that the West Coast was the vanguard of innovation in the college football community. Half the Heisman Trophy winners from 1963 to 1970 came from the West Coast. The game was evolving, and the eyes of college football fans—and Heisman Trophy voters—were becoming less myopic. There was a good reason for this. Gone was the day when fans and Heisman voters got all their news of games and players from reading newspaper stories on Sunday mornings.

Back then, reporters from the largest newspapers in the East, Midwest, and South did not travel much to the West Coast for games. It was not just provincialism. Those West Coast games started too late to make it into many editions of those plump Sunday papers on the East Coast, or in Chicago, St. Louis, and Atlanta. So editors of those newspapers did not dispatch reporters to those games; it was not cost effective.

National television networks changed all that. By the late 1960s and early 1970s, television was paying the NCAA hundreds of thousands of dollars in rights fees for college football, and with it, the networks could demand that a West Coast school move its scheduled kickoff up to 11:00 A.M. Saturday so the game could be broadcast at 2:00 P.M. in the East and 1:00 P.M. in the Midwest. The networks could even show late afternoon or, occasionally, evening games from the West Coast. Now everyone could see college football players from places that once seemed as distant as the Orient, and see them every week. That included eastern-based writers, coaches, and broadcasters, the bulk of Heisman Trophy voters in 1970.

Sports reporters from all regions flocked westward, and those earlier-timed games now would make the earliest editions of eastern and midwestern Sunday newspapers.

(Years later, when cable giant ESPN came along, the eastern voting bloc bias was entirely upended. Everyone who cared about college football could see the telecast of just about any major college game, especially with specialty satellite packages beamed to individual homes. One can usually watch college football nonstop from 11:00 A.M. Saturday to 2:00 A.M. Sunday, and all of it is live. The Heisman Trophy race is now a reality television contest.)

In 1970, things had not yet changed that dramatically, but Plunkett was an early beneficiary of increased exposure in the Heisman balloting.

In mid-December that year, Plunkett was in New York to appear on comedian Bob Hope's television special celebrating the All-America team when he was informed he had won the Heisman Trophy. It was an unusual coincidence to have the Heisman winner in New York on the day his selec-

tion was announced, and it sent the New York–based media into a tizzy to get what was then a rare interview—the new Heisman winner on the day he joined the most exclusive fraternity in sports. Plunkett, awaiting the taping of the Bob Hope show, suddenly faced a deluge of reporters and cameras.

It was at this juncture that Plunkett met a man who would become a lifelong friend: Rudy Riska, the executive director of the Downtown Athletic Club. As reporters swarmed Plunkett and the Bob Hope television studio, Riska appeared with one hand on Plunkett's shoulder, guiding him expertly through the room after a few brief interviews. Riska smiled at the crowd of his friends and associates and explained that a press conference had been set up at the DAC for later in the day.

Plunkett completed his part during the taping of the Hope special, and then Riska whisked the new Heisman winner by limousine to the club. Riska fluently and courteously went about getting Plunkett whatever he needed, including a new necktie and a room at the Downtown Athletic Club to help Jim relax and prepare for his major media appearance. Riska also arranged for Plunkett to talk to his mother by telephone to share the good news, and he had the DAC forward Carmen Plunkett a bouquet of congratulatory flowers.

"Rudy is the embodiment of the Heisman to winners of the trophy," says Plunkett. Riska, who in the 1940s was raised in a lower Manhattan neighborhood adjacent to the DAC, has been the caretaker of the trophy and its winners for more than forty years.

"I walked into the room for the press conference a bit nervous," says Plunkett, recalling his 1970 media appearance. "But just as I got through the door, from behind me I felt Rudy's hand on my shoulder. He walked with me through the room, smiling at everyone as he introduced me. I knew everything was going to be just fine."

Within hours Plunkett was flying back to San Francisco. In those days, the actual awards dinner was a week later in New York.

"I remember that on the trip back to San Francisco, the pilot announced that the Heisman Trophy winner was on the plane," Plunkett says. "It was the first time I was introduced like that. It was certainly not the last. I won a lot of other awards in the next few years in the pros, but from that day forward, the first part of my name has always been 'Heisman Trophy winner.'

"On the plane, people came by to shake my hand and they served me champagne and cake. And then when I landed, there were hundreds of people from Stanford greeting the plane. I was overwhelmed at that."

He returned to New York for the official awards dinner with his coaches.

"To win the Heisman from my background, I was pretty proud of myself," Plunkett says. "My mom couldn't travel to the ceremony and that was too bad, but she was happy for me. She didn't really follow sports, but she knew this was something special because she said to me: 'Jimmy, this must be a big deal; everyone keeps stopping to talk to me about it.'

"I brought the trophy home and she would run her hands over it. She liked that."

Ohio State came into the Rose Bowl that New Year's Day 1971 with thirty-one victories in its last thirty-two games. In the Midwest, they had been dubbed the "Team of the Century." The Buckeyes had six players who would be first-round draft picks in the next NFL college draft. Heisman winner or not, Plunkett and Stanford were thirteen-point underdogs.

"And we knew why," Plunkett says. "We weren't as good man-for-man as Ohio State. But we were pretty sure they hadn't faced a passing attack like ours either. So we thought we'd move the football on them. And we had a lot of guys on our team playing their last college game. Unlike Ohio State, our guys weren't going anywhere in football. This was it for their football career and they banded together and played a notch above their normal levels that day."

But Plunkett's teammates later said they believed they could play above their customary level for a different reason: They had the best quarterback in the nation. And Plunkett did not let them down, engineering two drives that gave Stanford an early 10–0 lead in the game. Ohio State, however, roared back to take a 14–10 halftime lead.

The teams exchanged third-quarter field goals before the Cardinals defense made a pivotal stop, tackling the Buckeyes' All-American fullback John Brockington for a loss on a fourth-down-and-one play at the Stanford 20-yard line. The first play of the fourth quarter, it defied in the most corporal way Ohio State's once accepted invincibility.

One Stanford player later said he gazed across the line of scrimmage into the eyes of Brockington and saw "the unexpected fear of losing."

The tenor of the game changed, and Plunkett sprinted onto the field aware of the opportunity presented him. Plunkett methodically led the Cardinals on a thirteen-play, eighty-yard touchdown drive. Later, he added a ten-yard touchdown strike to Vataha and Stanford had a 27–17 victory that is still considered to be among the greatest upsets in Rose Bowl history.

It was a performance that probably made Plunkett the first overall pick of the ensuing NFL draft. Taken by the New England Patriots, he was their starting quarterback in his first game as a rookie, a rarity then and even rarer now. Desperate for a savior, the woebegone Patriots thrust their top draft pick onto the big stage and asked him to perform magic.

Plunkett was the 1971 NFL Rookie of the Year, though the Patriots' revival was short-lived. Plunkett, who never had good pass protection in New England, took a beating—in the pocket and in the Boston press.

After five years, he was traded to his hometown 49ers, another franchise desperate for a savior after three consecutive losing seasons. The whole organization was reeling, about to be sold to a new owner and re-made by Coach Bill Walsh. Before Plunkett's arrival, the 49ers had turned to a different Heisman Trophy–winning quarterback, Steve Spurrier, who could not revive the stumbling team.

Plunkett's efforts for the 49ers would be lost in the disorder, too. In two seasons in San Francisco, Plunkett led the 49ers to an indifferent 13–15 record. Pass protection was not a 49er strength either, and Plunkett began to play tentatively, always a mistake for a quarterback whose primary responsibility is to make the right and decisive choices. All the collisions with charging defensive linemen over the years in New England and San Francisco had made him fidgety in the pocket, which is like being fidgety in a Wild West gunfight. You will lose.

His accuracy, once a strong point, was gone. With few other skilled players around him, he had started to press, doing too much and accomplishing less.

Finally, in 1978, the 49ers tried to trade Plunkett, but surprisingly, received no interest from other clubs. Eight years after the dramatic Rose Bowl upset of Ohio State and a charmed Heisman Trophy–winning season, Plunkett was released by the 49ers. As a free agent, he had no suitors anywhere in pro football.

"Certainly, there was a feeling of having hit rock bottom," Plunkett says. "In athletics, I had been on top all my life. I considered retiring. But I had friends, my guys from Stanford, who told me I was a victim of circumstances, that I still had the same ability. I just needed time, and a chance, to get it all back.

"They had more confidence in me than I did, but it worked. I was willing to try again."

He called the Oakland Raiders, just across the bay, and asked for a tryout.

"It was humbling because I don't think I had ever tried out for anything, even in high school," Plunkett says. "But you know, I had to do it. And they liked me enough to sign me as the back-up quarterback to Ken Stabler."

Plunkett did not play a single second during the 1978 season for the Raiders. In 1979, he attempted only fifteen passes in a sixteen-game season. In 1980, the Raiders had traded Stabler to the Houston Oilers for Dan Pastorini. At this point, Plunkett asked to be traded.

"I had worked hard and gotten my tools back," he says. "I was confident again."

But Raiders owner Al Davis knew a team needed more than one capable quarterback, and he declined Plunkett's trade request. Plunkett was in despair again, but five games into the 1980 season, Pastorini broke his leg.

In the movies, Plunkett would have thrown off his sideline cape, pulled on his helmet, and led the Raiders to a last-second victory. But if Plunkett's return to the starting lineup with Oakland were a movie, it would have starred Moe, Larry, and Curly.

Plunkett threw five interceptions against Kansas City in a 31–17 loss. Dumbfounded, he wondered if, at thirty-three, maybe he was finished.

"But I started to think about all the things I had overcome," he says, "going all the way back to my childhood. I thought what I needed to do was show some resolve. I had played that first game back with a lot of butterflies. It wasn't physical inability; I had just made a lot of mental mistakes. I hadn't been tough enough in the pocket. I didn't stand in there to deliver the pass even if it meant taking a hit after the throw.

"So I started playing little head games with myself. I went to the next game and talked myself into remembering how to do the gritty things. You know, 'Stand in there. Don't start running around. Look downfield. Find your receiver despite the rush in your face.' I fought it internally. It was all about finding the mental toughness."

The Raiders won their next game against San Diego, then had a game on Monday Night Football at Pittsburgh against the Steelers, their usual playoff nemesis. There was more feuding and bad blood in a Raiders–Steelers nationally televised football game than on the other prime-time giants of the time: *Dallas, Dynasty,* and *Knots Landing.*

It would be a pivotal game of the season, and a make-or-break point in Plunkett's comeback. And he knew it.

"We were losing at halftime and Howard Cosell was getting on me pretty good already," Plunkett says. "I knew this could be it for my career. And later I found out that Cosell was going on about me, saying I don't have the ability to play anymore. I couldn't hear him but I didn't have to. I could feel it. At one point he said, 'He's done. He's had his chance but he can't do it.'"

In 1980, Monday Night Football was an American institution and Cosell was its ringmaster. People tuned in week after week just to see how Cosell would anger them. Monday Night Football had become something new, the ultimate saloon-gathering event, an excuse to get out of the house on the deadest night of the week in any city or town; and bars used the game as an attraction—with added effects.

Understanding Cosell's position as the cynosure of the show, a bar in western Pennsylvania began raffling off a brick before the Monday night telecast. In a corner of the bar, they would set up an old black-and-white television. The winner of the raffle would have the honor of throwing the brick through the television as soon as Howard Cosell's visage appeared on the screen.

Other bars across the nation copied the ritual.

But what made Cosell a distinctive personality was his ability to define the game. He did not do commentary as much as he announced a story line every week. And then he would harp at it ceaselessly. It was a football game-as-television show and Cosell drafted the script. People at home or in saloons would spend the night rooting for Cosell to be wrong.

And so, that evening in 1980, a nation started rooting for Plunkett to bring the Raiders back in the second half. And he did, winning a thrilling 45–34 game. Life was good: Cosell had been wrong.

Plunkett, long forgotten three weeks ago, was suddenly everybody's favorite NFL quarterback and an irresistible comeback story.

The Raiders won their next four games and seven of their last nine. An underdog wild-card playoff team, they won back-to-back road games to reach Super Bowl XV. Then, in America's most-watched sports event, Oakland whipped the Philadelphia Eagles, 27–10.

Plunkett passed for each of the Raiders' three touchdowns, completing thirteen of twenty-one passes for 261 yards.

"I felt a sense of redemption," says Plunkett, who was named the game's most valuable player. "It was important to me. I had worked very hard to get it back, and now people couldn't say my professional career was a failure. It was a success."

And he was not yet done.

Plunkett returned to the Super Bowl in 1983, quarterbacking the Raiders to a 38–9 rout of the Washington Redskins.

Plunkett continued with the Raiders for a few more seasons, but by 1987 he sensed that his body had delivered all the football magic it had to offer, and with a mix of regret and appreciation, Plunkett retired.

"That was very hard, too, but I couldn't ask for more from myself," Plunkett says. "Fortunately, my kids were young and there was plenty to do with them."

Plunkett and his wife, Gerry, now have a college-aged son and daughter. He owns a Coors beer distributorship and appears on several Raiders radio and television pre- and postgame shows. He has raised more than $1 million for Stanford University athletics, money dedicated to scholarships and women's sports. A guest house adjacent to his home in Atherton, which is minutes from the Stanford campus, is occupied yearly by a different Stanford football player or athlete.

"Just a way to help out," Plunkett says. "I got so much help growing up."

He returns to his old neighborhood periodically, shaking his head to reflect on what it took to make it out.

"I had great parents who never took anything that happened to them as a setback," he says. "As a kid watching that, it will sit with you forever. I don't think my life is any different than anyone else's. We all have things to rise above. That is life. I learned that early. I saw it every day."

Carmen Plunkett died in 2002 at the age of eighty-nine.

"Towards the end of my pro football career, she actually started paying close attention to what I was doing," Jim says of his mother. "For years, I would call her the night before a game and all she would say was, 'Don't get hurt.' But in the Super Bowl years, she was hearing so much on the newscasts and listening to people talk on the street and in the shops. So when I would call she would say: 'Jimmy, I think you're going to have to hold onto the football.' She'd say, 'They're going to try to take it away from you.' I remember she said, 'It's all in your hands.'

"And at the time, I would laugh. But I think about that sometimes."

"The Heisman Is a Privilege, Not a Free Pass"

JOHNNY RODGERS, 1972

When he was fourteen, Johnny Rodgers stole a car, left home, and did not return for a year. When he was fifteen, he was stabbed in the back outside a drug store. At seventeen, he met his father for the first time. At eighteen, he sat at the wheel of the getaway car while two friends robbed a gas station. At twenty-one, he won the Heisman Trophy.

Johnny Rodgers is the living, corporeal proof that the Heisman Trophy balloting is not a contest recognizing civic responsibility or citizenship. Rodgers, whose life as late as 1987 was tangled enough to include a brief imprisonment, is the sobering evidence that the noted Heisman Trophy mystique does not automatically bless each winner's life.

Any history of the Heisman fraternity must acknowledge a subsociety, a gallery of Heisman winners whose designation as recipients of college football's ultimate honor only underscored their ignoble, public falls from grace in later years.

The 1959 Heisman Trophy winner, Louisiana State's Billy Cannon, served two and a half years in a federal penitentiary for his role as leader of a counterfeiting ring that printed $6 million in phony $100 bills.

The 1978 winner, Billy Sims, served jail time as a deadbeat dad who failed to make child support payments.

The 1979 Heisman Trophy winner, Southern Cal's Charles White, battled cocaine addiction for several years during his professional football career, which led to a National Football League suspension before he retired at the age of 31.

The 1980 Heisman winner, George Rogers of South Carolina, also had drug problems that cast a stigma over an eight-year NFL career.

The grand marshal of this subgroup is 1968 Heisman winner O.J. Simpson, the man who may be the most notorious innocent man—by court decree—of the twentieth century.

In a bit of irony, Simpson, acquitted of two murders in a California courtroom but forever convicted by public opinion, spent decades prior to his arrest trumpeting the sense of moral order and responsibility that most Heisman winners see as an accompaniment to the award.

Just a few years before his high-profile arrest, Simpson wrote an essay for the Downtown Athletic Club's *Heisman Journal*, the periodical published annually on the eve of the award's presentation.

The Heisman Trophy, Simpson wrote, "signifies a great citizen. A couple of winners have had their problems, but I'll argue that among our winners are some of this country's leading citizens. . . . I think a Heisman Trophy winner has an obligation to all of college football—to every guy who ever played football—to be an outstanding citizen."

Each winner of the most recognizable trophy in American sport quickly comes to understand, usually within hours of accepting the award, that forevermore there were three words attached to the front of his name, "Heisman Trophy winner . . ."

It can be spoken to distinguish a man of achievement, or it can be spoken to register a distinction misspent.

In the same essay, Simpson wrote: "I think if you look at Johnny Rodgers—perhaps more than any of the other winners I can recall—you see a man who has accepted the responsibility that goes with the Heisman. Rodgers had some troubles before he won the Trophy, but since he won the Heisman he has carried the banner very well."

But here is what sets Rodgers apart from O.J., and it has much to do with a modest sense of discretion on the topic of citizenship. One can talk to Johnny Rodgers for days and he will never deny anything about his rocky past. He has his take on it, and insists he was not as bad as he might have been portrayed at times—something many of his coaches and friends said at the time as well. But today, Rodgers admits to his failures, saying:

"I was wrong many, many times. I made mistakes. I call them childhood mistakes. I may have been a teenager or adolescent but I was one of those guys who saw the light late. But the important thing to add is that every time I did something wrong, I was eager to try and do good the next time. Nowadays, I tell kids and teenagers who have made mistakes that it is not over until it is over. You can make mistakes. But you can correct them. You can do good in the end."

Rodgers lives and understands his words, even as they relate to his greatest athletic accomplishment.

"The Heisman," he said, "is a privilege, not a free pass."

The lessons of Johnny Rodgers's life are highly practical even if they are as complex as the Heisman Trophy's famed symbolism. In that perspective, the life of Johnny Rodgers is as good and deserving an example of the Heisman in context as any.

This is a man who on the day he was enshrined into the hall of Heisman Trophy winners, was immediately cast as its most disreputable beneficiary ever, which is saying something in a subgroup that includes a counterfeiting felon.

As Rodgers said looking back on that day more than thirty years later, "I was called college football's bad boy even before I won the Heisman. There wasn't so much conversation about whether I earned it, but whether they should let me have it. I was like, 'What?' I never thought I was bad."

Born in Omaha's roughest downtown district, Rodgers lived on the corner of Twenty-seventh Street and Pinckney Avenue, the city's high-crime crossroads.

"From the time I was about ten years old, I went to school before the sun came up and I went home after the sun went down," Rodgers said. "In the dark I figured I had a chance to get home without getting jumped. I would walk right down the middle of the street, that way I figured I had a 50–50 chance to run in the direction they couldn't catch me.

"There just seemed to always be somebody out there who wanted to beat you up or cut you. They didn't shoot you like they do now. I grew up seven blocks from where Malcolm X grew up on Thirty-fourth and Pinckney. It was truly the Wild Wild West. You didn't live, man, you survived."

Dick Christie, Rodgers's high school football coach at Omaha Tech, said he remembered taking knives from Rodgers, who would plead, "Coach, how am I going to get home now?"

Christie said: "The thing you have to understand is that he was honest about it. He was honest about everything. He accepted any discipline. There was never an argument. He has never shrugged any kind of responsibility. He is in many ways everything a person would want in a son. He would tell you: 'I'm not kidding. I need that knife to survive.'"

Rodgers, his teachers said, was a dutiful if overtaxed student who would try his best when inside the school. Then he returned to what might as well have been another planet: Twenty-seventh and Pinckney.

Rodgers, however, does not blame his neighborhood for the troubles that followed him in a multitude of ways along the way. He is a realist.

"There was a lot going on. I mean, let's just say I went through the early parts of my life unbalanced," Rodgers said. "Look, when I was fourteen, I ran away from home and went all the way to Detroit. Now if that isn't the act of an unbalanced individual I don't know what is. In 1965, who leaves anyplace else to go to Detroit?"

Rodgers lived a Detroit street life for a year.

"When you get to Detroit, you realize you didn't mean to be there," he said. "I thought Omaha was tough because somebody was getting killed every week. In Detroit, it seemed like somebody was getting killed every hour."

While he was away, Rodgers learned that he had become a father for the first time and returned to Omaha. "It was still a rough life on Twenty-seventh Street," he said.

But he was a star athlete, fleet and nimble, with the kind of cutback instincts that define so many great backs. He wasn't big, no more than 175 pounds, but he could play running back, wide receiver, and throw passes. Most of all, he was electrifying as a return man on punts and kickoffs.

The University of Nebraska at Lincoln was a natural choice, and Rodgers was nearly an immediate attraction as a return man. During his three seasons on the varsity, no one left his Nebraska Stadium seat, and no one watching Cornhuskers games on television left the room, whenever the opposition was getting ready to kick the football to Johnny Rodgers. The street kid was like the ultimate street performer, improvising, entertaining, and always demanding your attention. Rodgers had a knack for saving his biggest plays for the end of games, when he would extract himself from the most precarious situations with his own brand of death-defying moves. It was a talent, one could uncomfortably conclude in retrospect, that Rodgers may have honed in truly death-defying circumstances—like nighttime walks down the middle of the street.

But on the football field, the opposition was in the most danger as soon as it surrounded Johnny Rodgers. He was number 20, "Johnny the Jet," a wingback in an otherwise staid Nebraska offense. Rodgers was often used in reverses, flashing around the corner where he would deftly plant his outside leg in the sticky, hard artificial turf of the day and cut back across the grain as if propelled by slingshot. Bodies of defenders would clatter, collide, and collapse at Rodgers's feet trying to change direction as fast as Johnny had, but it would be pointless. Faster still, Johnny would run until faced with another wall of defenders, where he would slide his hips in one direction when in fact he was about to head in the other, a classic upper body/lower body fake that fools all but a very few.

And Johnny the Jet would be gone again.

"Johnny probably could impact a football game more ways than anybody I've ever coached or been affiliated with," said Nebraska's longtime Coach Tom Osborne, who was an assistant under Nebraska Head Coach Bob Devaney during Rodgers's college career. "That versatility and explosiveness was something else. You never knew where he might be next."

Nebraska did not lose a game in Rodgers's sophomore and junior seasons, when the Huskers won back-to-back national championships. In 1971, he scored one of the more memorable touchdowns in modern college football history on what everyone in Nebraska will forever call "The Punt Return of the Century." It came during what is still billed in the heart of the cornbelt as "The Game of the Century."

It was a gray, forty-nine-degree Thanksgiving Day in Norman, Oklahoma, when top-ranked Nebraska, unbeaten in its last twenty-nine games, visited the second-ranked Sooners, an undefeated team that was averaging nearly forty points a game. Nebraska had the top-rated defense in the country. And it had Johnny Rodgers.

In the first quarter, Rodgers took a Sooner punt seventy-two yards from the end zone and launched himself upfield in a dash through Oklahoma's onrushing eleven. It was Oklahoma running back Greg Pruitt, a Heisman candidate himself, who would have the best shot at Rodgers, but Pruitt could not stop the churning legs beneath Rodgers's swiveling hips. With a bounce off Pruitt's shoulder pads, Rodgers put one hand down to the turf for balance, spun and stutter-stepped and headed for the middle of the field. He faced a gaggle of Nebraska defenders and broke for the sideline, and then he was gone, a streak of red and white sprinting to the end zone. The state of Nebraska was never the same.

The punt return was the signature moment in a classic game. Fifty-five million Americans enjoying their Thanksgiving holiday watched the seesaw battle that ensued on television, an astonishing total for a sporting event in the days before the Super Bowl had gained widespread cultural consequence. The lead changed hands several times until Nebraska mounted a last, long drive, one kept alive when Rodgers made a gritty eleven-yard, third-down reception that picked up a first down.

"Everyone remembers my punt return," Rodgers said. "But in my mind, the third down catch was the biggest play of the game."

Nebraska's Jeff Kinney scored the last of his four touchdowns on a one-yard run and the Cornhuskers held on for an electrifying 35–31 victory.

The game put Nebraska at the epicenter of a college football world that had long overlooked the flat Nebraska plains as a hotbed of the game. The Cornhuskers were often disregarded because of an offensive style that featured a pulverizing, if maddeningly unvarying, running attack. Now they had something truly unstoppable, a speed and an agility that none of the teams from the Big Eight Conference or the Southeastern Conference of the time could match. Johnny Rodgers of Omaha added spice to the dependability of the Nebraska Cornhuskers.

In the Orange Bowl game at the conclusion of the 1971 season, number one and undefeated Nebraska faced number two Alabama, which took an 11–0 record into the game. In a 38–6 rout by Nebraska, Rodgers fielded a punt on the Nebraska 29-yard line and dashed up the sideline. As Rodgers ran, too fast for his pursuers in the historic and elegant uniforms of the University of Alabama, he passed directly in front of the bench of the Alabama Crimson Tide. And as Rodgers ran, he passed just a few feet in front of Alabama Coach Bear Bryant.

Bryant glared at Rodgers, motionless, turning his eyes but not his head to follow Rodgers's charge toward the end zone. The famed coach then dropped his hands to his side, watching his players in pursuit, none closer than ten yards as Rodgers sprinted across the goal line for a memorable seventy-one-yard touchdown.

"For the last twenty years, when I'm traveling down South I have people come up to me and thank me for being the one to get Alabama to desegregate its football team," Rodgers said. "I don't know if it's true but people down South tell me that my run right past Coach Bryant caused him to change."

In fact, there was one African-American player on Alabama's roster in 1971, a tight end named Wilbur Jackson. Earlier that season, Jackson had become the first black player to step on the football field for the Crimson Tide. But the comments Rodgers has heard over the years are understandable in a historic context.

Bryant himself was frequently quoted as saying it was the performance of Southern California's black running back Sam Cunningham, who in 1970 scored three touchdowns in a twenty-one-point victory at Alabama, that had the biggest influence on his decision to urge the university to add black players to its roster.

Perhaps most telling, while Alabama had never played against black players until the mid-1960s, it was becoming more common late in that decade, and Alabama's record in 1969 was a stunning 6–5. In 1970, the Crimson Tide did not rebound. Their record was more disturbing: 6–5–1.

Speed was changing the game all around Bryant, and he was quick to react. Jackson was his first black recruit, and it would be fair to speculate that Bryant saw the necessity to do more than just break the color barrier as Rodgers, a blur of Nebraska red-and-white, whizzed by him in a thirty-two-point defeat. Bryant historians say the coach had been lobbying the university to allow black players for years. By the time Coach Bryant had retired after the 1982 season, hundreds of African-Americans had played for him, helping the coach to three of his six career national championships.

In Rodgers's senior year, Nebraska lost twice, ruining the Cornhuskers' chances for a third successive national title, but Johnny had not lost his flair for the dramatic or his ability to play his best in the biggest games. In his last game for Nebraska, against Notre Dame in the 1973 Orange Bowl, Rodgers scored four touchdowns and threw a touchdown pass during a 40–6 romp.

Weeks earlier, he had been voted the 1972 recipient of the Heisman Trophy. In his career, he had scored forty-five touchdowns and returned seven punts for touchdowns, tying an NCAA record. Rodgers had 5,586 career all-purpose yards, gaining an average of 13.6 yards every time he touched the football. He was the school's leading receiver in career receptions with 143 for 2,479 yards, a record he still held more than thirty years after his last Nebraska game.

Rodgers was drafted in the first round by the San Diego Chargers, but he felt San Diego's salary offer was too low, so he instead became the biggest name from American college football to ever bolt for the Canadian Football League.

"I was the first one to take the Heisman out of the country, at least as a football player," Rodgers said. "After I went to Canada, a bunch of other guys in the next few years came north, too. And the NFL had to start offering bigger contracts. I started a trend."

It is not a trend that fans will likely celebrate, but the era of high-salaried athletes was about to overtake every American sport. In 1972, baseball had just endured its first mass strike of players. Losses in court had whittled away the legitimacy of baseball's reserve clause, which had bound players to their clubs in perpetuity. Two years later, when the average baseball salary was $44,000, Atlanta owner Ted Turner signed the first baseball "free agent," Andy Messersmith, to a $1.7 million contract.

Pro football followed along, albeit much more slowly.

Rodgers played four seasons in Canada for the Montreal Alouettes, where he was named rookie of the year and was the runner-up for player of the year two other times. He was a popular star in eastern Canada, busy with product endorsements and public appearances. He had not, though, smoothed all the rough edges from an erratic lifestyle. Because he was frequently late for team meetings, or missed them entirely, Rodgers was less than popular with his coach in Montreal, Marv Levy, who would later make his fame as the coach of the Buffalo Bills. In 1976, Levy cut Rodgers, who took that demotion as a sign that it was time to turn back to the NFL. He signed with San Diego. A host of injuries, one after another and usually in training camp, kept Rodgers from ever donning a Chargers uniform in a regular season game.

"It's one of the great regrets I have as a player," Rodgers said. "That I never played in the NFL. I was in shape, the best shape of my life. But I kept getting hurt."

Retired as a player, he remained in San Diego and started a cable television magazine called *Tuned In*, which thrived for a while. Rodgers had other business ventures but a spotty record when it came to making them endure. In 1987, in what Rodgers calls a monumental misunderstanding, he was arrested for allegedly threatening a cable television repairman who came to his house to disconnect his cable TV.

Rodgers, who had received probation as an accomplice in the gas station robbery in 1970, acted as his own attorney when his 1987 assault case went to court. One day, he placed his Heisman Trophy on the defendant's table next to him, hoping it would influence the judge. Rodgers learned, not for the first time but perhaps for the last, the limits of the Heisman's noted aura.

"For a while, they were talking about sentencing me to nine years in jail," Rodgers said. "That's what you get for representing yourself."

He was briefly jailed awaiting his appeal, which, with the help of an attorney, he won and had his conviction overturned. By then, Rodgers had all but officially returned to Nebraska, where he was still admired and accepted. Rodgers had also commenced on a new course for his life.

It is one of Rodgers's life canons that there is always time to make amends. Rodgers has an unrelenting dedication to that principle, and in the early 1990s, he had a moment of revelation that spurred him to the next path in his life.

On his return to Nebraska, Rodgers was frequently asked to address school groups.

"I would tell the kids that they can be whatever they want to be if they get an education," Rodgers said. "And all the while, I knew I had quit school before I had received a college degree. I decided then and there that I either had to take that stuff out of my speech or get a degree. You can't just say what you say, you have to do like you say."

So Johnny Rodgers, with financial aid from the state university, re-enrolled at the University of Nebraska, living in Lincoln as a full-time student.

"It's not easy to start over like that," said Rodgers, who was a forty-two-year-old in class with eighteen-year-olds. "You have to break a lot of bad habits, in the classroom and outside the classroom. You have to study. I had to be more disciplined than ever before. It was a great experience. Maybe the smartest thing I ever did."

It took four years, but Rodgers graduated from Nebraska with two degrees, in advertising and broadcasting.

A year earlier, at forty-five, Johnny was married inside the Heisman Room of the Downtown Athletic Club. Today, he and his wife of nine years, Jawana, have a seven-year-old daughter, Jewel.

Johnny and Jawana have since started two business ventures, one in juvenile bedding, the other in sports memorabilia. And the couple decided to move back to Johnny's former Omaha neighborhood.

"I didn't want to run from it," he says. "We work in it. We work to make it better, to make it work for everyone. I love telling my daughter, 'Hey, this is my neighborhood. This is your neighborhood.' "

Recently, Rodgers was voted the Husker of the Century after a statewide poll in football-mad Nebraska asked respondents to name the greatest University of Nebraska players ever. Rodgers was the runaway winner.

In 2002, Rodgers started a youth foundation, which he funds in part by money he receives from motivational speaking engagements. Rodgers has also been active in various charitable enterprises related to the Heisman Foundation, a connection that especially pleases Rodgers because he came into the group in 1972 labeled as a scandalous choice.

"One of the great things is that the Heisman fraternity of winners has always been willing to help me, even in the toughest times," he said. "I owe a lot to them. When I was getting married, they were the ones who said, 'Why not do it at the club on Heisman weekend?' "

There had never been a wedding in the Heisman Room. But Rudy Riska of the Downtown Athletic Club, the majordomo of the Heisman Trophy, arranged not only for a ceremony in the stately wood-paneled Heisman Room, he arranged for a reception for the newlyweds at the club as well.

"I have a great allegiance to the Heisman, to Rudy and all the winners who stood with me," Rodgers said. "I would never want to do anything that would turn out bad and make it look bad for the group. I think I got a slow start in this game of life. I was running the wrong way, but I proved you can change direction in the game. You don't have to keep running the wrong way."

He is not alone in this business of changing one's course in life, even among the Heisman Trophy winners who have so notably stumbled.

Billy Cannon served his time for counterfeiting and returned to his practice as an orthodontist. While somewhat of a reclusive, enigmatic figure, Cannon has lived a quiet life in his native Louisiana for several decades now.

Charles White overcame his drug problems, rebounded in 1987 to lead the NFL in rushing, and returned to the University of Southern California to work in a variety of capacities, including helping current and former players complete their studies. White now monitors the school's computer systems. In a 2002 interview with the *Los Angeles Times*, he explained his drug woes thusly: "Dumbness and stupidity and immaturity."[9]

George Rogers also rose above his troubles, and he took work at his alma mater, the University of South Carolina, in the athletic department. He hosts a golf tournament in South Carolina benefiting the Heisman Foundation and other community charities, including one Rogers started.

"I just wish I had grown up a lot sooner," Rogers said in a 1998 interview.

The vast majority of Heisman Trophy winners, at an early age, harness the resolve that made them athletic successes and use it for the next challenges of life, including Heisman celebrity. Other Heisman Trophy winners are less prepared, a condition no doubt made worse by a modern sporting culture all too willing to coddle star athletes from the fields of peewee football to the grand arenas of pro football.

But even Heisman Trophy winners eventually get older and slower. They are deposited on the street of life, and as they search for their next steps in a world that plays by different rules, for some, the Heisman that once defined them becomes more a weighty trophy of burden.

Johnny Rodgers didn't have it easy. He did not make it easy on some around him. In 1972 he was the most troubling selection ever to emerge first from the tally of Heisman votes, but no one is more proud of his Heisman Trophy now than Rodgers. And within the fraternity of Heisman Trophy winners, there are few as well liked.

---

[9]*The Los Angeles Times*, November 30, 2002.

When these Heisman Trophy winners gather, usually once a year at the time of the Heisman selection in December, the more recent winners defer to the earlier winners, like children looking up to their grandparents. Together, the assembled winners fill the room with a spark, a charge of accomplishment with their timeline of stories that span eight decades. It is a room that seems to hold the entire history of college football and America with it. And in this room, one man is the most active.

Johnny Rodgers, who won his Heisman nearly at the midpoint of the award's history to date, is the bridge between the winners of the war years and the winners of the modern era. Rodgers is well known to both groups, the former who once welcomed him warily and the latter who as children watched, mouths agape, as he dashed across their television screens. Even the most recent winners know of Johnny the Jet, number 20 from Nebraska.

Vivacious, unpretentious, and ever grateful to his colleagues, Rodgers helps bring the room to life. No one seems happier to be in that setting than Rodgers. And his fellow winners accept him as a shining example of the complex and diverse effect the award can have on a life. Unlike many before him, Johnny Rodgers did not win the Heisman and ride happily ever after into succeeding sunsets of greater triumph. Rodgers stumbled, fell, got up, and stumbled again.

The player embodied on the Heisman Trophy is a solid, strong, and balanced figure—sturdy, poised, and confident as he stares ahead. That did not begin to describe the young Johnny Rodgers. Rodgers remembers that when he was presented the trophy, he was surprised at how heavy it was. He picked it up with some effort and took hold of it. He concedes he did not, at the time, grasp it.

"No, and there are a lot of things I probably didn't understand back then but that's okay," he said. "When I make a speech now, my number one theme is perseverance. There is nothing more important, no quality in life that will help you more. Some people figure things out sooner than others. They make fewer mistakes or maybe they choose the smoother road. Then there's the rest of us. We have to dig ourselves out of things at some point.

"But it's not important how you do it; it's important that you try."

For thirty years, Rodgers has taken his Heisman Trophy with him to speeches and appearances. Naturally, he is often asked to pose for photographs with the trophy.

"I get down low with my head next to it and hug it tight like a best friend," Rodgers said. "Sometimes I feel like that guy on my trophy is putting his arm out and around me, like he's hugging me back. Sounds crazy, I know. But then, we've been through a lot together."

"Everyone Is Here
for Their Moment"

JOHN CAPPELLETTI, 1973

John Cappelletti was alone in his New York City hotel, scribbling a few thoughts on stationery he found in the room's desk drawer. It was Monday, December 13, 1973, and the evening to come would provide the pivotal sequence of his life. He would soon complete one of the most famous off-the-field acts in American sports history, an unpremeditated deed of compassion that soothed and touched the country in a period of deep upheaval. It would spawn a best-selling book and a television movie, making Cappelletti and his family forever renowned.

Two days earlier, Cappelletti had been an accomplished college football player at Penn State University, but far from a national personality. On that Saturday afternoon, it was announced Cappelletti had won the Heisman Trophy, the first player from Penn State to do so.

"Then, before you know it," Cappelletti says, "it is Monday and you're getting ready for that night's Heisman acceptance dinner at the Waldorf-Astoria. Vice President Gerald Ford will be there, fifteen hundred other people will be there. They are waiting for your speech."

Faced with the speech of his life, Cappelletti started listing the people he wanted to thank.

"I thought: 'How did I get here?'" Cappelletti says. "So I wrote down my coaches, teachers, my family. I was moving in a logical order. It was easy.

"And then, I just wrote down Joey's name. I made no other notes. I left it open. I just wrote 'Joey' on a little sheet of paper and stopped writing."

John Cappelletti grew up in south Philadelphia, the setting for the movie "Rocky," which opened three years after Cappelletti won his Heisman. His parents, John Sr. and Anne, were born in Italy, each having immigrated to America as children to settle in south Philly, a bustling, gritty neighborhood of mostly first-generation Italian-Americans.

John Sr. had served in the U.S. Army and on his return to south Philly met and married Anne. He found work as a tradesman, part carpenter, part mechanic. In his off hours, John made things in his own workshop that he would sell on the streets of his neighborhood. Handmade Christmas tree stands were a particularly popular Cappelletti ware. Anne Cappelletti sewed for extra income and worked at a cleaner's.

The elder Cappellettis were not interested in sports, but their three sons and one daughter played them voraciously. It was what all the kids in south Philly did. When John was in grade school, his parents left the city for nearby Upper Darby, Pennsylvania, where sports were no less a passion.

"Most every family then believed that athletics funneled you into a positive atmosphere," John Cappelletti says. "And they were right. My parents weren't sports people but they liked the passion it brought out in us."

John was a star high school running back who naturally migrated several hours west to Penn State. As a freshman, Cappelletti was a running back and linebacker, but as a sophomore, Coach Joe Paterno asked him to try defensive back. Though he considered himself a running back, Cappelletti knew that the starting Penn State backfield at the time was Franco Harris and Lydell Mitchell, a successful duo and two future NFL stars. There was no running room for Cappelletti.

"The argument was that I could start playing varsity as a sophomore and I did play a lot," Cappelletti says. "But then in my junior year, when I switched back to running back, I had lost a whole season as an offensive player. I struggled to get comfortable, to handle the football again. I was worried I wasn't going to find my running instincts again.

"But then, almost like a light bulb went off, it all clicked again."

As a junior, Cappelletti rushed for 1,117 yards, a prelude to a stunning senior season. Cappelletti was not the Heisman favorite heading into his fi-

nal college season, though, perhaps because Penn State had never produced a Heisman winner.

But Cappelletti would be the driving force on a 12–0 Penn State team.
Twenty-four of the twenty-five freshman football players who came to
Penn State with Cappelletti had matured into a steady, veteran team. In
Penn State's classically generic—simple is beautiful—uniforms, the 1973
team mowed through its early schedule of opponents, winning by an average of twenty-six points in games at Stanford, Navy, Air Force, and Syracuse. At home, Iowa fell by 27–8 and Army was defeated 54–3. Penn State
was 7–0 as the season wound into November.

But the Heisman race was still a mix of names. Ohio State had three
candidates in John Hicks, a mountain of a tackle; linebacker Randy
Gradishar; and sophomore running back, Archie Griffin. Elsewhere, quar-
terback Danny White was leading a resurgence at Arizona State and the
University of Texas's Roosevelt Leaks was the best running back in the
Southwestern Conference.

As for Cappelletti, he was perceived as just another capable, somewhat faceless back on another methodically brilliant Penn State team.
Didn't all those hard-charging Penn State backs look alike in those look-
alike uniforms?

But Cappelletti was different. Neither a true speed back nor a pure
power runner, Cappelletti was a mix of skills and possessed one unique ap-
titude: He was hard to knock off his feet. Balance may be the elite athlete's
most treasured faculty and Cappelletti was remarkably steady even after
absorbing a myriad of blows or after he was spun around on a tackle. He
could run through tacklers and still have the agility to find another opening
in the defense—and the speed to burst through it. He was a determined
runner who rarely made the wrong decision following his blockers, the result of another inimitable, natural gift: precise game-time concentration.

When his younger brother Joey, on the eve of Joey's birthday, asked
him, as a present, to score four touchdowns in the next game John was
playing, Cappelletti did so even though he had never before scored four
touchdowns in any game. When Joey asked him to do it again later in the
season, John scored four touchdowns in the first half alone.

In November of his senior season in 1973, Cappelletti ran for 200 or
more yards in three successive games, the first running back in the history

of college football to do so. In a 42–22 victory over Maryland, he gained 202 yards. The following week, against Lou Holtz's surprisingly strong North Carolina State Wolf Pack, Cappelletti had 220 rushing yards in a 35–29 victory. On November 17, though playing in only the first half of a 49–10 Penn State win over Ohio University, Cappelletti had 204 yards.

The Heisman was Cappelletti's from that moment forward. This was a Penn State team carving out new territory. It had been said before, mostly on the rambling campus in State College, Pennsylvania, but the group of Nittany Lions rumbling through its season might be college football's best team. And it had college football's best player.

There was considerable debate when it came to Penn State's claim to a national title—thirty years later, there still is. At the conclusion of that season, Notre Dame was recognized, generally, as a consensus national champ after the Fighting Irish defeated Alabama in the Sugar Bowl. Undefeated Penn State had dearly wanted to face Alabama in the Sugar Bowl, but there was no Bowl Championship Series system and no way for an Eastern team to leverage its way into a national championship matchup. Penn State was relegated to the Orange Bowl where it defeated Louisiana State University.

"Joe Paterno was upset and made a big deal about it, mostly, I think, trying to have it rectified in the future," Cappelletti says of his coach. "In the end, that is how a better system probably came about, although it doesn't eliminate the arguments.

"In our case, we were all kind of disappointed at not getting the chance to play for the national championship. At the end of that season, I think we all felt certain that we could have played with anybody in the country. Over the years, it's something you come to accept, even if in most of the minds at Penn State, we were at least co-national champions that year."

When it came to the Heisman vote, however, there was near unanimity on the top choice.

Cappelletti became the first Penn State Heisman Trophy winner in a landslide. His life changed immediately; indeed, the Heisman has been all around Cappelletti's life ever since. In one of the great curiosities of the award, John's brother Michael later married the daughter of 1954 Heisman

Trophy winner Alan Ameche. Cathy Ameche met Michael Cappelletti through her brothers, who played football with Michael at a Pennsylvania prep school.

Noting that Ameche's widow Yvonne married 1946 Heisman Trophy winner Glenn Davis, Cappelletti says: "That means my nephews and nieces—my brother Michael's children—have an uncle, a grandfather, and a step-grandfather who are all Heisman Trophy winners. Figure the odds of that. It makes you wonder about how things really work out, if everything is really left to chance."

Over the years now, John Cappelletti has decided some of the events of his life were not simple happenstance. He views his winning of the Heisman—even his acceptance speech of the award—with a fateful eye.

"It seemed a time when people needed a lift. I know within our family that was certainly true," he says. "It was the kind of situation where we needed a break for one reason, and others maybe needed it for other reasons."

The times were tangled in America in 1973. A year that began with the announcement of a truce in the Vietnam War nonetheless seemed to lead to nonstop, worldwide conflict. Maybe it was the joylessness of the truce announcement, with its focus on these numbers: more than 46,000 Americans already dead.

Within weeks, FBI agents and a group of Native Americans faced off at Wounded Knee in South Dakota. There was a growing sense of national distrust, a sentiment disturbingly evident all around America. For example, in 1973, scarred by the spate of airline hijackings, U.S. authorities announced that the nation's 531 airports would begin to inspect and x-ray all passengers' baggage and require passengers to pass through metal detectors.

But there was one disquieting drama dominating the American culture in 1973 that was like no other. The summer of 1973 was the summer of Senator Sam Ervin's Watergate hearings. Four of President Richard Nixon's top aides had already quit. On a steamy Monday in June, John Dean accused Nixon of vigorously participating in the Watergate break-in cover-up. In a separate investigation, Vice President Spiro Agnew was forced to resign.

When Penn State's football team defeated West Virginia on Saturday,

October 23, 1973, it was hardly big news in the following morning's papers. The news pages were filled with the account of a startling misuse of power: President Nixon had suddenly dismissed the special Watergate prosecutor Archibald Cox, attorney general Elliot Richardson, and deputy attorney general William Ruckelshouse. It was instantly labeled the Saturday Night Massacre.

The country's financial health was no more settled. There was an oil shortage, then a full-fledged Arab oil embargo, which led to gas rationing and lengthy lines at gas stations.

New York City, meanwhile, was seemingly expanding and imploding at the same time. The twin towers of the World Trade Center opened in 1973, the same year New York, crippled by debt, first considered filing for bankruptcy and defaulting on hundreds of city loans. In fact, it was this monetary crisis that brought Vice President Ford to New York on the eve of that year's Heisman dinner. The former Michigan All-American decided to attend the Heisman banquet after meeting with New York City officials.

In these times, steps away from the gleaming new World Trade Center, John Cappelletti first grasped his Heisman Trophy in a Saturday reception with the media at the Downtown Athletic Club. He toured the Statue of Liberty, nearby Wall Street, and lower Manhattan. He awaited the official dinner presentation, when he would make his speech, on Monday night.

"If you believe in a greater power in your life," Cappelletti says, recalling that weekend in December 1973, "at that moment in time, I was where I was for a specific reason. Things were happening for a specific reason."

With brother Joey, the Cappellettis were enjoying their sight-seeing in New York, enjoying the recognition and accomplishment of big brother John.

"For us, knowing what we went through and what our family experienced, it was a moment in time when the pressure was off—even if for just a few days," Cappelletti says. "For a little while at least, we did not have to worry about every little thing. Joey smiled the whole weekend and I can't tell you what that meant to all of us."

In December 1973, John Cappelletti's eleven-year-old brother Joey was dying of leukemia. His illness, first diagnosed when Joey was five, had been an ongoing ordeal for the Cappelletti family—unending days and nights of pain, helplessness, and unrelenting uncertainty. Little in their lives proved an escape from dueling emotions: heartbreak over Joey's condition and inspiration derived from the determination he exhibited battling each debilitating stage.

Day after day, year by year, the lessons of a young life to all those around him had been stored away, constants within the Cappelletti household. Four years earlier, when college coaches came to recruit John, they invariably sat across from the living room couch where Joey lay resting. There was no avoiding the impact of a terminally ill young child on a family. In Joey's life, a simple case of chickenpox was nearly fatal. Monthly spinal taps brought excruciating pain. The steady interchange of medications meant ever-changing side effects—hair loss, blurred vision, frightening hemorrhages. And throughout, the Cappellettis wrestled with a dilemma: Was the intense, problematic therapy that held the promise of a recovery worth the discomfort it caused their son?

Joey endured it all, then got up and went to school, played Little League baseball, and if asked, revealed that he held onto a dream of one day following his brother John to Penn State.

Alone in his hotel room as he prepared his acceptance speech on that Monday afternoon, between lunch and the donning of a rented tuxedo, John Cappelletti made no attempt to sum up in words what Joey meant to him and his family. That evening, when he approached the lectern at the Waldorf-Astoria in midtown Manhattan, he had only a few sparse jottings on hotel stationery.

Beginning his remarks, Cappelletti thanked his coaches, teachers, and family. He rambled briefly, looking about the large ballroom, until he found the compass for his speech with a glance at the final four letters scrawled in his hotel that afternoon.

Briefly and directly, he explained to the audience about Joey: "He has leukemia." With his head raised, John said: "Joey lives with pain all the time. His courage is around the clock. If I could dedicate this trophy to him, if it could buy him one day of happiness, it would all be worthwhile."

John turned to Joey, who was seated nearby. Tears rolled down John's cheeks, falling to the lapels of his tuxedo. "This trophy is more his than mine and I want him to have it," he said, "because he has been my inspiration."

John Cappelletti sat down.

Archbishop Fulton J. Sheen had been told to follow Cappelletti to the microphone to deliver a benediction. The bishop rose to announce that his blessing was no longer necessary.

"Maybe for the first time in your lives," Sheen said, "you have heard a speech from the heart and not from the lips. Part of John's triumph was made by Joseph's sorrow. You don't need a blessing. God has already blessed you in John Cappelletti."

Joey Cappelletti died less than three years later, on April 8, 1976. His brother John was at his side.

Thirty years later, John Cappelletti acknowledges that he is frequently asked how he came up with the words for his speech, especially without a script of any kind.

"You have to understand," he says, "that everyone in my family lived with this situation for six years. It was never going to be difficult to give an account of what my brother went through and what it had meant to our family. We lived this. All I needed was to get started. It never occurred to me to pick words out ahead of time for how I felt about Joey."

In the years since, John Cappelletti has raised three sons of his own and built a successful biotechnical business in California where he lives with his wife Betty. After Penn State, he spent nine years as a dependable running back in the National Football League, but when his football career ended, he adopted a certain purposeful anonymity. The closest he has come to involvement in organized sports is as a Little League coach.

"Especially when my sons were playing sports, I figured the less visible I was, the more visible they were," he says.

But his life has remained connected to those few minutes at the Waldorf-Astoria in midtown Manhattan, something he regards as almost a public trust. The inspirational story of Joey Cappelletti is no longer something quietly and selflessly understood within one family. John's speech produced a television movie in 1977, *Something for Joey*, which inspired a book of the same name that continues to be read, inspiring a worldwide audience.

"Every month, still to this day, I will get a bundle of letters from a class of fourth or fifth graders in the United States or Japan or Canada, who are writing to me about the book and Joey," Cappelletti says. "Their teacher will have put together all their letters. I read them and I see how it touches them. Lifestyles change in thirty years, but to young kids, the story is the same.

CAPPELLETTI AND VICE PRESIDENT GERALD
FORD AT THE HEISMAN CEREMONY IN 1973

"Now as then, family units struggle. You argue with your brother or squabble with your sister. Families have tragedies and deaths. I am amazed how I'll get these letters from kids vowing not to argue with their siblings anymore after reading the book. They'll vow to be better children to their parents. People relate to our family and the situation we were in because coming together as a family in times of need is still the basis of a family."

Over time, Cappelletti has grasped the notion that his words at the 1973 Heisman ceremony, one of the most famous speeches in sports history, were predestined to have meaning beyond his own household, beyond that hotel ballroom, and beyond 1973.

"I believe everyone is here to do certain things with their life," Cappelletti says. "Without that one moment in time, my life is completely different. Looking back, it feels like it was set out ahead of time—it was supposed to happen. On the face of it, there was meaning for my family in that speech, but because of it, afterward I could do a lot of good things for other people.

"And at the time, it seemed like there were a lot of people who needed help, who needed something to raise them up. Because of that moment in time, people came to me for years, and still do, asking for things I am able and willing to do to help. There have been speeches and appearances for so many charities and good causes. There have been so many people moved and lifted by Joey's story, through the book and the movie. The good graces have extended around the world for decades now.

"There are days I still wish they had been able to cure Joey, that the story ended differently and he was still here. I wish I was talking to him on the phone every night. He isn't here but look what his life has been able to do.

"None of it happens if some power doesn't put me in front of that microphone on that night. And Joey, and my family's will to help him, lets it all come out. So I believe I was meant to be there at that moment. There are things in life worth striving for, and those are the things that lead you through life. It is for the things you are meant to do for the good of others.

"I believe that. I believe everyone is here for their moment."

16.

Paying Forward

ARCHIE GRIFFIN, 1974, 1975

There was no mistaking who was in charge, who was in control—and who was not—during their first game-time meeting as coach and player.

"Griffin!" Woody Hayes, Ohio State's larger than life coach, snarled. "Griffin! Griffin, where are you?"

Archie Griffin, a freshman fifth-string halfback, didn't move from the bench. Although he knew he was the only Griffin on the Ohio State roster, he still thought Coach Hayes had to be summoning someone else.

He couldn't, Archie thought, be calling for this Griffin. This Griffin was not even listed in the game program distributed to 86,000 fans that day at Ohio Stadium. This Griffin had been given one opportunity to play the week before, and in that first college running attempt, had fumbled away the football, the ultimate, inexcusable sin in the Ohio football planet ruled by Woody Hayes.

This Griffin figured it could be a year before he was granted a second running attempt. He had not been invited to the off-campus hotel where the varsity customarily stayed the night before games to ward off distractions. He had not accompanied the team to its pregame meal. He was lucky to be in uniform at all.

Still, there was that large man, with his trademark white short-sleeved shirt, thin dark tie, and big black baseball cap bearing the wide red "O" above the rim, glaring his way and growling his name: "Griffin, get over here."

Hayes was acting on a hunch, one put in his head by running backs coach Rudy Hubbard, who believed in Griffin's potential.

So Archie finally ran to Hayes.

"Yes, Coach," he said.

"Get in there. Now!"

And Archie Griffin ran onto the field.

One problem.

He did so without his helmet.

Now they were yelling at him again.

"Griffin, get back here," his teammates screamed. "You forgot your helmet. Here! Take it! Now go!"

Retrieving his helmet, Archie Griffin entered the game, which Ohio State was surprisingly losing 7–0 to North Carolina.

"I was in a daze for a few plays," Griffin said of that first quarter. "My eyes were as wide as saucers."

He did not hear his name shouted much for a few hours after that. But they called it repeatedly in the huddle. This was 1972 and an Ohio State football team could go weeks without throwing more than twenty passes. Running the football was not just some game-planning option, it was a state-sponsored religion. Buckeyes running backs had already won three Heisman Trophies: Les Horvath in 1944, Vic Janowicz in 1950, and Howard "Hopalong" Cassady in 1955. They had not won those trophies catching things thrown in the air. Hayes, like many of his contemporaries, had helped coin the saying, "When you pass, three things can happen and two of them are bad."

And in Ohio, especially in 1972, whatever Woody Hayes said was gospel. He was the state's best-known citizen and its most respected. For years, tour buses would stop by Hayes's A-frame house two miles from the football stadium so visitors could spill out and pose to have their picture taken in front of Coach Hayes's lawn and neatly trimmed hedges.

So when Coach Hayes said to run the football, and then said to run it again, his players listened. On this day, the football was increasingly in the hands of number 45, who could not be found in the game program.

For Archie Griffin, the five-foot-eight, 175-pound back born in the state capital city of Columbus and home to the Ohio State Buckeyes, this first game in the historic bowl of Ohio Stadium was evolving into a dream come true. He would leave the field with only a few minutes remaining in Ohio State's 29–14 victory having run for 239 yards, a school record for rushing yards in one game. He had done something neither Horvath, Janowicz, nor Cassady had done.

On the sideline, when he pulled off his helmet—safely putting it aside—he heard the cheering.

Ohio Stadium is a steeply pitched, double-decker concrete horseshoe with decorative arches all around the outside that give it a feel of ancient Rome. In the rotunda of the front entrance, there is a seventy-foot ceiling decorated with tiles and stained glass windows that are illuminated with flood lights at night.

If the setting sounds like a house of worship, it is not completely by accident. Ohio State football is almost a calling to some in the state. It is a common, if unsanctioned, tradition for fans to bring small urns containing the remains of recently departed loved ones who asked to have their ashes spread across the football field.

Ohio State officials understand and look the other way.

When Archie Griffin looked up at the end of his first game in Ohio Stadium, he saw row after row of Ohio State fans rising from their seats to applaud. And then, it was section after section until it was clear the entire 86,000 were offering a standing ovation meant for him.

"It was one of the most incredible sights of my life," Griffin said. "Amazing how your life can change in a day. From sunup to sundown."

His extraordinary debut would not be the last bit of record-setting for Archie Griffin. In 1974 and 1975 he became the first and only player to win two Heisman Trophies. As part of the first college freshman class allowed to play varsity football, he went on to become the first and only player to start in four successive Rose Bowl games.

And Hayes, who was once skeptical of Griffin's ability to compete at the Division I football level, had a player he warded over like a son. "He is a better young man than he is a football player," Hayes said of Griffin as Archie's senior season was winding down. "And he is the best football player I've ever seen."

Hayes and Griffin had a remarkable relationship, one born not so much through football but through matters that weighed off the field. They were a constant in middle America in the mid-1970s, national sporting touchstones. Saturday afternoons were for Archie and Woody, Saturday nights were for the most watched television show of the times, featuring Archie and Edith.

Griffin and Hayes were forever linked, and yet, they could not have seemed more different. Appearances, in this case, were deceiving.

An aficionado of military history, Hayes was a loud, imposing disciplinarian, the kind of willful public figure who was admired for his leadership in the 1950s and early 1960s. But in the burgeoning counterculture of the Vietnam War era, his drill sergeant style was increasingly challenged and condemned. To some, Hayes became a symbol of the kind of combative authoritarian that a changing, freethinking America was leaving behind. His supporters, and there were millions, said the image of an intractable tyrant was a caricature and missed the true measure of the man.

Hayes, who won five national titles and compiled a 205–61–10 record at Ohio State, succeeded for many years, smiling and winning through the worst of the backlash, though he tussled famously with writers, officials, faculty, and administrators. There were many frustrations, especially in the pursuit of national championships in the mid-1970s. And then, in a shocking end, came a downfall of public self-destruction, a Shakespearean tumble from grace.

The ultimate ball-control coach lost it all with a spasm of temper in the 1978 Gator Bowl. An opposing player intercepted an Ohio State pass and then happened to be pushed out of bounds on the sideline next to Hayes. The interception was going to cost Ohio State the game, and suddenly in the crush of jostling bodies—some upset, some beginning to celebrate— Hayes snapped and punched the player. A nation's television screens displayed an iron-willed coach who had lost his bearing.

Ohio State fired Hayes shortly thereafter—he refused to resign—but his popularity in Ohio barely waned. He was forgiven and those who knew him best believed, and still believe, he was widely misunderstood. The punch was a one-second oversight in an otherwise exemplary life.

In 1986, a year before his death, Hayes was asked to deliver Ohio State's winter session graduation address. Referring to himself, he said: "A lot of great men have been fired—Douglas MacArthur, Richard Nixon. There is no shame in it." Hayes is buried not far from the Ohio State campus, and his gravesite is a frequent stop for Ohio State fans on football weekends. They leave notes, Buckeye mementos, and roses, to acknowledge Hayes's thirteen Big Ten champions.

"He was a man with a huge and generous heart," Griffin said. "I am fortunate to have known the real man but I am by no means alone in that. I just happened, lucky for me, to be in the right place at the right time."

Providence and opportunity combined to bring Archie Griffin to Ohio. His father, a coal miner in Logan, West Virginia, was growing tired of his backbreaking job and its manifest hazards.

"My father didn't like working in the mines; I don't know anyone who did," Griffin said. "It was tough and dangerous. In 1953, my father heard there was work in central Ohio and he moved the family to Columbus."

Archie was the fourth of eight children born to James and Margaret Griffin and the first born in Ohio, at University Hospital, in 1955.

"My father was the hardest-working person I knew," Archie said. James Griffin worked three jobs: at Ohio Malleable, a steel casing company; at the city sanitation department; and on weekends, as a custodian.

"He took his vacation time one day at a time, not to go anywhere or to relax, but so he could be off on Friday nights to watch my brothers and I play high school football," Archie said. "He wanted us to play sports; he believed it taught values useful in other walks of life and he believed it taught discipline."

Archie Griffin and his siblings were told that athletics might be a way to pay for college, but that it was important for them to understand that athletics was a vehicle for the ultimate goal: a college education. Six sons of James and Margaret Griffin received college athletic scholarships and a seventh received a financial aid package to attend college. Archie's only sister also went to college on an athletic scholarship. The Griffin offspring were scattered all over the region: Kent State, Muskingum College, the University of Louisville, Ohio State.

"But schoolwork remained the priority; I was told that all the time by my mom and dad," said Archie, who graduated with a degree in industrial relations.

Archie Griffin recalls his first meeting with Woody Hayes. Several Big Ten schools were interested in Griffin, who had good grades and a host of rushing records at Columbus's Eastmoor High School. But Hayes wasn't sure if the plucky Griffin was big enough.

Northwestern and the Naval Academy had showed interest in Griffin, but then so had the University of Michigan. It irked everyone in Columbus that one of their own football stars might go to their hated arch-rivals in Michigan. It even irked Columbus resident Woody Hayes, who immediately called Archie and invited him to dinner.

"We talked for ninety minutes but he never mentioned football," Griffin said of Hayes, who was the son of a school superintendent. "He talked to me about what I wanted to study. He asked me to tell him what I wanted to do with my life. He talked to me about what I wanted to do for my family. He asked me what I wanted to contribute to society.

"I had never had a conversation with a football coach about what I thought I could do to make the rest of the world a better place. But that first night, he asked me if anyone had helped me, and I of course mentioned about ten people in particular. And he looked at me and said: 'You may not be able to help those people that helped you, but it's your obligation to help out others as you were helped.'

"I went home and told my father that I didn't think Coach Hayes wanted me to play football for him, because he never brought the game up. My father said, 'Maybe he cares more about you, the person, than you, the football player.' And my father was right."

Griffin, like others close to Hayes, feels the coach's legacy has been sullied by the violent episode that ended his coaching career, a punch caught on videotape and replayed now for more than twenty-five years.

"You know, during games he was a tough, gruff guy, that's true," Griffin said. "But football is a tough game. That didn't come close to describing the entire man. I believe he didn't want people to know the truth about him. I went with him to visit some children's hospitals. He would go in a back door so nobody would see him.

"And everyone always talked about how he loved military history. He played that up but he was open-minded in general and more flexible than people knew."

When Hayes took over as coach at Ohio State in 1951, his predecessor, Wes Fesler, offered Woody one piece of advice—get an unlisted telephone number. Woody ignored the admonition. All his life, his number and address were published in the Columbus telephone directory.

"He was a straightforward guy," Griffin said. "He wasn't afraid of criticism. He didn't believe in running from anything. He thought we should spend more time face-to-face with the public.

"He would grab guys and order them to go to the local elementary schools and make speeches about studying and working hard to the schoolkids. He would say, 'We can help and it will teach you something.' He was such a mentor and role model for all of us. He made me more than a football player."

In following Hayes's example, Griffin has spearheaded the establishment of several charitable organizations, including the Archie Griffin Sportsmanship Award for Ohio high school athletes and the Archie Griffin Scholarship Fund, which helps athletes competing in Olympic-level sports, as well as other Ohio State sports programs and local Little Leagues.

"Woody called it paying forward," Griffin said. "Put yourself out first; do something good to help people. He said you can't always pay back but you can pay forward and it will lead to something good."

The introduction to these life lessons came during Griffin's first dinner with Hayes, an occasion that involved little football talk, and perhaps with good reason. Archie was right to surmise that Hayes had misgivings about his ability to play in the Big Ten Conference. There were a lot of football coaches who did not think any 5-foot-8 back could succeed in a game that was beginning to feature 270-pound tackles.

Still, Hayes listened to his staff, who cautioned that Griffin was not to be underestimated, and by Archie's junior and senior seasons in 1974 and 1975 what unfolded became college football history. Archie had a powerfully built, compact body that turned out to be perfectly suited for combating and confounding the ever larger defensive linemen and linebackers of the mid-1970s. Griffin's low-to-the-ground running style made him a hard target to find in the scrum at the line of scrimmage. He would get lost behind blockers and he knew how to exploit that advantage.

Having a low shoulder pad level is always beneficial to running backs because it helps them avoid head-on collisions with defenders attempting tackles with a low shoulder pad level of their own. Running backs who stand erect, with shoulders square, don't usually last long in the upper echelons of football. It helps to know how to dip and dart, with a slashing technique. This allows the running back to see the play unfold from his perspective and occasionally keep the defender from seeing him. He can come around a teammate's block and be the one delivering the crunching blow on the defender, rather than absorbing a sudden unexpected blow.

Griffin understood these principles of his craft. He also had a naturally low center of balance, which made it easier for him to exhibit his quickness. He could run for power and he knew how to make linebackers and defensive backs miss in the open field. It did not hurt that he played behind a massive offensive line that often helped him get three to five yards downfield before he would encounter that first defensive player with a genuine shot at a tackle.

But Griffin was more than smallish (by college football standards) and elusive. He was the whole package as a running back—wily, prepared, and gifted, with great vision and reflexes.

After two solid seasons as a freshman and sophomore, Griffin's abilities and experience coalesced to produce a breakthrough season. Ohio State rolled over opponent after opponent in 1974, Oregon State by 51–10, Washington State fell 42–7, then Indiana (49–9), Northwestern (55–7), and Illinois (49–7).

Griffin was consistently dominating. In a span that reached from his sophomore season to his senior season, he rushed for 100 or more yards in thirty-one successive regular season games. In 1974, he ran for 1,695 yards and twelve touchdowns even though he frequently sat out the second half of games that Ohio State led by a wide margin. He never had more than twenty-five rushing attempts in any game and averaged 6.6 yards per carry.

Griffin won the 1974 Heisman Trophy in a landslide, winning the balloting in every region and getting more than four times the number of first place votes as runner-up Anthony Davis of Southern California.

Before flying to New York to accept the Heisman that year, Griffin remembers being warned by Woody Hayes and others that he might be overcome by emotion as he made his acceptance speech in New York City.

"It was just one year after John Cappelletti's very moving speech," Griffin said. "But when people told me that I might be emotional, I thought: 'I don't know why I would break down. Why should that happen?'

"Well, I got up there and I didn't get more than five or six words out of my mouth when something just overtook me. I looked at my brothers and sister, and Coach Hayes, and I just started crying like a baby."

Entering his senior season in 1975, Griffin was the favorite to win a second Heisman. He was in the position of others who had won the trophy as a junior, like Army's Doc Blanchard and Navy's Roger Staubach, but no one had been able to produce back-to-back magical seasons. There had always been injuries, or bad luck, or sometimes other players simply played superiorly to the reigning Heisman Trophy winner.

"I put a lot of pressure on myself in 1975," Griffin said. "I really wanted to win it twice. I worked very hard that summer to be sure I was prepared and hopefully be in the kind of shape that would keep me injury-free."

That fall and winter, Griffin was no less spectacular, although occasionally in more subtle ways. Behind one of the most talented and skilled offensive lines in college football history, he led Ohio State to an 11–1 record and its seventh Big Ten title in the last eight seasons. Statistically, Griffin did not match his junior year, rushing for 1,450 yards and only four touchdowns. Michigan broke his streak of 100-yard games when the Wolverines held him to forty-six yards in his final game of the storied series. But as Michigan focused on stopping Griffin, late in the game, his Buckeye teammates found ways to cut loose, overcoming a touchdown deficit to rally for a 21–14 victory.

Ohio State was 40–5–1 in Griffin's four seasons as the starting halfback. He finished with a school and conference record 5,589 rushing yards, a mark not surpassed until 1999 Heisman Trophy winner Ron Dayne of Wisconsin ran for 6,397 yards in four seasons.

In New York in 1975, Griffin accepted his second Heisman. "I was determined not to cry and I didn't," he said.

Griffin has spent decades now as the only two-time Heisman winner, a standing he relishes, even if he expects to someday have company in the most exclusive wing of the most exclusive fraternity in sport.

"It does have great meaning to have two Heismans," Griffin said. "I knew that when I was going for my second trophy. It's an honor to win one. To win two only magnifies all the things the trophy means and symbolizes. I know how it has impacted my life. It changed my name. For a long time now I've been 'Two-time Heisman winner Archie Griffin.'

"But I do think someone else will win two again and that's fine with me."

The best Ohio State teams in the Archie Griffin era (1974, 1975) never won a national championship because of consecutive upset losses in the Rose Bowl. But it is a measure of the significance of the Ohio State–

Michigan rivalry that Archie considers it a weighty consolation that he never lost to Michigan.

Like coach, like player. On a recruiting trip to Michigan, Hayes once refused to let his assistant coaches stop to get gas in the state. He said he would push the car to the Ohio border before he would buy Michigan gas.

The rivalry is no less intense years later. When the good folks of New-comerstown, Ohio, where Hayes was raised, elected a new mayor in the 1990s, it was a minor controversy, and the locals had some explaining to do to their fellow Ohioans when it was uncovered that the new mayor was a Michigan native.

While he had a commendable pro football career, Archie Griffin's best football days remained in Columbus. Griffin was the first pick of the NFL's Cincinnati Bengals, but he was miscast in Cincinnati. If Hayes's Buckeyes loved the run, the Bengals of the late 1970s loved to pass.

"I had a good career on a passing team," said Griffin of his eight capa-ble seasons with the Bengals, which included a trip to the Super Bowl. "I averaged over four yards per running attempt for my career, but I never had 200 rushing attempts in any season like some of the big backs back then. I still look at it as a successful time in my life."

Griffin is now the associate athletic director at Ohio State, where he supervises fourteen sports, including football.

He still attends football games at Ohio Stadium, that cathedral of col-lege football built in 1922, and the place where eighteen-year-old Archie Griffin heard his coach call his name but did not move, and when he did, he did so without his helmet. In many ways, Archie Griffin hasn't stopped moving since.

On October 30, 1999, the stadium, The Horseshoe, as it is called, was nearly filled with more than 96,000 fans awaiting a halftime ceremony hon-oring many of Ohio State's great teams from the 1970s and 1980s. Archie Griffin was waiting for the festivities to commence.

To his surprise, a large framed replica of his number 45 jersey was brought onto the field. That day, twenty-five years after Griffin won his first Heisman Trophy, Ohio State retired a player's jersey.

Griffin was joined by his wife, Bonita, and family, which included An-dre, a sophomore running back for Ohio State in 1999.

"For me, it was kind of like the first Heisman Trophy presentation," Griffin said. "I started to cry. But I pulled myself together."

Later that day, Griffin was seated in his Ohio State office, which is dominated by a drawing of Coach Woody Hayes looking out from beneath his trademark baseball cap with the signature "O." He was asked what Coach Hayes would have said had he been there for the ceremony.

Answered Archie Griffin: "He would have told me, 'Congratulations. Now don't get a big head. There's still a lot of good work for you to do.'"

"I Wouldn't Have Asked You to Do Something if I Didn't Know You Could Do It"

HERSCHEL WALKER, 1982

In 1970, Herschel Walker was a short, self-conscious, overweight eight-year-old who stuttered when he spoke. As if to add to his unease, the world around him was changing.

Christine and Willis Walker raised Herschel and his six brothers and sisters in a small tenant farmer's house perched on a hill in the tiny town of Wrightsville, in southeastern Georgia's Johnson County. Christine and Willis began life there picking cotton in the surrounding fields, returning nightly to their simple house with the tin roof. In time, Willis got a job working double shifts at a nearby chalk mine. Christine was a seamstress and housekeeper. By 1970, the couple had saved enough money to move to a one-story house down the hill from the cotton fields.

The governor of Georgia was Lester Maddox, an avowed segregation-ist who just that year, while addressing Congress, had called a black representative from Michigan a baboon. In the same visit to Washington, Maddox had distributed small axes, his way of commemorating the event that had brought him to prominence, when Maddox and his supporters used axe handles to prevent blacks from entering his Atlanta restaurant.

But in 1970, Maddox's efforts notwithstanding, Johnson County's schools were finally forced to desegregate—five years after the federal education commissioner had prohibited all public schools from separating blacks and whites. Most African-Americans in Wrightsville had virtually no interaction with white children. There were, for example, no public parks in town. If the white children needed recreation, they usually congregated at private clubs.

Now all the children in Wrightsville, population 2,200, would be in the same school buildings.

A new school and new classmates meant new opportunities for Herschel to be teased about his physique, and most especially, about his speech impediment.

"It was hard," Walker says more than thirty years later. "The other kids made fun of me real bad."

Herschel had two older brothers who had been athletes, and if the new school had one thing going for it, it was shiny new athletic facilities. Athletes were respected leaders in the school and, Herschel noticed, were fawned over by other students and teachers alike. He vowed to become an athlete himself, but he was still runtish and plump. He appealed to his parents and received this advice: Don't complain; do something about it.

"My mother and my father are my heroes," Herschel says. "And that's because their answer to everything was hard work. They used to say, 'Don't make excuses, just get it done.' They would say, 'I wouldn't have asked you to do something if I didn't know you could do it. So don't tell me why you can't do something. Figure out a way to do it.'"

This is how a legendary training regimen was born. At the age of ten, Herschel began sleeping no more than four hours every night and every day did 3,000 sit-ups and roughly 750 push-ups. Decades later, roommates in college, and later in the dormitories of pro football training camps, would wake to find Herschel doing sit-ups and push-ups in the middle of the night.

"People laugh at my sit-ups and push-ups like it's some sort of gimmick," Walker says now. "It wasn't a gimmick. When I was a kid losing weight and trying to become a strong athlete, it was the only way I could exercise. I didn't have the money for fancy stuff like weights or dumbbells. I did sit-ups, push-ups, and pull-ups. I was figuring out a way."

He also began to run everywhere he needed to go. Everywhere.

"I didn't have a bike," Walker says. "And we lived a long way from anything. When I tell people I never had a bike as a little kid, they ask me if I wasn't sad about that. Listen, we lived in the country. We went to the blacks-only school. I'm not kidding, I didn't know what a bike was until I was nine."

Herschel's self-discipline extended to other parts of his life. He had, for example, always been a bright student and a good reader, but his grades suffered because he never spoke out in class. He was terrified he would stutter so he remained quiet, even if he knew the answers to teacher's queries.

"My mom went out and got me all these library books," Herschel says. "And I began to sit in a chair in front of a mirror that I would hold in my lap. I would read the books, one after another, reading to myself. I would watch my lips and realize I could speak just fine. Somehow, reading those books in front of that mirror gave me confidence.

"My stuttering was going away. I was rising to speak in class."

It may have helped that the young boy who stood up had grown stronger physically and more confident, too. By the ninth grade, Herschel was becoming an accomplished athlete. The running was paying off. He was fast, faster than anyone in the high school as a freshman. The local coaches came to Christine and Willis and asked if they could take Herschel to statewide track meets.

"My biggest dream in the world as a kid was to see Atlanta," Herschel says. "It was two hours and forty-five minutes away. There are still some people in my town who will never see Atlanta. I saw it earlier than I thought, through track."

The poor black child from the country home outside of town was now being squired around the state by white coaches and administrators. So were other African-American athletes. This did not sit well with everyone in both the white and black communities. Wrightsville might have been changing, but whites still controlled all the avenues of power and it made some whites uncomfortable that black children were at the vanguard of the town's athletic programs. Some blacks bristled at the perception that their offspring were accepted by town leaders only when they were good enough to help predominantly white teams, with white coaches, win track meets.

"I didn't like to see it that way," Walker says. "I saw a lot of people trying to create divisions in the school. People are afraid of what they don't understand. But if you ask me, sports definitely made the adjustment of whites and blacks mixing together much easier. I'm not saying there still weren't racial prejudices. Of course there were. I was aware of it, we all were. But I do think playing sports gave us all a simple, unjudgmental way to come together.

"There were tensions, but my parents told me to focus on my education and on doing the right thing. We were all raised Christians, which means there is no such thing as color. I was also taught early on to ignore those that try to divide."

Crowds of organized black demonstrators had started making weekly marches on the county courthouse demanding that more blacks be hired for county jobs and that more county money be spent on infrastructure improvements (sewers, paved roads) for the decaying black neighborhoods.

On occasion, white groups gathered in protest of the black demonstrators. The two sides frequently clashed, spawning dangerous skirmishes that bordered on riots. The county police were accused of aiding the white demonstrators, and off and on for several weeks, 200 state troopers were called to duty in Wrightsville.

The one place Wrightsville blacks and whites congregated peacefully was at the Friday night Johnson County High football games. In this setting, Herschel was a leading figure. By the time he was a junior in high school, he was 6-foot-2 and a muscular 222 pounds. He was also on his way to becoming the valedictorian of his class.

"I don't think it's naïve to say that the football team helped keep the town together," Walker says. "We were winning and that somehow did some good things for everybody. We were playing together. But obviously, it was a very difficult time in a lot of towns like Wrightsville back then.

"My parents told me my best contribution would be making something of myself. I was a poor black child from the country. They said, 'Go out and be a role model. Show respect for others and expect respect from others. Be a good student, a good player, and a good teammate. Do that, and you can do a lot of good.'"

Football was king in Johnson County, as it was, and is, in most southern towns. And by the time he was a senior, Herschel was the most sought-after high school football player in the country. College coaches from across the nation landed their helicopters next to the cotton fields so they could see Herschel play for Johnson County High School on Friday nights.

Assistant coaches from some colleges stayed in town for months to court Herschel. An assistant from the University of Georgia bunked in a Wrightsville house owned by a Georgia alumnus.

Herschel was a prospect like none other before him, perhaps the first of a kind of super-back. He was the proof of a nascent generation in America that was more than just culturally fifty years removed from the Great Depression. Treatment for dozens of childhood diseases had been developed, parents were better equipped and better educated to feed and care for their young, and almost universally people were living longer. By the 1980s, the most fit, robust Americans were significantly bigger and faster than their parents. In the 1980s, the national average height for men was creeping toward six feet. In World War II it was 5-foot-8.

Athletes were also more highly trained. World records in Olympic events—judged in time, distance, weight lifted, and height jumped—toppled year after year, nonstop for ten to fifteen years. And while the 1980s were also the decade that saw the proliferation of performance-enhancing drugs, the same records were being obliterated at the high school level nationwide, which steroids had yet to infiltrate.

In football, especially college football, there had not been many 220-pound, strapping football running backs who also qualified for the United States Olympic Trials in the 100-meter dash as Walker would later do. In the 1980 Georgia high school outdoor track championships, Walker did something that illustrated his heretofore uncommon combination of skills and abilities. He won the 100-yard dash and the shot put event.

So in the fall of his senior football season, when eighteen-year-old Herschel Walker took the football in the backfield for Johnson County High, he knew he had the choice of either running swiftly past all eleven defenders on the field or using his mighty thighs and powerful, wide shoulders to brutally run over all eleven defenders. In the eleven games of his last high school football season, he rushed for 3,167 yards and scored forty-five touchdowns. No one had seen anything like him.

Walker was the first high school football player that college recruiters and professional scouts alike believed could have gone straight into the National Football League, as Moses Malone had done in basketball six years earlier.

Walker instead went on to Athens, Georgia, and the state university. And soon, he was even bigger in Athens than he had been in Wrightsville.

On the road for the opening game of the 1980 season against Tennessee, Georgia trailed 15–2 late in the third quarter. Walker had been told he would not play in the game as there were two upperclassmen ahead of him on the depth chart. But as the Georgia offense continued to sputter, Coach Vince Dooley turned to the nation's most renowned college freshman.

Walker gained only eight yards on his first two carries.

"But you could see the difference right away. It was like night and day," Dooley later said. "Herschel didn't know where he was running yet but he was running there in a hurry."

Georgia moved the football to Tennessee's 16-yard line where Walker took a pitch on a sweep to the right. Rounding the corner, Walker cut back to his left, flattened a defensive end and dashed through four arm tackles to the 5-yard line, where Tennessee safety Bill Bates waited directly in Walker's path.

Herschel lowered his broad shoulders and ran right through Bates, stepping on his chest as he continued toward the goal line. Two Tennessee cornerbacks then converged from either side, and each clearly expected to get a hand on him, but a lightning-quick step put Walker into another gear and neither Tennessee cornerback so much as touched him.

It was the kind of run that stirs a team, a university, a state. For weeks and months thereafter, it was shown on televisions throughout Georgia, slowed down so people could more closely examine what little Wrightsville had bestowed on grateful Georgians everywhere. It was the moment Herschel Walker announced his arrival. No one alive in Georgia that weekend will ever forget Herschel's first touchdown run, or that he scored a second touchdown in the game, giving Georgia a stunning, come-from-behind 16–15 victory at Tennessee.

Tennessee Coach Johnny Majors, who finished second in the 1956 Heisman balloting when he starred at Tennessee and later coached 1976 Heisman Trophy winner Tony Dorsett at the University of Pittsburgh, said of Walker: "That running back is something God puts on this earth every several decades or so. He has more power, speed, and strength than anyone I've ever seen. He's got more going for him than any player that's ever played this game."

Walker scored three touchdowns the next week against Texas A&M and then had four successive games with more than 200 rushing yards, in-

cluding a 283-yard effort against Vanderbilt. That year, he set a freshman collegiate rushing record with 1,616 rushing yards for the season.

On New Year's Day 1981, the undefeated Georgia Bulldogs went to the Sugar Bowl to face Notre Dame, with the national championship on the line. On the second play of the game, Walker was tackled and felt a stabbing pain in his left shoulder.

"I was on the sideline and I heard the doctor say it was a dislocated shoulder," Walker says. "He told Coach Dooley I couldn't play. Well, to me, dislocated meant it can be put back in. The doctor said it would painful and I said, 'Well, do that.' We had come too far at that point. I wasn't going to stop."

Walker returned to the game, and carrying the football exclusively under his right arm, gained 150 yards on thirty-six rushing attempts. He scored two touchdowns in a 17–10 victory that earned 12–0 Georgia its first national title after nearly eighty-nine years of playing football. Without Walker, the Bulldogs' offensive output against Notre Dame would have totaled minus twenty-three yards.

"That was the best season of my life," Walker says. "We were a true team. We loved each other and everyone sacrificed. It was wonderful."

Georgia had its chances to win the national championship again in the next two years as Walker continued to dominate, but an upset at Clemson in 1981 and losses in the next two Sugar Bowls helped keep Georgia from a second title. Still, the Bulldogs had an incredible run, winning all but one of their thirty-three regular season games from 1980 to 1982. Walker's Georgia teams won the Southeastern Conference championship each of those seasons, a title they did not win again until twenty years later.

The Heisman Trophy balloting of 1982 was a who's who of football luminaries, with Stanford quarterback John Elway finishing second and Southern Methodist University running back Eric Dickerson third.

Walker won the Heisman not only because he had another outstanding season in 1982, but because of the cumulative effect of his three seasons at Georgia. He had already rushed for 5,259 yards, which placed him among the career leaders in college football history, even though the other leaders at the time had played four seasons, not three. He had broken eleven NCAA records, sixteen conference records, and forty-one school records. To a majority of the voters, who cast their ballots before the bowl season, Walker and Georgia might still win a second national championship, and

Walker had had another great year. But most of all, it was becoming apparent that Walker's time in college football might be nearing an end, and it was incomprehensible that Herschel Walker could leave without having won at least one Heisman Trophy. After all, he had been the first freshman to finish as high as third in the 1980 balloting. He had been the second-place finisher as a sophomore.

"I have to say I almost felt bad because there were some very, very good guys at other schools that year," Walker says of 1982. "Some of my friends said I really deserved the Heisman my freshman year. But I earned it my junior year, too."

Leading up to his junior season, Walker had made it plain he planned to challenge the NFL's dictum that no player could leave college early to sign a pro contract. He had already spurned an offer to play in the Canadian Football League.

"No offense to Canada," he said at the time, "but I'm an American. I want to play in America."

But after his third year at Georgia, if the U.S. courts didn't help him in his fight with the NFL, there was also the upstart United States Football League, which was willing to sign college underclassmen. Walker signed with Donald Trump's New Jersey Generals of the USFL on February 25, 1983, in what was literally and figuratively a rainy night in Georgia. Walker played three seasons for the Generals with 1984 Heisman Trophy winner Doug Flutie and was the league's most valuable player twice. He became a favorite pass receiver for Flutie, though catching passes was something he had rarely done at Georgia. All told, Walker amassed more than 7,000 all-purpose yards for the Generals.

When the USFL shut down in financial ruins, Walker signed with the Dallas Cowboys in 1986, the first of 15 seasons in the NFL. His career in the league was hard to define since he always seemed on the move—not just from team to team, but from offensive system to offensive system and position to position.

He played three seasons for undertalented Cowboys teams but remained a prized running back in the eyes of most NFL talent evaluators, leading to the blockbuster trade that sent him to the Minnesota Vikings. Minnesota gave the Cowboys five players and eight future draft picks for Walker. Initially, many thought it was going to be a deal that made the Vikings Super Bowl contenders. Instead, over time, the Cowboys under

Coach Jimmy Johnson shrewdly used their haul from the Vikings to acquire nineteen new players in all—the backbone of what became three Super Bowl winning teams in the 1990s.

The Vikings never made the playoffs in the three seasons Walker played for them. He was also never the dominant ball carrier he had been in college. NFL defenses successfully keyed in on Walker. As a free agent in 1992, Walker signed with the Philadelphia Eagles, where he became a versatile back, catching passes, running the football, and returning kickoffs. He was the team's offensive MVP in 1994 when he had a rushing attempt, a pass reception, and a kickoff return of ninety yards or more. No one in the seventy-five-year history of the league had ever done that in one season. Only one player before Walker had ever done all three in a career.

Herschel's last three NFL seasons were with the New York Giants and the Cowboys, time spent as a special teams player, kick returner, and blocking back.

Like many great college players who were the cynosure of their team's offense, Walker never quite found the perfect fit in the NFL. But that should not understate his contribution in the league. His 18,168 all-purpose yards rank fifth in NFL history, and if Walker's 7,115 all-purpose yards from the USFL were counted, he would surpass the NFL all-purpose leader by nearly 3,500 yards. But the USFL stats are not included in NFL totals.

"Combine my stats from both leagues and they are untouchable," Walker says now. "People say the competition in the USFL wasn't as good as in the NFL and that may be true, but it was a professional league and dozens of USFL guys went on to be record-setters and Pro Bowlers in the NFL. It counts for something."

While some wonder why Herschel Walker, a player so unstoppable in college, did not become that kind of force in the pros, Herschel feels his pro career is underrated.

"What I became is a complete football player," he says. "Even simply in NFL stats, I'm among the leaders in all-purpose yards, rushing, pass receptions, and kick returns. Do you judge someone for how well he played one position, or do you acknowledge that he was a good all-around player?"

Besides, Walker says the final statistics on his career haven't been tabulated yet.

"People think I'm crazy but I'm going to be the George Foreman of football," he says. "I'm going to come back and play at fifty years old."

That would be in 2012.

"I still do my 3,000 sit-ups and the 750 push-ups," Walker said. "I could play right now, no problem."

And as a family man with young children, it comes in handy that he still needs no more than four hours' sleep.

"A guy asked me just the other day if I'm tired," he says. "I said: 'Sir, I am fine.'"

He operates two companies in Dallas where he lives; one sells food appetizers and the other supplies draperies and bedspreads for hotels. He is planning a third business enterprise.

"I love to work," Walker says. "It's in my blood."

His parents still live in Johnson County, and they have his Heisman Trophy.

"They have a big trophy room," Walker says. "But for a while they thought the Heisman was too showy and they didn't want to leave it out. They put it in the attic.

"But people kept coming over and asking where the Heisman was. And they would go to the attic and get it, and then put it back in the attic. This went on for a while, but people kept coming around and they got tired of climbing up and down to that attic. So now they put it out front in the trophy case. You can't keep the Heisman Trophy away from people. They are just drawn to it."

Walker returns to Johnson County frequently.

"There are some things about you that are always home," he says. "I've been to a lot of places but that is where I learned what mattered."

The small tenant farmer's house he was raised in as a young child is now used to store hay.

"I'll bring people back and they'll say, 'You lived there? All of you?'" Walker says. "But you know, we were happy. It made me understand the rest of my life so much better. We had everything we needed.

"We didn't have the best of things, but we loved each other, and that is the best of things."

"I Feel Bigger"

DOUG FLUTIE, 1984

Forget "The Pass" against Miami on Thanksgiving weekend in 1984. Forget Donald Trump's United States Football League. Forget the six most valuable player awards and the three championships in the Canadian Football League. Forget the 50,000 yards of completed passes in three professional leagues. Forget the Flutie Flakes and the amazing comeback as a 36-year-old dashing hither and dither in Buffalo. Forget that ten days past his forty-first birthday, Doug Flutie was still a quarterback in the National Football League, leading his team to a come-from-behind victory.

Forget all that. Once, Doug Flutie was an eighteen-year-old freshman and the ninth-string quarterback at Boston College. Actually, Doug Flutie was the ninth-string quarterback in his mind only. Boston College did not have a nine-player quarterback depth chart. There was no ninth-string quarterback. Or a seventh-string or an eighth-string quarterback.

What Flutie really was in 1981 was the third-string punt returner and something like the fifth-string flanker. Flutie knew the actual quarterback depth chart ended at six players, and when he examined the roster, he came across two other freshmen he knew the coaches liked as quarterbacks better than him.

"So I started calling myself the ninth-string quarterback," Flutie says now, looking back to the fall of 1981. "And I started pleading to play quarterback in practice. They let me run the scout team, the scrubs imitating the other team's offense, but even that was only against the first-string freshman team. I was as low on the totem pole as you could be. I was under the totem pole. I wasn't even dressing in the same locker room as everyone else."

He did not even have a quarterback's jersey number and never would. Flutie wore number 22. At 5-foot-8¾ and 175 pounds, Flutie was at Boston College only by happenstance, because other high school recruits, at the last minute, had turned down scholarship offers from the school.

There had been a coaching change the year before at BC, which had chased off some recruits who didn't know what to make of the new coach with the radical, free-form ideas about modern college football offense. The coach's name was Jack Bicknell, known as "Cowboy Jack."

With recruits shunning BC, Bicknell and his staff were suddenly left with a few unused football scholarships. So they went back to their files and looked at the discard pile. In it was a smallish kid from nearby Natick, Massachusetts, who as a high school quarterback had won a lot, scrambling around, throwing on the run. He drove defenses nuts trying to catch him, but he was way too small to play football at the Division I level.

BC was trying to move up in the college world, playing mighty Penn State, Notre Dame, and Alabama nearly every year in the early 1980s, and soon the University of Miami would be on the schedule, too. Quarterbacks were getting bigger, not smaller, in this brave new college football world. When Boston College's coaches looked at Flutie, they saw why he was slated to go to either Harvard or the University of New Hampshire, football programs that played a notch below the Division I levels.

But they couldn't just waste a scholarship either. Maybe, the BC coaches thought, Flutie could be transformed into a wide receiver or a scatback kick returner. They offered the kid from Natick a scholarship. Except now, in his freshman year, he insisted he was a quarterback.

"And they let me try and I did pretty good," Flutie says. "I jumped over a couple of freshmen that had been ahead of me. Then, the starter on the varsity got hurt and a couple of guys below him got to play and they didn't do very good. So I kept moving up. By October, I figure I was actually the fourth-string quarterback."

On October 10, there were 84,473 spectators inside Penn State University's football stadium watching the home team, ranked second in the land, pummel Boston College as they had always done. In ten games across thirty-two years, BC had never beaten Penn State, and now, losing 31–0 at halftime, BC was desperate.

In the locker room at the game's intermission, Tom Coughlin, the quarterbacks coach who would in succeeding years be instrumental in Flutie's development (and would also go on to several successful seasons as a head coach in the NFL), approached Bicknell and suggested it was time they thought about a change at quarterback. BC to that point had completed one of fifteen passes in the game for two yards. There were two other backups officially ahead of Flutie, but they had already seen playing time as a quarterback earlier in the season and had been unimpressive.

Coughlin told Bicknell he would like to see what Flutie could do.

"Flutie?" Bicknell asked. "He's a special teams player."

And indeed, Doug had not played on anything but the kickoff team. Bicknell, however, relented because he trusted the no-nonsense, hard-nosed Coughlin.

"So Tom Coughlin comes to me and says: 'Be ready,'" Flutie says, retelling the story of the day. "And I was like, 'Yeah, right.' Honestly, I thought he was joking."

In the third quarter, BC continued to struggle and the Penn State lead grew to 38–0. Coughlin and Bicknell turned to Flutie on the sideline and told him to take over the offense on the next possession.

"I was amazed," Flutie says. "I was excited. But I was amazed."

It is common for football coaches making a quarterback change, especially when the new quarterback is an eighteen-year-old freshman, to call a running play on the first sequence. That eases the pressure on the sure-to-be-nervous quarterback.

Bicknell did call a run on Flutie's first play, but when Flutie went to the line and saw a weakness in the pass defense, he changed the play at the line of scrimmage, dropped back, and completed the pass for a first down.

Flutie went into the huddle and called another pass. Another first down. Coughlin and Bicknell were trying to signal plays into the game, and Flutie was heeding their advice. Sort of. Coughlin would later note that even routine, established plays looked a little different when Flutie ran them, frequently with some measure of improvisation.

Five passes and five completions later, Doug Flutie had thrown his first college touchdown pass. BC would still lose, 38–7, but Doug Flutie, the self-estimated ninth string quarterback around Labor Day 1981, would start, at quarterback, each of the next forty-two games for Boston College, right through the 1985 Cotton Bowl.

"When I look back at the Penn State game, it's the first time I realized I might have something to work with that won't go away," Flutie says. "Everybody had been making so much about my size and I knew from our college practices that they were right about a couple of things. There were lots of guys who could throw it better than me. There were lots of guys who were faster than me. But when they got into the games, when the bright lights came on, I saw those same guys play differently than they did in practice.

"They saw the distractions, they made mistakes. You could see they seemed rattled. I can honestly say that I went in that day against Penn State and to me it felt just like being a high school quarterback again. I saw no change; it didn't matter how bright the lights were or whether there were 84,000 people watching. I took the snap, I made my reads, and I threw the football. It was no big deal.

"People wanted to talk about my size. Well, some guys shrink in big moments. I don't shrink. I feel bigger."

Eventually, significantly, people would come to see Doug Flutie as he saw himself.

Though he did not win his first college football start as a freshman, BC won four of its last six games in 1981. As a sophomore, Flutie led the Boston College Eagles to an 8–3 record and a trip to their first bowl game in forty years.

As a junior, BC finally defeated Penn State and eight other teams on their way to a one-point loss to Notre Dame in the Liberty Bowl. At the end of that season, Flutie finished third in the balloting for the 1983 Heisman Trophy.

"When I finished third, and I knew the two guys ahead of me were graduating (Heisman winner Mike Rozier and runner-up Steve Young)," Flutie says, "I thought, 'Holy mackerel.' I wasn't even supposed to play major college football and now I'm a top Heisman candidate. I sat down in my dorm room and said: 'You've got to be kidding me.'"

Roughly four years earlier, when Boston College had come back to him with their scholarship offer, Doug had found his girlfriend in the hallways at Natick High and told her he was going to try to make it at Division

I Boston College rather than attend Harvard, where he felt certain he would play.

"Laurie and I had met as sophomores in high school," Doug says of his future wife. "So by now she knew how competitive I was about everything. So when I told her about BC, she said to me: 'What the hell. Go win the Heisman Trophy.' It was a joke, but that's what she said. And I can tell you, I definitely laughed."

Now look who was laughing. Flutie was not only close to an inconceivable dream, he was becoming a Boston, and New England, athletic legend—something not often done by a collegian in that region and without parallel in football since Joe Bellino in 1960. While Flutie was popular for his boy-next-door charm and because he was resurrecting the notion that the traditional small, Northeastern, Catholic colleges could once again compete nationally, Flutie was not actually a native son of the area. Born outside Baltimore, he had been raised in southern Florida and did not move to the Boston area until he was thirteen.

"I grew up on the beach playing every conceivable game night and day for hours on end," Flutie says. "It was a great place to be a young athlete."

But Flutie was not like most of the other kids, which he acknowledges decades later.

"It is true that I was pretty intense about winning," he says. "Other parents were dropping their kids off at games saying, 'Have fun, Johnny.' And I would be like, 'Johnny, it's not about fun. We have to win today.'

"Even as a ten-year-old Little Leaguer. The coach would be saying, 'Everyone gets to play at least three innings.' And I would ask why. And the coach would say: 'Because that's fair.' And I would answer: 'Well, that makes us lose sometimes. What's fair about that?'

"I was serious about winning. I'm not sure where that came from. My parents weren't really like that."

Richard and Joan Flutie had not even made athletics a priority for Doug or their three other children. The Fluties had other concerns. They were not a well-to-do family, something Doug grasped as a youngster when he saw how his mother's face would brighten on Dad's payday. Richard Flutie changed jobs frequently, but a constant was his interest in whatever activity his children pursued. And the Fluties, on their own, all became athletes.

"I remember he always volunteered to coach because he said that was the one way we would always have a bat and ball at home," Doug says. "The coach gets to take the equipment bag home."

When Richard moved his family to Natick in the mid-1970s, Doug played three sports at his new high school: football, basketball, and baseball.

"I liked eastern Massachusetts because there were a lot of competitive people," Flutie says. "I always felt there was a strong sense of the underdog athletically in everything we did. It was definitely there on our BC teams. We had a bunch of guys like me, guys who on the face of it were probably more qualified to be in the Ivy League. We had wide receivers that only ran 4.7 in the forty. We had an undersized fullback and an undersized tailback.

"But there was a magic because we were so much the same and very close as a group. We trusted each other. We knew we were all overachievers."

There is no question that the allure of watching an underdog beating the odds was a big part of the Flutie phenomenon, and it became a cultural phenomenon in New England and the Boston area. Boston may be the vanguard of American higher education, a grand, vibrant, and sophisticated city, but when it comes to athletics it suffers from an all-consuming, even celebrated, inferiority complex. This comes in large part from its most prized team, baseball's Boston Red Sox, who have spent nearly a century in well-documented atonement for selling Babe Ruth to the New York Yankees in 1919.

Moreover, Boston, with no more than 700,000 residents, has always chafed at being perceived as the little sister to New York, the megalopolis roughly 200 miles to its south. So in their very soul, Bostonians know about underdogs.

And no one who ever watched Doug Flutie play, especially as a collegian with his trademark number 22 jersey flapping behind him as he ran from sideline to sideline on his way to another Boston College upset victory, ever lost sight of the fact that the little guy out there was beating the odds. Bostonians made him a godlike figure for it.

At the start of Flutie's senior year in 1984, Boston College had high hopes for a last magical season. Early that year, the Eagles went to Birmingham, Alabama, and shocked the host Crimson Tide 38–31, with Flutie leading BC to the winning score on its final possession. Immediately, Flutie's Eagles were the focus of the national college football press. There was even talk of a national championship, something that hadn't been discussed—even in jest—in New England for forty years.

But a one-point loss to West Virginia derailed BC's route to a national title and a devastating defeat to their old nemesis, Penn State, buried the title dreams. Still, BC was 8–2 heading to Miami's Orange Bowl on November 23, the day after Thanksgiving. The Miami Hurricanes were the defending national champions with quarterback Bernie Kosar, who was about to become a top NFL draft pick.

The Hurricanes were also in a testy mood. They had just blown a 31–0 lead in a two-point loss to Maryland two weeks earlier. Miami needed a blowout victory over BC, whom they traditionally dominated, to put them back on the path to a national championship. And that is exactly what seemed likely.

The game that unfolded, however, fit none of the usual models. In the history of college football, there had never been a game in which both quarterbacks threw for more than three hundred yards. In the November 23 game at the Orange Bowl, Kosar threw for 447 yards and Flutie for 472.

"That's the thing people forget about that game," said Flutie, who threw for three touchdowns and ran for another. "People always talk about The Pass. The rest of the game was unbelievable, too."

Several times during the game, which was played in a drizzle and ended in a shadowy dusk, Miami seemed to put Boston College away. The Hurricanes led 38–34 with three minutes left, but BC's Steve Strachman scored to give the Eagles a 41–38 lead. Kosar then brought Miami seventy-eight yards down the field, calling time-out at the Boston College 1-yard line with half a minute remaining in the game.

In the seconds preceding what figured to be the pivotal play of the game, Kosar went to the sideline to consult with Miami Coach Jimmy Johnson. The national network television cameras caught the normally contemplative Kosar, his uniform muddy and his breath labored, barking at Johnson that the Hurricanes should "just ram it down their throats." (Kosar added a particularly salty profanity just before "throats.")

Johnson nodded in agreement, and running back Melvin Bratton did that, ramming his way over the BC line to give Miami a 45–41 lead.

BC took the kickoff at its 22-yard line and Flutie immediately threw for nineteen yards. Another pass netted eleven yards to the Miami 48-yard line, and Flutie then stopped the clock with six seconds by intentionally throwing away a pass.

What happened next has been a constant in Doug Flutie's life ever since. "Not a day has gone by," Flutie says, "unless I don't go out of the house, without someone mentioning it to me in some way."

In the huddle, Flutie called the one play designed for the situation: "Flood Tip." Three receivers were to run fly patterns down the right side with Stradford and Kelvin Martin assigned to stop at the 5-yard line hoping to entice Miami's deep defensive backs to stay with them. Meanwhile, the third receiver, Gerald Phelan, was instructed to keep going, hoping to drift behind the Miami defense—or to be in a position to catch a pass tipped back to him by his teammates at the 5-yard line.

Flutie took the snap and started scrambling backward. He had to buy time for his receivers to run half the length of the field. At his own 35-yard line, he moved to his right.

"I looked toward the end zone," Flutie says. "I saw Gerald, not necessarily open, but heading to a spot where he might be. I wasn't trying to get the ball tipped to him. I was trying to reach him in the end zone."

Flutie planted his right foot at the 36-yard line as the game clock showed :01. He cocked his right arm like a center fielder, which he had been, trying to throw the ball all the way to home plate.

Seeing Flutie wind up sixty-four yards from the end zone, Miami defenders Darrell Fullington and Reggie Sutton moved up, apparently deciding Flutie could not throw the ball all the way to the end zone.

Flutie let the football fly, and with the network cameras following the ball in flight, the game clock went to :00.

Phelan was a step behind the last Miami player when the pass settled into his stomach and the football's point struck him right in the belly button. He clutched his arms around it and fell backward into the end zone. The referee signaled touchdown. Boston College 47, Miami 45.

The broadcast call of the play has become among the most recognized of the century: "Caught by Boston College! It's a touchdown! I don't believe it! Doug Flutie has done it!"

The Pass became one of those touchstone moments in American athletics. Across most of the country that day, it had been overcast and gloomy. It was late in the day after a holiday. Few people were working. No one was in school. Everyone, it seemed, had retired to the living room or

den and settled in front of the television to watch this game that seemingly would not end—until it ended in the most unlikely fashion ever.

Flutie was being carried off the field by his teammates, arms raised, and Kosar was literally staggering off the field, his eyes glassy.

The Pass became a signature sports moment of the decade, a period piece of 1980s Americana like Michael Jackson's *Thriller* album, Steven Spielberg's Indiana Jones movies, or Ronald Reagan's Morning in America. Even people who did not follow college football were dragged into the happening of when and where they were when Doug Flutie let fly with his "Hail Mary" bomb, a desperate prayer that was answered.

If Doug Flutie was a regional hero before The Pass, he became a national icon afterward. He played with a free-form charm, the little man scrambling to evade wide-body peril to win, smile, and wink at the end of the day.

Eight days later, Flutie led Boston College to a 45–10 rout of in-state rival Holy Cross, throwing a touchdown pass to his younger brother, Darren, who was a BC underclassman. He immediately flew to New York's LaGuardia Airport, and from there was taken by helicopter to Manhattan island, setting down at a West Side heliport a few miles north of the Downtown Athletic Club. Flutie, who had thrown for 3,454 yards in 1984 to set the all-time major college career passing record (10,579 yards), was the prohibitive favorite to win the Heisman, and his selection came in one of the largest voting margins of victory ever. He was the first choice in each of the Heisman's six regional voting blocs.

Flutie was gracious in his acceptance, thanking teammates, coaches, and family. But he conceded later that what he really wanted to do was get back to Boston. And Flutie, via helicopter, airplane, and limousine, was back on the BC campus that evening, where he took his Heisman Trophy into his dormitory room—already the site of a raucous party.

"I just kind of put it up on my bureau and we all stared at it," Flutie says. "That was a lot fun. Just hanging out with my teammates and friends. You could kind of take it in then—it had been quite a trip to that moment."

What sportswriters had taken to calling "Flutie-mania" came to an end, at least in its college version, with a 45–28 Cotton Bowl victory over the University of Houston.

Then came Flutie's pro football career, which has been almost as unpredictable or unforeseen as his college career. Before he had even graduated from BC with two degrees, personnel managers in the National Football League had made it plain they felt Flutie had no future whatsoever in their league. The NFL is an arena of technical assessment, a place highly prejudiced when it comes to the merits of a player's physical attributes. At the NFL combine before its annual draft, players are tested, poked, and prodded like cattle at auction, and the tangible statistics of height, weight, arm strength, and foot speed are the only measures of consequence. Flutie arrived with a distinct computer printout disadvantage.

There was another knock against Flutie. Everyone knew that Jack Bicknell let his creative quarterback improvise, designing the offense around Flutie's abilities. But the NFL is a coach's league through and through. Coaches generally find players to fit their strategic schemes, and no coach in 1985 schemed for a 5-foot-9, 175-pound quarterback who likes to change plays at the line of scrimmage, ad-lib, and run around a lot.

So with the handwriting on the wall, Flutie decided to break ground in another way, signing with Trump's upstart New Jersey Generals of the United States Football League. Flutie played well for Trump on a good team that would include 1982 Heisman winner Herschel Walker, but the USFL eventually went bankrupt and Flutie was back wondering if the NFL would want him. The Chicago Bears and the New England Patriots each took Flutie for two seasons, but Flutie struggled to exhibit the freeform offensive genius he displayed naturally in college. By 1990, Flutie had decided to play in the Canadian Football League, first in British Columbia, followed by stops in Calgary and Toronto.

In eight seasons in Canada, Flutie found a second football home. He became the greatest player in the history of CFL. On a wider field in a league that favored passing, Flutie was nearly unstoppable. He won three championships: one in Calgary and consecutive titles in 1996 and 1997 in Toronto.

Flutie's Canadian numbers were astounding: fifty-two touchdowns in one season, more than 6,000 passing yards in a season, 556 yards passing in one game, another season when he ran for 756 yards and passed for 5,720. He was named the league's Most Outstanding Player six times.

But after the 1997 season, Flutie, at thirty-five years old, decided he wanted one last shot at the NFL. His agent contacted twenty teams that said "no" to Doug Flutie, and one, the Buffalo Bills, who offered the league minimum salary. Flutie accepted the deal and the Bills went out of their way to say that Flutie was their back-up quarterback.

In August 1998, seventeen years after his freshman year at Boston College, Flutie was at the back of the quarterback depth chart again. To Flutie fans, it was no surprise when 1998 turned into another storybook season. Five games into that season, Flutie took over a losing team and led the Bills to a playoff berth with victories in seven of their remaining ten games. Once spurned by a host of NFL coaches in the 1980s and 1990s, Flutie was now a Pro Bowl quarterback. At the end of the season, he was thirty-six years old, and voted the NFL Comeback Player of the Year.

"I never look at it as redemption," he says. "It was another chance and I made something of it. There isn't time in life for worrying about slights and things like that. There are other things that matter so much more."

It was this perspective that may have aided Doug and Laurie Flutie in 1995 when their three-year-old son Dougie was diagnosed with autism. Once an outgoing, jovial young boy who loved to sing and play with his sister Alexa and his mother and father, Dougie had begun to go into a shell. He stopped saying his ABCs and his other verbal skills dwindled. He became less active and withdrew more and more from those around him.

Told about their son's autism, the Fluties were thunderstruck. "I love being a father," Flutie says, "so it was very hard. It was very hard on everyone in our family. But something like this is very hard on many, many families. Not just ours."

Raising an autistic child, Flutie says, requires constant therapy and attention, which can lead to great expense and other ancillary side effects on a family. In 1998, realizing that other families may not have the financial resources that the Fluties have to raise their child, Doug and Laurie created the Doug Flutie Jr. Foundation for Autism.

They provided the start-up donation and have spent years organizing and hosting dinners, functions, and golf outings for the foundation, which helps disadvantaged families who need assistance in caring for their children with autism and helps to fund research into finding a cure for the neurological disorder.

In 1998, in the midst of the Bills' playoff run, Flutie launched "Flutie Flakes" cereal to benefit the foundation and sold more than 1.5 million boxes.

"The foundation has been a great thing," Flutie says. "It has helped a lot of people, and frankly, it has helped us, too. We have raised four and a half million dollars. And that's not corporate donations. That's the good graces of a lot of individuals and a lot of hard work."

In 2000, Flutie was on the professional move again, leaving the Bills for the San Diego Chargers. After two seasons as the starter, he lost his job to the Chargers' first-round draft pick, Drew Brees. But in the 2003 season, when San Diego lost seven of its first eight games, there was Flutie back in the saddle again, a forty-one-year-old putting new life into another team.

"I am basically still a kid at heart," Flutie says. "My basic attitude about this is, if I slow down, then I'll feel old. So I don't let myself slow down. I have the same routine I had when I was twenty-five. It's a little tougher on me some days, I might be a little more sore, but for the most part it's the same."

He does not consider retirement. Why?

"Because if I so-called retired," he says, "I would instead sign up to play in three adult basketball leagues, play in a flag football league on Sunday morning and a hockey league on Sunday night. I mean, playing in the NFL might be easier."

So forget retirement for now. In the final days of his football career—even Flutie concedes those are at least nearer—what does he think will be his enduring football legacy?

"You mean, what will people think of my football career?" he asks, then answers: "They will probably think, 'He looked like he was having fun.'

"And they will be right. I have had a blast."

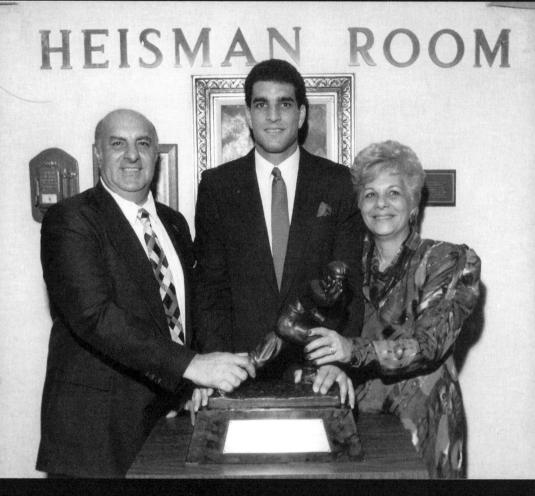

VINNIE TESTAVERDE WITH HIS PARENTS,
AL AND JOSIE TESTAVERDE

"We Won This Together"
VINNY TESTAVERDE, 1986

It first came to him on a Saturday afternoon in 1960, an idle notion, without forethought, spurred by the smile on another man's face. Al Testaverde was watching the 1960 Army–Navy game on television when the network cameras found Michele Bellino in the crowd as he watched his son Joe, the star Navy halfback.

The television announcers identified Michele Bellino as the father of the likely winner of the next Heisman Trophy, a selection to be revealed in less than a week.

"No wonder he's smiling," Al Testaverde said. But there was something in the joy Al observed in the face of the elder Bellino, something beyond the patent sense of pride. There was an acknowledgment, an understanding that a place in time would forevermore be marked for the Bellino family.

Al Testaverde, twenty-seven at the time, saw that smile and knew it was something he wanted. And though his first and only son would not be born for several years, as he watched television that day Al said: "I'd like to be that guy some day. I'd like to have a son win the Heisman Trophy."

More than a decade later, Al Testaverde, a construction foreman working on a job in lower Manhattan, would take his lunch break on the steps of an imposing brick building next door. He would shade himself beneath the awning that read, "Home of the Heisman Trophy," by the back entrance to the Downtown Athletic Club.

Al watched the businessmen, shipping magnates, and Wall Street brokers shuttle in and out of the club. One day when his construction boots were not too dusty or crusted with the residue of mixed cement, Al hurriedly darted inside to the club's lobby to view a replica of the Heisman Trophy statuette enclosed in glass along one wall.

Again, Al Testaverde had a thought, a dream of the grandeur he saw in the trophy and what it symbolized.

"Someday I am going to walk through these doors as a guest of honor," he said. "I won't have to sneak in. Things will be different. And one of those trophies will be coming out with me."

Al Testaverde lived his life with the deep belief that his dreams had power. He saw them as the currency that opened the door to happiness. He worked hard every day to support his family of four daughters, one son, and his wife Josie. He dreamed big and he told the world about his dreams. It was in his blood. Josie and Al, whose parents each came from Palermo, Sicily, and settled in Brooklyn, saw dreams come true up and down the streets of their neighborhood in the borough's Red Hook section.

All it took was perseverance, Al told his children or anyone who asked. Had he and Josie not built a life on a quiet, neat street in the middle-class town of Elmont, New York? Were they not living, flourishing examples of a prosperous, growing Long Island? He worked the tough, dangerous construction jobs in New York City, but he came home each night to a peaceful suburban street to enjoy the embrace of a warm community of other first-generation Americans happily making better lives for their children, just as their parents had done for them.

Some nights Al Testaverde would come home from the construction job so late there was only time to take his boots off, head in for a quick shower and a hot meal, and then get right into bed. He would, after all, have to rise by 4:30 A.M. the next day to beat the city traffic to the construction site. But there were many other days when the job was less demanding and Al would be headed home before rush hour, and there, waiting for him on the front steps of the simple Testaverde home, was Vinny.

"I'd be there with the football and we would start having a catch,"

Vinny said in 2003, sitting in the locker room of the New York Jets, the third of three teams for which Testaverde would play in his first sixteen years as an NFL quarterback. "Then he would work with me on things. I loved that. I ate it up. And certainly I understood that some days he probably might have found it more relaxing to go inside and put his feet up. But my dad would make any sacrifice for us."

Football was the game that appealed to Al, a strapping man at 6-foot-1 and 280 pounds. It had been Al who placed a miniature football in five-day-old Vinny's bassinet.

His son was well on his way to his eventual height of 6-foot-5 when, as a high school sophomore, he played in his first high school game. Vinny's high school coach, Bill Piner, remembers sending young Vinny, who was then the back-up quarterback, into the game as a wide receiver.

The play called, however, was actually a double-pass play, designed to have Testaverde catch the ball behind the line of scrimmage and then loft it to a tight end sprinting behind a drawn-in defense. On the first high school pass of his career, Testaverde executed the play perfectly, throwing a forty-five-yard touchdown.

Most of the rest of Vinny's high school football career was as gracefully unforced and as triumphant. As a high school senior, he was among the most sought-after young quarterbacks in the land.

"My Dad and I had always talked about getting a college football scholarship," Vinny said, "and it was going to happen. But frankly, I hadn't taken my high school classes seriously. I tried to get all my grades in order my senior year, but it was too late. College coaches were interested, but most thought I would have trouble getting into their schools. I was stuck. It was all my fault, but I was stuck."

Al Testaverde had a solution. It began with a long drive from Long Island to central Virginia, to the Fork Union Military Academy, a prep school noted for its football and its discipline. One year of good grades at Fork Union could rehabilitate Vinny's academic standing.

"I remember when we first went to check out Fork Union," Vinny said. "I was in the back seat as we pulled into this big archway at the entrance. The place was all walled in and gray. Students were marching around. It was a tough place. It was the military without the real weapons."

The Testaverdes completed their tour and talked with school officials, who told Al they would have room for their son in next year's class. Vinny, Al, and Josie got back in the car for the return trip to Long Island.

"My dad asked me, 'What do you think?'" Vinny said. "And I said, 'I don't like it, Dad. I don't want to go there.' And he looked at me in the rearview mirror and he said: 'Oh, you're going all right.'

"And I said: 'No, I'm not.' And he looked at me again and said very slowly, 'Yes, you are.' Needless to say, it was a very long ride back to Long Island. And, of course, I went. It saved my football dreams."

But it was not the football at Fork Union that changed Testaverde. He learned the strength of his own resolve and he acquired strong study habits.

"I remember that from 7:30 to 9:45 every night, the entire school was studying," Vinny said. "Talking wasn't allowed. Everywhere inside those walls, for those two hours and fifteen minutes there wasn't a peep. And it made a difference. I learned what you can accomplish when you focus."

The University of Miami, college football's great bastion for future NFL quarterbacks, awaited Testaverde after his single year at Fork Union, and Testaverde was delirious to be there. The Miami campus in the 1980s was the unquestioned kingdom of college football, a time when the Hurricanes won four national championships, and finished second twice and third twice. But Miami was also the kind of place that could attract a host of top quarterbacks, and Testaverde quickly found himself in competition for the starting position with Bernie Kosar.

It was a close battle but Miami Coach Jimmy Johnson chose Kosar on merits Johnson could never entirely explain except to cite Kosar's extraordinary leadership skills and heady approach to Miami's sophisticated pro-style offense. Kosar did indeed thrive that season, leading Miami to the 1983 national championship. The 1984 season was spoiled by Doug Flutie's last-second heroics in the legendary day-after-Thanksgiving 47–45 victory by Boston College, but Kosar had been nearly as impressive as Flutie in that game. Kosar was considered the odds-on favorite to win the award the next season.

It was at this time that Testaverde pondered transferring from Miami. He had two seasons of eligibility remaining but he could see his college career disappearing entirely in Kosar's long, successful shadow.

"Then Bernie came to my dorm room one evening that winter," Testaverde said. "And he says to me, 'I hear you might transfer.' And he tells me that I might not want to do that because he's thinking about leaving early for the NFL draft. I really appreciated that because he didn't have to tell me. He was looking out for me."

Kosar was soon the star of the resurgent Cleveland Browns and Vinny Testaverde was at the controls of the Miami Hurricanes football juggernaut. He did not disappoint, leading Miami to victory in twenty-one of twenty-three games in the next two seasons. Now 220 pounds, Testaverde had the size and the arm strength to overpower college defensive units. Bill Parcells, his coach with the Jets twelve years later, would say of Vinny, "He can throw every type of pass: touch, short, middle, over the top, and long. Physically, as a thrower, there is nothing he cannot do."

The 1985 and 1986 seasons were grand times for all the Testaverdes. Al and Josie did not miss a game, no matter where it was played.

"I remember looking up at my father in the stands and he was quite a sight," Vinny told the Fox television network when they did a biography of his career in 2001. "He would be jumping around and gesturing. I'm sure there were people afraid to sit next to him. Not because he was going to start a fight or something, but he got so excited, you might accidentally catch an elbow in the head."

Vinny led Miami to the first 11–0 record in the history of the program during his senior season. They were the top-ranked team in the nation, and Vinny was the runaway favorite to win the Heisman Trophy.

In the early evening of December 6, 1986, Al and Josie Testaverde, their four daughters, Vinny, and another dozen or so cousins and friends bypassed the back entrance to the Downtown Athletic Club and strode through the ceremonial, more formal, art deco entranceway on West Street. On the lapel of the camel-haired sport coat that Al wore was a small button that read, in the bright orange of Miami's home jersey, "Vinny Wins!"

Inside the lobby, the Testaverde contingent glanced at the Heisman Trophy on display, which Al pointed out, and then were greeted by club officers, who escorted them to an elevator that took them to the thirteenth floor. It was there that the Testaverdes were led to the Heisman Room, a stately place of dark-wood paneling upon whose walls hung paintings of the fifty winners that preceded the 1986 Heisman Trophy announcement.

THE HEISMAN ROOM AT THE DOWNTOWN
ATHLETIC CLUB, 1982

Since 1981, the Heisman Trophy winner had been announced live on national television from the Heisman Room. A handful of finalists for the award were invited to the made-for-TV presentation ceremony, which was also attended by dozens of reporters and the families, coaches, and friends of the finalists.

Inside the Heisman Room in 1986, Vinny took a seat in the first round of chairs. Al and Josie were seated a row behind their son. When club president Eugene V. Meyer proclaimed Vinny the winner, members of the Testaverde family squealed as they bounced in their seats.

Smiling briefly, Testaverde, then twenty-three years old, stood at the podium with the trophy and stared at his father. In an even, full voice, he said:

"I just want to say to my dad, 'Dad, we dreamed this together, we lived this together, and tonight we won this together.'"

Al smiled back at Vinny, wiping away tears.

Father and son, trailed by a rather loud and rowdy gaggle of family, spent the rest of the night side by side.

"He did all the work," Al told reporters. "It wasn't me. I couldn't be prouder of him."

Vinny deferred all praise to his father. "I've had sports role models," he said, "but he is my life role model. I owe it to him." When Vinny was asked if it seemed as if his father had won the Heisman as much as he had won it, he answered: "Well, there is an old saying, 'What you are, I was. What I was, you will be.'"

The football days and nights that followed for Vinny Testaverde were far more inglorious. Miami lost the national championship in a New Year's Day upset to Penn State. He was drafted by the Tampa Bay Buccaneers, a franchise whose futility had devoured talented quarterbacks before him, most notably future Pro Football Hall of Famer Steve Young. Nothing about his stay at Tampa Bay seemed to come out right.

In the Tampa Bay stadium during Vinny's first start as a professional, Al Testaverde had a heart attack, turning to Josie to say his chest pained him and that he was having trouble breathing. Not long afterward, Al's doctors told him he could no longer watch his son play football; it was too taxing on an already weak heart.

"That was really hard on me," Vinny said. "He was the guy I couldn't wait to see after every game just to give him a hug and talk to him. Now, I had to call him somewhere. It wasn't the same."

After six seasons, Vinny was released from Tampa. He found a new home in Cleveland, where he had a measure of success and rebuilt his reputation as a quarterback. When the Cleveland franchise moved to Baltimore, Vinny had a Pro Bowl season in 1996 for the new Ravens. In 1998, Parcells and the Jets signed Testaverde, who was a free agent.

Under Parcells's tutelage, Testaverde had another Pro Bowl season, setting club records and resurrecting the Jets, who two years earlier had won just one game. Testaverde was the hometown boy made good, practicing at the Jets complex in Hempstead, New York, just a twenty-minute drive from his father and mother's home in Elmont. Al, whom other Jets players started to call "Big Al," would come to Jets practices and drive Vinny home for lunch. Although Al still could not watch Vinny's games live, he could get an in-person visit and account from his son not long after many games.

As Testaverde led the 1998 Jets into the American Football Conference championship, putting them one victory from a Super Bowl berth, Al told Vinny he was planning to make an exception to his doctor's orders.

"If you're in the Super Bowl," Al said, "I'm going. No one is stopping me."

The Jets led the Denver Broncos 10–0 at the half of that AFC championship game, but lost the lead and the game in the second half. It turned out to be the first in a series of setbacks for the entire Testaverde family.

On vacation in southern Florida with Josie in February 1999, Al suffered a fatal heart attack. He was sixty-six.

"He was an irreplaceable man in all our lives," Vinny said at the time. "All who knew my father knew how much he relished his life. And he did not squander a day of that life."

"You know, most people don't know how special their father is when he's around," Paul Muscarelli, Vinny's friend since high school, told the Fox Network in their Testaverde biography. "Vinny knew all that when Al was alive."

In 2003, sitting quietly inside the Jets locker room, Vinny gently nodded his head when his friend's statement was read to him.

"I am now a parent of three," he said, referring to the family he and his wife, Mitzi, are raising in a small Long Island town. "And you appreciate what your parents did more than ever. I remember that we used to eat lunch together just about every Saturday afternoon. My mom would go out and get all these cold cuts and Italian salads. And we would have a big Sunday dinner with all the kids.

"I try to do the same thing. And I go back to my Mom's house, too. You learn by example. Kids learn by example. I know I did."

Vinny Testaverde has had to remake his football career several times now, even in what would seem its waning days.

"Perseverence," he said on this day in 2003, "I think it's my biggest strength. My father wouldn't have wanted it any other way. He never gave up. He dreamed and dreamed and made me dream big with him. I owe it to him to live up to that. And I always will."

Inside Vinny Testaverde's Long Island home, in a den lit with track lighting, is the Heisman Trophy awarded for the most outstanding college football player of 1986. On the wall above the Heisman, enlarged and placed in an elegant frame, is a photograph.

"The night of the Heisman presentation, we were back in our hotel room at the Downtown Athletic Club," Vinny said. "We had put the trophy on a coffee table and my Dad and I were sitting next to each other on the couch behind the table. We leaned forward together, next to the Heisman, and someone took our picture.

"That's the picture I have over the Heisman Trophy at my house. To know what his dreams were back then, and now that he's not here, to know how much it had meant to him, it is just a great thing to look at."

And there is an aspect of the photograph that everyone who gazes at it notices immediately. Al Testaverde is smiling broadly.

It is the look of a man whose dream came true.

"I Didn't Know Everything Like I Thought I Knew Everything"

EDDIE GEORGE, 1995

Eddie George wasn't sure what he was going to do, but he knew one thing: He wasn't going to salute this pipsqueak standing in front of him. There was no chance of that.

Eddie stood still, looking down at the smaller student before him, the one in uniform barking orders in his face. How in the world, Eddie thought, did I get here anyway? Okay, so it was his Mom's orange 1981 Mustang that had made the trip from downtown Philadelphia to the Fork Union Military Academy in central Virginia, with Eddie in the front seat and all of his belongings in the trunk, but really, now what?

Salute? Say "Yes, sir"?

Not to this little man. You got the wrong guy, Eddie thought.

Just a few hours earlier Eddie had been back on North Hills Avenue in Philly. In these last days of August 1989, Eddie could often be found on the street corner with his friends, the usual crowd. They weren't bad guys, high school football players every one of them. They were a gang of sorts, though not the kind that gave the law any real trouble. This gang specialized in simple, unorganized disobedience: Defy authority, and don't suck up to anyone, least of all your teachers. Hang out with a clear attitude. Theirs was hardly an atypical response for teenage boys.

Eddie's friends wore their pants backward. They cut their football uniform numbers in the side of their hair. In their high school classes that year—or those they attended—they sat at the back and never raised a hand. If called upon, on a good day, they would mumble an answer. If they had felt mouthy that day, which was not infrequent, they might include a veiled slight to the teacher. They weren't bad guys; their C average kept them eligible for the football games they lived for. But they weren't playing the model student for any teacher or any parent. They weren't living by those rules. They had their pride.

This was the Eddie George who stood before a fellow student on the parade grounds at Fork Union in late August 1989. The student was at least a head shorter than Eddie and a bit younger, too, but he had been at the academy for two years already, and as a company commander, he vastly outranked this new arrival. Six-foot-three-inch Eddie George may have been a star running back as a sophomore at Philadelphia's Abington High School, but he was a complete nobody on his first day at Fork Union.

They had already cut his hair and taken all of his personal belongings and put them in storage. The kid who had once worn the same pair of jeans every day of the week (backward, of course) now had a specific uniform for every part of his day, including bedtime.

"I fought the whole thing from the minute I got there," Eddie George says now. "I couldn't take it, to tell you the truth. I thought it was stupid. I mean, who cares if my shoes are shined or if my clothes are folded just right? And how was I supposed to take orders from these young kids just because they had taken it, because they had sucked up and rose up the ladder first? I kept thinking: 'Man, I'm not even supposed to be here. I'd lay in bed thinking that this was all a bad dream and it would end soon.'"

Back in Philadelphia Donna George was not sleeping well either. It had been her decision to send her only son to Fork Union. Ten years earlier, her parents had sent her brother, who had also been a wayward student spending too much time on the streets of Philadelphia, to Fork Union. Donna George had seen the change in her brother, had seen him learn to study, focus, set goals, and redirect his life.

But that did not make it any easier when Donna George saw her Eddie exhibiting much the same behavior as her brother at the same age. "He could be antagonistic, rebellious, but most of all, he wasn't doing anything with his studies," Donna George would say in interviews years later. "He skipped classes, walked out on classes. He didn't do his homework. He thought the whole thing was a waste of his time."

Eddie had once been a devoted student, a curious kid in elementary school who pleased teachers, parents, and grandparents alike. Divorced when Eddie was five years old, Donna George had been raising him and his older sister, Leslie, by working three jobs: flight attendant, model, and waitress. Eddie and his sister frequently lived with Donna George's mother, especially when Donna was working cross-country flights. This arrangement worked when Eddie was younger, but eventually Donna sensed that Eddie lacked a father figure in his life, and she found it difficult to discipline a teenager who towered over her and was growing more and more unfocused by the day.

Donna George mailed away for the applications to Fork Union and applied for the loans she would need to pay Eddie's hefty tuition and board at the academy. Then she sat Eddie down in the North Hills Avenue living room and informed him of her decision.

"He literally threw himself to the floor crying," Donna George said in a 1995 interview. "He said: 'Mom, you can't do this to me. Mom, I'll dry up down there. Mom, I'm going to be the starting running back this year and college scouts are coming to see me. They'll never find me in Virginia.'

"And I said: 'Son, I love you and you need this or you will have no future. Not at the rate you're going. You might have college scouts look at you, but they won't be able to give you a scholarship, not with the grades you're getting in school.' He kept saying I was killing his football career and I kept saying I didn't care about his football career, I cared about him and his education and his ability to discipline himself."

The argument went on for days, although Eddie knew he never had any choice in the matter, which is not to say that Donna George did not waver from time to time.

"As a mother watching your son cry, some part of you wants to just hug him and say, 'It's okay, you can stay, just try harder,'" Donna said. "I cried, too, wondering if I was doing the right thing. I could have not let him go but I knew deep down that the only way I could get my son back the way I wanted him back was to let him go. I had to sacrifice in a sense, and he had to sacrifice, too."

Donna George packed for Eddie, loaded the suitcases in her Mustang, and drove to Fork Union, Virginia. Eddie had little to say on the trip. There was little contact between son and mother in the first few weeks of Eddie's term at Fork Union Military Academy. Students were allowed only a brief weekly telephone call.

"I didn't say much," Eddie says. "What was the point?"

He was too busy walking extra tours of guard duty. He was too busy polishing every pew in the chapel. Twice. He was too busy working in the kitchen, washing and stacking dishes as his classmates relaxed and played sports.

"I was rebelling against it all but I sure wasn't winning the rebellion," Eddie says. "Slowly I started to see that I had to change for my own good. You know, I had a lot of ambitions and dreams but I had no drive. I really didn't know how to work for what I wanted. I didn't understand the sacrifice of joining a group working toward something. I realized I didn't know everything like I thought I knew everything.

"I was a streetwise kid with a lot of talk. An atmosphere like Fork Union humbles you and redirects you. And I needed that."

It did not take long for Eddie to expunge his list of demerits. He saluted his younger, smaller classmates and learned to say, "Yes, sir." He came to thrive in—if not enjoy—the environment of discipline, marching, and drilling.

"Well, I enjoyed it enough to understand its worth," he says, laughing. "And I got to know the guys I was around. A good bunch of guys with ambitions, too. We would sit around and talk about our dreams. It was a great experience, without question, the most important thing I ever did in my life."

Donna George came back for Parents Weekend late in October of 1989. She did not know what to expect, and was shaken when Eddie's company of students, Alpha Company, marched past and Eddie was not with them. Then came an honor guard bearing three ceremonial flags. Hoisting one of the flags was Eddie. He shot a brief glance toward the grandstand, where his mother covered her surprise with a hand over her mouth, an expression that quickly changed to a beaming smile and wave.

"She knew I was on my way," Eddie says.

Eddie George's first season of football at Fork Union was part of the learning experience as well. He played sparingly.

"Again, I learned I wasn't as good as I thought," Eddie says. "I was tall but only about 175 pounds. I asked the coach what I could do to make myself a starter by next season and he pointed to the weight room."

Eddie was nearly 200 pounds when he ran for twenty-two touchdowns and more than 1,200 yards as Fork Union's first-string tailback the next season. He was eligible to graduate, having completed four years of high school, but the only offer Eddie had after his senior season at Fork Union was from Division II Edinboro State near Erie, Pennsylvania.

"I could have taken it," Eddie says. "I would have been through with military school, which was still a demanding schedule. But I could also stay another year, a fifth, prep school year."

It is a common choice of many football recruits hoping to improve their standing with major football schools, but for Eddie, it meant another year of getting up at 5:30 A.M. to march, another year when every minute of his day was consumed by an exhausting regimen. Another year of a uniform for everything, even sleeping.

"I decided that nothing worth achieving comes easily," Eddie says. "I had been told that when I got to Fork Union. I didn't believe them then. I believed them now."

His rushing totals as a fifth-year player were his best at the school, 1,372 yards, and several schools paid visits to Fork Union. Penn State offered Eddie a scholarship but said they would turn him into a linebacker. Eddie wanted no part of that.

Why? Because a linebacker, Eddie knew, had never won the Heisman Trophy. And since he was a young boy, Eddie George had planned to win the Heisman Trophy.

"I used to watch Marcus Allen and Herschel Walker play and I remember watching the Heisman Trophy ceremony when they won it," Eddie says. "I stood up and said, 'Mom, that's going to be me.' Then I would go into my bedroom and stand in front of the mirror so I could practice my Heisman Trophy acceptance speech. It was pretty funny, this skinny little kid in Philadelphia dreaming of the Heisman. But I wanted to win it, and I knew linebackers didn't win it. I was going to be a running back."

At Ohio State, the coaching staff did not know a thing about Eddie George until Dan Osman, an assistant trainer at the school, approached the recruiting coordinator Bill Conley and asked him if he had heard about a running back named Eddie George at Fork Union Military Academy. Conley knew the school but not the player. Since the student assistant trainer had been polite and zealous about this Eddie George, as a courtesy, Conley called Fork Union the next day and asked for a tape of their star tailback. Conley liked what he saw and asked for more tape and then invited Eddie for a visit to the campus. Suitably impressed, especially with his poise and unruffled demeanor, Ohio State offered Eddie a full scholarship.

And who was Osman? He was Eddie George's company commander during that first year at Fork Union, the first high-ranking student to confront Eddie. Osman spent many of those early days handing out demerits to Eddie, especially for insubordination, since the towering Eddie seemed to have a problem saluting the much shorter Osman.

"Yeah, another of those life coincidences," Eddie says. "He goes off to Ohio State and happens to be there to say something."

As a freshman in 1991, Eddie George was an instant contributor. He scored three short-yardage touchdowns in a win over Syracuse, and two weeks later was about to score another one-yard touchdown against Illinois when a defender knocked the football from Eddie's grasp just before the goal line. An Illinois player scooped up the fumble at the Illinois 4-yard line and ran ninety-six yards for a touchdown.

By the fourth quarter, Ohio State had a two-point lead and was on the verge of a game-clinching touchdown. Again, the powerfully built George, now 225 pounds, charged toward the end zone with the football under his arm. Again, at the 1-yard line, he fumbled. Illinois took that possession and drove into Ohio State territory for what would prove to be the game-winning touchdown.

Donna George was at the game (she had attended all of Eddie's games since high school, even at Fork Union) and she met Eddie outside the locker room afterward. When she noticed tears rolling down Eddie's face as they walked, she turned him back toward the massive Ohio Stadium, where fans had booed Eddie off the field after the second fumble.

"We sat in the empty stands and cried," Donna George said in 1995. "I told him to get it all out and then forget it. He had many more games to play. Three more years and more."

But his coaches did not give Eddie George a chance at redemption that season. Before the Illinois game, Eddie had carried the football twenty-five times for five touchdowns. After the Illinois game, he received only twelve carries and never scored again. In eleven games of the next season, behind two seniors on the running back depth chart, Eddie had just forty-two carries, mostly in mop-up duty of games the Ohio State Buckeyes were winning by wide margins.

Despite what seemed like two years of punishment for his two crushing fumbles, Eddie views the Illinois game as a pivotal afternoon in his collegiate career.

"I think I won the Heisman Trophy that day," he says. "I mean it. Most successful things in life are shaped by some amount of adversity. Maybe good things were coming to me too soon as a freshman. The Illinois game was a devastating experience but it steeled me to be ready when my chance came again. Maybe I wouldn't have been ready without it."

Which is not to say that he didn't have other thoughts as well. He considered transferring to another college. Donna George disapproved.

"She said I would get another chance," Eddie says. "And this was the place to wait for that chance. My Mom told me not to run away."

As a junior, Eddie was Ohio State's top running back, rushing for 1,442 yards and twelve touchdowns, but his head coach John Cooper told reporters at the end of the season that he thought Eddie George was using only a fraction of his ability. Cooper was convinced that with off-season work, Eddie could get faster at hitting the holes that Ohio State's legendary offensive line was so good at opening.

"I did work harder that off-season than any other in college," Eddie says. "I think I always worked hard but I pushed it beyond those standards. I'm not saying I thought I could win the Heisman Trophy. But I could dream."

Most who watched Eddie George gallop through the Big Ten Conference in his senior season agreed they saw a twenty-one-year-old who had somehow learned to run faster. While he had few long scoring runs as a junior, as a senior in 1995, Eddie had touchdown runs of 87, 64, and 51 yards and five more touchdown runs that were of more than ten yards. Overall, Eddie scored twenty-four touchdowns, doubling his total as a junior. He rushed for a school record 1,826 yards, quite an accomplishment considering that more than a few quality running backs preceded Eddie George at Ohio State, including five whose seasons were rewarded with a Heisman Trophy.

Eddie George's 1995 Heisman candidacy blossomed in a nationally televised game against Notre Dame when he ran for 207 yards in a 45–26

Ohio State upset. It was his third 200-yard rushing game of the season. Then, in a fitting bit of redemption, Eddie rushed for 314 yards in a victory over Illinois. In the three seasons since the two fumbles against Illinois in 1991, Eddie George had carried the football more than 600 times and fumbled just six times.

A 31–23 loss to Michigan in his final Big Ten game was the only blemish in Ohio State's regular season, which concluded with an 11–1 record. That loss brought more tears outside the Ohio State locker room between mother and son as Eddie would never get a chance to play in the Rose Bowl. But a few weeks later, in the closest vote in the history of the award to that point, Eddie won the Heisman Trophy, by 264 balloting points over Nebraska's Tommie Frazier. It was Ohio State's sixth Heisman Trophy, one fewer than Notre Dame, which has the most of any college or university.

Accepting the trophy, Eddie thanked his teammates and family, especially his mother. It was a gracious, thoughtful speech inside the Heisman Room of the Downtown Athletic Club, one that he had been practicing for nearly twenty years and delivered with aplomb. During the weekend of activities in New York City, Eddie George went to a jazz club where he met Tamara Johnson, to whom he was engaged to be married in 2002.

"You could say I picked up two trophies that weekend," Eddie says.

Eddie George's pro football career blossomed in Tennessee, where he played for the Titans, the state's first NFL team. Eddie was the landmark star of the team, formerly the Houston Oilers, and he won the 1996 NFL rookie of the year award. He compiled a succession of Pro Bowl seasons, helping lead the Titans into the 2000 Super Bowl, where they narrowly lost to the St. Louis Rams.

Eddie's pro career has been a model of durability and dependability. In the three-game run to the 2000 Super Bowl, he rushed for 354 yards, then added another ninety-five yards in the Super Bowl. A punishing runner between the tackles, the roughest quadrant of the field in any football game, Eddie never missed a professional start in his first eight NFL seasons. The defiant kid from the late 1980s has become an admired personality in Tennessee, active in charity work and sponsoring college scholarships for inner-city high school students in Tennessee and Ohio.

"You cannot stand in the Heisman Room of the Downtown Athletic Club, put your hands on that trophy, and not feel the responsibility to handle yourself properly from then on," he says. "I try not to get in any trouble and I want to help kids as I was helped."

In 2001, Donna and Eddie George were uncomfortably in the spotlight when Donna was arrested and charged with drunken driving as she drove to a Titans Monday Night Football game in Nashville. Eddie's four-year-old son was in the back seat of the car.

"My mother and I have worked through many things," Eddie says. "This is an unfortunate situation but it's something we worked through, too. We are still very close. Obviously, I owe so much to her."

And to Eddie George, no decision was more imperative than his mother's resolve for her son to be challenged by a demanding environment, a sink-or-swim moment in a life.

"I believe my life would have turned out all right but I wouldn't be where I am today," Eddie says. "I didn't believe in myself. I was setting myself up for failure somewhere along the way. I would have survived but I did not have the confidence to come back and excel. Military school showed me the way to make the most of me. And I have been blessed with determination.

"I've always said football was a test of faith because it takes great patience. It took patience for me to get what I wanted out of Fork Union, to graduate and to get a scholarship to Ohio State. It took patience to rise back to the top at Ohio State after the fumbles as a freshman. In the NFL, it takes enormous patience; you get knocked down on every play waiting for that big game-breaking run.

"It can be draining at times, but you remember that this is how life works. You work, you wait, and you believe."

You soldier on.

"That's right," Eddie says. "You do your job and pay your respect. You don't think you're above it or anybody. And you will be better for it. I tell people, I am the living proof."

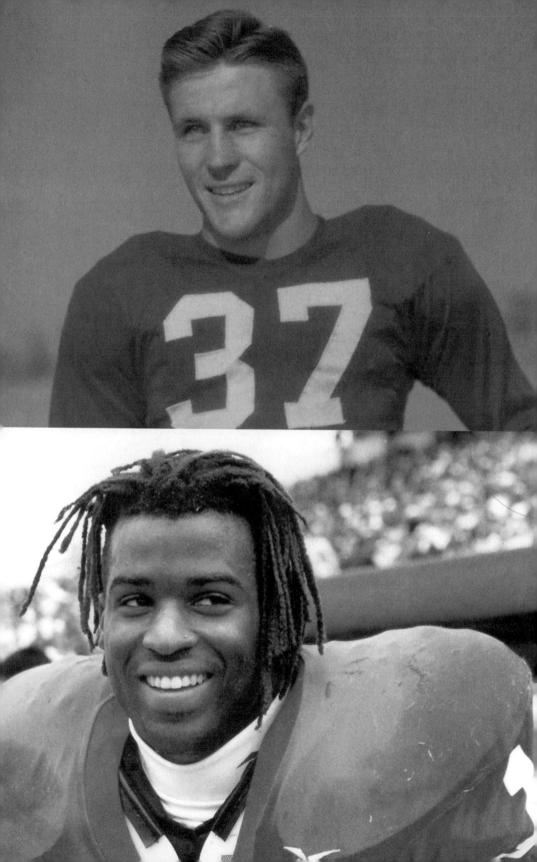

"Kindred Spirits"

RICKY WILLIAMS, 1998; AND

DOAK WALKER, 1948

Doak Walker, Heisman Trophy winner from 1948, was on a mission. He had to find Ricky Williams and look him in the eye.

It might have been easier to tackle Ricky Williams, especially for Walker, three times an All-American.

On this day, January 20, 1998, the two men were in the same Dallas hotel ballroom: Williams, the fleet and powerful star of the University of Texas, the greatest college football running back of his time; and Walker, a dashing, stylish football icon from Southern Methodist University, a man who exactly fifty years earlier had been an American matinee idol and revered in Texas only slightly less than the Alamo.

Williams wore his hair in dreadlocks and sported body piercings and tattoos that made him stand out in most football crowds, but he was extraordinarily shy, indeed, almost unbearably uncomfortable in public settings. Williams was known for staring at his feet in such gatherings, often declining to look up at those he met. But on this day, the twenty-one-year-old Williams was to receive the Doak Walker Award, given to America's top

(TOP) DOAK WALKER

(BOTTOM) RICKY WILLIAMS

running back each year. And here, on this day, with a broad smile on his face, came the gray-haired, seventy-one-year-old Doak Walker, approaching Williams with his right hand extended.

"I was awed but he had a selfless way that was genuinely comforting," Ricky said later. "Doak Walker had a way to make you feel special. He could do it to anyone. He was humble, he looked at you, and it was like he was searching for how to make you at ease. But he was still reserved and quiet. After a while, I couldn't stop looking at him, watching and trying to learn from watching him."

Others, meanwhile, were watching Walker and Williams.

"They were like kindred spirits separated by all those years and generations," Doak Walker's wife, Skeeter Werner Walker, told reporters afterward. "They were close friends in a short period of time. It was an unbelievable thing to see."

Williams and Walker had actually met for the first time a few weeks earlier in Orlando, Florida, during a made-for-TV presentation of the Doak Walker Award. In Dallas, they renewed a relationship that led to a lengthy conversation after the ceremony. Williams stayed overnight and the two had lunch. They went for a walk together. They talked some more at the home of a mutual friend.

Said Doak: "We were fast friends. I believe you look somebody in the eye and you shake their hand and you go from there. And what I saw was a fine, caring young man. A real person."

Williams had spent the days leading up to the Dallas function reading Walker's biography, the kind of thing the studious, serious Williams often did, trying to prepare himself for any setting. Williams took the book out of the University of Texas library and sat at home reading, his eyes growing wider as he turned each page.

Ewell "Doak" Walker, father of the future Heisman Trophy winner, had walked into his North Dallas High School English class on the morning after New Year's Day in 1927 and announced to his pupils: "Great news! Yesterday, an All-American quarterback was born."

When one student asked how he knew the newborn baby would be an All-American quarterback, the proud father responded: "Well, I can't be sure he'll be a quarterback, but I'm sure he'll be All-American."

WALKER ARRIVING IN NEW YORK TO ACCEPT THE HEISMAN

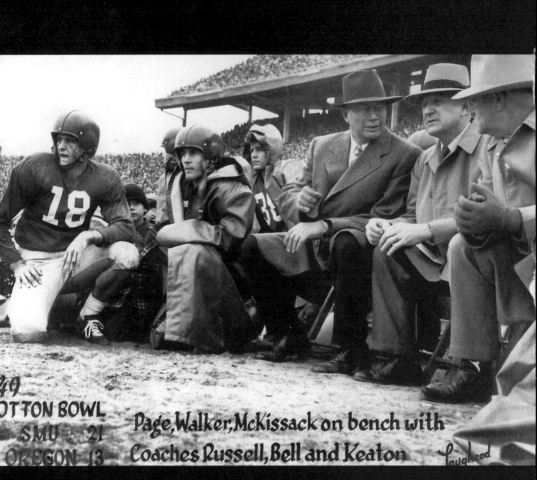

'49
OTTON BOWL
SMU   21
OREGON 13

Page, Walker, McKissack on bench with
Coaches Russell, Bell and Keaton

WALKER (SECOND FROM LEFT) DURING
THE 1949 COTTON BOWL

The younger Ewell Doak Walker, who would come to be known in Texas and the rest of the nation as "The Doaker," was an athlete like few before him in Dallas, or anywhere else. At SMU, in 1947, when Walker blossomed into national prominence as a sophomore, school officials could not contain the crowds at the university's on-campus football stadium. So they began playing at Dallas's Cotton Bowl, inside the sprawling state fairgrounds. That, however, seemed to only invite more fans to witness the Doak Walker phenomenon, and the crowds surging to watch Walker's exploits—he was both a running back and ball-hawking defensive back—were so great they had to expand the seating at the Cotton Bowl.

Before Walker's senior season, anticipating an even greater rush of Doaker-mania in booming postwar Texas, state officials decided to expand the Cotton Bowl again. They added a second, upper tier to the grandstand, hence the nickname for the venerable bowl south of downtown Dallas: The House That Doak Built.

Walker led SMU to consecutive Southwestern Conference championships, finishing first in the league in rushing, passing, punting, punt returns, kickoff returns, field goals, and extra points. He won the Heisman as a junior in 1948, when SMU was unbeaten and ranked third nationally, and people said Walker was both the best offensive and the best defensive player in the nation. Injuries and illness hampered his senior season, although he still finished third in the Heisman voting.

Walker then signed with the Detroit Lions, and as a two-way back, was the pivotal player on consecutive NFL championship teams. Though he retired after just six pro seasons, Walker was inducted into the Pro Football Hall of Fame, to go along with his selection to the College Football Hall of Fame, and of course, the Texas Hall of Fame. Walker later met and married Gladys "Skeeter" Warner, a pioneering American Olympic alpine skier who had established a ski school and business in Steamboat Springs, Colorado. That is where the Walkers settled as Doak tended to a variety of interests, many of them charitable.

"But what impressed me was how respected he had been wherever he went," Williams said. "His teammates all loved him, despite the attention he received. Everyone interviewed for his biography just seemed drawn to him. Then, I met him and found out why. I could not get enough information from him whenever I was with him. I asked a million questions about football in the 1940s and 1950s, about how he handled all the accolades. We talked and talked.

"And I remember when I left that night in Dallas with my family, he turned and said goodbye to each one of them by name. He remembered everybody's first name. He looked my two sisters in the eye, said their name, and smiled his goodbye. I just left feeling like I had a role model. I told myself, Doak Walker is who I want to be.'"

Ten days after the Doak Walker Award banquet, Walker, who had become an expert skier in his decades with Skeeter, was traversing an intermediate ski slope near his home in Steamboat Springs when he made a simple miscalculation. Those skiing with Walker that day said he was not going overly fast, but he misjudged the drop on the other side of a small rise in the terrain and suddenly was airborne, soaring above the snow for twenty-five feet.

Walker landed hard, fell, and somersaulted down the trail another seventy feet. When he came to a stop, Doak Walker had a broken vertebra in his neck. His breathing and heart stopped. A dentist skiing nearby stopped and revived Walker, who was then rushed to a hospital. He was paralyzed from the chest down.

In the next three months, hundreds of letters found their way to Walker's hospital room. Walker had always written thank-you notes or responses to every fan letter he had ever received. In his football prime, he was known to write sportswriters thank-you notes after they praised him in their articles. Now, at her husband's hospital bedside, Skeeter Walker tried to answer the letters flooding the room.

And roughly every ten days, she opened a letter from Ricky Williams.

"Here was a young man getting ready for his senior season in college," Skeeter Walker said in a 1998 interview. "It's the greatest time of his life and he is sitting down writing letters of encouragement to someone he met once. He's pouring out his thoughts and explaining how much Doak and his recovery will mean to him. It has been really touching for the both of us. I've seen the tears in Doak's eyes when I read the letters to him."

Five years later, when asked about his correspondence to Walker in early 1998, Williams said it was a subject he would rather not discuss.

"Sometimes you know what the right thing to do is," he said. "We are all raised to know what to do."

WALKER (FAR RIGHT) RUNNING FOR THE
DETROIT LIONS

Ricky Williams was six years old when his parents divorced and he lost virtually all touch with his father. His mother Sandy went to work as a U.S. Navy purchasing agent. She also attended college classes at night after work. It was Ricky's job to watch over the house and his twin sister, Cassie, and younger sister, Nisey, until Sandy got out of school at 10 P.M.

Ricky had to remind his sisters to do their homework, to review it, and to make sure they went to bed on time. Ricky made the macaroni and cheese or a special recipe of his mother's: Ramen noodles, which Ricky still remembers as coming eight to a pack for $1, mixed with a can of peas and a can of green beans. Ricky did the laundry and answered the telephone only when he knew it was Sandy executing a prearranged secret ring. On weekend mornings before the local Jack-in-the-Box opened, Ricky scrubbed its bathrooms and floors for $5 a day.

"I had more responsibility than some kids, but nothing I couldn't handle," Ricky said years later. "My mom needed the help."

There were concealed frustrations. Some who knew Ricky felt he was annoyed by his father's exit and demonstrated it outside Sandy Williams's home. He was getting into neighborhood fights and developing a reputation as a kid with a temper. Sandy sent him to anger management sessions, then to karate lessons, hoping structured aggression would give vent to Ricky's frustrations.

"All the karate did was make him a better fighter," Sandy said. "He was upset; Ricky took things personally. But he was never in trouble and he did calm down and come to better understand the things going on around him. I think being the man of the house at so young an age was hard on him. But Ricky is a kind and generous person and he accepted it."

Williams soon sought father figures in athletics. As a teenager, he had developed into a superior athlete, one of the most highly sought-after high school running backs in America and a good enough baseball player to sign a professional contract with the Philadelphia Phillies. He played minor league baseball in his summers between football seasons. A good student, he nonetheless rarely raised his hand in class, his teachers noticed, even though his test scores revealed he usually knew the right answers to the questions. Around this time, he began wearing his now-trademark dreadlocks because his favorite musician was reggae star Bob Marley.

Ricky chose to attend the University of Texas for its tradition and because he wanted to live in a true college town, Austin, Texas. His mother and sisters moved to Austin with him, and Williams used his $50,000 signing bonus from the Phillies, and his summer paychecks from baseball, to pay for his sisters' education as students at Texas.

Ricky was initially converted into a fullback at Texas but was still an exceptional ball carrier for some uneven Longhorn teams. When he was finally made the featured back as a junior, he responded by leading the nation in rushing with 1,893 yards. Since Texas had won only four of its eleven games that season, he was expected to turn pro and enter the NFL draft. Williams would have immediately earned millions as a certain first-round draft pick, but he shocked everyone, even his Texas supporters, by announcing he would stay for another season.

He said he had come to Texas to get a college degree that he had not yet earned and he had many friends on the football team he did not want to leave behind. Added Ricky: "You can't put a price on loyalty."

Doak Walker had no input in Williams's decision, but he offered an opinion afterward.

"He said he didn't think too many guys would still do that," Williams said. "I think he was proud I did."

Williams entered the 1998 season the runaway favorite to win the Heisman Trophy. He needed 1,928 yards to pass 1976 Heisman Trophy winner Tony Dorsett's all-time college rushing total of 6,082 yards, a record that had stood for twenty-two years.

Williams's season got off to a good start before Kansas State, then the second-ranked team in the nation, held him to forty-three yards rushing in the Longhorns' third game of the year, a 48–3 Kansas State rout. But Williams had not returned for his final college season without preparation. He had curtailed his final season of professional baseball with the Phillies' farm team to return to Austin and subject himself to a grueling regimen under the hot Texas sun that included forty-yard sprints up a steep on-campus hill while wearing a forty-pound weighted vest.

And so in Texas's fourth game Williams rebounded from the Kansas State setback with 318 rushing yards in a 59–21 victory over Rice University.

The next day, September 27, 1998, after several months attempting to recover from the skiing injury that had brought complete stillness to nearly his entire body, Doak Walker succumbed to complications from his paralysis. Eulogized as "an uncommon common man," Walker was buried in Steamboat Springs after a ceremony that featured readings from letters sent from around the nation, including a five-paragraph missive composed by Ricky Williams that lauded Doak Walker for "his gentleness of spirit."

At the hour-long funeral/prayer service, five loose-leaf notebooks containing more than 6,000 letters and faxes sent to Walker in the previous ten months rested next to his coffin, alongside his 1948 Heisman Trophy and a cowboy hat.

In Texas, Ricky Williams put a picture of Walker inside his locker and announced he would wear a decal with the number 37—Walker's jersey number at SMU—on the back of his helmet for the rest of the season. The following weekend he rushed for 350 yards in a twenty-one-point victory over Iowa State. Then, Williams received permission from the National Collegiate Athletic Association to switch his jersey from number 34 to number 37 for Texas's October 10 game, which was the annual grudge match with Oklahoma at the Cotton Bowl, the House That Doak Built.

In a 34–3 Texas victory, Williams rushed for 139 yards (and had another seventy-eight yards nullified by a holding penalty called on a teammate thirty yards behind the play). He scored two touchdowns, pointing to the sky in the end zone and shouting: "That's for you, Doak." In the locker room afterward, Ricky gave the number 37 jersey to eight members of Walker's family who attended the game.

"You have no idea what that young man means to our family," Skeeter Walker said.

Williams's spectacular run through the 1998 season was now a Texas phenomenon akin to the commotion Walker brought to the state half a century earlier. There were billboards of Williams throughout Austin, including one that counted down the yardage he needed to pass Dorsett. As Texas won six straight games, Williams was mobbed wherever he went, and asked to autograph anything and everything, even the sonogram of a pregnant woman who said she planned to name her son Ricky.

And there was a website, run-ricky-run.com, a prescient designation in a dual life of ever-accelerating public accomplishment and ever-escalating hidden turmoil. Texas loves its heroes, especially its football heroes, and while Ricky was not Texas-born, his polite, reserved nature made him welcome in a mannered society. But it was during the crush of his senior-year celebrity that Ricky Williams came face-to-face with a personal crisis he knew existed but did not know how to handle. In fact, he did not understand it in the least.

Ricky had known since his high school days that, in his words, he was wired differently than his friends. Ricky Williams was not just shy in public gatherings; sometimes they made his heart race and his blood pressure skyrocket. His mind would be swimming in a thousand nervous thoughts as he fought the one he seemed to hear the loudest: flee!

Sometimes, at a party, the mall, or a fast-food restaurant, Ricky wanted nothing more than to get up and run out of the building, go home, and sit alone in his bedroom. And yet, when Ricky did that, he would feel empty and alone. It was a quandary that Ricky wrestled with for years, and along the way he learned to survive and mask his distress in a myriad of ways. He would get others to fill in at personal appearances and often made sure friends never left his side at a party. He would walk through a crowded room without making eye contact, because that might bring on a conversation and he was afraid he might give in to the urge to flee the conversation in mid-sentence.

These feelings were not a constant for Ricky, especially in his heyday at Texas, but they were never too distant. And later, when he was drafted into professional football, and felt the stress and strain of injuries, expectations, professional setbacks, and an increasingly intense media scrutiny, Williams's anxiety in public settings began to overtake him. Famously, he did interviews with reporters with his helmet on because the helmet had a tinted visor that kept him from having to make eye contact with his interviewers. He shunned all social settings, declining to so much as use the drive-thru window of the local Burger King because it would mean talking to the stranger operating the drive-thru. Williams locked himself in his house for hours on end. In the off-season, he might go weeks without talking to anyone, even by telephone. Then, in 2001, he began to dread leaving his house even for football practice or games.

"It's hard to describe how scared you are," Williams said in a 2003 interview. "You don't really know what's going on, but you know something is wrong. You don't know yourself anymore, and don't know why. And since you're a 235-pound football player, you feel added pressure because you know people will view anything other than a physical injury as a weakness, a lack of mental toughness. It starts to race and race.

"But when I just didn't want to play football anymore, I knew I had to do something. Because now this thing, whatever it was, was affecting what I used to love to do."

Williams sought the advice of a psychologist, and he did so with an assist from another burly football player from the University of Texas, Earl Campbell, the 1977 Heisman Trophy winner. If ever there was someone considered indestructible, it was Campbell. Once, during his Texas career, he had run out of bounds and collided with Bevo, the university's massive longhorn mascot. Campbell went down, but so did the steer.

During his tenure at Texas, Williams had occasionally been compared to Campbell; he was even called "Little Earl." The two were similar in more ways than anyone could have known.

Shortly after his football career was over in the 1980s, Campbell had suddenly suffered from bouts of overwhelming anxiety, crippling episodes that drove Campbell to believe he was having a heart attack or about to die. Campbell's troubles were diagnosed as a panic disorder, and in 1999 he wrote a book about his struggles to live with the disorder and occasionally made speeches to groups hoping to help others with the disease. Campbell's situation comforted Williams, which made him feel less alone in his anxiety.

"It was a wonderful thing for me to know," Williams said, "because the scariest part is when something is going wrong and you don't know what the problem is. But when you have something to call it, and you learn there is something you can do about it, then there is hope."

Williams was told he suffered from social phobia, or a social anxiety disorder.

"I have to say I can completely understand how many people—coaches, teammates, media—must have felt frustrated with me," Williams said in a 2003 interview, a year after he had led all NFL running backs in rushing during the 2002 season. "But I can tell them I'm taking care of that now."

With psychotherapy sessions and a daily medication aimed at easing his uneasiness in social settings, Williams said he rarely feels the disquieting nervousness he felt for years.

"I can go to a mall or walk through a crowded room with my head up," Williams said. "And I can't tell you how nice that feels. It had been a while, at least back to college, since I could do that."

The final weeks of Ricky Williams's collegiate football career were indeed idyllic, and they remain that way in Williams's recollection and that of fans throughout Texas. Williams left the state with a historic sendoff. He entered the final game of Texas's 1998 regular season against arch-rival Texas A&M needing sixty-two yards to overtake Dorsett in the all-time rushing total. Williams's teammates seemed to want the record as much as Ricky did. He had earned their respect with his choice to come back for his senior season, which gave many of them the chance to make their own senior seasons more memorable. He had earned their respect with his grueling workouts in the summer sun. Most of all, despite all the attention he had received, he had earned their respect with his humility.

And so in that final regular season game, before a sold-out crowd on the Texas campus, Williams's offensive linemen opened massive holes for him to run through. In the game's opening minutes, he quickly accumulated fifty-two rushing yards. Then, late in the first quarter, Williams took a handoff, bounced off two tackles at the line of scrimmage, cut outside, and ran sixty yards down the left sideline. He deftly waited for a downfield block, then cut back at the 5-yard line and carried a Texas A&M safety who had jumped on his back into the end zone with him. He had established an NCAA rushing record, and Campbell, Dorsett, and John David Crow, Texas A&M's Heisman Trophy winner from 1957, joined him on the field in celebration. Ricky would rush for 259 yards in Texas's 26–24 victory over Texas A&M to finish with a record 6,279 yards, a total compiled in sixty-three fewer rushing attempts than Dorsett.

"You just dream of days like that," Williams said. "I accomplished everything I had wanted in staying for another year at school."

On December 12, 1998, with his mother and sisters, Ricky traveled to New York City. His selection as the Heisman Trophy winner was a certainly, but Ricky Williams felt the focus of more than just that achievement as he entered the Downtown Athletic Club building. He walked through the art deco entrance on West Street and stopped flat-footed as he gazed around the lobby.

He took in the rich, regal paneling, the elegant lighting and carpeting, the massive pillars that held up thirty-four more floors, props to nearly seven decades of college football history.

"I just wanted to soak it all in," Williams said years later, recalling the moment.

From Jay Berwanger to Nile Kinnick, Blanchard and Davis to Leahy's Notre Dame lads, they had all walked through this room. Roger Staubach, Archie Griffin, and Marcus Allen, too, who was Ricky's hero growing up in San Diego, Allen's hometown. This was, as the awning outside read, the home of the Heisman Trophy. This is where Barry Sanders had come, Ricky thought, and Johnny Rodgers, too. And Mike Garrett and Ernie Davis.

This is where Doak Walker had accepted his award. He had walked through the same lobby door, wearing a double-breasted suit, white shirt, and stylish print tie, with a jaunty white handkerchief propped up in the breast pocket. The wide Walker smile, the one that had graced forty-seven magazine covers in the late 1940s, flashed in the lobby that day, an unaffected response to dozens of camera bulbs greeting his arrival.

"I love college football history," Williams said. "I love the mystique, the symbols. I was once a kid dreaming of this award so I know what it means. I looked around. I wanted to feel it."

Welcomed formally by club officials in the lobby, Williams and his family were escorted to their rooms at the club. There were a few hours to kill and Williams took an extended tour of the club.

"I really don't think it had sunk in that I was going to be part of the history of the Heisman," Williams said. "I began to feel a strong sense of duty to the other players who won it. It kind of hits you when you're there. It is not just another football award."

It is *the* football award.

Williams went back to his room to dress for the ceremony that would officially recognize him as that season's Heisman Trophy winner. He put on a three-piece blue suit. From the inside vest pocket, he removed a slip of paper upon which he had written a phone number. Dialing it in his hotel room, Ricky Williams waited for Skeeter Walker to answer. The two talked briefly, Skeeter telling Ricky that she knew he would win and that Doak was proud of him, and Ricky responding that he wanted Skeeter to know he would be thinking of her and her late husband no matter what the night held.

Then, with his family, Ricky walked down the hotel hall to a waiting elevator where an attendant pushed a button marked not with a floor number but with a black "H" circled in gold and bronze. This led the Williams entourage to the thirteenth floor of the Downtown Athletic Club and the Heisman Room.

The portraits of every previous Heisman Trophy winner adorned the walls of the Heisman Room, giving it the feel of a college football sanctum. Williams strolled from image to image.

"You start to wonder how you got here, looking at all the players before you," Williams said. "You start to wonder how you can possibly add to that history. I wondered how I would say the right things, how I would know how to handle myself, how I would live up to the responsibility that goes with the award."

Williams kept walking through the Heisman Room. He came to the portrait recently draped with a dark memorial ribbon. Ricky Williams stared into the eyes of Doak Walker.

"I'm ready," he thought to himself, turning from his friend's portrait to take his seat next to the podium microphone, through which his name would soon be announced.

Ricky Williams smiled.

"I'm ready now," he said.

Afterword

On September, 11, 2001, the terrorist attacks on the World Trade Center occurred just blocks from the Downtown Athletic Club, the ancestral home of the Heisman Trophy. The force of the explosions and the collapse of adjacent buildings nearly tumbled the club's skyscraper edifice. Within minutes, debris and a gray cloud of smoke and dust began to fill the club lobby. Then, spilling through the doors by the dozens, came the injured—office workers, pedestrians, police, and firefighters. Club employees quickly turned the lobby into a mock emergency room. Drapes were torn off the walls to serve as blankets, water hoses doused the dust from gasping, caked faces, and dining tables served as stretchers. Tablecloths and napkins were shredded then fashioned into masks, bandages, compresses, and slings.

Like much of lower Manhattan, the Downtown Athletic Club never recovered from the catastrophe of September 11. Sadly, the attacks have shuttered the club building, its future uncertain. The Heisman Trophy, however, is not in search of a new home.

Its home is its mythic stature in the American imagination. Each year, the members of the Downtown Athletic Club continue to award the trophy to one shining example of America's finest athletes. The Heisman and its legacy endure as a powerful symbol of the grandeur of one man—and the grandeur of thousands.

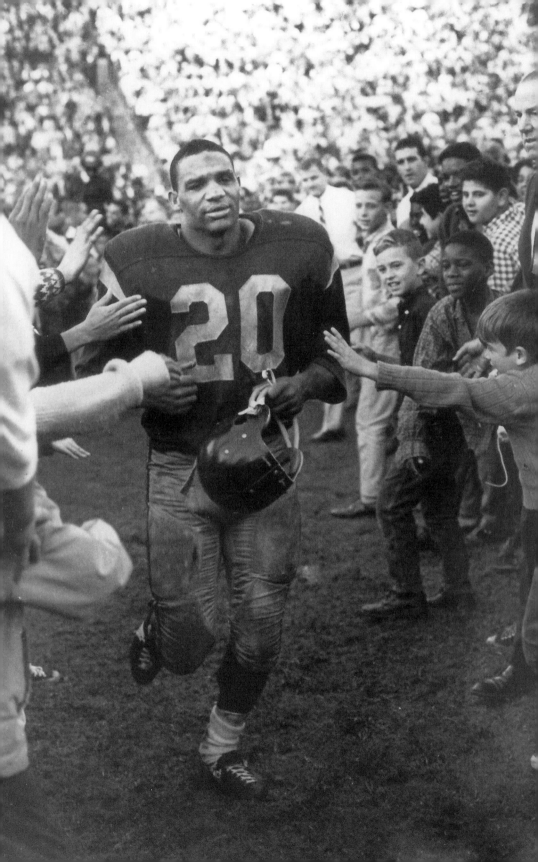

Complete List of
Heisman Trophy Winners

1935 JAY BERWANGER, University of Chicago
1936 LARRY KELLEY, Yale University
1937 CLINTON FRANK, Yale University
1938 DAVEY O'BRIEN, Texas Christian University
1939 NILE KINNICK, University of Iowa
1940 TOM HARMON, University of Michigan
1941 BRUCE SMITH, University of Minnesota
1942 FRANK SINKWICH, University of Georgia
1943 ANGELO BERTELLI, University of Notre Dame
1944 LESLIE HORVATH, Ohio State University
1945 FELIX BLANCHARD, U.S. Military Academy
1946 GLENN DAVIS, U.S. Military Academy
1947 JOHN LUJACK, University of Notre Dame
1948 DOAK WALKER, So. Methodist University
1949 LEON HART, University of Notre Dame
1950 VICTOR JANOWICZ, Ohio State University
1951 RICHARD KAZMAIER, Princeton University
1952 BILLY VESSELS, Oklahoma University
1953 JOHN LATTNER, University of Notre Dame
1954 ALAN AMECHE, University of Wisconsin
1955 HOWARD CASSADY, Ohio State University
1956 PAUL HORNUNG, University of Notre Dame
1957 JOHN DAVID CROW, Texas A&M University
1958 PETER DAWKINS, U.S. Military Academy
1959 BILLY CANNON, Louisiana State University
1960 JOSEPH BELLINO, U.S. Naval Academy

1961 ERNIE DAVIS, Syracuse University
1962 TERRY BAKER, University of Oregon
1963 ROGER STAUBACH, U.S. Naval Academy
1964 JOHN HUARTE, University of Notre Dame
1965 MIKE GARRETT, University of So. California
1966 STEVE SPURRIER, University of Florida
1967 GARY BEBAN, U.C.L.A.
1968 O.J. SIMPSON, University of So. California
1969 STEVE OWENS, Oklahoma University
1970 JIM PLUNKETT, Stanford University
1971 PAT SULLIVAN, Auburn University
1972 JOHNNY RODGERS, Nebraska University
1973 JOHN CAPPELLETTI, Penn State University
1974 ARCHIE GRIFFIN, Ohio State University
1975 ARCHIE GRIFFIN, Ohio State University
1976 ANTHONY DORSETT, University of Pittsburgh
1977 EARL CAMPBELL, University of Texas
1978 BILLY SIMS, Oklahoma University
1979 CHARLES WHITE, University of So. California
1980 GEORGE ROGERS, University of So. California
1981 MARCUS ALLEN, University of So. California
1982 HERSCHEL WALKER, University of Georgia
1983 MIKE ROZIER, Nebraska University
1984 DOUG FLUTIE, Boston College
1985 VINCENT JACKSON, Auburn University
1986 VINNY TESTAVERDE, University of Miami
1987 TIM BROWN, University of Notre Dame
1988 BARRY SANDERS, Oklahoma State University
1989 ANDRE WARE, University of Houston
1990 TY DETMER, Brigham Young University
1991 DESMOND HOWARD, University of Michigan
1992 GINO TORRETTA, University of Miami
1993 CHARLIE WARD, Florida State University
1994 RASHAAN SALAAM, University of Colorado
1995 EDDIE GEORGE, Ohio State University
1996 DANNY WUERFFEL, University of Florida
1997 CHARLES WOODSON, University of Michigan
1998 RICKY WILLIAMS, University of Texas
1999 RON DAYNE, University of Wisconsin
2000 CHRIS WEINKE, Florida State
2001 ERIC CROUCH, Nebraska
2002 CARSON PALMER, University of So. California
2003 JASON WHITE, Oklahoma University

Index